Dedication

To the Seven Glenmoriston Men
Padruig Dubh Grant
Hugh Chisholm
Grigor MacGregor
Donald Chisholm
Alexander MacDonald
Alexander Chisholm
John Campbell MacDonald
from 1746...
...and their descendants to this day
in whatever part of the world they may now
be living.

Mac Nachten Enterprises

Bruce

Marion

Malcolm

Ailsa

Cherry

Padruig

Zahra

Grigor

Grigor Og

Kenneth

Ivy

Aonghus

Alex

Matilda

Alexander

Hugh Mohr

Helen

The Eccentric Family

Hugh and Hamish

Secrets of the Braes and Glens

Zaynab El-Fatah

Art by Brisbane Artist Halima Karger

Contents

Contents

38. Loch Garry Ranch
39. Loch Garry Forest
40. Donald Chisholm #1
41. Donald Chisholm #2
42. Isobel-Mairi, Ewen and Nachtain MacNachten
43. The Blacksmith's Forge
44. Ewen MacNachten
45. Bruce MacKay
46. Duncan MacDonnell #1
47. Helen MacGregor with sheep
48. Morag-Freya MacLachlan
49. Morag-Freya and Gillcrest MacLachlan by Loch Fyne
50. Helen MacGregor
51. Grigor Og MacGregor – older
52. Henry MacKichan
53. Malcolm MacNachten #1
54. Alexandria MacKichan
55. Marion MacNachten #2
56. Bruce MacDonald
57. Malcolm MacNachten #2
58. James Grant
59. Family Tree of Patrick and Henrietta Grant
60. Murdoch MacLean
61. Bruce MacDonald #2
62. Cherry MacNachten Dancing
63. Cherry and Malcolm MacNachten
64. Malcolm's Prize Bull
65. Kenneth MacNachten young
66. Padruig and Isobel Grant Portraits
67. The MacNachten Twins
68. Ivy Fraser
69. Duncan Mohr MacDonnell
70. Ivy and Kenneth MacNachten
71. Loch Insh Bell
72. Druid Stone, Loch Insh
73. Family Tree of Alexander Grant
74. Aonghus MacGregor Lawyer #1
75. Aonghus MacGregor #2
76. Grigor Mohr MacGregor
77. Goat kid
78. Isobel Teamster
79. Malcolm MacNachten
80. Marion MacNachten #3
81. A Loch Garry Home
82. Loch Garry
83. Malcolm and Cherry
84. Wolf in Heather
85. Duncan's Irish Wolf Hound
86. Stook of oats
87. Malcolm MacNachten and Padruig Grant
88. The Wolf Hunt
89. Padruig Grant and Malcolm MacNachten
90. Family Tree of Marion Grant
91. King George IV 1822

List of Maps

Isobel of Glenmoriston Series of Books — Zaynab El-Fatah
Secrets of the Braes and Glens

Family Tree of Isobel and Padruig Grant

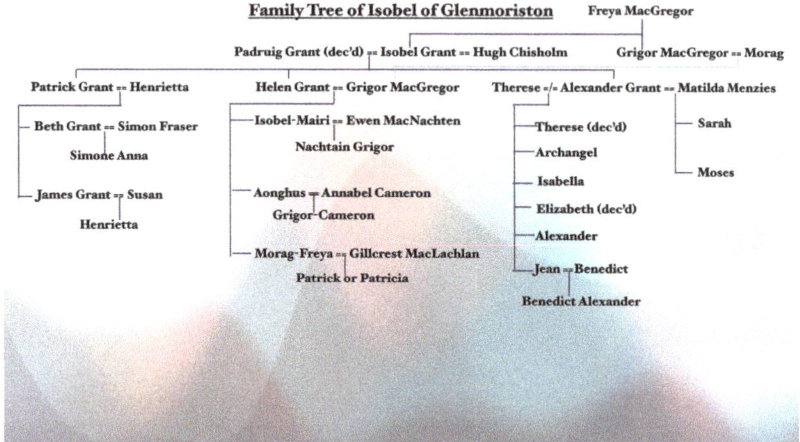

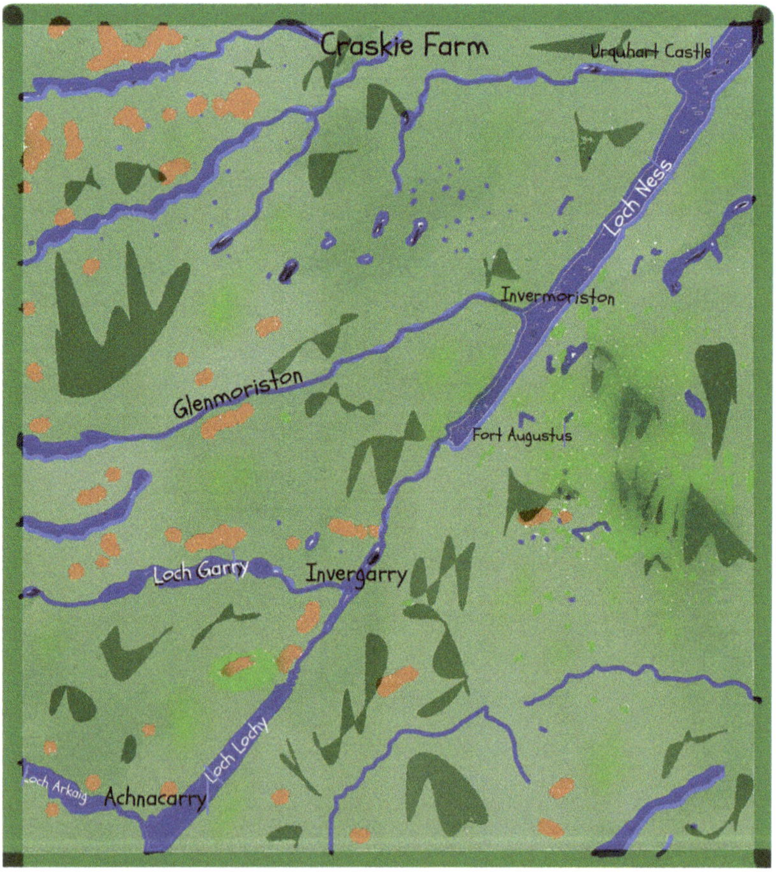

Map 1. Map of Glenmoriston and Glengarry

Map 2: Highland Scottish Clan Lands in the 1700s

Clan lands featured in the story include Grant, Chisholm, Urquhart, MacDonnell of Glengarry, Cameron, MacLachlan and Menzies

Prologue

Have you wondered what happened to everyone else in the Braes and Glens of Glenmoriston?

Who was Fleur? Buried deep in Isobel's Forest is the biggest secret of all, having been concealed by both Hugh Chisholm and Isobel Grant from that dark Badenoch night, as the Prince's army had prepared to depart for Edinburgh in 1745. Passion, secrecy and forbidden love made life both enthralling and dangerous for them both.

Grigor Og MacGregor tells of his rebellious youth and his story of the day that all of Glenmoriston was rummaged and set on fire by the British troops and local militia from Skye.

What were Uncle Allan's true motives from the day that Isobel was born? Her younger son, Alex, finds out that he has a twin, while their paternity is still in question and Isobel's family learn secrets long buried that are revealed, one by one. Why did John Grant remove one of the twins?

Their old lawyer ponders over a letter addressed to Marion Grant and decides whether he should leave it to Aonghus and Helen to deal with, or just deliver it himself before both Padruig and Isobel pass away.

Who are Marion's handsome sons, Malcolm and Kenneth MacNachten from Loch Insh?

Scotland changes over time after Padruig's death in 1786, but the family keeps on growing and making their own mark on the world as they now find it and Isobel's own death followed soon after her husband's.

Who is the mysterious Zara and how had she ended up in this world and time and who is her infamous husband of the Otherworld? Padruig Dubh speaks from beyond the grave to communicate with his grandson Malcolm, uncannily like him in appearance. The two of them form a close bond, while wolves are discovered to be present again in the Aird.

Introduction

As I was about to climb up onto the carriage, I felt a warm hand about my waist.

"Will you come with me out of sight?" the voice quietly asked.

I was taken by his voice and moved to the back of the carriage. He was young, blonde and extremely handsome.

"Was it your hand?" I asked. "Aye," he admitted.

Suddenly, we were one, as he began to thrust his large, hard manhood, while I just held onto the back of the carriage. It was a beautiful experience that I did not object to. I could have pulled away but didn't, then I turned and kissed him lovingly and passionately.

Up close, he had the most beautiful blue eyes, chiselled features and soft, sensual lips with an innocence about him.

We weren't to expect that, from this, we would create new life and that it could so easily be taken away from us.

I watched on as he disappeared into the dark Badenoch night.

Book 1

Secrets of the Braes and Glens

Book 1 – Short Stories

Isobel Grant

Hugh Chisholm

Grigor Og
MacGregor

Padruig
Dubh Grant

Alexander
Malcolm David

Annabel
MacGregor

Alexander
Grant

Matilda
Grant

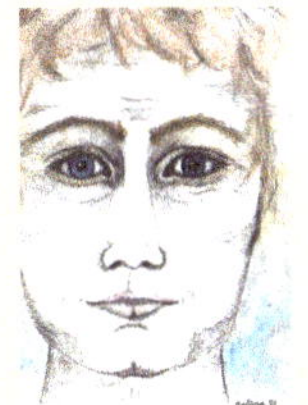

Donald
Chisholm

Isobel-Mairi
MacNachten

Morag-Freya
MacLachlan

Helen
MacGregor

Isobel Grant Chisholm's Story

"Fleur"

By Zaynab El-Fatah

Illustration by Halima Karger

Glenmoriston
Scotland, 1763

I had never been smiled at so broadly by such a tall and handsome young lad until my first day of school at Glenmoriston, when Padruig Grant did just that. My heart missed a beat and I was so excited that he could think that I was worth such a beautiful broad smile. He captured my heart from the age of six and for most of my life. I married him when I was just fourteen years old, when he was training to be a soldier with the Independent Highland Companies and later with Lord Lovat, Simon Fraser.

We all lived on Craskie Farm in the Braes of Glenmoriston in the Highlands of Scotland and my Mither's name was Freya MacGregor Grant and my Father's name was John Grant. My name is Isobel MacGregor Grant.

My Mither never spoke of her Clan because her Grandmother had been one of those falsely accused of being a witch in 1661 when she was a healer and a midwife. She was tortured in the tollbooth in Edinburgh, then hung until unconscious and then burned at the stake. She had been innocent. The ancient remedies she had known were still written in a wee book, which was passed down to my Mither, who gave it to me. She taught me the names of the medicinal herbs and plants and their purposes.

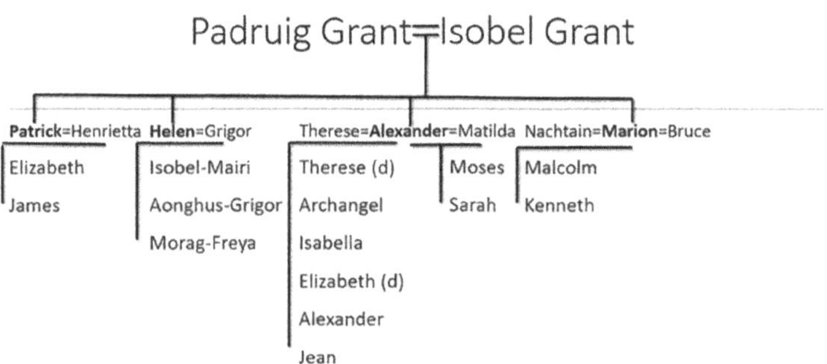

On the day that the dragoons came to Craskie Farm in 1746, it was the only book that I escaped with into the shieling with my three bairns. I was teaching my daughter, Helen, the healing properties of various herbs and plants. My bairns hadn't been sick for one day in their lives due to those plants.

I had four living bairns, Patrick, Helen, Alexander and Marion, then Fleur, whom I miscarried. The paternity to the twins was in question because I had been raped by my Uncle Allan, of

MacDonald Farm, whom I struggled to forgive and Alex's twin sister was kept in hiding from Uncle Allan in Loch Insh into adulthood. My husband didn't learn of her existence for a long time. My younger daughter, Fleur, was conceived with Hugh Chisholm, but was tragically miscarried at five months. The grief of it threatened to overwhelm me. I had always denied that Alex and Marion were offspring of Allan MacDonald, or he would have taken either or both of them from us. Twins were born to us that terrible night and out of dread of losing one or both of them, my Father John Grant, removed one of the twins and hid her in Loch Insh with my Mither's clan.

It may not have been the best solution, but it protected at least one of the twins. Alex's paternity was questioned as a MacDonald. It could never be known for certain if the twins were Allan's bairns or their Father's without doubt, but I believed that Alex and Marion's Father was definitely Padruig Grant. I also never believed that the rape would be found out, but it was eventually and I just thank God that my husband never knew of Fleur in his lifetime. I wouldn't want to have hurt him that much, despite my great love for Hugh.

I had a choice to admit to the rape by Uncle Allan or to having made love with Hugh Chisholm on the day before Padruig's return from his almost four-year long absence in Quebec. In protecting both Hugh and I, I had to endure the consequences of not having told Padruig about Uncle Allan and the rape. His relationship with my younger son, Alex had always been poor, but it only then became worse, and so my favourite son left for Nova Scotia with his wife Therese and their bairns.

I wouldn't see him again for almost twenty-two agonising more years.

I saw Alex's twin sister frequently, while she was growing up in Loch Insh when we had the team of Clydesdales and could give the family there enough money to raise her. I always made her clothes, allowing for her growth, as time went by. It broke my heart every time we had to leave her behind, but Allan always threatened to take the child born of rape. He never knew that

I'd given birth to twins. Marion grew up healthy and strong in Loch Insh and loved Mr MacNachten, whom she called Da. I never adopted her to them legally. I hadn't anticipated the Rising to occur in Scotland and the subsequent burnings after 1746 and thereby losing our only way to visit her with the Clydesdales, as well as losing my own Mither.

All our horses were gone and I wasn't even sure if Marion had survived that period. Word did reach me eventually that no harm had come to her, but Mrs MacNachten had passed away. Eventually, I saw Marion again after she was long married and widowed with two beautiful lads of her own, Malcolm and Kenneth many years later when I was visited by Mr MacNachten under the sole guise of looking into my ancestry. Later, I visited them with the excuse of building a wee Chapel on Craskie Farm, which we did build. I wanted them all back home. However, I became ill from that journey alone along the Great Glen at night, which slowed down my chance to tell Padruig that he had another daughter, as well as two more Grandsons and the hopes of moving them all back to Craskie.

My lawyer still had the letter addressed to her from my Da about an inheritance.

My twin daughter's name was Marion Grant, but at her local school in Loch Insh, she was always known as Marion MacNachten. Having married within the clan, her husband's name was also MacNachten, but when he became ill with pneumonia, he passed away suddenly. I was desperate to move Marion back to Craskie Farm with both of her unmarried lads, but I had still never told Padruig. She met her Father before he passed away and both twins not only enjoyed their love of each other, but they both also had the opportunity to not only meet Padruig but for him to know why she had been so carefully hidden and well protected.

It wasn't because of Padruig that she had been concealed, it was because of his Uncle Allan. Padruig was blessed to meet her before his death and was pleased she had been protected.

A house was made available for Marion and her sons temporarily, as Helen built two new houses at the rear of New Farm where Ewen, Isobel-Mairi and their son Nachtain would live. I had completed all of the arrangements when Ewen made his final visit to see his adoptive Father. Mr MacNachten's wife was long in the ground and he had raised my wee lass for all that time and had patiently taught my Grandsons his trade of beautifully decorating grave slabs and stone masonry. He had gone without good shoes himself, just to give them all what they needed.

My dear Gillcrest passed away as he watched the only family he had known, other than Ewen, depart Loch Insh. His grave is in our cemetery. My husband, Padruig followed soon after.

I wasn't expecting that my wee Alex, who was 6'6" would come home from Nova Scotia to meet his twin sister, but he did, and praise be to the Almighty God, my twins were overjoyed to be reunited. Marion was a sweet looking and quietly spoken lass and very polite to the man whom she had revered all that time, so Padruig took to his sweet new daughter and it was nice to see that something made him happy before he passed from this earth.

Early on in my marriage my husband rarely came home from his military training and was constantly annoyed with me that I wasn't living with his Father, which was what he had wanted. He detested having to visit both farms and would complain to me every time he came home to Craskie Farm, reiterating that it hadn't been his choice. He felt that a wee lass like me, had no right to override his desires. The first time I was punished by my husband was over this issue and he took out his wide leather belt and buckle and strapped me with it about ten times. He believed it was his duty to punish me, as most men did in those times and for most of my adult life. It was awfully painful, but I dared not cry in fear of him doing it again. He satisfied himself sexually several times during that same night and I knew that my marriage was one of strict obedience and was very glad of my round bottom.

In the morning following the strapping, I wanted to appease Padruig desperately and knowing that the upcoming week wasn't busy with any deliveries with the Team, I asked my husband if it would please both himself and his Father if I could spend a week over at their farm, despite disliking them, then return home and continue with my work with my Father. He told me that his Mither was long in the ground and his Da had needs, like cooking his meals and helping him to get around with his arthritis. I then asked Da for his permission, which annoyed Padruig, who thought only his permission needed to be sought, but Da agreed unwillingly. He said he would pick me up in one week, so I could go back to work. Da picked me up as promised from an uneventful week of hard work at the Grant farm and my Da didn't even look at Mr Grant, let alone speak any niceties.

"You're not going back there Isobel," Da said. "That old coot might ravish you, not having a wife," he said. And that was how it was to be.

Whenever Padruig came home, thereafter, I was extremely cautious to never displease him. I think I had made things worse by spending one week at their farm. It was hard to imagine that he was that same lad who had smiled broadly at me when I was wee and at times, I wept quietly to myself in bed, while still loving the man of my dreams. I'd only been punished once by my Father at the age of three, when I was in the wrong. His words were then, "take your punishment," at that time and then remembering those words, as Padruig's wife, made the frequent punishments much easier to cope with.

I had never stopped loving Padruig Grant, but loving our Clydesdale horses made it all the easier. That was until I met Hugh. My dear old Da had taught me the Erse language from a young age to talk to the horses and I became his trained offsider because I was his only bairn. His first wife and bairn had died in childbirth and his second wife, my Mither, wasn't young enough to have more than I. She did have a son born to her first deceased husband, of whom I knew nothing and neither did my half brother know of me. Clan Gregor disallowed my Da to become his Stepfather. We discovered each other many years later by accident. Coincidentally, my daughter, Helen, was betrothed to his son, Grigor, whom I adored, as my wee Alex was no longer living at home.

It seemed that I would never get with child and it was fifteen years before I had my first bairn, Patrick and then Helen was easy to conceive and unfortunately, so were my twins, Alex and Marion. I was a very small person and I didn't grow beyond four feet and eleven inches. My Mither said that most of the women in her family were tiny and even smaller than me. Da wasn't tall for a Grant either, so I was destined to be small and that was the reason the Doctor gave me for not yet being with child. When I was still not yet with child at twenty-five years of age, Padruig came home drunk and blamed me for not yet having had his son. He accused me of being barren, but I didn't believe that I was barren, just small and my Mither blamed him for being unkind to me. My Mither was growing to dislike him, as he became more bloodthirsty and gruesome with all of his military talk. At bedtime he started saying,

"You had better get pregnant this time Isobel, or I'll have to divorce you!" I was longing for love from him when I look back on it, but I didn't feel loved, although in context he had the weight of the world on his young shoulders, as Scotland entered a calamitous phase in its history.

Da and I kept working the Clydesdale team over the years and it became busier and busier with the distances becoming longer. The eight horses could carry very heavy loads and I was able to manage them, while speaking Erse to them. Da's old fingers were becoming more and more crippled with arthritis and it was left to me to accomplish the difficult tasks. Local people called me "Isobel of Glenmoriston" [2]. Da would load and unload and threaten any men to keep their eyes off me, reminding them whose wife I was, which had a strong impact. They all seemed to know who Padruig Dubh was and were frightened at the thought of upsetting him, which was surprising. I kept my arisaid over my head and I noticed only a few of the people. My job was to keep the horses calm when we were stationary, while Da unloaded or was receiving his payment. Sometimes foolish people would do things to frighten the team deliberately, but my lead horse and I worked well together, so that the younger ones didn't fret.

When we had to deliver to the Jacobites in '45, it became much harder with more men leering at me. All those men were away from their wives and with a lass in their midst, it would always cause a murmuring amongst the gathering of men. It was lucky that Padruig didn't know that I was out there many times at night, I thought and I trusted Cluny MacPherson would have it all under control. I was neither a Jacobite nor a Hanoverian. I had no clue that my husband was actually amongst the Jacobites in Badenoch, who were gaining in number and he had no idea that I was there, I thought.

John Grant-Da

Padruig had never asked me what we did on our farm, which meant he also didn't know about the Team and my teamstering. I'd often want to tell him, just in conversation, but he would talk non-stop about the Military. He was first with Lord Lovat for a long time and then with other Highland Independent Companies[2]. I'd always admired Lord Lovat and had no desire to interrupt and so I didn't and Padruig never learned of Da's Team, until the horses were stolen in May and June '46 during the burnings in Glenmoriston and he still didn't imagine that I was a teamster.

I missed him, being away so much and eventually when Patrick was finally born, my husband didn't even come to see our new wee bairn right away. He went to tell his Father first.

There was no gift for the bairn or me, so I was being trained too, as a wife who was not to expect much from her husband. I loved his beautiful black hair and at times in bed, I'd touch his hair and caress his face that I loved and he'd respond and call me Dar'Thula from Erse poetry. I loved his beautiful body, especially his long legs and would bathe him and wash his gorgeous long, black hair and kiss his lips. When he was in those moods, he was the most beautiful man in the world, who I hated parting with. He loved wee Helen when she was born too, with our trademark jet black hair and she loved him. Helen was his favourite child and he'd recite Erse poetry in length to the wee bairn, who would look into his dark blue eyes. It was a touching scene. My first two children had started to soften my husband's heart and for the first time in our marriage, I had started to feel like a real wife, despite our sex life never being enjoyable.

One Dark Badenoch Night

On one of the deliveries to the Jacobites in Badenoch, it was a difficult haul. There were many sealed drums to deliver there. I never asked Da what was in them. There were rules to our partnership, one of which was 'don't ask what's in a sealed delivery' and 'how much coin that he was paid each time', as well as the obvious care and responsibility for the horses. Da's arthritis in his fingers meant that I would always do the tricky turns of the larger teams, like the eight horse teams in smaller spaces, and one of those was Badenoch.

It was raining heavily that day on the narrow old Drover's Road, when a lad wanted a ride to Fort Augustus, which we gave him. There was a familiarity about him and he really liked our Clydesdale horses. He was signing up with John Campbell at Fort Augustus. John Campbell later became Lord Louden who fought on the Hanoverian side.

It seemed like forever after we dropped the lad off before we reached our destination in Badenoch.

It was very dark by the time we arrived, but there were lanterns hung all around, as well as fires here and there and it was teeming with men and much busier than before. I looked for Ewen MacPherson of Cluny, but couldn't see him at first, until I finally spotted him huddled around and talking with three big, young men, much taller than himself. He looked my way then waved and I waved back. I quite liked and admired Cluny, but there was a sense of urgency in the air and the energy had changed.

I wondered then where my husband was.

I covered my head as it started to rain again, but I had a need to relieve myself, which I told Da upon the completion of the unloading. He told me to make it quick and get down from the carriage and pish behind a tree. As I was finishing, I felt a man's hand slide quickly under my big skirt onto my private parts, to finger my womanhood, despite just having pished. I jumped up in shock and then responded to a sound in front of me. There stood a really tall, broad, blonde, unsmiling and rather scary looking man, who was about to do more than the hand had done, I feared. Then another blonde, younger man emerged from out of the sheets of rain, pulling down his big blue bonnet over his head. He asked me if I needed any help and I said to that man that I needed to be taken back to the Team.

He delivered me to Da saying,

"My name is Donald Chisholm. This is your lassie delivered safely to your Team, Mr Grant," he said. Da had not looked up and just acknowledged him with a nod, as he was entering notes into his wee book taking care for it to stay dry. I was then about to climb up onto the carriage, when I felt a warm hand about my waist.

"Will you come with me out of sight?" the voice asked.

I was taken by the warmth of his hand and his voice and moved to the back of the carriage as asked. He was young and very handsome.

"Was it your hand?" I asked. "Aye," he said.

"Here's water that you might want to wash with," he said smiling. I washed myself, having overlooked that with the shock of his hand on my private area.

"Can you look away please?" I asked. I washed myself, having lifted up my skirt when I noticed that the rain had finally stopped.

Then suddenly, he was inside me and thrusting his large, hard appendage, holding my skirt and me firmly at the hips while I was holding onto the carriage just hoping that no one would see us, especially my Da. There was no escape from his strong grasp. His brothers then stood one on each side of the carriage, like sentries, to protect their brother, but it was a beautiful experience that I did not object to and I didn't feel raped. I could have pulled away, but additionally when he had finished, spontaneously I turned and kissed him lovingly and passionately. It had been the first time that I'd ever experienced an orgasm. Up close, he had the most beautiful blue eyes, but his hair was covered over with a blue bonnet. He was so handsome with chiselled features, beautiful clear skin and he had an innocence about him that I loved.

"Are you marching to Edinburgh, Holyrood House?" I asked him.

"Aye, then onto London we think," the young man replied. He needed God on his side and more courage to keep him going on such a horrible journey with the Jacobites, against the Hanoverians.

"Are you prepared, my young friend?" I asked seriously, but in trying to reply, his throat choked up with emotion. He allowed me to take his hand and I recited:

"May you have a good journey, May the sun not burn you, May the Almighty God keep you warm and dry, May He keep stones out from under your feet, May you go like water and return to your Clan like water, May strength and bravery be your friend, May your horse fly you to your destination and back to your Clan, May you return back to Scotland," I said impulsively from a poem that I'd read. I gave him my silver necklace that my Mither gave me that was for protection. He stood staring into my eyes for a moment pleadingly, wanting tenderness and affection, or an escape from his impending doom.

One of his brothers then said, "Hugh, hurry it up. Her Da is coming down off the carriage." The beautiful young man then disappeared into the dark Badenoch night and Donald returned me to my Father.

"About time Isobel. We have to get going. Thank you, lad," he said to Donald.

"Come and see us anytime at Craskie Farm in Glenmoriston," my Father said, even letting the brothers know where we lived.

I then had the difficult job negotiating the tight turn with the eight horses, while Da yelled an obscenity at the men who hadn't moved out of the way. "Good job lassie," my Da would always say if he knew he couldn't accomplish a task, now as his fingers became more and more crippled.

I was with child after that night in Badenoch. Our farmhouse was very crowded then with both of my growing sons, Patrick and Alex as well as lovely Helen, Ma and Da. Helen and I slept very closely next to each other in the same bed, which kept us both warm. No one suspected that I was with child, not even either of my parents when I would frequently 'reach' each morning outside. I barely had time to ask myself what I was going to do once the pregnancy would be obvious to all. One day when I needed to wash in the burn, I was about five months with child and not revealing much under my big dresses, but when naked, it was clearly obvious. So, I chose to bathe alone. Suddenly, I felt an agonising pain in my lower abdomen and blood floated up to the surface of the water. Panicking, I immediately got out of the burn to wrap myself in my plaid, trying to hold my wee bairn in when the pain became too much to bear. There was a lot of blood.

I had never had a miscarriage before, but I had the dreaded realisation that I was losing this bairn and I could only lie down in agony by the side of the burn. Da came running, seeing that I was in trouble and lifted up my tiny wee bairn from between my legs and cried, "Oh Isobel, I am so sorry. You have lost your tiny wee lass" and passing her to me. I held her in my arms, crying my heart out, as did he and couldn't stop. Da held me there a while then said, "She has some blonde hair, Isobel. Is she Padruig's?" he asked cautiously. "Nae Da, the lad in Badenoch. Hugh Chisholm." His blue eyes and handsome face came back to me hauntingly and I had to tell him. What sorrow this young man would feel too, as well as myself and I hadn't yet told him. Why hadn't I written to him before now? He should have been told, but I hadn't expected a tragedy would befall us. I berated myself for he was surely marching into England by now, I thought.

Da and I secretly buried Fleur Chisholm beside my Pict stone in my forest

and no one else was told. I asked my Da where the Jacobite troops were and he answered, "Edinburgh or departing Edinburgh."

"How will I get word to him Da?" I asked pleadingly.

"By mail Isobel, but write it in English, so that Padruig can't read it should he come by your letter. But what will you say to the poor lad in his circumstances? What if it upsets him too much and he gets himself killed?" Da asked.

"So, should I not tell him that Fleur has already passed? Just that I am with child?" I asked. "Don't tell him she's passed already," he suggested. "Just that you'd like to see him upon his return," he added.

"Then, Da can you please post the letter if I write to him now?" I asked.

"Aye, I will, my poor darling lass. And every time I light a candle for my deceased wife and bairn, I will also light one for wee Fleur," he said with tears in his eyes. Fleur was also his wee Grandchild and he chose not to tell my Mither. I was grateful he didn't judge me for what had happened with the handsome lad or maybe it had just been his fear of my Mither's judgement on him.

I wrote the letter to the lad from that dark Badenoch night, remembering how fearful and young he had looked and the Turkish poem that I'd recited to him. I couldn't mislead him, even though Da's reasoning was sound and so I did tell him that I was sorry that our wee bairn that I'd been carrying, sadly passed. I told him that I'd named her Fleur and to please come and meet with her at her graveside upon his return from his long journeying. God willing. I wasn't to know that my trusted Da would open the letter to see what I'd written and then burn it.

Both Padruig and Hugh and his friends and brothers, Donald and Alexander Chisholm, came home safe, as I had prayed constantly for.

Their next destination had been Inverness, Drumossie Moor.

The day that Padruig and his six friends were escaping the battlefield of Culloden, the only man to turn and wave to me was the youngest of the group of the Seven Glenmoriston Men, Hugh Chisholm. I waved back slowly in recognition of the Father of my lost wee bairn, but I had learned to accept my loss. My heart was yearning to see him and show him where his bairn was now in the ground.

That was April 16th, 1746. Hugh Chisholm and my husband, Padruig Dubh Grant were not only together, but hiding in the same cave, with his brothers too, out of necessity and the Redcoats weren't far behind them.

We were all in danger.

The next time that Fleur's Father and Alexander Chisholm would see me was in May or June 1746, when my life was departing me, after having been ravished repeatedly by the troops of the Duke of Cumberland, then bayoneted on my bottom by local Militia at Fort Augustus. I was later dropped by dragoons at the entrance of our burnt out Craskie Farm, with my then deceased Aunty Margaret. Ma had already been killed by them, as well as some of our crofters, the remainder of whom had left. Life looked like it was all over for me when Da, Uncle Allan and Morag did their best, before deciding that it was over and I was taken to my husband's secret location in a cave, wherein at that time were Hugh and Alexander Chisholm and Alexander MacDonald. It was by some miracle of God that both Hugh and Alexander used their Grandfather's traditional remedies, as well as using their cat gut stitching kit, that my life was miraculously restored.

Hugh returned me to the shieling, without my husband, nor I having known that I had ever been there. I had no memory of it. They hadn't wanted Padruig to see me naked in front of them as they worked, repairing such delicate feminine areas as was necessary, or else their lives too would be at risk.

Alexander Chisholm was extremely skilful and he had seen some terrible wounds in his lifetime. His loss to the world shortly afterwards was enormous. In their cave, I was unaware of my surroundings, as I floated in and out of consciousness. I was told that I was too close to death to know what was real. Sometimes in the following years, I would have flashbacks, like the smell of the bed of heather upon which they had me lay, the frigid, icy cold water of the burn in which they had bathed me in their cave to stem the blood flow and a strange chanting sound, which made me think that I was already dead, when it was just the prayers that Hugh and Alexander used when performing their healing rituals.

Alexander MacDonald

I owed both of those men my life, as well as Alexander MacDonald, now also deceased. When I was taken back to the shieling by Hugh, I was wrapped in his plaids. I couldn't part with them and would inhale the aroma that they emitted. I felt a strong need to be with that young and beautiful man from Badenoch, but I hadn't known why. It was very hard to try and walk again after all of the injuries that I'd received and I still don't remember when it was that I saw my husband again or if he had indeed even been told. All I wanted to do was to walk to the wee grave beside my Pict stone and to be reunited with that part of myself. I chiselled our daughter's name into a stone, reading Fleur Chisholm, daughter of Isobel and Hugh Chisholm, even though I was Isobel Grant. I didn't want to think of her as being born out of wedlock and I would pray there often.

When I was finally able to introduce Fleur's Father to her, he was first in disbelief that he had fathered a child, let alone lost her and he was naturally, devastated. It was hard not to arouse Padruig's attention after they had all returned home, when the amnesty was finally declared in 1747, it may have been August. Hugh then was a frequent visitor to Fleur's grave. I was still unaware that he had never received my letter and he asked me why I hadn't told him that I was with his child or that I'd lost his child before he had left on the march to England with Prince Charles Edward Stuart's army.[2]

I told him that I did write to him on the day that I had lost her, when I was with child for nearly five months, by the side of the burn and I concluded then that my Da had never posted the letter that I'd penned to him.

"I would have come back to you if I had known," he said very emotively. "I feel I've lost my life's only bairn and you are her Mither, Isobel," Hugh said.

It was a tragic moment for Hugh with all of the death and destruction around him that he had seen. The most precious thing in the world was that wee bairn, that I'd lost. I was overcome with grief, unable to express it to anyone who could understand and the two of us just held each other for comfort over her loss, unable to make sense out of any of it.

I explained to him that she was buried in a wee wooden casket that Da had made for her, so that in the future if we were ever married, she could join us in the cemetery. I wanted to be buried with her.

"When I saw you out the front of this farm as we escaped from Culloden Field, I was in love with you and wanted you, even though you were Padruig's wife. I loved you without knowing you were the Mither of my bairn," he said. Hugh poured out his heart and asked me to marry him if ever Padruig passed away or just left.

"I am so sorry I did what I did to you at Badenoch," Hugh added.

"I never imagined it would become a bairn, I was just afraid and I needed you to give me strength and you did. I couldn't have pulled through all of that death and destruction, without your kind words and your tenderness. Please forgive me Isobel. Maybe the Almighty God did not reward us with this bairn because of what we did that dark night in Badenoch?" he said.

"I don't believe that Hugh, our God does not punish wee bairns like that," I added. Hugh disagreed.

"You haven't seen what I've seen done to bairns and pregnant women alike. Cruelty doesn't even begin to describe it," he said and never spoke again of those atrocities, but he didn't need to, he always carried it with him.

"Is our bairn wrapped in tartan, Isobel, is she warm enough do you think?" Hugh asked. "Aye, sweet man, she is wrapped in my tartan that my Mither gave me, but she didn't tell me her clan. I'll find out if you like. It's very pretty though and also, I knitted a wee blue bonnet for Fleur to keep her warm. The wee wooden box is also lined with a warm blanket," I said. I started to cry all over again, imagining her tiny wee body in there, cold and alone. "I am so sorry that I lost her Hugh, please forgive me and now I am unable to have any more bairns," I begged and wept.

"Isobel, it's true, I would have wanted more bairns with you. But now with this new reality, please do not disclose the whereabouts of our bairn's resting place, else the government forces will dig up her grave and strip her tiny body of the tartan, as they have done everywhere else," [3] he said. Stunned, I just nodded. He then wrapped his arms around me to both console and caress.

"You're mine Isobel. I know you are Catholic like me and cannot divorce Padruig, but one day. Please agree to marry me?" he begged as we both continued to grieve for the loss of Fleur. I agreed to marry Hugh Chisholm one day in the future when Padruig would release me. I needed to be truthful to Hugh, concerning my other daughter, Marion, hidden in Loch Insh and the reason why she was hidden there. He was horrified to hear the rape story, but agreed with Da that protecting the lass was all we could have done, so long as she was being raised well, which she was, but not to tell Padruig.

The mist became thicker and dense as my Ancestors joined us and then we lay close to her grave at first, but then he asked me if we could make love nearer her. And we did and the emotion of it was unlike anything that I had ever felt before and his voice gave out in ecstasy that was quickly replaced again by grief. He sobbed like a child into my breast. We talked in length about what it could have been like if Fleur had lived and he took my hand and placed it on his large appendage, which was a joyous experience of both his flesh and his acceptance of me as his lover and on that day. I did things I had never imagined doing sexually and it gave us both joy, over and over again. It sunk in that this man was mine as my hand explored his arms and chest and his beautiful blonde hair. Even the hair on his arms and his legs and chest were blonde too. Running my fingers through his soft chest hair was scintillating to the senses. He loved me exploring his body because he hadn't belonged to anyone before. He had only had a flirtatious relationship with a young lass named Emily who had passed away also. I was quick to become jealous and I hoped that he wouldn't take another from that moment on or I couldn't bear it. He was so gorgeous. How did God create such a beautiful looking man to throw into my path this way, only to lose his bairn?

I was half expecting his brother to come and get him, but we were both left in peace. He told me that he would make a better stone for Fleur and I agreed. He wanted my name to be Isobel Chisholm and I was very happy about that. He also found that special place on my body that allows us to transcend this world, unable to keep silent, my voice became part of the musical sounds of the old growth forest and my fingernails dug deep into his flesh and I kissed his neck and face passionately. We both loved the intensity of oral sex when he stopped and looked me in the eyes asking, "Do you remember this?"

"Nae," I answered quizzically.

"You don't recall being in the cave after you were ravished then?" Hugh asked.

"Nae, I wasn't there. I think I was at Uncle Allan's farm. Why do you ask that? How did you know about that? I don't want it widely known please Hugh. Padruig doesn't know," I pleaded.

"I know he doesn't know, but why doesn't he know?" Hugh asked.

"I don't want him looking at me differently as his wife and if he had known on that day, he would have gone there and been killed, of that I am certain. The Duke of Cumberland was there, with all of his troops and there was local militia too. It was local militia who caused the wounds on my bottom with bayonets. Padruig wouldn't have survived going to Fort Augustus, which is what we knew he would do. They were saying terrible things about Padruig. They did what they did to me out of hatred for him because they couldn't catch him. I kept praying that God would protect Padruig. It was Uncle Allan's idea to say that the wounds on my bottom were from his coos, if I survived," I explained. "How did you know, please Hugh? Tell me," I pleaded.

He told me the whole story, how Allan believed I would die, so he thought to take me to Padruig, who should know and Hugh said, "Up to that point, if you hadn't met my brother and I, you would be dead with all of that blood loss that still hadn't stopped. We stopped the bleeding first, then located the other injuries, which my brother, Alexander repaired," he explained.

"Did you chant something?" I asked.

"Aye, it's part of the healing from our auld ways from our grandfather," he answered.

"I thought I was already dead," I said and he smiled for the first time. "You're still wearing the necklace I gave you, Hugh," I said, as I rested my hand amongst the soft hairs of his chest.

"Aye, I have never taken it off since that night and I never will. I love you, Isobel," Hugh said.

Then he caressed my face gently, placed his hand over mine and then I gave in to crying inconsolably.

"I love you too and I am married. Oh God, Hugh," I cried.

I think our bairn held us tightly together for the rest of our lives and I am grateful for that dark Badenoch night that God gave to us both, for different reasons.

We both then heard the sound of the breaking of a tiny twig on the forest floor and wondered then if Donald was coming to get us. We both put our clothes back on reluctantly and he continuously caressed me and said that I was his. I brushed off the dirt from our clothes, then saw Donald urgently ushering to us. Hugh kissed me again and placed a stone atop Fleur's grave, then picked me up in his big strong arms and carried me towards Donald. Solemnly, he told Donald, "We had a wee bairn. Her name is Fleur," he said with both sadness and pride and Donald's eyes welled up with tears.

"Oh Sister," he said. "I am so sorry" and we three all walked slowly back to the house where Padruig appeared annoyed about something. He had hurt his hand lifting rocks to start to build our new house and I treated it with comfrey leaves and only one finger was dislocated, which I pulled back into place.

"Where have you two been anyway and what have you been doing?" Padruig asked me angrily.

Lying to my spouse of thirty-one years so blatantly, weighed heavily on my conscience. Asking for God's forgiveness, I had to think of something very quickly, or face imminent death and commenced an elaborate story.

"I was aware recently that I'd need a full inventory of my native forest plants and trees, shrubs, lichens and so on and so I asked Hugh, who knows his plants, to help me to identify some of them. Then I can start to gather their seeds and pot them with their correct names in readiness for those who are wanting to replant their native forests. My intention is to build a wee nursery, especially for them. Hugh said that he would build a palisade around them to keep the deer out," I answered.

Shooting a quick look at Hugh, I had hoped that he would back up my incredulous story, but it was Donald who interjected and said that he would help Hugh do that when they finished their current job, then went on to ask me for the usual herbs for Eilidh to assist her with her poor health. I then hurriedly went to collect the herbs to strengthen Eilidh's constitution and battle her colds and flus.

"You know where she got those remedies from, don't you Donald?" asked Padruig. "Her Grandmother was a witch for doing that and was burned at the stake in 1661," he added for effect, to put down any value that I might have obtained in his absence, while he had lived in the cave and Chisholm country, as well as marching with the Prince's Army.

"1661 you say? A lot of the MacGregor women were wrongfully accused of those crimes and tortured and killed horribly around that time and before that. Was your Grandmother Clan Gregor sister?" Donald asked genuinely.

"My Mither didn't tell me, Donald. I wish I knew and she has now passed away. She was killed by dragoons when they came to Craskie to burn it all down, looking for the Prince in June last year," I answered. "I have her wee book with all of the recipes to help in healing, but obviously not like your God gifted brother, Alexander. Please send him my regards. I hope Eilidh gets well with these herbs or at least gets some relief and if she needs me, please call on me and I'll come over, but please don't think of me as a witch," I requested.

Both Alexander Chisholm and Alexander MacDonald were killed in 1751, well after the pardon was issued.

"God bless you, Isobel. I don't and nor were they probably," Donald said.

Grigor Og was listening, as he had come down from the field from which he was collecting rocks and looked interested that I could be Clan Gregor, like him.

"You're such a good lad," I said patting him warmly on his skinny shoulder. "Good work lad, I can help you now. 'Himself' has hurt his hand." And I bade farewell to both Fleur's Father and his brother, Donald and didn't know when we would see each other again.

I looked around the farm at how little work Padruig had done since his return and was worried that we would not have enough food to eat soon, if he didn't get more crops into the ground. Grigor Og told me that day that he was leaving to do a course on farming to improve crop yield and he would be gone for two years. My heart sank to be without this sweet lad for all that time.

"Your Ma will miss you lad and so will Helen and I. Don't forget to write," I said a bit sadly. I was accustomed to the sweet lad and he was the only one working hard on the farm and now with Padruig's hand injured, that left my two lazy sons, whom I could not motivate. 'God please grant me patience and a forgiving heart' was my prayer. "Have you read about Prophet Ayub, or some say the name in English is Job?" I asked Grigor. "Nae," he answered. "It teaches patience and I do believe we need a lot of that now, my dear lad, but I still want you to think of me as your second Ma when you are away at your course and please come back to Craskie at the end of it, even if "Himself" is grumpy at times, he is still Helen's Father," I said.

Grigor Og stayed on for dinner, then left us to go away for two years. I missed him like he was my own lad and was so sorry for Helen waiting for that long time and encouraged her to write long love letters to him. "My dear sweet Helen," I would say to her when we were working in the corn fields, "when you are missing Grigor, just imagine us all becoming a huge happy family with your children and your Grandchildren, all loving one another, still here on Craskie Farm in Glenmoriston. Alex's children might come back too and we'll need help to cook enough food to be on time for dinner," I said. I was forever hopeful that I would see my twin son Alex again with however many bairns he had by now.

Patience was indeed needed to endure the years to come, but God had given me Hugh Chisholm, who became my great love, while Padruig Grant would always be my first love meeting with such innocence at school. I had learned that men needed to know that you would follow them and in my brief second marriage with Hugh, it gave me wonderful happiness, especially in our sex life and he gave me a serenity that I had never known. We shared a life and a unique love, like no other and every night I thanked God for my life's great love and thanked Hugh for loving me, albiet for such a brief time.

Alex's twin sister, Marion was moved to Ewen's house at first, and she also took over from Meredith as part time home help when the work was too hard during Meredith's pregnancy. Marion then took casual work at her twin brother's farm in Loch Garry. She preferred it over at Alex's farm and her oldest son, Malcolm went there too, to work on building the stone perimeter fencing and he remained living there with his Uncle Alex. Malcolm had an uncanny likeness to his grandfather, with exactly the same hair, his height and he even had those long legs that Padruig had. Sometimes when I saw him out of the corner of my eye, I thought it was Padruig, only when he was younger. His brother, Kenneth worked on Craskie Farm assisting Hugh Mohr and dug graves when needed, as well as engraving the tombstones. Kenneth was then moved into the big house semi permanently. Hugh needed the help, he said.

Their Clan name was MacNachten and so the brothers were split up by their Aunty Helen for the first time in their young lives. I couldn't help but feel that this wouldn't have happened if Padruig had still been alive. Helen ensured that her sister, Marion and the older brother, Malcolm were removed permanently to Loch Garry to live with Alex. I rarely saw Marion again after that and I had to ask myself if I had done the right thing by my twin daughter and her sons in having made that hasty decision on that night of Marion's birth.

What was obvious was that Helen hadn't warmed to an unknown sister, let alone her sons as well. I still kept forgetting to remind Helen to give Marion that letter, thinking it couldn't be too important.

29

Hugh Chisholm's Story

"My Great Love"

By Zaynab El-Fatah

Illustrations by Halima Karger & Fatima Zayn al-Abidin

Glenmoriston
Scotland, 1759

"Donald," called Eilidh. "Aye," he said. "It's Isobel from Craskie Farm wanting to talk to ye," she said.

"Oh aye? I wonder what for. Isobel, come in lass. Do you want a cup of tea?" I heard my brother Donald enquire.

31

"Nae, thank ye Donald. I am just here to ask if you've seen Padruig around anywhere. He left for Leith you see and was due back yesterday," Isobel said sounding worried.

"Come on in and sit down. Relax and tell us the whole story," said my kindly older brother. Reluctantly, she entered our homely abode, as I came out of my bedroom and walked into the kitchen.

"Isobel, what a nice surprise to see you here. We can be your hosts for a change," I said cheerfully, hoping to enjoy her company for a while.

"Thank you. Then I will," she said and sat down. She explained that Padruig had written out a requested document in Erse for it to be translated into English for the Reverend Robert Forbes in Leith and had ridden down to Leith just to drop it off, so he said, because the Reverend didn't trust the Post Office. He hadn't returned home yet.

"I fear something's amiss, or he'd be home by now," Isobel said. "It's been days now and no word," she said.

"Have you not seen him at all?" Donald asked.

"Nae," she answered.

"Hugh, have you seen Padruig?" asked Donald.

"Nae, not for over a week when I dropped the hart around. I've been busy, so I haven't had time to visit either," I answered. "I haven't seen him either Isobel, so I am sorry, but I will put the word around and will ask Grigor Mohr too. Maybe he's seen him? But none of us had any plans together this week, so it is unlikely," I replied. Eilidh's tea was delicious and she tried to make everyone feel better by giving Isobel a hug and a kiss on both cheeks and said, "He'll be fine Isobel. If anyone can ride to Leith and back without trouble, it is Padruig Dubh. He's a tough man. Even if his horse threw a shoe, he could fix it and he wouldn't fall off his horse. What could go wrong, really?" she asked.

"I don't know, but it is not like him. It's like he has just vanished," Isobel said. I made a guttural sound automatically and said, "Not much chance of Padruig vanishing." I'd been secretly hoping for that for many years now. Donald's face said something different, after all, our oldest brother, Alexander had been killed in Glenmoriston only eight years earlier. Donald promised to search for Padruig himself and said,

"If he is nearby in an alehouse, he'll get a mouthful from me for sure Isobel, so go on home and be reassured that we'll locate him," he said.

Isobel still looked worried as she left and said she needed to attend to the wee garden that she and Helen had and there were seeds to plant.

I talked it over with Donald and my sister-in-law, Eilidh, over breakfast as to what could've happened and said, "What if he's taken off to France to find the Prince like he said he wanted to?"

Listening on Eilidh said, "He was going to do what? Does Isobel know he could've gone to France? Afterall, he was in Leith where all the big ships are."

"I don't think she knows how fanatical he was in wanting to achieve that. That having been said, she would still love him anyway and live on as if he had never said it. She is dignified like that," said Donald. "As if it was yesterday, I can still hear Padruig say, 'For if he (the Prince) be on the face of the earth, I'll find him out, as I hear they are good Christians on the other side of the seas. And meet when we will, the Prince and I shall never part again'." [3]

"Oh, poor Isobel," lamented Eilidh. "I hope you find him Donald. Her house still isn't finished. It's been thirteen years and Padruig hasn't finished it yet and with only three crops – neeps, kale and corn. They can't live on that. No wonder both Patrick and Alex left. They would've been hungry all the time," she said.

"Alex has left?" I asked.

"Aye, the day before yesterday. Isobel was heartbroken. Her Da and Alex had a stramash," said Eilidh.

Donald then stood up and with having made up his mind to do something about the situation, he said, "Hugh, put on something warm and we'll go around and see Grigor Mohr first. Eilidh, will you be alright today, mo cridhe, if I leave you to go look for him?" he asked compassionately of his wife. Hugging one another, she said, "Oh my darling man, this is important. I'll prepare a big stew in case it is needed and bannocks too," she said. Kissing each other in a loving embrace, the lovers from childhood said their farewells.

"Are you taking your Collies Hugh?" she then asked.

"Aye, come on my beauties," I called to my beloved dogs. I was aware that Eilidh's house would be quiet after we left, while she got to cleaning and cooking before her energy levels dropped, as they always did.

Entering Craskie Farm, Isobel had wondered if her Uncle Allan had seen Padruig and went up to the MacDonald property that overlooked her farm, to ask him if Padruig had been there and as usual, she found Allan tending to his coos, he told me afterwards and she had asked him the same questions that she had asked of us. He told her, "I saw him ride out of your place a few days ago and I haven't seen him since and there are other things you should know too, Isobel. He borrowed money from me before that, to pay off a debt," he had said. Isobel had asked about the debt. So, in relating the story, Allan told me that he asked her if she had known Paul Chisholm, my Father. She had responded that she had only known him by reputation but had never met him.

So, Allan had told her that when the Prince was living in the cave with us, Padruig had opened up an account with my Da, who sold things from our house, like a shop does. The debt belonged to all seven of us Glenmoriston Men and Grigor had already paid his share, Da had relieved my brothers Alex, Donald and myself of our debts because he was our Father and John Campbell MacDonald claimed he was in poverty and couldn't pay it, so that left only Alexander MacDonald and Padruig. Alexander, passed away, so Padruig had to pay both his own debt as well as Alexander's. That's why he asked Allan for help, given the MacDonald kinship. That left fifty guineas owed to my Father, Paul, who had creditors pursuing him after his place was burned down by British forces and local militia. Neither Da nor Padruig had the money to pay off those debts.

Allan also suggested to Isobel that Padruig could have abandoned her, with no plan to return or maybe had signed up for a Commission with the British Armed Forces, who pay a wage with a pension at the end, in order for the debt to be repaid. "Could he have left you for good this time to do this?" Allan had asked her. Isobel had been patting one of the coos on the head apparently but stopped suddenly. She was obviously hungry, tired, upset and shocked at this revelation, she fainted. "Isobel, Isobel, oh God, Isobel, wake up," he said to her frantically. Having lost a lot of weight, Isobel didn't weigh much and Allan was able to carry her back to the shieling. Helen, upon seeing her Mither like that, cried and cried, trying to wake her up and eventually she awoke, much to Allan's relief.

The following morning, Isobel had awoken weeping and Helen heard her begging the Almighty God not to challenge her like before and convinced Helen to go to her garden without her. Helen told me that Isobel feared that Padruig had left her for good, as he had wanted to before in order to follow the Prince. That reality had finally sunken in. Having lost her wee bairn, her own Mither in '46 and then with her sons abandoning her, Helen told me later that the despair began to take its terrible hold on her Mither, like in those days when she had wanted to drown herself in the loch if Padruig was executed by the Redcoats. Helen was old enough now to manage without her, Isobel had tried to justify to herself and planned to walk down to the loch. Being unable to swim, it wouldn't take long, she had hoped, so she dressed prepared to walk to the loch to drown.

Her heart was inconsolable to be parted again from her husband, despite his many flaws, especially if the reason was all over a secret debt, when he could have at least built the house before it snowed, yet again. Her daughter, Helen, had Grigor Og, a loving and trustworthy lad. Isobel told herself that the world didn't need her anymore. She had endured losing Fleur, being raped by Uncle Allan, the ravishing at the fort and had kept them all a secret. At least six dragoons had raped both her and her Aunty Margaret, then local Militia slashed Isobel five times with their bayonets agonisingly on the buttocks, before forcing her naked onto horseback for their own recreational races[3]. It was fortunate that she'd already had her family of three bairns because it wasn't going to be possible to have any more bairns after all of that internal damage and days of bleeding.

Isobel was lucky, except her husband was rarely at home. She had counted the years apart and together and while understanding that he was a soldier, she had hoped that farming would become his passion one day, but it still hadn't. Uncle Allan was probably right. He had left her for good this time. Isobel put on her shoes, while Helen was tending to her garden and she calmly planned her long walk to the loch. John Grant was at his late wife's graveside, as usual. He had more interest in the dead than the living, which Isobel could relate to, with her lost bairn Fleur buried still beneath the cold earth.

Isobel loved Helen dearly and wrote her a note and left her the Grant brooch that Padruig had given to her on their wedding day. As she departed the shieling, I saw her walking outside along the Drover's Road.

"Isobel, Isobel," I called. "What are you doing here? Where are you going?" I asked. Isobel's face was easy to read in her shocking condition.

"Hugh," she said. "He has left me. I am sure," she said. "Uncle Allan said he borrowed money from him to pay back your Da for a debt owed from when the Prince was with you all. Grigor had paid up his debt, he explained and your Da relieved all of you of your debt and that just left Alexander, Padruig and Oes Iain. Oes Iain couldn't pay, he said. Then Alexander died, so Padruig asked for money from Uncle Allan for Alex's share and I haven't seen him since," she said. "He may have gone to France. I have no reason to live now Hugh. Please let me go?" Isobel continued her walk to the loch.

Cautiously, I followed behind her, then gently took her arm and reassured her that we would do everything we could do to locate him and find the real reason for his departure. My opinion was that Allan would try to blacken Padruig's name, whom he had always hated, as well as the Chisholms.

"Come back with me Isobel," I pleaded. My heart was pounding. I was scared to death that this woman, whom I'd loved for so long, the Mither of my only bairn, could slip through my fingers in such a tragic way. "All three of us Glenmoriston men have met and discussed the situation about you and decided to finish your house for you before the next snows start. We will build it beautifully for you and will even enlarge it, so you will be happy, warm and safe. We will look after you. If Padruig never returns, I vow before God that I will marry you," I said. "You will have respectability. Please come back to the farm, so that we can all talk with Donald and Grigor too?" I implored.

Isobel pulled away, too burdened with grief and I had to pick her up and carry her sobbing and crying all the way back.

"But I can't give you another bairn. Please Hugh," she said. Holding back my own tears with that knowledge, I carried the love of my life, Isobel, to her shieling of too many years now. To hear her berate herself was more than sad. "Hugh, Hugh, I am nothing to anyone. I am useless now," she said. Her pleading was so tragic, I had to clarify to her just how much I loved her and I couldn't bear life without her in it, even if we were not yet married or if she couldn't give me bairns because Fleur meant the world to me, so her Mither had to, for my sake, live on. I had to beg Isobel to stay alive and she allowed me to carry her into her shieling, as she clutched onto me, grateful for the one human being who needed her.

Eilidh had brought food with her, but Isobel wouldn't eat. She was still inconsolable and as we sat on the shieling floor, she clung on to me and onto life. Grigor Og then ran to get Allan and Morag. The next few days were spent in both preventing Isobel from drowning herself and trying to obtain information on Padruig's whereabouts. Morag sat beside us knitting and I let the others know what had happened and that she was going to drown herself and drastic measures were needed.

"I am happy to finish building the house," I said. "Me too," said Donald. "Me too," said Grigor.

The whole time this discussion was taking place inside the wee shieling, all of the adults were crammed in as Isobel kept clinging onto me. Allan watched on at the scene, as did Isobel's Da in disbelief and Da spoke roughly to Allan. "You shouldn't have said that 'he might have left her for good'. We've all thought it a thousand times, but he's come back to her. He'll come back and there'll be a logical reason, even if it's just to pay Paul and you back," Da said. "You're right John, I am sorry. I didn't know that she would become suicidal. Isobel has always been so strong," he replied.

"It doesn't matter now," I said. "What's done is done and it is better that she knows Padruig was hiding something. It is not the first time he's hidden things from her, like when he was going to go to France. We all had to talk him out of that, but I'll do everything I can for her as well as you and Helen. We'll all build the family a nice house," I said.

Grigor Mohr then asked, "Why is she clinging onto you, Hugh? If Padruig was here, you'd be dead meat," he asked.

"She's trying to stay alive, which is something and she is not really conscious of it. It has knocked her badly. I could kill Padruig. I really could," I replied. Grigor had never known of our past association, or our wee bairn buried deep in the forest.

"Grigor, if Hugh is keeping her alive, leave them be, love," said Morag trying to keep the peace.

"I'll say this though, Hugh, if he really doesn't return or he's found dead or some such, I'll hold you to your word and you will marry her, despite your age difference," Grigor Mohr said, and I once again agreed to that. I knew that Grigor Mohr meant every word he said with that particular, severe MacGregor expression of his.

Grigor Og watched on worried about what the future held for all of them, including his and Helen's wedding plans.

"Da, what about our wedding plans, now that he's gone?" Grigor Og asked. Isobel's Father butted in and answered that question.

"Hand fast lad, hand fast, then one day when all is settled, we'll go to the Kirk before a Priest, but Helen is still yours," he said very defiantly. Helen moved over closer to her Grandda and said, "Thank you, Grandda." He then put his arm around her warmly. Donald had his arm around Eilidh, so Grigor Mohr put his arm around Morag, who looked very happy to have her husband's attention.

"Alright," said Donald, "when do we start work? First, I think we need to draw up a new floor plan of the house and its dimensions, rooms, chimneys, stairs and so on and work off the sketch. The current house that Padruig has started, in my opinion, is far too small, so it will need to be much larger," he added.

"Aye, I agree," I said.

"So, we'll need more stones. Grigor Og, can you cart more stones for us?" Donald asked.

"Aye," he responded.

"There's a storm coming in Eilidh. Can we eat now?" asked Donald. "We won't be able to start building today, but we can do the drawings at my place, where we have better light," he said conclusively.

After finishing the meal, the grateful men went on talking about sending someone up to Inverness to seek Padruig out.

"I can't leave Isobel in this storm," I said.

"We have to get going and start on that floor plan," Donald objected. Isobel had finally stopped sobbing and had fallen asleep on my lap, so I lifted her gently and placed her on her mattress, discovering that she still had my plaids and covered her over with a warm blanket. "Helen, can you sleep beside your Ma?" I asked. She agreed and climbed in for comfort and warmth.

Standing up in the wee shieling, my head was touching the ceiling and I hated having to leave Isobel. Donald asked Grigor if Morag could come over first thing in the morning and comfort Isobel and told Allan to ensure that she went nowhere near that damn loch. As I walked away from the shieling, my heart was breaking for the woman I'd loved since I was seventeen years old. After lengthy discussions over the house plan drawings, as I lay in bed that night, the storm came over and all I could see when I closed my eyes were the dead bodies, stripped naked at the edge of Culloden Field, thrown into a pile like lots of rubbish, one on top of the other, waiting to be burned [4]. One of them was my sixteen-year-old sweetheart, Emily. I had jumped down from my horse, recognising the coloured ribbon in her hair that I'd given her. She had gone there to watch the battle, to see her hero on the winning side. As I approached her on that dreaded pile, her eyes opened in recognition of me and then she died. I'd lost my virginity to Emily and we were going to marry one day. Frozen on the spot, Donald had grabbed me to leave the field immediately to escape, which I did, but in shock.

After having escaped from the battlefield, arriving at Craskie Farm with the other six of the Glenmoriston Men, Padruig Dubh's wife stood out the front on Drover's Road, holding her youngest lad. She was smaller than I had remembered from that night in Badenoch and she had the most beautiful, long flowing jet-black silken hair. Her beauty was like none I'd ever seen before in the Highlands or in our travels to England. Her eyes were really large and penetratingly pale blue. The sight of her again made my heart race in recognition and remembrance of that night that we had made love in Badenoch. I had desperately needed her and held her up against the carriage. It seems barbaric to think of it now like that, but we had an instant attraction. Most importantly, after Culloden, she was alive and her husband was leaving her and her bairns to save himself. His wife was alive. It went over and over in my mind. Why couldn't he appreciate that, for how much time did she have before the Redcoats came?

They were close behind us as we galloped off and I turned to see the expression on her face. Nothing but silent resignation. She raised a hand to me to wave, ever so slowly and I've loved her ever since. Maybe just because she was replacing the horrors of what I'd just seen in losing Emily and the horrors of Culloden, but me loving Isobel had never stopped after finding out that she had miscarried our bairn and I knew it never would.

She had willingly taken me into herself that night in Badenoch, which I had never quite understood. I was trying to annoy the woman pointed out to us by Cluny not to look at, nor go near, as she was Padruig's wife, so of course I had to slide my hand underneath her, after she had relieved herself. My brother Alexander had other ideas, so thank God for Donald, who knew what was going on and took her back to the carriage. It was my fault that it hadn't stopped there and I continued to pursue her. I had to have her. I was drawn to her, I needed her, I was no longer thinking with my head and I was scared of what battles lay ahead. She had given me strength and tenderness and yet here we all were, safe and abandoning such a soul, and of all people, I was hiding out with her husband.

Arguing with Padruig in our place of hiding, which was a very large cave with a small burn that ran through it, I accused him of neglecting his husbandly duties and we had a huge row. He justified his decision by saying we could all be hung or worse if we were caught, but his wife would be fine on the farm with her parents. Of course, she wasn't fine. The farm was burned down including all of the crops, her coos stolen and her father's Clydesdales were taken as well. All six of their crofters were burned out also. We had it confirmed, whilst living in the cave through my father, Paul Chisholm, that Padruig's farm had all been burned down with no knowledge of the where-abouts of his bairns or his wife. He only knew that a few of the crofter's wives had been ravished and a few men killed, as well as burned out. The survivors had all left for the coast where there was work in the kelp industry.

This news hit Padruig hard, but I had warned him and no one knew if Isobel was still alive until Grigor went down there to check on his wife, Morag and his only son, Grigor. He came back much relieved that both his wife and son were alive and fairly well. His house wasn't burned down and his son had been out with friends at the time that it had all happened and was able to give a full report of where the Militia were from and how many government soldiers accompanied them. His son had told him that the militia were from the Isle of Skye.[3] He'd gone on to report details of the damage and knowing of some people living in a shieling, not far from his house and in between both properties. He had seen a young girl, about twelve years old, with very long black hair, whose Mither appeared to be also inside the shieling, who sounded like Helen and Isobel.

When Grigor Mohr reported all of this back to Padruig, he was relieved to know that his daughter Helen was alive and pos-sibly Isobel too, but that was all. He didn't go himself to be certain that they were alive or in what condition. Surprisingly, he hadn't even enquired about his sons or his parents-in-law. His main ambitions were still to harass the Redcoats, wher-ever they were. He and Alexander MacDonald were a vicious fighting team of one mind and family didn't come first. We all, as the Seven Glenmoriston Men, were indeed a terror to any Englishmen or traitor to us Highlanders and that was our goal and, in a way, our own war continued against the mon-grels who had destroyed the Highlands. We hated them and I don't have any remorse for my part against the English and the Militiamen, especially the MacLeods from the Isle of Skye, not Raasay.

Eventually, the time came when we checked on our families, so we Chisholms checked on our parents in Chisholm lands. On one occasion, it wasn't Redcoats attacking Da, it was people we knew – the MacLeods. On one of those trips, either to check on Da or to get provisions later for the Prince when he turned up, we had to open an account with Da, because the Prince had a big appetite [3] and insisted on bread, so, the account was in Padruig's name. I sincerely hoped that my Father has had nothing to do with Padruig's disappearance. Da had lost everything and we had to help both him and Ma. The outstanding debts were all forgotten for a time, but as years passed and creditors began asking for their money back, he was then asking in turn for people to pay their debts back to him. He didn't say anything to me about approaching Padruig, but I knew Grigor had already paid his share of the debt. Partly from what Cluny gave us each and partly from his wages that he'd stashed somewhere from the time he had been with Lord Louden. Grigor didn't like debt for sure and Padruig would've expected Da to write it off, given that it was for the Prince, but we knew that he couldn't.

After everybody had been pardoned for their part in the Rising with the 1747 Act of Amnesty, we were all free to go back home, back to where most of us had no home to go to. Donald and I chose to be tenants in Grant country, close by to Padruig and Grigor's wee croft. Isobel's family were the only actual landowners out of the surviving members. Donald and I started a building contracting business because there was so much building to do and despite people still being cleared off their land, we stayed. We always thought that if Grant land was cleared too, we'd go back to Chisholm country and build a house there, but that never eventuated.

The problem was Eilidh. She wasn't strong anymore. She'd been ravished severely and yet Donald insisted on marrying her to care for her and didn't want to cause her any stress or overwork. They'd always loved each other, and he couldn't part with her, despite her now being unable to have bairns. The tenderness between them was always good for my heart, although I'd wanted a woman for myself and even with Padruig back at Craskie Farm, I had the constant desire for his wife, Isobel. We'd all sworn an oath to one another, to never surrender, but it did not include an unconditional allegiance to one another, even though that was how our gang operated. When my older brother Alex and Alexander MacDonald were set upon and killed, I felt differently. Both Donald and I had always looked up to our oldest brother and we felt lost without him. Donald then felt more responsibility towards me and we both feared who was around the next corner. Sometimes I still couldn't believe that Alex was actually dead, as well as Alexander MacDonald. They had seemed so indestructible. I wanted to know who had committed such a horrible crime against us all.

The odd coincidence was that two of those who saved Padruig Dubh's wife were dead and I was the only other one there that day, so I was especially defensive. It wasn't safe anywhere and despite the law against carrying weapons, I always carried my long rifle and my skein dubh and I got dogs. Two breeding Collies to appear innocent enough, but they were loyal and I bred from them too, for the coin. More people were getting sheep and needed sheep dogs, so every litter sold out before they were born. I stopped naming the puppies, so I wouldn't get too attached to them. I know that Eilidh did and would sometimes cry when each puppy went to a new home. Isobel was very attached to whichever pair I had at the time and was very interested in getting a trained dog, but Padruig wasn't. She loved my Collies.

We didn't hear much from Padruig when he went home to his farm, so I approached Allan MacDonald, whose farm overlooks Craskie, to get an overview. At first, we just chatted, but then I asked him directly how things were at Craskie with Isobel's family. His face altered and I knew there was a story.

"Padruig has financial woes," he said, "And he is slow to get crops into the ground to feed his family. Without the crofters' income from their rent, like it used to be and without John's teamstering income, I don't know how he'll manage," he said. "He's not a farmer's bootlace I'm afraid, no sense of the weather and when to plant things and he's not increasing his livestock. He might go under and lose the place. Poor Isobel," he said.

I hadn't known the stories behind what had happened with the crofters that had lived on Craskie and he filled me in, including the ravishing of a few of the crofter women and Isobel's Mither's death. I hadn't known that she'd lost her Mither, so Allan, seeing that I was interested, told me more. He was full of information and then he said,

"I suppose you've heard about my wife Margaret and what happened to both her and Isobel?" he said.

"Nae," I answered. "What happened?" I asked.

"My wife was killed by those cursed Redcoats, while you were plying that damn Prince with wine," he said.

He described the whole scene of negotiation of the forty coos to save Isobel's bairns, while they held Isobel by her arms behind her back and they weren't going to release her.

"After taking the coos for the lives of Margaret and the bairns, they then suddenly broke their word and snatched my wife, as well as Isobel and galloped off with both women, leaving me with the bairns," Allan said.

"I cared for them up at my house, because John was in no condition to care for them, but it wasn't until the next morning, wandering down with the three of them to John at Craskie, that two English soldiers came again and dropped what looked like two sacks of salt. It was Margaret and Isobel, stripped naked, but Margaret had a broken neck and was clearly dead with her head lolling around on her shoulders. I told John to take the bairns where they couldn't see their Mither, back to the shieling, then Grigor Og arrived and he was asked to keep them there. Margaret had to just be left for a time, while John and I desperately attended to Isobel, as her life was fast departing her. We both tended to Isobel's injuries up at my house, where we washed the dreadful wounds with water and whiskey and dressed her in some of Margaret's warm clothes. She was semi-conscious but the blood loss was awful," he said, remembering the scene.

"We didn't know how to stop the flow of blood and we just used touls and cloths and whatever we had to soak it up. She was as white as a ghost, her lips were going blue and John was getting panicky that she could die if the bleeding didn't stop, so we sent for Morag to help us," he said

"Isobel just kept repeating, 'Don't tell Padruig,' over and over. God, it was awful. Losing my wife. Trying to save Padruig's bairns. Trying to save Padruig's wife. It was the worse day of my life. Freya's death was bad enough with her decapitation and her arm chopped off. A nightmare for John to live with. I didn't ever think I'd see our lovely women in that condition. Freya, so dignified as she was, Margaret always caring for others and then Isobel, my special Isobel. My heart was breaking and I couldn't take it anymore and I fell to the floor weeping when finally, Morag came. When I finally collected myself, I saw that she was grey faced and weak herself, but she knew what to do. Isobel was still repeating, 'Don't tell Padruig.' God, I don't want to remember," he said as he wiped his face with a cloth.

"Isobel mumbled something about a white horse with blood on its back that she thought was an injury at first, but it wasn't and then the Militiamen suddenly slashed her bare buttocks with their bayonets, saying they wanted to see what the French would look like dead with the red blood against their white uniforms. She had been the first woman stripped naked in front of all those men. There were gashes, big, deep gashes on Isobel's buttocks," he said and wiped his face with his cloth again.

Isobel said again "Don't tell Padruig." We all promised Isobel, so you have to promise too," Allan said, almost crying with the memory.

"Aye," I said, "he'll nae hear it from me."

"It were those damn horse races at the fort. They stripped the women naked, then forced them onto the horses, bareback. Isobel was put on the white one, so the blood would seep all over its back. They enjoyed the spectacle, as well as who won. My poor wife couldn't ride a horse and fell off and split her head open on a rock and her neck was broken instantly. The dead women are all buried under a big tree out the back of the fort, apparently," he continued.

"We were lucky we got our wives bodies back at all. Isobel tried hard to recover from her injuries. She tried hard to smile at her bairns, but she couldn't walk for more than two weeks," he said with tears in his eyes.

"I'd taken her to your cave to be with Padruig, as I believed she was dying, so he was supposed to know of her being near to death, but one of your own must have known how to better treat her than any of us, so Padruig wasn't informed, as he wasn't there and she was moved before he returned. I suppose he'd have raided the Fort and been killed in the process, so it was important that he didn't know. More than anything, Isobel wanted Padruig alive. He'll never know what a gem of wife he has. Government forces were still looking for him, so they thought it a fair bonus to snatch his wife to please the Black Prince," said Allan.

He then went back to his farm after getting it all off his chest, but looking miserable, as was I.

It had been confirmed then that Isobel had been ravished, even though that's what we had assumed. I never told Allan of my brother Alexander, myself and Alexander MacDonald's role in saving Isobel. I had returned her to her shieling that day, wrapped in my plaids. Padruig would have killed us for sure, just for seeing her naked. I killed a hart that day after talking with Allan and took it around to Padruig, who just asked why.

"Just had one too many," I said. "Can you help me out and eat it?" I asked.

"Oh aye, well thanks Hugh," he said and he skinned and gutted it. I saw the woman I loved and all I could feel was deep sorrow, so I understood why she didn't want people to know. She didn't want anyone to start looking at her with pity in their eyes.

"How's the house coming on?" I asked. "Good enough. Time consuming business, house building," he said.

That was the last time I had spoken to Padruig before he vanished.

The storm of that first night was terrible. I heard several trees falling and I only hoped that they were oak trees for Isobel's new home. I started planning Isobel's house and I wanted it to be perfect. I couldn't stop feeling that she would be my wife and I was aroused every time I thought of her in bed. 'Could I imagine her sleeping beside me?' I asked myself. Her lovely long silken black hair, her beautiful face and enormous blue eyes and her slim legs and body next to mine? Could I imagine her nakedness being happily up against mine, with her large breasts pressed into my chest or her lovely small hand on my manhood delicately wanting to arouse me? Would she ever reach out to me in the middle of the night? I wanted to know what she smelled like up close, now she wasn't in the throes of death that she has no memory of. More than anything, I had to keep her alive for my own selfish reasons, to feel her, to smell her and to hear her beautiful voice telling me that she felt love for me. Even if she felt a tiny fraction of what I felt for her, I'd be a happy man.

I recalled that awful day Alexander and I had to work on her most delicate of feminine parts, missed by Morag, with Alexander MacDonald holding her so gently. Alexander, my brother with the seriousness of a surgeon, would never repeat what we had to do after first immersing her into that freezing cold water in the cave to stem the blood flow. An old Chisholm remedy taught to us by my grandfather with the knowledge handed down through generations of Chisholm's using herbs, and compresses, as well as our prayers chanted quietly. Alexander MacDonald, may God rest his soul, had never had to be involved in anything like this and I learned a compassionate side to him that he kept well hidden.

When I first lived in the cave, I was seventeen years old and keen to compare male genitalia and I was pleased that mine was bigger than Padruig's. All the Chisholms were well endowered, even Donald, although Grigor was close second then Alexander MacDonald third, then Padruig, then Oes Iain last. A few of us were circumcised and the rest weren't. I am not sure of the reason. It wasn't a religious thing because Padruig and I were both Catholic. I'd sometimes stand up against him when he was doing a pish, just to measure his size compared to mine and I was a good inch longer. Then he'd push me away from him for being too close, while expressing some Gaelic obscenities, of which he knew many. I enjoyed challenging the older man of our group. It always got him riled up. My brothers would enjoy the sport too, but Grigor used to shake his head as if to say I was acting too stupidly.

The pleasure I got from upsetting Padruig was worth the judgement.

Now, in this new situation with him gone, I could actually start to imagine Isobel beside me as my wife. She'd find me more handsome, I was sure of that, especially when she finds that I've got beautiful, soft blonde hair and much bigger manhood. I had more chest hair and I thought she'd like the feel of that. But first, the house. Donald and I went by Grigor's place to get the tools and we all went around to Craskie and it began. The oak trees that had fallen were going to be used for an addition onto the back of the current house and a veranda, as well as beds. Grigor Og's job was stripping down the trees, as well as carting stone. We had two new stone rooms built in no time, with chimneys and the roof covering part of the house that was to become Isobel's bedroom.

I overheard Helen offer her Mither a hot bath and she joyously lit a fire in the new fireplace to boil up enough hot water for her bath. I was stationed up on the roof, where I could peak at Isobel's nakedness without them knowing it. Isobel's skin was milky white and pure, but she had scars across her buttocks from that time at the fort when the Militiamen slashed her, but it wasn't ugly because her bottom was such a beautiful shape. Defying her age, she had a perfect body shape and her muscles were fit and strong. Her beautiful long hair fell to her waist now, mostly all black with only streaks of shining silver.

She was indescribably gorgeous. Her breasts were large, firm and round for such a wee lady, with dark brown nipples. I estimated each breast would fit comfortably one in each hand. Her bush was plentiful and pitch black and that was when I remembered again having to shave it all off in the cave that day, for my brother Alexander, to seek out all of her other injuries, finding that she was badly split from side to side. Alexander's cat gut stitches repaired all of the damage that we found and he poured a stinging whisky over it. It must have been excruciating. I was glad of her lack of consciousness at the time or surely, she could not have been able to bear it.

Then as she climbed into the bath water, my heart was racing, I felt a hand fall on my shoulder. It was Donald shaking his head and I subsequently moved away obediently from my vantage point. We had to carefully manoeuvre across the slate rooftop, so as not to be heard climbing off the roof and down the ladder. He took me further away from our house building project, so no one could hear us.

"What are you doing Hugh?" he asked.

"If I am to marry her, I want to see what I'm marrying," I candidly replied.

"I think you should work on the privies tomorrow and I'll finish the roof," Donald responded. He wasn't angry because he could never get angry with me being the youngest of the family, but he did also have curiosity and I could see that in his eyes.

When we were eating the food that Eilidh had prepared for us, Grigor was still working on the big oak front door. Donald, unsurprisingly, asked me,

"So, what does she look like?" I described her body, her taught milky skin, her curvy legs and inner thighs, her arms, her gorgeous breasts and her hair in detail.

"Nice body for sure. Is she too small for you?" Donald asked. I hadn't expected that he'd think my appendage was too big for Isobel, as I had always been proud of its size.

"Nae, she loved it in Badenoch," I answered. Donald cringed remembering the reality of that night, patted me on the thigh and said,

"I hope so brother, for your sake, but it won't hurt to take it nice and slow. But first she has to overcome the loss of her husband and the reason for his departure. That's what takes time. She first needs to overcome the pain of his departure and she's loyal to him as well as religious," he said.

"Religious?" I said.

"Aye. Both spiritual and religious. Being Catholic, she can't divorce him even if she wanted to and there's no cause for annulment," said Donald.

"You'd be doing us all a favour if you married her, if Padruig dies or never returns because Grigor and I are already married, but if he does come back, you'll have to face giving up your dream of marrying Isobel. She's too special to hurt in any way brother. Please don't compromise her faith again. You know how important that is. Us Catholics have copped it left, right and centre from the Presbyterian fanatics and the last thing we should do is harm each other, okay?" Donald said.

"You really know how to make a man feel bad for peaking at the woman of his dreams, but okay. The terms remain, if

Padruig dies or never returns," I said disappointingly. "I want to take her as my woman right now," I declared. With a sympathetic tone, Donald answered,

"I know and I understand, but you'll need to control your lust or find another," he said.

"Another?" I said. "Nae, I'll wait for her and I say that he deserves to lose her."

The oak trees that had fallen were perfect for my plans. Isobel would have a two-story wooden extension at the rear of the stone home, as well as an attic, all with slate rooves. I made my own nails and John went into Inverness with Grigor to get the rest of the stained-glass windows that Isobel had chosen and the door latches. Grigor's door was beautiful. I didn't know he could build a masterpiece like that. He had widened the entrance and the door was two meters wide. He finished it off with a polish, while waiting to hang it and I reminded him that there was a back door too that was needed, but not so large and shutters as well for all of the windows. He was happy to do those finicky things, so that they became a feature. Isobel was going to be happy now, we were sure of it.

Each day that passed, her health improved and both Allan and Morag ceased worrying about the loch duty. One day Morag said an odd thing to me.

"To think that she used to be so confident that she'd ride that yellow horse of hers into the loch without her Mither even knowing, those years ago. She was the best rider out of all of us," she said.

"What yellow horse would that be?" I asked.

"It was while she was teamstering with Da in the years before Patrick was born. Her Da bought her a beautiful yellow horse with a long flowing mane and tail. She named him Custard. She loved that horse. Poor thing," she said sadly.

"Who? The horse or Isobel?" I asked.

"The horse of course. The Redcoats killed it, then set it on fire. The smell was awful all around here and I heard that the hungry crofters ate some of her too," she said. "Isobel buried her Mither and what remained of her horse on the same day and she never talks of it. I think it is too painful. I don't think Padruig even knows she can ride a horse and with her being famous in these parts as the only woman teamster, there is so much he doesn't even know about his own wife. He was only interested in the Highland Independent Companies, first Lord Lovat then I lost count of who. His only interest was in fighting and he talked about it non-stop," she said.

"I know Isobel is aware of all his gifts in that way and she respects him for it, although it's not her way, but her Mither had begun to judge how blood thirsty he was becoming. Isobel always admired his leadership qualities and his acute awareness of his surroundings. She always thought that he was special. Don't tell anyone I said that to you, Hugh," Morag said. "I won't repeat it Morag, but how can she be herself without her horses?" I asked. "Aye. Good question. Da can't live happily without his Clydesdales, as well as his beautiful wife, but I have faith in Isobel. She's not just made up of horses or religion or farm work or finances, community, bairns or any one thing in particular because she has had to spread herself out over her world, as she knows it and is unafraid to learn a new skill, like making goat's cheese," she said with a smile.

"It helps that she was raised by John and Freya with so much love and she can give that love back to the world and who is living in it, including Padruig, who most women would find impossible to love and very boring," she added.

The news Isobel had waited for, finally came by way of a rider who'd come all the way on horseback from Inverness. I was both happy and sad to hear that Padruig was alive and well, but on board a ship bound for New France. He had signed up with the British Armed Forces after all and God only knows for how long he'd be gone. The story was that he was forced or pressed into service, but I knew him, if he didn't want to do something, you couldn't force him to do it. I also received a letter from my Mither around the same time, still in Chisholm lands, to tell me that my Father, Paul Chisholm, was also on his way to New France having also signed up for service, so that he could pay his bills. I had a horrible feeling that they were on the same ship to fight for the 78th Fraser Highlanders. The difference between them was that my Father wasn't a trained soldier and could easily die over there. Da was going to send Ma his wages for both her and his creditors. Isobel received no such assurance. I was really starting to lose the respect that I once had for one of our group.

I discussed Ma's letter with Donald and we both thought that Padruig and Da had somehow met up in Leith and left on the same ship together, both to repay their respective debts. I really hoped that Isobel had a miraculous gift to get her through this current situation, both financially and emotionally. We weren't sure whether to tell Grigor Mohr at first, but we did and although very disappointed in his friend, he accepted it as a reality that we were all going to have to live with, possibly for many years, with a strong chance that neither man may return. We all felt the burden of his absence. Isobel wrote frantically to Padruig to acknowledge receiving the message and knowing where he was and that he was alive. Of course, she blamed a third party for 'kidnapping' Padruig, which made her feel better, but Donald and I were feeling guiltier by the day if it was indeed on our Father's insistence.

All we could do was to help Isobel and her family, but without Padruig's death, my personal hopes were temporarily dashed at having her as my wife, unless he was killed in battle or if the ship somehow fell foul of the French navy.

It was going to get harder for me being so near to Isobel, smelling her glorious scent, hearing her soft, sweet voice and watching her fluid way of walking, without ever having sex with her. God help me. If I stood still for a moment to observe her beauty, my appendage would respond and I confess to wanting to make passionate love with her every day. I imagined lifting her dress and feeling all of her femininity. I wondered if her body was responding to my presence again like she did in Badenoch, when I had her on that night before the army marched to Edinburgh. I had to have her again was all I could think of.

Helen and Grigor Og were hand fasted at a wee celebration that Isobel held at her new home that we had all had finally finished. I tried to be happy for them, but I had wanted it to be me and Isobel. Our bairn lay dead in a lonely grave in her forest by the Pict stone, 'why couldn't God give Isobel to me?' was a constant question. That night I was close to tears all over again. Allan had provided the beef for the celebration and miraculously, Isobel and Allan had moved both Patrick and his wife, Henrietta back home to re-join their bairns, who had already been living there without their parents. Isobel had staged an intervention by first visiting the Reverend John Stewart to ask what was happening over at Henrietta's parents' farm. Isobel had made her first move at reclaiming her life and Patrick her son, was a big part of it.

Now with more coos, she had also taken on a wee cottage industry, sewing and selling the product or in our case, being gifted a beautiful linen shirt. My old shirt was a rag, I admit and I felt handsome again in the new one that she'd made me with her own hands. Donald and Grigor too looked smart in theirs, as did Da and Allan. She was definitely better. It felt very special to wear a garment made with her own hands and it was such a perfect fit. She must have looked at me occasionally, I thought, to get the size so perfect. She had to have measured across my big broad shoulders and my chest.

There was a donkey bought with the money she earned selling dresses and men's shirts, as well as two highland ponies, three goats, geese, an ox and eventually, black faced sheep. I admit, the black-faced sheep were a shock and for someone that knew nothing about sheep or goats, I was impressed. She had Grigor Og working harder than I've ever seen a lad that age work and he was totally dedicated to Helen, to Isobel and the dirt that he wanted to grow the oats in. Eventually, he had a beautiful summer crop of oats. The potatoes that we'd all recommended, were all flourishing, as was her corn, kale and neeps and a lot of herbs that I've never seen or heard of before. For medicine, she said, or flavouring the stews. Donald would still ask her for medicine for his wife, so I suppose it must have been medicinal.

Isobel's stews were addictive. I much preferred her food to Eilidh's, so I tried to eat over with her as often as possible and she loved my Collies, who loved her back. She'd fuss over them and rub them dry if they were wet, in turn they'd lick her face and for the first time in months, I actually heard her giggle when playing with the Collies. It put a smile on my face and she kept on sewing and selling, sewing and selling to prepare for a clipping season and she'd even bought the right pair of clippers for me to clip the sheep. I think that meant that I was now working, at least for one clipping season, at Craskie Farm, while she and her lady friends started up the wool waulking. The atmosphere around Craskie was wonderful and communal with the singing voices of the ladies. I felt happy for the first time in years.

I couldn't stop myself from feeling her femininity and on one occasion as she walked close to me, I held her in my hand hoping she wouldn't pull away, and she didn't. Her hand went up underneath my kilt to feel my manhood, as hard as it was. Holding each other's, we looked into each other's eyes like as if to say that's enough time now that has passed. There was no one around and we kissed passionately before I was inside her up against the wall. Her body was ready for me to enter again and again and she kept on kissing me frantically, making joyful sounds. I was happy then knowing I could do it again.

There were lads there who had been selling Isobel some fish from the loch, Hugh and Hamish Chisholm were their names. I taught Hamish how to wash the sheep in the burn and how to clip the sheep. There were a few sheep that wrestled out of his control, and we had to set the dogs on to them to bring them back. It was worth the laugh that we heard from the ladies, who were all watching on. Hamish had an interested young lass, I thought and would go bright red whenever he saw her or if she smiled at him. She was a homely lass, whose

Mither was with her, so nothing happened with them at first. Her Mither, Mairi, was the lead singer of the wool waulking group and she was teaching Cora, her lass, all of the many songs. It helped the time pass by quickly, as each lady had brought their own sheep and paid us coin separately before they left each time with their shorn sheep.

I was happy to be a part of Craskie Farm and watching it grow because of Isobel's new-found inner strength. Sometimes, I'd remember those awful gashes, now scars, on her buttocks and felt a bit guilty for spying again on her nudity, but that never measured against the guilt and shame I felt for what I did to her on that dark night in Badenoch. Wee Fleur was miscarried because of me, I thought and I felt God was not happy to give me another bairn. I couldn't help wanting to know just who had slashed her like that and if I knew, I'd kill them for sure. Equally, if Padruig knew of what I had done to his wife, one of us would no longer be alive. One of Isobel's scars was very deep and long and it must have been extremely painful at the time. Morag had to have stitched the skin back together without pain relief on that day. I'd want to run my hand down each scar on her luscious buttocks just the same. Then I'd try and put it out of my mind and stay focussed on the present.

The letters from Padruig were infrequent, but the battle in Quebec had been won and he was trying to return home to Scotland, he said. I estimated it would just be a few months, but it was much longer. Thank goodness Grigor Og was on the farm every day to help her, while Donald and I completed our building tasks nearby. She loved Grigor Og dearly as her own son and Patrick took over the role of taking care of the growing herd of coos. They were all following Isobel's orders, even Da, except when he decided independently to have more trees taken down for an additional oat field.

Allan was still worried about the status of her land and was taking her in to see a lawyer in Inverness. I had wanted to go too, but thought I'd better not make it too obvious to her family that I was in love with her. She has no memory of the day that she had clung onto me, hanging on to dear life, let alone the cave. I would rub my waist sometimes where she had held me just to remember how it had felt and I missed her physically and I never removed the necklace she gave me. God, how much I missed her. Even if I saw her every day, I'd miss her when going back to Donald's place. I think she loved me, but I needed to hear it. I wanted to live on Craskie Farm somehow as a permanent employee, when it would be possible. That was my goal so I could be nearer to her every day and night.

I had to have sex with her again after that day against the wall, or I'd go mad. I remembered exactly what it had felt like on that night, so warm, so welcoming, so loving and in the forest near our wee Fleur. Could we make love again near our wee Fleur? Would she come with me and agree to that? Then unexpectedly, one day as I worked, Isobel asked me to join her to visit Fleur with yellow wildflowers she had picked from beside the burn. We strolled slowly deep into the forest after Grigor Mohr had left for the day and I knew I wasn't going to be able to control myself alone with my woman. Donald's words had been forgotten and I lay my plaid near the wee grave and asked Isobel if she would have me again. My love for her was never going to abate, which I told her.

She reached out her small hand for me first and I knew then that I would always be accepted. We made love that day and many other days in the whole time Padruig was gone with only Donald knowing on occasion. Our passionate love making could only be dreamed of, I had thought, as I lifted her dress and kissed and sucked her most delicious spot, while lifting her from her buttocks. I was like a ravenous wolf and I had to have every part of her. I wouldn't wash my face after those days, so her fragrance could sleep alongside me on the nights alone at my brother's house. She loved our sex together and was equally hungry for anything I had wanted to do or asked of her.

I got along well with the fisher lads, as she called them, Hugh and Hamish and wished that they too would always remain on the farm. Both lads called me Uncle Hugh, which was nice and so too did Helen and Grigor Og. We were a family of sorts, who frequently breakfasted, lunched and dined together. At every opportunity I would hold her femininity in my hand, even when others were around, but where they could not see and it felt good to challenge our boundaries. Similarly, she would stand in front with her back to me and move her buttocks over my erection side to side with Grigor Mohr in the room, because he was always the biggest challenge. She knew it would be nearly impossible for me to make no sound, but somehow, I managed to suppress it. We would always try to make love afterwards in private after one of those occasions. One day she put her hand straight up my kilt and started to massage my member and as she was kissing me, just as I was embracing her, we were then seen by my brother. The expressions on our faces gave us both away. He asked me that night after that if Isobel had fallen in love with me and I answered honestly that I thought so, but I didn't elaborate. Of course, he wanted details, but I simply told him that I would not ask him about himself with Eilidh.

Another dog had been introduced onto the property. It may have been an Irish Setter, but I wasn't sure and Isobel seemed keen to have him with Grigor Og whenever he was alone. After being in town again today, she bought Grigor Og a much-needed ox for ploughing the new field and he was in love with that ox. I was going to have fun with Grigor Og over that one day. She had sorted out the land apparently. Grigor Og and Helen, as well as Patrick, would inherit Craskie after both her and Padruig died, which really pleased the young couple. Grigor Mohr had a bit of an attitude because they could not yet use the MacGregor name on the title but would do in time. It was one way of Isobel paying a dowry, I suppose because she had nothing to give to Grigor Mohr and they all did not want to lose Grigor Og.

I'd often see Isobel wandering into the deepest part of her woodland and I wouldn't usually follow her, unless we were going to make love, but I was curious, and I was becoming very protective too. She'd never come back with mushrooms, and I knew she must be visiting Fleur, but there was something else that I knew I hadn't yet understood. I stealthily followed her one day until she reached her Pict stone, near our wee bairn's grave and all she did was sit down in front of it and at first, she was peaceful and quiet, but then it became strangely misty and I could barely see her. I could hear her speaking in Gaelic, and I wanted to know who she was talking to. Was she talking to Fleur? So, I got closer, but she was still alone at the Pict stone and she was conversing and listening, as you do when you are talking with someone else. As she spoke, it became hypnotic and there were misty figures all around her. It seemed like she was thanking them and in a prayerful way, asking them for their continued support. She then fell into a deep sleep and while she slept, they formed an impenetrable force about her. I decided it was time I left this forest. I was definitely in the wrong place and wrong for having invaded her privacy again. Maybe she was one of those who connected with the ancestors of Auld and I saw her in a different way as I departed.

Grigor Mohr had been acting strangely while he'd been continuing teaching Padruig's and Isobel's grandchildren how to ride. There was something on his mind. Isobel's abilities with the horses had been kept a secret in case Padruig had caught on about the races at the fort. I put it down to Isobel having horse riding abilities all along, that he may have found out about. 'She couldn't bear Padruig looking at her differently,' is what Allan had said. So, it had to be a secret for now. On top of that, I think the loss of that yellow horse and the Clydesdales was too heartbreaking to speak of. One day, I wanted to buy her a yellow horse too. She had written Grigor Mohr a letter before going to that lawyer in Inverness about his son's inheritance on Craskie Farm and I knew he hated the topic of Proscription against the MacGregor name. She might have offended him. He was easy to offend, like most MacGregors, but I liked that about Grigor. I had always been able to trust him. Maybe he thought that he should have inherited too because there was no dowry for himself, but that would have been impossible for Isobel.

Then one evening when we were all at Isobel's while standing right in front of Donald and I, Grigor Mohr intentionally put his arm around Isobel. I panicked for a moment. Had he made love to her? Was he in love with her too? I told him very seriously to take his arm off her, but he said that she was his sister. Of course, both Donald and I didn't believe it and said it was a good lie.

Then Donald told him that Padruig was due back soon and he'd better not do that or someone might die. Grigor Mohr then defiantly wrapped his arms around her and just as I was going to hit him, Da had to intervene. "She is his half-sister," he said. "He's Freya's son, my stepson," he said, proudly looking upon Grigor Mohr. It was all explained to us and Donald understood first because my emotions were running too high.

"It's okay brother," he said. "They are half brother and sister and didn't know until last night when Isobel was singing a song that her Mither had taught her, that he recognised, and Grigor pulled out a wee carved wooden Clydesdale from his sporran." Grigor then told us, "Da made this for me when I was wee and he wanted to raise me as his own, but my MacGregor family disallowed it and so I lost my Ma and possible stepfather. One day, I saw Isobel driving the team, but I didn't know that she was Da's bairn and later when she married Padruig, I didn't recognise her as that same teamster lass. She'd had a plaid over her head when I saw her before that," he said. Grigor was glowing, knowing he had a sister. Donald stood up and hugged him. "Congratulations, Brother. I am so happy for you both," he said. I realised just how jealous I had been, but I had to congratulate him too. "Was Freya Clan Gregor then?" I asked. "Aye, she was the widow MacGregor when Da married her, but she was born to a different branch of Clan Gregor who lived at Loch Insh. She was never to tell Isobel that she was half Clan Gregor," he said. "Isobel is not at all like a MacGregor," mentioned Donald.

"Nae, she's got the ancestors in her, I guess. We'll never know which one," Grigor Mohr said. "Which ancestors?" I asked. "Pict," he replied. "Could be from King Bridei from Inverness, or some further back in time to near Urquhart Castle," he said. Jokingly, I said, "So, she could be like a Princess of Auld?" "Aye," Grigor Mohr replied, "she's my princess," kissing her on the cheek and she kissed him back. My blood began to boil and Donald held my leg and I knew that this wasn't a fight that I could win. When I went to bed that night, I wept. It was stupid, I know, because I didn't want to be her brother, but he could openly kiss her in public and touch her, over and over. I tossed and turned that night and it was driving me crazy. It was bad enough that Padruig was now in London and coming back to Scotland, but one of my best friends was smooching my precious Isobel in public. More than ever, I just wanted to snatch her for myself. Elopement came into my mind or killing Padruig. Lots of crazy stuff. I had to get her.

The following morning, I saw Grigor Mohr and Isobel embracing by the tree line and they went into the forest together and I decided to follow them out of curiosity. I was jealous seeing them embrace and looking so happy to see each other, even though they had told me that they were brother and sister on Isobel's Mither's side. I suddenly came to an abrupt stop in the forest when I saw that someone else had followed them in too. A tall, skinny English looking fellow, wearing big grey coat and grey breeks with a cap that covered his hair, was hiding behind a large oak tree. Then I saw that he was carrying a dirk.

His hand then fell on the dirk, as he watched both Isobel and Grigor Mohr intensely. He was going to either kill them both or rob them, as I saw they were fiddling with each other's hair, unaware that they were being observed. I knew I'd have to rush this fellow and grab him before he grabbed that dirk. Then, in a flash I was on him and held a tight grip around his neck and dragged him out of the forest. The dirk had fallen on the ground where he had been standing and he was gasping for air as I dropped him on the ground to kill him, only to see that it was Padruig.

"Hugh!" he said. "Stop, it's me!" he yelled.

"God. Padruig, what are you doing creeping around like that? I was going to kill ye," I said.

"It's Isobel," he said. "She's with Grigor Mohr. I'll kill them both, so don't get in my way you idiot," he said.

"You're the idiot, they're brother and sister. The MacGregors wouldn't give him to John to raise when he was wee. They only just found out themselves," I explained. "'Twas lucky I stopped ye. Now, what are we going to do?" I asked. "How bout you go back out to the Drover's Road and leave it a while before you come back in? You're a day early anyway," I suggested.

"Aye, I'll go back out. Maybe stay the night at James Grant's place and come back tomorrow," he added.

"Maybe he could lend you some clothes too. You look ridiculous," I added.

I noticed he was much thinner than he used to be and was looking pale.

"You alright?" I enquired.

"Aye. See you tomorrow, probably," he said and he left. Misunderstandings in this case could have cost them their lives, as well as his. We agreed we wouldn't mention it to anyone. I noticed as he was leaving that he had a slight limp and was slouching, feeling stupid I suppose. His homecoming not being what any of us could have expected, but I thought I'd better get that dirk before it was noticed. Picking it up, the two of them were embracing again. 'Lucky for some,' I thought.

I went back to my place to wash before returning to Craskie when Donald entered the house calling out to his wife.

"Eilidh's not here," I said.

"I haven't seen Padruig yet," Donald said.

"I have," I said. "Nearly bloody killed him. He was going to kill Isobel and Grigor with this," I said as I produced the dirk.

"Why?" Donald asked. Telling him the story, I remembered that I wasn't supposed to mention it, so I asked him not to mention it.

"Aye," Donald agreed, "So, he is coming back tomorrow then?" he asked.

"Hope so," I said.

"That gives us time to build another stable. Grigor and I have bought him a horse to replace that old thing that he had, which must have been left in Leith," said Donald.

Padruig's early return wasn't revealed to anyone other than Donald and Padruig who loved the horse we gave him, despite forgetting to feed it. That night, he abused Isobel horribly in order to restore his role as head of the family, he thought, but no one forgave him for his methods. He and his 78th Fraser Highlander friends had overheard militia conversation on the ship about their inability to catch him in '46 and so had taken his wife instead, referring to Isobel. His friends and Padruig slit their throats and threw them overboard that night. Obtaining this information from Isobel, involved both Grigor and Padruig and it made me sick to the stomach and I was even more determined to marry her. She could have disclosed our love, but she didn't. The plans went ahead to get my house on Craskie Farm and I became a permanent employee as an overseer, but it is quite a story. I ended up just about running the place and security became very important.

After old Allan died, he left his place to Padruig, probably because of a guilty conscience, which gave Padruig more land for oats and Grigor Og was thrilled with that. After his Da passed away too, we were all terribly sad, especially young Grigor, but the strangest thing was that Isobel was seeing him as a ghost. She had always confided in me and I would keep a watchful eye on her all those years and never stopped loving her. I wasn't going to allow Padruig to hurt her again.

Later that day, she came up to me and she said that she had had a dream and wanted to know if something in the dream had actually happened. She asked me if she had clung to me when Padruig had disappeared because she couldn't remember it. "Aye," I said. And I told her how I had stopped her from going to the loch and I'd carried her back to the shieling, sobbing and crying.

"Oh Hugh," she said. "I am so sorry. Please forgive me," she said.

"Isobel, you know that you can cling to me anytime and I would be a happy man," I had jested and she smiled at me coyly.

"Do you love me really, Hugh?" she asked me directly. I answered honestly.

"I have loved you since I first saw you and even more when we both shared the loss of wee Fleur. You clung to me after Padruig's disappearance and we all agreed that I would marry you if Padruig died or failed to return. I still love you, Isobel. One day, you will marry me, you'll see," I said with a smile. She reached out her hand to me and I took her small hand and kissed it.

"Won't I be too old to marry, Hugh," she asked.

"You'll never be too old for me," I said, and I held her tightly to me. The feeling was sorrow for a love lost. I kissed her forehead, I knew that Padruig was away for the day, then kissed

her cheeks. "I have coffee inside my house if you'd like some," I said, and she followed me inside.

No one was around and as soon as we walked in the door, I couldn't control myself and rubbed my hands up and down her back and then across her buttocks without any objection. "Hugh, oh Hugh," she said without resisting me. "I know about the scars on your buttocks," I said. I caressed her buttocks partly to make the pain of the day it had happened go away, but mostly because the love of my life was once again in my arms. Lifting up her long dress, I kneeled and gently kissed each scar and fondled her beautiful round bottom, then my hand slipped between her thighs and immediately found the part of every woman's secret desires because I knew every centimetre of that part of her body. I stood massaging it and she was instantly in another world with her arms wrapped around me. "Hugh," she screamed reaching her height of pleasure. I didn't know that a woman could reach that peak of pleasure and my heart was racing. Entering her this time had a different quality about it, as we made love on the kitchen table. She began to cry and the tears rolled freely down her face. I wiped them away, but we were thinking the same thing. Padruig was back.

Then with sadness in her eyes, she said, "My husband will be reunited with us all, which makes me happy, but it also makes me sad. I was loyal all those years to an oft times absent husband, almost imaginary husband as you know and my wedding vows have only been threatened by you. For the first and only time in my lonely life, I have been so tempted only with you, even though you are younger and far more beautiful than I. I would miss you too much if you stopped coming to Craskie and stopped eating meals with us. We have all become a happy family. It hit me hard that maybe I would never see you again and I don't know what to do. I am married, but I love you so much Hugh. Please tell me what we can do?" she said with tears in her eyes.

Wiping her hair from her face, I was ecstatic to hear her say that she also loved me and so I began, "I will never love another but you, Isobel, but we can't break up your marriage. I will wait for you your whole life and live on Craskie. Give me land there to live on, so I can be a permanent employee. I will build the house, so long as I have a lifelong contract from you both rent free. Hugh Og can live with me and pay rent. Put me in your wee pay book before Grigor Og or Padruig sees it, as an overseer. Then, I can eat with you as often as you like. I can help you with your sheep. You can keep playing with my Collies. We won't be married legally or before God, but we won't ever need to be apart," I said sadly, almost choking.

"You won't take another woman?" she asked, looking afraid of the answer.

"Nae, I will never take another woman on one condition," I said. "Aye?" she said. "Kiss me Isobel and touch me and there will be no other woman," and she did, passionately.

Her lips were so soft and sensual and her lovely warm hand wrapping around my manhood sent me into those realms of delight unable not to vocalise the joy. She kneeled down and kissed my member and I asked her to take the fullness of it into her mouth, which she did. Gently caressing her beautiful head, her tongue unexpectedly searched each part of my member and I was unable to stop the inevitable groaning at the extremes of pleasure that I reached. I then raised her up, then holding her up by her knees and in the standing position, I entered my beloved, hard once again and she squealed a joy that gave me goose bumps, thrusting as I reached my peak again. In some peculiar way she was now vowed to me, as well as Padruig. She always satisfied me and gave me whatever I asked of her and I know that I always satisfied her. She believed that I was the most beautiful man on this earth and she especially loved my yellow hair. That always felt good to know because I had often been teased by other men about my yellow, blonde hair. To Isobel I was like a Celtic God and that was good for my male ego.

My life then was on Craskie Farm with all of the farms' comings and goings and I was aroused at the sight of Isobel every day. Donald departed for Canada which made my life lonelier and in more need of her. We'd meet in so many places on that property and often I would meet up with her in the goat shed and make passionate love with her there, exploring each other's bodies and needs even before slaughtering a sheep and my hands never stopped wandering over my beloved Isobel, squeezing and sucking her beautiful full breasts. Chisholm House was the only place where we were nearly caught out, as Padruig was coming up there to see me. Having fallen asleep, we were both naked after love making when Grigor Og unexpectedly came to warn us and he helped his mother-in-law dress and pretended to Padruig that we were having smoko and made the tea.

He had known about us since the day in the shieling and the loch and the goathouse but said nothing to either his Father or Padruig because of what would happen to Isobel if he did. We even made love many times beside her precious stone and Fleur's grave in the forest and on those days, it was like a small death and entering Heaven, only to wake up to the mist all around us as she began to talk to the misty figures in another language. It wasn't Erse or Gaelic, I do believe she had finally learned the language her Mither knew when she spoke to the swans. I knew that my Isobel was very special and I never stopped appreciating her in so many ways.

Isobel stayed married to Padruig and cared for him until his last breath and then we hand fasted before the Priests had even left after Padruig's funeral. She was finally my wife. Mrs Chisholm. As old as we both were, she clung to me in that same way every night until the night of the Art Gallery Opening, when she passed away. She had longed for love and I do believe I gave her that, every moment of every day of what remained of her life. Grigor Og had always loved his Mother in Law and wanted me to stay in the main house because all of their hearts were broken as well, at her passing.

Her beloved son Alex had returned to live nearby in Loch Garry and he loved his Mither too, that was obvious and surprisingly, he loved me too. He had a twin sister, whose name was Marion, who was carefully protected from the likes of Allan. She had been raised in Loch Insh, married a man of Clan Nachten and had two lads before her husband passed away from illness. Alex met her on his return and Padruig learned of her and met her shortly before his death. Ewen loaned the family his home after his family moved.

Marion occasionally worked in the main house when Meredith was tired. The rest of the time she was at her new-found twins' farm in Loch Garry working in the house, cooking and cleaning. Her oldest son, Malcolm, ended up working with Alex permanently at Glengarry, but Kenneth remained at Craskie working with me on the graves and whatever else was needed and then moved into the big house.

It's impossible to describe the loss of such a one as Isobel of Glenmoriston, my great love. I wept all day long, while I waited for them to bring her to me to take her to her grave, after I had to dig up my wee bairn, Fleur, in her casket. I carried Fleur. Isobel wore the gold wedding band that I gave to her on our wedding day and she wanted to be buried with it, as well as with our wee bairn Fleur. It was the only wedding ring that she had ever worn and she told me she would always wait for me in her Afterlife. Her tombstone now reading, 'Isobel MacGregor Grant Chisholm, wife of Hugh Chisholm', with Marion Grant and Fleur Chisholm's names added to her list of children.

John Fraser and his wife Anna, along with Beth and Simon, had come that day to install free standing lamps and candles for the Chapel, only to be greeted with the terrible news. When Grigor, Patrick, Helen, Alex, Marion, Henrietta and all of her grandchildren were ready, as well as Gillcrest MacLachlan, Ewen MacNachten, Hugh Og and Meredith, Hamish and Cora, Dougal, Milread and Bruce MacKay, John and Anna Fraser and Matilda MacMartin, I led them all to her wee Chapel to her favourite piped tune. She didn't want fuss, were her clear instructions and to be buried within twenty-four hours after her passing, with Fleur.

After lowering my wife into the ground, the hardest part was closing it over with the decorative tombstone. Unable to stop weeping, I sat in one of her pews and I just hoped that it wouldn't be too long for me to join her in her world, if she would allow it. Alex and Grigor, whom I'd grown to love as my family, sat with me and we all wept together, accompanied, one by one, by the rest of the family. I would still need to arrange the newspaper notice and the Priest for the formal mass.

At least Isobel would be at peace now, knowing our wee Fleur was finally buried in a House of God and despite everything, I knew that I was her great love and I could feel the love from their grave.

Meredith and Marion had cooked up some beautiful food, sufficient to feed us all in the main house. When I looked to our bedroom door, I saw Isobel smiling at me with her hair long and black once again and she was beckoning me to our bedroom and I lay on our bed reaching for her.

The great love of my whole adult life, Isobel.

Grigor Og Macgregor's Story

"Glenmoriston on Fire"

By Zaynab El-Fatah

Illustration by Halima Karger

Glenmoriston,
Scotland, 1746

I had just turned thirteen and two of my rebellious young friends and I, whose Fathers like mine, were absent, decided to steal tobacco from English dragoons and MacLeod Militia, who had come to the Braes of Glenmoriston. A group of them were taking a break at an alehouse, when we snuck up behind them and relieved them of what was in their pockets, while they sat and drank unawares. I heard the militia saying they were from the Isle of Skye who planned to break into three groups. [3]

Not yet having tried tobacco rolled into a cigarette, I thought it was going to be an adventure, knowing Da was far away in a cave, hiding out from the government soldiers, so we all had good reason to feel rebellious, in following in our Fathers' footsteps. It was quite the walk from our house, but it was worth it, even though the air was already smoky. We thought that this would be to our advantage because no one would see the smoke rising from our hand rolled cigarettes that we'd roll and smoke. It was a grab and run exercise and then we hid behind a rock wall, Bruce, me and Dougal.

My name is Grigor Og MacGregor, son of Grigor MacGregor of Glenmoriston.

What these dragoons and militia's purpose was in Glenmoriston wasn't really on our minds, so long as we got the tobacco. Bruce also relieved one soldier of his wee purse. It contained coin, amounting to 10 pounds Scots, which we shared between us three.

We untied the dragoon's horses, that were tethered nearby and loosened the girths on all of their saddles. We hoped we'd see a few soldiers fall from their horses, which we did and at least four horses just wandered off to eat greener grass, far away from the alehouse. It was a laugh and an enjoyable morning out, as we all wanted to contribute in some way against the English and the Scots who fought alongside with them against us in the Highlands.

After we'd smoked as much as we could without feeling sick, I noticed that the air was getting even thicker with smoke and all of the soldiers had gone. Looking down the narrow Drover's Road, there were fires erupting everywhere, as far as the eye could see. Glenmoriston was on fire. Bruce panicked about his Mither and ran as fast as he could to check on her, knowing she was alone and his Father had told him to mind his Mither in his absence.

The three parties of MacLeods from the Isle of Skye were rummaging up and down the glen. They destroyed the ploughs and harrows from the farms, as well as pots and pans and all household furniture, even the stone querns on which to grind corn, breaking them to pieces[3]. It was an unbelievable sight that I could not comprehend and cringed at the value of those items being destroyed.

Dougal and I, not panicking, walked cautiously taking in the scene, amidst smoke and fires, were just too blasé to fear for our Mithers and watched Bruce until he was out of sight. The scene was a bit surreal. The smoke became thicker and thicker and I was beginning to regret having inhaled the cigarette smoke, as it was becoming harder to breathe in the air. I decided on that day that I would never smoke again. The further we walked down Drover's Road, we saw that more farms and crops were on fire and when we reached our immediate neighbour, Craskie Farm, we witnessed those same English soldiers and MacLeod Militia from the alehouse, noisily pouring out of there, with at least forty coos and all eight of John Grant's Clydesdale horses and his carriage. We regretted not having taken this day more seriously then. Observing Craskie Farm from behind a rock wall, I thought I saw a headless body laying on the ground and a woman being chased up and down between the fires with a look of sheer terror on her face.

Both of us then ran to our Mithers' crofts next door and as we entered, Dougal's Mither called us over to her home just when I was going to check on Ma, but she insisted. "Nae lad, your Ma is sick. Stay here wi' me a while," she said. We had a piece of bread each and a cup of tea. I had to check Ma, so I excused myself even though the door appeared locked, which it never was except at night-time. I tried to open the front door, but it was locked and I called out to her and there was no answer. I couldn't get in, when I heard Bruce calling out to me for help from his croft. His Ma had a terrible facial injury, where one side of her face had been sliced off and her cheek was hanging by just a few sinews and she was bleeding pro-fusely. Her eyes rolled and she died right in front of us. I had never seen anyone die before and I had only heard the grue-some stories from my Father, Grigor MacGregor and I prayed that he was here. We all helped dig a grave for Bruce's Mither, while Dougal's Mither had us all stay with her. "Where's my Mither?" I asked her. "She is not well lad. Stay wi' me until she is well," was her answer.

The following morning, I awoke early having slept outside with a blanket in the cold at Dougal's house. I was grateful that it wasn't winter. Feeling hungry, I glanced across at our house and the door was still locked and there was no sign of a fire being lit. I decided to go for a walk behind our house, passed the peat mounds, where there was an old pathway leading to an unused old shieling which led then onto Craskie Farm. On my way there, a beautiful girl stood on the path in front of the wee shieling. It was like a dream. The wind blew her black shimmering hair as she turned toward me. It was like seeing an 'other worldly being' or a fairy. She was so beautiful with big blue eyes and she looked straight at me. I stood still, not sure of what to say or do because I didn't know her or if she was even real.

Then coming out of the shieling was her Mither, I think, asking her to empty a chamber pot and calling her Helen. My beauty's name was Helen and I was relieved that she was real, I wanted to marry her, have bairns with her and be a farmer alongside her.

It was a dream, but then I realised that my male appendage had become hard and my pants had become wet. How I hated these accursed English breeks that we had been forced to wear, where your wetness would show. I longed for my tartan plaid and ran back home, determined to break in if I had to, in order to change my dirty clothes. I went around the side of my house and climbed through my bedroom window, when I saw that inside there was the old doctor, standing in our hallway, who ushered me to be quiet. I threw my dirty clothes under my bed and put on new ones, where I could hear the voices of at least two other women, talking to my Mither, who was sobbing. That doctor ushered me out quickly and I jumped back out the window.

I don't know what was happening with Mither, but I was determined to find my Father, so I went around to the front of the house just as he was entering the property. I ran towards him and held him tightly around his waist.

"Da, we need you," I said. "Ma is sick and Bruce's Ma is dead and Craskie…" I didn't finish my sentence when he asked me,

"Alright son. Have you seen the Mistress and her daughter from Craskie Farm?" he asked. I told him that I had seen a girl named Helen living in a shieling with, who I thought, was her Mither. He looked relieved at that and said,

"Give Bruce my sincere condolences," he expressed and handed me some coin to give to him.

The doctor left our house, as did the two ladies, unknown to me and Da entered to see Ma. She was standing up in the bedroom and was trying to sound happy to see him, but she was very pale. Da was pleased that the house wasn't burnt down and wanted something to eat, and so did I. And so, we waited for Ma to make us some food. He told us his news and we told him ours, but I begged him to come home. He said he wanted to, but it was still too dangerous for him, especially being a deserter from Lord Louden's regiment and so he'd have to go back to the cave, but he'd be home soon, he said. "I'll be back soon." Da had already been in prison for desertion [3] and knew what it was like and was fortunate to have been broken out by his friends that time, before he faced hanging. We all ate some of Ma's food together, as I was really hungry and Da promised to bring Ma a hart next time, so we would have enough food to eat and to give some to Bruce.

"Ma, can I sleep here tonight?" I asked. "Aye, lad," she answered.

I wanted my Father to explain to me what had happened to my male appendage that morning, because I hadn't experienced that before, but he was too quick to leave, in case the Redcoats were still around. He kissed my Ma gently on the lips, then she held him and began to cry, but he left anyway. My Father was a tall, handsome man and he'd grown a beard, making him even more handsome. My Mither used to cut his hair to keep it neat and tidy, she'd said. But without her and her clippers, he had grown it long since living apart. We both shared the same jet-black hair, while my Mither had brown hair. Mither was a buxom woman, who my Father had always been devoted to and I was always glad of that. Even I would still want to touch her bosoms and found every excuse to brush up against them or lie in her bed before she awoke.

When Da left that day, I decided to follow him on foot to see where he was hiding, as it was all just too secretive. I couldn't keep up with his big bay gelding, no matter how fast I ran, so when he was out of sight, I followed the hoof prints made in the muddy ground. Eventually, his horse's hoof prints stopped and he may have concealed the tracks or hidden the horse, so I just looked for the most likely cave dwelling big enough for seven men, but to no avail. I had to keep walking along peaks and dangerous slopes for many miles and I was getting lost. Da was one of the notorious Seven Glenmoriston Men, known for harassing Redcoats wherever they could find them. All seven of them were formidable in their own rights as fighters, who'd only just managed to escape captivity after the Battle of Culloden. The downside was that their families, like mine and Craskie, were left without the primary protector of the family, their crops and crofters. Searching diligently for Da, as I hid behind rocks, I saw movement finally when our neighbour, Padruig Dubh Grant could be seen at the entrance of Coiraghoth Cave, which was on the Hill of Lundy, between Corri Dho and Glen Affaric.[3] Then I knew where Da was if

I ever needed him, so I eventually made it back home, satisfied with my sleuthing but totally exhausted and freezing cold and a sore ankle from a slip I had made. I don't know how he lived in those conditions for so long but he was fit and strong and always seemed to know where to go in the wilderness of our Highlands.

The vision of the lovely Helen, that I'd seen on the path that day, wouldn't depart from my mind or from my manhood. I kept wetting the bed at night in my dreams of her and so, I decided to watch over that family too, just to get another glimpse of her, maybe even catch them bathing in the burn. My strongest desire was to see her naked, of course. When I cautiously walked down that path again, it was very quiet, but I waited to see how many of the family were living there, after all Da did ask 'had I seen them?' so I could report to him as an excuse because Padruig Dubh wasn't himself coming to check on his own family. I didn't know how many there were in the family, or if Helen had sisters or brothers. I only knew for certain that Padruig Grant wasn't with them.

I waited behind a large oak tree for several hours when I finally saw Helen shaking out their bedding and preparing to sweep out the wee shieling. Her Mither looked barely older than Helen and even more beautiful, with very long black hair and huge blue eyes, even bigger than Helen's. Then I heard male voices approaching from the Craskie end of the old path and I recognised John Grant, Mrs Grant's Father, who wasn't a very tall man and he was very lean. He was accompanied by what looked like Helen's brothers, one older, one younger. The younger one looked a little different in his facial features. More like a MacDonald, I thought, but handsome for a young lad. John Grant looked miserable but gave out instructions to the older of the two lads. When in front of the shieling, Helen's Mither held her youngest lad in her arms and kissed and hugged him with such love. It was touching to see and I heard her calling him, wee Alex, even though he wasn't really wee.

The oldest lad held two rabbits and Mr Grant began to show him and Helen how to skin them, gut them and prepare them for cooking. I concluded that they didn't have much food and were trapping their own. Suddenly, I became aware that Mrs Grant was coming my way with a shovel and carrying a basket over her shoulder, probably to dig up the peat just near where I was standing, so I came out as if I had just arrived and said hello to her and asked her if I could help.

"Aye lad, you can," she said. She was so lovely and I carried it back for her and then I introduced myself.

"I'm Grigor MacGregor, son of Grigor MacGregor and Morag MacGregor," I said. Helen was so shy. I knew that she liked me, as I liked her and I wanted her so badly. I knew this family would be mine one day.

There came an unexpected addition to our number, who was quite a tall man with a goatee, whom I recognised as the Highland coo breeder from MacDonald Farm further up the mountain. His name was Allan MacDonald. Both men looked relieved to see each other, after having endured the haunting sounds of the Crofters' departure. I was introduced to him as Grigor MacGregor's son, Grigor, who lives nearby. He nodded a kind of approval of my carrying the peat for Mrs Grant, whom he called Isobel. I had never known her name until that moment, but I started piecing things together, like the theft of the Clydesdale horses, how tiny she was, but clearly strong and capable, and loved by both men.

Was she 'Isobel of Glenmoriston', the famous lady teamster? I wondered. She called Mr MacDonald 'Uncle Allan', and they exchanged a brief hug and kiss.

Then he addressed John Grant saying, "I am so sorry about Freya, John."

Mr Grant's face was immediately grief stricken and he began to weep. I had never seen a man weep before. I was hoping it wasn't his wife that I saw headless on the ground, Mrs Grant's Mither, but it was.

Mr MacDonald invited them all up to his farmhouse that night for a good feed and he was going to slaughter a coo. He invited me and my Mither as well and I thanked him for the invitation. I really wanted to go, but I doubted that Ma would want to go to the MacDonald Farm, none of us in our family had ever been up there.

After he left, Helen said, "Ma, we'll have to take a bath in the burn."

This was my opportunity to see her and her Mither naked, so I departed for my home, leaving them to prepare to bathe, but I turned around and skulked back through the woods and watched them all bathing naked in that freezing cold water. Her older brother's name was Patrick, and he was a bit fat, I thought. Helen's breasts, even as a twelve-year-old, were already plump and round with light brown nipples, but not much pubic hair, but a lovely large bottom. Her Mither was gorgeous with large round breasts, dark brown nipples, a slim waistline, a large bottom and perfect milky skin and a real bush of pubic hair like my Ma's. Once again, my manhood responded even bigger and harder this time and I could only relieve myself in the woods.

I then went home to ask Ma if she wanted to go to the MacDonald Farm, trying to hide any ulterior motive. Reluctantly, she agreed and we washed and dressed and quickly went down the path to meet up with them before they left. We were only just on time. My Mither knew Mrs Grant, who was unexpectantly very happy to see her and warmly hugged her, as did the youngest lad, whose name was Alex.

Once again at dinner, I noticed Helen's younger brother, who was seated near Allan, looked a lot like the MacDonalds, not a Grant at all. In fact, I thought he looked like Allan MacDonald, but maybe it was just because they were related through Helen's Father, Padruig. The big lad climbed on Uncle Allan's lap before we departed and threw his arms around Uncle Allan's neck and kissed his face, to which he seemed to be accustomed and to like from the young lad. The older lad, Patrick, barely spoke to him or looked at him, other than with polite manners to thank him for the dinner.

That night at the MacDonald Farm was the last time any of us would see either Mrs MacDonald alive again or Mrs Grant in the same condition.

The following day brought new horrors to Craskie Farm. Aunty Margaret, Mrs MacDonald, died from an attack from the dragoons and Mrs Grant, Isobel, was near death, but I was asked to keep her bairns away from their Mither in the shieling for a time. It was hours before my Mither came to fetch me from there and then she took me home, looking very weak and pale herself. I asked her what had happened to Mrs Grant.

"Farm accident lad. It was Uncle Allan's coos that have injured Mrs Grant," she said. I knew that was a lie.

"What about Mrs MacDonald?" I asked.

"I don't know lad, why?" she asked. That was the first time that Mither knew that Mrs MacDonald was ailing too, until we both attended her funeral.

I was later informed by my new beloved, Helen, that after Ma and I had left the shieling, Hugh Chisholm arrived carrying Mrs Grant on horseback wrapped in his plaids, alive but very pale. He handed Helen the wet clothes he had washed and gave Helen instructions on how to care for her, according to his brother, Alexander and himself. He handed her ointments for various farm injuries that she was to apply after a wash in the burn daily, but if Mrs Grant's bleeding commenced again, she was to take her to the cold burn and immerse her immediately, then apply the ointment afterwards. He told her to keep up her fluids with honey and some salt. Hopefully, soup or food with gravy as she became stronger and above all, not to upset her in any way or ask her what had happened.

'Love and prayer,' he had said. A devout Papist, I knew I would really grow to admire Hugh Chisholm for his role in saving Ma's life, but I hadn't expected just how much he would feature in the family that I had just adopted as my own. Just the same, that day, I thanked God for Hugh. The absence of Mrs Grant's husband and their Father was something we were all growing accustomed to and I just hoped it wasn't always going to be like that for Helen's sake. Mrs Grant's Father was ageing fast and I couldn't help but feel that crops should be the priority and I wanted to start work on their soil. There was nothing left at mine, with no direction. Craskie was where I could make the difference. Helen and I were nearly old enough to hand fast, but I wanted to work on it and I decided to tell my Mither of my decision that night.

Over dinner that night, my Mither appeared unwell still and disinterested in the world in general. She missed my Father, I knew that, but what else ailed her was a mystery to me until well after she had passed away, as well as my Father who had died of a broken heart. I approached the subject of wanting to work on Craskie Farm and to help them restore the land for crops. She just made a sound like, "Hmm".

"I also wish to marry Helen if you and Da both approve and Mrs Grant too," I said with a definite decision clearly having already been made. Ma was accustomed to MacGregors, so it wasn't as hard to discuss things with her as I had thought, so we went through everything. She thought that soon the men would all be home again and that needed factoring in.

"Ideally," she had said, "It would be better at first if you were the only man in the household to start with, so Isobel would rely on you and you would have to be a loving son, as well as a reliable hard worker. Alex and Patrick will leave eventually, so you could replace them in a way. Then that only leaves Padruig if he ever returns from the cave. Even then, he may not stay long. He wants to follow the Prince, your Da told me. They're trying to talk him out of it, but you know him, he's not the 'stay at home' type, let alone the farming type and also wouldn't like competition from another male as young and handsome as you are," she said smiling.

Finally, my Mither smiled. "Ma, you are so pretty when you smile," I said. Then her sadness returned. "Son," she said, "you have my full support. The lass you have chosen is indeed lovely and an obedient daughter. But please wait a while longer when we can also talk to your Father and he can talk to Padruig to obtain his permission to court his daughter. I can talk to Isobel, she would be so happy to have you in her family and I trust her implicitly," she said. "You have asked Helen, haven't you?" Ma asked.

Not yet having asked Helen, I planned that for the following day. Early in the morning was when Helen was out of the shieling and possibly cleaning up, while her brothers were off trying to trap a wee squirrel or rabbit with their grandfather. I hoped to get her alone to talk, which I did and waved her over to that big oak tree where I would usually hide.

"Helen, I have to talk to you," I said. "Can we go to another part of the forest in the heather to talk? So long as it's not where your brothers are." I knew a quiet place nearer Craskie, but no one was there now, so it was okay to go there.

We sat down in the heather and I asked her if she would like to hand fast with me soon, if she liked me enough to marry me and live out our whole lives together, having bairns and farming. To my surprise her first response was,

"Did you want to look at mine first?" she asked. "My friends said they looked at each other's first and I'd like to look at yours first," she said.

I lifted up my kilt, not expecting her to be so bold, but she had a good look at mine and thought it was quite big.

"Now can I look at yours then?" I asked. She didn't wear any underwear and she lay down in the heather, lifting up her dress. I asked to see her breasts too, so she took her dress off completely and lay naked in the heather. I'll never forget that day. I asked her if I could touch her and she said to touch it all until I was happy enough and then she'd touch all of mine too. My man part went hard and I had to stand to one side to empty it. She asked me what I was doing with it and I just told her it was doing this lately since seeing her.

She almost decided to get up, when I begged her to just wait a moment, then I began the search all over her naked body. I loved her breasts.

"Do you want to suck them?" she asked. "I've seen Da do that to Ma," she added. So, I sucked her breasts and I couldn't believe she was allowing me, so I touched her woman part. "I don't have much hair there yet, but its growing. Ma has lots, so maybe one day I'll have lots too," she said. Opening up Helen's femininity to look at, I was fascinated at what it appeared like up close, so I fondled the folds and found a part that made her squeal. I thought I'd hurt her and stopped and apologised feeling nervous. She told me that it wasn't pain, it was pleasure and could I do it again, so finding the part that made her squeal, I rubbed it over and over and she was really loving it. I didn't know that girls loved this kind of thing, so I was happy to ask her to play with mine, which she did, all of it. It happened again and then mine became hard again and I was making a noise I've not made before, then to my surprise, she put mine up between her legs. She said it was where it had to go. Putting it into the warm comfortable hole in her body, the wet stuff came out again, but this time into Helen. I apologised again.

"That's how Da does it and then he pushes back and forth. Have you seen your Ma and Da do that?" she asked. "Aye," I replied because I had often watched on to see what they were doing in bed. "Then try to push back and forth when it gets hard again," she suggested and I was keen to try once more.

So, just as I was about to do that, I heard a familiar voice above us saying,

"Hello you two. Best put that away or it'll turn into a bairn." It was Hugh Chisholm, carrying his long rifle over his shoulder. We dressed quickly, while he watched on.

"How often have you done this lad?" he asked. He didn't believe us when we said it was our first time.

"We were wanting to be sure before we got married or hand fasted, so we were just looking at each other's," I said lamely.

"What I saw was more than looking lad, but let's hope Helen isn't with child or you'll be getting married sooner than you expected to," he said.

Of course, I didn't know that was how bairns were made, but I wanted to marry her, so it only gave me ideas of how to hurry that process along. He kept our secret for us or my Da would have come down again from his cave, but angry this time. On one condition, Hugh had said that we had to get married, or hand fast as soon as possible. Helen then said to Hugh that while the family was still living in the shieling, it wouldn't be possible to marry or hand fast.

"Da still hasn't even started building us a new home," she said, "but I do want to marry Grigor or hand fast. I'm sorry Grigor, I do want to marry you," she said, starting to cry.

"I didn't know that's how bairns were made," I told her. I put my arm around Helen to console her, when Hugh asked Helen how Mrs Grant was today. Then she looked panicked again and ran off to check on her Mither as Hugh had instructed her to do.

"Alright lad," Hugh said, "pray your lovely lass isn't with child and when the time is right, you will hand fast properly, then marry. We can keep each other's secrets until then, can't we?" the big man said.

"If you need advice on how it all works, you can ask me if your Da is unavailable. You have chosen well. I do wish you every happiness, but do not draw Padruig's attention to this until you have his permission," then he vanished into the woods as he frequently did. I was getting the picture that Helen was Mr Grant's favourite bairn and it wouldn't look good for me if I upset him.

That night, Bruce, Dougal and I had planned to be at Dougal's house where Bruce lived now since his Mither's death, to play a card game called 'Ombre'. Bruce's Father had been sent to the colonies in the Americas as an indentured servant for an unknown period of time, or permanently, so it left Bruce an orphan really and we also helped Dougal's Ma feed and clothe him. All the books had been burned in the fires, so there wasn't much in the way of reading materials. I disclosed to my friends how I loved the lass with the long black hair and they were surprised and asked how I was going to care for anyone now with us Highlanders persecuted at every turn.

"My dream is to perfect the soil, so we will not have the famines to which we are accustomed," I said. The answer was in the soil and I asked them if they knew anyone who I could learn from. Bruce had heard of a Professor in Inverness, who worked at the hospital there, who was involved in researching soil and was looking for volunteers to work on soil with him. Both of my friends came with me into Inverness to look for that man and I decided to make myself an asset to Craskie Farm, so Padruig Dubh would approve of me. He wasn't an easy man to impress. All three of us were doing the course, but part way through the course, Bruce decided to move to the Americas to find his only remaining family. He had been missing his Father too much and I understood that.

Dougal and I completed the course over two years, while boarding with the Professor, and in that time, he had started up an entire Science department attached to the hospital focussing on soil for crop yields to improve in the Highlands. He was a really dedicated man. We were sent from farm to farm and worked on different crops. I focussed on oats and in order to pass my course, I had to succeed in that crop on one of the farms, which was in Nairn. I rarely went home in that whole time because it was unaffordable and Da was now home caring for Ma again. The Science department had then moved and was established in Invermoriston for when I collected my certificate, which I had then intended to present to my future Father-in-law. Da saw it first and was very proud.

The Science department had grown and the old Professor was retiring and a younger man was taking his place. I was nearly sixteen by the time I saw Helen again and I'd hoped her love letters were as truthful as the real thing. I loved reading them over and over again, but it did make me homesick. I never wanted to return to Nairn. I was nervous to meet with her again and she had obviously never been with child since that day we had been caught in the woods by Hugh Chisholm. I was grateful for his silence. As the day approached when Padruig Grant would be consulted about me by my Mither and Father, I wasn't sure if he would accept or reject me.

Entering Craskie Farm, I observed that it was only slightly improved to how I remembered it with a half completed, stone home. He walked from the shieling.

"Are they still living in the shieling?" I asked Da. He kicked me to be silent, which meant 'yes they are'. Helen was walking silently behind her Father with her head tilted down, followed by her Mither, now looking as beautiful as she had when I first met her when collecting the peat, two years before. I was a lot taller now and stronger from all of the heavy farm work, but I now had a good reputation and a letter of recommendation from the old Professor.

Helen looked at me coyly and a bit shyly, remembering what we did that day in the woods and we knew that we were already promised to each other, even if her Father didn't. We sat in front of the partially completed home and I was a bit surprised at the lack of crops or new home for my wife to be. My Father still continued as was requested of him to put me forward to marry Helen Grant, his daughter without anything but my certificate. There was going to be a lot of hard work ahead. Mr Grant also had no dowry for Helen, I heard him tell my Da, to which my Da was none too pleased. This problem was later resolved by her Mither.

Mr Grant tried hard to intimidate me that day and I had to repeat myself more than three times. I answered all his fierce and fast questions without baulking and was always calm and polite to him. He had expected me to fold, but I knew what I wanted and I was, after all, a MacGregor. Mr Grant then walked over to my Father and said that he accepted me to court his daughter if she wanted me to, so he asked Helen if she wanted me to. Thank God she answered, "Aye" to her intimidating Father and then Mrs Grant was asked, almost as an afterthought, but she said she knew me and my Mither well and she would love to welcome me into her family when we all decided that we would marry. She gave me a warm and encouraging smile.

Helen and I knew we had Hugh Chisholm, who I'd called Uncle Hugh by then, watching our backs and so there were times that the two of us snuck into the vacant teacher's house behind the old schoolhouse, long closed. Uncle Hugh told me where to find the key to the cottage, which I always replaced. We hand fasted without anyone's knowledge several times and practised safe sex with a myriad of herbs to prevent pregnancy that my Ma provided. This we continued for almost ten years, as I built up the fields intended for oats and drew up a Master Plan for the farm with my Mither in law, who was a marvellous intelligence. Her husband had no idea how to farm and his sons had never assisted building up the farm.

With her sewing, Helen's Ma managed to sell dresses, which in turn purchased me an ox, who I named Charlotte. Later, Charlotte was retired when Ma recovered her Clydesdales and she finally made it known that she had in fact been Isobel of Glenmoriston, teamster with her Father, John Grant. I'd seen her mistreated too often and carefully kept the secrets of the great love in her life, Hugh Chisholm. I'd also promised him all those years ago when Helen I were discovered that I would keep all of his as he kept mine.

When the time came that Helen's Da was pressed into service, on my part, I felt only relief, but for Ma it was yet another misery to endure. This time I wasn't sure if she could endure it alone. I suspected it had become my turn to cover for Hugh, but finding out that he was in love with my Mither in law to be, was indeed dangerous for me. Eventually, as time passed with her careful financial management of the farm, what was one farm became two and multiplied. The Art Gallery was Mr Grant's idea, having purchased the old school and my wife's artwork was a huge success. Ma gave me an apprentice to work with me on the farm's soil and his name was Charlie MacKichan, whose Father was long in the ground and his Mither, Widow MacKichan, did odd jobs washing and ironing in the district. He had a younger brother named Henry. Charlie was putting himself through school and was only eleven years old when he first started at Craskie. When he completed

Charlie MacKichan

his schooling, I also sent him to the soil course, now held in Invermoriston with my son in law, Gillcrest MacLachlan in charge. I needed Charlie to be part time on the course, so that he could work with me as well, considering how much land had now been inherited from Allan MacDonald. I wondered if his brother Henry could later join us, if it was an interest he might develop. Both lads certainly needed the guidance and the work as Scotland's troubles were not yet over, according to Ma.

Eventually, in their old ages when Da was facing his death, he actually asked Uncle Hugh to look after Ma when he had passed away. Uncle Hugh then married Ma and became my Da and they were very happy for a time. He had waited patiently for her for forty years and was inconsolable at her funeral. I had grown so attached to the big man over the years, that I couldn't part with him and begged him to stay in the main house with us, or my own heart would break at the loss of my Mither in law as well as him. I always remembered her telling me that we would indeed need patience.

When he placed her gently into her grave that day, he also placed a tiny wee coffin in with her, with Fleur Chisholm, daughter of Isobel and Hugh Chisholm 1746, written on the top. Then both the names of Isobel Chisholm and Fleur Chisholm were etched into the black marble plaques on the wall, thereby being memorialised. It was an untold tragedy, yet to be discussed one day, if ever he felt he could. Both of them had had a miscarried daughter, but he didn't wish to speak of it. Alex and I frequented our Chapel that Ma had built us all and I learned some new prayers and when Da began to give his occasional sermons, it wasn't a surprise and we all learned a lot from him. The numbers attending began to grow. We didn't ask the Priests if it could be done that way because after all, the Chapel belonged to us.

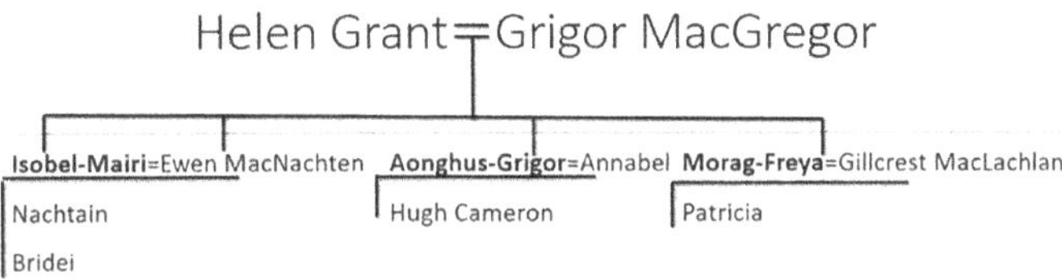

From my rebellious youth to becoming a dedicated farmer, husband, father and grandfather, we had to overcome a lot, it's true. Craskie had indeed been left a veritable waste land, but with the absolute dedication to making the farms recover and work again, fed not only ourselves but many others and it had been worth the effort. When I first saw my wife Helen, I had thought she was a fairy. Bruce had married an Indian lass in South Carolina and owned land there and had a lot of bairns before returning to Scotland. Dougal, like me, married an heiress to a large property near Uncle Alex in MacDonnell lands in Glengarry, whose Father was known by Uncle Alex's new wife Matilda. Uncle Alex also had a twin sister named Marion, who had two sons. One of the lads, named Kenneth, stayed and worked on Craskie with Da then went on to learn accounting in Inverness. Her older son, Malcolm lived and worked for Alex.

Dougal, Bruce and I meet up on occasion and remember that day, looking around at Glenmoriston on fire and we thank God for helping us get through those days and enabling us to hold fast onto some of our Scottish lands. Our homeland. I want my grandchildren to look up to me with respect and not disappointment, despite Helen's unexpected exit from life, then this world. Not everyone had coped. My most important ambition had been the ability to feed everyone well and maybe I had expected too much from the fairy I thought I saw on the path that day.

Padruig Dubh Grant's Story

"The Sharpness of my Blade"

By Zaynab El-Fatah

Illustrations by Halima Karger.

78th Highlanders based on inspiration from J.R. Harper's "The 78th Fighting Frasers"[5]

The Atlantic Ocean, somewhere.

1759

John Fraser and I were just sitting on the creaking deck of the ship, occasionally looking up at the masts reaching high up into the sky as the ship rocked from side to side, when a group of the 78th Highlander Regiment, unknown to us both, had begun to gather in growing numbers, enjoying their story telling. Seasickness was starting to kick in after watching the masts. I estimated that they were Highlanders like us, but with one big difference, they'd fought on the side with the English at Culloden and this was probably their last military campaign. I recognised some facial features common to a clan and I knew John was trying to guess that too. One MacKenzie, one Fraser, three Campbells, one Grant and so on.

John and I had been talking quietly, Bible in hand, about what was in Isobel's latest letter from the Braes of Glenmoriston and he commented on how lovely her handwriting was. John was teaching me English with only a Bible to use as a text and translating my letters from English into Gaelic, so I could read what my wife had written to me. God only knows why she had written to me in English?

We hadn't been interested in that group of men until I heard one of them say, "That white horse," which for some reason, took my attention. I felt my old, heightened awareness kicking back in, as if I was back amongst my fellow Glenmoriston Men. Then one of them laughed saying,

"I got her good as she was put on the horse, a deep gash. And did you see the blood dripping all the way down to her feet? Then I was pleased wi' me work."

He laughed some more and was obviously proud of his handiwork. They were all Highlanders and guessing, he appeared and sounded like Clan Grant, judging by his height, features, frame and ruthlessness and then he went on to say,

"If I wasn't going to capture him, I'd get his wife and we all did. Didn't we fellas? We did that Padruig Dubh by doin' his wee wife." he said in the most ruthless sounding voice that he could summons. But he wasn't Padruig Dubh Grant and he was yet to meet the meaning of 'ruthless to an innocent', head on.

John and I were aware of what we were hearing and Robert Fraser came over to us also having overheard it and the three of us concocted a deadly plan. Firstly, we ascertained how many of them were involved in any injury or ravishing of my wife, Isobel Grant, then we decided we'd kill them all that night and throw their bodies overboard to the sharks. Any coin on their person was just an added benefit of ridding humanity of this garbage. I'd deal with my wife and her lying compatriots later, back in Scotland.

At roll call the next day, there were eight names called that were not responding. "Good work men. We despatched those mongrels in the way they deserved," I said, as John and Robert sat with a knowing smirk on their faces. Our night's work had been productive. We had gone under their hammocks and stabbed them in their kidneys with our dirks, then quickly slit their throats, one by one. It niggled at me the next day as to why Isobel had never told me that she'd been ravished and why I was given the elaborate story of Allan's coos having caused the scars on her backside. It had all been a lie. It made me feel stupid and angry and I was made to look the fool. 'What were Allan's motives in all of this? What was Allan up to? Men are supposed to stick together and there he was spinning lies just for me.' I then planned to do harm to Allan and anyone else who'd kept it from me. 'What else has he done that I don't know about and why is he so interested in what happens to my wife?'

John's opinion was that she must have felt too ashamed to tell me such an horrific story. "Your wife is heroic in my eyes Padruig and you should support her and her reasons," said John.

"So, John, you wouldn't help me kill my wife then?" I asked him.

"Not without meeting her and making my own assessment," he said and so it was decided, we would both meet again in the future under the guise of his son Simon needing a wife and we had one of those, my granddaughter Beth.

In the coming days on that boring sea journey to New France, John began to ask questions about my life with Isobel, starting with my Father and his brothers, who were my uncles. He asked whether they had been regular supporters of Isobel's family, while I was unable to be with them. Of course, I knew my Father had never been back to that farm after Isobel and I were married, when she was not yet fourteen. His reason was his anger towards John Grant, who had disallowed his daughter to live on his Father's farm, after he had approved of the union between myself and her. I gave Isobel her first strapping with my leather belt for upsetting my family and I probably shouldn't have strapped her quite as many times as I did that night, but it felt good.

John Grant's condition on approving of me as her future husband was that she stay living with him and her Mither Freya, where she would continue her farm work with him. They only had one bairn and she was essential to the running of the farm with her as his offsider, he claimed. Not having a son, he relied on his lass and so did her Mither, from whom she learned sewing, spinning, cooking and all of the skills needed to raise a family. Their opinion was that my family would only see her as a servant to wash the floors and their clothes and cook and serve them when I was or wasn't there, with no voice that gave the farm its essential qualities.

He never mentioned to my Father that he was training her in any specific field of farm work, but I confess to never asking her, nor her parents when I went home before or after I married her.

However, sadly I remember one night in Badenoch, as the Prince's army was preparing to depart and we had received the last of the deliveries that we needed and all of those men who were going to join us there, had already done so. Then Cluny came up to me and told me my wife was there with the eight horse Clydesdale team and was departing.

"What's she doing here?" I asked him.

"She's the teamster mate. Old John's arthritis is too bad now to do all the tricky stuff. Isobel does it. She always waves to me when they deliver here and smiles. Lovely lass, your wife. Didn't you know?" Cluny said incredulously.

So, I dashed down to where they would depart from and sure enough, Isobel was driving the team away from our Jacobite camp with John Grant yelling at the young fellas to move out of the way. I couldn't believe my eyes.

"Married for thirty years at that time and it was the first that I knew of my wife's involvement in teamstering. So, John, what do you think of that? All those years of marriage and she didn't bother to mention it. She hadn't sought me out amongst the soldiers there either, so I asked Cluny if I could catch up. I needed to see my wife. In the morning, I arrived at Craskie Farm, after resting for a while and went down to the back of the farm, where I had never been before, where John stabled his Clydesdales, as it turned out. I stood at the opening of their big stable, having stealthily approached in order to not be heard. Inside, sitting on a wee stool was my wife brushing the big old Clydesdale stallion's tail and trimming the long length of it with clippers and washing the mud off it with soapy water and speaking quietly to him in Erse. Most people would not try to get near that stallion. She then moved on to clean out his enormous hooves that he willingly lifted for her, speaking to him, ever so gently, then washed the feathery hair around each leg. I just watched knowingly that she was washing off Badenoch mud," I added

"My tiny wife was a Teamster of gigantic horses, who loved her and obeyed her. When she finally turned in my direction, I had already gone to re-join Cluny. She had her secrets and so did I," I said.

"I was hurt by Isobel's deception if I'm honest. On the side of their carriage it said, 'John Grant Teamster'. It made me angry thinking then that I must be the butt of everybody's jokes," I said. "Farming had always been so boring to me, so I wasn't particularly interested in the answer even if I had asked, so not knowing about the teamstering was probably my fault. The farm was, however, well run and very neat and tidy from outward appearances and everyone seemed to know their roles there, including the crofters. Once it was all burned down, that all changed with the crofters' departure and the tragic death of her Mither. She wouldn't talk about any of it but maintained a positive attitude in order to rebuild the farm. I looked around at the disastrous state of it, even after they'd been working at it for a long time and could envisage myself having to return to farming, which was my life's dread. I wasn't a builder either, so trying to build a house took forever and it was still incomplete when I left, but I had expected that my sons would take over, but they left as well," I lamented.

"Alex was very close to his Mither, so that bemused me. I had actually thought they'd all be happier with me gone. Patrick had always criticised me for leaving them all alone when I was hiding in the cave after the Battle of Culloden. Helen missed me and still would and so, for her, I had remorse, but not Alex, whom I was never sure was even my bairn. Many people would comment on how much like the MacDonalds Alex looked and comparing the two brothers, you'd never think they were related, except for their hair. I'd strap Isobel often regarding my son Alex and I always blamed her for the many times that he was rude to me or yell at me for no reason. She'd stand between him and me, so as to protect him, which made me even angrier. I wish I hadn't hit her quite so much, being so small as she is. Her Mither had grown to hate me, I think and both her parents disapproved of the strap, but never once interfered," I said.

I told John Fraser that it has only been due to my unexpected departure, that in her letters she had become remorseful for the things that she had never spoken of to me in all those years. It was more than thirteen years before I finally learned exactly how her Mither had died.

"I know why it's a hard story to speak of, but I was her husband and surely, she should tell me, I thought, but she couldn't. I realise now that I was resentful towards them all, including Da with his adoring love for her, my Uncle and his similar adoration of my wife, which I never understood. Even my best friends had a peculiar respect and empathy towards Isobel that, to this day, I still do not understand. In fact, I cannot name one person who thought ill of my wife, which should make me happy and proud, but it irritates me to hell and back," I complained.

"I can't say that she ever disrespected me or disobeyed me and she always gave me sex when I demanded it and I'd not always intended to please her. I just wanted it and that was my selfish approach to love making and I'm too old to change now. Being a virgin when I married her, she had no adventurous techniques in love making and on our first night she cried in pain. It put me right off and I left the farm earlier than necessary to re-join the company the next day, hoping she wouldn't cry the next time," I said.

I think John just took it all in without judgement, then he asked more questions about when my first son, Patrick was born.

"Did your parents visit your first-born bairn?" he asked.

"Mither died when I was fifteen and of course, Da didn't visit them. He just sent his congratulations along with me. He still resented that she chose to live with her parents and not him because he needed a cook. I would see him first when I was home in the Braes of Glenmoriston, then go to my wife's home at Craskie. Isobel has only seen some of my family once for a week since the day they scared her to death, then her Father wouldn't allow her to return, in case my Father ravaged her, given my Mither had passed. She didn't like them, so she would never miss them, especially my uncles, whom she thought were very mean, she said. The physical appearance of my family and hers was strikingly different also. Her Father wasn't even tall like my line of Grants. He was actually lean and of average height, while still having our jet-black hair.

John's wife, however, when she was alive was a true beauty and that's why Isobel is so beautiful with enormous blue eyes. Even my daughter, Helen has a similar beauty, but not quite as striking as her Mither and grandmother. I suppose that was because I was her Father and while I'd always thought myself braw, it really does reveal itself in your bairns. Isobel was the better looking of the two of us, though it is sad for me to admit it. Patrick wasn't as tall as I'd hoped he would grow to be because of how small Isobel is, but Alex did for some strange reason and he was a good-looking lad, although he was a right nuisance, disobedient and rude. He only had time for his Mither, whom he adored like her Da did, as well as Helen who would fuss over her, although I can't complain about my dear lassie. She was always obedient and well-mannered, unlike Alex, who had no manners at all. I blame Isobel for that," I concluded.

"Did you take your new bairns presents each time they were born?" John asked.

"What for? Bairns only need breast milk," I replied.

"Did you buy your wife a wee gift for giving you new bairns?" he asked.

"Nae, that's what wives are expected to do and it had taken Isobel years to be with child. Why are you asking about presents?" I asked him. It was all John's idea that I buy everyone presents back in Scotland after the Quebec battle was over. 'Why should I buy her anything?' I thought. It took Isobel years to be with child and I was almost ready to divorce her if she hadn't finally got with child and she certainly didn't deserve a gold wedding band, so I only gave her the Clan Grant brooch to wear on her arisaid.

When we eventually reached the River St Lawrence, it was realised that us Highlanders were going to have to go down the river in wee boats, speak French to the locals, then scale a 150ft cliff, lugging up both the English and their weaponry. 'Not too much to ask,' I thought, at fifty-eight years of age. That was before we all started to kill the French and the Indians, when they'd finally got out of bed. Naturally, the idiot Wolfe got himself shot twice and died. He had tuberculosis anyway, so it was a quicker death than what he'd otherwise have to face. Naturally, we won that battle at Abraham's Field and despite orders to burn out all the crofters, John, Robert and I obtained spoils of war legally. Isobel had asked for French silk and French silk I got loads of, as well as linen for men's shirts and hundreds of different coloured buttons.

We also enjoyed the company of the ladies, who thought us kilted heroes were braw and they wanted our company. I enjoyed that attention. Robert had himself a French lass for a whole night and decided to stay on for the offer of land, as he had lost his land back in Scotland. John and I bought land in Nova Scotia with the government handout and met up with the Indians and I was tempted to stay there, but I knew Isobel would never leave the braes and glens of Glenmoriston. She only loved her country. It was there that we met up with some very friendly Indians, who sold us their wares and also thought we were braw, but for John's hair, which is bright ginger red, like a sunset.

The ladies didn't want to give birth to a bairn with that red coloured hair, for which he was obviously grateful, even though they laughed at him. Mine being black like theirs, meant that I was in high demand from the young and the old. It was hard to resist their attention and after all those years of loyalty to my wife, I enjoyed a night with Indian women, one of whom wept when I left and so began a life of deception, having broken my wedding vows. I bought a polar bear rug from the Indians to compensate them for my enjoyable night, to give to Helen and Grigor for their wedding day. I wasn't sure then how I would look into the eyes of my wife, who often narrated the first day that we had met at the Glenmoriston School where we fell in love. I must admit that I pursued her and got her to promise herself to me, while I was away training with the military, so none of my mates would get her. That's when I arranged for my Father to be involved and make sure that she was stitched up.

John Fraser had a generosity about him, unlike most Scots and still insisted on the various gifts for family and the friends who were building my house back in Scotland.

"You must be pleased about having such a wonderful son in law like Grigor. I'm guessing he's Clan Gregor?" he said out of the blue.

"Aye, good lad. He's Grigor MacGregor's son, who is a close friend of mine. We could get him some weapons free of charge if we lie a bit," I replied.

And so, we acquired a replacement kit claimed to have been lost or broken and Robert made a false bottom on the sea trunk to carry them safely back to Scotland. I asked him how it was going with his French lover and it was already over, but he'd enjoyed a lot of love making with his mouth and tongue, he said. He had still decided to stay and take up the land offer and get another lassie.

He asked me about the Indian lassies and it shocked me what I'd done for the first time, in having made passionate love with more than one lass, all night. I didn't have to do any work at all. I just lay there while they mounted me like a horse, until I felt like it and then I really went for it. I had never done that before and now I didn't know how I'd be able to face Isobel. All that time after Culloden living in the cave, the only temptation was to follow the Prince to France, but no women, even though I enjoyed their admiration. I knew too that my faithful wife had no temptation, there was only the dreadful revelation of the ravishing.

Maybe I wouldn't find my wife appealing anymore knowing how many men had been inside of her, even though I had already killed them. Those wounds on her buttocks still niggled at me. How did I not know they were from bayonets?

I felt like a bit of an idiot, I have to admit, like how I felt finding out she was a famous teamster and I was the only clod who didn't know. I didn't once consider the pain and humiliation that she had endured with those kinds of injuries, then was put on to a horse, naked just to entertain the soldiers.

Then it occurred to me, how was it that she'd lived through it? Surely Da and Allan couldn't have repaired all that damage without her bleeding out or getting an infection, so I asked John and Robert. "How then did my wife survive? How could Isobel have survived with all that blood loss?" Robert then commented, "Now, do you really want to know my opinion? Because if you do, I will give it to you, but you have got to be willing to listen. You're onto something, asking that question.

On Abraham's Field, I saw a Frenchman die of just one bayonet wound, with half of his face missing, mind. I picked his pockets and got a snuff box made of silver, no coin though." "Aye," said John, "I surveyed that field at the end of the battle and I saw that most of the dead and dying were like sheep after a mauling and had fewer than two sword or bayonet wounds, bleeding profusely. You can assume that Isobel was bleeding profusely from both vaginal and buttock wounds, aggravated further by the horse race." Then Robert went on, "That's without considering the injuries from the ravishing. A lot of women have died from that alone," he said.

Padruig Dubh

"In Isobel's case," he went on, "If eight dragoons each took a turn, it could have caused irreparable harm, external splitting and multiple abrasions, all likely to become infected because she was put onto a dirty horse, then dropped into the dirt, naked out the front of Craskie Farm. Is that right Padruig? That's not even considering the diseases that she could have caught from those men," he added.

I should have been cringing, but it was all just a matter of fact.

"That's right. So, she must have been with Aunty Margaret, who died from a broken neck, which gives us the date at least that we can work around," I said. "Okay," said Robert, "That explains Allan MacDonald's involvement, but it doesn't explain their positive genius at saving your wife, which is the question that you are asking isn't it?" continued Robert. "So, is there anyone else in the Braes of Glenmoriston that could have helped? A lady friend perhaps, that could keep quiet?" he asked. It was then that I realised that Grigor's wife, Morag, must have been involved.

"Morag had a wee stitching kit for sewing up small wounds with cat gut and she had also been ravished and Grigor was never told. I've only just been told in one of these letters that you've translated to me, John. That was the first that I learned of Morag having been ravished," I said.

"It's got to be their decision," said Robert. "In my experience, women like that are far too damaged to have high expectations of. If Isobel ever tells you, I'd be surprised and it would only be if she felt safe enough and strong enough to tell you. What I am saying is, forget your arrogance and the rights of a husband to know everything. This is a whole different arena of savagery that she has lived through. You've done your part now by killing exactly who was involved and not an innocent. Your Uncle didn't want to see you killed at the Fort, which may explain his motives. However, she was dying, in my opinion and that is where your rights would apply. Was Isobel ever taken to the cave where you lived at that time?" he asked.

"Nae, never. She didn't know where it was," I responded.

"Who did know, out of those three people?" he asked.

"Allan. Uncle Allan," I said.

"Okay. Was there a day when there were fewer of you than usual minding the cave?" Robert asked. "Thinking back on it is hard, being so long ago, but those early days are quite clear in my mind, as they were before Glenalladale arrived needing help for the Prince. Therefore, I think if I write it down,

I can tell you who was where and when and what date it was, in relation to Margaret's death," I answered. "Okay, what do you have written down?" he asked impatiently. "There was a day when four of us went a foraging instead of three and we left the older Chisholm brother, Alexander, the youngest, Hugh and Alexander MacDonald because they had needed the rest," I said.

"How long were you gone for?" asked Robert.

"We were gone for about four or five hours," I replied.

"When you got back, was there any evidence at all that there had been anyone else in the cave? Any signs of blood? Any signs of cleaning up from such a thing?" asked Robert.

"It was cleaner than usual when we got back and that's all. The older Chisholm brother Alexander, who rarely smiled at the best of times, certainly wasn't smiling. Young Hugh, despite his usual cheerful nature, also wasn't cheerful and Alex MacDonald was their spokesman, who welcomed us back. Admittedly, looking a little pale, but that's all. I thought they were all still just tired," I said.

"Does the older Chisholm brother, Alexander, have any particular skills other than sword fighting?" asked Robert. "Aye, we called him 'the doctor'. He had his own box of medicinals, as well as a stitching kit," I answered.

"But you say that he's dead now and so is Alexander MacDonald? So, that only leaves Hugh who might know if your wife was ever there. My advice to you, Padruig, when you get back, is to talk with Hugh and ask him plainly if Isobel was in the cave at any time for any reason," said Robert.

"Then you'll eventually get to the bottom of it without hurting anyone, especially your wife or a friend that just built your house," he added.

Eventually, arriving back in Scotland in 1762, after a lengthy and disgusting sea journey, severe illness kept me in London to rehabilitate there with the Reverend Gordon of the Episcopalian Church. The parishioners were very kind in donating my fare back to Leith in Scotland by ship and then onto Glenmoriston by coach, wearing fine English clothes. Our Scottish tartan was still banned. The sea chest only just made it, with so many thieves trying to steal from it. I arrived at Craskie Farm one day early and observed Isobel greeting Grigor Mohr MacGregor with an amorous hug and I was instantly angry all over again and I followed the two of them into the forest. They were far too friendly for my liking and so I reached for my dirk with intent.

Immediately, I was grabbed from behind and the knife fell to the ground.

I had been going to kill both Grigor Mohr and Isobel, only to have it explained by the now beefy and stronger Hugh Chisholm, that they were brother and sister. My wife was also Clan Gregor and had never known it. Her Mither had had another child, Grigor, whom John Grant had wanted to adopt, but was disallowed by her family. Grigor lost his Mither at aged two and she was thirty. So, Isobel was born to Freya and John Grant and the truth of their relationship had only just been found out two nights before my return. Grigor Mohr and Isobel were half brother and sister.

Thank God, Hugh had stopped me from killing my best friend and my wife. I re-entered the farm the following day after staying the night with a neighbour. My emotions, however, were heightened once again to the act of killing and as a killing machine, I had once been effective, but now I was faced with the superior strength of the younger man who overcame me easily, the reality of farming, my estranged son Alex and the guilt of having slept with other women. Worst of all, as I surveyed the property, was my wife's obvious success without me or my wages that I'd given to Paul Chisholm to repay my debt.

My son Alex had always thought he was better looking than me and he must have inherited his looks from his Mither and the MacGregors with that fire that he had in his belly. I think I was always jealous of Isobel's love for him, especially when she was breastfeeding him. I'd want to take the bairn off her breast and have both breasts to myself and I sometimes did just that. But then he wouldn't stop screaming until she put him back on her breast, suckling away ravenously at the milk. I hadn't been jealous of Patrick or Helen, but Isobel's love for Alex annoyed me somehow and made me angry. Alex and I were never compatible, so sending him to Nova Scotia was a brilliant solution after the Quebec campaign, I had thought. He'd be out of sight completely and then there'd be no competition for Isobel's attention, but I hadn't intended on making her quite so miserable without her youngest bairn. I don't think she ever forgave me for giving him my land in Nova Scotia, where she'd never see him again.

There was a part of her that never stopped grieving for him. I didn't understand how women felt about their bairns. When Isobel told me that she'd written to him to come back and see me in my remaining days, I'd responded very negatively and told her he wouldn't come. She was so heart broken and crawled up into a ball in front of the fire, so I wrote to him and asked him to come home to see his Mither, maybe bring a couple of his bairns with him and hopefully I'd see him before I died, I thought. Which I did and Isobel then had her wee Alex to adore when I left this world. The sooky lad would probably still suckle on his Mither's breasts, if he had the chance and share her bed. She was still breast feeding him until he was nearly five years old and he would just walk up to her and take her breast out of her blouse to have a drink, which horrified me and it was stopped the minute that I knew. I gave her a beating that night that may have injured her ribs, as she clutched her right side, but she never complained to any of us. Her breathing at night had changed to a raspy sound and she couldn't sleep on the painful side.

Alex wasn't the only man in her life who I had wanted to kill more than once, the other one being Hugh Chisholm. So much for our oath to one another. The only reason he was allowed in our gang was because of his psycho brother Alexander and Donald, but they only did things in threes. Damn Chisholms. I couldn't believe that she could ever love him in return, but

I knew he loved her and was going to marry her if I had died or if I just decided to not return. However, she always loved seeing him and his damn Collie dogs. It made me sick, the way she fussed over those dogs and rubbed them down if they were wet.

"Oh, poor Collies," she'd say. Then they'd lick her face and even if I told her that was unhygienic, she'd still let them lick her and she'd kiss them both. The final straw with the last litter of Collies he had, was that Hugh allowed her to name them, so she named the two male dogs Charlie and Louis and the bitch was Pompidou, after that French woman. She wanted to bring Charlie home to round up her sheep and sleep on our bed, but I put my foot down at that. It was an insult to his majestic self, and she knew it, just like Grigor calling his fat ox, Charlotte, but at least that witch was Hanoverian, God curse them. Hugh thought it was hilarious of course, as he would. She was developing that Chisholm sense of humour that wasn't funny at all. I concluded they were seeing far too much of each other if she was naming his Collies, so one day I went up there to talk to him at Chisholm House to address a few unhealthy habits like that one, only to find Grigor Og, my wife and Hugh all enjoying smoko by themselves without me.

"Are you here to see Charlie?" I asked Isobel and she almost choked on her tea.

"Charlie's taking a wee rest before he has to work again," she said, "Isn't he Hugh?"

"Aye," Hugh replied.

"Well," I said to them, "While the House of Stuart is taking their rest, you can come home wi' me to take a wee rest beside your husband, Isobel," I demanded.

"Aye, Padruig," she said or some such and followed me back home. I didn't just rest on the bed, I wanted sex with her, so I did, which exhausted me, then rested. She was my wife, not his and I wasn't about to share her. He still thought he was brawer than me and with my silvering hair, he probably is now. I'd never been an adventurous lover in my whole life and it was too exhausting to contemplate now, but I did ask her if I satisfied her sexually and she said that she was always satisfied.

Then I asked the delicate question of whether she had ever been in the cave all those years ago and she was momentarily quiet. Both Robert and John Fraser had encouraged me to enquire about how she had survived the ravishing. I'd put it off because of how things happened when I arrived back home, then I gave her a beating anyway, so she had been punished if she had been there, whether taken by Allan, unconscious or not.

"Why do you ask me that? Of course not," she said in earnest. "I still don't know where your cave is to this day and what purpose would I have to go there, even if I did know where it was?" she asked. "It would have been very uncomfortable amongst all those men," she added.

I was satisfied that she actually had no recollection of being there, which made me pleased. At least she wasn't hiding that too.

I asked more questions, which she didn't like answering about that day and said she had already been punished and wanted to sleep. She was about to roll over when I asked her to look me in the eyes and tell me about the bayonet injuries and insisted on examining them again with fresh eyes. I had been told they were from Allan's coo horns, so for years I believed it, until I heard to the contrary on board the ship. I rolled her over to examine each scar and to my surprise she began to weep. I had never acknowledged the trauma or the pain that she had suffered, only exhibited anger at not having been told.

"I'm sorry Padruig," she said, "I couldn't stop them," Isobel said.

My heart had been so hardened to the event, then to see her weeping and say that for the first time, I was sorry and felt her pain.

"Was it very painful?" I asked.

"Aye," she answered, "But my life was departing me and in each of those minutes it was less painful, I suppose," she said intentionally not looking at me.

"Who saved you Isobel?" I asked.

"Da and Uncle Allan and maybe Morag, but I'm not sure about that. I want to sleep now," she said. And she rolled away from me to sleep. I had left it too late to show sympathy or turn back what I had done to her. I knew her love for me still existed, but she had never been the same person after I had beaten her in front of the whole family with a guest present and just left her there on the floor unconscious. In the family's eyes, I was a bit of a monster from that night and it had never changed, no matter what I did for them.

My arrogance wouldn't allow me to take the blame for all of my mistakes, but I asked her for forgiveness knowing how close to death that I was and how close to those in the other world she was.

"Please forgive me Isobel," I asked.

I thanked God that night that Isobel had forgiven me then and a weight was lifted as we embraced for one of the last times. I had never appreciated my wife and I knew that I had driven her away from the lad she had once loved so much at the Glenmoriston School. I fell asleep remembering her as a young thirteen-year-old lass, herding her coos up the mountain, when I followed her to ask her to wait for me. She was coy, loving and so beautiful and she still is beautiful. My Father had been a big reason for our early fights and it didn't change with Isobel, even when he was long in the ground.

If I'm honest with myself, my problem with Alex was that he was so much like her. He even walked like her in that fluid way that they both do, as if they're walking on water. I met his secret twin, Marion, hidden for her own safety in Loch Insh and raised by Gillcrest MacNachten and his wife. She too had that same fluid way of walking, only she was an angel who spoke sweetly and kindly and had raised two sons after marrying another MacNachten who had passed away. My usual response to these secrets of the Braes of Glenmoriston, is to go into a blind rage and almost kill someone, but too close to death myself, that wasn't going to happen this time.

I am too tired. Afterall, I had gained a daughter. I welcomed them all to Craskie farm.

I prayed to God for forgiveness for all of my multiple sins, but not for the British that I had killed during and after Culloden. I know Isobel had supported all of us men in the Rising, despite not being a Jacobite herself and for that, I've always been grateful. We would meet again on the other side one day and I wished her well.

"Thou Shalt Not Covet"

By Zaynab El-Fatah

Illustrations by Fatima Zayn al-Abidin and Halima Karger

Glenmoriston

Scotland, 1700

The day that I married Margaret Grant was the happiest day of my life, both of us in our respective tartans, Margaret's was handmade beautifully. We were both young, good looking and had inherited the land from Margaret's Father. I bred Highland coos and we were making a lot of money droving them into the markets regularly. My wife couldn't ride a horse, so she'd help on foot or I'd just take temporary help. The mountains behind us were enormous as they rose up to the skies and it snowed every winter, so the weather was cold, but one gets used to it and our house seemed to keep warm enough.

Margaret had had wealthy parents, so we had been left beautiful china, as well as furnishings and ancient Turkish floor rugs and we regularly spoke of how many bairns we would have one day. She wanted a wee lass and name her Gobnait and I wanted a lad, maybe two lads and I wanted to name my first lad Alexander and the second son, Kenneth.

Our neighbours below us were farmers with oat crops among many others, as well as crofters, goats, chickens and a dozen coos. They were Grants and this was Grant country. John Grant was his name and his first wife and child had both died in childbirth.

My name is Allan MacDonald of MacDonald farm in Glenmoriston.

As the years passed, it was obvious that Margaret was unable to conceive and neither one of us knew who was the infertile one. All my dreams of a son had to be forgotten and I was shattered. The sadness never left me when I saw the crofter's boys on Craskie Farm running around and I couldn't help but feel cheated. Why were they able to have so many bairns and we couldn't even have one?

John Grant brought home a beautiful new wife one day and she too gave birth to a wee lass within the first year of their marriage. It was as easy as that. Margaret couldn't feel happy for them and she took it really hard. I'd see her looking down at Craskie once the wee lass had started playing outside and especially once the wee lass could walk and then I was given regular updates at the bairn's development. The day she told me the tiny wee lass could run, I suggested that she introduce herself to John's wife, Freya, and maybe take some of our meat to them as a gesture in order to meet her.

Her name was Isobel. We would call her 'Isobel of Glenmoriston' and the name stuck, as she was called that until she was old and still living on Craskie Farm having married my nephew, Padruig Dubh Grant. She had always called me Uncle Allan, respected me and had taken my advice about farming, despite what I had done.

My wife wanted the wee bairn to visit us on MacDonald Farm out of longing for our own bairn. Thinking that it could fill that void, we invited them to dinner, which surprised them. Up close, John's wife was even more beautiful than I had realised and it was obvious that Isobel was going to be even more beautiful than her Mither. They all had jet-black hair and John wasn't a tall man, he was as lean as can be. He was kindly towards his wife and his beloved lass.

Isobel would jump into his arms and put her wee arms around his neck and she'd kiss her Da and readily fall asleep on his lap. At our house, I offered to lay her down in our bed, but he declined and he thanked us for the meal that we'd given them with a gift of their home-grown honey and they went back down to their farm.

Margaret cried that night, wishing she'd had a bairn like wee Isobel. She desperately wanted the bairn back to our house and she asked me to arrange it with John to have her eat, bathe and sleep here with us, as extended family, if they'd allow it. I know if it had been me and someone asked for my child to sleep at their house, I'd be suspicious and definitely decline, but I had to ask for my wife's sake. I was hoping that if she could experience Motherhood alone with her, that she would overcome the yearning for her own wee lass.

The following day, I strolled down to Craskie, wary of our boundaries, when I saw John working with two of his Clydesdale horses. He was pleased to see me and we'd started a friendship, I had believed. I quite liked the man, as he was unlike most Grants. Being a Teamster, he had to get along with everyone and he was a wonderful horseman. It was an awkward question to ask for your neighbour's bairn to stay overnight, so I confided with him upfront that Margaret and I were unable to have bairns, which shocked him at first, but I think he guessed what I was going to ask.

"Do you think wee Isobel could stay with us for dinner, bathe and sleep overnight with us, so that Margaret could feel like a real Mither?" I asked.

John said that if both his wife Freya and Margaret were happy with that arrangement, then we could have her there as he trusted me, but there was a condition. He explained that he was building up his horse team to eventually number eight horses.

"Could you help me acquire six more horses if we lent Isobel to you?" he asked.

"Do you mean pay for Isobel to stay?" I asked at first, a bit shocked.

"Aye," he said. "You have a need and so do I. What do you say, you help me to buy six Clydesdale horses and Isobel stays with you, two nights at a time?" John said.

That was the arrangement and both women agreed and Isobel was thrilled at coming to our house. We were now family friends. They said that she often felt lonely, not having more family and so she'd love it. They gave us a change of clothes for the following day for her to stay two days.

The sweet bairn wasn't big enough for our dining room chairs, so at first, we put one cushion for her to sit on in order to reach her dinner, but she still couldn't reach her food. She was so tiny I thought. When I picked her up, she was as light as a feather and she would automatically put her wee arms around my neck and kiss my face a lot. I had never been kissed by a bairn before and it was a new experience for me. Margaret was touched by the sight.

"I've prepared her bath, Allan. I am not sure how they do it, but I have put lots of bubbles in it for her. Can you take her clothes off please darling?" she asked.

And sweet Isobel just lifted her arms up, so I could take her clothes off over her head. Her skin was perfect and a milky colour. When Margaret came in, I told her what beautiful skin she had.

"Oh aye, she is so perfect Allan. I wish she was ours," Margaret said and placed her small body into the bath to wash, but she reached out her arms to me.

"What does she want?" I asked.

"She wants you to wash her, I think. Isobel, do you want Uncle Allan to wash you?" Margaret asked.

"Aye," she replied.

"Margaret, are you sure?" I asked.

"Aye, come on Allan. She'll get cold," she said. And so, I took the soapy sponge and washed her all over.

"Her privates," said Margaret. So, I even sponged her privates, which was a first for me in my life. The sweet bairn giggled at the washing of her privates and wanted me to get into the bath too, so I did or the water would be cold soon. She sat on my lap and washed my toes, talking away in what I think was Gaelic, but I wasn't sure.

"Is she speaking Gaelic?" I asked Margaret.

"I am not sure, maybe it's Erse," she replied. "Your turn Margaret and we'll get out," I said. Towelling the wee bairn dry was so enjoyable. I didn't know that parenting could be so enjoyable. I didn't dry her privates, so once again, she pointed to them for me to dry, which was embarrassing at first, but as I started doing it, I felt like a parent, I suppose. Margaret had a wee night dress laying on the bed for her, that she'd made, but Isobel just climbed into bed naked and said, "Unca Allan," indicating for me to get into bed. When Margaret came in, she put on her nightdress, neck to ankles and underwear too, then climbed into bed with us both.

Our nakedness seemed so natural to her and she obviously slept like that at home.

The nights spent with sweet Isobel were so special to us both and unforgettable. It made us both desperate to have our own bairn more than ever. During those nights, the sweet bairn would put her tiny hands on my face and often curl into my arms to keep warm. I loved sweet Isobel and we paid John again for our last two nights. It was all I could afford and John was training his Clydesdales well. He was a very good horse-man and Teamster and he could even make all of his own leatherwork. I judged him for how he'd obtained the horses, but at least Isobel was safe with us. The Grants around these parts thought I was an intruder, being a MacDonald, so it didn't bother him taking the money from me. I doubt that he'd have taken the money from a Grant.

Wee Isobel played with Margaret's new litter of kittens and wanted to take one home and helped feed the chickens and collected the eggs into her tiny wee hands. When I watched Margaret brush her lustrous, black hair, I noticed that it was dead straight on one side, but a bit curly on the other, just like her Mither Freya. There was no doubt who her Mither was. Margaret would read books to her in English that she wouldn't understand, so she'd point to the drawings and illustrations and tried to understand the English. She was about two at that time, we thought. If the coos came up close to the house, she'd get giggly and excited and jump up and down on the spot. It was so cute, so I'd take her outside and pick her up to pat them and she'd giggle again. One of my docile female coos allowed her to sit on her back and she played with the hair, with a preference for the orange colour.

Isobel loved staying with us and I tried out increasing her chair to two cushions, so she could reach for her food, but sometimes it was just easier to sit her on my lap to eat. It was all new to me what wee bairns did, so I allowed it all and Margaret frowned, but Isobel liked it that way and at least then she ate all of her dinner. She had definitely grown attached to me and she would frequently touch my face. She was a clever little thing and was determining a person's mood when she touched, to get a feel of what she could say or do. I believe she had never been hit in any way or even yelled at, so we let her do whatever she wanted to do because we didn't want to tell her that there was something that she couldn't do, unless it was unsafe. I was raised with very strict boundaries, but I wasn't aware of there being boundaries at all with wee Isobel.

Bath time was once again up to Margaret, I thought, but I had thought wrong. John had obviously been involved in every part of this bairn's life. I think helping Margaret to help her overcome her desire to become a Mither was having the reverse effect on me. I was then more desperate to have a child, more each day and was going over every which way I could get one for ourselves. Kidnapping came to mind, but not just any child, this child and I had to suppress those thoughts. John was trusting me with his bairn. Adoption maybe, surrogacy maybe, but we didn't know if it was me or Margaret that was sterile. None of the MacDonald's were sterile and none of Margaret's family had been sterile either.

When she turned three, I asked John if I could be betrothed to Isobel and wait until she was thirteen, perhaps, when I could marry her to have a son. At first, he was horrified, but it was still done in the Highlands and I needed a son.

"What will happen to Margaret?" John asked. "We will have to annul the marriage," I said. "She is Catholic, so divorce is not an option, but annulment based on her inability to bear a child is a legal option for me," I said. Both John and Freya did end up agreeing, whereby she could still see them and be trained as a teamster as he had planned for her, but eventually be my bride and give me my son. With everyone in agreement except Isobel, it was in writing and we were betrothed and we could then see her more often without having to pay and she slept in our bed on occasion.

I was devastated when all those years of planning were dashed, as betrothal to Isobel was no longer an option and she would instead marry my ghastly nephew, Padruig Dubh Grant. He was known to be a really difficult lad, after his Mither's death, so his Father was sending him to a Highland Independent Company of Foot, but the clever lad knew their number and got to Isobel before he was sent away. Isobel agreed to marry him and to wait for him indefinitely. She was barely thirteen, but looked ten years old and he was barely fourteen, but they both knew their own minds.

She was always going to be tiny and he towered over her, even when he was just fourteen.

The minute the lad was sent away, his Father and Uncles did as was expected in 'assessing' the lass for suitability in marriage. The Grants had poured onto John Grant's farm in force. Isobel Grant had wanted him, which even surprised them and she hadn't known of any other prior arrangement between John Grant and myself. Despite running away from them and hiding at first, they caught her and examined her. The poor wee thing had all four of those big, mean looking men insisting on her lifting up her dress, opening up her wee legs to look inside to guarantee that she was a virgin.

I think they enjoyed stripping her naked eventually, holding her down and opening her up, so they saw all of her most intimate parts before Padruig ever did. Poor Freya was beside herself. We regretted not telling Isobel of our arrangement then, but it was too late. No-one was going to deny the Grants what they wanted. She would be his wife within the year and my hopes of a son with Isobel were gone.

Of course, Isobel had never known that my motives had shifted from Fatherly love for her, to just a way to eventually provide me with a son. I felt like an idiot when the two youngsters got married, as youngsters do, but I feigned happiness for them.

I still played a role in their lives because it wasn't possible to roll back all those years of involvement with them and just suddenly stop seeing her when she genuinely loved me as her uncle. So, Uncle it had to be and I watched on as she eventually gave birth to her first son, without her husband even being there or his family. He came to see Patrick, the bairn, a week later. Then we waited for her to have her next bairn, a wee lass, Helen, who was nearly as pretty as her Mither.

There were still occasions when I'd be asked to take Isobel up to Inverness for shopping with my pony and cart and over the many years, we did that quite a lot and I really enjoyed her company, as the Mither that she had become. She breastfed both of her first two children and I expected that that would continue and I confess to frequently looking at her breasts when she fed them. They had grown beautifully, I had thought. Big and round for such a wee Mither. Her skin was still as perfect as it had been all those years ago in the bath and I'd want to touch her with any excuse. Without the bairns there, I was aroused as I brushed up against her breasts or her thighs. I even apologised for brushing up against her breasts. I wanted to do a lot more than get a feel for her beautiful body.

Of course, in her naivety she trusted me completely.

On one of these trips, one evening, Isobel and I were coming back home through the Great Glen. I still had the urge to Father a son and I am ashamed to say it, I think I may have Fathered Isobel's third child, Alex. I feigned tiredness and asked Isobel if she didn't mind if we could rest for fifteen minutes and lay down in the back of the cart. I told her that it had been a long day and my shoulders were aching. Naturally, she felt sorry for me and she massaged my shoulders and I asked her to lay beside me like we used to do at home. Her tiny frame was pressed up against mine, then I lost complete control of myself and entered Isobel and ejaculated immediately.

"Oh Uncle!" she said. "What have you done?" she said and wept. I kept on apologising and said that it had 'just happened' and how sorry I was. But I knew when her courses were and had calculated the days when she could fall with child and today was one of those days.

"When I get home, if I wash in the burn Uncle, will that stop a baby from coming?" she asked.

"Of course, just wash," I said, "And don't tell anyone about this or we'll both be in a lot of trouble, especially you from Padruig when you tell him you were massaging me," I said.

She looked terrified at the thought that Padruig could blame her.

We agreed to never disclose this mistake to anyone and damage our otherwise good family relationship. I begged her forgiveness and she forgave me, but I insisted she ask me to forgive her too, as she had tempted me and so she begged forgiveness for her mistake. She was convinced it was all her fault, after a bit of talking. I insisted she let me finger her too because of the temptation that she had presented. She obediently opened herself up, while she wept as she apologised and I enjoyed the fingering and wanted more.

I told her what a good girl she was and I was surprised at how submissive she was and I knew I could do anything then. So, I sucked both breasts, enjoying the wee lass who once shared my bed as a two-year-old. I insisted on full penetration, while she cried and I raped her again. I had to admit it was the best sexual experience of my life. I enjoyed her submissiveness, ignorance and her absolute terror.

Padruig arrived home later that night and despite her having washed in the burn, she did fall pregnant, then the paternity of the newborn was going to be in doubt. The wee bairn was different, the birth was different, the pregnancy had been different and the wee lad was a breech birth. It was fortunate that Freya could still deliver the bairn. Padruig was notified that she was in a bit of trouble and he came home to only a new baby boy, Alex, who looked a lot like a MacDonald, in my opinion.

I rushed down to see the new bairn with a wee gift in anticipation that it was mine and a boy. I took one look at his wee face and saw MacDonald from my family in this bairn. I knew he was mine and so I wasn't the sterile one, Margaret was. When everyone had left the room briefly, leaving the two of us alone with the bairn, I asked her plainly,

"Isobel, is he mine?" I asked. She looked shocked and said, "Nae Uncle, of course not. Padruig is his Da." Not even the lawyer had been supportive of challenging the loss of the lass, who was supposed to become my wife. I left the gift, then went home feeling miserable and defeated.

He was mine, I knew it, but I did not deserve it. I didn't like to admit to myself that I'd raped Isobel twice.

Wee Alex and I still had a good relationship and I think the bairn liked me. He would do the same thing that Isobel had done when she was wee and wrap his arms around my neck and kiss me. I had eventually given up having my own child and it was enough to see Alex once in a while. As he grew into himself, he became more difficult towards his Father, Padruig, but most especially to John Grant. There were flaming rows between wee Alex and one or other of the men and his manners were frightful towards them with only love towards his Mither, with whom he slept most nights until Padruig objected, which broke his little heart. He was a sensitive wee thing and I felt responsible for making his life worse than it should have been. I even offered to adopt him one day to Padruig to help out and he was horrified and I thought he was going to hit me that day or worse. I'd had to save them from the dragoons one day after the failed Rising and it was an opportunity to keep one of the children, but I vowed then to never mention it again. Padruig had become nastier than any of his uncles could ever have been and I wondered how Isobel could still love him.

He had become a blood thirsty killer, along with his friends after Culloden.

Wee Alex is handsome like our family, nothing like the Grants, but he would always have the sensitivity of his Mither with the fire of the MacGregors in there from his Mither too. When his Father returned from Quebec finally, after years of having abandoned Isobel, Alex decided to take up his Father's land in Nova Scotia, which meant neither Isobel nor I would ever see him again. I knew it must have broken her heart knowing how the poor lad had been conceived that night in the back of the pony cart.

Somehow, she would endure when others would have died of a broken heart, with all that had happened to her, but I suspected she had found new love that was giving her strength. I just didn't know who it was. John was long in the ground, as was Freya and Margaret.

When I married the widow Chisholm, I decided to not see any of that family again and to die in relative peace, but my guilt overwhelmed me and I left my entire property and my Highland coos to Padruig Dubh Grant and hoped he would care for Isobel.

There was no way that the Chisholm Stepsons were going to get it.

Alexander Malcolm David's Story

"What the Wig has Witnessed"

By Zaynab El-Fatah

Illustrations by Halima Karger and Fatima Zayn al-Abidin

Inverness
Scotland, 1715

Born to wealthy parents in Inverness, Scotland, my Mither thought the best thing that they could do for me was to send me to England to complete my law degree and board at the University. Of course, my Scottish accent wasn't going to win over the ladies, who thought I wasn't even speaking English. The lads were all very involved in sport, as well as studies, but being short and not sporty minded, there wasn't a sport that I fitted into without making a fool out of myself.

I really missed Scotland and the people that I knew in Inverness. In London, I was a nobody with a peculiar accent. My Mither was sure that I would bring home an English rose to introduce to her circle of snobby friends, but there weren't many English roses here where I was studying and they also didn't like me. I heard them laughing at me one day at my odd, short, box-like shape and so I decided to improve my looks with a wig. I went to many wig shops in London, trying many of them on until I was happy with one. It had cost nearly six months of my allowance. I looked in the mirror and saw a handsome Highland lad, but what they saw was a ridiculous short law student, trying too hard.

Eventually, the degree was completed and I specialised in fields such as Contract Law, which drew my first client to me when my parents opened my Law Rooms in Inverness. They put a sign up saying, "Malcolm Law Rooms." Of course, that confused people who thought that my first name was Malcolm, but it stayed that way.

My Mither thought it humorous to put this poem on the wall:

The Beggar's Opera
A Fox may steal your hens, sir,
A whore your health and pence, sir,
Your daughter may rob your
chest, sir,
Your wife may steal your rest, sir,
A thief your goods and plate,
But this is all but picking,
With rest, pence, chest, and chicken;
It ever was decreed, sir,
If Lawyer's hand is fee'd, sir,
He steals your whole estate.

- John Gay [4]

My first client's name was Allan MacDonald, who had had a betrothal contract drawn up between himself and Mr John Grant of Craskie Farm in Glenmoriston, for John Grant's daughter. So, my first question to Mr MacDonald had been if he was single because he wasn't a young man, he wore a wedding ring and the person referred to in the document was only three years old at the time of signing between her parents and himself. I wasn't sure if the lady he was with was his wife or not, but she was and she had agreed to an annulment, so he could have a son with the bairn, who was now thirteen years old and her name was Isobel Grant.

"So, what are you wanting from me?" I asked. He explained that they had broken the agreement and Isobel was now promised to a lad called Padruig Grant. The area where they lived was all Grant country and my first thoughts were that he was stepping on Clan Grant toes if the lad's family were involved, as they were and living amongst them would be awkward if he rocked the boat. The Highlands frequently had Clan rivalries that could erupt over anything at any time.

"Are you wanting to avoid a Clan feud between the Grants and the MacDonalds, who aren't very far away, or is the priority the young lady or do you want compensation for the broken contract?" I asked. His wife, being Clan Grant herself, did say it would be unwise to start a Clan feud with those Grants.

"They are not known for their kind-heartedness. I know them and have grown up with them and they are mean-hearted," she said. They had wanted to take Isobel home with them, but John Grant had refused them that request.

"He is teaching her teamstering, so she is his offsider," Margaret said.

"So, you do want to avoid a Clan feud, especially in these times with Queen Ann not leaving an heir and there is to be another Rising, is what I'm hearing. That might put the lad in the middle of that, if he's military. Is he?" I asked.

"Aye, he has heard that Lord Lovat is returning from France. Meanwhile, he is with the MacDonalds of Keppoch in Grant lands [4] who are Jacobite," Allan said.

"The Stuarts are trying for the throne again, so my advice to you both is to stay away from the Rising and don't poke the bear, so to speak. The MacDonalds and the Grants will have to watch themselves if one of those Germans takes the throne and you might need each other, especially if you are door neighbours, like yourselves and John Grant. I can ask for compensation for you from John Grant, but if he challenged it in a court of law, it could always be argued that the lass had never been consulted, nor did she know about your arrangement and therefore made her own choice of husband. Are you related to her betrothed, Mrs MacDonald?" I asked.

"Aye, he's our nephew," she said.

"Alternatively, I can ask Padruig and Isobel to come into my office and ask them myself who they wish to marry, whilst not disclosing the name of the challenger," I said. Allan MacDonald sat rubbing his hands together, like he wanted to do harm to young Padruig and wasn't pleased at the picture that I was painting of adding to Highland disruption. "Compensation then from John Grant is what I'll settle for. I want at least a thousand pounds Scots," Allan said. I asked them both if that's what they'd be happy with and they both agreed and my secretary wrote it all down.

"Alright Mr MacDonald, Mrs MacDonald, I'll send the letter today and we will be in touch when I receive a response," I said.

As they left, my secretary said, "It's lucky that lass is marrying into the meanest family in the district. He'll never get her off them and John Grant doesn't have that kind of money."

Much to my surprise, John Grant and his lovely wife Freya, came to see me, letter in hand, explaining their side of the story and said that the young couple had made their agreements behind everyone's backs, which the Grants acted upon.

"I don't see how I'm up for one thousand pounds. We weren't due to present it to Isobel until she was old enough to understand the betrothal agreement, which Allan and I had decided together, was in six months time," he said.

"Padruig Dubh outsmarted us and my daughter loves him. I don't know why, only they know that, but I am happy to marry them both. Can you explain that to Mr MacDonald please?" he asked.

As she was departing that day, the beautiful Mrs John Grant handed me an envelope and asked me to give it to her son, Grigor MacGregor if ever he tried finding her, now that she is no longer in Loch Insh.

"He has a sister, but doesn't yet know it," she said. I carefully filed it in the cabinet for those rare Loch Insh cases.

"Was he adopted?" I asked.

"Nae, he is my son to my first husband, who died two years into my marriage, then I had to move in with the other Clan Gregor as I had no way of supporting myself. John saw me from afar one day while delivering to Loch Insh and I knew I would marry him. He came and proposed, but the Clan disallowed my wee son Grigor to go with us, only me. If ever he comes here to look for me, please tell him I love him, we both love him," she said.

"I'll do that Mrs Grant," I said, but the lad never came by my office.

They departed, just saying 'Have a nice day.' Nothing was heard about it from that day on and I was right, the Earl of Marr did raise the Standard of James III and VIII in Braemar in September of 1715.

Craskie Farm, Glenmoriston, 1764

I did, however, find his son one day, purely by accident many years later after I had become great friends with Padruig and Isobel Grant from Craskie Farm in the Braes of Glenmoriston and I was staying there overnight and there he was, Grigor

MacGregor, son of Grigor Mohr MacGregor. By then he had married Helen and his Father, Grigor Mohr had only just found out that Isobel was his half sister.

Anxiously, I mentioned that the now late Freya Grant had left a letter in my safe keeping, to be held at my office at Inverness, in the off chance that her son, Grigor, may try and look for her. She had explained that she was no longer living in Loch Insh and wanted him to know where she was and that he had a sister. Naturally, I couldn't explain why else Freya was in my office, but Padruig was giving me side glances at the untold story. Padruig had recently arrived back from Quebec, looking thinner, so life was still unsettled, but I asked Grigor Og to give his father the message for me about the letter still being there and waiting for him to collect at my office, Malcolm Law Rooms, in Inverness.

Surprise would not describe the reaction to all and sundry, not even shock, it was a mixture of disbelief, shock and disappointment that I hadn't confided it to the Grants, which of course was against all of the confidentiality rules, but I'd hoped our friendship hadn't been harmed in any way.

"I'll go now and tell him," said Grigor Og, sensing some peculiarity in the whole scenario. "I'm coming too," said Helen. Both of them left running as fast as they could, for some reason, and gave the message to Grigor Mohr, who lived not too far away obviously and came over then with his wife, Morag, to ascertain exactly what I had and why.

Isobel's front door was a beautiful huge oak door and I had always admired it. She made us coffee in the hope that we could relax again, but there wasn't much chance of that as Padruig anxiously watched his front door until his friend walked in with Grigor Og, Helen and Morag. Upon entering, he greeted everyone.

"Padruig, Isobel, hope I'm not disturbing you all. Apparently, there is a letter for me from my late Mither in Inverness?" he said.

I stood up then, feeling the emotion from his side for the first time as a two-year-old bairn, whose Mither had since been murdered brutally and who then hears that there's a message from beyond the grave and I felt the weight of it.

"Mr MacGregor, I'm Alexander David, Padruig's lawyer," I explained. "Can you please sit down and enjoy Isobel's coffee and I'll convey to you all that I know?" I said.

I could see that Mr MacGregor's face could switch from joy at seeing his sister, to sternness at anyone who displeased him, so caution was necessary, but just the same, I liked him at first, as well as his son.

"I apologise that this may come to you as a shock that I'm holding a letter for you in Inverness. What your Mither's instructions at the time were to keep it there, filed amongst the Loch Insh files, for you if ever you came to my rooms looking for her, which, I am afraid, you didn't do. So, the letter is still there and that was a very long time ago. The letter would be fifty years old now lad and I am aware that your Mither has since passed away and so none of it may be relevant in terms of information, but you might like it to keep and I'd like to give it to you, as I might be going to sell my business one day. Would you like to come and get it or would you like me to bring it out myself?" I asked.

"Why was my Mither there in your rooms?" Grigor Mohr asked.

"Och. At the time, my rooms were fairly new. My parents had set it up for me and I'd only had about three clients and your Mither came in with Mr John Grant, Isobel's Da, and they left that letter with me. There weren't any other instructions to search for you, or anything like that," I said.

"Alright, we'll come in and get it, Grigor and I. Is that alright Isobel? Can you spare Grigor tomorrow?" Grigor Mohr asked.

"Aye," replied Isobel.

"Alright, we'll follow you to Inverness tomorrow morning. Will this cost us anything? Any money?" he asked.

"Nae, of course not," I responded, "May I give you my sincere condolences on the death of your Mither," I added.

I saw Morag and Isobel both retiring to chairs by the fire, looking both weary and confused knowing that something didn't add up. Isobel appeared to question why her parents would go into Inverness to see a lawyer when they knew where the family lived. I was worried, then, that as clever as Isobel was, that she was going to make more enquiries with Padruig who had already become acutely sensitised to this topic. When John Grant came out of his bedroom, having heard it all, he gave me a look as if to say, 'You'd better not say why we were there. After all, Allan still lives on MacDonald Farm.' This was uncomfortable and I was beginning to regret mentioning the letter, but I had to. It wasn't mine to keep. I just had to cooperate with everyone but hoped that Isobel was not going to be compromised in any way. Apparently, Allan was supposed to come over for dinner that night, but had cancelled at the last minute, then I arrived with their land titles that had all been legalised.

Isobel was then ushered over to her brother Grigor Mohr, who apparently had 'brotherly rights' that I guessed he was going to assert. He asked her to lie across his lap and the room went silent as she gazed hypnotically into his blue eyes, identical to hers.

"You know that after Padruig, I am the guardian of this," he said, referring to her modesty and she nodded in understanding as his face became stern. I looked across at Padruig to see if he approved of what was taking place and he did. He almost had expectations of her brother to get results from his line of enquiry. I must confess that I've seen many old customs still practised in the Highlands since I had become a lawyer in Inverness, but a revived MacGregor custom such as this one, I had yet to see with my own eyes. I wondered if I should leave them in privacy, but was too riveted to my chair. Padruig just stood watching, Helen and Grigor too, but his wife looked away, careful to avert her husband's eyes. Isobel's Father, seated next to me, didn't say a word and was similarly riveted.

I noticed Hugh Chisholm had been quiet most of the night and sat in the corner of the room and shifted awkwardly in his seat, then cast his eyes downwards in sympathy for Isobel. I wondered then if he had had an affection for her beyond just house building, while Padruig was away.

It was obvious that both Grigor Mohr and Isobel shared an affection borne from brotherly and sisterly love, but that had its responsibilities and my heart was pounding, thinking of that dreaded betrothal agreement that John Grant had agreed to with Allan MacDonald all those years ago. I had to follow John Grant because he had been the client on that day and just hoped Grigor had his limitations. I was wrong. The whole room seemed to be in an hypnotic state, excluding myself, who was never susceptible to hypnosis. Grigor stated his rights after Padruig once more and asked her if she understood that and she nodded, still staring into his eyes.

"Has anyone entered here recently other than your husband Padruig?" Grigor Mohr asked. She shook her head and said, "Nae," in a voice that seemed distant, very quiet and completely submissive, unlike the confident Isobel that I had grown to know. Grigor went on, "Has anyone entered here since you married Padruig?" he asked. Then her eyes grew wide and tears welled up and rolled down her cheeks.

'Oh my God, I had hoped Isobel was never unfaithful to such a man as Padruig Dubh or we'd be burying her in the morning', was my immediate thought and I didn't want to be witness to such a thing. Grigor went on to ascertain when and who.

"Was it before Patrick's birth?" he asked. She answered 'Nae'.

"Was it before Helen's birth?" he asked. She answered 'Nae'. Thank God, with Helen in the room listening to every word, I was relieved that it hadn't been, but then he asked,

"Was it before Alex's birth?" and she nodded with tears still rolling down her face.

"Who was it Isobel and where?" he then demanded. Her feeble voice said, "The Great Glen," His hand then pressed harder to remind her, which must have hurt because she winced.

"Who?" Grigor Mohr repeated.

"Alex is Padruig's bairn," Isobel answered.

I concluded then that she had been raped by a family member. He asked again, looking very displeased. I then saw Padruig take down a horse whip from the wall, where it had previously hung.

I thought it was going to be all over for Isobel and so did Helen, who sent the Grandchildren to bed, as well as herself and Morag followed her. Hugh's head hung in sadness, but stayed as did Grigor Og. Then unexpectedly, John Grant spoke up.

"It was my fault. I trusted Allan to take her into Inverness, but he'd never overcome being unable to marry Isobel after she had agreed to marry Padruig. My wife and I had a betrothal arrangement in place on Allan's request when she was three years old, unknown to Isobel because she was too young to understand. I hadn't known of her agreement with Padruig and she hadn't known of ours with Allan, but when the Grants came here to check on her suitability for marriage to Padruig, I knew then that the betrothal with Allan was over. Isobel was completely innocent, because she thought Allan had just loved her as an uncle. He was desperate for a bairn and Margaret was barren, he thought and wanted to have a bairn with Isobel once she turned fourteen years old, but not until we had explained it all to her and only then if Isobel agreed would it have then converted into a marriage contract," he blurted out to the shocked audience.

"I can vouch for the story concerning the contract," I said. "But questioning Alex's parentage is new to me," I added.

Grigor then asked Isobel, "Were you raped sister?" She then sat up and looked at him through dazed eyes and said, "Aye, but he'd told me that it was all my fault," Then she kept saying,

"I'm sorry brother," it was all too sad. Then she told the story of Allan wanting to rest a while in the Great Glen because of his sore shoulders, which she had massaged. "He said I massaged his shoulders and therefore tempted him, so it was all my fault and if Padruig found out about the rape, he would blame me," she said. Then Padruig asked plainly who Alex's Father was. She looked horrified that it could be anyone but him and told him so.

"You are Alex's Father, I know, but Allan kept badgering me saying that Alex was his and he wanted to take him," she said and she couldn't stop sobbing. "He's just better looking than Patrick and not tubby like him and much taller, like you. He doesn't look like Allan. He's my wee Alex," she said and threw herself to the floor yowling a grief so deep for her son Alex. I was near tears, as was her Father and Grigor Og and I wasn't sure how much longer Hugh could control himself, as his face grew redder and redder.

"You'll still need punishment, Isobel, for not disclosing this information to me," Padruig said.

Hugh stood up at that point and said he could do it, which shocked Grigor Og, who would like to have rescued his Mother-in-law by this stage, I thought. He was a good lad. Padruig considered the idea for a moment, but was going to decline when Grigor Og then said, "That would save some of your energy Da."

"Do I look too tired to beat my own wife when there's still the ravishing and the bayonet injuries to explain that she's lied about? Look at me Isobel. I've killed the men responsible for that. They were on the same ship as me, then we threw their bodies overboard to the sharks. You didn't care to tell me about that either, did you? You will get a beating from me for all of the lies, including the teamstering. You and your co-conspirators told me that the injuries on your buttocks were from coo horns, but oh no, another lie you told when that was local Militia from down at the fort and it was Cluny who told me you were at the Jacobite camp teamstering, with not so much as any acknowledgement to your husband," Padruig bellowed.

"She was protecting you son," said John Grant. "You would have gone down there to the fort, all angry like you are now and got yourself killed because she knew who was down there. None of us, even Allan, wanted to see you harmed. We know how much Isobel loves you and to have that on her conscience would have killed her and the teamstering wasn't a secret until after the ravishing. You weren't interested in the farm or my horses," he said sincerely and with judgement.

"We've all been doing our best around here in your very many absences, most of the time throughout your entire marriage. These past few years have nearly done us all in and if it hadn't been for Hugh, Donald and Grigor, God bless them all, we couldn't have pulled through," John said sadly, then appeared too sad to continue.

"I'm going to bed now and I'll leave you to decide what the future will hold for you and Isobel," he said and left the room and so did I, as I didn't wish to embarrass Isobel.

Her husband was about to beat her. Grigor Mohr fetched his wife and left quickly and his son Grigor Og went to bed leaving just Hugh, Isobel and Padruig.

"I can do it Padruig," from the guest room I heard Hugh offer again and decided to listen in to whatever transpired, but Padruig declined his offer. He dragged her up off the floor and made her lean over the dining table with her dress lifted up in front of Hugh, which surprised me and first began hitting her with his bare hand from what I could hear, the full length of her body, except her head at first, as he had grabbed her by the hair. Then, he took the whip to continue, when Hugh said it was enough. Hugh had saved her life many times and to see her small frame being beaten must have been agonising.

"Your turn then without the whip," said Padruig, but Hugh turned and left through the big front door in disgust and I heard it slam behind him. Without an audience, Padruig dropped her to the floor as she had been held up by her hair and 'himself' went to bed, just leaving her on the cold stone floor, unconscious and ominously silent. I waited a while to ensure he wasn't coming back out, then I quietly lifted Isobel up and placed her carefully in the guest room bed and I slept on the floor beside her, hoping she'd be alright throughout the night. Her breathing was raspy, but at least she was still breathing. I prayed more that night than I ever have in my life before.

I was glad to leave Craskie Farm after breakfast the following morning with my wee pony and cart. I had never married, nor was I ever likely to, but Isobel was an unappreciated intelligence and from now, I wouldn't blame her if she looked for another man in her life and although Hugh was by no means gentlefolk, he did have a religious and spiritual side to him that would better suit Isobel, even though there was a wide age difference. And he was strong enough to combat Padruig. What must it have felt like for her, waking up after that beating? Women have to suffer rape and ravishing and then they are punished for it, blamed for it, despite their obvious innocence. I respected a husband's rights in a marriage, but if I had married, even if my wife had committed a crime, I couldn't personally lift a finger to a woman, especially such a small woman. Despite all of my judgements towards Padruig, it had been Grigor that had drawn it out of his sister.

She would feel isolated, alone, rejected, humiliated, judged and may never look at her husband in the same way or with the same trust again. Poor Isobel.

Grigor Mohr decided he would ride with me on the cart into Inverness, leaving his son leading his horse behind us. 'He may want to explain himself on the long journey into Inverness or he was going to try to get me onside as another man to support his actions,' I thought. He started our conversation by thanking me for keeping his Mither's letter for all this time and was looking forward to seeing her handwriting, even if it said little. I told him that I was happy for him but asked him why he had to extract all of that dreadful information the night before from Isobel, knowing what Padruig would have to do in front of his family to restore his role after having been gone for nearly four years. I told him that I had picked up Isobel from the floor, where he'd left her unconscious.

"So, why?" I asked. "Couldn't you have waited until you were alone with her?" I asked.

I knew I was pushing the boundaries with a MacGregor, but at first, he accepted my criticism. "Because Padruig is back and he is the head of the household," he said. "There are too many secrets and she wasn't going to disclose them," Grigor said.

"Isobel doesn't have to," was my response. "She has been severely traumatised, but survived somehow and now you've made it worse by removing her support pillar, the man she loved. What can she do now with feeling that no one loves her after surviving for all those years with such hardship? She is revered in these parts as 'Isobel of Glenmoriston.' She has given other people hope. You of all people, her brother, a love found late in her lonely life. I do not know you personally, but I really wish that you'd left this problem up to the husband to sort out with his wife, to build up her trust and then one day, she would have felt safe enough to tell him everything. Now do you really think that she will ever feel safe enough to tell him anything else? That goes for all of the family watching on, especially poor Helen," I said.

"Then there's the example that you are setting the younger men, like your son Grigor Og and that other younger man, Hugh. Will they all feel that hypnosis and violence is always the solution to family matters? When you ushered Isobel over to you, she trusted you completely. Will you ever enjoy that same trust again? I'm a lawyer, as you know and I hear horrific stories, every day of my working life and there are few people who I actually look forward to seeing and Isobel is one of them. She has an intelligence unlike any other woman I've met here in the north, she has a decency and a kindness rarely found, she has a spirituality not found any more, with complete devotion to her family, especially Padruig, who is a formidable person if you are on the wrong side of him. Why would anyone want to further damage such a kind-hearted soul? But you have and that's on you, before your Maker," I concluded.

Grigor didn't much like the comments that I'd made and indicated that he'd ride his horse for the rest of the way into Inverness. I obliged and stopped the wee pony for him to alight to ride his horse. He believed his role was to aid his friend of many years to bring his wife into line, with some secrets that he'd obviously been made aware of and chose his old friend over his sister, despite what might happen to her. I doubted from then on that she would enjoy her loving relationship with Grigor Mohr again, despite her deep love for him.

I gave Grigor Mohr MacGregor his letter that day after we had arrived back at my office. Duly grateful, he went on his way, reflectively with his son, Grigor Og, who was still looking pale and badly affected from the previous night's horrors. My secretary asked me what on earth had happened, because apparently, I looked as though I'd seen a ghost. I had asked her to help me out a bit, as I prepared for my first client's arrival by getting my bath ready and some clean clothes out.

She obliged and as I was dressing, I looked in the mirror and didn't like what I saw. I should've helped Isobel, but what could I do up against a force like Padruig Grant? My hands wouldn't stop shaking. I prayed Isobel would find a man strong enough to compete with Padruig. One thing Padruig Grant could count on now was that the family would take forever to recover, if they ever did. Now it's known that she was raped by her uncle, I hoped that poor Alex Grant would never know that there was a question over his paternity.

Perusing the Loch Insh files again, the other letter there then stood out to me was Marion Grant MacNachten. I had never been told who she was.

Annabel Cameron MacGregor's Story

"So Many Good-Looking People"

By Zaynab El-Fatah

Illustrations by Halima Karger

Invermoriston

Scotland, 1784

My name is Annabel Cameron, I am eighteen years old and I was born at home on a farm in Cameron country in the Highlands.

My friend, Morag-Freya Grant and I would often meet to eat our lunch together at the hospital, where we were both doing our Nursing Training in Inverness, Scotland. We had planned to play doubles tennis together on the weekend with her brother and Gillcrest.

She would tell me funny stories about the lawyer's cases with whom she boarded and I lived with my Aunty Maud, so I had nothing of much interest to say. We had both hoped to be placed in the same hospital once we had finished our training and she wanted to be closer to her parents, who were in Glenmoriston.

So, when we filled in our placement forms, we both wrote Invermoriston.

She would often spend a lot of time in the Science department of the hospital and naively, I believed it was to do with her studies and it probably was the first time that she went there on an errand. After that, she often spoke of a young Scientist whose name was Gillcrest Lachlan MacLachlan, who was originally from the Lachlan lands at Loch Fyne, Argyle. I just thought he was too close to the Campbells for my liking, but when she had invited him to dinner at the old lawyer's house, I thought it was more than science that interested them both in each other.

I asked her to point him out to me at the canteen and I thought that he wasn't that good looking and he was a bad dresser for sure, not tall, bit round with fluffy red hair. Not my type at all, but she really liked him. I couldn't see what she saw in him, but I couldn't be nasty and so I supported her. She was afraid to tell her family about him because they were Clan Grant and Clan Gregor, who were known for their harshness, except for her Grandma she said.

So, in announcing her affection for Gillcrest to them, I advised her to sit near her Grandma then and follow tradition, being that they were a traditional family. I advised her if he owned a kilt, that he should wear it with a nice contrasting waistcoat and jacket and to go dressed much better than he usually does.

I also suggested that she cut his hair very neatly, before he was due to meet them. Ideally also, the old lawyer should accompany him on his cart and pony to give him better credentials.

Of course, neither of us knew that he already had good credentials because he was a Laird somewhere in Argyle on Loch Fyne.

We were both successful in our nursing applications and were sent to Invermoriston Hospital and while I had to board at the nurse's accommodation, she was going to marry Gillcrest MacLachlan over the holidays after all and live in his house, provided by the hospital. He was promoted to Head of the Science Department specialising in soil, or something as boring as that. She was so happy and proud to be marrying him and she adored him and he adored her. It was kind of cute to see them together.

At least Morag-Freya's brother, Aonghus MacGregor wasn't a scientist, he was a lawyer, but if he was anything like my good friend, he may be good looking but a bit dull, in a good way. Her hair was jet black, so I imagined his hair would be jet black too. Aonghus MacGregor was anything but dull, not great at tennis, but neither was I, so Gillcrest and Morag-Freya won that game. They suggested we all go back to their place for afternoon tea and dinner which we accepted, although I was aware Aonghus was staying there overnight anyway, which meant I was going to be the only lonely one at the end of the night.

When the time came to leave, Aonghus offered to escort me back to my lodgings. I hadn't noticed that he liked me in the time we were all together, but I'm not very intuitive in that way, so it was a surprise when we arrived at the nurses' accommodation to be kissed passionately by the very handsome young lawyer. I hate to admit it, but I had never even been kissed, let alone like that, tongue and all.

I was hoping he would leave then, so I could recover from that kiss, but his hands were all over me too like an octopus, which caught me by surprise. I had to call a halt to it and ask for some dialogue, as I was still a virgin, in every way and I had never indulged like this before, which I told him. He apologised for any offence, but found me particularly striking and attractive, intelligent and unlike those with whom he'd studied. He was glad about that because he was looking for a suitable wife and hadn't come across anyone who had met his criteria. He wanted to be able to proudly introduce the woman he would marry to his Father.

He knew his Mither would accept his choice, whoever she was, but his Da would only accept the best and frankly, he said, I was the best.

With great confidence in himself, Aonghus MacGregor asked if he could see me again or whether that required parental permission, then we could think about marriage because he had been offered a business to take over in Inverness with house attached, then all we needed to do was give up my nursing career in order to work with him in his law office. I was familiar with that office in the year that Morag-Freya had boarded there. The poor old lawyer had become too old and tired with the sometimes-dreadful things he'd had to deal with and had offered his business to the strong, young MacGregor, capable of taking it all on.

So, the word 'marriage' was mentioned and I think I may have been in shock.

"I would like to meet all of your family at Morag-Freya's wedding, especially your Grandma and I would like to meet them all before I give a definite answer if that's okay. Involving my parents is really a traditional affair and we would need to be familiar with each other and all of our plans, as well as the agreement of your entire family, before my Da makes me lose confidence," I explained a little shyly.

"Aonghus, may I say this? I do like you too, but could we please slow down? I have never met anyone like you before and you are very handsome," I said.

With that, my new man kissed me again with no sign of slowing down, as the word handsome did it for his male ego, so I tried my hardest to kiss him back, not knowing if I was doing it right.

"I love you Annabel Cameron, you'll be mine," he declared, then strode back to his accommodation.

Morag-Freya's wedding was lovely and I did get to meet everyone except his Grandma, whom I'd heard so much about. Aonghus was a gentleman and a lovely partner for such an event. He was then more insistent on us also getting married, but I asked him if we could please meet his Grandma. He thought I'd be bored there on the farm, so he asked if he could be excused and leave partway to go and visit Isobel-Mairi, his sister and then meet back up with me. I didn't find it boring at all and I even got along well with his Grandda, Padruig Grant, as well as his Grandma. His Grandda walked me all around the whole farm, showing me where everything was and where Aonghus' Father grew his oat crops. So, he took me over to Aonghus' Da, who I had only met the one time and he was pleased to see me again and asked where his son was. He apologised if his son wasn't looking after me.

I was introduced to a farm worker named Hugh Chisholm and shown the stables that belonged to Mr Grant's wife, Isobel, he called her. I was introduced to another Hugh there also, Hugh Chisholm. I asked Mr Grant if it was confusing with two Hugh Chisholms on staff and he explained that the older one was called Hugh Mohr and the younger one was Hugh Og and so no, he answered, it was never confusing, especially when you got to know their personalities. He said that with a story behind it.

Then another Chisholm arrived at the stables whose name was Hamish and then I was sure I would confuse all of these people. Mr Grant pointed at a lovely stone home on the property called 'Chisholm House', so I was getting the picture that the Grants, the Chisholms and the MacGregors all had a very close association. He pointed up the mountain to a Manor

House that he was building and maybe when we got married it would be complete.

He was certain that we were going to marry and I became rather shy.

Mr Grant and I enjoyed our walk back to the house and he told me about the Chapel and pointed it out to me and how his wife had had it built and that everyone who is buried in the cemetery have their names engraved on the inside walls. It was called Chapel of Saint Columba at Craskie. His wife's good friend, Gillcrest MacNachten, now deceased, built it for her.

"That's an old name," I remarked. "MacNachten. That's Pict isn't it?" I asked. He didn't know that, but I could ask his wife. Aonghus was coming back with Isobel-Mairi and her farrier husband, who was gorgeous looking.

"There are so many good-looking people on this farm, including Aonghus," I remarked. "How did you all get to be so handsome?" I asked.

Mr Grant liked that remark, with his long silver hair. He was old, but still good looking and Aonghus' Da was really lovely looking and all of those Chisholms too. He didn't agree about the Chisholms, I think, but liked that I thought that all of the family were handsome, even Ewen the farrier.

Walking back inside their lovely home, Grandma was looking impatient.

"Well, have you decided if you're marrying Aonghus or not dear?" she asked.

"Aye, Mistress. I'd like it if we could please ask my parents if we can have a meeting here together," I answered. It was finally said. I would marry Aonghus if my parents agreed. Out came her trusty calendar that she always carried in a leather satchel.

"When then?" she asked, as Aonghus walked in and we all agreed on a date to meet my parents on Craskie Farm.

"Where will you live?" asked Mr Grant. Aonghus told him that we would be living in Inverness, taking over the old Lawyer's Rooms, unless he wanted money for it.

I wasn't looking forward to the meeting with my parents and my grandfather and it was predictably ghastly with Da even involving Lochiel of the Camerons. It was so embarrassing, but I did draw closer to Grandma that day. She could be a hard woman to get to know or understand, I thought, and she didn't disclose much of herself, her life, her history or even Clan conversation. On the other hand, Mr Grant spoke a lot, as he was a veteran of Culloden, like my grandfather, so bringing him along, annoying though he was, kept the two of them busy.

I knew my Father would disapprove of Aonghus and for no reason, but in the end, I was awarded £4000 Scots dowry, thanks to Lochiel. Ma and I had a lovely time shopping to upgrade the Inverness house, but at first, we bought a new horse and a carriage for my new home, as well as drapes, new furniture and wallpaper. I also had the laundry upgraded and I made sure the guest room was particularly pretty. Aonghus' Uncle Alex was back from Nova Scotia and his lovely daughter Jean decided to stay with us after we were married for two days a week while working in Inverness. Uncle Alex would stay one night and then she would work for five days on his farm, with her equally handsome Father.

I was lucky to have met Aonghus and his family and I really loved him. Kissing became one of my favourite occupations in life, but once we were married, love making was thoroughly exciting. I worked in the office with my husband and that's when we heard the terrible news of Grandda's death. I had loved him deeply and I was so sad.

I'd been to a few funerals in my life, but nothing prepared me for that funeral. It was enormous. I lost count of how many people came to farewell Mr Grant, with all of the Clan flags flying, I felt rather ignorant as to the reason that I had never known he'd been a hero during and after Culloden and was one of the Seven Glenmoriston Men. My husband used the excuse that he thought it was just a folk story and not really true. It reached the newspapers and both Grandda and Grandma were spoken very highly of. It was very good for business and we did so much more business after Grandda's death, once they knew we were related to Padruig Dubh Grant, but what I wasn't expecting was that Grandma was famous too, as 'Isobel of Glenmoriston', the only teamster lady in the Highlands.

I asked my husband, "Why didn't you tell me?"

"I thought you knew," Aonghus said, "You were friends with Morag-Freya after all." Finding out all of the family history, I was kind of proud. What an achievement that was for a small woman in those difficult times. What I wasn't expecting though was that Grandma married again soon after the funeral, to one of those good looking Chisholms. One of the Hughs, I don't remember which one, but I think it was the one with the yellow hair.

"How nice is that?" I said to Aonghus, "Your Grandma getting remarried," I said and was very surprised at his response.

"Are you kidding? At her age? Getting married to someone younger? Nae, I don't think it's nice. She should have just remained a widow. That's my opinion," he said

"Oh, Aonghus. Come on darling. Your Grandma would be happy to have a new husband," I protested. Aonghus then said,

"How can she replace Grandda just like that? They even hand fasted without me being there. They didn't even wait for the whole family and the Priests to come back," he said pouting.

"So," I replied, "There's going to be another wedding, is there, that we can attend?" I asked "Aye, this Sunday there's the formal wedding and we're invited," he added.

"Weren't you going to tell me?" I asked.

"Of course, I was going to tell you, I just didn't get around to it," he said.

My husband had his MacGregor face on, so I kissed him, cuddled him and teased him until we were in the bedroom together and he was happy again and I asked him to be happy for Grandma and he agreed just for me.

"But Annabel," he went on to say, "What must people think? What must people be saying?" he asked.

"It doesn't matter," I replied, "They're very mature adults. They don't need our permission and since when have you cared what people thought? They've clearly known each other for a very long time. I think it's sweet. I am going to go buy them a gift today," I said, which I did. My grumpy faced husband couldn't improve his grumpy face, even on the day of their formal wedding either, but his Grandma didn't care. They were in a world of their own and Hugh Chisholm was clearly devoted to her.

"By the way darling, I have some news that might brighten you up," I said and he made some kind of grumpy, gutteral noise.

"Do you want some good news?" I asked.

"Aye," he said.

"You're going to be a Daddy," I said grinning. The smile finally returned to his face and he was overjoyed.

"You'll be able to tell your new Grandda," I teased.

The three Collie dogs were even at the wedding inside the Chapel, all washed, brushed and clean, wearing their new collars that I had bought them as a wedding gift with ribbons. Grandma had named this litter Charlie, Louis and Pompidou. She really loved new Grandda's Collies and she was the only person he trusted with them. I looked around to see if his long rifle was far away and it was only leaning up against the Priest's pulpit at arms distance. I had married into a character family for sure and I couldn't wait to see how my wee bairn was going to turn out with all the strong characters from this family, especially my darling Aonghus with all of that MacGregor fire. I wondered if a wee lass would be as fiery as a wee lad, then interrupting my thoughts came the cries of baby

Nachtain, who could really make a noise. It was his turn to be baptised and he didn't much like the cold water splashed on his face and it looked like if he could yell a Gaelic obscenity at the Priest at that age, he would. He was adorably cute and my baby would grow up with Nachtain.

Nachtain had MacGregor and Armstrong genes.

This was going to be an interesting life and I asked Aonghus if we could come more often to the farm for the bairns to see each other once ours was born and surprisingly he agreed. Cora's baby Donald was walking now, so he would probably assume the boss bairn role, I had guessed. I had to encourage Morag-Freya to have a baby too, so there'd be more of the same generation, as soon as the ceremony in the Chapel was over. Beth's baby was due soon too by the look of her and he or she would be the only red head. Simon was more ginger really, but if it was watered down a bit by Beth's hair colour, maybe it could even be auburn like Gillcrest's hair. Obsessing over hair and bairns, I realised I wasn't paying attention as everyone was due to go down to the house, when I heard that the other Hugh's wife, Meredith, was also with child and I wanted to chat with her.

I had the opportunity to tell Beth that I was with child and asked her when her bairn was due and what she was going to call him or her.

"Congratulations. The Doctor is unsure, but it may be twins," she said, "And it appears we do have twins in our family now. I've chosen names for boys and girls depending on what it or they turn out to be, which isn't far off. Simone Joanna for a girl to respect both my husband and his Father and Ma's Father John. Then for a boy, Simon Patrick. If there's twin girls Isobel Freya from my family and Anna Simone. Other names I've chosen are Grigor Hugh after Uncle Grigor, but you didn't meet him did you Annabel?" she said.

"So, you're naming him Hugh after Grandma's new husband?" I asked. "Aye, I like new Grandda Hugh, he has always been kind to both me and James when we both lived here before

Grandda returned from Quebec," she said and then went to help her husband Simon to get some food to eat. Beth could be a bit snobby at times for some reason.

"Aonghus darling, what names do you have in mind for our baby?" I asked.

"It might surprise you, my sweetness, that baby names hadn't entered my mind yet because you only just told me you were with child," he said a bit too sarcastically, but it was overheard.

"You're with child?" Grandma asked. "Hugh darling," she exclaimed. "Annabel's with child, isn't that wonderful? Another baptism for you to arrange," she said with a big smile. He took her into his arms and kissed her and she giggled. I decided to call my lad Hugh too and Isobel if it was a lass. My Grandparents on this side of the family had a way about them that brought happiness into the room wherever you were. Even the Collies started making cute "hooroo" sounds.

Seeking out Meredith was harder than I'd anticipated, as I went from room to room because she was so busy cleaning, serving and working hard. She was still employed as Grandma's house help. I felt sorry for her and when I did find her, I asked first if I could assist. Naturally, she was glad of the help, when I noticed she was at least six months pregnant. When others saw that I was helping Meredith, they also joined in to assist, especially her husband, Hugh Og. I had to get his name right and add the "Og" part. He was a sweetie too and I wondered about the character of the Chisholm Clan on Craskie, being a mixture of real toughness and sweetness, immeasurable.

I heard later that the sometimes difficult, MacKenzie family had to behave themselves on the property as a condition of her lease on the house on New Farm and while they did attend Grandda's funeral without fuss, they didn't trust themselves or Grandda didn't, in attending the wedding, which they expressed disapproval of. Her mood might have reflected that, as well as Hugh Mohr's rifle being close by in the Chapel. Testing my theory, I checked again to see where it was in relation to Grandda Hugh Mohr and he was holding his rifle behind his back with one hand and holding Grandma Isobel with the other.

Eventually, while bringing a pale of water in from the burn for Meredith, I was able to ask her when her bairn was due and tell her that I was also with child. Finally, she loosened up and told me that the wee bairn was due soon, according to the new doctor who had just moved into Glenmoriston. I asked her if he would also see me, as I didn't like any of the doctors in Inverness.

"Of course," she said, "He's only new, so he's looking for more patients and he has been given instructions by Grandma about delivering bairns our way. He is also unmarried though, so take Aonghus in case the husband becomes jealous. I always take Hugh Og," she said.

I didn't know what 'our way' was, so we chatted in length and she told me how Isobel-Mairi's bairn was delivered by Grandma and her washer lady with her and Helen assisting. Men have their limits though, poor Master Grigor fainted on the floor when his daughter was at the peak of her pain, she told me.

"We could all have our bairns play together, don't you think? I really want my bairn to be totally involved with his or her family," I expressed to my new-found friend Meredith.

"Aye, that would be lovely. Can you come out often then?" she asked, as my husband came up behind me to ask us ladies what we were gossiping about.

"Not gossip my love. Can I see the new doctor in Glenmoriston instead of Inverness and when he's born, can all the cousins play here together on the farm?" I asked.

"That's a fine idea, but I'll have to ask Grandma and Hugh Mohr first and my Ma and Da. Wait a while though, I don't think today is the right time," he said. "The wedding and the baptism are the priority today, then we'll make a proper visit when you are due to see the doctor again. How does that sound? By the way, I'm coming with you, seeing it's a man delivering the bairn. They're cutting the cake darling. Best come and join in and try and look interested," he said.

"I'm sorry, I am interested," I added.

"They want us to stay the night and the room is ready for us for whenever you are tired," he added.

"How lovely, I was hoping we could stay so I could take another look at the farm tomorrow. Do you think they'd let me?" I asked.

"Probably not. They're too busy. They have to catch up with what was left out today and feed the Priest and farewell him," my husband explained.

He could be so sensible and I was being selfish.

Anyhow, I was feeling tired after all that housework. We watched the happy couple cut the cake and new Grandda Hugh gave a nice speech to us all. Then my Father-in-law, Grigor, who I call Da, also gave a speech welcoming his new Da into the family and embraced him and so did Uncle Alex. I felt like crying, it was so touching and so I impulsively went to them and hugged both Grandma and my new Grandda and asked him if I could call him Grandda. He agreed with his wife proudly watching on and he kissed me gently on my forehead.

Aonghus, from that moment on, accepted Grandda Hugh as well as I and I couldn't wait to show them all our bairn. My parents disapproved of them marrying so soon after the funeral and chose not to come to their wedding, which was so sad for me. Grandma just took it in her stride and Grandda took his rifle. I had no doubt that he would kill someone for his newly beloved wife and that's a lot of emotion. I think to find each other at that age is a gift from God, in Grandda's case, his patience was a gift from God and I admired them for it, but others are entitled to their opinions too.

The next time Aonghus's cousin, Jean was staying over with us at first with Uncle Alex, I told her about the new Doctor in Glenmoriston and asked if she had met him yet. My plan being to see him frequently during the whole time that I was with child and that he would then deliver the wee bairn. I was increasingly feeling that it was a lass. Neither Jean nor Uncle Alex knew of the new doctor and wanted to meet him when we were due to see him. Dr Browne hadn't yet bought property on which to build a new practice as well as a house and was only working out of the old doctors' rooms near the new post office. I had heard that he wasn't Scottish and asked them if they knew.

"I know," said my husband appearing so unassuming.

"Oh Aonghus, how much do you know about him?" I asked.

"He's English! Do you still want him to deliver our bairn?" he asked. "Evidently, it was his Father, Dr Browne Snr. who saved Grandda in London from that awful, infected wound on his leg after the Quebec campaign and his son was expected to take over the London practise from his Father? As yet, he still doesn't know that his son has purchased a practice in Scotland. So, don't get your hopes up or Dr Benedict Browne might be packed off back to London," Aonghus said.

Uncle Alex responded saying, "I have to confess ignorance to all of those happenings. I hadn't yet restored a semblance of a relationship with my Father when he dropped around a wee gift from Nova Scotia. He was riding on a big black horse and it was like seeing a ghost. He didn't stay, so I thought he still hated me, as did Grandda. It was then that we decided to leave Scotland," Uncle Alex said. "I knew it was hopeless to try anymore and at first, we both thought that obtaining land in Virginia would be a good idea, until Da offered me his own land in Nova Scotia, not thinking of the wildlife and just how cold it was there. It seemed like a wonderful idea and I did make many good friends there, most of whom were Scots, namely Frasers," he said.

"I can't imagine you, Uncle Alex being unable to get on with old Grandda, I really loved him. When he showed me around Craskie Farm, he stood so straight and proud, not like most older men and he just grinned at me with a smiley face.

He was so pleased that Aonghus had someone who liked him," I said.

"It's true he liked the pretty young lassies, but he'd keep his distance, did you notice that?" Uncle Alex said.

"Aye, I did, he stood about six paces away from me," I said.

"What do you mean that he was so pleased that I'd found someone who liked me? Didn't he think that I was likeable?" asked my now offended husband.

"Maybe he found you opinionated and difficult to get along with, as well as argumentative, like all lawyers are supposed to be," answered Jean.

"It has nothing to do with being likeable, you are very likeable or Annabel wouldn't have married you, isn't that right Annabel?" Jean said in order to save this situation.

"That's right, my husband is gorgeous and Grandda was pleased that he could go to his grave knowing that you had found happiness with me," I said smiling.

"Oh well that's alright then. But why did he hate you then Uncle Alex?" Aonghus asked.

"I was badly affected by the English and the Militia ravishing the women on and near our farms and couldn't get over it, then one stupid night in the shieling, I sucked on Ma's breast, as I had done as a wee bairn, being breast fed for five years during a famine. Grandda kicked me and Therese both out and I was unwelcome from then on. It was one mistake that I had made in my sleep and even though Ma understood, no one else did.

In addition, Allan MacDonald had raped my Mither and even though my Father and Mither were both sexually active at the same time, paternity was then questioned if I was a MacDonald, not a Grant, because I was better looking than my brother Patrick. It's not hard to be better looking than Patrick, besides I had an equally gorgeous twin sister. Look how beautiful my Mither is, of course I was going to be handsome.

My Mither has explained everything to me and I am a Grant not a MacDonald," said Uncle Alex. "My nephew, Malcolm, who lives with me now, is the spitting image of Grandda as a younger man, so there's the proof, in Malcolm," he said.

"All the Indian women in Nova Scotia suckled their young for as long as they wanted and they did just what Da did reach out and try to suckle at any age. It was natural. Great Grandda was wrong what he did to you Da, in breaking up the family unit," Jean said in her Father's defence. Aonghus seemed satisfied with that answer if not only a little surprised.

"By the way family, we are all going to see Morag-Freya over the weekend if you were wanting to come with us. We have to discuss some amazing ideas that Jean has had with her cousin's scientist husband Gillcrest," said Uncle Alex.

"We are also meeting up with Isobel-Mairi and Ewen who have news, if we were interested to discuss that too," added Uncle Alex. They asked us to keep them informed about the new doctor, so we could meet him before they both went to bed and Uncle Alex left early in the morning to buy geese in Inverness. He also was dropping in to see Grandda and Grandma on his way home to Loch Garry to ask about hunting hart on his property. He was hoping new Grandda could teach him the ropes.

I was wondering whether the new doctor might want to stay in Glenmoriston if he met a lovely local lady like Jean. She was well educated like he was and a very interesting person and unafraid of hard work and they both had funny accents. Most of all, she had those good looks that only that family could produce. The downside was that he was English, so he would have to be dedicated to Scotland to pass their test. He wouldn't wear tartan, I suppose although there are kilts in plain colours like the Irish or clan adoption was an option, so I asked if he'd wear Grant tartan. I forgot to ask what colour his hair was, maybe brown with a surname like Browne and his age. I was too caught up in all that juicy gossip.

I'd have to filter that when my Mither came to visit the following day. I wanted to buy a new crib for our wee bairn and wee bairn blankets and wee bairn baths and all of the bairn clothes. Mummy was going to buy me books for the bairns too. What fun it was going to be.

My darling husband wanted some more loving before sleeping that night and I was only too happy to do that again and again as I found it very exciting and I just hoped my noises weren't waking up our guests.

Aonghus found a spot that always made me squeal, he was an amazing lover and he was all mine.

Alexander Grant's Story

"Loch Garry Ranch"

By Zaynab El-Fatah

Illustrations by Halima Karger and Fatima Zayn al-Abidin

Glenmoriston
Scotland, 1740

I've adored my Mither for as long as I can remember. I rarely saw my Father growing up and my Grandparents were Freya and John Grant. My Mither's name is Isobel MacGregor Grant and my Father's name is Padruig Dubh Grant, one of the infamous Seven Glenmoriston Men.

My name is Alexander Grant, the youngest son and one of twins, to Isobel and Padruig Grant of Glenmoriston. My twin's name is Marion MacNachten.

My earliest recollection of my Father was being on our front porch of the old farm in Craskie in the Braes of Glenmoriston,

Marion MacNachten

Scotland when a horse rider came in, sporting longish jet-black hair, sitting very straight and upright atop that big horse and I asked Mither who it was. "It's your Da," she said, looking pleased to see that man on the horse. I didn't remember my Da looking like that, in fact I'd forgotten what he looked like. I was clinging to my Ma's legs, as I often did if I felt threatened, but he wasn't looking for me, he wanted Ma.

I felt protective of my Mither and I thought he was a threat, even though she said it was my Da. He was about to take my Ma into the house and I tried to push him away from her, so he shoved me aside and I fell onto the wooden floor of the porch and I hit my lip on something, which made it bleed. I called out to Ma crying, but she didn't come. Grandma came and she told me to be quiet. She took me inside to wash my face and tended to my lip, when I heard Ma making sounds from her bedroom like Da was hurting her, so I tried to get in there, but the door was locked. I called out to her and banged on the door with my fists so many times that Grandda came and took me outside to go and play with Patrick, my brother, who was with the crofters' lads.

Grandda told my brother and Helen, my sister, that my Da had come home and to wash up and be quiet and most of all, be respectful to him or we'd all get the strap from him. Patrick kept on playing with his friends and said it didn't matter if our father was here or not and kept playing. Helen was disappointed to stop her game but did go inside the house to wash up and help Grandma with dinner and anything else she had needed. I was just left standing there with Patrick calling me a sook to the other boys. They teased me anyway, because I was still drinking milk from my Mither's breasts when they had already stopped, and younger siblings had taken their places at their Mithers' breasts. When I think of it now, it was the only sensible way to feed me when famine was rife and my Father had stopped sending money for us all on the farm.

Patrick's friends didn't want me to play with them and told me to go away that day, which was expected, so I looked for Grandda and his horses. I thought I could hide there with them in the stables until he had left, but by nightfall, asleep on the hay, I was awoken by Grandda to go and eat dinner. He was kind to me when I was really wee, but it changed as time passed and he also grew to dislike me, I thought and the dislike grew to complete lack of acceptance after I made a mistake. I just wanted my Ma and I was so thirsty from not having anything to drink from her. When he took me inside, Ma was at the kitchen table, and she was alright and in no pain. I was so relieved that she was alright.

"Wash up lad with your brother and sister," she said. So, we all bathed in the same cooling bath water, not knowing what to expect.

"Have you seen him?" I asked. Helen answered that she had and he was sweet to her when she gave him his tea and sandwiches. She said that he had even kissed her on each cheek and told her what a good girl she was.

"Ass kisser," said Patrick. Of course, I had to ask what an 'ass kisser' was right at the moment that he came into the room and I was dragged out of the bath and strapped for using bad language and on wet skin. That was painful.

We had never been compatible for as long as I can remember, but the worst was yet to come, when I wanted a drink from Ma, which was usually to just put my hand down her blouse to take out her breast to drink from it frantically, out of pure thirst. To my Father's horror, he grabbed me and belted me again without waiting for an explanation. I was confused. Ma was trying to stop him and to explain that I had to keep drinking breast milk, as it was free and available and we had run out of money.

"Please let him drink some milk darling?" she begged, "Or my breasts will become engorged and wee Alex needs it," she said.

"Were the other two bairns breast fed for this long?" he bellowed.

"They were fed until I was with child again, so one year and two years, but we had more food to give them," she answered.

"You'll turn him into a sook Isobel," he yelled and was very unhappy with Ma.

"I'm sorry Padruig, what do you want me to do then?" Ma asked through tears.

"Stop this for a start and make him eat his meat and vegetables and drink water from the burn if he's thirsty," he ordered.

He had spoken and that was how it was, until he predictably left again having hunted a hart for us all to eat and his wages were then given to Grandda. That didn't solve Ma's problem of her breasts then becoming engorged and painful with so much milk in them that I was no longer allowed to drink. They would leak sometimes through her clothes and he'd be annoyed if he saw that, so most of what I recall of him as a bairn was an angry and selfish man who had a lot of difficulty reining in the violent part of himself that he was trained to be.

I didn't understand then that the Highlands were about to be obliterated and life as a Highlander, especially a Jacobite, would become an unacceptable part of human society and not unlike the wolves and bears, would be completely wiped out of Scotland, if possible and sent to all the corners of the world, unknown to them. We were then living right on the edge of a volcano just prior to its eruption. I thought that I had the right to complain about losing Mither's breast milk at the age of five, but it had been a luxury that like everything, was about to end and Da's skills therefore were to become what the

Highlands needed for any of us to survive. Ma had known that all along, even though it wasn't her way, but Grandma was increasingly sickened by her ruthless son in law and wished Ma had never met him at all at the Glenmoriston School and all those Grants whom she disliked, especially my Father's own Father and his brothers.

The only Clan Grant individual she loved was her husband, John Grant, the very clever Teamster whose skills I had never appreciated as a bairn and all of his Clydesdale horses were stolen before I had the chance to really understand his skills and his love for those horses, let alone appreciate that he passed his skill onto my Mither, who spoke Erse to them. Grandma was killed by the British troops who burned down our farm in 1746. I was reminded that Ma was 'Isobel of Glenmoriston' at my Father's funeral because she drove a team of eight Clydesdale horses leading the cortege, at her advanced age, that carried his coffin.

Both of my parents had written to me to return to Scotland giving each other as the excuse. Ma wanted me to see Da before he passed away and Nova Scotia was a long way from Scotland. Da wanted me to return for my Mither's sake, he had said. He said he couldn't bear to see her suffer anymore without me, her favourite son and felt responsible for some of her unhappiness and begged me to not only visit but return to live nearby my Mither.

My ex-wife Therese, despite being Catholic, was able to divorce me under the laws in Nova Scotia and had met a new-found love. She had never forgiven me for taking us there to that frozen land, then held me responsible for one of our children's deaths by a black bear. I was with my daughter at the time and although I had shot the bear, I didn't succeed in killing it, only angering it further. Although our business in Nova Scotia was successful and we had two more children, she told me of her new love and her intention to replace me. I was devastated at the time that she told me because I couldn't have stopped that bear on that day, but she held it against me and so we first separated and then split the land in half, so I had half and she had half with her new husband.

I was at my wits end when first Ma's letter came, followed by Da's letter, so I sold my half of the land and obtained my ex-wife's permission to legally have two of my children reside with me permanently, Jean and Alexander and I left for Scotland. Seeing the letters as a sign from God, we three left. Never having had another woman except Therese, I couldn't imagine pursuing that life yet anyway, so first I was to see my Father, hopefully to reconcile before his death and to ease both my Mither's and my heart. I had no idea that I was also to meet my twin Marion for the first time who had been hidden for her own safety in Loch Insh. At least my Grandfather had already passed away, so he wouldn't be there to stir up trouble again.

Both Jean and Alexander were sick of the bickering in Nova Scotia and had an intense dislike for their Mither's new husband, so they were very keen to move 'home', they called it.

It was most fortunate that Jean was an interpreter and spoke Gaelic fluently along with Latin, French, German, Dutch, English and many First Nations languages. She was going to need Gaelic with mostly the older generation and there could be a need for her in the Courts system now with English being more widely spoken, I had thought. My dear son, Alexander, was dedicated to farming and animal husbandry and I was hoping to buy a farm near Craskie, hopefully still in Grant country. Many emigrants moving to Nova Scotia regretted having left Scotland but could not afford their return tickets. My Father was kind enough to include the money for however many fares we needed, not knowing any of what my family had gone through. It was the first letter that I had ever received from him, as I thought he still had no English.

I spent days speaking with my Father and my twin Marion before his passing, for which I am grateful to the Almighty God. Surprisingly, I also met Marion's two sons, Malcolm and Kenneth. I had never been told that I had a twin, but I was ecstatic to meet her and to know that I had another like myself to love. Ma had explained that when we were born, the neighbour wanted one of her bairns, which was a really bizarre story, so her Father made the decision to hide Marion for her own protection in Loch Insh, not anticipating the Rising. After Grandda lost the horses during the burnings, they were unable to see her for a very long time.

Marion's foster Father married her to a member of his Clan, who was a nice man of Clan Nachten with whom she had the two lads, but sadly he died of pneumonia when they were both young and she went back to live with Mr MacNachten who had raised her. He then contacted Lochiel of the Camerons to find Ma after an article appeared in the newspaper with both my parents in it. He thought she must have died. They were re-united, but Da had never been told about his other child, until just before his death. I didn't tell Marion that she was the lucky one because she revered Da. It was clear that she had only ever been told good things about Padruig Dubh, our Father, so I didn't want to spoil it. Luckily, for all of us he understood why she had been hidden from that neighbour, so that was a story I was yet to learn. It was Malcolm who told me what Grandma had told him in Loch Insh many years ago.

Marion also spent time talking to Da before his passing and on the day of his huge funeral I was able to carry our Clan Grant Nova Scotia flag alongside my brother, Patrick, who carried the Clan Grant Glenmoriston flag. Glenmoriston men had their own tartan colour, unlike that of other Grants and there were few of us left now after 'the great deception', as Da called it. I don't know if my deep sorrow that day was for my lost culture and people from Glenmoriston, or my Father or both, but for my Mither I held the flag high and followed all of her instructions to the letter. Ma had become a general type of figure, whose instructions Highland men, twice her size, obeyed and it had to be seen to be believed.

Long before Therese and I thought to go to the Colonies, we had known Helen's husband Grigor MacGregor, but I wouldn't say that I knew him well, only that he was the son of one of

Da's best friends and Ma loved him, so that was good enough for me. Apparently, according to Helen, being Da's favourite child went against her when it came time to marrying or hand fast with Grigor MacGregor. Da essentially approved that they could marry while they were still young, but he kept putting it off, so Grigor Og spent two years improving his knowledge on farming, particularly the soil in which oat crops are planted and of course when to plant and harvest and so on.

Apparently now he's quite the genius about soil and has linked up with the Science Department of the hospital in Invermoriston, who teach the course now. The idea being to prevent further famines. Co-incidentally, his daughter Morag-Freya, my beautiful niece, married the man in charge, Gillcrest Lachlan MacLachlan, which helped Craskie Farm's reputation and it appeared in the papers.

Poor Grigor, I often imagine their sorry scene with Da when I am feeling sorry for myself, but Da still disallowed the union until they were much older. Being so in love, they had a secret love affair, repeatedly hand fasting, for nearly ten years although it didn't help my sister in the end as she tragically committed suicide. I doubt that they knew that it had become common knowledge that was kept secret from Da, or all hell would have broken loose. Isobel-Mairi, Aonghus-Grigor and Morag-Freya were lucky to have ever been born. Hugh Chisholm especially, watched out for them, as if they were his own children. I didn't expect that they and their children would become his responsibility one day, any more than I would be calling him Da, the day after my Father's funeral.

While still living in the dreaded wee shieling down the pathway between us and our neighbours, I had met and married my now ex-wife, Therese. I won't pretend that it was easy to squeeze all those growing adults into such a small home, but I am still grateful for it having provided us with safety on the day that the dragoons came to our farm in 1746 when Grandma was killed by one of them. Da had ridden on horseback to let Ma know that the Battle of Culloden, had failed and to stay and look after us bairns. Being a hunted man, he would need to hide somewhere, but didn't say where. There were seven of them and all armed. One of them turned as they galloped off and Ma waved slowly back. She was crying, but I thought it was because she was missing my Da or feared for his life.

Later, Ma told me that it was Hugh who looked back. It was from that day when the dragoons first came to our farm when I heard the screams of women being raped or ravished or murdered. The groans of their husbands too were horrific. It was the most terrible sound that I could ever have imagined hearing, so I tried to close over my ears to not hear it, but it then became closer as a lady we knew as Aunty Morag, was screaming in utter agony and terror. I couldn't shut out the sound, no matter how hard I tried and I couldn't help her either because we had to be silent or be killed too. In all of my remaining childhood, I could still hear the screams and groans in my head and I would try ways of not hearing it, like yelling at my Father when he eventually came back to our burned-out farm. This often resulted in brutal bashings of both myself and Ma, but at least for a while I could shut out the screams.

It wasn't until I left Scotland for Nova Scotia in my late twenties with my own family, that finally the screams were gone. Just the whooshing, windy sounds of snow and ice could be heard, but I was grateful for that. Finally, they had gone. Upon re-entry to Scotland, I prayed those screaming voices would not return and they haven't. Aunty Morag is buried in Ma's graveyard and her name is engraved onto a plaque on the wall of Ma's newly built Chapel, as are the other ladies who died in that way. Ma has created peace for those ladies. She has planted roses for each of those, whom she knew died that way and had all their names engraved on little wooden plaques and they line the entry to Craskie Farm. She calls them the silent heroines of that time. I explained to my Father before he died the reason why I would yell at him so much and he was shocked to know, but pleased now that the screams and I were at peace.

We had embraced lovingly for the first and only time in my whole life and was finally accepted as a Grant.

He also told me that he thought I was another man's child because Ma had been raped and he wasn't sure if he was really my Father, especially when I'd not recognise him or kick him and tell him to go away. It was really quite amusing relating some of the stories, but sad at the same time, especially now knowing that we were twins. When he found out about Ma being raped and ravished many years later, he killed the men who ravished her and threw them off the ship he was on. But sadly, he still punished my Ma for it, which Highland men did then and he still regretted having beaten her up so badly and asked me not to beat my future wife because it changed Ma. She was still an obedient and good wife to him, but he worried that she had found love elsewhere. It was too late now for him, he said, but not me, so he gave me a lot of good advice in seeking a good woman, but more than anything caring for and loving her.

He really did love my Ma but had slept with Indian women in Nova Scotia and he asked me not to disclose that to Ma, as it would still hurt her. She had been loyal to him, while he was in the British Armed Forces and had rebuilt the farm, but he had never appreciated what she had done or what Grigor and Helen had done either. I confess to feeling deeply hurt that he had slept with Indian women, knowing what my Mither had gone through and knowing how that felt. "Oh Da, no you didn't!" I exclaimed. It just blurted out of my mouth. He wanted to make up for everything and so he then wanted my Mither to marry Hugh Chisholm, who loved her, after his death and asked me to support it, no matter how much opposition there might be. Despite the initial shock, I promised to do that and was looking forward to a new Father figure, but I didn't tell him that.

I still felt sad about him bashing her up into unconsciousness and that I should have been here, but no-one could have stopped him with the Indian women.

Being back at home, I really wanted to jump into bed with my Ma and cuddle her the way it used to be. Ma was sound asleep and so peaceful.

"Alex darling," she said stirring. "Come into bed with me," she said. I lay beside her and I caressed her. "You know there's no milk there now sweetheart," she said smiling.

"Aye, I know," I said. "I just wanted to remember how it felt before Grandda kicked me out of the shieling for suckling you again while Da was still away. I am so sorry for that Ma and I've never apologised for it, but it had all felt so natural. I didn't think of it as wrong and I've missed you so much and felt as if I was an evildoer somehow, even as a wee child when Da would take me off your breasts. I'd be so upset, but hungry all the time and your breast milk was the only thing that could quench my thirst, stop the hunger and make me feel loved all at the same time. It was a magic drink from you Ma and I know he beat you too, so please forgive me. I didn't mean you any harm. I didn't want to leave you alone when Da left you, but Grandda wouldn't allow me back after having done that. I heard word around Glenmoriston that Da had abandoned the whole family and I blamed myself and worried you'd suffer another freezing cold winter in that shieling," I said

"Grandda believed I wasn't Da's bairn, but I was, wasn't I?" I asked

"Aye," she said. "You and Marion are both Clan Grant to Padruig Grant, but on his side of the family there are MacDonalds, so there are some facial similarities to the MacDonalds. You are just more handsome than your brother Patrick, but tall and lean now that you are fully grown, like your Father. Nova Scotia has done amazing things for your physical health and strength and you can easily see both likenesses. I can't see any MacGregor in you from my Mither's family, physically, but your sensitivity is from my family. The Grants are very harsh people, my darling son, not at all like you and Helen with her artwork. You have done no wrong to me and you are not and have never been an evildoer, but

I must follow the men in my life who believe we women are their property. I should apologise to you but come with me now to my place in the forest to talk with me a while and maybe Hugh will join us," Ma said.

My Mither never ceased to surprise me and I became accustomed to Hugh Mohr following us around. In Ma's old forest was a beautiful Pict stone where she sought solace, which was always necessary in her life. As we walked there, the mist became quite thick, but it wasn't cold or wet.

"It's okay," she said out loud, "It's only wee Alex," she said to someone.

"Ma, who are you talking to?" I asked.

"Son," she said, "Do not ever disclose the location of this stone to anyone, but you may sit here and speak to our ancestors if you ever feel the need," she said.

We sat in front of that lovely comforting stone and the mist was thick, but Hugh Mohr still made his way to us carrying his long rifle and sat down too beside her protectively. I was glad this man was in her life, I really liked him. She automatically took his hand.

"Alex, this is my husband when your Da passes," she said. "He will need to be asked first if you want to be alone with me, because I will then belong to him," she said. "Grigor knows of our planned hand fasting just after the funeral and he will need you to support him. Has your Da explained that already?" she asked.

"Aye, he has and supports your marriage to Hugh after his death and he asked me to also support it. Hugh, I am ever so happy to have you as my new Da," I said sincerely.

I was happy for them both and as we three sat there, it felt very comforting and peaceful and I embraced my new Da to be and he embraced me back. I think he liked me. I felt emotional that this man accepted and liked me. The future wasn't going to be so bad here in Scotland. I bought a really nice farm with Ma's help, after Da's death and my son Alexander

Og and I ran it. The farmhand was all sorted out with Gillcrest MacLachlan's students, who stayed on the property for a year at a time and I didn't have to pay them. I got to know Lochiel of the Camerons really well, as he found the property for me on the border of both Grant and MacDonald lands, north of Cameron territory and I named it "Loch Garry Ranch" and had a sign made for it. I loved my new farm and told Marion, my new found twin sister, to move in with me as well as her son Malcolm whom I loved. Things were not great at Craskie for her or Malcolm. Helen had rejected them. It was only Kenneth who stayed on which I felt was a mistake.

Everyone was busy. Helen was busy preparing for her Art Gallery Opening and her art was amazing and it was a great success. She was going to then invest her money in a few proj-ects. Patrick and Henrietta having moved into the Manor House that Da built, ran that business well with his son James and his wife Susan. My daughter Jean's part time job meant she would stay in Inverness for two nights per week with her cousin

Jacobite Stone

The Old
Castle Lachlan

Aonghus and his wife Annabel, whom she liked and they would occasionally go shopping together or go sightseeing around Inverness. Not having been born there, Jean was taken to the Culloden battlefield with Annabel and shown places that disturbed her, such as all the places where imprisoned Jacobite Prisoners in 1746 were shot in the back in the High Church graveyard or sent to the ship 'The Furnace'. Annabel was full of knowledge on the topic because her Grandfather fought in that battle, as did my Father, Grigor's father, Hugh Chisholm and Gillcrest's Grandfather, who was killed on the battlefield. It was on one of those days when I was picking her up, that Jean came home on our wee horse and cart to Loch Garry saying,

"Did you know that Morag-Freya's husband is a Laird from Argyle and their castle is haunted?" she asked.

"What's for dinner?" I asked my sweetie pie.

Loch Garry, Scotland

It was quite a cold night and my daughter cuddled up to me on the way home, while we were trotting home to Loch Garry, she said something both clever but challenging that really appealed.

"Da," she said, "Can we please set aside a part or percentage of our farm, maybe 10% or more of the total land that's in current usage, to regrow the native forest, the way Grandma has? One difference being that she never took down all the original native forest. She has kept the original forest, like the Caledonian pines" Jean said.,

Without waiting for my answer Jean went on.

"You have to admit that the land around here has been cleared too much for sheep. The trees provide us with so many habitats for rare lichens and moss, as well as homes for all of the wild birds who live either in the trees or on the ground. The trees keep the air pure as well as the waterways, which has to in turn affect the fish life," she added quite passionately.

"Aye, is my answer, if Alexander Og agrees, but my question is who has influenced you on this matter?" I asked.

"Da, please don't insult my intelligence. You know I'm well educated. You paid for it. I can see it with my own eyes and I think we could contribute," she said vehemently. "Oh and

there's something else I want to ask you too Da. Annabel and Aonghus are going to meet with the new Doctor in Glenmoriston the next time she's expected to see a doctor and I've asked to go with them in order to meet him. Is that okay? His name is Dr Benedict Browne," she asked.

"I know that name," I said. "Is he related to the Doctor that treated your Grandda in London back in '64?" I asked. Jean said she didn't know that, but that he is English and there was a question over whether he would stay in Scotland or not because of his Father and he could only stay if he had enough patients, but she would find out. The day Jean met Dr Browne, I knew that he was definitely staying and had plans to build a two-story home and by the look on my daughter's face, she'd be moving in.

"Fancy him, did you love?" I asked, which embarrassed her.

"Aye. I did. He's so handsome Da, even though he's English, but I am sorry about his hair. It is kind of light brown, not like ours at all, but at least he won't go bald, so he said. Oh, and by the way, his Father was the Doctor who treated old Grandda in London. Did you know old Grandda was covered in lice too?" she asked.

With regards the rewilding of our ranch, my dearest daughter was very keen on her brother agreeing, so it could become a project with our current student involved also and maybe the Science Department at Invermoriston could even fund it by first  obtaining the seeds or wee plants by creating their own nursery there, somewhere near the hospital.

"We have to first make up a complete list of all of the original wild forest species, then obtain those and care for them, while we set aside the land and build a solid perimeter around it to keep out the deer, or else the deer would eat it all darling," I added.

"The deer just need a natural predator don't you think Da? Learn to hunt hart from new Grandda and we can all eat it. I've never tried it, but you all grew up on it, so that's what kept their population down and now there's too many deer since the Clearances of the people who ate them. I'll try to eat it, Da," Jean said. "The important thing is to build a new habitat, so that the birds and animals, that are now close to extinction or extinct, can return. If you and my brother Alexander can manage the grazing for the coos with the exclusion of some of your land, I believe we would be doing a good thing for the Highlands, like Granny does. I want to be like her, can we do it please Da?" she implored.

"Jean darling, only if your brother agrees. Aye, but I'll have to get out the plans of the property and see how much land can be spared and where. The perimeter of the whole property should be the priority. A tall rock wall is needed to keep out the deer as well as the English. Maybe my nephew, Malcolm could build that. Your first job is to get the list of trees and plants, lichens and whatever else grows there. That's what is needed for this native forest from Grandma. Okay? Then, when we are armed with solid information, we can approach my other nephew Gillcrest, in Invermoriston. While you're seeing Grandma about that list of plants, perhaps you could take Annabel and Aonghus with you on the same day that you see the doctor?" I suggested

The mature age student at 'Loch Garry Ranch' was very enthusiastic and mentioned a lady botanist, who was on their team growing oats, but she hated it because it wasn't really her field.

"This was her field," he said. So, I obtained her name and address in Invermoriston and I told them I'd also get her advice and maybe she could manage it. I was busy with my farm work, as well as preparation to grow potatoes, like Ma does and build bigger storage for them, as well as build a bigger chicken coup with shelter for the coming winter. I had a lot of work ahead. My storage shed for grain was only just big enough, but ideally it could be bigger too.

"Jean darling, can you please start a vegetable and herb garden near the house? I was thinking it might need to be a glass house. We really need more food growing, like those tomatoes your Granny has. Can you ask Aunty Helen for some seeds from all of their herbs as well as the tomatoes?" I asked. "By the way, save all of the horse, chicken and coo manure for the crops," I said.

"Da, Alex is already saving all the manure and he's getting kelp too from Uncle Grigor. Young Charlie, his assistant, can help us if we need more and can tell us how to get the kelp, but I will ask Aunty Helen for those seeds," she answered.

"Does Grigor have an assistant?" I asked.

"Aye, he's such a sweet lad. We might have to do that one day too, Da," she said.

"Hmm," I answered in response. There was too much already to think about.

Jean needed specialised stabling and an exercise yard for her young yearling too. I needed more staff to start building the perimeter wall and if we went ahead with the reforesting, we would need that botanist woman as a manager. It was fortunate that there was already an onsite home for staff that was currently unused, that she could live in. I would need to see how much I could afford to pay her, or preferably get the Science Department to fund it. All the coos were doing well and calving. The geese settled in and started to harass everyone, as I expected, but that was a goose's job.

"I also needed to ask Ma's new husband if he could put aside one of his Collies from his next litter. Pompidou looked ready to give birth when I saw her last don't you think?" I asked.

"Aye, that would be so nice to have Collies too. Can we have two please Da?" Jean asked. "Aye, if Da can sell us two," I replied.

"Out of interest, how old is this botanist woman? Is she good looking and is she married, hand fasted or betrothed and so on?" I asked Joe, my student.

"Oh, look who's interested now," he said very cheekily and they all laughed.

"Sorry boss, she's a real scrag," he added. My adult student's name was Joe who was cleared off one of the islands and he had his own peculiar sense of humour, but it made him very likeable. He had a wife and family who were living in Edinburgh with her parents. I thought all three of them were having me on and I regretted asking that question about that lady botanist, when my lad came up to me later while I was washing up dishes with the accurate details.

"Da, she's forty-one, has a degree in Biological Sciences specialising in Botany obtained in London, is unmarried or not betrothed or hand fasted and has no children. She's Clan Menzies, but was adopted. Her name is Matilda, she has long brownish, reddish curly hair and green eyes, but she's Episcopalian," he informed me, then took over the cleaning up.

"Thank you, son. Jean, help your brother, he did all the cooking," I said and both Jean and Joe cleaned up the kitchen and put it all away.

"Episcopalian you say? That's disappointing. Would she convert to Catholicism do you think you can find that out son?" I asked.

"If she met you, she'd convert to whatever you were, Da," he said smiling.

My son Alex Og was a sensitive lad, who was a lot like me and needed love and reassurance, so I hugged my lad and prepared the bath after we had all eaten a huge dinner that he had cooked so well. Jean, being the cleanest, could go first, then Alexander, myself, then

Joseph MacFie

the student definitely last, who looked filthy from all of the farm work.

"Have you fed my chestnut mare?" I asked Joe before my bath.

"Aye, relax, it's all done boss and all the animals are fed and away for the night," he replied. He was the best student so far and I wanted to get him back, so I locked it away in my mind to mention to Gillcrest. His name was Joseph MacFie, whom we just called Joe.

Grandma and Helen had given me sheets and touls, pillows and goose down doonas that they were no longer using, so all of our bedrooms beckoned to us all, after such a long day, with a lot to go over. I couldn't help but feel guilty for not having been here for Ma on her farms when she needed me the most. I thanked God for bringing us all back together again, just the same and hoped that I could do half as well as Ma did in building up my farm to leave to my precious lad, Alexander.

Hugh Mohr came over unexpectedly one day on his big horse and let himself in through the gate in his usual confident manner. He had a loud voice and would always call out, "Yay Alex lad." That day it sounded a little urgent, so instead of standing around outside in the cold, I greeted him warmly and I invited him in for coffee to talk over whatever was on his mind. He explained 'the year of the sheep' coming on earlier than expected and Grigor's apprentice family were going to be cleared from their croft and the poor lady didn't even know. Helen had already lost five more pupils from her school and I knew Helen was already struggling in trying to learn Ma's bookkeeping from her. At the heart of it, Helen was an artist, not a mathematician or bookkeeper and Isobel-Mairi was talking of leaving which would break her heart with both of her daughters leaving Craskie Farm. Helen had never left Ma and couldn't quite understand why all three of her children would leave her as she got older. I had wondered why Helen hadn't become closer to Marion as a sister, the way I had, but it didn't appear that Helen was encouraging any closeness and poor Marion was a very shy lady.

Da wanted me to accommodate Marion on Loch Garry Ranch permanently, if possible, as she was unmarried, as well as one of her sons, but he had a preference to keep Kenneth on Craskie for grave digging. He said his back wasn't up to that task anymore, but I suspected it was another issue he had with graves in general. He said that they would need to accommodate and employ the MacKichans because the oldest boy was Grigor's apprentice who was near the end of his course. Naturally, I wanted my twin sister, Marion to live with me, if there was no issue with her willingness in leaving Craskie Farm, or with the biologist lady.

I distinctly remembered, however, my Father had promised her permanent free accommodation on Craskie before he died and I had wondered why she hadn't been living in the main house. I happily agreed to employ the older of the two lads, Malcolm, if one brother was happy enough to part company with his other brother.

"I do need a fence builder. Actually, a rock wall builder to keep out the deer and the English," I said to Da.

"Sounds like Malcolm could have that job then," Da said.

He was going home to organise it all and I offered to go too, so I could bring both Marion and Malcolm back to their new home, if they both wanted to and I took two spare horses for Marion and Malcolm to ride. They both agreed to living with me, although I sensed a sadness in Malcolm being moved again, so I felt my new life was going to be both exciting, as well as challenging. Matilda arrived on that same day and I think I fell in love with her but was too busy to talk. Her beauty was captivating, but she didn't even seem to be aware of it. It was obvious that she had a quick intelligence, but despite being born in Scotland, she had no knowledge of how to act around us and her accent was English.

A dinner had been pre-arranged for the following night at Ma's farm to which Matilda was then invited. Apparently, it had been Hugh Mohr's idea because of something Matilda had told him after he observed her just seated beside Loch Ness taking down notes on the local environment. I asked her if we could deal with the forestry matters on the following day, as dealing with family concerns was the priority and she agreed. She arrived at the family dinner, wearing the same clothes, just a cleaner version and tall boots, accompanied by both Gillcrest and Morag-Freya MacLachlan. I took both Marion and Malcolm as well as Jean and Alexander along and the night turned out to be more eventful than any of us had expected. I noted that neither James nor Patrick or their wives had been invited, for some reason. Matilda was in for a shock that night, but so was I when Ma encouraged us both to marry. Ma was well known for marrying everyone off, or as she would say 'it was pure match making whose partners were sent by God.'

That night of shocks unveiled that I would marry Matilda Menzies very soon.

I had only been watching on that night to observe whether Malcolm had been happy to be the one brother that was moved out of Craskie Farm and was concerned that his feelings may have been hurt. I hadn't concentrated at all on marriage to a complete stranger. I knew that if it had been me in Malcolm's place, I would have cried myself to sleep. Helen, once again looked disinterested in her sister Marion, so I was pleased that I had my twin sister under my protective wing for her sake and decided to deal with any issues that came up with Malcolm for my twin's best interests and to treat him more like a son than a nephew. I loved him anyway and despite being a bit rough around the edges, he was a strong and handsome lad. It felt wonderful to have a big family again that I was responsible for, in actual fact.

Both Joe and Malcolm got along so well that he met up with other Islanders and married Joe's niece, Cherry MacLean. For a while my house was bursting at the seams, but I loved it and even Cherry and Malcolm's first wee lass was born under our roof. They named her Islay and she was the bonniest wee bairn I'd ever seen, other than our own of course. Their second bairn was born after they moved onto their new farm, right on my border. Malcolm still felt like my son and so I loved having him and the Islanders coming and going. The Islanders were all a very capable group of people, who had the funniest sense of humour which lifted the atmosphere at times.

Matilda loved being the head lady of our ranch and a more devoted woman you could never find. Loyal, honest and intelligent, hardworking and kind. Everyone in our neighbourhood respected my wife and I was proud to stand beside her wherever we went with our bairns, Sarah and Moses.

Matilda MacMartin Grant's Story

"Riding my Horse with Map in Hand"

By Zaynab El-Fatah

Illustration by Halima Karger

London, 1786

I was born into a poor crofter's family in 1745, somewhere in the Highlands of Scotland. They were Catholic and lived with one set of their parents and five bairns, in the lead up to the time when Prince Charles Edward Stuart was forming a Highland Army of Jacobites. Therefore, when I was born it was decided that they couldn't afford another bairn to raise, so predictably, I was adopted out to a childless and wealthy family in the village of Weem, near Aberfeldy in the Highlands of Perthshire.

The only name I knew growing up was Matilda Menzies.

It wasn't long before my adoptive parents felt it was too dangerous for their new wee bairn to remain in Scotland with Jacobite fervour gaining momentum. I was then sent to live in London indefinitely, where I went to boarding school and later obtained a university degree in Biological Sciences, specialising in Botany, having also learned French, Latin, Dutch and German. My interest was specifically old growth forests in Scotland that were being decimated to make way for sheep. My extracurricular activities included mostly Equestrian activities, but also fencing. I learned not only how to ride a horse, but also show jumping, dressage and horse breeding involving the Scottish Highland Ponies and the Scottish Clydesdale horses and how the blood lines all worked and how to perfect certain attributes of the breeds. My parents advised me to stay in London for as long as possible, while they were putting money aside for my dowry, which looked doubtful at forty-one years of age when I finally returned home.

When I returned to Scotland, I barely knew my adoptive parents, although they'd always sent me Christmas gifts, which wasn't done in Scotland and they had paid for my education. In London, being Catholic was disallowed where I was educated, so I chose to be Episcopalian without having a strong loyalty to it. I did, however, get to hear about the atrocities that took place after Culloden in 1746 and the Clearances, due to the Episcopalians caring for the Jacobite prisoners in London. It was them who advised me to learn Gaelic before returning home, which I endeavoured to do through one of the men whom they were assisting. My payments for the lessons enabled him to eventually return home to his family from whom he had been separated for many years.

His name was Killian MacDonnell from Glengarry in the Highlands and he was nearly sixty years old, a polite gentleman who said to look him up if ever I was in the vicinity. One day I asked him if it wasn't impolite, why he was imprisoned in London and he told me the story that in May 1746, a party of Cumberland's army had shot three Camerons, two of them were brothers carrying a letter of protection. "I happened to be in the vicinity," he said, "at that time in Tommadow in Glenkengie and was arrested by association." [3]

Little did I know then that Mr MacDonnell would be one of my door neighbours one day. I gave him a wee gift on his departure and was sad to see him leave.

Weem, Scotland, 1787

I wasn't expecting much on my return to Scotland, which I travelled to by train as far as it took me, then horse drawn carriage to the village of Weem, with its association to Clan Menzies, (pronounced meng-is). The Castle Menzies, in the Valley of the Tay, was yet to be rebuilt for the Clan. I didn't feel any attachment to Clan Menzies or Weem, so being in Scotland, I first needed a job and then I had a passion to find the name of the Clan of my birth. My adoptive Mummy gave me a wee box that I came with as an adopted bairn. In it, was a tiny knitted blue bonnet and an equally tiny bracelet made of some kind of plaited vine, which, being a Botanist, gave me a clue at least.

I applied for an advertised job at the Science Department of the Invermoriston Hospital. Naturally, I had never been there, so I asked Daddy for a good map and a good horse with saddle and bridle, to ride there. My equestrian abilities were unequalled in London and I gave my Mummy a small port full of my equestrian ribbons for her to keep. She was thrilled to have something for the money they had paid out. She didn't much like my masculine looking clothing that I wore, but it was work related and necessary, as were my knee-high leather boots and an oiled, waterproof jacket with hood. My long pants were a type of soft leather to protect my skin when walking through the brushes. I had leather gloves to ride with also, as well as saddle bags for my food, a journal, water and blanket and a hairbrush for my messy long hair.

One look at my clothes and Mummy took me shopping, just in case I needed to look more like a lady and she spent a small fortune on long dresses, slippers and jewellery that I believed I would never wear.

"It's Scotland, Mummy. I'll get cold in these," I had complained. So, woollen tartan dresses and arisaids in the Menzies tartan also became the feature in my port and I was regretting complaining because I did not want to represent Clan Menzies. Just the same, I gratefully accepted her gifts and sent them ahead of myself in a port to Invermoriston, certain of my success with the job application.

'Anywhere was better than Weem', I thought. Of course, she reminded me that I was forty one and that was old for marriage now, so not to get my hopes up, but to never stop trying. She even went so far as to estimate how many children that it was possible to have now in these modern times, if there was a good doctor close by. I had no plans to marry. Being adopted had put me off producing offspring. When I rode my lovely big, black five-year-old horse out of Weem, I felt liberated, map in hand and on my way to a new life, centred on Invermoriston.

I took my time and stopped if the horse, who I'd named Clancy, or if I needed to stop. If there were people to chat to, I would, but my main interest was in observing the countryside to see just how much of the land was in fact degraded and to what degree and noted it all down in my journal. I was shocked to see huge hillsides barren of all their trees and the seriousness of Scotland's situation really sunk in. 'What were these various governments thinking, to destroy the myriad habitats lost?' I thought. The further I rode, approaching Loch Ness, I was almost in tears as I wrote in the journal to the extensive needs of the Highlands, to prevent even further extinction of the wildlife and wild birds.

On one of those days, I was sitting on a rock to make entries in my journal beside the huge Loch Ness, I believe it was called the Great Glen. I was approached by a tall older man on a large bay gelding, who asked me what I was doing alone in the Great Glen. He had a strong Scottish accent and was obviously only accustomed to speaking Gaelic.

"Thank you for asking. I will be on my way soon. I am taking notes first of my observations of the forest and the wildlife situation," I explained.

Frowning, he introduced himself as Hugh Chisholm, a kindly older gentleman, who appeared trustworthy.

"Matilda Menzies," I said. "On my way to Invermoriston Hospital. I've applied for a job there at the Science Department," I added. That seemed to take his attention.

"So, that would be with Gillcrest Lachlan MacLachlan? Tell him that you have met Hugh Chisholm and to give you the job, and he will," Mr Chisholm said. "Then lass, be on your way. It's not safe to stay here alone, especially as it gets dark. I can escort you to Invermoriston now, if you like and you'll be safe," he added.

"Alright, thank you," I said, suddenly feeling insecure.

He was silent most of the way, unless I spoke, so I told him that I'd been adopted out in 1746 by poor folk and was hoping to trace them and find out my actual Clan name.

"Poor folk? Do you mean crofters?" he asked.

"I don't know what they did, but maybe?" I replied.

"You may never find them. Where I live, the crofters were all burned out in '46 or killed. Those that left went to the coast, some to the Isle of Skye. There was a small group though that split and went to Letter Finlay on Loch Lochy. Do ye know the name of your birth family?" he asked. "No," I said. "I only have a small box with a tiny, knitted bonnet and a wooden plaited bracelet, with Matilda written on it," I said. He then looked at me thoughtfully.

"It might help to talk to my wife, Mrs Chisholm. She delivered bairns back then, as did her Mither and might know something that could help. Once you get settled in at

Invermoriston, tell Gillcrest to give you good accommodation or he'll answer to me. Then come and see my wife at Craskie Farm in Glenmoriston," Mr Chisholm said seriously.

I was grateful to Mr Chisholm when he dropped me to the front of the hospital and I was successful with my qualifications and I mentioned Mr Chisholm, riding a bay gelding with a white star, to Gillcrest and asked for good accommodation.

"Hugh Chisholm?" he asked, almost panicking.

"Yes. So, you do know him? I met him in the Great Glen by Loch Ness and he brought me here and that is when he suggested that I also meet with his wife," I said.

"Grandma? My wife and I are going to go see Grandma tomorrow evening for dinner. We can take you with us in our carriage and if there's anything that we can do for you..." he started to say

"Well, there is," I interjected.

"Aye?" he asked.

"I don't want to work on oat crops, for long anyway. I want to work on the regeneration of the wild forests. Do you have any jobs going in that area?" I asked.

"My Uncle Alex is looking for someone in that field," he admitted. "However, I want you to start tomorrow on the oat crops and meet everyone and become part of our team and then I'll ask my Uncle Alex, who wants to regenerate about 10% of his land or more from its current condition of having been cleared, back to the native forest," he explained

The team were a lovely bunch of young and enthusiastic students, but it wasn't my ultimate aim, only a start, a wage and good accommodation. I was given the best house that was empty and on that first night, Gillcrest invited me to dine with him and his wife at their house and I'd be picked up and dropped back safely. I was getting the hint that safety was an issue. I was introduced to his wife, Morag-Freya MacLachlan, who was so lovely and welcoming. I admit that I was hungry and she was a great cook. It all tasted so good and I complemented her and admitted that I was lacking in culinary skills. Gillcrest also told Morag-Freya that I was accompanying them both to Grandma's house, which was a surprise to her.

"That's good, Uncle Alex will be there with Marion, Malcolm, Jean and Alex Og, so you can meet him and ask about that other job. Can't she darling?" she said.

"Aye, but Matilda needs to work with the team for at least two weeks first and settle in and get to know everyone on the team," he said.

"Why? You can advertise the job again. There were lots of applicants," Morag-Freya said, interferingly.

"I'm happy to work with the team first, Gillcrest and become part of your Science Department and then if it works out with your Uncle later, then maybe I can move to that job if it is my area of expertise," I added.

"It's definitely your area, but he's divorced. Would you be uncomfortable, knowing that he is single?" he asked.

"And Catholic," added Morag-Freya.

"I am sure that his religion won't matter," I said.

"Why then are you Episcopalian?" she asked, which embarrassed Gillcrest.

"It wasn't really that I had a choice, having been adopted and being sent off to London, where Catholicism was disallowed, so there was a choice between two Churches," I answered.

"If you ever were to marry, would you convert to Catholicism then?" she asked.

"Yes, but I haven't got marriage in mind at this point in my life," I answered.

After a well-earned night's sleep, I joined the team and I well understood the aims of that group, studying and improving the soil and working on oat crops, some were barley crops as well, but truth be known, I hated that kind of work.

I respected it, however, the end goal being greater crop yields, as starvation was a very real and scary prospect that many Scots had faced. Gillcrest was definitely that kind of Scientist, but I longed to be outside in a forest even if it was raining or snowing, so I could listen to the wind blowing through the leaves of the old-growth forest because the music spoke to me and I knew I could make a difference here in Scotland. I just needed the opportunity and the seeds. God help me.

As promised the following evening, I was picked up in a small carriage by a very well-dressed Morag-Freya and Gillcrest MacLachlan and I was still wearing a pair of clean long trousers. My shirt was clean, but that was all I could say about it. I was hoping Grandma wasn't fussy about what I was wearing and I kept thinking, 'Maybe I should've worn that damn tartan.' I hadn't done anything with my wild hair, other than brush it and tie it back in my usual ponytail, which came to my waist. The horse and carriage pulled into a brightly lit farm. 'That was unusual,' I thought, but I started to become quite nervous, wondering then who Grandma was, so I asked Morag-Freya,

"What should I call Grandma when you introduce me?" I asked

"Mrs Chisholm," she said.

"Oh, yes," I responded.

"How do you want to be introduced, Matilda?" she asked.

"Just Matilda," I answered.

I was much taller than Morag-Freya. She was barely five-foot tall and for a woman, I suppose, if I compared myself to the students, I was the tallest. I was even taller than Gillcrest, so I was hoping this wasn't going to be a family of tiny people, or I would really feel embarrassed. Apart from the lights, the first thing that strikes you about Craskie Farmhouse is the wide oak front door on the house. It was stunning. Gillcrest made a gentle tapping sound on the door and walked in saying, "Granny, we're here," and it seemed like we were greeted by a whole group of people. Morag- Freya's Mither Helen, her

Father Grigor and of course Grandma and Grandpa, Mr and Mrs Chisholm. Then, under the front window on the couch were three lovely looking youngsters, Malcolm, Jean and Alexander Og, seated with an older man who was an absolute dish, sporting a goatee, with a woman his age who looked like his sister.

Then, I was embarrassed in my knee-high boots and long trousers as Mr Chisholm called me over to the fireside.

"Matilda, come sit down here and meet my wife. Dinner is not quite yet ready," he said. There was home help in the kitchen, cooking busily with her husband. The house was spotless and there were beautiful paintings on the walls. One was a different version of Grandma with a different man and another one was with a team of Clydesdales. That's all I had a chance to look at before I sat down.

"Matilda, meet my wife, Mrs Chisholm," he said. Mrs Chisholm slowly turned her head towards me, looking to assess me from head to toe, like as if to say, 'Who on earth has Gillcrest brought here tonight?' She was a very direct woman and just said plainly.

"Who are you dear?" I went to extend my hand, as if to shake her hand, but she didn't extend hers, so I withdrew mine.

"My name is Matilda Menzies, Mistress," I said. Her huge blue eyes penetrated deeply into my soul and I don't think I've ever felt quite that uncomfortable. Mr Chisholm was obviously accustomed to her mannerisms in dealing with new people and he clearly respected his wife, which I'd never encountered between husbands and wives before then.

"Why are you here?" she asked.

I took out my wee box and decided to get straight to the point.

"I have this small box Mistress, from when I was adopted out to a family in the village of Weem in Perthshire. That's why my name is Menzies, but I wasn't born Menzies and I was wondering if you could help me find any clue as to who my parents could've been," I asked nervously. Opening the small box,

Mrs Chisholm took out the tiny blue bonnet and her facial expression completely altered and then she took out the tiny bracelet, looking familiar with it.

"Well, my dear, I can tell you this. I made both of these items for you when you were born and I delivered you into this world and for every bairn that I delivered, this is what I gave them all. Pink for a boy, blue for a girl. And the bracelet is from my forest and for me to have delivered you as a bairn, you would have been born here on Craskie Farm," she said.

I wasn't expecting to find a clue to my birth, just hoping for direction. I certainly hadn't expected the resulting flood of tears, knowing that I was standing on the land where I was born and this woman, Mrs Chisholm, was the lady who first saw me.

"Can you tell me please if you know what croft I came from?" I asked her through tears.

"There was only one croft who gave away one of their bairns, that is why I remember it clearly. Your father was a Jacobite and feared for the safety of his family. Once he left to go and fight with the Jacobites, he had you adopted out. I can tell you the family's Clan name because they were also the only Clan group that split up when they left. If you are hoping to find them, you may not be successful, but I don't know if you came from the group that went to the Isle of Skye or the group that went to Letter Finlay on Loch Lochy in Cameron lands, so you'd need to make enquiries in both of those places, notably speak to Lochiel of the Camerons. Your Clan name was Martin, MacMartin, a sept of the Cameron Clan. So, your name is Matilda MacMartin. I was devastated that they gave you away and you were one of the last bairns that I ever delivered of the crofters, before they were all burned out of their homes and then they all left," she said reflectively.

With that, she put the two items back into the box and said it had been wise for me to have kept the two items.

"Welcome home Matilda," she said meaningfully.

Mrs Chisholm then stood up, as did I and she hugged me and then introduced me to the entire family as 'one of those born on Craskie Farm, who had come home' as Matilda MacMartin. Then, one by one, the family came and introduced themselves and said, "Welcome home." By then, the home help, whose name was Meredith, called out impatiently, "Dinner is ready!" The man that was with her was clearly her husband and helped her put all of the food out. Mrs Chisholm had asked me to call her Grandma and said to Meredith and her husband to stay for dinner also and they did. So, there was a table of sixteen people, after Morag-Freya disappeared and came back with whom I presumed was her sister, brother-in-law and nephew and I was similarly introduced to them. This is what I had dreamed of my whole life. A big family all talking loudly to each other and loving each other.

Over dinner, Gillcrest finally had an opportunity through the conversation to speak and told them all that he'd employed me at the hospital on his science team, when in actual fact my qualifications were the regeneration of the old growth forests.

"Really?" said Jean.

"Are you the Episcopalian?" asked Alex Og.

"Not really," I said a little surprised. "If I ever get married, I'd just go to whatever religion he was," I said and everyone turned and looked at Alexander Mohr.

"Uncle Alex," spoke up Isobel-Mairi. "You are unmarried, you need a wife who will convert to Catholicism and you needed someone who could work on the old growth forests project. I think your wife is already sitting at the table," she said enthusiastically. Alexander Mohr blushed and I felt acutely shy for the first time in my life and I really wished I'd worn something better on this occasion.

I then noticed Mr Chisholm smiling and looking very pleased with himself.

"So, Alex," he said. "You helped me hand-fast with my wife. When's it going to happen? And just so you know, I am available to help and no doubt Grigor will help too. Won't we Grigor?" he said. Alexander Mohr then looked to his Mither for support.

"Son. It's a good idea. You do need a wife and this lass was born here. She's as pretty as a picture. Helen can help her with her clothes and with her wedding dress. Before that, if you just want to hand-fast we could do it now," Grandma said.

I interrupted, "Excuse me? What's hand-fasting?" I asked.

Grigor responded, "Sister, if you hand-fast with Alex, it is a simple ceremony done in your own home, you can do it with or without witnesses. The ultimate outcome of which means marriage for one year and one day."

Morag-Freya unexpectedly jumped out of her chair and put her arms around me. "Poor Aunty, don't put so much pressure on her. What say, you have a look at Uncle Alex's farm in a few days' time maybe, when you've had time to think about it. But you might lose your oats lady, Gillcrest," she said, smiling as she turned to her husband.

"Hand-fasting was good enough for me and Isobel, so it's good enough for you too Alex and it's about time you got remarried. You need a wife, son and you're not getting any younger Matilda, to have bairns," he said.

"Aye, Da. Ma, do you really think this is a good idea?" Alex asked.

"Look at her son, she's gorgeous and educated and Scottish and she was born here, just like you were, son. Yes, it's a good idea," Mrs Chisholm insisted.

I was feeling sorry for Alex, who was under a lot of pressure and so I thought to change the subject and asked where my parent's croft had been located on the property. Granny put on her big coat and boots and her husband and her, with their collie dogs, took me outside to where all of the crofts used to be.

"There used to be six crofts in a row along here that were all burned to the ground. All that was left were a ring of stones that the families cooked with. Those stones are still here in the order of the crofts. Your family was the third croft," she said.

It was clearly a sad story that she would not ordinarily discuss and I sensed that there was a lot more to it that she would ever tell me, unless it related directly with the MacMartins. We all went behind the stables with Mr Chisholm holding the big lantern and holding his wife's arm, being very protective of her and she showed me which stones were from my parents' croft. I asked her if I could have those stones to keep, wherever I decided to live one day and she agreed.

"Hugh darling, could you make sure that happens?" she said.

"Aye," he responded. The love between them was obvious and I did hope to have that one day. On her trusty calendar, Grandma also pointed out a date that was very important to them all, being the opening of the Art Gallery belonging to Morag-Freya's Mither, Helen. I was invited, as was Alex, Marion with Alexander Og, Malcolm and Jean and Malcolm's brother Kenneth. Eventually we would just become the Glengarry branch of the family.

Granny also helped me on that same night that I was there and told me that they already had an entire nursery of the trees that were needed for the reforesting that I needed on Alex's farm and that Mr Chisholm knew all of their common names. He had memorised them all. He showed Alex where they all were because he had built the palisades for them and they were all very mature now. There were trees of many types, including oak, shrubs, lichens and every kind of plant that grows in an old-growth forest and she had prepared it forty years ago.

"See those trees over there, son? That's your forest. They're all there. They're all the trees from my forest here and I'd be really glad of the room if you could take them all," she said finally smiling to her son.

I helped Alex to achieve the removal of the readymade forest from Craskie with Isobel-Mairi and Hugh Og delivering them to Alex's property with their beautiful team of four Clydesdale horses. We had the entire forest ready to plant after multiple trips from Craskie to Loch Garry Ranch. I was too tired at the end of that day to do any planting and accepted the kind invitation of dinner cooked by Alexander Og, a hot bath and a sleepover in Jean's bed.

I was invited by Alex Mohr to Loch Garry Ranch on the following weekend to discuss the forest and I rode my horse, Clancy, there. I was better dressed this time, as Helen had given me a lovely crimson coloured blouse and a mustard coloured ari-said, which accentuated many of the different highlights in my hair. I even coloured my lips to match the blouse. When

Loch Garry Ranch

I arrived at Alex's gate, he was waiting on his chestnut horse and he liked what he saw, which made me awfully shy. In his own environment, he was especially gorgeous. I didn't think plants were going to be discussed after all. We hand-fasted with Malcolm, Jean and Alexander Og and Joe, their student, as our witnesses that day.

I had been a virgin, which surprised him, given that I had spent my youth in London. After making love for the first time at that age made me quite emotional and I just held on tight to my new man. I moved permanently to Loch Garry Ranch to live with my husband and we now have two bairns, who are beautiful wee darlings. After our first bairn, Sarah, was born, we decided to marry properly with the Priests at Chapel St. Columba at Craskie after I converted to Catholicism and they helped me with lessons. Killian MacDonnell, my Gaelic tutor from London, did end up being our nearest door neighbour and he and his wife and family attended our wedding. I had never envisaged that moving home to Scotland would bring so much happiness into my life, as well as to Alex and his children and I thanked God for it. I had prayed to find my family and this was the family whom I was given.

My love for Ma was very deep, but the time with her was too brief, because Ma was lost to us on the night of the opening of the Art Gallery. My husband was heartbroken and I was glad of his twin sister Marion, being there too to help to console him. She was so quiet most of the time, but her feelings went very deep and her loss was the loss of hardly ever knowing them, but in meeting me and seeing that I had found no blood relations, she felt glad of the time that she did have with her Mither. Marion chose to hide behind her big, protective son, Malcolm and my husband Alex, who all cared and loved her. She was luckier than me in that her adoptive parents were always there for her and had loved her dearly and she was never sent away. Marion and I got along very well, despite our many differences.

I was unlucky in finding any other relatives. They had either been killed at Culloden, were cleared from the land or transported to the Colonies, although I hadn't given up hope that maybe one day from the Americas, or Nova Scotia or even Ireland, that someone would be found. My family now are my bairns with my darling husband Alex, his children, Jean and Alexander Og and his other children in Nova Scotia, his family on Craskie Farm, as well as Malcolm and Cherry and their two new bairns. When we all have a gathering, it is quite a tribe and the bairns have their own little group, organised by Annabel, where they meet every week at Craskie Farm and Nachtain is now the leader of the group. I can't see our children ever trying to overtake

Nachtain, he's way too big, strong and bossy, but we love him.

My adoptive Mummy and Daddy have visited a few times to Glenmoriston and Loch Garry Ranch to join one of our gatherings in order to meet everyone. They attended our wedding and the two baptisms, both held at Craskie Farm. They know that they are welcome to return anytime. They also provided my dowry of five thousand pounds which went directly to my husband Alex. Alex then discussed it with me and we decided to replace the roof with slate on the farmhouse and install internal plumbing on the lower floor, as well as upgrade my laundry. Mummy also sends lovely presents to our bairns, Sarah and Moses, as well as to Jean and Alex Og on their birthdays and New Year. They've also set up an education fund for both Sarah and Moses, in case we had overlooked that. They also funded the purchase of the Clydesdale bloodlines from Isobel-Mairi for Hugh Og and refused any payment for it. For now, while our children are young, they will be attending the Glenmoriston School and learning Gaelic from their half-sister Jean, who is expecting her first bairn with Dr Benedict

Browne, an unpopular English man whom she married, shortly after we married.

My happiest achievement on Loch Garry Ranch thanks to Ma, was our native forest.

In my latter years, I published my journal on the Highlands of Scotland and its lost habitats and bird and animal species, with the assistance of Professors from the Edinburgh University, who had access to the current numbers of birds and animals, either extinct like the wolves and bears, or facing extinction, like the Scottish wild cat. My husband Alex supported me to enter into a doctorate with the university before his early death. Other farms around us in Glengarry and Glenmoriston had started also to replant the native species of the original forests and the wild birds have already begun to return, despite the never-ending clearances and the influx of so many sheep. With Alex gone, I left the ranch to my stepson Alex and his wife Siobhan and returned to Weem after Mummy and Daddy left the estate to me upon their deaths. It was too sad to stay in Glengarry with the constant reminder of my late husband Alex whom I adored with all my heart.

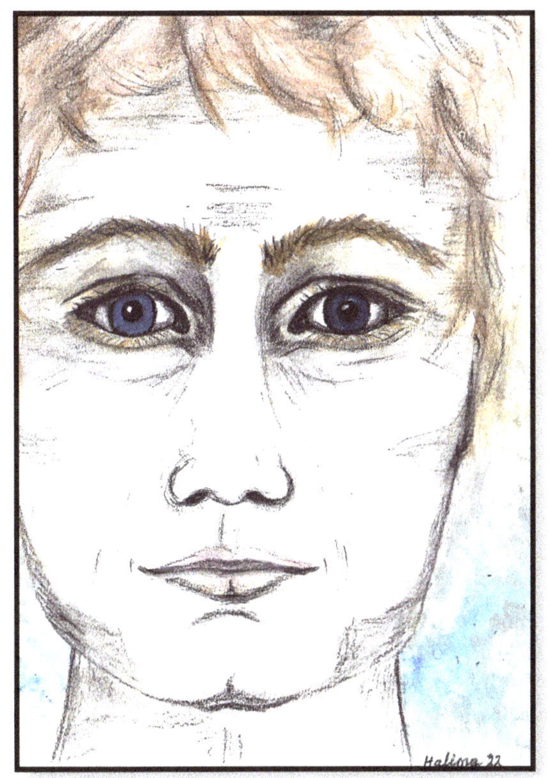

Donald Chisholm's Story

"I Could Have Entered the Priesthood"

By Zaynab El-Fatah

Illustrations by Halima Karger

Chisholm Lands
Scotland, 1734

My Father was Paul Chisholm from Clan Chisholm and my Mither was Clan Grant and brutal, but my Father was even more brutal, common to that era with lads as big as us and as adventurous as us. My Father was born in the Lowlands. Our Aunties remained behind with their husbands when the

197

family departed the Lowlands due to my Grandfather's advantageous new marriage and we joined the rest of our family, who already lived in the Highlands of Scotland. My older brother, Alexander and I would compare welts to see who'd had the worst punishment, but the one lad who was not to be touched by anyone other than God was our youngest brother, Hugh and we'd be severely punished if any harm came to him when he was in our care.

My name is Donald (Mc Paul) Chisholm from Chisholm lands in the Highlands.

My older brother, Alexander, felt very responsible for the two of us when we were out hunting for a hart. We learned most of our hunting skills from him and he had learned them from our Grandfather, John Chisholm, whose name actually had been 'Jean de Chisholme', so our name was adapted to become Chisholm.

All three of us Chisholm lads were born in Chisholm country. Right beside Grant lands.

Upon arrival, my newly re-married Grandfather realised that the farm was severely depleted of all its stock and commenced to arrange a raiding party involving my father on a Grant property stealing Highland coos, goats, sheep and even chickens and geese. Da's job was chasing the chickens around and catching them. Our Grandfather didn't quite get away with it and was taken to Court over it for compensation. It wasn't the best start to the family reputation in the Highlands, but it must have attracted the attention of those higher in the Highland Independent Companies when it came time to join in the Jacobite rebellion.

Alexander learned healing with herbs and other bush remedies accompanied with our Papist chants because our Father could not afford to send him to Medical School in Edinburgh. The chants were a bit hypnotic and quite beautiful, as my family were all devout Papists. It was always an option for any one of us lads to enter the Priesthood and I had considered it just before The Prince arrived. When the Presbyterians took control of religion in Scotland, we didn't make our religion obvious, let alone the knowledge, prayers, chants and healing crafts. We blended, as most Papist clans' people had to do, as no doubt the Pict people before us had to.

We never questioned why God had singled out Hugh to go untouched and unpunished in our family, even though he always knew when he'd been in the wrong. We loved him too much to even hit him once, let alone be angry with him and even protected him from himself. He insisted on annoying Isobel Grant when we were all gathered to march to Edinburgh with the Prince's army and she arrived leading an eight-horse team of Clydesdales with her Father. With the delivery unloaded, she wanted to go behind a tree to pish and Hugh was hoping if he slid his hand where one should not, that she would be sufficiently angry to report it to Ewen MacPherson of Cluny, who would then tell her husband Padruig Dubh, who would be angry with him. But she didn't complain. I could never be angry with him, even when I caught him peaking on the nudity of Padruig Grant's beautiful wife, during his long absence many years later.

We all used love as our strongest weapon with a character as strong as his and it worked. I think Da knew he was going to suffer longer than any of us and he was right. As brothers, we all loved each other dearly and were loyal and devoted to one another and the only time Alexander would laugh was when the three of us were alone together and Hugh would always make us laugh. The rest of the time, Alexander never smiled and maintained a serious demeanour. Alexander and I grew to 6'7" and Hugh just kept growing. I thought he would stop at 6'7", but he grew wider than both of us and very strong. Da thought it was the mountain air, because we all outgrew him, but maybe it was eating hart and Highland coos too.

We Chisholms all had blonde hair that was popular in the Lowlands apparently, but near us in the Highlands were a lot of local people with black hair. Hugh's hair was particularly striking, as it was a kind of yellow blonde and soft and wavy. He would take particular care of his hair and frequently washed it and always carried a comb with him. He would then cover it over with a large blue bonnet, so that no-one could see that he was blonde.

We all grew large appendages and we would compare them to one another's to see which one of us had the largest. Hugh did and he liked to compare his to other men, like Padruig's, to know that his appendage was the biggest. He enjoyed annoying Padruig when we were all together living in the cave after the battle of Culloden and enjoyed upsetting him, which was really funny to watch. He even cut off Padruig's black hair while he slept, just to prove how stealthy he was and how much better looking we blondies were to those with that black hair, who thought themselves braw.

I fell deeply in love with my childhood sweetheart Eilidh, when I was around ten years of age and she may have been a year younger. We'd met at a Kirk function in Chisholm lands and we both agreed then that we would marry one day. I'd ask Alexander about my body functions rather than my Father, who would become angry at the mere mention of genitalia, when mine began to respond to my girlfriend in Kirk. Alexander always seemed to know everything about a girl's body, including how babies were made, so he would talk in length to us both, with us listening intently. Hugh liked a young lass named Emily and I asked Alexander about Eilidh. He also told us both of a trick our Grandfather taught him to do with his tongue, which he'd teach us one day because of a secret part in a lassie's body that was well concealed.

I thought talk about women and their body parts was left behind after Culloden, but instead of that it seemed to have had the opposite effect and the men talked constantly about every inch of a woman's body. There were those of us who preferred women's breasts and there were many comparisons made as to who had the best and most alluring breasts for a man, as well as for feeding the bairns. Padruig's wife's name frequently came up if breasts were talked about. Isobel may have had the best breasts if we had taken a vote on it when Padruig wasn't around. I know Hugh wanted to see them with his own eyes and hold them in his two hands. Alexander MacDonald would never say in case we repeated it to Padruig. I think Grigor Mohr might have thought that his own wife's were the best.

We Chisholms were all big, tall, bulky, broad and blonde and we ate a lot when we were at home in Chisholm lands. I really don't know how Mither kept up with the food we all needed. Living off the land in that cave and foraging for ourselves was a whole other experience in making sure we all had enough food to eat. At home Hugh would tease everyone, even our Mither, who would never chastise him, but that wasn't the case in the cave. He wasn't told off at home, even if he pinched Ma on her large bottom, but amongst men like Padruig, he was in another league and could be killed if he upset someone.

At home, Da would simply speak to him in his childhood about the dignity of women, but now amongst the foul-mouthed men we were living with, he had to change. It was preferable that he didn't pinch Ma on the bottom at home, but now he faced knives for any offence. Eventually, he had stopped upsetting Ma because there wasn't the reaction he had hoped for, but he always got the reaction he wanted from Padruig, so it never stopped and it was dangerous at times. Especially in Badenoch, on one dark Badenoch night, when there came a teamster delivery.

Cluny MacPherson told everyone to keep their eyes off the teamster lass, who was accompanied by her Da, John Grant. Her name was Isobel Grant, the wife of Padruig Dubh and Hugh couldn't wait to do the opposite to what he'd been told. And so, he did. We brothers had to protect him from being caught and we were thankful that Isobel liked him a lot. We weren't expecting that.

At home I just got on with my studies, learning French, Erse, including the figures, as well as Gaelic and Latin. I considered the Church but chose not to enter as many of my relatives had done. So, I did want higher education, but Da could not afford that as he only sold wares from his home to the locals. Da would sometimes get deliveries from John Grant, the teamster, with his Clydesdale horses, so our house was full of stuff to sell. I was disappointed about many things growing up, if I think about it, but education was the main one. My looks were one too, as I wasn't as good looking as both of my brothers. I wasn't the oldest, so I didn't have that responsibility, so I tried to be as good as my younger brother with his rifle. My accuracy never matched his, although I was quite good. All three of us competed for accuracy and even Alexander wasn't as good as Hugh. We threw knives too and Hugh was even better at that. I didn't have a skill that was better than anyone else's, so I wrote poetry sometimes to get it off my chest as to how I felt.

I would yearn to see Eilidh every day, so we'd meet sometimes at a waterfall, where we started up kissing. My manhood wasn't as big then as it became when I filled out fully with broad shoulders and height. Her parents were Clan Grant, so I knew I'd be in trouble if we were ever caught, but as we got older, we hand fasted until we were brave enough to tell them of our intention to marry. She wanted to live in Grant country, so eventually we did, but by then she had been badly injured by the dragoons and

Donald Chisholm

left for dead. Although she was saved by local people, Eilidh was left unable to bear children. She was completely honest with me about what had happened when the dragoons arrived, but that was to relieve me of my promise to her, knowing we would be childless and I had wanted bairns.

I loved Eilidh so much and had promised myself to her and to care for her until her death, which I did. She was frequently unwell and caught colds easily and died young. No matter how young or old a person may be, love is the key and my love and her love disallowed separation, but soon after her death, I was introduced to another Grant lassie with whom I remained married until my own death in Canada. We had many bairns and one of them I named Hugh. We had stayed in Scotland and enjoyed the good company of friends for as long as possible, so I can't complain. I had wanted to be with Eilidh in the Otherworld.

So much happened in Scotland in those years that it would not fit on these humble pages, suffice it to say that I fought on the side of Bonny Prince Charlie and would've died for him. Our wee band of terrors, in escaping Culloden, became known as the Seven Glenmoriston Men because we continued to kill the Redcoats after Culloden and they were indeed terrified of us. We had to hide first in a cave called Coiraghoth, then when it was suspected that we were becoming too well known, we moved to the Chisholm lands. We were then able to get goods for the Prince, who was with us for some time. It cost us a pretty penny and it nearly cost us our lives, but we were devoted to him and getting him to safety, as we were asked to do, was our priority.

My older brother, Alexander, when he came looming out of the shadows of our cave, could look intimidating and with his height and unsmiling appearance, combined with his quick wit and intelligence, scared most people. He adopted a serious unsmiling demeanour because his task was also medical, as well as his skilful, sword fighting abilities. We all had a role over and above our fighting abilities that we all shared and his role was his incredible healing abilities.

Both Alexander and my younger brother, Hugh, and Alexander MacDonald assisted Padruig's wife, Isobel, after her ravishing, but Padruig was never made aware of it because if he had known that three of our men had all seen his wife naked and needing stitches in her most tender parts, he would have killed us all. He had no logic in that way. He was an extremely jealous man, who couldn't see the need for anyone to see her undressed, even if it was to save her life. I sometimes think that he would have preferred that she died, rather than any other option, so we chose not to ever tell him. My brothers told me and it remained a secret. Thank God Isobel herself was dying and had no memory of it.

I wondered if Hugh would tell her after he married her once Padruig died, which was his plan. I'd hoped so, as it weighed on Hugh's mind that it could be a deception. I suspected that Isobel knew somehow. She had Hugh build a home for himself on her farm, so he would be secure and wouldn't be another victim of the clearances. I had never felt adequate as the older brother after Alexander was murdered and his loss was enormous. All that skill and knowledge was all gone. I was then in charge of keeping Hugh on track, according to my Father and I knew that it was a task only angels were capable of, but I had tried.

Isobel was an incredible woman and I didn't blame my brother for loving her, but he had to wait forty years for Isobel and that is patience. My life after we left the cave was with Hugh and Eilidh and Hugh's Collie dogs. He loved his dogs and his rifle and they all slept with him. I wondered what it would be like for Isobel when she did marry Hugh having to sleep with his dogs and his rifle, but I suppose by then she wouldn't have cared. I was all wrapped up in enjoying the little life I had left with Eilidh, as her health steadily worsened. I lost her to grief and ill health. She had never really recovered from the ravishing and nightmares that kept her awake at night.

Isobel admired me, as I admired her in our different ways. I was very worried about her when Padruig vanished and had gone into military service again without telling her. We three remaining of the Glenmoriston Men aided her then because despair had set in and she was going to kill herself had Hugh not found her and taken her home. I had never seen her like that and she was inconsolable to be faced with losing him again. Padruig had gone too far this time, was our general opinion and we built her house for her.

After an almost four-year long absence, he still decided to beat her upon his return, declaring that he had found out about the ravishing that had been kept a secret from him, of all places on the ship that he was on. He and two Highlander friends despatched them all and threw them overboard. I had to feel for Isobel and knew then that my brother was the only one who could save her. One day Isobel said to me, "Donald, you are such a sweetie. I wish you were my family." I knew my brother had loved her since he was seventeen years old, but I had hoped that he'd grow out of it, but he never did and they were having an affair, undisclosed to me, well before Padruig died. She had found a way to save herself from the many miseries in Scotland and Padruig. I loved her as my sister, but I wish that I'd had the chance to actually be her brother, like Grigor Mohr had, which he squandered.

Isobel had cared for all of us Glenmoriston Men, defended us, forgiven us, fed us, overlooked our failings, cared for our wives, kept our memories alive and provided graves for us, when no one else cared. Once Padruig had returned, my new wife and I departed for Canada to take up land there and to continue raising my family, although it was conditional on being a loyalist when the war of Independence came. I hated having to fight on the side of the British as Padruig had had to do and I then understood how he must have felt all those years earlier. John MacDonald and his family, who were in poverty, followed me there too and we settled in Glengarry, Canada.

We are all able to meet in Isobel's wee Chapel as the spectres that we all are now, waiting for Hugh, seeing our names written on plaques on the walls and I then understood why she built it. Even as a spectre, Padruig is exactly the same with his eagle eyes and his intense alertness. We Six Glenmoriston Men, one by one, meet in there to talk of old times, protected from the snow, wind and rain. God bless Isobel, who joined us briefly and then left, while waiting for Hugh and for the first time Padruig had accepted their love.

Isobel-Mairi MacNachten's Story

"MacKnight Tartan"

By Zaynab El-Fatah

Illustrations by Halima Karger

Braes of Glenmoriston,

Scotland, 1784

My name is Isobel-Mairi MacNachten now, because I married Ewen MacNachten. I was born Isobel-Mairi MacGregor with my hyphenated name in 1764, similar to my sister, who was named Morag-Freya, but our brother was Aonghus-Grigor and refused to use his hyphenated name for his whole life. That's what started the problems between our Father, Grigor and my brother.

I loved where I was born on Craskie Farm in Glenmoriston, Scotland and never wanted to leave, although I did eventually, unlike Grandma who had never left Craskie. Not having much of a mind for education other than home learning, I chose to learn farming, but most especially the management of the Clydesdale team because I wanted to be just like Grandma, who was famous as Isobel of Glenmoriston, the only lady teamster at that time.

Unfortunately, being the fool that I am, I was influenced by my cousin Beth, one day when Grandma was sick and took out the team without Grandma's knowledge. That resulted in Beth being sent back to her family in Stratherick, but worse for me, I was unable to do any teamster work for a month. Delegated to goats, sheep, chickens and helping Da in the oat fields. For me that was a step down and I lost all of my confidence in doing teamstering, even though I had been going to inherit the whole team when Grandma passed away.

My Mither and Father then also insisted that I get married, considering that I was already twenty years of age. The man they put forward was a big bulky giant of a man and I couldn't imagine even having a husband, let alone that man at that time. Of course, he'd say all of the right things and call me Isobel-Mairi, taking care not to shorten my name and complementing me like, 'What a pretty name', 'what a pretty dress you're wearing' and so on. He was just a 'sheep clipper'. 'What were they thinking?' was how I used to think about my husband.

Then one of my Grandma's friends, Mr MacNachten, saw that Ewen's proposal of marriage wasn't going well due to his poor connections in the border lands and offered to adopt him. I'd never heard of an adult being adopted and being given the name of that parent, but that is what happened and the elderly Gillcrest MacNachten adopted my suitor in order for him to try again to propose to me with success.

It was starting to seem like a good idea and he was growing on me bit by bit, even though he was such a hulk. He was even bigger than the Chisholms. My Ma thought that he was very handsome and so did Grandma and so I tried to look at his face to see if he was indeed handsome and I guess he was. His features were chiselled, his eyes were blue, he had brown hair and a soft voice.

Aye, he was handsome, but it wasn't until I found out that he was a farrier without all of his equipment, that he really became appealing. I tried then to watch him work, making horseshoes in the forge that my Grandda arranged and he had no trouble shoeing all of the Clydesdales, being so big as he was. I still couldn't imagine marriage to him though. I was a virgin and had never kissed anyone except my Da on the cheek and Grandma, of course, but not a lad. No one had dared to try to come near me because my Da is a MacGregor and a bit protective of his daughters and could be scary if anyone came near one of us two lassies.

My young sister, Morag-Freya, decided to become a nurse, so she lived in Inverness for a time with the old lawyer, who Aonghus had trained with. The lawyer was unmarried and couldn't cook. All my sister had to do was cook a meal for him each night and listen to his boring conversation and her board with him was free. She then went on to marry a Scientist, whom she'd met at that same hospital where she'd trained. So, my younger sister married before me and I helped Grandma make her wedding dress. I did feel a bit jealous then that she had married before me.

I didn't ask her about what it was like to share a house with her husband Gillcrest, who was a Laird as it turned out, let alone the same bed and I most certainly didn't dare ask about how bairns were made, although I thought I knew how in watching all of the farm animals. I was hoping it wasn't how horses and dogs did it.

Eventually, once Ewen was earning a good wage with his farrier work, he bought himself some new clothes and shoes in order to propose to me again and up until then, I hadn't accepted, but on that day, I accepted. He did look rather smart. My work with the horses was due to start up again with Hugh Og Chisholm and when Ewen proposed, the whole family were present when it finally happened. Ewen and I were then to get married and Grandma set the date in her special calendar. It was a weird sensation, putting myself and marriage in the same sentence, especially given that I didn't know what it involved exactly. I was grateful of the love my Ma and Da obviously had for each other and hoped it would be like that.

Ewen built us a beautiful home beside Cora and Hamish's cottage on Ma's land behind the school that would be a rented property at first and everyone helped us decorate it and fit it out. So, we were ready and I was as nervous as could be. I'd never been so nervous. Once Ma earned her money from the Art Gallery opening, she gifted that house and land to us both as well as an additional rented home on New Farm to protect us from the Clearances.

We married in Grandma's new wee Chapel on Craskie Farm and Ewen sang songs because he had a really big singing voice and could play the Hurdy Girdy. There wasn't much Ewen couldn't do. Up until the day we were married, neither one of us had ever touched the other or anyone else. Not a handshake or a pat on the back, nothing. I didn't know what it felt like to touch Ewen MacNachten. I didn't get advice on the first night either, so it was really awkward, especially because he too was a virgin, I was told. We were going to have to try hard not to die of embarrassment on the first night.

Standing on each side of the nice bed we'd been given, with sheets that Grandma had given me and a beautiful doona that Ma had made, I didn't know what to do. He stood on one side of the bed, fully clothed, and I stood on the other, also fully clothed. At first, I couldn't even look at him, but he didn't even speak, which made it even worse. So, I decided to break the ice.

"Ewen," I said, "I don't know what to do. Do you?" I asked

"Nae," he said, "I don't know either, but I've listened to Uncle Hugh's advice, who told me a few things that his brother Alexander told him," he said. And that was the awkward beginning of our marriage. In hindsight, though, I am so pleased that neither one of us knew anyone else, nor did we ever develop any interest in anyone else.

Awkwardly, we both climbed into the bed, a little afraid to touch each other.

"Isobel-Mairi," he said. "Can I please kiss you?" he bravely asked. I had to think about that for a moment because I didn't know if there was a particular way that one kissed a husband. "Aye," I said eventually. He put his huge, muscly arms around me, which gave me a shock at first, then he kissed me on the lips, but stopped.

"Was that alright?" he asked. I quite liked it, especially with his arms around me and I said, "Aye. Can we cuddle too?" So, with his arms around me, he gently lay me down and we cuddled and kissed. I found myself smiling and the nervousness had passed, but he asked if he could do more.

"More what?" I asked. "Can we get to know each other as husband and wife?" he asked shyly. My husband was shy and when I rolled over to kiss him, I realised there was hardness in his lower body.

I think his appendage was bigger and harder than it had been before and so I asked,

"Ewen, is it supposed to be like that?"

"Aye," he said, "if you want to, it can go inside of you."

I couldn't imagine a big thing like that going inside of me, so I asked where.

"Do you want me to show you where?" he offered. So, he did, with his finger seeking out the spot, then he touched a part of my body down there and I screamed. Of course, it all stopped and he sat up and begged forgiveness, saying how sorry he was for hurting me.

"No, Ewen, it wasn't pain. You touched something that was ecstatic that I've never felt before and I didn't know it could be. Can you find it again with your fingers?" I asked, so we both took off all our clothes and he looked for that spot again.

Ewan MacNachten

Once again, I was screaming too loudly, which made him happy. He asked then, could he try to enter his appendage into my body, but if I wanted him to stop, then he would, he promised. He asked me to put my hand on it and to feel if it was too big and immediately, I wanted him to put it in, but slowly in case it hurt. I lay on my back and he took it really slowly and there was just a moment of pain and a bit of blood and he kissed my cheeks and my tears of joy rolled down my face.

"You are my wife Isobel-Mairi. This is the most joyous moment of my life," he said. He penetrated deeply and thrusted slowly, while using his hand to massage the earlier spot that he said was called the "Jean de Chisholme." He then gave out the loudest of noises when his body gave way to the joy of the moment. I guessed by how loud we both were that Cora and Hamish, our neighbours, would have heard us and I hoped they wouldn't come to the door.

I fell pregnant that night, counting the days according to Grandma, so she set up a chart for me to keep a watch if my courses returned or not. If not, the bairn had a due date. Our neighbours, Cora and Hamish, at one time had thought the noises that we made were an indication of a problem, but no, it was like that every night.

The main house at Craskie Farm was still very busy when Grandda died. People were still coming and going. Both of my grandparents and my parents had worked very hard at their respective tasks and I was proud of my Da and I loved him lots. He was a handsome man, I thought and he never seemed to age because of his physical fitness. My parents met when they were young. Grandma's story was a lot more complicated and it was only Ewen's Da and her second husband, our new Grandda, who seemed to really understand her and love her in a really spiritual and deep way. Ewen's Da, Mr MacNachten had known of "the man who loved her," as he said, long before any of us knew, that at Grandma's age, she'd been having a love affair. She went on to marry the best-looking Chisholm on the farm, who became my new Grandda after my real Grandda's death.

They didn't even wait a day after Grandda was in the ground when they hand fasted and married with the Priest two weeks later. New Grandda moved in with Grandma and I don't think I'd ever seen her happy because she was a changed woman with both new Grandda and her favourite son, Uncle Alex, returning home from Nova Scotia and his mysterious twin Aunty Marion, his sister from Loch Insh who appeared out of nowhere it seemed with two sons. I then had additional cousins from both twins, being Malcolm and Kenneth from Loch Insh and Jean and Alexander from Nova Scotia. The farm house was packed and busy and noisy. According to Ma, Grandma and new Grandda were making a lot of love making noises every night and my Da was then asking my Ma for more sex which she wasn't too keen on any more, it seemed.

Aonghus' new wife, Annabel Cameron MacGregor, commented that she had never seen so many good-looking people in one place in the Highlands and it was true. As the farm had grown, it had only attracted handsome people like my husband, Ewen. Annabel had liked old Grandda, but accepted new Grandda before Aonghus could. The old lawyer who sold his business to him explained something to Aonghus, which completely turned him around and he became one of their strongest supporters because there were a few folks in the community who were critical of Grandma for re-marrying immediately after her first husband's death. There was a story there, but I wasn't told the details.

Grandma had to deliver my wee bairn in her house with the help of the washer lady, Mairi, Ma and Meredith. We named him Nachtain Grigor MacNachten and he was a big lad with fluffy brown hair and big red, round cheeks. He loved his breastmilk, as I am told most of our family did. All our women folk had large breasts that became even larger when lactating and when feeding my bairn, Nachtain, he would scream like mad if I took him off one breast to put him onto the other one. Then he would suck furiously with milk coming down the side of his cute little mouth.

My husband always watched on in fascination of the whole feeding process and even tried to drink my milk too, just to see what it tasted like. He didn't much like the taste of it but was a bit jealous that Nachtain had my breasts to himself until he fell asleep. Then Ewen had them back again for himself. Before I ever married, I couldn't imagine one of my body parts being in such demand. One day, Morag-Freya came to talk to me and asked what it was like being a Mither because she hadn't yet fallen pregnant, even though they were trying.

I told her about the secret "Jean de Chisholme" and she was pregnant within the next few months and doing the "Jean de Chisholme" over and over because she loved it so much. Her husband had been too scientific, she thought, instead of focussing on pure pleasure. New Grandda's advice to newlyweds was spreading like wildfire. Ma's Art Gallery finally opened and Grandma paid for the artwork from Loch Insh for Ewen in memory of his adopted Da, but sadly Grandma passed away the same night. My husband tried to make me feel better by saying that her work was finally completed on this earth as another tiny coffin was placed in there with her. New Grandda was inconsolable at her loss and the wee coffin had been his bairn with Grandma.

Ewen frequently went there with him to the Chapel and they'd pray together the prayers that they both knew. There were two candles lit. One for Grandma and one for the wee bairn Fleur Chisholm. We all understood new Grandda so much better then with that tragic knowledge that Grandma had taken to her grave with her wee bairn she had with Hugh Chisholm, not my actual Grandda. I didn't ask questions.

Ewen devoted a part of every week to new Grandda and they formed a strong bond with each other and my Da too, who all lit candles for Grandma, old Grandda, his Da and all those people Grandma had memorialised in plaques on the wall of the wee Chapel. The Frasers brought candles for the interior of the Chapel, so more of us prayed there at night and before long, new Grandda gave sermons to whoever would listen. Of course, 'obedience to the husband' was one of his sermons, but dealing with grief and loss was another meaningful and heart-felt sermon.

I then had the idea to diversify as Grandma had always recommended. I had to ask for my husband's patience to hear out my long-term plan for our family, so I began. I suggested that given the popularity and high demand now on tartan, I wanted to open a Mill in Inverness with the machinery obtained from the Lowlands. It would involve building a Mill with Ma's money and buying a shop as the retail outlet for the tartan in Inverness. As it grew, other large towns would need a shop too. We would also need to take Milread and her husband Bruce MacKay with us, as well as Ewen because the blacksmithing would also need to be moved from the farm to the rear of the Mill, where stabling of the

Bruce MacKay

215

team would be catered for with deliveries to and from the farm and all outer lying areas except during ploughing season.

Ewen's blacksmithing skills would be needed for each time the machinery broke down and he would do good business in Inverness in farrier work alone. Our own Clydesdales would be shod when they came up to Inverness if needed. The accommodation for both families would be Bruce and Milread above the stable nearest the Mill where she would work with two other rooms available for women workers, if the wool waulking women were willing to move. Ewen and I would live above the shop not far from there and we would employ Annabel one day per week and Jean one day and my cousin Alexander Og was very keen to work selling kilts to the gentlemen two days a week as a man was needed for that in measuring up the gentlemen. He could either stay with Annabel or us. So, I needed one more person for two

Duncan MacDonnell

days. Cora was staying in Glenmoriston because the school had grown so much and Ma was helping her out. The farm might need to look for more staff with us taking Bruce. Dougal then would be the head groom on the farm and Da had suggested a recommendation from his friend, also named Dougal in Glengarry and that young groomsman's name was Duncan MacDonnell and was twenty-three years old.

It would be called "MacNachten's Mill" and the shop would be just "MacNachten Tartan," which would also make ladies tartan dresses, skirts and sashes, as well as tartan kilts in the current Clan colours and begin designing new tartans for specific Clans and Military groups, like the 78th Fraser Regiment old Grandda used to be in. We could promote the military uniforms by putting Grandda's certificate of valour on the wall.

We'd need Ma's help with all the dyes and colours. Both Ewen and Da agreed to the new idea, bold though it was and Ma agreed to fund it all with the knowledge of the wool waulking group, who could be employed too.

Before we had left the farm, Annabel had started up a special bairn gathering just for the bairns at Craskie and at the end of one of those frantic days, Ewen and I were finishing up at Cora and Hamish's house next door. Annabel had decided to call it 'the gathering of the bairns' no matter how old the wee bairn was and no matter how many the numbers grew to. Annabel and Aonghus had decided to sleep over at Grandma's house that night, where it was a little quieter. The Fathers to be were getting all kinds of ideas of what they wanted to do with the bairns, like running races when they were old enough. Ewen was impatient to go home and the look on his face said he wanted some loving himself, so we were about to depart Cora's house, when Nachtain put his hands on the doorframe, screamed and stomped his feet refusing to leave. It was fortunate for us that Hamish and Cora both adored Nachtain. Hamish picked him up in his big arms and said,

"Do ye want to stay longer lad?" "Aye, Unca Mish," he replied. Nachtain couldn't say Hamish and so it had to be 'Mish'.

Being delayed and knowing that Ewen wanted some loving with me after the long day was disappointing for him, but then Hamish said Nachtain could stay as long as he liked and he'd bring him home when he was ready.

"We're spoiling him Isobel-Mairi," Ewen said, but he was so keen to get me home that he agreed. Hamish asked if we wanted him to sleep over with his son Donald, but wee Donald had had enough, we could see that. I said to bring him home in about an hour if it suited them. Our son Nachtain stayed in Hamish's arms, he clearly loved Unca Mish. Unlocking our front door, I knew it was straight to the bedroom, but I really needed a bath first and so asked my beloved if he could be patient while I bathed.

"Okay then. Only if I can wash you all over," he said with the happiest face I'd seen all day.

Boiling the water took a little time, but his hands were all over me, while we waited and I suggested we get in together, but with his size we both didn't fit, but it was nice to see him naked I admit. He did what he said he'd do and bathed me all over with a soaped-up sponge and tickled me to death and I could barely lie still, until he got to my private area when he slowed down and began to explore for my "Jean De Chisholme," which he found and massaged it until I gave out my usual scream like I was being murdered.

"I've never seen you from above and what you look like in that state of ecstasy. You look heavenly wife," he said.

He then pulled me out of the bath, towelling me and said, "I can't wait any longer." My husband's large appendage determinedly entered my body, then he groaned with the fulfilment of a husband being kept too long from his wife. "I'll wash again," I said and immediately came back to him. Then he asked,

"Will you always obey me Isobel-Mairi?" "What a strange question, but yes of course I will obey you my darling husband," I answered as I caressed his beautiful body.

"I hope I never make you unhappy, Ewen," I said looking into his big blue eyes when he said, "Then can I ask you to do things we haven't yet done as husband and wife?" he asked.

"What do you mean?" I asked. "If I ask you to take my appendage into your mouth for a while, would you obey me?"

Slowly, I replied, "Aye, I'll do my best Ewen," as tears rolled down my cheeks, knowing I had no experience of what to do. He was a gentle lover most often and whatever his desires were, he approached it in a kind way, but he knew what he wanted and so I accommodated him, as he gave instructions along the way, wiping away my tears. He wanted me to love his member that way and more often, hold it and massage it for him, testing my love for him and I did everything he asked me to do. Hamish had been knocking on our door, but we hadn't heard him and he came in holding Nachtain, so he may have seen Ewen and I in the newly discovered way to enjoy marriage.

"Hello Mummy and Daddy," he said with the biggest smile on his face. It definitely had that Chisholm ring of humour to what he had seen. We were a huge family now and I was with child again thanks to Ewen's special night with me, so was Morag-Freya and Annabel and Cora was expecting her third bairn. Meredith had had a pretty wee lass. All the bairns and their parents would attend 'the gathering of the bairns' each week organised by Annabel. The bairns and their parents were:

Cora and Hamish – bairns Donald, David and Mairi
My husband Ewen and I – Nachtain and Bridei
Morag-Freya and Gillcrest – Patricia Helen
Meredith and Hugh Og – Ferne
James and Susan – Henrietta
Milread and Bruce MacKay – Robert
Annabel and Aonghus – Hugh Cameron
Beth and Simon Fraser – Simone-Anna
Jean and Dr Benedict Browne – Benedict Alexander
Uncle Alex and Aunty Matilda – Sarah and Moses
Malcolm and Cherry – Islay and Alexander-Nachtain

I think we were all dedicated to repopulating our wee part of the Highlands and educating them all and Donald was the boss bairn, until Nachtain took over by splitting Donald's lip. Uncle Alex had gone on to marry the lady Scientist who specialised in Botany, Matilda MacMartin and they had two bairns, one girl and one boy, Sarah and Moses and remained living in Glengarry, building up his ranch and planting their patch of wild forest.

By that time, she had been unable to locate her biological parents. It was Grandma who assisted her and told her that she had, in actual fact, delivered her on Craskie Farm and her biological name was Clan Martin. When the crofters left, the

Helen MacGregor

Martins split into two groups and left with the bulk of the crofters to the coast. They went to Skye. The other group went to their homeland, which was Letter Finlay. It was known that they were Jacobites and were part of the Cameron Clan. Most of the Martins in her family would've been killed at Culloden and those that weren't would've been cleared since. Grandma suggested that she speak to the current Lochiel to get the details as to what happened to the Martins to find any relatives that she still might have. Despite my Uncle Alex having been told that she was Episcopalian, she was very happy to convert to Catholicism in order to marry him before a Priest.

Ma paid for two more homes to be built on New Farm, next door to Meredith and Hugh Og for Ewen and myself and Hamish and Cora. Our home was gifted to us by Ma with its land and owned with no rent to be paid, but we could rent it out. The other two were permanent leases with wee rent to Craskie Farm. Ewen and I would then be able to pass both of our homes onto Bridei and Nachtain when they came of age or if we passed away. Ma's investment in our Mill and shop meant that our sons were also going to inherit the new business of MacNachten Mill and MacNachten Tartan in Inverness and that's where we hung her picture on the wall as the Patron. Four new teachers moved into the teacher's house as the student numbers grew, but my husband kept his home there rented to Craskie Farm employees in the interim with the intention to leave it to our son, Nachtain.

The Art gallery was reduced in size to accommodate the students at the school, but Ma was happy to see children being educated and she wasn't sure the numbers would stay high. They were even learning Donald Chisholm's poetry from his own privately written work that was later published by new Grandda Chisholm before his brother's death. One of the poems was 'Grigor in the Mist', read out at Grigor Mohr's funeral about him not having known about his sister, my Grandma, when he was growing up. My Ma wasn't too fond of Erse poetry, like old Grandda was, so she preferred Uncle Donald's poetry to be taught in Gaelic at the school and all of our bairns liked it. I feel privileged to have lived on our beautiful farms and to breathe in our fresh mountain air. All our bairns inherited strong personalities from their great-grandparents that had fought to stay here and each one of them proudly wears tartan.

Hugh Og mostly manages the Clydesdale team, if Da doesn't need them, whether they are needed for crops or deliveries and I changed the name of the teamster business to "Isobel of Glenmoriston – Teamster." Hugh Og was not happy with that name change and was looking into it. He wanted a more modern name or one including his name. I was expecting a letter from Aonghus any day now to see what he preferred. The move to Inverness was successful and we could barely keep up with the tartan orders once more, despite a small hiccup with the name of our business. My other cousin Malcolm, whose Mither married a Clan Nachten from Loch Insh, objected to us using our name.

So, the business names became MacKnight Mill and MacKnight Tartan.

He is a really painful relative that I wish I had never met. We employed more of our wool waulking women and finally were able to employ a permanent gentleman salesman in the shop, whose name was Gabriel and was a bit effeminate. He got along well with my cousin, Alexander Og when they first met and they went out for tea occasionally. My husband Ewen and I pay my Mither back a little at a time for the huge cost of setting up the Mill and the shop, which was working well for us, but Ma was wanting us to pay her back more from her Art Gallery earnings.

Ma was starting to complain that we had taken too much out of Craskie Farm, even the forge which was meant to stay there. As far as Ewen was concerned, it was a gift to him and so he owned it, not Craskie Farm.

The letter finally arrived from Aonghus regarding the name change of the teamster business. Hugh Og Chisholme wants it called 'Chisholm Clydesdale Team, Glenmoriston'. On every letter head for a bill it will read, Hugh Og Chisholm and Grigor MacGregor, Craskie Farm, Glenmoriston. I couldn't see the harm in that name change and took Ewen's advice in avoiding court proceedings and just agreed to it in writing. So, I hoped Hugh Og was happy with that.

'Who does he think he is?' I thought. 'He was just a fisher lad, not even family.' But I held the high ground and agreed and I even sent him a new kilt in the Chisholm hunting tartan. Good will, Da would say. Hugh Og's wife was a MacKenzie and still the home help at the farm, but the stirring in the background made me think that she was behind it because she also doesn't want her husband staying overnight in Inverness with the Team, unless she came too. What fun, having Meredith here at the Mill. But my choice was to hire another firm or get our own Team. Another firm was wanting our business because Hugh had refused to go any further than Inverness. A lot of our business was to Edinburgh and he wouldn't go there, not even to Ross-shire.

Then Ewen suggested I sell the bloodlines to Hugh Og, so we could afford another company who would go anywhere that we asked them to go. I was getting tired of annoying relatives when we were invited to a family meeting up at the Manor House in Glenmoriston, regarding Aunty Marion's inheritance. That was fairly uneventful and thank goodness that woman only got five thousand pounds out of us. Ewen noticed also that all of the stone carving tools from Loch Insh were all gone, as well as the stone. Apparently, Malcolm said that they were his, not Ewen's.

I thought the inheritance issue had ended that night, but I heard later that there had been some fiddling with Aunty Marion's inheritance and she received a lot more money as did her bairns, those annoying rough, Loch Insh lads. At least one of them was educating himself in accountancy, so he was an option to employ if he was any good. He was still living with poor Annabel, who was really sick of him. I asked Ewen to find him a proper professional accountancy room with house attached, which he found for him, then visited Kenneth at Aonghus Law Rooms. It wasn't too long before he moved and then we employed him so he could pay his rent.

Annabel had never been happier. Apparently, he smacked her on the bottom when Aonghus was out of the room and she was a bit upset by it, even though it was apparently a 'Loch Insh thing' to differentiate real men from effeminite men. His older brother, Malcolm was deadly in my opinion and he split my husband's lip over our business name, so Malcolm is not my favourite relative and I heard that he is married now. Just because he thought he was the real MacNachten and we weren't.

'Who would marry him?' I thought. Her name was Cherry. What kind of name was Cherry I thought? It sounded made up? She was an Islander, so maybe her judgement wasn't as good as ours we concluded. Now they've got two bairns. They really didn't waste time and he bought a nice farm adjacent to Uncle Alex, who seemed to love them all. That was a puzzle. Then I heard by mail that Hugh Og did want to buy the Clydesdale bloodlines. What to do and how much?

"It'll cost him," said Ewen. "How much do you think?" I asked. "Offer him two thousand Pounds Scots. He doesn't have that kind of money," Ewen said. Our offer was accepted via Aonghus and the full payment waiting for my signature, signing it all over to him with the books on the blood lines carefully maintained by Grandma and her Father John Grant. I signed over all that history for said amount, which was supposed to go towards our debt to Ma, but Ewen wanted it to improve the mill machines.

I wasn't looking forward to the next 'gathering of the bairns' at Craskie Farm.

Ma might not be pleased to see me.

Morag-Freya MacLachlan's Story

"A Laird's Lady"

By Zaynab El-Fatah

Illustrations by Halima Karger and Fatima Zayn al-Abidin

Invermoriston,
Scotland, 1788

My parents were Grigor MacGregor and Helen Grant, from the Braes of Glenmoriston in the Highlands of Scotland and I was born in June 1766. I was delivered at home by my Grandma, who was known as Isobel of Glenmoriston.

My name is Morag-Freya MacGregor, later to become Morag-Freya MacLachlan when I married Gillcrest Lachlan MacLachlan, whom I adored.

I loved the farm life in which I grew up and am forever grateful that I enjoy good health due to the fresh and adequate food that I grew up on. Many others in Scotland died of starvation and my Father was a pioneer in ensuring that Scotland's crop yields were adequate to feed its people. I am very proud of my Father's legacy and my husband, who went on to run the Science Department in Invermoriston to ensure that there were many students going from farm to farm, improving the soil. They are both heroes in my eyes. How can you do better than to feed the people?

I loved being with my Father in his oat fields and helping him in all of the stages of producing the oats, right through to harvesting. Even when I was in Inverness, studying nursing, I would go home to help during the busy periods, like harvesting, when nearly the whole family was involved to get the oats into storage. This was always followed by an enormous family dinner over a traditional goose or geese that we all shared together.

As a wee bairn, I would hide in the oat fields and play around, which can't have been helpful, but Da loved my company anyway. At smoko, he'd pick me up onto his shoulders and carry me down to the house for coffee and cake. My Grandma was really the boss over the farms, but she let Grandda think that he was important on the farm. He was an important historical figure, I believe, just not much of a farmer like Da was, but all of us felt safe because of Grandda's reputation, as well as all the others that Grandma employed. Both my Da and Grandda were tall men, compared to many and they both had black hair. I thought I had the best-looking family in the Braes of Glenmoriston, but I grew up a little self-conscious that my nose was a bit too big. My husband never thought so though. He said he thought I looked a little bit Spanish, but I am sure there are no Spanish people in our family tree.

My Grandma had trouble getting with child at first and so did I. Eventually, I had a discussion with my older sister, Isobel-Mairi, who'd had no trouble getting with child. Their son, Nachtain, is really big, strong and healthy and yet she was married after me. Gillcrest and I were under some pressure to reproduce because he's a Laird of the Lachlan lands in Argyle, while not living there. His Mither still lives there and is constantly asked who the next Laird will be after my husband. She has invited us back to Loch Fyne to meet up with all of the people of the Lachlan lands, who were unable to attend our wedding and I am now really under pressure to be with child. I hadn't known that Gillcrest was a Laird when I first met him, so I didn't know what I was letting myself in for.

When I first married Gillcrest, I could never have been happier and I do take some credit for introducing my brother Aonghus to Annabel Cameron, with whom I'd studied nursing. When they married, Annabel was with child within the first year and was telling everyone at Grandma's wedding to new Grandda. Annabel was enthusiastic to have all of the next generation from the family to get together every week and we loved the idea for the social aspect. She may have also been thinking of the two middle aged twins Alex, newly arrived from Nova Scotia and his two adult bairns and his sister Marion, as well as her two big lads. I just wish that I hadn't been the last to be with child. Annabel had a lovely wee lad who they named Grigor Cameron MacGregor.

We planned to call our lad Patrick Lachlan, or if it was a lass, we'd call her Patricia Fleur, with Grandda's permission for the name Fleur and now that I am with child finally, we are going to Loch Fyne for that visit. However, that was our plan before Ma's Art Gallery Opening and we both dressed to look like a Laird and Lady and had all of our clothes in preparedness for the journey.

Preparing to leave the next day, the terrible news came that Grandma had passed away during the night and I was so shocked and saddened. I couldn't imagine a world without Grandma in it. It seemed like she'd been alive forever and she was such a force for good and I loved her so much, even though she could be a bit mysterious at times. The braes have their secrets and people do die with their secrets, but on that day, one of those secrets was revealed when Grandda led us all to the Chapel carrying a tiny wee old coffin. It was so sad to learn that Grandma and new Grandda had had a wee bairn miscarried at five months, decades before.

Their love story went back much further than any of us had ever known and wee Fleur was buried with Grandma. I can't imagine what that was like for Grandda Grant, if he had ever known, but apparently, he never knew and that was a blessing for him. If Fleur Chisholm had lived, she would've been my Aunty. After the very sad funeral, Gillcrest and I didn't feel like we could go to Loch Fyne for at least another week, so my husband wrote to his Mither and postponed our visit and explained the reason. There was so much going on in the family and in the district.

I wondered about our safety going that close to the Campbells in Argyle and despite having my husband's hounds that could protect us, I still felt the need for additional company. We didn't want to risk any other members of the family after just losing Grandma, despite thinking of Isobel-Mairi and Ewen as both being safe and enjoyable company. Ewen was such a big strong man, but I didn't want to risk my sister and Nachtain near the Campbells. My husband understood my deep concern because we are MacGregors, after all and Ewen had taken on MacNachten. Both Clans are unpopular with the Campbells. We therefore ruled out family, even though we did think of Grandda, but he was going to take time to recover from the loss of his adored wife. If any man obviously loved his wife, it was new Grandda. He hadn't inherited any one of the farms because that was always planned to go to both Helen and Grigor, so all he inherited was ownership of the land upon which Chisholm House sat and so I hoped this wasn't going to be an issue in the future. Being Ma's husband, it didn't sit right with me.

Anyway, Aonghus, my brother, suggested his old friend from university in the Pict Club, whose name was Fergus MacDougal to accompany us to Argyle. I had met him one night on the farm when Ma and I put on a play about Saint Columba and the Loch Ness Monster [2]. He had an interest in

Loch Fyne and had already been there with Aonghus to view Kilmartin Glen. We decided to get Aonghus to ask him if he would accompany us with a plus-one if he wished and we would pay for all of his expenses and his accommodation was Mrs MacLachlan's own home in Argyle. Because we would be gone for three weeks, we also offered a small wage that he and his plus-one were currently earning.

We anxiously waited on the answer from Fergus, who understood that I was with child and nervous about the Campbells. Despite taking two hound dogs with our enclosed horse carriage, it could be a difficult journey with many stops along the way. When we finally heard back from Fergus, he was at our front door with a pleasant looking male friend and his port, telling us that he was ready to go. He explained that he wanted to explore the burial Cairns again and if possible, learn as much from Gillcrest about the history of Argyle. He asked if he would be able to see the family Chapel in Argyle, as well as the family castle, which was bombed in 1746 by the English after the Battle of Culloden. Gillcrest had grown up in a house, not a castle, but Clan Lachlan didn't lose their lands.

Finances were all sorted out and agreements were made between us all, which included helping me when necessary. The men would take it in turns to drive our horse, enabling us all to get some rest along the way. We also had a spare horse tied to the back of the carriage, who trotted behind in case of any incidents with the lead horse.

We needn't have been so worried and the journey and the scenery was pleasant enough. Often, Gillcrest and Fergus sat together on the carriage seat and talked endlessly about the history of Argyle without the animosity that my brother has on that topic. Fergus' friend's name was Patrick Hamilton and we all got along well and he explained that his family were originally from the southern end of Argyle. When it was just Patrick and I inside our carriage, he asked me about our expected bairn and he said that his wife, Joanna, wasn't yet with child and was having difficulty falling pregnant like I had been. I didn't dare tell him what Isobel-Mairi told me about the 'Jean de Chisholme', so I said to talk to Grandda when we got back and he could explain it. I wrote the name down and told him that I'd recommended him to explain it. Then I would say a prayer for him and his wife in our wee Chapel when we got back home.

At least it took my mind off having to meet the sixty people, who were all judging me once I arrived in Argyle as Gillcrest's choice of wife, given that I was a MacGregor. In time, I think, with carrying myself with dignity, despite their thoughts, things improved from the first days. Fergus visited his Cairns, but Patrick wanted to stay with me and Gillcrest. He found it all so fascinating meet-ing new people, who were so different from anyone he had known. Like Grandma had said, the Clan Lachlan folk all had that weath-ered look about them and were old for their ages.

Morag-Freya and Gillcrest at Loch Fyne

I was glad to be heading home but pleased too for my husband that he had performed all of his Laird duties, including dealing with the finances of all of his lands. Fergus talked a lot about the Cairns and mentioned that I would have Pict blood too. I didn't want to get into that discussion, so I just nodded like 'if you say so.' We decided to travel up to Craskie Farm first on our way home, to let everyone know that we were back and safe with the hounds. We must have looked a bit dishevelled, tired and hungry because young Dougal, our groomsman, first took the horses to care for and then Ma invited all four of us in for baths, clean clothes, dinner and good night's rest.

I had forgotten what sleeping at Craskie was like. I fell into the deepest sleep after bathing, clean clothes and a generous meal. There was no other place on earth that I slept so peacefully at, than in our Braes of Glenmoriston. The following morn-ing, I visited Grandma's grave in our Chapel, where I lit three candles, one for Grandda, one for Grandma and one for wee Fleur. As I had promised, I then went to pray for Patrick and his wife, when I saw Patrick speaking with new Grandda, who had a rather surprised look on his face, but I nodded for him to tell Patrick about the 'Jean de Chisholme', which he did. He didn't mind really. He is such a big sweetie and I do love him.

Patrick's wife, Joanna, was with child within three months of speaking with my Grandda. Whoever Jean de Chisholme was, really knew his women. When our bairn was due, I asked Grandda for permission if our bairn was a lassie, could she be named Patricia Fleur after his wee bairn and he agreed. One of the secrets of the Braes had indeed been unearthed. Poor wee Fleur had to be dug up from her forest grave to be interred with Grandma and I am grateful that it is no longer a secret for their sakes.

I had taken leave from my nursing job in Invermoriston. Being the Head Sister of my Department, I needed to return back to work and reapply, in a few weeks' time, for leave to have my bairn. My husband was worried about me working whilst with child and I think I was too. I was keen to get back and start the following day, when Aonghus and Annabel arrived at Craskie Farm on their new horse and cart to welcome home us travellers. It was so nice to see my handsome brother, who was looking more and more like Da as he was maturing. I threw my arms around him when he alighted and kissed his face. I was glad to be amongst familiar people again and I hoped that Gillcrest would never suggest that we move to Loch Fyne. Annabel was as sweet as ever and thrilled about my pregnancy.

Then Aonghus, Gillcrest, Fergus and Patrick all sat around the dining room table, rather seriously going over details and the inevitable dialogue concerning Pict people came up. Ma had a really bad idea and suggested that the four of them team up and go to Mr Menzies, the Editor at the Inverness Newspaper, telling him of their travels and their theories and ask for members of the public to write into the newspaper, giving any information that they had on the Pict people or if they themselves knew they were from the Pict lineage and then it could go into print, Ma had suggested. I was so glad Grandda was there to be a voice of reason, because even Gillcrest was keen on the idea and I really wasn't. I was with child, who had Pict blood and it felt threatening.

"Ma, I don't wish to be disrespectful, but first of all," I said, "hold on please. There are only a few of us here in this room with that ancestry, in varying degrees. Da, because of his Grandma Freya, Isobel-Mairi, me, my bairn, Nachtain, Aonghus and his baby Grigor and you too, Ma. What if this is an unpopular identity to have and we bring harm to both ourselves and our children?" I said. Ma was looking surprised, when Grandda then said,

"Morag-Freya is right. Hear me out family, for a while and let me ask you this question. After the battle of Culloden, when your Grandfather and your Father, Grigor and I were hiding in the cave, would any of you have disclosed our location to the English or the Militia?" he asked.

"None of us knew where you were, Da," said Ma.

"One of you did, didn't you Grigor? I saw you skulking around, looking for your Father. I don't blame you but would you have ever disclosed our location?" he asked again. Looking horrified at the thought, my Da said,

"Nae Da. Never. But can you explain the connection?" he asked. "What would have happened if the English knew where we were? Ask yourself that. We'd all be dead," Grandda said, answering his own question.

"So, what I am saying in relation to the Pict story is this. If your Grandma had wanted you to know what she knew, she would've told you all, but she has died with her secrets for good reason. Those that remained of the descendants of the original people who ran this entire land for centuries, slipped quietly into the Septs of Clans and did not reveal themselves for good reason. They'd have been hunted down and killed like dogs. Who's to say that that still isn't the case now, if people felt threatened enough, that you are indeed related to King

Bridei? Be like Grandma and take it to your grave and don't disclose family member's names who could become targets. You are lucky to have this ancestry. I don't have it. Why not enjoy it, instead of exploiting it? Let alone endangering yourselves or other members of your family and other people who may write into the newspaper," he said with a very compelling argument.

"Let me suggest this," he went on. "You four could write a joint academic paper, after all, you are all educated, that just says where the Pict sites are, who the Kings and Queens were and their battles but without mentioning this family by name and location. You are my family. I won't allow that. Have you all understood that?" Grandda said and I had never seen him like this. He was serious and no one argued back, even Aonghus, who apologised to Grandda. That was quite a revealing discussion on so many levels and I think I appreciated, for the first time, the dangers that Grandda's generation had lived through. I hugged him and thanked him. He kissed me on the forehead.

"Helen, how about we have a cup of tea together?" he suggested. She smiled and they drank tea together with Da. Our family has definitely not lost its character and as we waved goodbye that day, I was sorry that I lived far away in Invermoriston. I really missed the farm.

"You've got that look," Gillcrest said.

"What look?" I asked.

"That one. Now I can identify it. You get home sick. No wonder Annabel brings Aonghus here once a week. Would you like to come here more often, darling?" he asked.

"If it's with you love, aye I would," I said feeling happier.

"Okay, we will. Then I can go fishing with the men," he said smiling.

Our journey home then was lovely. Coming back to Craskie will draw me closer to my Grandda and I can visit both

Grandda Grant's grave and Grandma's grave more often as well as poor wee Fleur, may God rest their souls. I loved my husband and my family and our new baby, who had started to kick furiously. According to the pendulum reveal, it was going to be a lassie, Patricia Fleur MacLachlan.

Helen MacGregor's Story

"Bliadhna nan Caorach - The Year of the Sheep"

By Zaynab El-Fatah

Illustrations by Halima Karger
Caution: suicide theme.

Glenmoriston,
Scotland, 1792

It was no secret that I wasn't running the farms as well as Ma had, even with my husband's and Da's help. We had all suffered too much from the loss of my Mither and I wasn't inspired to do my artwork to assist with our income either. Half of the

235

old school had been dedicated to the needs of students at the school, although I had noticed a slight decline in numbers recently, so I wandered down to ask Cora how the school was going and what her enrolment numbers were. Much to my surprise, there were fewer pupils than the previous time that I had visited her. On top of that, my daughter Isobel-Mairi and her husband Ewen were leaving the farm to embark on their new business venture in Inverness, that I have funded. So far, I have purchased land there, built them a Mill and paid for the equipment. The Mill was going to be called MacNachten's Mill and a shop called MacNachten's Tartan. They said they would pay me back over time. It was still non-operational while they bought the machinery from the Lowlands. Craskie had lost its farrier, our head groom, the weavers and a clipper to their new venture. My Ma would be worried looking down from heaven and so was I.

We had all met at Isobel-Mairi's home before this had all happened with Annabel, Aonghus, Alex, Matilda, Jean, Gillcrest, Morag-Freya, Patrick, James, Grigor, Hugh Og, Hamish, Da and myself. It was quite the crowd and a very animated conversation. None of us were expecting to hear that the farm would be losing so many people in one move, including the head groom Bruce and his wife Milread, who was our head spinner. It also meant the end of the wool waulking at home, as those women moved into Inverness to work for them too.

My name is Helen MacGregor, wife to Grigor MacGregor and I run three farms with my husband Grigor MacGregor in the Braes of Glenmoriston.

"Och, Helen," Cora said, "We've lost another five pupils this week, due to the Clearances. The parents, who are tenants are all being thrown off their land, whether large or small and from what I hear, they're being forced to live in the Colonies," she said with fear in her voice.

"Ma warned us about this. Do you know who's next?" I asked.

"Aye, according to Hamish, Charlie MacKichan and his younger brother Henry with their Mither, Widow MacKichan," Cora answered.

"Send Henry to me at the house when you finish your lessons Cora, please, with their Mither, if she comes to pick Henry up," I asked.

"Henry doesn't come to school often, but he is here today," she said. "Henry!" she yelled. "You have to visit the Mistress at her house, with your Mither and Charlie after school," The poor child looked afraid of whatever that was about, but he agreed to see me after school with his family.

Grigor MacGregor

It was me who was panicking at the thought of my husband losing our apprentice, Charlie, who my husband was relying on for when he got too old. His work was labour intensive, so I would frequently massage his shoulders. Grigor had grown a wee beard like his Da and was looking as handsome as ever. I greatly enjoyed running my fingers through his beard along his strong jaw line to caress his beautiful face. The massage would frequently become much more than that and I remembered when it was more than just us who were making all of the lovely love making sounds that came out of the bedrooms when Alex first returned from Nova Scotia. I hadn't thought that I'd ever be in charge of more than the care for the chickens, cooking for Ma, the staff and my husband. The wool waulking had been a once-a-year thing, but now we had even lost the wool waulking to Isobel-Mairi, so that left me with the pay book and all three farms, without so many of my staff. Diversifying for the future, my daughter reminded me. It was a daunting task and my Mither was a hard act to follow. I prayed that Da would never leave. None of us even knew how to slaughter and skin a large beast. A squirrel was as big as I had ever slaughtered. I reminded myself to ask him to teach a young man how to do all the things he did too. Kenneth came to mind.

When I approached our lovely home, Grigor and Charlie were coming down for lunch together, so it gave me the opportunity to talk to them about the MacKichan's situation. Charlie was sixteen now and he was Grigor's hard-working apprentice and the only one on the farm interested in the soil's condition, along with Grigor, as well as the only one who valued manure and tolerated being called names for collecting any amount of animal droppings for miles around. He had paid to put himself through school, which he had completed and was currently doing the soil course, part time, borrowing our donkey to go to Invermoriston. Grigor was horrified to hear that Charlie's family were ear marked to be cleared and wanted to rescue all three of them immediately.

Firstly, I explained that there was Alex's twin, Marion, her sons Malcolm and Kenneth to consider, so we needed to talk to Alex in order for both the MacKichan's and the MacNachten's to be housed and in suitable work, so that both farms could afford to care for them all. Currently, Marion and her lads were in Ewan's house. Craskie could not afford to take on both families, so we arranged to ask Alex and his wife, Matilda to come over to discuss the issue. I'm sure Ma would have done it better with her trusty calendar, but clumsily, I did my best. I hadn't appreciated just how much Ma had actually done in running the farms. Da came in for lunch too, so Grigor explained it all to him as well and he offered up Chisholm House for Charlie's family with wee rent.

"Helen, why don't you have a trusty calendar like your Ma?" he asked. From that day on, I had to use Ma's method with her trusty calendar to keep everything in order.

"It looks like you need me after all," said Da, finally smiling for the first time since Ma's death. "You know what they're calling it?" he said. "The year of the sheep. 'Bliadhna nan Caorach'. I'll ride down to see Alex and Matilda and explain it all and invite them to dinner and we can go over it all with both families here. Can Meredith cook up a storm at late notice? We can't lose your apprentice, Grigor. You keep the Widow MacKichan and Henry here for dinner too," said Da and he saddled up his horse with a purpose in mind. He was going to Loch Garry Ranch to see Alex. As he rode off, there was a loneliness about him that never went away, even if he was working or busy. He always thought he was riding alongside Ma. Maybe these additional folks on the farms might make him feel less lonely, I hoped.

Meredith was happy to stay back and cook for us all, so long as Hugh Og and her could stay to eat as well. He also had some things to update us all with about the Team, which worried me. Isobel-Mairi wanted stables built in Inverness as well, for when the team was staying overnight there, which meant that he had to stay with them and Meredith wasn't pleased about that. This was going to be a long and hard conversation without the wisdom of both Ma and old Da. Fortunately there was enough money to build her the stables.

Henry MacKichan

Mrs MacKichan and Henry arrived late after he had finished his lessons and were greeted heartily by Charlie, who had never seen them both on Craskie Farm, so he was positively excited without the adult understanding of what a Clearance was. Their poor family lived in a wee croft not too far from Loch Craskie and after her Jacobite husband's death in Barbados, she did odd jobs to feed the family. She was obviously shy and unaccustomed to company, let alone loud company. Both Hugh Og and Hugh Mohr washed up from their work and were obviously prepared for dinner and a long conversation, like it used to be. The fire was lit in the lounge and the house was nice and warm. Grigor came in also from washing up and lighting another fire.

"It's going to be a cold one," he said. Around now, I was expected to ask if all of the animals were fed and put away, as Ma would have done and I could hear her voice prompting me, so instead of ignoring her voice, I asked if all the sheep were put away and the horses and if they were all fed. Grigor and Hugh Og both made some kind of sarcastic remark like, 'nae, we thought of letting them freeze tonight.' Then both laughed at me.

"Don't laugh at me," I said. "Ma would have asked you that," I said and they both apologised.

"Aye, Helen's even got a 'trusty calendar' like her Ma, so we can all be better organised, haven't you Helen?" Da said.

The twins, Marion and Alex then arrived and their horses were stabled by our senior groomsman, Dougal, who we also invited to stay along with the new junior groomsman, Duncan MacDonald. Alex's wife Matilda was with their first wee bairn, Moses and Marion was with her two lads, twenty-two-year-old, Malcolm and twenty-year-old, Kenneth. I could never become accustomed to seeing my brother, Alex with a twin sister, let alone her two sons as well. Da was becoming closer to Kenneth because of his great talents with the gravestones and slabs, so I knew he wanted him to stay on at Craskie to dig the graves, as he was no longer the young man he used to be.

Da had slaughtered a coo earlier, so there was a feast with about 14 people at the table. It made us all happy and we learned all about what was happening over at Alex's farm at first and Matilda was with child again. In a very nonchalant way, Alex just happened to mention that he needed one farm-hand to help out with the fencing, particularly a rock wall and now that Jean was married, he needed assistance in the house with cooking and cleaning. He offered either the empty house on his property to his sister Marion and Malcolm to live in, or his big house as a family, which was two storeys high with adequate bedrooms.

"That would work for me," Da said.

"I don't want to lose Kenneth, if he's happy to be separated from his Ma. I'll look after him. I promise you that, Marion and it's not like we don't see each other often anyway," he continued.

"So, Kenneth, do you want a good job on Craskie Farm and live here in the big house? Your Aunty will put you in her wee pay book. Can you part with your Ma and Malcolm? Is it settled then lad? Do you want to be my offsider?" Da asked.

"Aye alright, what do I call ye," Kenneth said quietly.

"Grandda," Da answered.

"Can I live wherever you live then, Grandda?" said Kenneth.

"Aye you can. Helen, can you put Kenneth in your wee pay book?" Da asked. I nodded in agreement.

"Then you'll live in the big house lad, you're one of the family," Da stated. I noticed his brother Malcolm wince when he said that.

I followed all of the instructions and then we had to deal with the obvious, wee Henry.

Malcolm MacNachten

"There's the Clearance issue of wee Henry, Charlie and their Mither, the Widow MacKichan," I said. "Grigor can you please address this topic?" I asked. More food was put in front of us all and Grigor began his ideas for the MacKichan family. If they all agreed, Chisholm House has been offered up by Hugh Mohr, so they could all live there, while both lads worked on Craskie Farm. On the days Meredith was busy with her bairn or was in Inverness, the Widow would cook and clean at the main house, if she agreed. What we needed was an agreement between the Widow and Mr Chisholm for the rent and other rental agreements he had. So, they were to stay in the servant's room that night, as it was too cold out and early in the morning, we were to collect their belongings.

"Our donkey and cart can bring your belongings back here," Grigor explained.

"Can I please ask why Master?" the widow asked.

"You're being cleared out of your wee croft and if you don't accept our offer, they'll send you to the colonies," Grigor said with urgency. Not having known, the poor woman then broke down and cried. I felt so sorry for her, I embraced her and confirmed the information that Cora gave me that day.

"You're lucky that my brother, Cora's husband Hamish, is in the security business and knows who is next," Hugh Og said.

"Do you accept Mrs MacKichan?" asked Hugh Mohr.

"Aye Master," she said, not daring to look him in the eye.

"Would you like to see the house now then? The lads might want to say what room they'd prefer," he suggested. Her shyness made it hard to communicate, but I said I could go with her and her lads as well as Grigor, Da and I, all went up to Chisholm House together in the cold and dark. We lit the torch from the Chapel and went on in. Da lit a few candles and as I had never been inside there before, I was impressed. It was a lovely home that he had kept immaculately clean and tidy with adequate furniture.

"Well lads, which rooms do you want?" Da asked. "That

Alexandria MacKichan

242

room there is the only one that is out of bounds because it's mine, but all the others are up to you," he said to them. She signed an agreement to rent it at a wee rent, if she cooked and cleaned with Meredith up at the big house as well and he emphasised how clean he expected Chisholm House to be kept, so both lads had to sign too to keep their rooms clean.

"Because the men Clearing you will be armed, you will all stay here in the morning, and we will empty your croft out because it's too risky for you. They might injure you, at the very least," Grigor said.

Charlie, however, insisted on going with both Grigor and Da to get his Mither's plants out of her garden to plant back at Craskie. He went along and came back with a black eye, as was expected, but at least he was happy to have saved his Mither's plants.

"You're such a good lad Charlie," I said. I was fond of Charlie. He reminded me a bit of Grigor when he was young.

The MacKichans became a part of Craskie, as did Kenneth at first, who was loved by his Grandda and both of their lives seemed to improve from that day forward. Marion and Malcolm left that night with Alex, with their arrangement to live on Loch Garry Ranch in Glengarry and I was pleased to see them leave if I'm honest. It freed up Ewen's house for renting to any other workers who we needed. I had built two more homes at the back of New Farm, one for Ewen when they came out from Inverness and one for Cora and Hamish because the teacher house needed to be freed up for a new teacher.

Hugh Og informed us all what was going on with the Team and the arrangements he had made with my daughter and therefore the Mill was up and running in no time. We suggested that he take Meredith with him to stay overnight when he was in Inverness, so she wouldn't be parted from her husband. There was plenty of wool for spinning and making into tartan in the Mill and it was no longer done by hand, although Milread was in charge of that department. All of Ma's secret dyes were given to Isobel-Mairi in a book and that made me cringe. In bed that night, my sweet husband actually made passionate love to me and congratulated me on sorting out the farms and saving one family at least. I hoped Ma was proud of me but I knew that family was a priority with Ma, so it worried me a bit about my sister Marion and Malcolm no longer living on Craskie, as she and Da had planned.

I had to admit, that I was jealous when I found out that I hadn't been the only daughter of Padruig Dubh Grant and so when Marion left for Loch Garry that night, I wasn't too disappointed. She was a lot prettier than me and a bit younger, but we shared the same long black hair. Mine, however, was becoming grey and hers was still all black.

What we hadn't noticed that night, was Dougal eyeing off the young shy, widow and being empathetic to the two lads. Within the month, the two of them came to Grigor, myself and Da to ask permission to marry. Naturally, we agreed. I must admit she was as pretty as a picture. Da asked for increased rent, of course, at Chisholm House given that Dougal's pay had gone up. The new Mrs MacDougal cooked at the big house when Meredith wasn't there and Dougal and the lads stayed over too and we got to know them better. Being so quiet all those years, Dougal really enjoyed being with the family and was proud of his new wife's cooking. His sister Milread had left him too. Both Charlie and Henry never looked happier. I remembered how it had all started with Hugh Og and Hamish, who Ma had called 'the fisher lads', when they sold her fish from the lochs and they have been with us ever since. I hoped Henry and Charlie, named after the princes, would follow and be a part of our family like Hugh Og and Hamish.

On Saturdays, when the gathering of the bairns took place, Henry and Charlie met the rest of the family and helped out with the games. It was wonderful when everyone was there all at once, with Annabel running that, at least. The young Mithers all exchanged information and Ewen shod a few horses, while we still had him there. I missed them all and introduced them to Kenneth. Once accommodation for all of the families was sorted out, I had thought it would be smooth sailing from there. After all, Da had Kenneth under his wing and he was a good lad. There was already talk of sending him to obtain a better education in Inverness, enabling him to do the books one day. In the meantime, I had to call on James, my nephew, so I could do a better job.

Over at Alex's place it was another story, however, as Malcolm was making his views known to both Alex and Matilda about their circumstances, as well as his objection to Isobel-Mairi using MacNachten as the name of the Mill and the shop when none of them were born MacNachten. As far as he was concerned, Ewen had no right to use their name, even though he was legally adopted by Gillcrest MacNachten and gave up his name of Armstrong and adopted MacNachten in order to be accepted by Isobel-Mairi's family. Malcolm was a strong character in body and in mind, unlike his brother Kenneth, who was compliant with Hugh, whom he called Grandda. He didn't like to rock the boat. Malcolm, however looked around at the wealth of all three land-owning families and felt very jilted. His Mither was the twin, after all, of his legitimate Uncle and in his opinion, his Mither was equal to inherit but hadn't.

'What to do?' was his angry question before Ewen left Craskie Farm to take up the Mill and the shop. It was explained to him that Helen was Isobel-Mairi's Mither and could give her finance for the new business in Inverness. Nothing would convince him that using his family name was legitimate, if his family were not involved. Despite Kenneth not verbalising any objection, he asked to borrow a horse to talk to Ewen before they were due to leave. So, Malcolm rode with his Uncle Alex to Craskie Farm, where Alex alerted me to what was going on. I sent a runner to Grigor to let him know, as it had that sound of the beginning of a stramash like we used to have a lot of, while Da was alive.

Unable to find Kenneth to accompany him to New Farm, Malcolm went alone, while my brother Alex stabled both horses. He looked for Ewen in the second house along, as they were loading up a pony driven cart for their new adventure into business. "Ewen!" he called out to him. It was an intimidating approach, not a friendly one. He made it known to Ewen that he had no right to use his birth and Clan name that he was born with.

"My Father's name was MacNachten, but yours was Armstrong," Malcolm said rather painfully to Ewen, who had worked hard to be a better person than his own parents had been. Just the same, Ewen asked permission of him to use the name that they all shared, explaining that his wife and son were also MacNachtens.

"Your wife and son have no right to use my name either in business," he stated. "My Father was born Clan Nachten, as were both Kenneth and I, yet you all get to own businesses in our name," he said very angrily and by then Isobel-Mairi came out holding Nachtain and asked if it would make a difference if they paid him for his permission to use the name exclusively.

"No!" he snapped. "It won't". Both men were strong physically and were now locked in a serious feud against each other, especially after Malcolm had snapped at Ewen's wife and his precious bairn.

"I am legally named MacNachten and I have the paperwork to prove it," Ewen said, as he seemed to grow in size like Da once did, as I had observed many times before a stramash.

Ewen then pulled his right shoulder back in a defence mechanism to strike Malcolm if needed. Malcolm, similarly, grew in size and lowered his stance to pounce on Ewen. This was not going to be an ordinary stramash. Both of these men were very strong and highly enraged and obviously skilled fighters. Thank God Grigor and Da, followed by Hugh Og arrived, but not quite on time. Malcolm ended up with a broken nose and Ewen's eye was swollen shut and his lip was bloodied and split, before Da could break them up. Grigor couldn't believe what was going on, then Alex appeared. Da's old fighting instincts kicked back in and he kneed both of them in the groin, whilst tearing off their bloodied shirts. Once on the ground Da screamed at them like a banshee with threats unheard of in my daily language, which chilled us all to the bone. My dearest late Ma had married herself a berserker and hadn't known it. Both men were suitably terrified that day of Hugh Chisholm.

Alex didn't seem surprised and arrived calmly by saying,

"Oh dear. Best get you home to your Ma lad or the Doctor," and helped him up as Malcolm limped painfully to his horse, holding his groin. Ewen was left moaning, holding his groin too and limped back into his house. The local Doctor was Alex's son in law but decided to make a few pounds Scots out of us that day, as he found more injuries, all explained as 'farm accidents. Jean's husband could have helped out I thought, but he was remembering all of the paintings that he had paid full price for, I suspected. So, I was going to keep charging him full price until he did us a favour. 'Damn English', I thought. We all knew that it wasn't the end of this thorny issue, while the two men's wounds were dealt with. I had enough money left for a wee farm or business if Malcolm wished it, but in the meantime the name of the shop and Mill was decided to be spelled MacKnight in case it was taken to Court. It helped to have a son who was a lawyer, from whom I could get some advice for free. My son Aonghus also advised me to suggest to both parties that either the Mill or the shop be run by one of the families and the other by the second of the families, in which case it could retain its original planned name. I left it with God at the end of an exhausting day and decided to sleep on my son's advice.

My nephew James was due over in the morning to assist me with the farm's books. I had been lazy with them and had looked for short cuts, consequently it had left holes in my understanding of where the farms were all situated financially. When I had taken over the books, I saw no need for each of the parts of the three farms, such as the oat crops, the teams and so on, all having their own separate book, which in turn was entered into the larger one for each farm, to submit for taxation purposes. Ma had said her way enabled her to see which parts of the farms were doing well or not and what was needed therefore to assist that area of the farms to become more productive. In having shut down those additional books, I had made a mistake, so I was going to ask James to help me re-instate Ma's old bookkeeping methods. Then, if Da agreed, we could send Kenneth to an accountancy or bookkeeping school, even if it was part time, so we knew there was someone to take over from me or better still replace me altogether. I prayed that Kenneth stayed on at Craskie, after the events of the day and didn't share his brother's strong held opinions. I prayed a lot that night and was left with the image of my Da as a berserker.

Then I remembered the letter.

"Grigor darling, please remind me in the morning to get out a letter for Marion that was left in the lawyer's office," I said to my husband, as we both were pulling up the warm bed covers.

"Oh God!" he exclaimed. "Not another letter from the lawyer's office. This time he was too afraid to even bring it to us and left it with poor Aonghus to deal with. How long have you had it?" Grigor asked.

"A while now, I didn't know who Marion was until she came here before Da passed away and then I was busy with the Art Gallery, then the funeral and then I forgot all about it," I replied.

"Oh Helen, how long have you had it?" Grigor asked, looking very worried.

"About six years, there abouts. I can't remember," I said.

"Listen to me my love. Do not give it to Marion directly. I'll tell Da in the morning and what I think you should do is go into Inverness with him early, then meet with Aonghus to ask for his legal opinion on it, without Annabel in the room, or anyone else for that matter. It has to be a secret. Do you understand me?" m husband said in the most serious of tones.

"But darling, I have a meeting with James arranged already to go over the books in the morning. I can't go into Inverness. Can you and Da please go?" I asked.

"Can I trust you not to tell James about this letter while I'm gone?" Grigor asked.

"Of course, you can. I'm disappointed that you even asked me that question," I replied.

"James has a cunning way of getting information from you and before you know it, you'll be telling him what we ate for breakfast," Grigor said.

"Would you prefer that I cancel James then?" I asked.

"Yes, frankly and I'm disappointed you didn't tell me about this letter before now. You know what happened the last time one of those letters came into this house. Da broke Ma's ribs and that's what killed her. The Doctor said she had a punctured lung from an old injury," my husband said with emotion long withheld.

He hadn't intended to ever tell me that my own Father was the actual cause of Ma's death. He sat on the edge of the bed holding his head in his hands, then asked for the letter and decided to open it himself without my reading it in case it was harmless enough, but it really wasn't.

Grigor strictly told me to never tell anyone about it, especially James and Marion's family and carry on as usual and he would talk it over with Da. They were talking for a long while and I eventually fell asleep. I only awoke to him climbing back into bed to get a few hours' sleep before the rooster announced the new day. He hadn't taken off all of his clothes and said they might be going to Inverness, or another location, but would be gone overnight, maybe two nights. I packed plenty of food and coffee for them both and included water, warm blankets and clothes in their saddle bags.

"You have to run the farm while I'm gone and get Kenneth to help, as well as Charlie's family and if you need, get Hugh Og and Meredith. Good luck with the books. I do love you, Helen," Grigor said as he and Da departed.

I saw they had a shovel on one of the horses, as well as strong hemp bags of varying sizes. Then they galloped off together rather mysteriously. Kenneth stood beside me as they left and told me he would do anything that I needed, so his first job was letting the chickens out and collecting the eggs. Delegating might be the way to go.

It was then that I saw my well dressed and well-groomed nephew, James, strolling down from the Manor House and he waved hello.

It was a hard task sorting out the books and James was rather surprised at how badly I was doing it all. He set up all the books Ma had, while she was alive and it was then that I missed her so much, all over again and the grief felt overwhelming.

"James, I can't do this like Ma did. I was hoping to send Kenneth to that same school you went to, so he could take over, but in the meantime can you please help me on a weekly basis including the payroll?" I asked.

He said they were in an off season for tourists, so while it was quiet, he could, but as soon as they were busy again, he would have to leave me to it. He gave me the name of the school and who to contact and also spoke to Kenneth and asked him if he had an interest in bookkeeping. He offered assistance to get him through the door easily because he had a good name and Kenneth was surprisingly interested. However, he would have to wait until his Grandda returned to get permission, Kenneth said.

James was curious then where Da and Grigor had gone, so I actually did what Ma would have done to avoid the truth and I lied.

"Hunting," I said. Kenneth had a knowing look about him, so Da must have given him a different story, but he didn't let on. God bless him. He was busy all day, while we attended to the books when a visitor arrived. It was John Fraser, Ma and old Da's old friend from the military.

"You look just like your Mither, Helen, working away on those books. She was a hard worker, your Ma," Uncle John said. "How are you managing?" he enquired. I told him I found bookkeeping hard and had made a mistake, so James was helping me sort it out. We all decided that it was time for lunch and Meredith had cooked up something nice, so I invited him, Kenneth, James and Charlie MacKichan in for lunch and coffee just as Hugh Og arrived.

"Where's the big man?" Uncle John asked. Kenneth then answered, he was out hunting with Grigor. "I was hoping to talk to them both about the Clearances. I heard you've taken in one family," he said. He asked if we were taking in more because he planned doing that too, over at his place in Stratherick. I told him to ask Cora or Hamish who might know who is next and how worried I was about the school losing pupils.

He then suggested I go back to my artwork once I wasn't too busy because he was always asked about the painting in his house called, "The Murder of Fraser of Inverallochy." He told me if he had ten more the same, he could have sold them. It made me so sad that I couldn't get back to my artwork, so I explained that to him and he suggested his accountant.

"What if I send over my accountant after James has finished here and get him to work free of charge for you for a few months while you paint?" he asked. I explained that I couldn't make that decision without both Da and my husband, which surprised him.

"Now Helen, Isobel just would have decided and that's what made her successful. A few fights along the way, but she got there in the end. Decide. Do you want my accountant?" he asked again.

James was prompting me to accept.

"I'm not sure what to do," I said.

"Then, I'll send him around tomorrow morning. All three of you can listen in and learn," Uncle John said.

Then Kenneth spoke up saying he wanted to learn it at a proper school.

"Good lad, I'll pay for it as a gift to you then son and organise that for you all. Your name is Kenneth MacNachten, isn't it? Your Grandma was a great friend of mine. You'd have to stay over in Inverness with Aonghus and Annabel," he said very matter of fact and told me he was off to organise it all.

"Tell the big man I've been here," he said as a last thought. The big man was in reference to Da. Maybe he had heard about the stramash.

I was busy still when Grigor and Da arrived home days later, looking very dirty and tired. I boiled up plenty of water for them both to have nice hot baths. Their hands and fingernails were filthy. I didn't ask what it was that they had been doing, but that I had told folks here the story that they were hunting and my husband was pleased with me and gave me a wet kiss.

"Do I get a kiss too Helen?" Da asked and I kissed and hugged Da. I washed both of their hair too and I confess to never seeing Da's blonde hair up close and it was truly beautiful hair. He enjoyed giving me instructions like scrub his fingernails, his toenails and feet, until I heard Grigor shout out a Gaelic obscenity to him, which meant 'stay away from my wife' or some such, which made him laugh. At least both men had obviously had success in their mission. Over dinner we all exchanged information like the accountant from Fraser's Trading Company.

I was then in a bit of bother for having made that decision. I knew it. I shouldn't have made that decision.

"Are you going to give your wife the strap Grigor?" Da asked.

"Aye Da," my husband answered, without even looking up at me. At bedtime that night in the privacy of our room, I was strapped for the first time in our marriage. It was so painful with his leather belt and then he wanted more sex than usual. He was so amorous and did things to me that he must have learned from Da, I thought. It was all new sexual activity to me, that was so wonderful that I forgot the strapping. In the morning when the accountant came, Da sent him away with feigned gratitude, but accepted John's offer of paying for Kenneth's schooling.

Da kissed me over breakfast and spanked my bottom where it hurt.

"Good girl," he said. "Your big ass is just like your Ma's." I was a bit embarrassed in front of Kenneth and just hoped he wasn't going to spank me too, when he said,

"Can I spank her too?" He did seem to think it was rather funny and he really admired Da, so anything he did he would emulate.

"Ask Grigor," Da said. "Can I spank Aunty Helen too, Uncle Grigor?" he asked when Grigor sat down.

"Nae lad. That's my job," answered Grigor. A little disappointed, Kenneth ate his breakfast, but I saw he had the same side to him that Malcolm had. There was fire in them both, but not like the MacGregors and the MacNachtens from Loch Insh, who, if anything, were docile. So, that left the Grant blood from Padruig Dubh. A wildness. I decided to be more cautious around him and when the opportunity arose, he would be better off in Chisholm House, eventually.

With my nephew's assistance, I eventually got all the books in order and gave each section of the farms their own book to complete, which Hugh Og was glad about, now that the farm and the Mill were going to have mixed finances. What he wanted was payment to the farm every time the team was required by the Mill. Meredith and Hugh were both due to leave for Inverness and Alexandria MacKichan was due to take over our house cooking and cleaning. Dougal and Alexandria were to marry on the weekend and the Priest was coming from Edinburgh.

John Fraser came over again and I apologised about his kind offer of the accountant, but Da had said no. He wasn't bothered at all but wanted me to know he had arranged the schooling for Kenneth. I heaved a sigh of relief and it must have been obvious.

"The lads are a bit wild, I have heard from living in Loch Insh without a Father," Uncle John said. "Kenneth will come good, if he marries as soon as he is earning money, in my opinion," he said. "The poor lads have missed out. Is there any inheritance left to Marion?" he asked.

"Uncle John, please don't ask me anything, or I might say the wrong thing," I implored, just as my husband and Da walked in the door.

"Asking you what?" said Da.

"Inheritance for Marion, so her sons are equal," John Fraser answered.

"Of course, there is. What do you think we were organising? Another Rising?" said Da with an attitude I'd not heard him use with Uncle John before. So poor Uncle John just gave me the name of the school where Kenneth was to attend, the dates and the duration, all at his cost.

"We have to help our own. Good luck Kenneth, I can take you this afternoon into Malcolm MacGregor Law Rooms in Inverness if you want to start tomorrow," he said.

Da was then struck with the realisation that he was losing Kenneth and looked morose. Kenneth asked permission to go to both Grigor and Da and left that afternoon with his meagre possessions. He proved to be quite clever and had no trouble passing all of his exams. Little Henry, Charlie's brother, was the delegated helper then for Da, much to his disappointment at first. He was a sensitive wee lad but obedient. He so wanted to please Da, but he was so young and not as strong as the older lads. Da was harsh at times with him and one day I said to him,

"You're starting to sound like a Grant, where's your sense of humour gone Da?" He didn't much like my remark and he wanted to talk to Grigor again to organise a talk with Alex, Patrick, Marion, James and me and Malcolm with Grigor and Matilda if she wanted to come.

Patrick agreed out of curiosity and offered The Manor House as the location for the meeting in two days' time, which I entered into my trusty calendar.

The Inheritance

On the evening of the meeting, we were all suitably dressed and left to attend the meeting at the Manor House where dinner was provided by Henrietta and Susan.

My husband was the Chairman of the meeting announcing something of importance. We were all very curious. I sat nearest Da on one side and on the other was Matilda. It was nice to have feminine company. Grigor gave us all a speech, first outlining what we had all inherited from John Grant, Isobel Chisholm formerly Isobel Grant and Padruig Grant. He carefully outlined what properties were owned and by whom and then, of course, mentioned that Alex had inherited the land owned by my Father, Padruig Grant, in Nova Scotia, now halved so that Therese Grant was still there with her family and Alex had bought Loch Garry Ranch with his share of the remaining and what was left over had been paid for by his Mither, Isobel. It was like a legal conversation and that was when my son Aonghus arrived late with Kenneth and sat down apologising for their lateness.

"It came to our attention that the late John Grant had left an inheritance for Marion Grant, who became Marion MacNachten and her family, separate to all other inheritances afore mentioned. He did this because Marion was removed from her family by necessity to protect her from a neighbour, who was trying to claim one of Ma's bairns, being Alex. Therefore, as they were twins, she was hidden in the off chance that Padruig did give up Alex to Mr MacDonald who raped Ma. Naturally, Da never did that and neither child was ever given to that rapist. Our new Da, Hugh Chisholm, whom Ma married after Da's death, accompanied me to unearth your inheritance, Marion. We have waited on its validation and authenticity, which I will pass to you Aonghus, and banked the amount in the Inverness Bank of Scotland in the sole

Marion MacNachten

name of Marion MacNachten. Naturally, we also needed to acquire your marriage certificate for the change of name and your husband's death certificate. I have to thank Da for all of his hard work to ensure all of these details were acquired. Can you please come to the front, Da and give your speech?" my husband said.

"My dearest family, I am not a man of fine words like Aonghus. The manager of the bank, Mr Gordon has written this letter of authenticity for Marion to keep. You have inherited a very hard earned 5,000 pounds Scots, to do with what you will. Congratulations. Your Grandfather and your Mither never forgot you," Da said, then choking with emotion.

"I knew about you in 1746 from your Mither when we lost our wee bairn Fleur, so I hope both Malcolm and Kenneth will feel as equals in this wonderful family, as I do," he said.

We all had a lovely night afterwards, getting to know Malcolm, Kenneth and Marion better, who had been overlooked and we caught up on each other's concerns. Kenneth was succeeding at his accountancy school and was staying overnight at the Manor House with Aonghus, then leaving first thing in the morning. Malcolm's nose was healing, but before leaving, he enquired about his Mither's letter that he had known about. Marion began to listen in to her protective son. My heart just about stopped. I told him to ask Uncle Grigor and Grandda. Malcolm took a confused looking Alex across to Grigor and Da and asked about the letter that he had been told about, when Ma had visited them in Loch Insh, before the wee Chapel was built.

Ma had told them that it was at a lawyer's office in Inverness.

Out of Da's pocket came a very dirty looking letter from John Grant, addressed to Marion Grant and privately explained what they had had to do in exchanging French bars of gold into usable currency, in following the map that John had written down for the location of Marion's money, enclosed in the letter saying,

"Lad, it's not a good idea to let people know that your Great Grandda had French gold, let alone your Ma, so if you want to cause an international stooshie, go ahead, but your Ma might lose her money. The French wanted it back, you see. Do you understand how much of a secret this has to remain?" Da tried to explain. I then understood why he didn't want that accountant snooping through our books too.

Malcolm understood and thanked them both, but still wanted the letter, just the same, because it wasn't addressed to them.

"Best destroy it," Da said. I think Da then looked worried that night.

"I'm sorry for your wee lassie, Fleur," Malcolm said to Da, "But I want Ma's letter before I leave with Alex tonight, as it belongs to us," he said. I saw Da handing it over to him reluctantly and he emphasised that there was no more money than what was in Marion's account.

I was then suspicious that my husband and Da may have taken some of Marion's inheritance. It was obvious on Malcolm's face that he had no trust for either my husband or Da, whom he had experienced as a berserker. 'How honest was a berserker after all?' was his expression and he showed no fear of this particular berserker anymore.

He just cared for his own Mither and now saw us all, except Alex, as the enemy.

Alex took his family home before anyone became upset. Alex was doing a wonderful job of caring for his big family, but we were all getting bigger families as the Clearances continued. But French gold? I got a beating over that when dishonesty was afoot! I let my husband know that night that he was never to beat me again, or we would part ways.

"On top of that, where is the rest of that gold you dug up, you rat bag?" I asked. "I never thought you could steal an inheritance, but you have, haven't you Grigor?" I asked. My husband sat on the edge of the bed, unsure at first what to do.

"And don't ask Da what to do because Ma left this property to you and I to manage, not Da. We own the three farms, and this could threaten our ownership of them, if you have stolen gold bars from Marion. Please explain," I demanded. "My Ma loved you so much and was devoted to you, as if you were her own and this action is out of character for you. You have never threatened Craskie or the other farms, until Da was in your head every day since Ma died. Can't you see what's happening? He has returned to being one of the Seven Glenmoriston Men, when they were thieves. I know you think of them all like they were always heroes, but they weren't. Maybe you don't want to think your Da was a thief too, I don't know because I only knew them all as good men, until Da told you to punish me," I said. "Now I want whatever gold it is you have, belonging to Marion and give it back to her and let her deal with the French authorities," I said.

Grigor had never heard me speak to him in that way and was shocked. He looked up at me like a child in trouble.

"Well, where is it?" I asked, with my hands on my hips.

"Under the bed," my husband confessed.

We went to the stables and saddled up two horses and rode all through the night to Loch Garry Ranch. It was dark as we opened their front gate, but there was a fire lit at least, as there was some smoke coming from their kitchen chimney. We were heard, as we closed up the gate again and a dog barked and there were distant sounds of geese honking, as Alex and his burly looking student came out onto his front porch. His student named Joe, was instructed to stable the horses, while we went inside. Thank goodness Marion and Matilda were asleep as was young Alexander, but the dreaded Malcolm was seated at the kitchen table, like as if he was expecting us. It was a bit weird.

As I walked in the door, he was looking straight at me.

I had the gold in two saddle bags and handed them to him, stating that it was Marion's to deal with, but to be aware that now French authorities might want it back unless they melted it down, so that it was still usable currency in modern day Scotland. Both bags were full, and I'd hate to know the actual value of the gold. I remembered that old man who came snooping for gold at our place, asking Ma about what she and my Grandda had been moving for the Jacobites in 1745. Looks like that old man might have known more about Grandda than we did. Malcolm just took the bags and opened them, then counted how many bars there were.

"Did the big fella take any of it?" Malcolm asked.

"No," answered Grigor, "He just planned it all," he replied. Alex was normally calm and quiet and not really judgemental, but he was horrified that Grigor had been complicit in stealing from his twin, Marion. Tears came to his eyes, as he sat at the table with his head in his hands.

"I am so sorry Malcolm, to both you and your Ma, that this has happened. I suppose you can never forgive any of us, after all of that long speech at the hotel. It was all shite," Alex said with such deep sorrow. "Whose idea was it, Grigor to steal from Marion's family?" Alex asked.

"The idea was Da's, but I can't claim innocence, as I went along with everything," he said. "I've been lost without Ma and I have only been able to follow Da, but I know now that it was wrong. Both Helen and I have been struggling with all the farms since Ma died," Grigor answered as he sat down.

Joe then came in taking in the scene.

"Well, who's been robbing King Louis XV," Joe jokingly remarked. "Hope you're not giving it back to that asshole, Malcolm?" he asked. "I can help you melt it down lad and they won't know, best you keep it quiet though or we'll have thieves turning up here and Alex won't want that, will you?" Joe said.

Malcolm had sat quietly, but after his friend Joe had spoken, his only few words were, "Thank you, Joe, I will need your help and I'll pay you for it," he said.

He picked up his mither's gold bars without looking at either of us and left the room, unsurprised by his relatives' dishonesty. I've never felt so judged in my life before and I too was to blame in forgetting to pass on the letter. I had really hurt my sister and my Mither's Grandchildren, when both of my parents were keen to see us all established, before they had both died. I had let my Mither and Father down too, as well as my Grandfather John Grant. I no longer felt so important to their lives, even though they were already dead. Somehow, they felt alive in that room, watching on and the only family they admired were Malcolm and Alex.

I'd forgotten how connected Ma was in spiritual matters and it occurred to me that she was channelling through Malcolm. I can't describe the disappointment I felt towards Da, who I felt like calling Hugh once again, as Da no longer fitted him. Maybe he should move back into Chisholm House.

"I would like Hugh Mohr to move back into his own house Grigor, he is a bad influence on you and my guess is, he is wanting money for their lost bairn too. I don't like him smacking me on my backside as well and he shouldn't want me to wash his hair," I added.

Joe poured us all more coffee upon hearing that and wanted to do him some damage, compared to my husband who accepted him smacking me or pinching me on the bottom.

"You need new staff over there and you can't take on more families who are being cleared, but you could get good workmen who are being cleared," he said. "I do know another sea dog like myself who's very good at everything. You name it, he can do it, but he won't expect you to take on his family. It's a matter of pride," Joe said.

Alex was too disappointed in both of us and just wanted to go to bed.

"Joe, I'll leave them with you to talk over that friend of yours to work at Craskie and please get their horses for them when they leave. It's been a long day. Good night everyone," said my disappointed brother as he went to bed. I'd never seen that saddened expression before on Alex's face.

Grigor had worked hard his whole life for it to reach this crossroad and he too wanted Hugh Mohr to move out of our house, which meant he had to live with the MacDougal family, so he would have a cook at least, but the idea of living with Henry would not be appealing. But he did move, realising he had outstayed his welcome or need. Joe was a wonder and organised his friend, Murdoch MacLean, within the space of a day and he was energetic, intelligent, fixed things I didn't know needed fixing, could slaughter any type of beast, helped with the horses, the oat fields and anything needing to be done. The farm was looking neat and tidy once again and he rented Ewen's house.

I sighed a sigh of relief and could do the books without worrying and then I painted my first painting in four years. The painting was of the Clearances, representing the day the MacKichans and neighbours who were cleared from their crofts, with buildings being burned down and women being beaten. This was described to me in detail by Charlie. John Fraser said he had a buyer immediately for my painting. An image of it ended up on the front page of the newspaper, letting people know just how bad and violent the Clearances had become. Out of interest, I asked him who had bought the painting and he said it was Mr Menzies from Inverness News. He has it hanging on the wall in his newspaper office.

Grigor was taking longer to recover from the disappointment in himself, so it was going to be personal effort on his part to improve matters with my nephew Malcolm, who still had long scruffy hair and was dressed like a ruffian, despite his new-found wealth from his Mither. He still resided with and worked for Alex with his friend Joe, by choice. They built a beautiful rock wall at the front of Alex's farm together, as well as the perimeter wall around the forest project and Alex put in a bigger gate and two pole lights like we had, near the entry of Loch Garry Ranch. Grigor was due to meet up with his old friend Dougal, who told him Bruce was back, so all three of them were going to go out together. He came home very late and a little drunk, but his amorous intentions were at least loving, even though it was short lived, and he fell asleep before he could even finish. Poor darling, I did love him with all my heart.

At breakfast before he left for his work on the oat fields, he whispered sorry to me for his lack lustre performance the previous night and he kissed me sweetly. Just as he was about to leave, he mentioned that his old friend Bruce, who was about our ages, had lost his wife to illness in the Americas and all of his bairns were well established there, so he had yearned to return to Scotland. He wanted us to find him a nice wife, who he wanted to be of the farming type, not too demanding, pretty, not too young and without young bairns. He'd had enough bairns he said and just wanted some company as he aged.

My mind went to Marion who could afford her own place, even though she had never left Alex, except to stay over with her son, Malcolm.

"What about Marion?" I asked. "That could mend things darling. If they liked each other," I said. "Talk to Alex first, he seems to speak for her," I suggested.

I saw Grigor shift in both embarrassment and sadness, but embraced the idea and rode up to Glengarry immediately. Alex was always wary now of my poor husband and so standing on Alex's front porch, Grigor stated his reason for visiting, he told me later, before they invited him in. He explained Bruce's circumstances with his wife, now passed and children, all married in South Carolina, who was looking for a wife, his age. Marion hadn't had anyone show any interest in her, for some reason, maybe because she was so quiet and stayed behind her brother, or her son. It was a surprise for them all to hear that there may be an interested party.

Alex was going to decline, when Matilda said Marion should at least meet him and be sure, because she understood why Marion was too shy to put herself forward. It was agreed that they meet at that same alehouse where Cherry used to work, but in the restaurant, not where

Bruce MacDonald

all the drinking men were. Alex only agreed if both he and Malcolm could accompany her and make their own assessment about him as well. Bruce agreed with no issue to that when he was told and was looking forward to the meal, which he offered to pay for. They seemed to like each other when they met, but it was hard to tell. It wasn't one of those 'let's hand fast now' moments like with Malcolm, but they did agree to meet again on the ranch, where he was introduced to everyone else, including Joe and Cherry, all hoping to pick fault with Grigor's suggestion.

They strolled around the new forest that had been planted by Matilda and he was very impressed with the wee burn flowing through it. He said it was a romantic setting. Maybe it was the word 'romantic', but she decided to see him often, until they were both sure of each other and had common interests and could get to know all about each other, including their offspring.

She was especially proud of Malcolm getting married. So, with Alex's permission for Bruce to see her granted, he went there weekly taking gifts each time or food or offered to cook fried chicken with some chickens he brought with him.

Alex was hooked then, if a man could cook him his favourite dish like his Ma once did, Alex was no longer a problem. Malcolm was the next hurdle and that was a high one, he told my husband. He was asked all kinds of questions about his life in Glenmoriston, then in the Americas and the War of Independence there, as well as his large property in South Carolina, which he sold part of for himself and left the rest for his offspring. He had enough money to purchase a farm in our region if one became available.

Eventually, he won their hearts through Malcolm's bairn, Islay. He bought her gifts from the Americas, including Indian artefacts, as well as a bow and arrow kit, which he taught her how to use, with strict instructions not to kill the farm animals or wild birds. Then he was accepted gradually by the family. But did Marion like him enough to marry? They decided to be good friends for as long as it took, before any commitment and so it was about a year before they were married. Marion was twenty years a widow to a man that she had obviously adored and so Mr MacNachten was a hard act for Bruce MacDonald to follow.

Finally accepting him first through friendship, then trust and kindness, Marion was a beautiful bride at her wedding to Bruce MacDonald and Grigor was finally forgiven. Thank God.

Our marriage, however was never the same again and I confess to my inability to cope as well as my many mistakes and my poor attitude towards Marion and her sons, when they first arrived.

After many fights, Grigor finally moved out and I was all alone with my ghosts. I took my own life hoping to join my Mither. I couldn't hold on any more. I am sorry to those who found me but I just couldn't go on for a moment longer.

Helen.

Book 2 – The Letter

Malcolm MacNachten's Story

"The Letter"

By Zaynab El-Fatah

Illustrations by Halima Karger

Glenmoriston,
Scotland, 1792

It came about after an argument I had with Ewen, who was opening a Mill using our family name when he hadn't even been born in the Highlands, let alone with our family name. I don't really blame his wife, let alone his baby Nachtain for having our name and if they were not exploiting it, the issue would not have reached the heights that eventuated. The issue was respect for Clan Nachten and they had no respect.

1. Loch Insh

My name is Malcolm MacNachten, son of the late Nachtain MacNachten and Marion Grant MacNachten of Loch Insh, Scotland.

I have been labelled 'wild and uncivilised' for being raised in Loch Insh because my Father died of pneumonia when I was four years old and my brother Kenneth was just two years old. In Loch Insh I was never called names. That only happened when we had to move to the Braes of Glenmoriston.

When Da died, we went back with our Ma to live with our Grandda, who had raised my Mither in Loch Insh. We were both told as young bairns that Grandda wasn't my Mither's real Father, but he was the only person willing to take us in after Da died. I wasn't told what happened to my Father's parents, but they were no longer living in Loch Insh. It was a heartbreaking time in our young lives, as we watched our Mither mourn our Father's death and I couldn't understand why he had died and why we had to live in another croft. It was all too confusing and my young brother was a gentle bairn, unlike me, because I was at least a bit tougher. Our Grandda never punished us or raised his voice to us. He taught us about the swans that lived on the lake and how to respect them and to not hunt them as some people did. I loved Grandda, but his impending death meant that we had to leave to live on Craskie Farm in Glenmoriston, eventually with the Grants.

Ma had taught us what she knew of Clan Grant from Grandma, which wasn't much because her Mither was unable to visit her beyond the age of ten. It wasn't explained to us why we were not living with our real family. The Grandda and Grandma that I knew growing up were not wealthy people, but related somehow to my Grandmither, Isobel Grant, who later became Isobel Chisholm. We two brothers met our real

Grandma when she came to see Grandda and my Mither when I was in my teens. She came alone on a huge Clydesdale horse, but she herself was a tiny, lean woman. In my mind, I had always imagined a big, strong and loud woman, not the sweet, tiny lady with a quiet voice, who was full of love for us. Apart from arranging for a Chapel to be built on her farm with Grandda, she wanted us back to live with them, so we could all be part of the Grant family. She was also Clan Gregor, she said. I asked why we hadn't been part of the family and she lowered her head in shame.

She must have thought that I was old enough to hear the terrible truth and said, "I was raped lad, by my neighbour who was a beloved Uncle and I had always thought his love was that of an Uncle, since I was wee, but I was mistaken. However, my husband came home that night also, so there was a question over who the Father was of what I thought was just one wee bairn when I was with child as a result of that night. The neighbour, Mr MacDonald, was desperate for a child to inherit his property, but in the end, he left it to my husband. Compensation for what he had done maybe? When your Mither was born, to our surprise, she was one of twins. We named them Marion and Alexander Grant. My Father, John Grant, knew the folk from Loch Insh well and begged Mr MacNachten to take Marion into their care because they were childless and we were desperate and my Da promised to pay for her upkeep. A promise that we were unable to keep due to unforeseen circumstances. I made your Ma clothes and for years it went well with seeing her, taking her books, new shoes, food from our farm to your Grandda, as well as money to raise her, but neither one of us had anticipated the Rising of 1745. We lost my Mither, all of our crofters, our home, our outbuildings and all of the crops, but worst of all, we lost the horses and the coos. So, we could no longer go to see your Mither," she explained in deep sorrow. As she left that day, she reminded us all that there was a letter waiting for my Mither, Marion, at the lawyer's office in Inverness when we wanted to get it. I don't remember Ma ever having gone there to get it.

2. The Move to Glenmoriston

We moved to Glenmoriston in 1786 because, despite Grandma's efforts to bring us home, she had been beaten by one of the men and then became ill and nearly died herself. My Grandda was a spiritual man who could hear voices and he awoke that night knowing that she was in trouble in trying to return home to Glenmoriston, alone on her horse. He said he was sent to her spiritually, as was another, her brother Grigor Mohr MacGregor, because she was falling asleep on her horse and nearly fell off. He would confide to me all that he knew of the spirit world and the old Druid religion, as well as what he knew of our ancestry connected to the Pict people. He went to Craskie Farm the next day and she was ill and remained ill for a time and had been beaten by the 'one who loved her'. My Grandda asked why and she explained that if it had been her husband, she would no longer be alive. They had objected to her going to Loch Insh alone for a trivial matter despite her having left a written note. He concluded she couldn't yet tell her husband about us all and so we stayed longer in Loch Insh. I had been looking forward to moving there, but after that happened, I wasn't sure what the future held for my brother and me.

My Ma was devastated and once more I watched her mourn for a lost loved one, her Mither.

I knew Grandda was old, but he taught us his craft of engraving grave slabs, many in the Pictish style.

"One way to see the farm lad," he said, "But without visiting your Grandma, would be to join the building team who are building the wee Chapel on Craskie Farm," he said. So that is what I did.

Without their knowledge, I just observed them all while I worked. I lived in a house called Chisholm House owned by Hugh Chisholm, who seemed awfully fond and worried about Grandma. However, he was the one who had beaten her, but the talk amongst the staff was that she had asked him to do it so she would survive the night. If Padruig Dubh had beaten his wife that night, they said we would all be digging her grave. When we met again later, after Grandda Grant died, Hugh Mohr didn't even recognise me. I had just been one of the workers and he didn't like me.

Grandma, knowing of us, gave Grandda her highland ponies, so his old pony could be retired on Craskie where it had died. During all of that time when Grandda was involved with the family, he offered to adopt an adult male wanting to marry Isobel-Mairi, Helen's daughter and gave him our name. Ewen seemed harmless enough at the time because his intention then was only to be the farm farrier. In 1786 our Grandda passed away in Loch Insh and we then had to move to Craskie Farm. Ewen had already taken back the highland ponies and all of our tools that we used to engrave the tombstones with, as well as all of the spare stones. He felt superior to us as the grandchildren of Mr MacNachten, overlooking that my Father also worked the stone and as his sons, he took away all of our tools of craft and our income. I found all of our old stone and tools on Craskie Farm, behind the Chapel when we moved there. It made my blood boil. Ewen was my enemy from then on.

Moving there was a long way from all things familiar or any of my friends growing up. Aunty Helen didn't seem to want us to be seen by anyone at first and so she didn't offer to have us live in the main house with her, despite Grandda Grant promising his daughter permanent accomadation in his house. Ewen had temporarily loaned us his house, while Ma met with old Grandda before he passed. When he invited us all to live on the farm, we all understood that to mean a permanent arrangement in the main house. I was mistaken about that. Grandda Grant's funeral was so enormous that we were swallowed up amidst the crowds of people there paying their respects. We hadn't known that he had been some kind of local hero, let alone how well-known Grandma was as well, as 'Isobel of Glenmoriston'. It made us both feel even more insignificant than we had already felt. Ma was only just handling it, but she was always so polite and sweet, especially to her elders, so hers was always a silent suffering.

3. Trouble Brewing

Hugh Chisholm didn't know who we were, even though I had lived in his house and then in Ewen's house. Uncle Alex was my Mither's twin by birth and like everyone else, he seemed to be doing well financially, compared to us, but at least he could look you in the eye and remember who you were, as well as your name. It was Ewen I hated. Although Granny was still alive for just over a year beyond that, she married Hugh Chisholm much to everyone's shock. They hand fasted before the Priests from the funeral had even left to return to Edinburgh. I admired that at least in my Granny. She was brave at that age to just announce it and do it. I was learning how it worked in Glenmoriston.

My hatred grew for Ewen when I discovered their plans for business with my Clan name. He had taken my tools, my stone, my livelihood, my ability to remain in Loch Insh and then my Clan. I wanted to kill him if he didn't return my tools of trade, the ponies and changed the name of their business. Only we could use MacNachten, we were the last and I owed it to my Clan to stop the deceit and get back my stone working tools. I wasn't moved off Craskie Farm for the remaining year of Granny's life and I made it known to her about the ponies and got both back at least, but I think the new Grandda Hugh Mohr didn't much like that about me, so I told him I was one of the builders of the wee chapel. He was shocked. I told him I wanted all of my tools and stone back also and not realising they had belonged to me, he apologised. "Ewen just helped himself," I said. "Think what you like of me, but it was wrong, which left both my brother and I unable to earn an income." I didn't care what he thought of me, I wanted what was ours.

4. Moved Again

I heard Aunty Helen mention another family being cleared off their land, so we were going to be moved – again. They had priority over us, despite us being family and Grandda's promise. It was no surprise that Kenneth, however, managed to get into the good books with new Grandda Hugh and he was staying on at Craskie and then had his education paid for, by some miracle. Only I was being moved to Uncle Alex's farm with my poor Ma. At least she felt a closeness to Uncle Alex as her twin, but I still couldn't understand why there wasn't equality between all of the children of both Isobel and Padruig Grant and their grandchildren. It was when Ewen and Isobel-Mairi announced they were going to use our family name on businesses in Inverness that I became riled.

He was then exploiting the name given to him out of the kindness of an old man's heart and I couldn't bear to see that kind of disrespect to our Clan and we had an awful stramash, resulting in my broken nose. Lucky my Aunty Helen paid the bill because the Dr charged full price to fix it. Uncle Alex was a fair and kind man, who married a very attractive but older woman, named Matilda and I don't think she had much time for me either, given that she was educated in London. I was dirt under her feet or that's how it felt. Maybe it was just a lack of trust, but we were never going to get along.

5. *Island Clearances*

The student, Joseph MacFie, was originally from the Isles. I'm not sure which Island that was, as I was unfamiliar with the sea, but he was a bit of a sea dog. He had been cleared from his land, as had all of his friends and family and the land had been taken over by a rich landowner from London who wanted no one who had lived there for centuries to live there anymore. There were many fights there, initially, in trying to keep their crofts, he said, as well as their grazing land, but to no avail. Troops were sent in and many of them were severely bashed up, including their women folk. Joe said he had to find somewhere to live where he could still earn an income and make a new life for himself, given he was no longer as young as the other students. He had a wife and three children, who were relying on his income each month. They were living with her parents somewhere in Edinburgh, who had a wee shop selling pottery. Uncle Alex found him to be very useful and wanted Joe to stay on permanently, beyond the usual one-year arrangement. We got along well and he often gave me advice, especially on which fights to pick, because some were not winnable. His advice, although good, did not take away my intentions where Ewen was concerned.

I received a letter addressed to Uncle Alex's farm, to my surprise, which was to inform me that Isobel-Mairi and Ewen's businesses were no longer going to be called MacNachten's Mill and MacNachten's Tartan. They were now going to be called MacKnight's Mill and MacKnight's Tartan, if I agreed to that alteration. The letter was from Aonghus MacGregor, Aunty Helen's son. He also welcomed me to join the family at a meeting to be held at 'The Hart of the Highland Manor House' with Uncle Alex and my Mither, Marion MacNachten and he would be there too with Kenneth. I replied to him by mail accepting the name change of their businesses and the invitation. I was very curious what the meeting could be all about. I went about building the wall my Uncle wanted, having retrieved all of my tools of trade from Craskie Farm, finally. I had the two old ponies as well, which were then stabled at Loch Garry Ranch.

6. Don't You Like Me Malcolm?

I made it clear to Uncle Alex what was mine and he didn't seem to mind. His son, Alexander, was more interested in cookery and art more than anything, but he still pulled his weight, especially with the livestock, and he tried to befriend me, but being a bit effeminate, I found him a bit creepy. I asked Joe if the lad had ever had a girlfriend, when a smile crept across his face and his reply was,

"Not likely to happen lad," he said and laughed his loud raucous laugh. Only he could laugh at his own jokes. "He's your cousin German too, hope it doesn't run in the family" he said and walked off still laughing at his own joke. I wasn't sure what the joke was, but I hoped it wasn't what he was insinuating. I decided to sit between Ma and Uncle Alex at the table from then on and avoided bathing with my cousin again. We had also been sharing a bedroom together, but I was hoping to move into another empty room. Then one day he asked me,

"Don't you like me, Malcolm?" he asked. It was hard to answer because he was a nice enough person who hadn't done me any harm, so I lied.

"Of course, I do. You're my first cousin," I said. Sometimes a lie was necessary, but I was foreign to lying.

The family gathered at a fine Manor House that my Grandda had built by himself and had given to his son Patrick to run as a business, renting rooms to tourists from England, playing golf and hunting hart. It was the off season, so we could all eat dinner there and Patrick's wife's name was Henrietta, who wasn't nice at all, but I understood why she wouldn't be nice amidst the Grants and the Chisholms, as well as the MacGregors. I admired her being able to stomach them all that time. Their son James was a decent young man, my cousin, who looked at me like he should take me shopping one day. His wife was Susan, who got along well with Henrietta it seemed, but not so well with both Patrick or her husband James. All being Catholic, they were stuck with each other. I thought their problem had to be bad sex.

There was no alcohol on offer, so this was going to be a dry night, no music, no dancing, let alone available lassies and I was wanting one of those for sure. If we were in Loch Insh, we would all be playing musical instruments

James Grant

and singing and I would have scored a few times already there. Sitting down near the only relative that I trusted, Uncle Alex, I was wondering where Kenneth and Aonghus were, but after some bullshit talk by Grigor about how rich they all were, my Mither's inheritance came up, which took my attention. A measly five thousand Pounds Scots when the crystal chandelier above my head would have cost that much, was all my Ma was getting. Without so much as an explanation as to how that sum of money had been arrived at and where it had come from and who had made all of those decisions, I had to know. 'The Letter'. The words came to me from my Grandda from Loch Insh.

7. Voices

I smelled a giant rat in the form of a berserker and his offsider, Grigor and asked for Ma's letter. It was like extracting teeth from that old bloke, but I got it and I had the strongest sense of the presence of both my Grandda MacNachten and my Grandma, Isobel of Glenmoriston. Their message to me was they would sort it out, but I had to be polite, patient and persistent. So, I was all three, listening as I had been taught by Grandda MacNachten and Grandma. Alex stood by my side in confusion but co-operated with me. Armed with Ma's letter, Alex and I went home and that room breathed a sigh of relief at our departure. I knew to just sit in Alex's kitchen with a beverage and wait patiently, as instructed by the voices. I knew to expect Grigor and Helen within hours and while small talk over the farm took place, I was holding the seat of my chair, trying my best to be as calm as Grandda would have been.

A dog barked, the geese honked as the front gate squeaked to its closure. They're here!

Joe and Alex stood on the porch, with Joe holding a concealed weapon behind his back and Alex asked Joe to stable the horses out of the cold night air, upon seeing who it was. It had started to snow with a light flurry of snowflakes on the ground. He was surprised to be visited so late at night by anyone, let alone by both his sister Helen and her husband

Grigor, carrying two saddle bags that looked very heavy. He looked worried in case there was another family death or illness. When he came inside his face was grave, but pleased that his wife and sister were asleep, as well as his precious son, whom he adored. I liked Alex. I would call him a man of honour. He invited them in and Helen looked straight at me, as I had anticipated and then so did her guilty husband. They put the saddle bags on the table and went through the whole story from how long Helen had had the letter passed to her from Aonghus when he had bought the old law business and had found it in the Loch Insh files, so he had passed it on to his Mither, Helen.

It was their farm address, but at first, she didn't know who Marion was and put it aside without asking Grandma, but even when she met Marion, she had forgotten about it in the confusion of her Da's death and the funeral followed by her Ma's marriage, the opening of her art gallery and then her Ma's eventual death. When she finally remembered the letter, as she was doing the bookwork, she was punished for some reason and the culprit for stealing Ma's actual inheritance was all Hugh Mohr's idea, according to them. Helen said that at the meeting, she also had the strange sensation that her Ma was there listening and judging and felt a dishonesty afoot with both her husband Grigor and Hugh Mohr. At their home, after the meeting she had insisted that Grigor tell her the truth concerning her sister Marion's, inheritance.

8. *Ma Gets Her Inheritance*

"It is, after all, quite a tragic tale of a family trying not only to save their wee bairn from a predatory neighbour, but with all the good intentions of equalising the offspring's inheritance," said Alex, who was so horrified at what was done by the family. "Then for all of that good to be undone by theft," he lamented. Alex was so apologetic to me and mine, which wasn't because of him, but it felt good to get an apology. He was as broken hearted as I was, only I refused to let them see it and was glad to see them leave out into the cold snowy night.

I hadn't forgiven them and I'm not sure yet if I can. One day maybe, but in the meantime Joe helped me melt down the gold with my astounded Mither and Alex with his clingy wife Matilda watching on. She no longer saw me as dirt under her shoe, I joked to Joe, maybe gold dust instead, as she more readily smiled to me and made my breakfast or brought us both smoko when we were both fence building.

"Women are fickle things," I commented to Joe.

"Just keep in good with the boss's Misses, but keep your distance is my rule, or next thing you'll lose your job," he replied.

"You don't trust her either?" I asked.

"She's more English than Highlander lad, that's what you can't trust," he replied. "She was born to a crofter family, but it ends there. Once she was sent off to the Menzies crowd, then on to England, there wasn't much hope for her. Poor lass lost her identity," he said with the wisdom of a sage in an old book. "She's a MacMartin, who are a really old clan branch, as they were one of the Camerons. It's a real shame so many of them died at Culloden or she'd have blood relations and she'd know how to act around us. The good news is their wee ones will carry that old clan with them, they were the most loyal to the Gentle Lochiel. Almost suicidal, some have said. Loyalty is what you should see in her, eventually, to her husband and to her wee ones and they'll be nice bairns, I'm sure of it with a Father like Alex and a Mither like her," said Joe.

"So, would my Grandda have known her Father?" I asked.

"Aye, she was born on Craskie and her Father was a Jacobite, so your Grandda would have fought alongside her Father. He escaped with Grigor's father and hid in a cave. Did you know that?" he asked.

I was going to get all the history lessons I needed from Joe when suddenly he exclaimed, "Lad, what you need is a lassie. My mate Murdoch, who is now working over at Craskie and I are going out Friday night to an alehouse that has a nice new cook with their wee restaurant. Come with us to eat and drink a few ales," he said.

"Last time I drank ale, it made me spew. Maybe a dram is all I can manage in the restaurant, and I can take a look at what you think is a nice-looking wee lassie. She could be a weathered and wrinkly old seadog like you two, with a fat ass, flat tits and a crooked nose," I replied, "but I'll come just to get away from Alexander and Matilda," I said.

"Last time we went there, we met two blokes named Hamish and his brother Hugh from Craskie Farm. Nice fellas. They know more about the lochs and rivers and burns of all sizes between here and the coast and what fish can be caught at what time of the year and when. They used to sell fish for a living. That's how they met your Granny. She called them 'the fisher lads' and gave them their first jobs and chances in life because their Father drowned in Loch Craskie. Their Father taught them how to swim too and I admit I can't swim. They talk no end about your Granny. It's one way to catch up on your family knowledge. You never know when knowledge is needed to help you in a bind, especially if you're dealing with that trickster, Hugh Chisholm. Your Granny loved him, so there's the mystery of love isn't it? Married to a superhero and she loved Hugh Chisholm. I've pondered on that one. Do you know why?" Joe asked.

"They miscarried a wee bairn, Fleur, in 1746 and she is buried with Granny," I answered.

"Wo, wo, wo, and her husband never knew?" he said looking shocked.

"He never knew with all of his contacts and she miraculously kept it from him. A brute like that would have killed them all, I suppose," I answered.

"Her life must have felt like she was walking on eggshells, but how crazy to be with child in the first place with one of his own traitorous colleagues. I hope he never knew when he was dying. Poor fella," Joe said.

"I think I will go with you and Murdoch on Friday. Will he mind?" I asked, as I was about to get back to work. All the talk about badly behaved relatives was doing me in.

"Nae, he's like me. Real sociable. I call him Bear. Can we borrow your old highland ponies? It's a distance from here and I can't promise to be sober at the end of the night," he asked grinning.

"Of course, we can use them, but not on slippery or treacherous ground. They're both getting old, but they have been recently shod," I answered.

"Malcolm, if you want to impress a lassie, get a new shirt and pants. A pair of new boots too won't hurt and one of those waistcoats that the lassies like, as well as a coat. It's getting cold," he advised and I thought of cousin James. He'd know what to wear and where to go to buy it.

9. Shopping with James

James was surprised to see me at the front door of their Manor House but was quick to invite me in hospitably. His Father, Uncle Patrick, saw me too and shook my hand.

"Nice to see you, Malcolm. Come here as often as you like, you're welcome," he said. When I explained what it was that I needed from James, they were both overly anxious to assist and offered up their carriage to take us all to a shop they frequented in Invermoriston, but if it didn't have all I needed, they'd gladly take me to Inverness as well. They were excited at their appointed role in my life. At the end of that day, I looked like the proverbial peacock and I was a bit embarrassed, so they included casual wear and my clan Kilt for the occasion, even a sporran. But my Friday night outfit was just casual, so even though I bought it all, including the leather knee-high boots as well as work boots, I got two types of caps and one beret for the cold evenings as well as a knee length coat. Stockings were suggested as well as underwear.

"No! Don't wear underwear, not even to bed," I said.

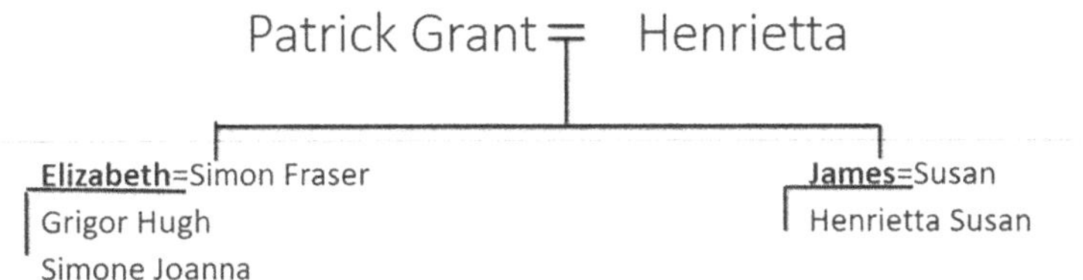

I told James I wanted myself a lassie, so he then took me to the barber also, who washed my hair and when he was about to cut off all of my black hair that I loved.

"No just a wee trim!" I said. The barber did all kinds of weird things like pluck my nose hairs and even my ear hairs and trimmed my facial hair, so it had a sculpted shape and then slapped on a stingy smelly perfumed substance that I hated. James was elated. He thought I looked really handsome, and he meant it.

"You should get your portrait done, but not by Aunty Helen," he said.

"I agree, she'd paint me with the devil's horns," and he laughed. He showed me where there was a public bathhouse if I needed it, but he always bathed in the burn because it was cleaner water.

"My advice before you try to attract this lassie you have in mind, is to bathe in the burn at your farm and then get dressed, so she can't say you stink of this or that. Women are funny like that," he advised. Then his accommodating Father, Uncle Patrick, unexpectedly bought me an Italian silk handkerchief, so if I had the sniffles, at least it would impress her. I think Uncle Patrick had been told about the gold.

Alex was excited to see me all dressed up and Joe burst into loud laughter.

"We're only meeting the wee cook, not Queen Mary of Scots," he said. Matilda surprisingly came to my defence.

"It's the effort, Joe. Be nice. He might be meeting his future wife. Then who'd be laughing...hmm?" Matilda said.

"I've a surprise for you lad," Uncle Alex said. He had bought me a beautiful grey mare with saddlery and proudly handed me the reins. I'm not a kisser unless it's for a lassie or my Ma, but on this occasion, I made an exception and kissed Alex for my lovely horse and he liked that. So, poor Joe was on the small pony and I was on my new horse, suitably dressed and not carrying too much money lest it attract thieves. We met up with Bear on his horse and went on to my destination. My new wife. I could feel it, but I didn't want to get too excited to believe it.

I saw the lights ahead coming from the alehouse restaurant and I had butterflies in my stomach, the nearer we got. As we entered the musical noisy alehouse, there were a few people there that my friends knew, so they pointed me in the direction of the kitchen attached to the restaurant where she worked. From behind, I saw a very small lassie about my age, who was a bit thin. She had her hair tied back because of her job, but it was long and jet black like mine. Her waist was tiny, but her bottom was round. The type you want to pinch or fondle or smack even. I was turned on without even seeing her face. Then I panicked, what if she turns around and she's ugly? She turned and looked straight at me. She was stunning with a perfect nose, tanned skin and her eyes were huge and green, like Matilda's.

"Can I help you?" she asked in a sweet voice.

"Yes, I'm hungry Ma'am. Can you please cook me a nice meal and make me a jug of coffee?" I asked.

"I can. Please come over to a comfortable place by the fire Sir," she said as she took me to the table. I wanted to pinch her bottom but felt too nervous. Arriving at the nice table by the fireside,

"My name is Malcolm, not Sir, what's your name?" I asked.

"Cherry. My name is Cherry, but I wish my parents had given me another name. I am always teased because of it," she said.

"I like it," I said. "Are you married Cherry?" I asked.

"Nae, I'm from the Islands, so I don't know anyone, except my Uncle Murdoch and Uncle Joe," she said.

"Murdoch MacLean?" I asked. "Aye, do you know him?" she asked seemingly surprised.

"Aye, we came here tonight together with Joe," I answered, catching on slowly.

Murdoch MacLean

"Uncle Joe. We are all family, and we were cleared off the Isles together. I'll go cook your dinner Malcolm," she said smiling. "Before you go," I said, "Can you eat dinner with me then come home with me and meet my family tonight?" I asked. I had to have her. I wanted to hand fast that night, if she agreed and we could live together as husband and wife. I'd like to have bairns with her. She was so lovely. I had never felt this way before and her penetrating green eyes seemed to look deeply into my very soul.

"I am very flattered indeed Malcolm. Can you please ask my uncles to come here to discuss this, as my parents are long in the ground?" Her face was shy, and her cheeks went pinkish red. I think she liked me, but how would I know? I went to get the uncles, hoping they weren't too drunk.

The slightly drunk Uncles wandered in with me to talk to Cherry and she asked them permission to marry me, hand fast first of course she explained, so I could take her home to meet my Uncle. Both had that very cheeky island sense of humour that I was learning to understand, looked at each other and laughed, which ordinarily I would be offended by, but culturally that meant 'damn good' or something like that. They patted each other on the shoulder to congratulate themselves, then came to me and congratulated me, then to her for getting herself a fine lad.

"So, is the answer yes then?" I asked.

"Aye," they seemed to answer in unison and asked if we wanted to hand fast now, so we could leave. Then Cherry was very embarrassed and shy, but in case she was going to back out of this fine opportunity, one of them said, "Do it now, after all what else will come to you, Cherry, in this environment with losing our farms. Do you like him?" he asked.

"Aye," Cherry said, eyes cast down.

One of the people sitting at a table nearby took out a ribbon to provide and we were hand fast just like that. It would be a story to tell the Grandchildren for sure, as people clapped and cheered.

10. Went Home Married

We went home on my new horse, a married couple to be introduced to my Ma, Uncle Alex and Matilda and whoever else was awake. Of course, they were all awake anxiously waiting up for me. Uncle Alex met us at the gate, and I introduced my new wife Cherry to him. "Cherry MacLean," she said smiling, "But now I suppose I'm whatever my husband is," she said.

"MacNachten," I responded proudly.

"So, I'm Cherry MacNachten, Uncle Alex, and I'm sorry I'm not dressed for this occasion. I was busy working you see. You should know too that Joe MacFie is my Uncle," she said.

"Welcome to the family, Cherry," Alex said smiling from ear to ear. My sweet wife was immediately welcomed by my Ma, who could not believe that I had found a wife in a matter of hours and Matilda also, after welcoming her, went busily up to that empty room to make it into a double room for us both and that's where we lived happily for a long time. Joe came home late that night very drunk but managed to stable the poor old pony.

I decided to buy our own place with Uncle Alex and Ma's help, as well as the Chief of the Camerons and Killian MacDonnell's assistance, whose influence was needed with the MacDonnells, as we were originally outsiders. They had lost clan land to the English, so were understandedbly cautious. Being related to Padruig Dubh always held sway. Our small farm was nearby Uncle Alex and we shared a border. Given the competition with the English buying up properties, I had to pay more than the land was worth, but it was worth it. Our first bairn was born in the first twelve months of marriage, so we made our union official at the Chapel on Craskie Farm and the reception was held at the Manor House, free of charge with a smiling James and Patrick, to whom I would always be grateful for giving me the courage to do what I did with my wee wife Cherry. The bairn was baptised on the same day as our wedding and we named her Islay, after some island that was important to my wife.

My son was born soon after we moved onto our new farm, so I named him Alexander Nachtain, after my Uncle Alex and my Father. I had to deliver him myself, as there was no time to get Cherry to the Doctor and I didn't like him anyway. If we had another son, he was going to be Gillcrest James after my Grandda, Gillcrest MacNachten and my cousin James Grant.

I had wanted many bairns, but I left that up to my wife, who was a wonderful Mither, great cook and a loyal wife with that same sense of humour as her unusual Uncles. I loved her so much, I didn't think it possible. Cherry's Uncles frequently came around to visit their 'little family,' which was what they called us. They bought ale with them, of course, which neither Cherry nor I could drink. I was glad that she didn't drink like her Uncles, so I asked them to bring highland coo milk next time. It's really delicious milk. I had bought a few Highland coos for our wee farm. Those men were both happy in their respective jobs and Joe sent all of his wages to his wife in Edinburgh, so his children could be well fed, clothed and well educated. He often complained that they were losing their Gaelic, as were Murdoch's family. We always spoke Gaelic at home and at work for that reason and Cherry wanted the bairns to know our language, as well as English, and not lose it like her Uncles' bairns were.

Their accents with some words were different and there were obscenities that I had never heard before, mostly related to the sea, but I learned how to use their bad language too. I wondered how many more of these competent people needed work in our area and for some reason I remembered the wee Chapel that Grandma built for everyone. The topic went back to fishing and the Uncles had teamed up with Hamish and Hugh Og to go fishing and I was invited, so that was great to have fish in our diets as well, and they were great fellas and full of knowledge. My young brother, Kenneth, rarely came to visit me, as he was more attuned to life in Inverness and was a bit envious of my new life and new wife. I doubted that he would ever do Aunty Helen's books, unless she went there to him, so she was relying on James, who she paid for his work to help her. I missed Kenneth just the same.

James and I would go shopping for ourselves and ate out in Invermoriston and caught up with each other, which was always an enjoyable day out. My wife asked me to bring home six breeding chickens and some geese too. James would complain about his wife Susan, who would sleep often at the Craskie main house when she was sick of him, so I felt sorry for him, but I did tell him a trick that pleased the ladies that might help. Cherry loved what I did in bed for sure. I was glad that I wasn't actually Catholic like them. We had never been given a religion, just taught the Auld ways by my Grandda. He told me where there was a Pict stone on Craskie to be kept secret, but Hugh Mohr was guarding it for now, but one day if we ever get to talking again, I hope to go there and pray. Apparently, we had Pict ancestry on both my parents' sides and Grandma could talk to the ancestors there. My Da, when he was alive, could speak to the swans too, like my Great Grandmother and Aonghus had a connection also that hadn't yet matured.

One day I planned to visit him if Kenneth ever moved out of his house, considering he was already a qualified accountant. Maybe he would buy an accountancy business in Inverness and do the books for that dreaded Mill, I thought.

11. Uncle Alex's Advice

Uncle Alex was the only one with real farming knowledge and he came over specifically to give me advice on getting my farm more established like his was.

"You never know when the next famine will come lad, so Cherry was right to get you to buy some chickens and I see you've built a fine enclosure for them, but you will need a rooster too, so they keep multiplying if you know what I mean. Well done getting the two coos and I'll give you a few of mine although you will need a big bull to increase your herd," he added.

After a few more suggestions like planting potatoes and building a potato storage shed, he left a list and a design where on the property it should all go. It included goats with their own shed for both milk and meat and Cherry loved the idea of goats because she used to have her own herd on the island. That was great because I didn't know anything about goats.

"Don't waste their hair too Cherry, for your pillows and your mattresses," he said to my wife.

We walked the full length of my farm, which he had mapped to my surprise at how much thought he had put into it and told me where to plant the oats and that there was enough land for a winter crop and a summer crop.

"Hugh Og might bring the Clydesdales over to plough it for you if you ask him nicely," he said.

He asked me if we had met yet and after I told him about the fishing trips, he then suggested we all pitch in to buy a boat together and then Hugh Og might do my ploughing every year. I started looking for boats in the newspaper, so that when we all went out fishing next, I had the information and a good price on the boat. I hoped they'd all be interested in sharing in the cost of it, but was a bit nervous because a lot was riding on getting those Clydesdales over to my place free of charge. I couldn't see myself hand ploughing at all, but he told me to remove all of the rocks, which I needed to do anyhow, for the fence that I had planned. It was coming together nicely, especially when both Hugh Og and Hamish and the Uncles were ecstatic at the idea of a boat. We had a boat within two weeks of negotiations and the shared cost was all written down by Uncle Alex and signed by all parties. Life was looking good in Glengarry now that I had my new wife, new bairns, my new grey mare, my beautiful farm with great neighbours, good friends and a boat. I called my farm 'Cherry Farm' and planted a dozen cherry trees too.

I asked Alex about the idea of a temporary stay house for folks from the Isles who were cleared off Islay and looking for work on a strictly 'no booze rule'. There was enough room in the furthest corner of my border with Alex for a stone cottage, which could accommodate up to four men, a kitchenette and an open fire on which to cook. The rear could have a wee veranda to do the washing. He said to ask Joe because of their pride and they may not accept charity if that's how they perceived it. So, I left it with God for a time.

12. *What's Grigor Up To?*

One cold wet day, I saw from my yard that Grigor was visiting Alex. This I had to know about and rode down there to ask how it was all going at Craskie Farm. He was obviously nervous and so my Uncle explained that Grigor was wanting my Ma to meet up with one of his old friends, Bruce MacDonald, newly arrived back from the Americas. Neither one of us would budge at first and declined any such meeting between my Ma and his friend Bruce. It was Matilda who suggested we allow them to meet in a supervised setting, like the alehouse where I had met Cherry, so we both finally agreed to that with Ma coming too. Eventually after putting Grigor's friend Bruce through the hoops with a million questions to answer, Matilda and Joe thought we were a bit too harsh, so long as her money was kept from Bruce. So, both Alex and I set up a Trust Fund in both our names for my Ma. It required both of us to sign any withdrawal. Ma was such a shy lady having only loved my Father and she was in no hurry to commit anyhow.

After my initial reaction, where I wanted to kill the man who would dare look at my Mither, I calmed down a bit. He was a patient and lonely man with good intentions. He had been through the War of Independence in the Americas, so there was a lot of history and it appeared that he had no intention to harm. Ma took her time and did marry Bruce MacDonald, but I wasn't going to call him Da or even Uncle. It was Bruce or nothing and he wasn't getting his hands on Ma's money.

She looked so pretty at her wedding and much younger than her age, that I felt protective all over again and was sure this man, Bruce wasn't up to the job of taking care of her, so I needed to talk to him again after they said their vows.

"Listen here Bruce, don't go thinking she's all yours because she isn't. She's mine too and you had better taken care of her or you'll wish you'd never left America. I'll not have you strap, whip, bash or strike my Mither in any way," I said emphatically.

"Who does that around here?" he asked looking shocked. "I'll protect your Mither with my life Malcolm, I swear on it. Can we live with you until I get my own place, so we would all share your lovely Mither?" he asked timidly.

"I'll work for my keep," he said. I was taken aback, but I needed staff and I'd love my Ma to live with me and so it was agreed if Ma agreed, which she did.

13. *Bruce and Ma Stay*

Surprisingly, we all got along better than expected and Bruce worked hard on my farm and even started the hand ploughing to get the summer oats into the ground. I told Hugh Og on one of our fishing trips that I had Bruce hand ploughing and the very next day, he bought his Clydesdale team around with Grigor's blessings to plough both fields for us. I could see the sigh of relief on Bruce's face at seeing the ground so well ploughed, but he then examined the soil and looked a bit disappointed. He then asked Hugh if their team was picking up any kelp from the coast any time soon, which they were at this time of the year and he offered to get us a load, but we would have to pay for that, he told Bruce. I agreed to the cost of the kelp and any spare manure if they had any, which they did and a very

Bruce MacDonald

smelly load of manure and kelp arrived a few days later for us all to spread over the large field and Cherry joined in to assist, adding her goat manure to it as she went.

There was no bill from Craskie Farm. It had taken me that long to realise that Grigor was trying to make up for his part in what had taken place over Mither's inheritance. I asked Uncle Alex for advice as to whether Grigor should now be forgiven and he was reluctant and hadn't yet replied, when Matilda said,

"Yes. He is family after all and at least you have family to ponder over that question. My advice is to forgive him as forgiveness is very powerful, way more so than unending acrimony," she said.

Then she took herself to bed before I could disagree. We both smiled at what a character he had married and I thanked him for his time. I passed Joe on my way out.

"Hello stranger. Been missing you, I have," he said.

"Well, that's good because I need to ask you something. Can you come over for lunch tomorrow with Murdoch if he's around?" I asked. He patted me on my shoulder saying,

"Aye, goodnight family," Joe said.

Arriving back home, Cherry opened the gate for me, God bless her and closed it. She was rounding up her small herd of goats and looked very cheerful.

"How's my darling man? So, any mystery down there?" she asked. Dismounting I took her in my arms, grateful once again for this gift from God, my wife.

"Matilda says to forgive Grigor, so we are both considering it. What do you think?" I asked.

"Och, I'm a forgiving person for sure even when its truly hard to do so, like on the Island when I was raped by two men who took my virginity. That's what hurt my heart the most that I couldn't give you that on our wedding night. Please forgive me Malcolm, but I wasn't strong enough to fight them off and Da was killed. My Uncles scooped up Ma and me with their families in their wee boat to go to Oban, but Ma killed herself there by hanging and so my Uncles felt responsible for me until you came along. So, can I forgive those men for the rape, my Da's murder and my Ma's suicide and still lead a normal life? Aye. I have to or I would go mad or do what Ma did, God forbid. So, it's up to you my husband, but if I were you, I would forgive him. There's more to gain in having him as an ally, now that we need his team of horses and there's other unanswered questions too, like why Helen kept you all out of the main house and kicked you off the farm instead of that other crofter family," she said.

"In Island culture, family is first. Now come on up my love, I've cooked you something special and Bruce and Marion are waiting for you so we can all eat," my wife said.

I was so shocked at her story of being raped and her Ma dying that way.

"Cherry darling, can you wait a minute. I am so sorry about what happened to you and with or without your virginity you have made me the happiest man alive. I thank God for you every day. I am so sorry about both your parents, but I have to say, your Uncles have risen to great heights in my eyes, as I too share that same philosophy. That's part of what I wanted to talk to you about," I said.

"You're a good man Malcolm MacNachten," she said, as she kissed me gently on the lips.

14. Helping the Islanders into Work

My beautiful Ma had set the table and both ladies had done an amazing job with the food. Cherry cooked us all fried chicken, boiled corn, potatoes and kale that I never liked, but ate anyway. The coffee was cooked up in a huge pot that Bruce had bought over from the Americas and it was enough for coffees all around. Ma had made my favourite bannocks with Cherry's goat's cheese. So, I began.

"My dear family, do you mind if I discuss an idea I have had for a while to get your opinions on it, especially you Cherry because you would know best if I was treading on anyone's toes?" I asked.

"I don't mind darling. What is it?" Cherry asked.

"We don't mind either Malcolm, go ahead," Bruce said.

I outlined my plan to build a rock-solid home on my border with Alex that would have twin purposes to start with. I decided that the home, now larger than I had originally planned, would be Bruce and Ma's home, if he helped to build it while I was busy. It would have windows, as I think there was no window tax anymore. If it suited them however, they would not live in it immediately as there are many Islanders needing short stay accommodation while they looked for work. It would house up to four men at any one time, no more, with a strict 'no booze' rule or they'd have to leave. After a maximum stay of five days, borrowing the ponies while looking for work, they'd clean up and leave to go, wherever the work took them.

Eventually, there won't be as many in need, so the home would then revert to Bruce and Ma if you want it Ma and if not, it could be for other farm workers or students because you are always welcome in this house with Cherry and me. What do you all think?" I asked.

"Is it just for Islanders Malcolm?" Bruce asked.

"Aye, they're good workers and multi skilled," I replied.

"Malcolm darling, you don't have to give Bruce and me part of your land. It's a nice idea though, so long as the land still belongs to you, but what do you think Bruce?" Ma asked.

"I'd like living here on Malcolm's farm Marion if you did too, in our own home, but not owning any part of Malcolm's land. And I can do all the work and keep an eye on the residents too if you like. I think the family is happier together," Bruce replied.

"Cherry, you are quiet. Do you think it's an insult to your fellow Islanders? We could advertise the available workers in the paper and put a sign on the gate," I said.

"I think Uncles Joe and Murdoch should give that answer Malcolm, but it sounds like it could work like as you say, so long as there's no booze and they stay away from us ladies here at the house, but it's important the workers are not exploited too and they go to good accommodation," she said.

"Can I ask both of your Uncles tomorrow then Cherry? If you or they don't like it, it can just be for Bruce and Ma or staff or another idea entirely," I added.

"Yes, Malcolm, whatever you and my Uncles agree on. I love you Malcolm and I have news too. I'm with child again," she said smiling and hugged me ever so tightly.

The next day's lunch and meeting with Cherry's Uncles went well and they decided they would have to run it for it to work, so they could not only recommend which worker for which job but be able to check out the job and the farmer and have any contract of wages and accommodation in writing to avoid exploitation as Cherry had said. Murdoch had his say and I learned a lot about Craskie farm in comparison to Loch Garry Ranch.

"There are assholes out there for sure, who think of us like we're rubbish folk and turn up their noses at us, so the younger workers would find that hard to take. We would need to check out each job and their accommodation and food and approve the wage that they're offered. There's a lot of workers needed which is on our side, so it goes both ways, we can't exploit a poor farmer either. It's all about keeping everyone honest," he said.

"That Hugh Chisholm is still a problem at Craskie Farm, as well as how poorly Helen runs it. I'm tempted to move to a different job if I'm honest, but for Hugh Og, I would have left already," Murdoch said.

"Hugh Og said he's been putting up with shite since he was wee and it was only your Granny and her Da who he'd thought highly of. That Isobel-Mairi was causing trouble now, all the time with his Team and he was going to do something about that this coming week and I've promised to stand by him. She's trying to get the Team moved to Inverness, so as he owns the team's horses and gear, he's refusing to do that and now he wants to buy her out entirely, acquiring the blood lines to be rid of her and she can find someone else to deliver her tartan," he said.

Asking the Uncles how they'd run it, they slapped each other's shoulders knowingly.

"Firstly, none of them will come up here to the houses to worry either Cherry and Marion and we will draw up a list of house rules like no booze and so on. Then we would take it in turns dealing with each client, so we could still do our own jobs. Permission might be required to leave our jobs for a while and I might need to borrow your pony, Malcolm. Alex won't mind if I'm gone for a wee while, but Murdoch's lot are a strange bunch. He might have to sneak off here and there," Joe said.

"Can I suggest you give this letter to Grigor giving you permission to attend to Islander concerns for a time, as he is on speaking terms now with me?" I asked.

"Also, concerning the Team, Grigor has a say during ploughing seasons, so his decisions can override Isobel-Mairi and I can ask him to have her sell the blood lines to Hugh Og, so she can get her own delivery team. Their business isn't conducive with our farming needs in my opinion," I said. I also asked Bruce to back me up with Grigor, now that I had a family member who could get into his head. Bruce was as keen as mustard and thought very little of Isobel-Mairi and what she had done to the farm. He agreed, she needed to sell Hugh Og the blood lines to give him full control and I offered to help Hugh Og to buy them, so long as he didn't tell her it was coming from me.

Bruce and I started on the house plan and had it approved by Alex on his border and he suggested we put in a gate half-way down our border, so Joe had easier access to this new responsibility. He was proud of Joe helping his Islander mates in trouble, especially with winter around the corner. We had the cottage built with three fireplaces and room for four, as we planned. Ma was planting wee flowers and an herb garden there too and organising the outside laundry. Neighbours like Killian MacDonnell turned up with donations of beds, blankets, pillows, sheets, pots and pans and even a larger washing copper for the laundry. There were even two couch chairs donated and warm clothing, which we put in a wardrobe as well as work boots and hose.

Then the men came.

Both Joe and Murdoch met the first four men at the gate, who looked thin and cold but hugged their Islander compatriots. They were taken with their meagre possessions to the new Islander home that we decided to call Islay House. It was a sad sight to see men who had been at the peak of health and strength, to be reduced to such misery, but the little glimmer of hope it gave them made me weep quietly and in private.

My wife cooked up huge meals for them at first and sent it down to build up their strength and the first job offer was one of Killian's relations, a MacDonnell, who needed a groom accompanied by Joe on my pony to ensure he had good accommodation and the right wages and witnessed their agreement. It was a success so far and we prayed the younger man would do a good job. Joe came up to the house that day to re-assure me.

"Don't worry about them doing a good job, they have to answer to me if they don't," he said.

"Joe, come in you look tired," I said.

"Tired? I'm bloody exhausted, but thanks lad, I've got me own work to do now. Can't let Alex down," he said. Then, just as he said that Alex appeared on the porch after letting himself through the wee gate.

"Don't be silly Joe, all the work's done. We'd both like a coffee and cake," he said. Joe told us all about where the lad had gone to work and Murdoch was due here tomorrow to meet another farmer looking for help with the ploughing, then seeding the oats. It was hand ploughing, so a job for a strong man. We suggested he ask Grigor to charge for his team to plough, if that was an option. Either way, it had begun and the men were dressing in the warm clothes provided and we sent down a hart for them to eat. Cherry was happy with me. "I went to school with some of these people, but they would be ashamed if I saw them, so I'll stay out of sight," she said.

Over two years, we saw at least one hundred men pass through our cottage with only one who returned to start again in another job. As the numbers dwindled, Bruce was able to do more work on the house with the finishing touches of a comfortable home and he bought themselves a new double bed and a couch. It was obvious my Ma and Bruce had decided to stay in the lovely home, full of the laughter of the Islanders. Both Joe and Murdoch came over to eat dinner with us all to bring it to an end with Killian and his wife, Alex, Matilda, Bruce, Ma, Alexander Og and a friend of his Peter who was around a lot lately.

I think I was right to stop bathing with my cousin, Alexander when I did.

Joe stood and gave a speech, thanking us all with lots of emotive language when Murdoch stopped him.

"My turn," then he sang a song from the Islands and Cherry cried into my shoulder.

"Come on Cherry, you're the best songstress of the Isles. Give us a song. Anyone got any uillean pipes?" he asked.

"We do," said Matilda and ran down to their place to get them. Handing them over to Murdoch, he admired them.

15. *Cherry Can Sing and Dance to the Pipes*

Cherry MacNachten

"These are nice ones. Okay, let's go Cherry my darling," he started up a haunting melody that took you to the sea and my wife gained her composure finally and stood next to her Uncle Joe with her hand on his shoulder at first. The song was unlike anything that I had ever heard. You could almost feel you were in a rocking boat on a stormy ocean with a mermaid calling out from the rocks to lure a sailor to his death, when she took her hand from her Uncle then swirled around like a wind whipped up on the sea, as the song made you feel the dread of imminent danger to the sailors. She raised her arms to the heavens, singing in a lilting begging sound to God to save them all at sea, as the pipes raised up and fell with the drama before us. I felt so worried that my wife was heading for the rocks in that wild sea, it was so realistic, then she took it down a crescendo as the pipes cried out. Then stopped. So did Cherry. The Gaelic was hard to understand, but I think it meant the boat sank. We all clapped and I arose to hold my wife in my arms.

"Cherry, you are such a beautiful artiste."

Before the night was over, there was a knock on the door, which both Joe and I attended. It was Grigor accompanied by Hugh Og. They excused themselves being late at night and asked to speak to both myself, Bruce and Alex. I asked Ma to go to bed with my wife and we would clean up later. I told them both Murdoch and Joe would be present. I knew Joe held a weapon and still could not trust Grigor.

"I have come for three reasons," he said.

"One reason is to apologise for my past transgressions and to ask forgiveness. Another reason is congratulations on the success of the care and employment of the Islanders, which we wish to celebrate up at the Manor to go into the papers. The third, concerns the team, which I promised Hugh Og I'd deal with and in my capacity, I would like to start the legal process to buy out Isobel-Mairi of the blood lines to be owned in full by Hugh Og Chisholm. The money for this part of this discussion I was hoping Malcolm could assist to pay. Can we please address each topic?" he asked and they both sat down. Cherry hadn't left earshot and came back in to ask one more thing of Grigor.

"Grigor, you are my family too now, so I forgive you, but there are some answers to some questions I need to know. May I?" she asked. She sat back down looking him in the eye.

"Why could ye not accept your sister-in-law, Marion, into your family? Why was she shunned out of sight with her two sons, my husband and Kenneth? Why were they disallowed accommodation in the family home? Why did your wife Helen ignore her and make her unwelcome and when it came to a choice between the crofters and family, you chose to allow the crofters to stay and kicked out your family, even though Padruig Dubh himself and Grandma promised them a life on Craskie Farm?" she asked.

The Uncles didn't look surprised at all of what she had said and took on a serious demeanour, not to mention protective, if Grigor spoke out of turn to Cherry. She meant so much to them and she had obviously always been an island favourite.

16. The Truth Revealed about Helen

Grigor's eyes cast down and he didn't seem to know where to start, but when he did, I regretted knowing it all, but not Cherry. Knowledge was all important to her with all of the gruesome details. He began,

"When Helen was told that she had a sister, she changed her usual 'kind Helen' act to an enraged jealous sibling," he explained. "'No, no, no!' she had screamed, 'I'm the only daughter of Padruig Dubh Grant. No one can take my place as the favourite child!' still screaming at me," Grigor lamented.

Once again, I observed that Alex looked like he was going to weep and I held his shoulder.

"It was her decision that few people would know about you all, after all it was going to raise all the reasons why Marion was hidden and Helen said it would humiliate us all that Uncle Allen had raped Ma," Grigor said of his wife Helen.

"The crofters then gave her the perfect exit from the situation where she would never see Marion again, she hoped. Hers was not theft, but she was concerned about our inheritance being challenged in Court, so she saw her son and rewrote her Will and updated the land deeds in our names, without Aonghus knowing of Marion's relationship to Alex, only Hugh Mohr knew all of those details. Ma separately had her Will redone two weeks before her death to protect us all from a challenge from Hugh Mohr, but none of us have seen that Will and whether it included Marion. We would have to ask Aonghus to see it and remind him of Marion's relationship to Alex. I know none of this is pleasant to hear, but there it is," Grigor said.

"Am I still forgiven or do you want us both to leave?" he asked.

"I don't wish to leave yet please Malcolm. Can you please help me acquire the Team?" stated Hugh Og. "I had nothing to do with what happened to your Ma, Malcolm, but I did recognise you as one of the workers on the Chapel, who stayed at

Chisholm House. I said nothing, as you had your reasons for remaining anonymous and I thought there was a lot of a younger Padruig Dubh in you, but the difference being that you were decent as well as tough. You looked a lot like him, even your long legs and straight posture and long black hair. You are obviously his Grandson, so I felt they were all a bit stupid to try and conceal a virtual replica of Padruig Dubh, just better looking," he stated. "I wondered what Helen was up to, but I can't influence the running of the farm, even though she is failing miserably. However, I am desperate to save the Clydesdale Team, that's why I'm here and I'll pay you back over a few years," Hugh Og stated.

"I am happy to help you Hugh with the Team. How much are we talking?" I asked.

"I'm not sure, maybe two thousand pounds thereabouts?" he said.

Matilda had been listening and said she had studied equine bloodlines at university and thought it may be more than that and made us an offer.

"My Mummy and Daddy will give us the money, don't worry Hugh. All they'll want is a wee ride on the Team when they come to visit, not repayment," she said boldly.

"Alright, thanks Matilda," I said accepting her offer.

"I'll go see Aonghus with you, Matilda and that money with Hugh and Grigor to deal with the legalities of the Team to buy out Isobel-Mairi. While we are there, I wish to ask Aonghus to see that other Will of Grandma's to see if Ma was in it and get a copy of it for Ma. If Ma was in it, that will obviously have to be dealt with too. Then Aonghus can write the letters needed. A letter to the newspaper requesting privacy for the Islanders and their employers is also needed," I stated.

I was starting to feel like the boss of a big company, not a wee family.

I continued, "As for the article in the paper and a shindig up at the Manor, I'm not in support. Are you Murdoch, Joe?" I asked.

"Nae, who do they think we are? That reeks of Craskie trying to take credit for all the work we have all done. Pass that on. These are human beings with families, so I'll not have them treated like second class citizens," said Murdoch. I asked if there were any other outstanding questions and by the look on Alex's face, he couldn't take any more, so I suggested Matilda take him home to bed, which she did. She asked if Murdoch wanted to keep the pipes a while, until we saw each other again and he cheered right up and asked if he could play his old songs for a week at least. Grigor offered Murdoch a ride back to Craskie on the Team and he left carrying the pipes. There was so much of that night that was so wonderful but ruined by the family problems.

"I am sorry Cherry that my family are a disappointment," I said to her, but she seemed satisfied that Helen was revealed as a major culprit in not bringing home Marion's family. Bruce was so disappointed in his friend and even asked me if I was still happy with him. Of course, I didn't associate Bruce with what happened, I just asked if he could support us going forward because his loyalty to us was everything. Joe had followed Alex home in case he became ill. My Ma was asleep, so both Bruce and Ma slept in my house again and the next day would be their big move to their new house that they both really loved.

17. *What the Will Really Said*

The lawyer's visit was eventful and worthwhile. We achieved all that we planned, including the letter to the newspaper requesting privacy for both the employees and the farmers. We left Grandma's Will until last. First, we dealt with buying the Team bloodlines, which he said was a good idea and handed over the money to him to pass on if they accepted the offer. Little did we know that Ewen had already suggested this plan of action to his wife. We just had to wait to hear back from Isobel-Mairi. Grigor made it clear that he didn't want Ewen back as a farrier on Craskie Farm, as they already had a new one and had bought a new forge. Ewen had taken the forge that Padruig Dubh had given him. Hugh Og was looking elated at the action already being taken to protect his precious horses. Then when the Will was read over, I noticed there was a clause that had been added. Much to our shock, Ma had been left 'New Farm' including any new homes built on it, who would have to pay rent to Marion MacNachten, except Hugh Og's, which was given to him by Grandma and he owned that parcel of land on which it stood.

I asked Aonghus why he hadn't had a Will reading after the death and he said Hugh Mohr asked him to read it alone privately as she was his wife. He read that he only inherited the land on which Chisholm House stood and said for me to not to read it aloud, so he filed it away without noticing there was a change in it concerning 'New Farm'. Hugh Mohr was none too pleased at how little he had received.

"Did he know Ma had paid for his painting of him and the Collie dogs?" Grigor asked.

"Nae, even I didn't know that," Aonghus replied.

"Poor Ma tried to be so fair and it was all mucked up," Grigor said.

Aonghus apologised profusely for the oversight in the Will and then offered all of his services free of charge because of his mistake. His opinion on the Team was important because it was clear that Isobel-Mairi was causing disruption to the farm and needed to get her own Team or her own delivery company without further disruption to Craskie. Her businesses were doing well he said, due to the popularity of tartan now and the Clans now all wanting their own particular tartan, which was held in a register of some kind.

"They have the new MacGregor tartan Da," he said.

I almost forgot that Grigor was his Father.

"Maybe we'll take a look at the shop while we're here. Is there a family discount son?" he asked.

"Aye, I got a sporran for free just last week," Aonghus said and he showed it to us proudly. "So, lad can you arrange for New Farm to be transferred into Marion's name, Marion MacNachten?" Grigor Og asked.

"Isn't it Marion MacDonald now Da?" Aonghus said. "When she inherited this land, she was MacNachten, so that's what it should read if Malcolm agrees," he said and I agreed. I didn't want Bruce getting his hands on it.

"Malcolm should take a copy for Marion to read, or maybe she won't believe it," he added.

"May I suggest you read it to your Ma in private, Malcolm, and then please keep it in a safe at home with your important documents?" he asked, thinking what I was thinking. Better that Bruce still thought of his wife as not being wealthy.

"Cora will have to move back into the teacher's house now that there are no new teachers coming, as was originally thought. The school is down to five pupils and Cora works for Helen. Hamish will still be paid by Craskie, Hugh so don't worry about your brother. His job is secure," Grigor said.

"Ewen and Isobel-Mairi will have to use their old place when they visit home, not the new one. Can you write to both those tenants to let them know to move back to their original homes?" Grigor added.

Aonghus had a few more letters to write, but the important one was to my Mither informing her that she was now the owner of 'New Farm' and if grazing was needed by Craskie on that property, then a payment would be required from Helen to Marion and that could be monetary or even a slaughtered beast or beasts each week. That would be up to them to negotiate.

"One last letter," I said, "Can you also write to Patrick please and thank him for the offer of a meal with our friends, but they prefer to live private lives. Maybe another time privately with no newspaper involvement," I said.

That left two empty homes on New Farm that sat on my Ma's land and my mind wandered to Murdoch and Joe's families and wondered if that would offend them or be a blessing.

18. The Tartan Shop

Afterwards, we did go into the tartan shop and Grigor got himself a new MacGregor tartan kilt, waistcoats and belts and charged it to his daughter and asked us all what shirts we wanted.

"Hugh, do you want a shirt?" I asked. We got both Hugh and I, new shirts, free of charge and that felt good.

"What about shirts for Murdoch and Joe?" I suggested and Grigor just added two more shirts to the pile that looked the right size and we walked out very happy with our parcels. Matilda had also put a nice arisaid in the Grant tartan on the pile too as well as a Grant kilt for Alex.

As we were leaving, Matilda mentioned to me that her Daddy, who was Clan Menzies wanted to talk to me when they came to visit next.

We'd ridden into Inverness on our horses so it was dark and late when I finally opened our squeaky gate. Immediately, I saw Cherry on the front veranda with a torch and she ran towards me, hugged and kissed me and offered to take my horse to the stable and I said I'd do that myself, but she came with me. We strolled hand-in-hand back to the house and it looked awfully dark.

"Have Bruce and Ma already moved?" I asked.

"Aye, they moved today," she answered.

"I have news for her, but I'll tell her tomorrow," I said. Cherry and I had a wonderful night together. She had cooked up all my favourite dishes, as well as a desert cake with coo's cream on it. It was all so delicious despite the lateness of the hour.

19. *Bath time Husband*

The bairns were all asleep. They had waited up for me but became too tired, she said, so she put them to bed. It had been so long since we'd had private time together and Cherry had boiled up a huge pot of bath water for me and dragged out the copper bathtub.

"Bath time husband," she said with the sweetest smile only Cherry could muster and I didn't think I could last that long and she undressed me rather sensually, I thought. I was glad that Ma would no longer walk into the room as I stepped into the lovely hot water, as my wife poured hot water over my head and scrubbed a soapy substance into my hair vigorously, rougher than the barber, I thought, but when she washed out the soap from my hair, her wee hands slipped suddenly down to my nether regions and I pulled her into the bath, clothes and all laughing hysterically. But my General, as Cherry called him, was stood upright and not wanting to wait any longer. She had him in her grasp. It was a slippery wet departure from the bath in her wet clothes as I pulled them off and threw her on our bed, while she continued to giggle happily, until she was at her optimum pleasure when she would make so much noise, I thought. Even Killian MacDonnell could hear us at it.

We continued for what remained of the night with brief intermissions, like we had been starved of one another, or something like that and we were now gluttonously making up for that lost privacy. Then it was her time. I asked her to spread her legs for me and hold them back, so I could just take my time sucking, licking and kissing my wife's most delicate areas. I loved to suck her juicy fluids and always imagined it was the power of every man to drink from this well of their wives, unknown by many. I called it her 'secret well of divine power' and without it I could not be a man for her. I knew my wife to be wee and so when I thrust my big 'General' into her I was always gentle and slow to start with, until she was wet again and comfortable and simultaneously would rub her clitoris with my hand or thumb to bring her up before I thrust too hard. When she screamed her maximum pleasure, I thrust hard again and again and I was in heaven with both of us making a lot of noise, but we didn't care.

That night the bairns did wake up and come to peek around our bedroom door then ran back to bed giggling, they told us the next day. Apparently, they saw my bare bum. Ma said she couldn't hear us over them and thank goodness Killian didn't say anything. His wife was sick anyway, so I guessed their sex life was over. We heard one week later that his wife passed away and poor Killian losing all his sons to violence and imprisonment, had no immediate relative to leave his farm to and it bordered on both Alex's and mine, so I was hoping he wasn't going to sell up to an English sheep farmer, worse still a pig farmer. I hated pigs and pork was forbidden in our house, as it was in many of Granny's families houses, strangely. No one knew where the no pork rule originated.

Most of us couldn't drink ale either, or if we did, we were sick. Ewen was the only one who could drink in the family because he was, after all, a border lander, an Armstrong.

20. *We Meet Mr and Mrs Menzies*

I was expecting Hugh Og to plough the second field again to plough in all the nutritious manure we had put on that field and I was looking forward to seeing him again. We were going fishing afterwards in the boat with Joe and Hamish. I saw that Matilda and Alex had visitors, while Hugh Og was ploughing. Matilda was pointing up at the horses and waved to me. 'This must be Daddy' I thought.

"Cherry, do you think that's Matilda's adoptive parents who paid for the Team?" I asked.

"They do look posh, don't they?" she said. "So, maybe that's them," she answered.

I waved for Matilda to bring them up if they wanted to look at the Team as Hugh Og was finishing up and there was no dust today after the rain we'd just had. The elderly, well dressed gentleman carried a book under one arm and what looked like a small painting as well and walked with a crook.

'Always wanted one of those things, they looked handy for hitting someone with, as well as walking,' I thought as they approached the gate and entered. He was followed by an equally well-dressed fine lady.

"Hey Malcolm," called out Matilda, "Cherry, this is Daddy and Mummy." 'Who called their parents Daddy and Mummy?' I thought. Alex and Joe followed from behind chatting to each other about farm business, I thought. I was introduced to Mr and Mrs Menzies, who didn't give their first names. He shook my hand saying how pleased he was to meet me and lots of flowery stuff in an accent halfway Scots and halfway English.

"I'll just get Hugh Og for you," I said, but as I was about to walk off, Mrs Menzies said,

"Oh, Malcolm dear, I am the only one wanting a ride up top on the Team if that's alright, but my husband wants to talk to you and show you something in a book, as well as a painting," she said.

Hugh was walking towards us and overheard Mrs Menzies.

"Oh, you must be the clever teamster man Hugh Og, how wonderful it is to meet a real teamster," she said.

Hugh was taken aback, but smiled at the sweet old lady and offered her his arm to take her for a ride. I could hear the old lady laughing and making comments the whole time they were walking the team around, but it was nice to see how happy it made her. What a strange life Matilda had lived. She was so lucky to have met Uncle Alex or she'd be like that as an old lady. Bruce had stopped his work on the goat house and both Ma and him came out to see the action. I could see it on Cherry's face, worrying then that she hadn't cooked up any cakes yet today, so she dashed inside to make cakes and coffee for everyone.

21. The Big Storm

Ma saw her run off with some urgency and went to help.

"Malcolm MacNachten is your name lad, is that right?" said the old man Menzies.

"Aye," I answered, watching the sky as it was changing and getting darker.

"Alex, there's a storm coming. Do you have your stock in?" I asked.

"You're getting better than us now lad," said Joe and said he'd deal with it. I asked Bruce to put Cherry's goats and chickens back away, as well as the geese.

"Come inside Mr Menzies," I asked.

"Hugh," I shouted pointing at the sky. "Storm. Do you want to stable the horses here until it passes and bring Mrs Menzies inside?" I asked.

With people and stock all sorted, I was glad of my wife and my Mither serving up cakes, bannocks and coffee in our small kitchen, suddenly full of guests. Cherry continued cooking in case this was going to go on for a while, now the storm was setting in.

"Malcolm. The shutters," she said.

"I'll do it," said Joe just arriving back from Alex's farm. Thank goodness he closed them all up as the wind came up just before the lightning strikes.

"So, Mr Menzies, sorry to keep you waiting. What is it you wish to ask me?" I said.

Alex was worried about the storm, but he was also worried to know what Mr Menzies had to say, so he sat close to hear all that was said.

"See this painting lad?" Mr Menzies asked. "This is one of your ancestors, whose name was MacNachten. Of course, the spelling has changed over time, but I see you have retained the old spelling. This man worked for my Father during the 1745 Rising and my Father, who was a Jacobite but a silent one, donated a fine horse for Prince Charles Edward Stuart and your ancestor through all the dangers before him, delivered that fine horse to the Prince. You are the Grandson, I think, of this fine gentleman. He had the same black hair like you do. I want you to have this painting, so you and your children can feel proud of your very brave ancestor. The horse was sadly injured in the Battle of Culloden and must have run away and died. The Prince was thrown from him when the musket fire hit the horse's shoulder, poor thing," he said with much enthusiasm.

"It is indeed an honour to meet his Grandson," he said. Cherry looked over my shoulder at the painting.

"Can you see any resemblance my darling?" I asked her. "Oh Aye, the hair, the eyes, the posture, the attitude. It's like an old-fashioned drawing of you," she said. "Hugh, what do you think?" I asked. "Both this man and Padruig Dubh are obviously your family, but this man has the dignity that you have that Padruig was lacking, so it's more of an expression. Those two men could have almost been cousins, to be so alike and to have offspring like you who resembles them both so much," he said.

"One day at Craskie when you were working on the Chapel incognito, I thought I was seeing a ghost when I saw you." Old Mr Menzies was enjoying himself immensely, while the storm raged on about us with lightning bolts striking the running water along the ground. I was glad of the lightning rod we had installed on the roof. It was unlikely that Alex and his guests would be going home anytime soon. "Bruce, Matilda can you please boil up bath water for the bairns and get them cleaned up, dressed then ready for bed after they've eaten?" I asked.

I was going to have to delegate. "Mr Menzies, can you leave the book for me to read when I have more time, then I'll return it to Matilda?" I asked. I could see his book was going to be next and there was plenty of interest but no time.

"Hugh, will Meredith or Grigor be worried that you are not back yet?" I asked. "Aye, they will, but when I saw that storm, you pointed at coming on, I thought it was right over Craskie then it has slowly moved this way. It's a big storm and my guess is that there's damage up there at Craskie. My opinion is they would have expected me to hold out in safety where I was last, which they knew was to be here," he answered.

"Good, I hope your horses over there are alright. Who's your head groom?" I asked.

"Dougal. If he is worried about any one of the horses, he will sleep all night with them. His wife has to take his breakfast over to him in the morning sometimes. I trust him," he replied. "Will my stables be strong enough to stable these Clydesdales if they fret?" I asked. "In my opinion, no. You need a stronger building and bigger stalls and higher rooves but hopefully this storm blows over soon and they don't start kicking out your walls," he answered.

"Bad luck about that fishing trip for sure. Another time," I said.

We had all been looking forward to the fishing trip, but glad we hadn't been on Loch Ness when the storm broke.

"We can help finance bigger and better stables son. It would be an honour," said Mr Menzies. "The best design is Grandma's design at Craskie. They're the best stables around these parts," Hugh Og said.

"They're too big for my wee farm. I'd have to get more land somehow to build something grand, like those stables," I added.

"But thank you anyway, Mr Menzies." Then remembering the Will from the previous day, I said,

"Ma, I must talk to you privately with Joe too, if that's alright Bruce. I meant to tell you last night, but you had moved already, then today got rather busy and it's looking like staying that way. Can we please be excused and leave you all with Uncle Alex and my wife and if we take too long, don't wait for us to eat. All of you can start without us. Bairns first is my only rule. Alex, can we put yours down to sleep here after they've eaten and had their baths, if this storm continues?" I asked.

"Aye lad, I'll take care of our guests," replied my kindly Uncle.

"Thank you for having us son," he said and patted me on my shoulder to relieve some tension, I thought.

"Joe, Ma, can you follow me into what I use as an office? It's not much, but better than nothing," I said. I explained everything about the unread Will from after Grandma's death due to Hugh Mohr's prevention of a reading. In the Will, my Ma inherited one of the farms, 'New Farm' with all of the buildings on it except Hugh Og's home and land, which was gifted to him by my Grandma. None of us, including Helen's son Aonghus, were aware that Grandma had made that change for my Mither. At least Aonghus wasn't charging his usual lawyer's fees due to his horrible mistake of not checking for changes and having a Will reading, but like he said, Hugh said Grandma was his wife and he didn't want it read out. It did sound intimidating and I knew how Hugh Mohr could get.

22. Ma, the Landowner

My poor Mither was too shocked to take it in at first and I had to repeat it three times and tell her over and over where that property was. The houses, except Hugh's, had already been emptied out of tenants including Isobel-Mairi as a temporary tenant when she visited. She was moved back into Ewen's old house, which was a lovely place. I gave her the copy of the Will to read, but I had bought a safe while in Inverness to keep that document secure as well as my own farm documents. I asked her not to tell Bruce that she now owned it, which may have been hurtful but necessary.

Helen was going to either pay rent on the grazing or give a number of coos per week slaughtered and butchered ready to eat, so that Ma could preserve some meat in readiness for the winter. I had also bought her the barrels and the salt so she could start preserving, so it was clear what I thought. The hides also were to be tanned and given to Ma. All of the coo would be used by Ma except its head, which I knew Hugh Mohr always ate the brains from. She agreed on three coos per week to feed all three of our families – Alex, myself and

Bruce and her. She didn't have to share the coos, but that was her decision and she wanted the role of the preservation of the meat through our winters. There were outstanding coos from the time when the Will was written and this had to be paid in cash by Helen, so Ma could upgrade her home.

23. *Murdoch and Joe's Families Moving*

Then came the hard topic of the two houses without offending Joe. So, I just said it boldly.

"Joe, do you and Murdoch want to pay a wee rent on the two houses Ma now owns on New Farm?" I asked.

Looking flabbergasted as he hadn't even imagined that he was on the radar, let alone his wee family, suddenly his head dropped and he concealed his face and eyes then stood with his back to us for a while to gain his composure. He sat back down looking manly again, of course and said to my Ma,

"Mistress, how much rent?" he asked. Ma hadn't taken money from anyone in her life and I offered to be her factor so she didn't have to and I suggested two Pounds Scots quarterly.

"Do you both agree, and will you both sign this rental agreement?" I had it pre-prepared because I knew I'd be nervous looking at my old mate Joe. They both thought it was a bonny figure and signed.

"Now remember, when you both go out, this is not for public knowledge except that the two houses are already rented to both you and Murdoch, no money mentioned nor who owns them," to which they both agreed and I felt tired.

I was hoping this storm would be over soon, but at least the bairns were all asleep despite the noise of the storm. All the adults ate their fill and my poor Cherry was looking tired too, so I said it was her turn for a bath and someone else could clean up. Miraculously, Alex and Mr Menzies started washing and wiping bowls and pots and glasses and tidied up the kitchen. I had eaten too and asked who else wanted a bath in cooling bath water, but no one took me up on it. So, I threw out the dirty water and saw the storm was moving away, thank

God. The stables were still in one piece and it was becoming quiet with just the sounds of dripping water all around. So, the Clydesdales can't have minded my stables too much.

"I think we can go now Malcolm, to give you some sleep," said Alex as he picked up his two sleepy bairns and the six of them wandered slowly back down to his house.

"Hugh, you can sleep on the spare bed. Did you want a bath?" I asked. "Nae, I'm tired like you. See you in the morning," as Cherry gave him his blankets, pillows and a doona.

Cherry didn't mind me coming to bed unwashed, but I always felt bad if I hadn't bathed with such a clean wee wife. "Just wash your feet darling. I'll help you," she offered. God bless her, she washed my feet and then collected more clean water to wash my face and arms and hands and the slippery wee love sponged 'the general' to my surprise and her wee giggle meant only one thing. We didn't have the energy of the night before, but we did have a lot of erotic fun and she thoroughly enjoyed it, as did I. Hugh was sleeping just on the other side of our bedroom wall, so I knew there'd be a few glances the next morning. I really needed to do some renovations, extensions as well. I prayed there wasn't too much damage all about us, but you could never tell until the daylight then you had to be careful walking under the larger trees.

24. More Land

I was visited later the next day after the big storm clean up by Killian MacDonnell on his old horse, who was looking older these days since his poor wife's death.

"I'm sorry to take up your time Malcolm, like everyone, you're busy cleaning up," he said.

"I have discussed my Will with your Uncle Alex and he has suggested to me if I can run it past you too. I know that you must be tired of dealing with inheritance issues and despite being such a young man, you're doing a mighty fine job," Killian said.

"Come in for coffee Killian, my wife has just put a fresh pot on," I said. I had never called him Mr MacDonnell or Uncle, as it wasn't my style. He was just Killian.

"I'll get straight to the point over your wife's lovely coffee," he said. Cherry had our home all clean from the night before and there wasn't a sign of any mud on her perfectly clean floors and the fire was raging to keep the bairns all warm. The temperature had dropped somewhat and even I had put on a woolly sweater.

"I want to divide my land into two halves, one half that will have the house on it with the outbuildings and big stables. Obviously, there's land with that too if its divided exactly in half and then the other half is mostly for cropping like oats, wheat, potatoes or barley," he explained.

"Aye," I said, a little confused as to what this had to do with me.

"As you know, my young sons all passed by violence before they had bairns and my wife was too old to have more bairns with me by the time I came out of prison," he explained a little sadly.

"So, I talked to Alex concerning the both of you, as I am not in favour of English sheep farmers moving in here to our corner of Glengarry. My house and stables are in line with your house, as well as that additional land for either crops or grazing for coos. The other half would more be in line with your crops and outbuildings, if I get the land division done this week. I'm getting too old to work the farm now, even with the great Islander staff I have now. But without my wife I have no interest left in it, other than to protect it from the English and to help my fellow Scotsmen. My question to you Malcolm is, would you agree to inheriting half of my farm and your Uncle Alex the other half and if so, which half would be your preference?" Killian asked.

I need to mention too that we have bedrock here in Glengarry and the wee road between us and yourselves is the marker for us locals where the bedrock becomes deep enough to grow crops. Therefore, it is only my property and Old John MacDonnell's property whose land can tolerate cropping. You must have noticed the absence of crops in Glengarry and the bedrock is the reason. If you are able to keep the soil healthy, you should be able to grow oats, otherwise like everyone else, potatoes are the last resort as cattle breeding has always been our mainstay, until they were all stolen by the English in in 1746.

"Killian, I am shocked at what you have proposed and you are a gentleman for sure, as well as a decent, honest man, but surely you have relatives to give your farm to?" I said.

"I can't just take someone's farm," I added.

"Malcolm son, I'd be dead already. You wouldn't be taking it from anyone, but if you could employ the two Islanders, I'd appreciate that, or Alex one and you one," he suggested.

"Of course, I'd keep the Islanders on. Can you give me some time to talk to my Uncle and my wife?" I asked.

"Aye, so you will give it consideration then?" he asked. "I need to create the land division this week. My house is huge, double stone and two storeys high with an attic up top. It has a library with lots of books, nice Turkish rugs that my wife bought, crystal chandeliers, a huge kitchen with plumbed water to the sink and a large dining room with fireplaces in every room. I have one year's supply of peat in an outbuilding. The bedrooms are all large with heavy drapes to keep out the cold and all furnished with double beds. The roof is new and made from slate in readiness for the snow. Your wife would love the laundry that my wife had built and I have a laundry lady too. If you still want to keep her, I can leave money too for her wages. Come and see it then talk to your Uncle," he said.

"This seems too good to be true, but I will get my wife and we'll take a look, then I'll talk to Alex," I responded, trying to keep my head.

Cherry left the bairns with Ma and we went with Killian across the wee road that separated our properties. His house was like a mansion to us humble folk, so it was hard to take in.

"Did Alex want the house?" I asked. "Nae he didn't. He needed more land for cropping," he said. Therefore it will be Alex who will need to be mindful of the soil.

"Thank you, Killian, you have been sent by God. Can I see your stables?" His stables were huge like Grandma's and big enough for Clydesdales. There was a separate tackle room as well as a separate room for feed and an area for a carriage.

"The same builder built Craskie's stables and I think you are going to need your own soon," he said.

I wondered why he said that, but we said our farewells and I went alone down to see Alex. By the end of that week the land division had taken place and one side of the property with the house was in my name and the other half was in Alex's name with Killian's Will newly written. We were both given a copy of his Will each, in case there was a challenge from some obscure corner of the MacDonnell Clan. His lawyer was from Edinburgh and very thorough. Killian said he would still work the farm until he died, so we relaxed thinking that was a way off, but it turned out poor Killian had terminal cancer and he passed away within the month, happy with what he had achieved and in joining his wife.

It was a big funeral. He was loved and admired by more than he knew as one of the last few veterans of the Rising of 45. Matilda cried her heart out as her friend was lowered into the ground. Both Alex and I to this day are still perplexed at his generosity and our new-found wealth. I was able to graze coos up to forty in number on my new land and Cherry felt like the lady of the house. We loved our first home and asked if Bruce and Ma wished to live in it or stay where they were. To our surprise they stayed in their love nest. The old house then became accommodation for all of the male staff, including the two Islanders named Joshua MacLean and Iain MacNeil and I employed a student so I could get him free for the year on offer from the government to work on my two oat crops. I couldn't afford to pay more staff. Luckily, there was money left from Killian to pay wages to the laundry lady who worked for four days per week leaving at 4pm on the dot. She washed all of our clothes, all the bed linen and ironed everything, even the sheets.

25. *The Moves Begin*

There was a fair amount of movement over the next month. First with the Islander families arriving from Edinburgh to move into their new homes on New Farm, which caused quite the stir over at Craskie. Both men had three bairns, two boys and four girls and so suddenly, the school had new enrolments when it was close to closing its doors. At least Helen could be happy that the school could stay open for a while longer. Cherry and I moved to the big house on my new land, which was daunting at first. I had never lived in a fine house, so I invited the only person I knew who had lived like that over to dinner to help us feel settled in. James and his wife Susan and their bairn Henrietta, as well as Patrick and his wife Henrietta, in case there had been hard feelings over the recent rejection of their offer of dinner with the Islanders. Of course, we invited Hugh Og and his wife Meredith and their beautiful wee lassie Ferne and Hugh's brother Hamish and his wife Cora with their three bairns, Donald, David and Mairi. We wanted to invite the whole family including Aonghus and Annabel, but we thought it better to start small and then increase the numbers as we were better at this entertaining thing in a fine house.

Hugh Og surprised me that evening and asked if he could move his Team to my farm, now also called Cherry Farm as the Team was no longer tied to Craskie Farm, even though all of the accounts were in both his name as well as Grigor's. I said he was welcome to, but to please ask Grigor's permission because of the accounts being still run by them both excluding Helen. When I asked him why he wanted to leave such a nice stable, he said the politics with Hugh Mohr had become intolerable and while he could live over at New Farm, Chisholm House was too close for comfort at the stables and he was being given a hard time for having befriended me. Our old house was also available to him to share with other staff if he wanted to move house and rent their other one out.

"I personally think you should talk first to Grigor and tell him what's going on with Hugh Mohr because maybe he could put a stop to it, but if not, then my stables wouldn't be free. I would have to charge a small fee if you can understand that," I said.

And he had intended paying a fee. He also wanted to bring Duncan MacDonnell, the junior Groomsman with him and come and go between both properties, with the work now requested of him from many farms. Duncan was originally from Glengarry, so he was welcome back and could live in our old house too if he wanted to. Murdoch had frequently said he was unhappy working there too, so I asked if that had improved and it hadn't. Hugh Mohr was unhappily living with the crofter family that he had put into his house and the youngest lad was working with him. The house was a bit too noisy for his liking, especially after the widow had married Dougal. He demanded that his food was cooked on time and piping hot and he always complained if the taste wasn't quite right.

"Tomatoes woman, tomatoes. Add tomatoes," he would say to the poor lady who had never known a tomato before, so was unsure how to cook them.

26. Craskie Gossip

That night we also learned a lot about nearly everyone you care to name with the gossipy Uncle Patrick, who was really enjoying himself. James loved my new home and he congratulated both Cherry and I and he let me know also that his wife was happier with him after my 'advice' and Susan was now with child. Hamish and Cora weren't gossips, but great company and we planned our next fishing trip if there wasn't another storm.

"Did you know Hugh Mohr lost his roof?" James asked. I couldn't stop the smile that came across my face.

"Nae, poor old man. Does he need help fixing it?" I asked insincerely, with a crooked smile James and I looked at each other knowing I didn't mean it.

"I think he can manage it just fine Malcolm," he said smirking.

"Was there any other damage?" I asked.

"We had a few broken shutters, but thank goodness we had shutters," said Patrick. "The main house forgot to close their shutters, meaning Helen and Meredith, while Grigor was busy putting livestock safely away with Murdoch, so they've lost a lot of those pretty windows that are being repaired now, as are the shutters just hanging on their hinges. It's not like it used to be with Ma ordering everyone around, so that everything and everyone was safe and sound. Even Hugh Mohr used to help, but he doesn't anymore. He only does the jobs he is paid to do and that's all," Patrick said. "He has become quite an embittered old man. Why do you think that is?" he asked.

"It might have something to do with Grandma's Will, but that's all I should say in company," I replied.

"Well lad, come over by the fire and have a private chat with me why don't you?" Patrick asked.

"It's all about New Farm. Ma owns it, but Hugh Mohr kept the Will from being read, so I only just found out a few weeks ago. She also owns the two new houses that Helen built there, so I am her factor to collect any rent from those two homes and ensure that weekly payment for the grazing occurs from Helen in the form of three coos per week slaughtered, butchered and delivered to my Mither's front wee door and the hides tanned. Just excluding the heads," I explained.

"Another issue over your Ma's inheritance then?" Patrick inquired sadly. "I am sorry lad. We are not all like that. I hope you'll always feel welcome at our place" Patrick added.

"One thing Patrick, this is a private matter and Ma doesn't want it widely known, so please do not repeat what I have just told you," I asked.

"She has never owned land nor taken money from anyone, so I am handling her affairs still as her factor," I explained.

"What about her husband, Bruce? Does he know about the land or mind that you handle his wife's affairs?" he asked.

"The less he knows the better at this stage. He is a friend of Grigor's and was recommended by him and while I like him well enough and he is a good worker, he came onto the scene late in all our lives and doesn't deserve to inherit anything of Ma's, unless they buy small things together. The land will go to both myself and Kenneth after Ma, as well as what is left of her finances. I suggested Bruce and Ma open a bank account together with an equal deposit from both of them and they're thinking of doing that. After all, he does earn a wage from me and he had his own money from America," I explained. "They also live in their own home on my land and given the choice to move into Cherry's and my old place, they wanted to stay in their wee cottage," I said.

Patrick said he understood and agreed with my responsible actions and wished that they had taken precautions with Hugh Mohr when he married Ma, but it had been all too quick and Aounghus wasn't forewarned for legal alertness.

"Alex knew that they were going to hand fast after the funeral and so did Grigor but no-one told me," Patrick said sadly. "I was left out of a lot of family discussions, which made Henrietta even harder to manage. James was left out too and he is so trustworthy. You were the first to come to us as family in so many years, that I can remember. Thank you, Malcolm, and thank you for inviting us to your home. We don't get invited to many places," Patrick said.

"Sometimes we are also misunderstood and so we are left out," I said. "I put up with that until we were kicked off Craskie and from then on I wasn't going to be kicked around like someone's football ever again," I explained. "Don't put up with it, Uncle," I advised.

"Oh, that's right, you had your nose broken by that awful farrier fellow, Ewen. That must have hurt, you poor thing," he said.

"Ewen wasn't the freaky bit of that fight Uncle, it was Hugh Mohr who turned into some kind of wild berserker, kicking and screaming, ripping up our shirts and red in the face, breaking us up," I said, feeling a bit embarrassed. "Can't say I have ever liked or trusted that Hugh Mohr. Maybe Grandma was raped by him and was with child afterwards and after the grief of losing the bairn, maybe her mind wasn't remembering what really happened on the night he got her with child. He must have only been sixteen or seventeen. He has been rotten for a long time," I said. "I don't think you have heard the last of him is my gut feeling," I added and the night was rounded off nicely with my wife singing an island song with no pipes this time.

The carriages clinked off into the dark night with their wheels squeaking.

"Well fine lady wife, how'd it go?" I asked.

"It was different, sort of calm, if you like and civilised," Cherry answered.

"Not too civilised I hope?" I asked, as I pinched her on the bottom and she let out a squeal and ran for the bedroom laughing. Of course, I chased her like a wee rabbit and caught my prey and she succumbed to my desires.

"Nae, not too civilised my darling," she said.

27. The Dream

That night we had great sex again, but then I fell into the deepest sleep after our first night of entertaining in the new house. I dreamed something very strange, which I had to tell Cherry when I awoke the next day. In the dream there was a very misty forest with a Pict stone in sight, then I saw a grave nearby. Fleur Chisholm was on the roughly engraved stone covered in foliage, but I forgot what else it said. Then, I saw someone's hands placing the wee casket in a hole in the ground there. There was a deep sadness for this wee child. I thought I saw Grandma, who looked young and pretty, weeping over it with an old man who must have been John Grant, her Father. He covered it over, but it had been too heavy for it to be just a wee bairn inside the casket. He had the face of a cunning old man, not evil, just cunning. Then I saw the same casket with 'Fleur' written on it, aged and dirty lying in the ground with Grandma inside the Chapel. There was more than the remains of poor wee Fleur in that locked casket.

I asked my wife what the dream meant. She said because I had been talking about Hugh Mohr with Patrick, deciding why he had become belligerent in his old age, Grandma had revealed to me that the child was a wanted child and that the sadness was shared between them, carefully hiding it from her husband, who was known to beat her, but known also as a hero. "His character, Padruig Dubh, is like a contradiction of nature," she said. "He loved his wife and might have known of the affection Hugh Mohr had for her. The Casket contains the bairn's remains, which would be dust by now," she said.

"If I were you, I'd go to the Chapel at Craskie and open Grandma's grave then open that small casket, but don't go alone. Take Uncle Murdoch in there with you and if they fire him because of it, he would be glad to leave and then we can hire him," she said smiling. "Hugh Mohr might be dishonest in some ways, but there can be no doubt that he loved your Grandma and that wee bairn. That's my opinion, beloved. Can I help somehow, like to distract people while you, do it?" she asked.

"Nae, you stay home. I don't want you hurt in any way, but I'm tough enough and so is Murdoch. Is he superstitious about graves?" I asked.

"Depends on the grave. But not this one. She was an innocent and might be happier with the foreign contents removed," she added.

"Are you thinking gold or rocks?" I asked.

"Gold definitely. Why would Granny trouble you over worthless rocks?" she answered.

"Not too much. Maybe a few bars, but before you dig it up have a meeting with my Uncles then decide who the gold was intended for and have someone recite prayers too. In my opinion, any gold was intended for Fleur's parents. Maybe giving it to Hugh Mohr will appease him and if he doesn't want the crofter family living with him, it's Helen's responsibility to find them a home, except the lad who works for Grigor who could move into their house. Simple really. I'll go get Joe now to chat," Cherry said as she ran off leaving me to watch over the bairns.

"Malcolm lad how are you?" asked Joe. "What is it I can do for your wee family? I'm in debt to you Malcolm, my family are really happy in the new house," he said. I gave him one of the old highland ponies to keep so he could come and go whenever he needed. Both Cherry and I told him about the dream and it became obvious that he was not a grave robber nor opener.

"Would that lady haunt us for opening her grave?" Joe asked.

"Nae, she contacted me, Uncle. It wasn't my idea," I said.

"Okay then, this is what we do lad. Tomorrow, we go fishing with all of the fellas, Murdoch, Hugh Og, Hamish you and me. We catch a batch of fish then go back to Craskie on horseback, then ask to talk to Grigor for the key to the Chapel but ask him to come with us to chat. Leave Helen out of course. Then, we all go together carrying a wee bag, in case you do get something from the grave. When inside the Chapel, one of us watches the door for Hugh Mohr and if he comes, we start lighting candles and praying and shit like that. If he doesn't snoop, then we just tell Grigor all about the plan to open Isobel's grave to retrieve what's in the wee casket other than remains. Murdoch is as superstitious as hell, so I hope this Isobel doesn't get mad about being disturbed," he said with the plan all in hand. Joe sounded confident, so I got Cherry's blessings to go fishing and do it and ask Ma and Bruce to keep her company.

She said no to the company, she just wanted some peace with the bairns and the goats.

28. *Fishermen Unite*

Our fishing trip was unusually quiet after we had all talked over the plan. Each man was contemplating his role in the opening of a grave, but they did agree to give all the gold, if it was gold, to the bairn's Father. After a reasonable catch for us all, there was some left over to give to Grigor to use as the excuse to knock on their door in the late evening. Hugh Og stood at the front with a few pike, I think they were, when Grigor was called to the door.

"Grigor mate, we've been fishing. Got some good pike for your family," Hugh Og said. Grigor called out to Meredith to take them and she was surprised to see her husband at the door. Knowingly, she knew to say nothing other than thank you.

"Grigor, can you come with us to the wee Chapel with the key? Light some candles, you know?" Hugh Og said. Grigor was aware that Hugh Og wasn't a serious Catholic, so he was catching on to a discussion needed in private away from his wife and agreed, so he let his wife know he was off to do his prayers with his friends. Few of them even knew their prayers.

Walking up to the Chapel, it felt eerie when it never had done before and I was sure I saw a small lady figure in white standing outside the Chapel. It was Granny waiting for us. I got goose bumps all over my body. She's a serious lady. Grigor unlocked the door and lit the candles and then looked at all of us, one by one and said,

"Okay, you have me curious this far. What's going on you lot?". After we all took turns at explaining it and wound up with me telling him that it was all in my dream. At first, I wasn't sure that he would take it seriously.

"Okay, do what you think you need to do, but I'll not touch Ma or what remains of poor wee Fleur. I'll wait at the door and keep watch. If anyone comes, close it up and pretend to pray," Grigor said.

Joe had the tools to open the casket, but as soon as we slid back the lid to what was revealed inside, he crossed himself, went away from it and sat by the wall, as white as a ghost.

Murdoch took the tools and handed them to Hamish, looked upon the graves interior and similarly nearly vomited and sat beside his friend saying some kind of prayer continuously.

"You lift her legs Hugh," I said.

"Nae, what if they fall apart?" Hugh Og said.

"Alright Hamish, how about you and I lift them in the tartan, so no bits fall out," I said boldly and Hamish, having more guts, lifted them with me saying,

"Sorry Granny, can we take wee Fleur for a while then put her back?" I could have sworn I saw her legs move away further to get to poor Fleur's casket.

"Thanks Granny," I said. Hugh Og was spooked as hell and stepped away and when he told Joe what he had seen, Joe passed out.

Both Islander men didn't move then from the wall after Joe woke up too afraid of Granny. I jimmied the casket open, checking Grigor was keeping watch and he was. I opened it away from my friends, now knowing their respect for the dead was one of absolute fear. Inside I took out four bars of French gold, identical to the ones Ma had been left by old John Grant. He must have stolen it from the Jacobites. I closed the wee casket quickly, then asked for Hamish's help again to get Granny to move her legs back, but this time they didn't move, so we carefully lifted them in the aged tartan to cover over the casket as it was before. I put out the candle and kicked both

Joe and Murdoch to get up and go before our luck ran out. I lit a candle for Granny and a candle for Fleur and said the only prayer I knew, then demanded we all leave.

We put out all the wall candles and locked up the door, then decided to knock on Hugh Mohr's door then and there. We had all agreed to get the job done. There were only four bars of gold, but enough to satisfy a disgruntled husband, I had surmised. Hugh Mohr came to his front door.

Cherry and Malcolm

"What do you pests want?" he asked. Grigor was the spokesman.

"I believe this is yours, from wee Fleur," he said and we began to depart when Hugh said.

"What do you mean?"

"You can thank Malcolm, who saw it in a dream and you're the bairn's Father, so it's yours. Hide it from your crofters. You can house Charlie up at my place if you like, starting tomorrow, as he is my responsibility. Get Helen to find alternative accommodation for the family if you prefer. Ewen's house is empty. Goodnight Hugh. Sorry for your loss," said Grigor.

29. Hugh's Grief

I turned to see that Hugh Mohr was crying, then beating his fists on the stone wall. His grief was very deep and maybe he will never recover from losing his one and only love, Isobel, my Granny. I wondered if I'd be like him when I got old, if I lost Cherry. I couldn't wait to see her after seeing an old Highlander crying like that. It must have hurt him that she had never given him a part of the farm or some money. I had to review my situation with Bruce after seeing the affect it had had on this one man.

I was so relieved to arrive home in Glengarry with our big fish and a story to tell Cherry. There was smoke coming from at least two chimneys as I opened the gate and as I closed it up, I heard my wife running up behind me. I don't think that I have ever held anyone so tightly and emotionally as I did when she reached out for me.

"I never want to let you go Cherry, please don't ever leave me, or even go away for a day. I couldn't bear to be parted with you in this life or the next," I said. I was weeping without realising it when she wiped her hands across my face.

"I'll never leave you my husband and I hope when we die, we die together. Now let's get your poor grey mare into the nice warm stables. Duncan's here already, so he can take care of her and her tackle," she said. We took her to the stables then I realised I'd held in a lot of built-up emotion. We left the mare with Duncan not even asking why Duncan was there already and went inside our new house where Cherry had a lovely meal waiting for me.

"Oh God Cherry, we opened her grave like we decided and there was gold in the casket," I said, confused why I was crying now and not then. "Sorry my darling, it's all the months of stress and revelations. It's all been a bit too much. I'd like a break and just get on with my farm," I said.

"Did you give it to Hugh Mohr then?" she asked.

"Aye and when he understood what it was, he cried like a baby and bashed his fists against the rock wall. He was devastated obviously that he wasn't left anything from Grandma," I said.

"But the dream was from Grandma telling you where it was and correcting your misunderstanding about Hugh Mohr.

She was telling you to give it to him and now you will see him change back to how he used to be, he might visit us darling so it's not over yet. You've done a good thing, all of you," she said.

Then I remembered her Uncles huddled against the wall and Joe fainting, but I didn't tell her. "She moved, Cherry, in her grave so we could get the wee casket. She moved her legs! She didn't feel dead at all. It was a bit scary. Grandma was a tough old lady. I saw her too outside the Chapel, waiting for us in a white lacy night dress. Don't ever wear a white lacy night dress or it'll scare me to death," I said.

"You're sounding more like an Islander everyday Malcolm. I won't wear one of those night dresses. Now come on and eat something after you wash your hands if you've touched a dead body," she implored.

"I didn't touch her body. No way," I said.

"The gold may have been contaminated by the wee bairn though," I realised.

"Scrub your hands then sweetie pie," she said ever so sweetly.

"Then after we have eaten, we can both have a bath together. I have the water already heating up and the bath is in our room waiting for us," she said temptingly to take my mind off the dead body.

So, we ate finally and she promised fish for breakfast. "This fish looks wonderful. Did you catch it?" she asked. "We just shared up what was caught, excluding what was for Grigor, so I don't know which ones I caught, but I never catch as many as Hamish and Hugh Og. One of the ones I caught looked big and fat, which I was pleased about. I could never catch this many fish at Loch Insh. Da would take me ice fishing with him at times in the winter. It was freezing cold. Maybe that's how he got sick by fishing over the ice so often," I said.

"You never mention your Da, that's nice to hear about the life you had in Loch Insh. Can we take our bairns there one day to that wee Chapel and maybe have a wee meal by the Loch when its swan season?" she asked. "That's a bonny idea. I miss Loch

Insh. I never thought when I was wee that I would ever leave Loch Insh until the day I met Grandma and she wanted us all to move to Craskie Farm," I said.

"Truth be known, I blamed her for what had happened to us, until I heard the whole story from the staff when I was on the Chapel building team and it was absolutely horrible. Can you imagine having to choose the lesser of two violent men to be beaten by one of them, preserving your life in the best way possible? I felt bad for blaming her, especially when she nearly died. I wish that ghost brother of hers would come back and help us all out. Why does a ghost decide to finally disappear and be dead?" I asked my wife.

"Don't bring him on, we don't know him and he doesn't know us. Who was he?" she asked. "He was Grigor Og's Father and one of the Seven Glenmoriston Men. Hugh Mohr is the last of them. He was Grandma's half-brother as they shared the same Mither, Freya MacGregor who married John Grant, after her first husband died who was Clan Gregor, so she died as Freya Grant. It's written on that black board on the wall in the Chapel," I answered.

"So, Granny was Clan Grant and Clan Gregor?" Cherry asked.

"Aye, that's right," I answered, "but Granny wasn't told about the Clan Gregor connection because of two reasons. The act of proscription against Clan Gregor and her Grandmither was burned at the stake as a witch in Edinburgh in 1661," I answered. "Cherry let's have that bath," I asked.

30. A Storm of Pleasure

My wife poured hot water into our bath and put more water on to boil.

"You first Cherry," I said. "I can watch you get undressed or help you get undressed," I added.

"Okay, undress me Malcolm, slowly," she said with something in mind and I could feel my man juices revving up when she added the word 'slowly 'and as I slowly took off each item of clothing, she just stood there while I admired her lovely skin, as it was revealed. Her skin had no blemishes and was so pure and a gorgeous colour, being of an olive complexion. When I reached her big skirts, she still stood there gaining my attention as the General was standing to attention as her skirt fell to the floor, so I couldn't wait for a bath and just had to throw my wife onto the bed and was surprisingly anxious to really go for it without stopping and ejaculated like a teenager. Then she said she was going to ride me, so I'd better get the General up again standing to attention, as she sat on top of me playing with him, as she pulled off all of my clothes rather quickly. She did everything that drove me crazy and the General responded like she had command over my penis. I wondered if she told him to stand to attention in a room full of people from across the room, if he would just obey my wife. 'Now there's a reason to wear a kilt with a big sporran occasionally in company, in case it happened,' I thought. After crazy sex, we finally wore each other out including my enjoyment of sucking her womanly essence. She was screaming in an uncontrollable deep measure of her desire, then when she came it was such a joy for me to see her face so relaxed after the storm of pleasure. God, how much I loved every inch of my wife. We still had the baths with more hot water and washed each other and our hair, which was both relaxing and sensual.

"Could you have ever imagined a life like this with me in this fancy house a few years ago?" I asked.

"Nae, my darling. I am so lucky to have you as my very own beautiful man. I love you so much Malcolm," she replied. "Every day, I thank God for you and our bairns and our life together," she said. We dried off and tried to dry our long hair by the fire with both of us naked, when Islay came in saying, "Ma, I'm thirsty" and didn't seem to notice we were both naked, so I calmly put on a sweater.

"Come on Islay, I'll get you a drink of milk," I said and picked her up to get her milk, then she was happy to pee as well and go back to bed and kissed me.

"Da you forgot to put on panties," she then said and giggled.

"Thank you, sweetie, I'll remember next time," I said.

31. Back to Work

The farm was as busy as it had to be, making up for lost

time and I was glad Duncan was there. My cousin's husband, Gillcrest MacLachlan, sent his student over, so I established him in the old house and introduced Bruce to him and led them both over to the soil for their opinions and it seemed there were a few issues according to the student. I still had a few too many rocks and he insisted that all rocks and stones, were to be removed due to how close the bedrock was, then he said the actual soil wasn't too bad but would yield more if we had another load of manure and kelp then plough it in again. At the same time, I saw my coos being slowly walked up the road to our property, so I left the two scientists arguing over the soil while I took possession of my thirty coos. Uncle Alex said it could only graze thirty in his opinion but I disagreed and even then, I may have to drove them once yearly up the hill further for the greener feed to give my land time to regrow as well. I had the one bull, so my herd was going to multiply rapidly and I wanted to prove Uncle Alex was wrong and I needed a bigger herd for this type of land as with the rainfall we had plenty of feed.

The builder arrived to build their shelter on the Drover Roadside of the grazing field, which to us looks huge, but they eat all day. I asked him also to reinforce the lower fencing and the gate, so the coos didn't get out and eat the crops. I also needed a dividing fence between my land and Alex's land, so the coos wouldn't eat his crops. I then saw Alex coming up fortunately, so he could agree on the border and the type of fencing we would both have as we were going halves in the cost. Setting up the builder, I also asked him to check the stables too for stability, thinking of the Clydesdales and add a window in the roof. I also asked if he could put in a flooring like Grandma had to keep the mud down and he knew exactly what I meant. We had too much mud needing attention.

"Bring me the quotes too by the end of day and if I'm busy, my wife Cherry will take it from you," I said.

32. I Get Blamed

Alex had something on his mind other than fencing and my coos, so I asked him what was up.

"I don't like to interfere but is it true that you were at Craskie last night?" he asked.

"Aye Uncle and you're not interfering. You can always ask me anything," I replied.

"I heard from my brother Patrick earlier today when we met at the Frasers Trading Post where he was buying more lighting for security that Hugh Mohr went on a rampage last night and kicked out his tenants and smashed up his own place after a group of you fishermen went to his door, including you," he said. "Is that true?" Alex asked.

"Aye, we were there for a good purpose, not to do him harm. Grigor did suggest that his apprentice, Charlie move to his big house and the other tenants go to Ewen's house. I don't know what Hugh did after we left, but he did look upset," I answered.

"Helen has put the family into Ewen's house and Charlie into their house, so that all adds up," he said looking worried.

"Are you blaming me for something Hugh Mohr has done?" I asked.

"I wanted your side of the story before Helen goes ballistic. She's already hopping mad about having to pay for grazing on New Farm," Alex added.

"You look too worried for Helen for my liking Alex, considering between Hugh Mohr, Grigor and Helen, my Mither, your sister, was going to be ripped off. Why aren't you more concerned about your twin sister and be blowed if Hugh Mohr smashes up his own house? He can fix it. And that family were lucky to have been saved from transportation at our expense, when we were kicked off Craskie. What's with you Alex? What has happened to the trust between us?" I demanded.

I had never spoken to him like that before, but I wasn't going to be blamed for some stupid shite happening over at Craskie.

33. *Hugh Mohr Visits*

"Speak of the devil, it's Hugh Mohr looking for you," Alex said.

"Let him look, I'm no coward. Now bugger off Alex before I say something I regret," I said.

"You don't want me to stay?" he asked.

"Not until you have apologised to me and Ma," I said and he strode off looking shocked at my rebuke. When Hugh Mohr led his horse through all of the gates from Loch Garry's gate and all in between, he didn't look like a man about to raise hell, but just in case, I sent my wife inside.

"Hugh, what can I do for you?" I asked.

"I just came to thank ye for last night," he said.

"Also, my late wife had me care for a particular stone for her," he said.

"Was it Pictish, by any chance?" I asked.

"Aye, how'd you know?" he asked.

"It was in the dream too," I answered.

"Well, she said not to reveal it to anyone unless one of the family showed that they were fae and that's you, so meet me next Monday, if it suits and I'll show it to ye," he said in a matter-of-fact manner.

"I'll ask my wife then if it suits," I replied.

"By the way Hugh, I've been blamed for whatever it was you did at Craskie Farm last night. I'd appreciate it if you dropped in to see Alex and cleared that up," I requested.

"You've been blamed. Why?" he asked.

"Good question, but I'll no be blamed for another's doings," I said.

"Well, I am sorry Malcolm, for many things, that to start with and your Ma's inheritance. Can you forgive me then?" Hugh Mohr asked.

"Aye, forgiven," I said and we both shook on it.

He left to go to Alex's door to have me free of blame for whatever happened there at Craskie. Alex then came up after talking to him and said,

"You asked for an apology from me and I sincerely apologise. I feel the fool and I do trust you, Malcolm. I've let you and Marion down. Please forgive me. I think I was influenced by Patrick, who was mighty annoyed at the racket last night and his guests left his hotel early today complaining about the noise at Hugh's house," Alex said.

"Why was I the target of his blame and not Grigor or one of the others?" I asked.

"He said that you had him over for dinner here and you gave him an opinion about Hugh Mohr, so that's why he blamed you," Alex answered.

34. Jealousy Between Brothers

"And you were upset that you weren't invited. Is that the truth?" I asked.

"I admit that when I saw their carriage up here, I was surprised that we weren't invited," he answered, looking childishly embarrassed.

"My wife and I were practicing as to how to entertain in a fine home and while we wanted to invite the whole family, we didn't know how to entertain in a fine way and it was James' opinion that I was wanting, but Patrick complained a lot about being left out of family dinners and family meetings and was grateful to me at the time, so I'm confused now as to whether he enjoyed the night or not. Obviously not," I concluded.

"You were practicing on Patrick? So, it wasn't that you didn't want us here?" he asked.

"Aye, we were practicing alright and of course it wasn't because we didn't want you here. Hamish and Hugh Og came too, but they're my fishing mates and they'll be honest if it was a shite night if you know what I mean. As for Matilda, we had to get it right before we invited you. Are you satisfied now that I'm completely humiliated?" I asked feeling really low.

Then suddenly he hugged me and apologised profusely and he understood and was honoured that we would try so hard to get it right for Matilda.

"I'm so sorry Malcolm, so sorry," Alex said.

"Okay, I've got work to do," I replied wondering then where our relationship stood. We both went back to work and he was obviously happier, but I couldn't say the same for me. Then why was Patrick pointing fingers at me after all the sweet talk.

He has had his last invitation, I decided.

35. *What's Up with Kenneth?*

A lot of work was accomplished in the one week that I dedicated to getting on top of everything and the beef, slaughtered and butchered, had started coming into Ma's house and she started her preserving and delivered one drum each to Alex's house, our house and of course theirs. The staff will get one the fol-lowing week. We had a Priest hole that was very cold and suit-able for preserving, so I built shelves and started to preserve. Our potato crop was prolific

Kenneth MacNachten

337

and we preserved those in their own potato shed, the corn was delicious and there was not too much wrong with the soil, I thought. Our neeps were also prolific and we stored some of those in the Priest hole too. Cherry was growing herbs and got tomato seeds from a neighbour to grow tomatoes. The first oat crop was coming on nicely, we'd had our first new-born kids and first newborn calves, so my books were the next thing to worry about when I thought of my brother, Kenneth. I missed him.

It had been months since I'd seen him or heard any news about him, so I decided to take Cherry and the family in the cart to Inverness to seek him out and maybe he could do our books or not, depending on what I found. I was good at books anyhow. The family loved the funny bumpy journey on the cart and we took raincoats, in case it rained. We finally found where his practice was supposed to be, but it looked very quiet. I asked Cherry to wait in the cart with the bairns, while I knocked on the door. It did have a sign saying, "Kenneth MacNachten Accountant". I waited and heard some sounds, so there was life inside, but I wasn't sure if it was respectable life. Finally, a bleary-eyed Kenneth opened the door half naked with only a towel covering his private parts.

"Cherry, take the bairns for ice-cream," I called.

My brother was alone as it turned out, but without customers and only a bottle of booze for a companion, which I knew made him ill. My brother was sick and he had no clients. I asked how much rent he owed. He said Ewen paid it, so he could do their books free of charge.

"Cancel your rental agreement. You're coming home with me, first to the Doctor's then home, but no booze," I said as I dressed him and packed up his few belongings and paperwork lying around that I just threw into a box. As my bairns were coming back with Cherry eating their ice-cream, they looked at their Uncle and asked who he was.

"That's Uncle Kenneth," I answered. "He is sick, so I'm taking him to the Glenmoriston Doctor, then he may have to come home with us to stay, or with Ma and Bruce," I said. I had given Ma and Bruce the money owed to them by Helen to jointly decide what to do with it and they bought a wee horse and cart and were very excited about kitchen curtains the last time I saw them.

She will be shocked at the condition of her son in misery and drunkenness. I felt guilty for not checking on him regularly, but it seemed like it had all been in hand. I'd forgotten what a weak bairn he was and he didn't have the same guts that I had. He was an artist really, way better than Aunty Helen, but more abstract. There was no evidence of a girlfriend. I told Cherry I would drop her and the bairns home first in case the Doctor took his time. The only cash I had on me was from egg money, so I had to ask Cherry if I could use the egg money that was usually for her household costs and I would pay her back and she agreed. She suggested that I take Uncle Joe, but after seeing him faint recently I didn't think it would be helpful.

"Maybe Duncan then?" she asked. So, Duncan it was, but on my way out I asked Matilda to keep my wife company until I returned and explained the situation quickly. She agreed and hurried up to my place and I took the unconscious Kenneth to Glenmoriston. Alex later joined his wife and they all ate together, while Duncan and I waited for the verdict in the Doctor's rooms.

The Doctor was Jean's husband and an asshole Englishman, who had charged me full price for my broken nose, so I wasn't expecting the bill to be cheap as I counted up the egg money. Finally, he came out.

"Mr MacNachten, is it? The broken nose lad I remember," he said.

"Get on with it. What's wrong with my brother?" I asked.

"He's a drunk lad is all, so he is going to have to sober up. I can keep him here in my medical emergency room over-night, which he can't escape from and if he can eat and keep food down in a few days then he will be on the mend, so long as you keep him away from the booze. How long has been an alcoholic?" he asked.

"He's not an alcoholic," I said.

"Oh, I can assure you he is, but not unusual for lost souls in these parts," the pompous arse said and I was close to punching him, when Jean walked in to talk to me.

"Malcolm, Kenneth is unwell it is true, but it's not incurable and after tonight we will transfer him to the Invermoriston Hospital, where they have Doctors there who specialise in the care of alcoholics and there's no charge there," Jean said.

"We will have a small fee for tonight," Jean continued, "But family discount applies, doesn't it darling?" she said helpfully for my wife's egg money.

"Do you want to see him before you leave and after tomorrow visit him at Invermoriston Hospital? Okay?" she said.

I walked in to see my brother clean and washed, but still bleary eyed. He recognised me at least, then tears came to his eyes.

"I'm sorry Malcolm. I'm a failure," Kenneth said.

"No, you're not. The world is full of assholes, so you have to toughen up is all," I said.

"I'm not like you Malcolm and what would Ma say if she saw me like this?" he asked.

"She would love you even more. You know our lovely Ma. She misses you. When you are better, you can move onto our farm and if you want to, you can do my books or paint pictures of rabbits, whatever you like, so long as you keep your eyes off my wife. If you don't want to live in our house there's another house you can live in, but there's a strict no booze rule for all of the staff and those who live there. Even the Islanders don't drink now on the farm," I said.

"Uncle Alex is there too next door with Matilda, so there's Bruce and Ma if you want to live with them in their wee stone home. Bruce is a nice fellow, who also doesn't drink. Ma would love to have you in her home," I said.

"Really, would she? I've been so lonely in Inverness, but Isobel-Mairi said to stay there and do their books," he said so sadly.

I was then asked to leave and Jean said she would fix the bill after all.

"Dr Thompson is who he'll be under at the hospital, so go there before lunch time okay?" she said.

"Tell, Sister Morag-Freya too, who is your cousin, to keep an eye out for him, so someone doesn't slip him a dram. The alcoholics can get cunning and when you do get him home don't even have anything with alcohol in it lying around or pills. He's an artist I heard you say, so take him in some drawing materials or paints and paper to record his life. Take time tonight to explain alcoholism to your wife and children, so they too can't be tricked into getting bottles of booze for him," she explained.

I thanked her profusely and asked again if she was taking care of him tonight, which she was.

36. Kenneth Going to Hospital

I was sad leaving him behind with relative strangers and hoped the move to the hospital would work out smoothly. I had no faith in these people. I decided that night to write down some childhood memories of Loch Insh to read out to him when I visited. He loved the swans. I prayed like mad, which is unlike me, for the Almighty to fix his alcoholism completely. Poor wee Islay asked what was wrong with Uncle Kenneth and I was reminded to tell them all about his illness. They sat up attentively listening and asked if Granny was going to the hospital too and I had dropped in to fill her in and got her agreement to come with me and Bruce and Cherry too, but leaving the wee ones with Matilda in case the ward was too daunting.

Ma was naturally upset, but supportive of her youngest son and took him flowers, chocolates, paper and writing and painting equipment, as Jean had suggested. Morag-Freya, a nursing sister and with child, caught up with us and was sorry to see Kenneth so ill, but she was going to do everything in her capacity to care for him and keep away the alcohol that somehow sneaks into these places, like sugar does onto the heart wards, she said with annoyance. Her husband Gillcrest came and took me to lunch for a wee break and talked about the student he had sent.

"He will be alright," he reassured me, "With the love of family like you all and the security of home," he said. He felt Kenneth would make a complete recovery, but not to expect too much of him academically. Art was a great way to start to get it all out of his head. No-one mentioned then that it may have shortened his life span.

He felt Isobel-Mairi had a case to answer to and was going to talk to her himself to take one burden from us and wished us all the best and offered any assistance including his wife, who could come around every two days to check on him, then as he improved it would be weekly and so on.

"I'm going to Craskie tonight," he said. "Were there any messages you needed passed on?" he asked. So, Kenneth's illness was passed on to Hugh Mohr, Murdoch and Grigor and a message from me was that I couldn't now visit Hugh Mohr as planned at Craskie and could he apologise to him for me. They also couldn't bring any form of alcohol to the hospital when visiting.

I did feel better after talking to Gillcrest and I hoped to have him over for dinner soon with Morag-Freya. 'He'll get better,' I kept telling myself and each day after completing my farm tasks, I would visit him and see he had improved if only a little at a time. He had lost so much weight, so the hospital had to work hard to feed him up. His diet was high in nutrients like for someone with malnutrition. His body couldn't have taken much more if I hadn't gone to see him that day when I did.

Apparently, he had been very close to death when I took him to the Doctors.

One month passed and he was still in hospital because they said he'd had alcohol poisoning, so actually he was lucky to be alive. In that time naturally, the farm kept on working and Hugh Og was more often keeping his Team at my place working with Duncan. They were all aware of my circumstances caring for Kenneth and even Joe would come up to my place and work as did Murdoch. Ma had opened up an old port from Loch Insh that contained all of Kenneth's artwork which was beautiful, so Bruce offered to build him a studio next to the farmhouse, if I paid for the building materials. With that knowledge, both Hugh Og, Hamish and the Islanders we had helped coming from miles around, built the beautiful studio with a fireplace for Kenneth. It was both aesthetically a lovely building, as well as sturdy.

Joe knew how to frame Kenneth's artwork and the drawings of Loch Insh and paintings of swans and rabbits and insects that I never knew existed, were all hung. Most of the interior of the building was log and one wall was double stone lined with wood on which to hang the paintings. Kenneth was also painting or drawing all kinds of things in hospital, including one of Morag-Freya in her nursing Sister's uniform. We would take the art from him each day, frame it and hang it. On Uncle Alex's gate he put a sign saying, 'Art gallery opening soon' and on all of my gates including my main gate. Hugh Mohr heard of our troubles and had always liked Kenneth, so he came and offered his services too when the slate roof was to go on, so thankfully we did not have to pay an expensive builder, as he built the entire roof. Gillcrest sent another student around also to look after the farm when I wasn't there and Matilda watched over my family continuously and had written to her Menzies parents filling them in.

37. *Frasers Back on the Scene*

In competition for doing good, John Fraser, now quite elderly with his son Simon Fraser, came around and asked to help by sending all his rich Fraser friends and relatives once the gallery opened and also gave a clothing voucher at my favourite shop in Invermoriston, so Kenneth could be well dressed coming out of hospital, as well as a lot of art supplies of many types he already had in his shop. I set up a desk with all of his supplies on it, as well as piles of canvas and paper in a big cupboard. Bruce fussed over all the finishing touches like the shutters covering the windows for storms, a lightning rod on the roof and added a porch to the front for bad weather and a hitching rail to the side with water for visiting horses. Access was going to be through two points, my end and Alex's end, so we widened the wee gate to allow a carriage, if necessary, but was not preferable. The preferable entry was the gate at the top of my old farm then their horse could fit through as well as carriages, but we were hopeful that this was going to be a success.

Matilda was making up flyers to send to everyone in the district awaiting the opening date, as well as anyone of importance in Inverness, Aberfeldy and Edinburgh and the MacGregor family of course, all of the Islanders, Loch Insh residents with a complete list of Kenneth's works, which amounted to over one hundred and fifty pieces. Some smaller ones made the total 200. He was also busy painting portraits, like one of Matilda, our Mither, Alex and me in Loch Insh.

James and I went shopping for Kenneth and it also gave me the chance to ask why his Father had blamed me for the stramash at Hugh Mohr's house. He apologised and said his Da could be disappointing in that way, even though he was well aware of all of the men who had been there, including Grigor and who were not present when it all happened.

"He wanted someone to blame and to be honest," he said. "Da was a bit jealous of your windfall and your lovely fine home, given that no one expected you to amount to anything being a hidden family of some kind for whatever lame reason," he added. James was sad to tell me that story, considering they had all been invited to my house to enjoy a pleasant night. "I just feel like we all have to continuously apologise to you for all our wrong doings and I'm sick of it. I really enjoyed that night at your house. It was such a treat, so Da has spoiled it for us all. So, now if there is anything I can do to help Kenneth and you, I'd be glad to," James said.

"There is, after we buy his clothes. Can we pick him up from the hospital in your nice carriage, without Patrick of course? He's a fraud, you know that?" I said.

"I do. He has never had a strong character and his Father had to set him up in business or he would have been a total failure in life. Granny warned me about that and ensured that we ran the business together, which is in writing in a legal document, or I might lose the business that I'm supposed to inherit," he said candidly.

"Okay cousin let's go shopping," I said. I bought Kenneth four shirts of different styles and colours, two long trousers, one formal in tweed and one casual in tough material. Tall knee-high boots for all our mud and a tweed waistcoat with a thick coat. I also got him two sets of underwear and socks to keep warm with the cold winter coming. Then James suggested four nice woolly jumpers and an apron to keep his clothes clean when he's painting. We were passing a bedding shop and I was worried Ma didn't have enough warm bedding and sheets, so I bought all of that with a big warm doonas and pillows.

38. Suicide Warning

I thanked James but asked him if Susan and he still wanted to come over one day for tea with Alex and Matilda, Ma and Bruce and Kenneth.

"Of course, we do," he said, emotively hugging me and wiping his tears away. "I am so sorry I've hurt you, Malcolm. I don't have many friends and you mean the world to me. Please don't leave me out," he said. "And I'll pass on the flyers to all of our guests to go to the opening when you decide on the date, with a no booze rule I presume? Kenneth won't be able to drink anything at all now, you know that don't you? Henrietta's Father was a terrible drunkard, but violent with it, so you are lucky that Kenneth isn't a violent alcoholic, but can I ask if he has ever been suicidal?" James asked.

"I am sorry to mention it, but there were a few suicides around our area that were kept under wraps, like fighting injuries are called farm accidents. My Granny was going to kill herself twice. Hugh Mohr saved her apparently the last time when Grandda disappeared and went to New France. He abandoned the whole family, just like that and people call him a hero, leaving them homeless. I never thought so. He was a violent asshole. Things are never as they seem at Craskie," said James.

"If you ever need clarity, I'll fill you in, don't worry. I'll tell you the truth. As for suicide, I think Granny ended up with mental illness, therefore wanted to die more than a few times and it could be a weakness that runs in the family. Although I don't blame her for wanting to die married to Padruig Dubh. Most of our ancestors were closely related, maybe too close in some cases they have been second cousins, even first cousins. There is something you need not get involved with though, but Hugh Mohr is currently dealing with Ewen and Isobel-Mairi for what they did to Kenneth. You must have won favour with him. He had been inactive until that night. He has missed Granny, that I know. He loved her deeply. She wasn't an ordinary woman our Granny," James said.

"No, that's for sure," I said, as the carriage rattled us along back to Glengarry.

"You sound like you knew her better than I realised," he said.

"Aye maybe I did James," I said. I was dropped off at my gate and waved off James smiling in gratitude. "I will let you know when we are to collect my brother," I yelled and waved.

My wife was pleased to see me.

"Oh Malcolm, I'm missing you too much," she said wrapping her arms around me.

"I am sorry my love. I've got Kenneth's clothes and bedding now, so I'll be able to be home more. Do you want to give the bedding to Ma and Bruce?" I asked.

"Not really. Can you stay with me?" she asked.

"Is something wrong sweetie?" I asked.

"Aye there is. Oh Malcolm," she said.

"Don't tell me its Kenneth. Has he died?" I asked in a moment of sheer panic.

"Oh God, no, I'm sorry, it's not that. I'm with child and I knew, but you were busy and now I need you to hold me please and tell me that you're happy to have another wee one," she wept into my shoulder.

"Oh, my dearest Cherry, of course I'm happy we're having another wee one. Clever Mither and clever wife. You are everything to me my love. I have to try to help my brother too my dearest. Our prayers are needed as he has been really sick. Perhaps come with me one day to the hospital with the bairns, to get used to him," I suggested.

"Oh yes, I'd like that," Cherry said.

39. *Hugh Mohr Bloodied*

I called Duncan and asked him a favour.

"Would you mind giving this all to my Ma in the stone cottage?" and I fetched a coin from my pocket for him. He was happy to run down the bedding that I had bought for Kenneth.

"Tell them it's for Kenneth and I'll bring him home soon to their place," I said. Cherry then looked guilty to interrupt all of my plans in motion, especially over something so important, but she did look pale.

"Come on darling," and I picked her up in case fainting ran in the family. "Where's' Islay and wee Alex?" I asked. "Your Ma came and took them for a visit down there for lunch. They'll be home soon," she said.

"So why didn't you want me to go to Ma's if my children were there Cherry? What are you not telling me?" I asked.

"Hugh Mohr's inside the house, a bit bloodied. I treated it, but I vomited and he realised that I was with child, so he treated it himself, but he wanted to tell you about what happened in Inverness," she said.

"What's going on in Inverness?" I asked.

"Come and listen, I'm due for a coffee or do you want me to make it?" I replied.

Hugh Mohr stood with his back to the door at first, so when he turned, I was surprised at how mangled his face was.

"Hugh, you need a Doctor," I said. "I don't need a pretty face anymore. It will heal," he said. When I took a look, I thought it was quite serious, so I suggested I take him to the Doctor.

"Is your horse here?" I asked "Aye, a stabled bay gelding. Duncan took care of him," he said "Okay, sorry Cherry, I'm taking Hugh to the Doctor's," I said,

"Do you need my egg money again?" she asked.

"Probably," I answered. "Keep feeding up those chickens sweetie pie," I said smiling and I told her to lie down and take a wee nap.

40. At the Doctor's

Dr Browne just made a guttural sound like 'Hmmmm'. "Run in the family, this facial trauma?" he asked.

"Did my cousin Jean ever tell you what an asshole you are?" I asked.

"Hmmm. How's your brother?" he asked.

"Much better now he's not with you," I replied.

"So, who's this bloodied fella the wind blew in. Another farm accident, I presume?" he asked. "Hugh Chisholm's my name and my job in the war was killing you English and we continued killing them. You had better do a good job on my face mate or Jeanie will be a widow," Hugh answered. Hugh had a broken nose and a broken eye socket, as well as cuts and abrasions. He had lost a lot of blood. One of the cuts on his cheek required stitches and he didn't wince. He didn't want pain killers either.

"My wife tolerated you English bayonetting her and it was stitched without pain relief, so I'll no have any either," he said. He was talking about Granny. No wonder she was a tough lady. 'God Granny, why were you bayonetted?' I thought. I went to the waiting room to sit down. I was feeling queasy, then started to feel tired and lay down on their chairs and fell asleep.

I dreamed of Granny. It was unclear what it meant, so I thought I'd ask Hugh. There was a sad looking white horse in it with blood all over its back, then Granny was thrown on her, then I woke up. Hugh was coming out looking grey, but at least his face was in place. Egg money was all I had, then I heard the Doctor ask Hugh if he was one of the Seven Glenmoriston Men.

"Aye. I'm the last," he answered. The Doctor changed his expression entirely.

"My Father, Dr Browne, was a fan of you all and has a painting down there in London of the Seven Glenmoriston Men and I saw the one of you with the Collie dogs at the Glenmoriston Art Gallery opening. I was told I couldn't buy it because Mrs Chisholm had bought it for you, so you saved me a small fortune. That Helen sure can charge, even for these farm animals in the waiting room. So, tonight's free of charge, but not the next time. I am an asshole because every day you Scots spit at me," he said.

"Oh, poor you. My wife died that night, but I think you knew that. You wrote out the death certificate, so why the pretence if you knew who I was already?" Hugh said as he turned his back on him and we left.

While leaving, Hugh said, "So, my wife did buy me something after all," he said looking pleased as we were walking off in the direction of Craskie. "I didn't know she paid for that painting. It was really expensive and Helen can charge," he said.

"What happened, in Inverness Hugh?" I asked.

"First Grigor and I went to Aonghus to get Isobel-Mairi to repay her debt. So, wait for the noise on that one. Then I excused myself from Grigor to go to Ewen's Mill, where the bastard was working with the forge he stole from Craskie and with what he did to Kenneth, it was the last straw, so I beat him up and he beat me up," he said.

"Was he badly injured?" I asked.

"Och, aye. Worse than me, then I went to your place to let you know, not thinking of your wee wife. I'm sorry about that. I think it frightened her," he said remorsefully.

"She's with child, so is very sensitive right now and with what has happened to Kenneth, it has put a lot of strain on us and to make it worse, I was blamed for whatever you did at Craskie by that asshole Patrick," I said.

"He's always been a right asshole," he responded.

"Thank you for defending my brother. He doesn't have the same strength as I have, but neither of us can take the drink. It makes me as sick as hell. Poor thing was led into a trap, but I didn't check on him, so it's also my fault as his older brother. I hope Ma doesn't blame me. We have things set up for him at home now and he'll live with Ma and Bruce and if they get sick of each other, there's my house or the staff house. James is coming with his carriage to pick him up from hospital and we bought him new clothes. I guess it's up to him now," I concluded.

"Padruig couldn't hold his drink either and your Grandma never drank," he added.

41. The White Horse

"Can I ask you about a dream I had at the surgery?" I asked.

"Aye," he answered curiously. "There was a white, sad looking mare with its head drooping down and on its back was a lot of blood, but not her own blood. Then I saw men throwing Grandma up onto her, then I woke up," I said. Hugh Mohr looked at me in shock and asked if I had been told of Granny's injuries.

"Nae, not injuries. She told me she was raped by her Uncle to explain why we were all in Loch Insh. That day she planned to go back to Craskie to arrange for us to return home, she had said, but she was beaten up by you I think, instead of Padruig Dubh, so she would survive the beating. I could not ever imagine ever beating my wife," I said.

"It was the way of Highland men, especially then, when loyalty was a matter of life and death. Your Grandma handed me the whip, aye, it's true. I never wanted to hit her, but Padruig said 'good, do it'. I agreed if I didn't use the horsewhip and held her in my arms afterwards. It was a nightmare of a night and a thing no one should ever have to do to a wee woman like she was and yours is. Keep an eye on yours, there are still violent men out there," he said.

"Cherry knows that. She was raped on the Isles by two soldiers, then her Father was killed. Her Uncles both scooped Cherry up with them into a wee boat to go to Oban on the mainland, but her Ma couldn't bear to lose her husband and hung herself. So, the Uncles took responsibility for her and brought her here with them and got her a job as a cook and wanted me to meet her. That's when I met her and married her that same night. I loved her on sight and knew she was going to be my forever wife and the Mither of my bairns," I explained. "The white horse Hugh. What do you know?" I asked again.

We were strolling up to Chisholm House with the farm all quiet. He stabled his horse without speaking and took his time answering, but I knew that he knew what it was.

"I don't know how you know these things, Malcolm. Your Granny, like many women in those times, was raped or ravaged and the Black Prince had Sunday races for his men, as well as the local militia from the Isle of Skye. Isobel was grabbed off of this farm, as well as all three of her bairns who were to be stripped naked and raped, maybe killed in that process, then put naked onto horses, bareback. The farmer, Allan MacDonald paid the soldiers for his wife and the three bairns with forty coos, as agreed with the soldiers to save the four of them, but they were not going to negotiate for your Granny because she was Padruig Dubh Grant's wife. They were angry at not finding Prince Charles Edward Stuart and not catching any one of us, but they knew where Padruig's farm was, even though it was already burned down and worthless. A spy had seen the bairns and Isobel and her Father and had reported it back that they were still alive because they were after the land," he said trying to hold in any emotion.

"Her Uncle saved the bairns with his coos, but his wife Margaret was taken at the last minute too, along with Isobel to Fort Augustus. Your Granny was stripped naked in front of an audience and was raped by six dragoons. Then, as they threw her on that white horse that you saw, they bayoneted her five times, one really deeply and it bled a lot and that was the spectacle they wanted of the red blood against the white of that poor horse to toughen up the younger English men who were being trained to fight the French, as their uniform is white. Does that answer your question?" he explained.

"Aye. More than enough. Now I'd best be getting home to my wife. Hope you feel better tomorrow, Hugh," I said. I left quietly, while not feeling too well thinking of all that blood and not wanting to attract attention again, then galloped home fast to Glengarry. By this time, I was genuinely worried about Cherry.

When I arrived home, all was quiet there too and peaceful, so I stabled my lovely grey horse and rubbed her down and fed her. I walked quietly up to my locked front door and unlocked it. I had to light a candle to see where I was going and put a log on the fire. I checked if the bairns were home in bed and to my surprise all three of them were asleep together. I went into the kitchen and ate like a horse. I was ravenous after such a day. 'My place needs pole lights', I thought, like Craskie and Uncle Alex had just bought. It could be so dark out here. But as I sat by the fire munching on bread, meat and cheese sandwiches, I noticed a note on the table from Cherry saying,

"Darling man, I'm in bed with the bairns. A messenger from the hospital came and said to pick up Kenneth before dinnertime tomorrow. Get Duncan to get James and his carriage here by eleven o'clock in the morning to pick him up. Ma knows already, Cherrypie."

After drinking coffee and eating another sandwich, I felt better and took a wash and went into our room and pulled back the covers and lit the fire, smoored the lounge room fire and put the bed warmer in our bed. I wished we had house help. Then I fetched my wee wife to sleep with me and I held her tightly, falling asleep thinking of poor Granny and sent her a prayer and asked her for help with Kenneth. Our early morning love making brought my darling back into her normal state of happiness and she went about getting breakfast for all of us, while we heard Duncan riding off to tell James. I was nervous.

42. *James Arrives in the Carriage*

Would he even like my farms and Ma's house and the Art Gallery that we built for him to tinker about with, let alone an opening to sell it all? I took a few deep breaths and went down to the horse. They usually made me feel calm. I checked on the coos and Duncan arrived back saying he'd given the message to James, who would be here by eleven o'clock. I went and collected up his clothes, so he could choose what he would like to wear and the clock seemed to be ticking louder than usual. Nerves, nerves. I concluded.

"Cherry, do you and the bairns want to come?" I asked.

"Aye. Come on, let's all get dressed," she said and then James arrived on the dot. Cherry and the bairns climbed in and I sat up with James driving the two-horse carriage.

"You are good at this too. Granny taught me as well when we got the Clydesdales back," he said. "I wasn't strong enough for the Clydesdales or cunning enough, I think it is. They are intelligent animals and Granny spoke to them in Erse, so they obeyed her, but they didn't obey me," he said accepting his weakness, but smiling like Granny was a heroic figure in his mind, who would never lose his respect.

"But you are mighty good at this just the same. I can't drive these horses," I said. "I'll show you one day. If I can, you can Malcolm. So, it's the big day. Are you nervous?" James asked "Aye, I am," I responded. "I don't know if he'll settle on our place and like it at all," I said.

James stabled the carriage and horses near the hospital and we all walked together with one bairn each on our shoulders and Cherry carrying his clothes. Walking into the hospital, this time was different. My brother was finally leaving and he was no longer their responsibility. 'Oh God', I prayed for help. We came to his locked-up ward and were let in by Sister Morag-Freya, who was very pleased to see us and she asked if I had his clothes. I then realised she was quite heavy now with child. She had stayed on longer at work because of Kenneth. When I saw my brother, I was so emotional I wept and so did he and I helped him dress.

"Whose clothes are these?" Kenneth asked. "Yours, you idiot, who else?" I combed his hair, then invited Cherry and James and the bairns in to meet him. "Kenneth, this is my wife Cherry, our cousin James, who has a carriage outside and my bairns, Islay and Alex." My wife shyly shook his hand gently and James just hugged him, which lasted a while.

"Hello Uncle Kenneth," said Islay then wee Alex said, "Hallo Uncle Kenneff." He smiled at being called Kenneff and we all left hugging our cousin Morag-Freya and thanked her very much. The carriage ride was a real treat and he wanted to ride up top and chat to James. James told him about his art studio and all the new things he had, so by the time we arrived home he was looking cheerful to be out of hospital and feeling better and anxious to see Ma and her new husband. James pulled the carriage into my old farm and I opened the gate.

43. *The Prodigal Son*

He stopped the carriage outside Ma's house and Ma rushed to her son crying and hugging him saying lots of lovey, dovey stuff before Bruce was introduced, but he just stood back smiling at his wife and very pleased with both me and James. My son Alex said to Ma, "This is Uncle Keneff Grandma," as my son held his hand. Impulsively, Kenneth picked him up and kissed him saying, "Aye, I'm your Uncle Kenneff," he said.

"You're mine too," said Islay as she muscled in for attention. Ma invited us in while we noticed all eyes from the farmhouse were on us, as well as from Alex's farm. Even Duncan from my new farm was hanging over the fence with the coos all around him. It seemed that everyone was welcoming home the poor lad, who had been tricked by Isobel-Mairi and had nearly died in the process. I called Duncan down to stable the horses, so James could stay. He didn't look like he was leaving anytime soon. It was almost like one of those old Biblical stories. So, with Duncan coming, so did all the staff pour out of the house, then Joe from Alex's Farm, then Matilda and Alex carrying both their bairns. I introduced Bruce quickly before he was bombarded. Then Ma had prepared a lovely homecoming feast, as we all squeezed into Ma's wee home.

Somehow Murdoch had been told and out came the uillean pipes and Cherry started her dance. This time with a chanting from everyone - 'Welcome home Kenneth' repeatedly, which made him cry. I had to hold him and get him to sit down. It was a bit overwhelming but once in a lifetime, so Ma and Bruce allowed it. Bruce had prepared his bedroom nicely with all the new bedding that I had bought him. As the pipes kept playing, the party spilled outside and Ma passed around small food items and drinks of goat's milk. I made sure Kenneth wasn't getting too tired by keeping him in a lounge chair and people came to him to introduce themselves. Joe was emotional seeing my poor brother and hugged him.

"I'm Cherry's Uncle Joe and if you ever need anything son, you can come to me if Malcolm's birthing a coo or something and that's me brother playing the pipes, you can consider us all family," he said. Islay finally got her chance at sitting on his lap and touched his face saying, "I can do things too Uncle Kenneth, like pass you your paints," she said. Matilda shook his hand which he kissed instead.

"I'm Matilda, horrible accent I know, but I am Scottish and Alex's wife," she said.

"I remember you. You wore big boots at Granny's dinner, then found out you were born on Craskie. Weird that eh?" Kenneth said clearly remembering more than anyone had expected, which was a good sign.

Bruce came up to me then and asked if he could put him to bed as he thought he was getting pale. I agreed and shut down the pipes. Bruce and Ma took him to bed, while all of his new friends slowly went back to work. James said he had better get the carriage back home, but wanted to kiss Kenneth first, so he did.

"I love your brother. He has such a gentle soul," he said to me and made his way to the carriage. I was so grateful to James, Ma, Bruce and Cherry, my bairns, the staff, the Uncles, Alex and Matilda and I felt a sadness leaving him with Ma. I was the last to leave and I too kissed my brother gently, as he fell into a much-needed rest. There were gifts left for him and I told Ma to go through each one to ensure that there was no alcohol. She did find one gift of chocolates that had alcohol in them, so she threw them out immediately.

"Come and get me anytime Ma, I always want to know if he's alright," I added and joined my wife and bairns to go back home with Duncan and waved in gratitude to everyone up at the house when one of them reassured me he would make sure no alcohol came onto the property. I thanked them all and sadly went home without my brother and for the first time in my life, I felt a strong absence of my only family, except Ma. I couldn't overcome the guilt in the days that followed and although I kept very busy with all the work needed doing, it kept creeping into my mind that I had neglected him.

44. The Future in Glengarry

I asked Cherry if one day we should build Kenneth his own home on either one of the farms when it became too much for Ma. Her answer was, "Don't wait for that day to come, for it surely will come. Start building it now. My Uncles will help you build a nice stone home like Ma's on this property. There's not enough room on the other one. Even Bruce will help if he isn't offended with the thought that Kenneth will leave them one day, but you have to think of his future like a wee wife for instance. Once his name is out there with his artwork, all kinds of lassies will want to know him and they may not be what he needs. I think an Islander lassie would be better. Joe's oldest lassie is old enough to marry. She's fifteen already. What do you think? She's real pretty, doesn't drink, a virgin of course, can cook really well like her Mither, she's artistic, but no fool. Can speak Gaelic and English and good with numbers. She'd be good with adding up his earnings," she said.

"Then we could say she is going to help him at the opening night for that purpose of adding up and keeping the money safe with Hamish," I said.

"Then if they like each other, maybe it can grow from there, but he may not feel capable of caring for a wife. She would have to be independent and not clingy nor expect too much and know how to care for him without him knowing she is making sure that no alcohol comes near him," I responded.

"She's no fool. Can we talk to Joe at least about Amelia working with him on the opening night with the money with the view of courtship? He won't want her to lose her virginity unless they marry, so do you know what his morals are like these days?" she asked.

"Nae, I don't but he wouldn't harm a young virgin, I think. The two of us both lost our virginity in Loch Insh with married women, who thought we were braw. Kenneth's also been known for smacking pretty women on the bottom, so watch your arse near him, he loves a fat arse especially. I wanted to smack your arse when I first saw it as you walked me to the table, but I controlled myself," I said.

"What is it about you Loch Insh boys and women's arses?" she asked. "None of us were inclined toward men there, not like in other places, like Uncle Alex's farm. Have you seen Peter hanging around there for cousin Alexander? I would prefer my son pinch a lady's bottom than do whatever they're doing," I said.

"Fair enough darling, I understand, so I'll just explain to her to be flattered if he smacks or pinches her arse?" she asked. "Aye, unless he has changed camps. That can happen too. James told me," I said.

"James is quite knowledgeable about these things. Why is that?" she asked.

"The guests up at that disgusting lodge sometimes just go there, leaving wives behind saying they're going hunting with their mates and instead they bonk each other," I answered. Poor Cherry vomited again.

My answer with her morning sickness was too explicit.

45. Amelia MacFie

"Sorry Cherry, I'll be more delicate in the future. You've got more morning sickness than before. Why is that?" I asked.

"That piggy doctor says its twins Malcolm, I'm sorry. Can I ask you for home help just for a few years?" she asked as she vomited again.

"You said Amelia was a good cook. Can she clean house and mind bairns too, light fires, smoor fires, scrub the step, clean all the shoes and boots and follow orders if a particular meal was needed?" I asked.

"Aye that's all normal stuff Malcolm," she answered. "Would that be a good way she and Kenneth could be introduced then if you think she could help you enough?" I asked.

"Aye, it would and she could live with us if Joe agreed. Would 6d per week be enough then?" I asked. "That's plenty for a young lass, who has never had money and that would include her room and food then too darling?" she asked.

"Okay, you are the lady of the house and you already manage the wash lady. You will have to train any house staff we get, love. I've got too much to do already," I said.

"Don't forget to write it in the wee pay book," I said as I left to work.

I also wanted to see how Kenneth was doing and so far, he was doing well and putting on weight. He was helping Ma with the beef that was delivered and she explained how we all had to preserve food for the coming winter. It was predicted to be a bad one. I told him about Amelia, who I wanted to introduce to him to see if he thought she could be helpful in pricing his work and dealing with his takings on the opening night. He looked relieved that he would have help and just agreed, without needing to meet her.

"Just send her down this afternoon if she has a break when I'll be in the Art Gallery," he said.

"I wanted to ask you too if you would be interested in a small stone house like this one, built just for you on my top property? If so, we can all start building it before it starts snowing," I asked

"Oh Malcolm," he said rather emotionally. "That would be so nice of you," Kenneth replied.

The team of us building his house were all experienced, including Bruce and Duncan and built it within the month, just before it got very cold but raining just the same. It had three chimneys for the added bedroom. Ma was sad to see her son move out but helped him set it all up giving back his bedding and planting flowers.

"Ma, they'll die when it starts snowing," I said but she planted them anyway.

46. The Bandits Return to Cannich

Amelia moved in, one week later after an unusually long dialogue with her Father wanting to know the real reason for choosing Amelia and he managed to get to know that Kenneth was at the heart of it. He didn't think Amelia capable of caring for an alcoholic if a relationship developed and his issue was having to give up the drink then himself, especially on the fishing boat. But he reluctantly agreed. When she finally did arrive, she was shyer than I had expected. She'd call me Master and curtsy and worked hard to help Cherry and the bairns. She was as pretty as a picture, so I had to protect two pretty women then and ordered those pole lights for the side gate and the gate between both properties. I had iron bars installed about the place and wall held torches too, so I could see any trouble coming. When I was at the Trading Post buying up the poles and the whale oil, I met Hugh Mohr.

"You missed all the fuss at Craskie last night," he said. "Those Irish bandits came back, returned from the colonies and were out for revenge wanting to kill my wife, who was already dead much to their disappointment, so they were stealing my horse as well as Hugh Og's and blow me if they weren't trying to steal the whole Clydesdale team too, so I blew his head right off and took them all bound and gagged with Hamish and Hugh Og up to Fort William with Grigor, whose house they was prowlin' 'round in. They admitted to looking for Isobel, but just stole Grigor's brooches, much to his horror. I said to that Captain up there, that he was going to shoot me, so I shot him in self-defence. They'll be hung this morning at Fort William, as a second offence, especially for horse thieving here in these parts," he said.

"Well done, Hugh," I said feeling queasy. I wouldn't have been any good if I'd lived in his era.

"I need a recommendation for security at mine and Alex's places. Can you recommend someone?" I asked.

"I can. You have young Duncan MacDonnell there, don't you? His Father and Grandfather all have the same name. His

Father runs the farm there at Glengarry, while his Grandfather shoots anything that moves when he's bored. Duncan, the docile groomsman you have, didn't much like his family and moved away from the violence, but that being said, his Grandfather is a brilliant marksman. Better than me even. Duncan MacDonnell that we knew back in the day, was a man to be feared by the English for sure, so we kept in touch often. Now I recommend him because his son doesn't need him at home now and if he gets bored, he might kill an innocent person. He needs his self-esteem restored is all, so if you and Alex meet him and ask young Duncan if he would be happy if his Grandda was there, he could patrol all three properties without being seen, as well as ensure the 'no booze rule' applied," he answered.

"When's opening night then?" Hugh asked.

"First November 6pm," I answered. "Do you need me on the door then?" he asked.

"How much would you charge?" I asked.

"Call it a favour," he replied.

"Then aye, thank you that would be helpful, but it won't be a big do like Aunty Helen's," I said.

"See you there, son," he said and left with his bits and pieces.

47. The Art Gallery Opening, Glengarry

The opening was something to remember and I dressed up for the occasion as did my wife and Morag Freya and Gillcrest, and a whole lot of people I was unfamiliar with, but I did recognise Mr Menzies, who raved about my brother's artwork and bought at least four pieces. The turnout was a lot bigger than we expected and we needed every bit of the security and the no booze patrol. Kenneth was shocked at the turnout, so it was lucky the wee lassie was there to give him confidence. I sat with him too for a time to give him a break.

"I didn't think anyone would come, let alone buy one of my paintings," he said. I thought he was starting to quiver a bit, so

I gave close-up time warnings a half hour earlier than planned. Amelia was indeed a wonder with her numbers and it was all counted up with Hamish standing over her once all the people had left, as well as their horses and carriages. It was one of those special events that no-one wanted to miss, not even Uncle Patrick, who bought a painting of Loch Insh. James smiled at me with that knowing look. I left the money with Hamish, Hugh Og and Amelia, who were going to bank it in the morning in Invermoriston. Morag-Freya offered to do that given it was so much with her dressed in her nurse's uniform. The total sum was five thousand pounds, which my brother was so happy with. He gifted me with a painting of myself in Loch Insh when I was about sixteen. I loved it. Aunty Helen didn't even come.

I walked Kenneth home to his new home but was worried about him being alone after all the fuss of the evening, so I suggested he sleep in our home for that night until he gets used to the idea of being alone in his wee cottage. Cherry wasn't going to argue, she felt too nauseous. Amelia made up the guest room and lit his fire and put the grate in front in case of sparks. She also put the bed warmer in his bed, a water jug beside his bed, wash water and a chamber pot to pee in. She even put out night clothes with underwear for him and said goodnight, Master. She even called Kenneth 'Master' until he stopped her and said, "Please call me Kenneth."

"Alright Kenneth," she said. "I am Amelia, Joe's daughter," she said.

"Thank you, Amelia, for your work on the takings. I'll pay you some when I get access to it," he said.

"Kenneth, before you sleep the worry now was security because the Irish bandits had returned to kill Granny but she was already dead, so Hugh Mohr shot one of them stealing all the Craskie horses, so now we have high security too. If you see an older man who looks like Duncan, but older with a long rifle and prowling around, don't worry he has been hired by both our farms. You can call him Mr MacDonnell and give him coffee if you see him and introduce yourself, so he knows you are family," I said.

Then Kenneth dozed off to sleep, exhausted. Amelia adjusted the fire to be safer and closed his door saying, "Goodnight, Mr Kenneth."

Once again, I took a trip to the Frasers Trading Store for some heavy paint recommended to use on all the buildings in preparation for the snows. I bought several huge drums, which cost too much, so I queried the cost when I was asked for my name. The staff looked me up and apologised and it was all free.

"Why?" I asked.

"A discount would be fine," I said.

"Boss's orders. See, its written here up to the amount of five hundred pounds Scots with an apology for non-attendance at the Art Gallery opening because your cousin Beth was having her second child," he said.

"Then I'll get more drums, as well as whale oil too please," I asked. "Those lights sure use a lot of oil," I said.

"They do, but you need it. You heard about the bandits coming back attempting to kill poor old Isobel if she had been alive, did you? Glad they hung the bastards," he said.

"Aye, I heard from Hugh Mohr," I responded.

"There's also a message here for you Malcolm from Hugh Og Chisholm, asking if he can keep the Clydesdales at your place because there is one bandit still on the loose," he said.

"Is there?" I replied. "Leave a message telling him he can bring them to my place anytime. We have Duncan MacDonnell senior as the security there now. Old bloke with a marksman history," I said.

"I know his history. No one will go near you once that's known. Better marksman than Hugh Mohr apparently," he said.

I arrived home proudly carrying huge drums of white paint to protect our buildings from the expected snow, as well as paint brushes. I had one tin for Ma and Bruce who were in my kitchen, as I walked in calling out to my beloved. She was lying down on the couch and I immediately panicked dropping my paint brushes.

"Are ye alright lass?" I asked.

"It's nothing darling, just the excessive vomiting. When I couldn't keep my breakfast down, Amelia ran to get Ma and Bruce," she answered.

"Where's Kenneth?" I asked.

"He's alright son, he's fussing over his new house. I think he likes it," Ma said pleased with that.

"I'll just give him the paint and brushes then Cherry. I'll be right back," I said. I found Kenneth rearranging his things and hanging paintings on his walls. "Brother," I called.

"Och Malcolm, I love you so much, thank you for this. On my life, thank you," and he held me tighter than ever before, which I reciprocated.

"You are my only family, other than Ma and Cherry and now my bairns, so you mean the world to me Kenneth. Anyway, I got you this for the outside before it snows," I said.

"How much?" he asked. "Nothing thanks to the Frasers not coming last night because Beth went into labour. Can't say I'd ever miss Beth, but Simon's okay. Bit effeminate, but decent. So, thanks to you we got free brushes and paint and whale oil for the lights. I'll show you how to use the lights later," I said. "By the way there's a tradesman coming today to put bars on your windows because there's one bandit on the loose, but because of the risk of fire, I have ordered the type of bars you can open from the inside and white in colour to match the paint, but if you don't like them, we can exchange them. I think you will like them. They have that twisted iron look to be prettier than the bars of a prison," I said laughing.

"Don't worry if you see Hugh Og coming today with his Clydesdales. He's going to keep them here a while. By the way, before I go back to Cherry, do you want to come fishing with our fishing group, Joe, Murdoch, Hamish and Hugh Og tomorrow evening? I have to ask them first because we are a fisherman group, but it should be okay. You'll have to wear those tough pants I got you and sandals and a woolly, with a raincoat and we all ride to Loch Ness to the boat that we all bought. I'll loan you one of our horses," I said.

"I'm no good at fishing Malcolm, but I'd like to come if they don't mind. Is Joe Amelia's Father?" he asked.

"Joseph MacFie, yes, the Father of Amelia MacFie from the Isles originally. His family rents one of Ma's houses on New Farm," I replied.

"Ma's houses?" he asked.

"I forgot to tell you because you were sick, but Ma inherited New Farm, so she owns two of those houses there now rented by Joe and Murdoch's families. Helen pays Ma for grazing her coos on that land with all that meat you saw at Ma's place. Three coos per week slaughtered, butchered, skinned with the hide tanned. Ma then preserves it in barrels that I bought her for this winter coming for Alex's house, Ma's house and our house and any leftover goes to the staff house. You'll eat ours," I explained.

"Now I'd better go. Do you want to come in for dinner? I am hungry," I said anxious to see my wife. When I walked back into the house, we had more visitors and Amelia was cooking up a big lunch for everyone and I could smell cake too. My poor Cherry was asleep looking heavy with child with dark rings under her eyes.

I gave Ma and Bruce their paint and brushes and greeted Matilda and Alex. The Menzies family had left with their paintings and Alex had bought the portrait of his wife Matilda, his front gate and his beautiful forest. He was proud of his wife's and Kenneth's achievements and had hung them on his walls that morning. He was so pleased to see Kenneth, who was still shy with Alex and Matilda, so even when Alex raved about the lovely work, Kenneth barely responded.

"He is a humble achiever," I explained. "Can you all stay to dinner?" I asked. Ma, Bruce, Alex, Kenneth, Cherry had a lovely dinner cooked by Amelia, so I asked her to sit with us all as family. Then we heard stories of the Island where she was from.

"No dance from me today," said Cherry, "but I have taught Amelia Irish dancing," she said. "Can you play the pipes yet Matilda?" I asked. Shyly she answered,

"A little bit. I know one about your Grandda's Seven Glenmoriston Men that has an Irish dance, once we have all finished dinner," she answered a bit coyly. "I've been practising," she said. "Murdoch taught me lots of things," she said. So, no sooner had we finished eating, she washed her hands and sat in a chair with the pipes that she just happened to have with her.

"Amelia, are you going to do the Irish dance?" I asked.

"Yes Sir," she replied.

"Please call me Malcolm and stop bowing and curtsying. No one should be curtsied to," I said.

"Yes Sir," she said. It was going to take a while to kick that habit. But dance she could.

Matilda did well to play an Irish sounding tune and it was enjoyable to listen to, as Alex clapped and smiled from ear to ear. I wondered if Padruig Dubh was aware there was a song being played about him in my house, as well as a dance. Then Kenneth tried to do the Irish dance too and it was so hilarious with his long legs going everywhere. He really can't dance, but he tried hard and she took his hand to show him the steps and I looked across at my wife, eyebrows raised and she was smiling and very pleased with her choice of partner for her brother-in-law. I might have been wrong, but I think they liked each other. I was glad he was sleeping in his own house tonight, in case people talked and we lost the home help if Joe became wary of a randy Loch Insh lad. And knowing him, when he was in Loch Insh, she would definitely need to keep her bottom a long way from him. Just as I was thinking that the tune came to an end and excitedly, he smacked her on the bottom.

"That's a nice thing from a Loch Insh boy Amelia, it means that they like girls not boys," said my wife covering it up quickly.

"Oh," she said and was smiling. I think she liked her bottom being smacked and looked all lovingly at him as a desired lovely young lady. 'Oh dear, I hope he does like her and hand fast soon in case they end up in bed together with Joe enraged with me,' I was thinking.

"Well family, this has been a real treat and a great meal Amelia, thank you. We have to go now with our paint so I can get started on that. You do keep us busy Malcolm. Duncan MacDonnell senior came to be paid today, Malcolm, so are we going halves?" Alex asked.

"Aye, how much did he charge for last night?" I asked.

"Fifty pence for one night, but if we employ him for seven days it's cheaper. I think we should take him on, do you?" he asked

"Aye I do, but there's still one bandit on the loose, so you may also need bars on your windows. Never let Matilda go out alone at the moment, no offence Matilda, until he is caught. You too Cherry and Amelia. He is dangerous. The others have already been hung, but they did go there to kill Grandma not knowing she had already passed, so the one on the loose is after both families on Craskie and Glengarry, so I want to keep the security fella. I'll pay you half what you paid him today, but are you seeing him again or do you want me to talk to his Grandson?" I asked.

"What Grandson?" Alex asked.

"Duncan, the groom. They all have the same name as does Duncan's Father," I answered.

"Well, I'll leave it all to you, I think. Security is more your thing. Is that okay?" he asked. "Okay, but you will still need to buy your own bars. I have a tradesman coming for Kenneth's house today. His house first because he is on his own, then Ma and Bruce, then us, then you, then the Art Gallery, then the old farmhouse for the staff. Do you agree?" I asked. "Each family will have to pay for their own bars, but I'll pay for my farmhouse and the Art Gallery," I said.

"Nae Malcolm. I'll pay for the Art Gallery and my house because I have the money now," said Kenneth.

"Well okay Kenneth. That's nice of you and it would be a good idea to keep a wooden bat behind your doors, if not a gun somewhere," I added.

"Not a gun please Alex," asked Matilda.

"Okay darling, security it is. I see you have pole lights too Malcolm," Alex observed.

"Aye, need more light. They do like the dark, these bad guys," And they left happily taking the pipes with them. I overheard him tell Matilda not to go out alone and keep the house locked up. Alex was worried.

48. The Fishing Trip with Kenneth

Asking Joe about Kenneth joining us to go fishing was a bit surprising. He seemed to think it unfair if he hadn't paid into our boat and also, he grumbled then about being unable to drink on the boat. He saw that I was a bit hurt, which I was and felt bad, but he ultimately agreed.

"I can give up the drink," he said unconvincingly. "Me and Bear should give it up anyway," he added. We all rode our horses to the boat and Kenneth was excited.

"Can you swim?" Murdoch asked. "Aye, best in Loch Insh, but don't know anything about boats," Kenneth replied.

"Murdoch, I don't think we should stay out long tonight because the weather is changing and the loch can whip up suddenly with bad weather," I said.

"Now who's the authority on Loch Ness, eh?" said Joe sarcastically. Both Hamish and Hugh Og agreed, but the other two Islander men were stubborn and wanted to go deep into the middle of the Loch.

"Luckily we can all swim, too bad about you two when that storm hits us then," Hugh Og said in jest.

"That's not funny young fella," said Joe and stood up causing the boat to almost go over but taking in water on one side.

"Sit down you idiot!" yelled Murdoch.

"This is far enough Hamish, I think, I don't have a death wish. If the weather was better, I'd love to go further, but not tonight," I said and both Hamish and Hugh Og agreed, so we put out lines and caught a heap of fish right away.

Kenneth screamed blue murder at whatever he had on his hook.

"It won't stop running away, I can't bring it in, it's too bloody big and strong. What is it, Malcolm?" he yelled.

"Suppose you wee loch people think it's the Loch Ness monster," said Joe sarcastically.

"Feel free to take over Joseph," he said and handed it to Joe, who was sure it was no more than a big catfish. Taking the line, he was almost pulled overboard and then Kenneth laughed at him.

"Believe me now old man?" Kenneth said. Then I knew this was no ordinary fish.

"Hamish," I asked. "What is that?"

His reply was to cut the line now before it dragged us out along the River Ness then out to sea.

"No!" said the now belligerent fisherman, determined to catch the monster at the end of the line. As the storm began to build over the loch, the wee boat was being towed towards the River Ness.

"Joe, please cut the line," I asked as well as Hugh Og and the now anxious Kenneth seeing how far the shore was away. Once again, his reply was like from a fictional book story about a whale where the men end up eating each other, so I took my knife and leaned over his shoulder and cut it.

"Turn the boat around!" yelled Hamish, as we rowed like mad to get back to the shoreline, as the thunder roared and lightning bolts hit the surface of the loch. The black sky was menacing, but we made it thanks to Hamish and Hugh Og's incredible strength. I was rowing like a madman too, as was Kenneth and Murdoch, but Joe sat silently embarrassed.

We pulled up our boat and tied it to the boat shed and ran to the horses worrying that they may have bolted, but they were still there, only just. They were very anxious to get out of the storm when a mysterious landowner came down the slope ushering us to his shelter, under his home.

"I was watching you all. Didn't think you'd make it. Hope you caught some fish for that stressful trip," he said. We had all forgotten the fish, so I ran down and picked them all up. Luckily, there was enough for all of us.

"Thank you for giving us shelter," Hamish said and the man just seemed to disappear. It was dark, so we put it down to the dark or one of the many mysteries of Loch Ness.

"So," said Kenneth to Joe. "We are wee loch people, are we? Do you mind explaining what that means when you don't even come from a loch? Do you think an Islander is better than a person from Loch Insh is that it?" he pressed.

"Aye, Joe, what is a wee loch person?" I asked. "You don't even come from Loch Ness, being what I suppose you call the big loch. Only Hamish and Hugh Og are experts on all these lochs, so who are you judging?" I added.

Suddenly, Joe clocked me one and my nose was sore again. Hopefully not broken again, but it wasn't good. Then Kenneth hit him back in my defence. Kenneth was definitely getting back to how he used to be in Loch Insh.

"You little shite. You fancy my daughter Amelia, I know you dirty little prick," he said rather rudely to Kenneth.

"Aye, I fancy her, so what? At least I'm not up someone's bum, like someone I could name," he replied.

"You have to ask my permission to see her," he screamed above the raging storm. Hamish was shaking his head. How could he not see her when she was working both for him and for me?

"Okay Joseph, can I see your daughter Amelia and hand fast?" Kenneth said boldly and I was proud of him.

"Nae, ye can't and she's coming back home wi' me tonight and she's not working at Malcolm's house anymore," he stated.

"Why?" I asked. "They haven't done anything wrong. And look how you pushed me and Cherry together. Why was that okay and not my brother?" I asked. Hugh Og grunted to Murdoch to stop the argument.

"You're not Cherry's real Father. Is that the difference? You just wanted to offload Cherry, was that why?" I demanded to know.

"One reason was we needed to find her a good husband, aye, but my daughter is only fifteen. She doesn't need to marry yet. My wife needs her to look after the younger ones, while she cooks and cleans," he said vehemently.

"So, if my brother asked you in one year's time, would the answer be different or are you the alcoholic that no one knows about and you can't keep your alcohol away from my brother because you're the actual addict?" I asked. Then I got hit again, this time by Murdoch and it made me lose my balance. I fell onto a bloody rock and I nearly knocked myself out.

"Kenneth," I said, "Best get me to the Doctor's," I asked and Hamish lifted me up like a wee child and put me on my horse and rode with me holding onto me as tight as ever with Kenneth following, leading Hamish's horse. Hugh Og followed us both with the fish that were ours and left the angry Islanders to their fate. I couldn't have ridden by myself, as I felt I was going in and out of consciousness.

Thank God for Hamish.

49. *The Sarcastic Doctor*

We arrived at the Doctor's and of course the sarcastic prick said,

"You again. More facial injuries and your brother too. Looks like you have a concussion lad, lie down." I felt sick, so I vomited on the doctor and into some bucket, then I lay down. Jean was there.

"Hello Malcolm, hello Kenneth. What happened tonight?" she asked.

"What's a wee loch person?" I asked, then I felt the doctor rearranging my nose and putting a cast on it. He examined my head and said he was worried about that. He stitched up the wound but said I would have to stay in bed either in hospital or at home, so long as I stayed in bed for several days. Hamish said he could take me home, explaining that my wife was ill with her pregnancy.

"Then why don't I pop in to see you both tomorrow?" he said.

"We can't afford you," I answered. Poor Kenneth had a nasty gash needing stitches, but his heart was wounded more than anything. He had been rejected from the family of the lassie he had taken a liking too. Then there was poor Amelia. How will she feel being dragged out of my home at night by her angry Father and the other problem was my wife who needed help herself and now has to help us after losing the help she had? What a disastrous night. But I suppose it could have been worse, if that monster fish was allowed to keep dragging us up the loch. All my planned painting would have to wait. I was as crook as a dog.

Hamish and Hugh Og had been loyal friends. Who else would ride you that far on horseback at night in a storm? The doctor took the fish as payment. Theirs as well as ours. He's such a prick, couldn't even leave us one fish to take home to Cherry. I think my son Alex should study medicine and replace this pommy bastard one day was my plan. I was still wobbly on my feet and Hamish then carried me inside my house with my wife squealing in horror at the sight of me and then Kenneth too, who lay on the other couch, both of us still bleeding.

"Can his Ma come and help them, Cherry? He has to be watched overnight. He has a concussion," said Hamish.

"Was it the storm that caused this trouble? Joe has already been and taken Amelia home. Why? I don't understand. Amelia was so upset," then my wife started to cry.

"I'll go and get Marion," said Hugh Og, "then she can watch over all three of you. The doctor might be coming over tomorrow," he said. "Then both Ma and Bruce were there suddenly in their night wear.

"Ma, take care of Cherry first," I said before I passed out. Hamish and Hugh Og left quietly. I stayed asleep covered in a blanket on one couch while Kenneth stayed asleep on the other one. I briefly saw Ma patting Kenneth's head and I think she was crying, as she wiped his bloodied wound on such a pretty face. He would have a scar now. My fishing idea was a bad one, but it shouldn't have been.

50. *Is Joe an Alcoholic?*

"Is Joe an alcoholic?" I asked in my half sleep to Bruce.

"Aye lad, I always thought so, but it was confirmed when the 'no booze rule' was introduced and I caught him sneaking a bottle of grog onto the property. He begged me not to say anything, but please forgive me Marion. If I had, then our boys would be alright," and he wept into his hands.

"Our boys you say?" Kenneth said. "Oh aye, sorry Kenneth, I didn't mean to offend you, but you feel like my boy is all I mean and I want to do those men an injury and I thought I was past that," Bruce said.

"He will still lose his job Da," I said half asleep. "Can you speak to Alex about it in the morning and let him go? Ma, do you still want them renting your house?" I asked.

"Nae, I don't," she answered. "He can't damage my children's hearts and bodies and almost kill them and still benefit from my lovely wee house. Both him and Murdoch can leave with two weeks' notice. Can you write them their eviction son when you're better?" she asked. "Or should Bruce, do it?"

"Bruce can Ma. I might clock him one for taking poor wee Amelia from Kenneth. They were just starting to love each other. That makes me so sad. I'm sorry brother," I said.

"I'll do it tomorrow with two weeks' notice," said Bruce.

"If Grigor wants to keep Murdoch, then he will have to house him and his family elsewhere. They might want to employ Joe, but it needs to be said by Alex that he is an alcoholic and we are dry farms. So, I'll talk to Alex first to see what he intends to act on," Bruce said.

"Ma, you and Bruce can sleep in the guest room," I said. "Nae son, we have to watch you all night. How about I light the fire in your room now, so you and Cherry can cuddle up and we can both watch over you and we'll drag in the couch, so Kenneth is with us all too. I'll get your spare blankets for us and we might all get some rest. In the morning we'll worry about baths and clothes and the like and get you both fed up well. What makes you sick Cherrypie?" Bruce asked my wife.

"No eggs or fish please Da," she answered following my lead. Suddenly, we were a proper family but I knew Cherry was feeling the loss of her Islander Uncles, knowing now who they really were. They had just wanted to offload her, was what really hurt her. I just hoped she still loved me because I adored her like no one else and it worried me that this pregnancy was taking its toll.

51. Another Scary Dream

I slipped into a deep sleep holding my Cherry around her big belly. This time I dreamed of first seeing the face of Padruig

Dubh looking at me himself, really intensely, like he was alive, then there was a glow or wee light of some kind highlighting the oval portrait of him on the wall at Craskie Farm. Then that same soft light moved to another oval portrait of my Grandma, "Isobel of Glenmoriston," looking severe on that same wall in the lounge room there and I could hear at least two foreign voices, as I saw hands removing the paintings from the wall. Then, as they took Granny's painting, there was a third voice talking about taking the painting of the Clydesdales! I woke up.

Someone was in Grigor's house and I couldn't go there.

"Bruce," I called. "Wake up now! Someone's stealing the paintings of our Grandparents inside the Craskie home. At least three men. Please get our security man Duncan MacDonnell, not the wee groom Duncan, by banging the bell outside that I have set up for this need to locate him wherever he is. Tell him this is an emergency and to go now on a fast horse to Craskie Farm to tell Hugh Mohr and Hamish that possibly three thieves are inside the main house stealing the paintings," I insisted.

Knowing my reputation by now for the dreams, he did as I asked and banged the bell like mad over and over until old Duncan came. "What is it?" he asked really concerned. Bruce passed on all that I had said including taking a gun, but I had forgotten saying that. Apparently, I was saying "take a long rifle, take a long rifle and a bat, they'll need Hugh Og too," before I slipped back into unconsciousness.

Over breakfast the following morning, I had forgotten the whole thing until Bruce reminded me. I was wondering why he was staring at me, but I thought maybe I wasn't looking well. "Son," he started, "Do you remember last night?" he asked. All the family were quiet including Kenneth, leaving it all up to Bruce, while Ma looked on compassionately.

"You did well son, setting up the security system, so Duncan Mohr MacDonnell came to the loud sound of the bell," he said.

"Why? What happened? Is everyone alright?" I asked. He decided to be clear and honest, while no one interrupted.

"Aye, we are alright here in Glengarry, so is Alex's family, so don't worry about us. You had one of those revealing dreams last night and asked me to get Duncan Mohr to gallop as fast as he could to Craskie Farm, as there was a robbery taking place inside Grigor's house. Three more Irish bandits were trying to steal the paintings of both of your Grandparents, which you saw in your dream and it was actually happening," Bruce said calmly and patiently.

"Hugh Mohr was told and he didn't doubt the message when he was told that it was your dream, son. He asked Hamish, Hugh Og and Duncan Mohr to assist. You said they'd need Hugh Og, but Hugh, not being a killer, was just armed with a bat. So, when one of the thieves came running out of the front door, he hit him on the head, but it didn't kill the Irish thief who was armed with a gun and aimed it at poor Hugh Og, so Hugh Mohr shot his head right off too, as well as the one of the others and Duncan shot the other one, but because it was on Craskie they're saying it was Hamish. Must be an insurance thing. They needed Hugh Og to move the bodies and Meredith to clean up the blood.

All three were shot dead by marksmen, Malcolm. Well, done son. I'm so proud of you. They could have killed both Grigor and Helen and stolen those valuable items. They even had a wall clock in their box with the paintings. Grigor told me too that they found a letter behind Padruig's painting. It was from Isobel when she thought she'd live a while longer with Hugh. But that's up to Grigor or Hugh to discuss with you," he explained.

"Anyway, they took the three bodies up to Fort William, but Duncan came back here to tell me what had happened and to thank you. It's all good, no charges against the staff at Craskie for defending themselves. He's billing Craskie for last night's work," he said.

"The soldiers were all very shocked because there was only one bandit supposedly on the loose, but there were three. No wonder you had us security minded son. These men were killers, as well as thieves," Da said.

"Did Hugh Mohr, Hamish or Duncan get shot?" I asked.

"Hamish was winged in the upper arm, but has been seen by the Doctor, who has given him a clean bill of health, so long as he doesn't move that arm for a while. He's on holiday pay now, Grigor told Duncan. He won't mind the rest and said he wanted to sort out the boat arrangement you currently have. I think that means he might suggest that you all buy the uncles out. If you include Kenneth, there will be enough money and if you needed one more, I could always join you all to help, then I guarantee there will be no fights on the boat or on shore," Bruce said smiling.

Then I remembered the previous evening on the loch.

"That might be a nice idea and it was obvious that it was no longer going to work with Joe and Murdoch. Cherry, darling, would you mind if we bought out your Uncles?" I asked.

"Nae, husband, you could have been killed last night and that's hard to reconcile. On top of that, they didn't really love me like I thought they did. Then there's the families needing money to move with, so they might need it in order to get accommodated before the snows. I think with his pride the way it is, that they might move to one of the Colonies like New Holland. Britain has lost Virginia and the Carolinas, so it has reduced the places they can now go to. I just wish he had left Amelia for hers and my sakes. I'm not doing so well this time husband. Maybe we can't have any more bairns after this," she said sadly, but truthfully. "I am proud of you for helping the family last night, my darling. Maybe we can all go to the 'gathering of the bairns' this Saturday. We haven't been in a long while, so it would be better to be more familiar with everyone. What do you think?" she said.

"Aye darling, if Kenneth, Bruce and Ma come too. Hugh Mohr wanted to talk to me weeks ago now, so maybe it will give me the chance to ask what that was about," I answered.

52. Bruce and Ma Move In

"Malcolm, I talked to your Mither and we want to move in here to help you and Kenneth while you're unwell and do your hard chores and help poor Cherry with her pregnancy. It'll take the two of us to achieve that and you have the extra rooms. Your Mither said she'd do all the cleaning and most of the cooking. We can just bring our bedding and clothing up here and redirect where the meat is delivered. Do you all agree? It'll mean Kenneth stays inside here, while he is unwell. I'm worried about this winter, lad and I want to get your stores of peat higher as well. Can we get a tradesman to do the painting now? You have the money to pay someone, as well as the window bars and it's all done. I know a friend who can do the painting and can arrange it today. Is that okay?" he said.

"Yes, Da, you both can, but as you know I have been Ma's factor. If Ma agrees it may be time to hand over to you to manage, which I ask you now for understanding and forgiveness," I said.

"Do you mean you have hidden your Ma's wealth? I wouldn't have respected you Malcolm if you hadn't, but you have my complete respect, understanding and forgiveness even though it is not needed, but yes if you both wish it. You are my son now, even if you feel otherwise. I love you boys," he answered with tears in his eyes.

"I have seen too much death, sickness, murder and war, so now all I want is to care for you all as best as I can in peace. I value your honesty Malcolm and Kenneth. You are both good lads," he said.

"Can your Ma now take my name Malcolm, Kenneth?" he asked. "We would both approve, but not if Ma doesn't want to depart from her first married name," I said. It was then that Kenneth asked to be excused and he would be right back, but

Bruce went with him to his wee house just a short distance from the main house. When they returned, the mystery was revealed. It was a beautiful painting of our Father fishing on the ice in Loch Insh. Grandda had painted it many years ago and it perfectly captured our Father's heart and physical appearance.

"Can we hang our Father on the wall, so he will always be in our permanent memory? I can hardly remember him now and that makes me sad," Kenneth said.

"Of course, Kenneth. Cherry, can you make a frame for this and I'll hang it. I love it," I said and I hugged my brother.

"I'm happy to stay in the house until I'm all good, Ma" he said. I'd really appreciate your help Ma," said Cherry.

My Ma was so pleased to be called Ma for the first time by Cherry that she held her tightly. It was all a bit emotional for me, so I asked to be excused and bathe, then get properly dressed in case Alex came over unexpectedly. Ma had already prepared it, God bless her, but insisted on helping me in case I was dizzy.

"Nae Ma. Get Bruce. I'm a man now. You can't see my manhood," I said.

"Don't be silly son. I'm your Mither. Lie down in the tub and I'll wash your hair. It smells like fish," she said. She washed my hair despite my protestations and soaped me up, but as she got closer to my privates, I insisted.

"Nae Ma!" I shouted.

"Need help darling?" I heard Bruce calling through the door.

"Och aye, Malcolm's a wee bit shy, so it looks like we need you to wash the rest of him." Blood started trickling down my neck and Bruce wiped it away quickly.

"Now son, it won't take long. Ye were on the boat with fish, so you want to smell good for Cherry or she'll vomit," then he laughed. My arms were weak so I couldn't even stop him if I wanted to, as he washed all my privates.

"Sorry son, you'll be better soon and I won't have to wash your balls," he said smiling.

"You had better not tell anyone you've washed my balls or you're done for Bruce," I said. Then he washed my legs and my filthy feet, as he called them. Helping me out of the hot bath, I really needed help to sit down on a chair, while Bruce rubbed me dry when Ma walked in again when my privates were exposed again.

"This is not okay Mither," she ignored me and helped Bruce rub me dry.

"You're a well-developed young man now, Malcolm. I don't blame you for hiding it away. Yours is like your Father's," she said.

"Ma, stop it!" I said. "You can't peek at my manhood." Then I heard Cherry. "Cherry help me," I asked.

"I can't darling, please let them. I have to lie down now. Come and join me," she said.

"This is harder than bathing wee bairns for sure," said Ma.

"Kenneth is next but the water is too filthy, Bruce. I've got water cooking, Bruce, if you can tip this water out," Ma said.

Ma was a very clean person and would have everyone lined up for a wash if she had her way. I heard similar protestations from Kenneth, but at least he had been handled a bit in the hospital, but it was his manhood too that he didn't want Ma to see, but she did and she even rubbed the area dry. "Nae Ma!" I heard him yelling. So, I guessed that was his balls. Bruce had to help her with Kenneth too, whom she accused smelled of fish. When it was all over, I was exhausted and couldn't dress myself. So, my modesty was out the window with Bruce pulling on my trousers and a clean shirt, then helped me lie down with Cherry for a while.

Luckily, Duncan Og and the student, whose name was lost to the ether, were doing the hard yards around the farm and nearly all of the potato crop was brought into storage and the winter oats crop went in by some miracle. The summer crop was due to harvest the next day. Several coos birthed wee calves and the new building for their warmth was doing well, it was reported. The tradesman came and installed Kenneth's decorative window bars and he liked them. The painting team consisted of three men, who started on the old farm first. Ma's house to be exact and the dividing fence between us and Uncle Alex, then Kenneth's Art Studio and the old farmhouse as well as the goat shed. It was looking like a whole new place and bit by bit, I was becoming healthier and the dizziness had passed, but I still had headaches from time to time. Bars were then installed into Ma's house the same as Kenneth's, as well as the Art Studio. Kenneth had huge bolts and locks put on that building too. The painters painted any surface that needed it then moved to the main "Cherry Farm" and painted the coo housing shed, then the huge stables, then Kenneth's house and any wooden fencing in between. Last was ours, which we were lucky to achieve on time before the weather became intolerable.

The team of three men painted each surface at least twice because there was so much paint, then when they were doing the lower level of my house, the weather was obviously going to be too hard to work with and the paint wouldn't dry unless they hurried, which they did when Bruce joined in to help them to ensure every tiny surface was covered. God Bless them. They earned their money and said it needed doing again next year, but to call on them earlier next time then three coats could go on. I paid them, Kenneth gave me his contribution for his house and Bruce for his.

More meat had been arriving each week keeping Ma busy then delivering it to the different houses. They were almost due to move back to their lovely home when the real winter hit us hard. Thank God we had harvested the oats, the neeps, the potatoes, the kale, the corn and well prepared the stables and the cattle sheds. We were the envy of our neighbours who could not grow the crops on their land, like we could. My numbers of coos were growing, so we were going to have to drove to a winter shieling in about a month. All of Cherry's goats were giving a lot of milk and while Cherry was too heavy with child, Matilda offered to milk them and bring them in each day. We had cheese and butter from that milk. Ma said she could also take over the goats once back in her own home.

My house had never been cleaner with Ma there. I think she cleaned back to old MacDonnell dirt. Poor Cherry felt a bit incapable, but she learned cleaning skills from Ma as well as new recipes. I was getting tired of bland Island food, but she hadn't known how to cook anything different, until Ma lived with us. Ma's food was always tasty because of the onions and the garlic and the tomatoes and all of her hundreds of herbs from her herb garden. She taught Cherry about them too and planted a new herb garden under cover near our house and Kenneth's, so we could both use them. It was a warm spot that always had sunlight when there was any.

Kenneth's face now only had a wee scar and he was painting again in his house. He moved out, but more often than not, he would still sleep in our house, so there was a room permanently set up for my brother Kenneth, who had recovered from losing Amelia. The Uncles and their families did all go to New Holland where there were free land holdings and both Joseph and Murdoch grew sheep. He was an alcoholic but stayed that way because there were a lot like himself in the Colony of New South Wales. We bought him and Murdoch out of the boat and the harmonious team was then Hamish, Hugh Og, myself, Kenneth and Bruce. We all helped each other out and respected each other's decisions and shared the fish at the end of an evening. We didn't speak again of the strange man who appeared and took us to shelter, then disappeared or the things that Joe said to both of us.

We did, however, still speak of the asshole Doctor, who my cousin Jean was thinking of divorcing. She'd had enough of his rough and unkind words to sick and vulnerable people and so it was before the courts. Her grounds for annulment were weak, so she was going for the big one, divorce without having had an affair and it was going to be hard to achieve. I noticed she was quite keen on my brother, but he didn't notice her attentions. Maybe he didn't think she was sexy enough. I was going to ask him about that to ensure she didn't use him to obtain that divorce. I also spoke to Alex and Ma about it to protect him from being caught up in her legal proceedings. After all, she would have to name someone if adultery was her way out. I insisted that Kenneth could only see Jean romantically after she was divorced.

53. *Chaotic Gathering of the Bairns*

The 'gathering of the bairns' that we had planned to go to weeks earlier ended up in another stramash, but this time it was between Ewen and Hugh Mohr and then Grigor joined in about the money he and Helen were owed. Poor Annabel was left trying to get the bairns interested in games, but all Nachtain wanted to do then was fight too like his Father, Ewen. I had rarely been seen at one of these events and at the time I was still recovering from the concussion, so I had decided to sit quietly with my bairns and Cherry, Kenneth, Ma and Bruce. We had become a tight unit. Do you think Helen thanked me for sending my security to her house the night three men had their heads blown off? Nae. 'Ungrateful witch', I thought, but Grigor was eternally grateful as he had been terrified by the dead bodies lying all about him with the stolen goods already packed in a box ready to go.

Apparently, the portrait of Padruig Dubh was splattered with blood. The letter found in his portrait was a letter to Hugh Mohr from his wife Isobel and it was strictly not to be read by anyone. The word on the gossip vine was it was full of lewd love suggestions and how many times they did it here and there and everywhere on the farm, so he could have the memory of her lust for him and it worked. He was back to normal.

Islay and Alex were a bit disturbed by the rough scenes at the gathering, so they didn't want to play in case they were hurt by Nachtain. I approached Annabel about him who said there was nothing she could do about him.

"He is now out of control," she said.

"Can one of the men give him a smack on the behind, better still a strapping?" I said. I was overheard of course by his Mither, who screamed blue murder at me for suggesting the child stop misbehaving. Morag-Freya was there and dragged me away for my own good. His Father was storming towards me. She summoned Hugh Mohr.

"Was there something you wanted to talk to Malcolm about?" she asked.

"Aye, come on young Malcolm. Are you up for a walk? I can't carry you, be warned. My back is not what it used to be," he said smiling. I told Kenneth, so he could come too and left Ma with Cherry, the bairns and Bruce, who looked worried. We walked off before Ewen reached us with his overbearing complaints.

"Someone will do that bloke in one day," I said. "He is an aggressive fellow with no self-control," I commented.

"Oh, and you do?" asked Hugh Mohr.

"I do. More than you, I believe," I said. "But I've got to hand it to you Hugh, that marksmanship of yours and Duncan's is incredible," I said.

"Your Grandmither, Isobel, would have wanted both of you to know about something here on Craskie Farm that is to be kept a secret from all of these morons. Got it?" he asked.

"Aye," I replied.

"Then follow me into the woods and keep respectful and quiet," he said. Before we entered the old forest, he checked that we were not being followed.

"Rule number one lads. Check you are not being followed. I nearly killed your Grandda once, thinking he was an Englishman right over there. Admittedly, he was going to kill both Grigor Mohr as well as Isobel, who had found out days earlier that they were actually brother and sister, so naturally they were affectionate towards each other. He misunderstood and would have killed them both had I not been following Grigor and Isobel myself," he said.

"What was he going to kill them with?" asked Kenneth.

"A dirk. Nasty one too," he added

"I don't own one of those. Where do I buy one?" Kenneth asked.

"I'll get you a nasty one each and a skein dubh," Hugh said.

The forest became mistier and mistier as it became thicker and thicker with an eerie presence. I felt that there was someone that I could speak to there, of the invisible kind.

"Now Malcolm, you understand the unseen world, so don't be surprised by things you feel or see here. Isobel prayed here to her ancestors, but I'll show you where and why, but both of you have to promise to keep this a secret from the rest of the family, but most especially from Museums," he said.

He confidently led us through a forest that he was very familiar with and it felt that they were familiar with him. Following Hugh Mohr gave us all a strange uniting emotion that I couldn't quite put a word to.

"You do look like Padruig Dubh, Malcolm, but you are nothing like him. The odd thing is you are more like my wife, but in a masculine form, like the ghost of Padruig and Isobel combined. These dreams you have, might not ever stop now you've come here to Craskie, but for your sake I hope they do. It can't be easy seeing the things you see. For me it's easier to deal with a killer, I just kill him. Easy. But you, what can I say? I haven't met anyone like you. I suppose Kenneth is used to you, are you?" he asked.

"It began in Loch Insh, but it was never blood and guts, was it Kenneth? Sometimes, I would just tell Kenneth where there was a rabbit he could paint, so we would run off to find it and he would paint it. Remember Kenneth?" I asked.

"Aye, that was normal for us," he responded. "Hmmm," was all I recall hearing then we went on further and stopped.

"Why have we stopped?" I asked.

"This," Hugh said.

"There it was. The Pict stone that I had seen in one of the dreams," I said.

"Aye. Isobel would sit there and pray or talk to them," Hugh Mohr said. "Did you want to pray here near the stone?" he asked. "I'll sit with you both for a while, then when you have finished, we will leave. Okay?" Hugh said.

We agreed and tried to do what Granny did. We brothers sat together then Hugh with us and we waited. Then the mist rolled over and over like waves on the ocean without the wetness. The mist formed into separate parts, then I felt the urge to talk to whatever it was.

"Are you our Pict relatives?" I asked. Surprisingly, the mists in many forms seemed to move about like people do when they laugh. Kenneth then laughed too, spontaneously and he really enjoyed their company and just started talking to them, as did I. It made me tired, but relaxed and my headache had gone.

"If you see Granny, please tell her I'm sorry we had to move her legs to put the wee casket back containing Hugh's gold?" I asked. Hugh looked at me shocked, as you would be not knowing how I came by his gold but accepted it. I just wondered if my message would be passed on to Granny.

"Can you please tell Grandda Padruig too not to come right up to my face while I'm sleeping? It scared me half to death," I said. Then I wanted to leave.

"I'm ready to go now Hugh, are you Kenneth?" I said and he was looking bright and happy. Enlivened even. So, we left. Hugh didn't ask me about Granny's legs, for which I was grateful.

The gathering of the bairns was still chaotic, so we arranged to leave. Not much point going to one of those meetings again until Nachtain is given a smack on the bottom. It was nice though seeing my cousins like Morag-Freya and Gillcrest and Aonghus and Annabel, who was a bit lacking in intelligence I thought, but Aonghus loved her, that was obvious. We had almost escaped the gathering when Aonghus came up to me and said how sorry he was about my recent injuries, as well as Kenneth's.

"It could have been worse," I said. "A bloody huge fish of some kind was dragging us out to the River Ness towards the sea in that storm we had. Kenneth hooked it and couldn't hold it, so the rest is history," I added. Deciding not to tell him, as my headache was coming back. "By the way Aonghus, can you ensure that my brother's name doesn't appear in Jean's divorce? He has had no interest or romantic activity with her. He likes her as his cousin even with her peculiar accent, but if they are to see each other romantically, it won't be until she gets that divorce and names someone else if she has to," I said.

54. Meredith Starts Work

"We could do each other favours Malcolm. A friend of mine, Fergus wants to meet you to talk about your Pict ancestry," he said.

"You are welcome at Cherry Farm with your friend, so long as you don't bring any alcohol or come inebriated. We are dry farms in Glengarry. However, I don't know what he thinks I can tell him about the Pict people," I answered recalling Hugh Mohr's words about not telling folk and who was Fergus? "You wouldn't mind if Morag-Freya came with Gillcrest too and maybe Hugh Mohr and his friend Duncan MacDonnell?" I asked even pre-arranging security. Maybe I was taking it too far having sharp shooters at a dinner party. So, I planned to invite Ma and Bruce, Alex and Matilda, and Hamish and Cora and Hugh Og and Meredith.

"By the way do you know if Meredith is happy working with Helen here at Craskie?" I asked. "Are you kidding? She hates it and cleaning up that blood did her in. I think she wants to quit," he said. I saw Hugh Og looking across at me and I waved to talk.

"I'll drop you a line when we can arrange a dinner party Aonghus," I said as I went across to my mate Hugh. I hugged the big brute then asked him if Hamish was alright, when Hamish appeared with a bandage on his arm.

"Thanks for this," he said sarcastically. He hugged me too. All of us glad to see each other alive and well enough. I showed them my head, then Kenneth came and showed them his facial scar.

"Hugh, I have a delicate question for you," I asked.

"Delicate, is it?" he said.

"Might be. Would your wife be interested in working at my house to help Cherry?" I asked. "I'd pay her well and food is included for you both, when you're there and it's up to you if you both move into my house and rent out yours or stay in yours. The horses are still good at mine, if it still suits you and I just need help for Cherry. Ma's moving back into her place soon, so it'll be tough on her and me. She's having twins," I added.

"Well, Meredith hates working here and has wanted to leave for some time, but because of the horses she hasn't moved away. How much will you pay her?" he asked.

"As much as you want. I'm desperate and I know her cooking is good. Aonghus wants a dinner party at mine with someone called Fergus, so hopefully before that night or we'll be eating dried fish," I jested.

"Would you pay her two shillings per week Malcolm?" he asked. "That's more than Craskie," he added.

"Yes, I would. Can she start soon?" I asked. "Aye, one week maybe to give Helen notice," he said. Hamish looked concerned about something and told me to watch out for Fergus.

"He's one of those history buffs, who thinks he knows it all about the Pict people. Granny hardly told him anything. She took it to her grave, so I would follow her lead if you know anything at all," he advised.

"Also, if Helen gets mad, she might just end Meredith's contract, then can she start tomorrow? I can bring her over whichever way it goes. I'd be happier knowing she was safer in your house Malcolm. Grigor slept through those criminals entering his house. He didn't wake up till the guns were being fired," he said.

"There must be an open door or one they have a key to," I said.

"Agnes! She must be back. She's behind this all and we'd have killed her boyfriend Rory," Hamish said.

"Sorry Malcolm, we have to go and pass this on to Hugh Mohr and you tell Duncan that Agnes is back. I'll get my wife to you no worries," he added and they both went searching for Hugh Mohr to tell him about whoever Agnes was. I was filled in on the way home by Ma, who knew the story. But that day I met Agnes sitting in my house soon after arriving home, with my wife wanting home help. My innocent wife was thrilled to think such a nice lassie could start work right away.

"I'm sorry my love, I've already employed someone," I said and I followed her all the way to the gate and waved her away and locked the gate. I sent word down to Matilda too, to warn her about a home help lass named Agnes. Of course, when I walked back into the house Cherry was a wee bit annoyed.

"I've got Meredith for you love. More experience, good cook and Hugh Og's wife," I explained.

"But you told me to employ the house staff Malcolm," she said.

"I did and normally this wouldn't have happened, but you have to know who Agnes is," I said. It was a very long story ending in her being sent to the colonies, losing her child to her husband or boyfriend, an Irishman, and the child was removed from her. That explains why there was revenge on Grandma and their intention to kill her, had she still been alive. Why they wanted their paintings is a mystery.

"Meredith, you say? She is a good cook and a really good cleaner. Sorry Malcolm," she said.

"If Agnes ever comes here again, do not let her in the house and tell her to leave immediately. She is a convict love and Hamish thinks that she's behind all that's been happening. Alex came up to my house very unhappy that a convict had been on our properties and decided he would report it to Fort William and got the whole story from Cherry, who had been taken in by her. He wrote it all down like a statement and asked my pregnant wife to sign it.

"Oh lass," he said sorrowfully, "You were in danger had it not been for your amazing husband. Did she steal anything?" he asked.

"No, I don't think so," she replied.

Thank God Meredith started work the next day as dishes and pots piled high in our kitchen and my wife was much worse.

"Meredith, can I leave you to do what you do and I think I'll take my wife to see the Doctor?" I said.

"There is a Midwife too here in Glengarry, Malcolm, would you prefer that she came? That Doctor is not nice to Scottish women giving birth," she said.

"I would," said Cherry, so she lay back down and I went to the address that Meredith gave me. An older but kindly and strong looking woman answered the door.

"You'd be Malcolm? I wondered when you'd finally get here," she said. There was no time for questions. I was worried the babies might come today. We rode together on my grey mare with her bits and pieces. I passed my horse to Duncan Og, who smiled a lot more lately and I took the old lady inside. Maybe he was no longer ashamed of his blood thirsty Grandfather.

"Are the bairns coming Malcolm?" he asked

"Maybe Duncan lad, maybe," I answered.

"I'll pray for you all," he said. I hadn't taken him for the religious type, but apparently, he was seen praying on a wee rug on the floor at least five times every day and that was the real reason his Papist family didn't want him at home. He didn't swear nor drink either. Perfect really. 'People are funny fish,' went through my mind.

55. *Cherry's in Labour*

Cherry was in labour, so I also sent for Ma to help the Midwife who said we would need Bruce too to hold Cherry up if she birthed them standing. Bruce had delivered all of his eleven children in the Americas and was very knowledgeable and followed the Midwife. Ma had water cooking immediately, working around Meredith.

"Let Hugh Og in and cook up dinner for all of us here if he comes, Meredith," I said.

She was already doing all of that and it was becoming clear that she wouldn't need to be told much at all, thank God. Hugh Og did come and was needed to help in one of the walks around the room while the bairns were crowning but refusing to come out with the midwife carefully attempting to catch them. Meredith placed down a thick doona under my wife for a softer landing and sheets over the couches. 'She has done this before,' I thought. I held Cherry under one arm giving her encouragement, while Bruce held her under the other. When one of us was tired, we swapped to Hugh Og excusing himself. Eventually, the first of the bairns came out like a wee fish slithering into the midwife's arms. She quickly passed her to

Meredith, who had the table pre-prepared for cleaning the wee bairns then wrapping him tightly in a small cotton blanket. She put a wee pink bonnet on his head, so we would know it was a boy then placed him so gently in his cradle that I had made. He had a shock of black hair like mine. Kenneth was too nervous to watch and he said he wanted to cry and Ma had to help him at one time when he looked poorly.

"My sweet Kenneth," she said. "It was just like this when you were born darling and your Da passed out. You are so like him, so sit down dearest or you might pass out," she said. The second wee bairn was slower and the contractions slowed.

The Midwife said, "Now Cherry, when you get your next contraction, push a bit harder so we can birth him or her," She did what the midwife told her to do, while Hugh Og and I were holding her up hoping not to bruise her delicate skin. "My Cherry, you can do it darling. You already have a son and he's so handsome like me with black hair," I said smiling to my wife then the contraction came and she pushed until she was red in the face and thank whatever God that Duncan prayed to, that he was alright. They were identical twin lads.

"You've got identical twins Master," said the Midwife. "Mistress congratulations," she said and asked me to place my wife on the couch to deal with the other matters, like clots and the placenta. "Any preference for the placentas?" she asked. Ma asked if she could plant it under two identical plants near our front door to remember the occasion and Cherry asked to keep a wee piece of the tube. Some Island superstition that she put in a jar and kept in the cupboard with the other two. Kenneth wanted to help in some way, so he dug the holes for the two plants and Ma planted Geraniums surrounded by marigold flowers.

"The Marigolds keep dogs away from the door," she said. "But Ma," I protested, "They will die in this weather," I said.

"Maybe they won't," she said and to this day they are still there, growing prolifically and we have no stray dogs near our front door, not even a friendly one. Meredith cleaned up everything, so you would never know a birthing had ever taken place and both Meredith and the Midwife took Cherry for a medium to warm bath, so as not to increase any bleeding. Cleanliness was all the midwife wanted to achieve, then check for any splits and there weren't any. Then she ordered soft, clean pillows be placed each side of my wife on which she would rest both arms. The twins were then given to Cherry at the same time to suckle on her breasts, while they lay on the pillows covered in another tight blanket so they wouldn't roll off. Ruth explained to her when her milk would come in, but to continue on the clear fluids until then. When I paid the Midwife, I asked her name again.

"Beaton lad. My name is Ruth Beaton. I'll be back to check on all three of them tomorrow morning, around eleven o'clock and if the lads are losing weight, I have a formula you can give them for a few days then I'll come once each week for one month to check things, like both bairn's eyes and hearing and so on. Only if I find a problem do I send families into the hospital. My cost is one shilling for all of that," she said.

I gave the sweet lady five shillings, but she gave it back.

"I do it for God, son," but asked if someone could ride her home and Hugh Og offered.

"Would ye accept me Mistress? My horse is right there awaiting ye," he said.

"Aye lad, that would be fine and thank ye for your kind assistance," she said.

"Kenneth, would you like to hold our first-born twin?" I asked him.

"Oh, aye Malcolm, I just want to cry. Can I name him?" he asked. What could I say. I looked at Cherry and she nodded.

"This is wee Malcolm," he said. Then I caved in crying and even Bruce had to put his arms around me.

"He does look like you son. They both do," Bruce said smiling and I stopped blubbing.

"I wish Hamish was here to see them," I said.

"I'm here. Came a voice from the shadows. I didn't want to get in the way," said Hamish. "Cherry, we should call our other bairn Hamish-Hugh. What do you think? Or Hugh-Hamish," I said jokingly.

"No. Hamish-Hugh MacNachten. That's a fine name. If it had been a girl, I wanted to name her Marion. Sorry Ma," I said.

"There will be other times won't there?" Ma said.

"Nae, I don't think I could do that again," Cherry said. "Then could Ma's name be added to my first son's name so he is Malcolm-Marion?" I asked.

"Why not?" said Bruce. "I like it. Malcolm-Marion MacNachten. Two fine lads," he said. "Now I am hungry." We were all seated to eat when Duncan Mohr arrived asking about Agnes.

"Sit down Duncan, eat with us. We are celebrating the twin's birth. These are my sons Malcolm and Hamish-Hugh. Handsome sons, aren't they?" he said. "Cute wee lads. Well done you two. Now Malcolm, I'll eat and run, but please fill me in about Agnes." I started the story with 'the gathering of the bairns' when I happened to mention that there must be a key that someone has or Grigor had left a door open, when Hamish and Hugh Og both then realised who that could be.[2]

"A servant girl to Isobel for a long time named Agnes fell in love with a fence builder claiming to be Scottish when he was actually Irish, by the name of Rory O'Rourke and over time built up a group of criminals, who were stealing from all the local farms and hiding the stuff in a wee croft. Isobel and Padruig, with guests and family, came across them by accident in the new stables and there was the whole gang in there. Hugh Mohr saved them all from certain death. The gang then were either hung or sent to the colonies. Agnes stayed in a prison hospital until her bairn was born, then the bairn was given up for adoption and Agnes was sent to the Colonies. I think. Her boyfriend was shot dead, the first time the men were raiding Craskie recently and that was when it was realised that the Irish bandits had come back with one missing that turned out to be three, not one. The rest died in the second raid, much to the embarrassment of Fort William, relying on local people to catch the criminals. There is talk of bravery awards for Hugh Mohr Chisholm, Hugh Og Chisholm and Hamish Chisholm but I can't say that I was there, so no awards for you or me I'm afraid Malcolm. And you were the hero of the day. It's only a certificate and well earned by Hamish, who was shot. Anyway, lovely meal thanks to Hugh's wife," he said.

"Meredith," she shouted, which made him smile.

"Now what Clan might you be lass?" he asked.

"MacKenzie," she answered.

"That explains it. Good job lass. Has Malcolm told you about how to reach me when I'm patrolling around all three proper-ties?" he asked.

"Not yet Uncle," she replied respectfully.

"Come here lass," he said. He showed Meredith the bell and showed her to bang it until he comes, if it's really urgent.

"If not too urgent just a few bangs," he said.

"What's not really urgent?" Meredith asked.

"Like you've lost your kitty or your doggy, that kind of thing and you think he has run away," he smiled. Those two were going to get along well, as she smiled back. She admired the old fella. I liked him too. He didn't treat me like a moron. Hugh Og wasn't too impressed though.

"Does he eat here all the time Malcolm?" he asked.

"Nae, first time today because of Agnes," I answered. "But I can't say he won't ever come back in. Is there a problem with your wee wife?" I asked.

"Well, I'll not have men perving on me wife. You know how that is and I sure wouldn't like to fight it out with him, but I would kill him if he touched her," he answered.

"Best you tell Meredith to keep the silver fox at bay then, so you both stay alive. He's no competition for you Hugh. Young, handsome, strong and gorgeous as you are really to any woman, so I wouldn't worry about dry leaves, like poor old Duncan, who kicked his own Grandson out of home because of some religious difference," I said.

"Did he?" Hugh asked.

"Aye, both his son and him. Poor wee Duncan. Such a nice lad. I hope you leave him here. I can pay half his wages or come to some better arrangement for him," I said.

56. *Hugh Og and Meredith in Glengarry*

"What if I rent out my house on New Farm and both Meredith, wee Ferne and I move in here with you as you suggested and we work out all the arrangements? Hamish needs a bigger house with his three bairns and he needs my house. Then I can keep a closer eye on the silver fox and work the Team from here. Grigor just needs to agree, so when I am needed there, I can still be relied on for the ploughing. Lots more farmers are wanting me for the ploughing and even though things are improved with Hugh Mohr, thanks to you miraculously, I am not happy there anymore. It doesn't feel safe now or friendly, like it used to be. Maybe I just miss Isobel? Can you show me what room you had in mind for us here?" said Hugh Og.

"It's on the top floor with a nice view. It's self-sufficient and no one else is up there at the moment. The smaller room next to you could be for wee Ferne, if you like. When Bruce and Ma come here and stay, they sleep on the first floor and Kenneth has his own room on the bottom floor nearest the door, so he can come and go." Hugh was stunned at the space and how lovely it all was.

"Aye, Ma cleaned up here just recently," I said. "Years of dirt," she said. "The outside is looking great too. I can't believe how nice you've made this place," Hugh Og said.

"It's all from God," I said.

57. The Dinner Party

After Meredith also approved the accommodation, they both went back home to pack up their belongings or at least make a start because Meredith was needed early with the Midwife due at eleven o'clock. Over the next few weeks friends and relatives visited to see our new bairns and drop in a wee gift and the twins were both well and gaining weight. James was overjoyed at his new second cousins, who culturally would call him Uncle.

"I'm Uncle James," he said many times and danced around the room and my twins liked their Uncle James. As my wife regained her strength and happiness after the birth of the twins, we began to organise the dinner party mentioned at the gathering by Aonghus with Fergus invited, with a no booze rule applied on each invitation. Duncan Mohr was asked to frisk them all for any hidden booze and that was how that night started. I asked Matilda to assist my wife in writing them out, as her English was better than Cherry's, but I didn't say that to her face.

The guest list was extensive with Alex and Matilda, James and Susan, Bruce and Ma, Aonghus and Annabel, Gillcrest and Morag-Freya, Fergus and wife, Patrick Hamilton and wife, Hamish and Cora, Hugh Og and Meredith, Kenneth and Hugh Mohr, but not Duncan Mohr who was on the original list, which read: "Please find a baby-sitter for any bairns, if possible, because of our new twins. Strictly bring no alcohol in any form. Bring any Celtic musical instruments you feel like playing and enjoy the night. From Cherry and Malcolm MacNachten, Cherry Farms, Glengarry. RSVP....." We added the date when we finally could decide on it working around work rosters as well.

I had to apologise to Meredith that she was both guest, as well as the cook, but Cherry and Ma were going to help. Bruce extended the table and Ma bought me a huge new tablecloth with table napkins.

"So posh," Cherry said. Hugh Og said it needed a candelabra, so when I was down at Frasers, I bought one of those fancy candle holders with red candles with the last of my credit.

"I heard about your wee dinner party," said the worker at Frasers. "John and Anna, Beth and Simon might be put out to not be invited," he said, "I know that Grigor is," he said. I decided a lie was in order.

"I had planned a special night just for the four of them after this particular dinner party full of noise. I wanted to introduce them to my new wee twins, but it wouldn't be as quality a night with so many. Hence, I hope they are not offended, but not forgotten, not at all. A quieter night was what I had planned for them. Please pass it on," I said. 'Why did everyone want to come to our place in snowy weather?' I was wondering. Even I was wearing that thick woollen coat that I bought with James that day in Invermoriston.

The weather was typical Highland Scotland in winter, bloody freezing, so every fire in our house was lit and it was cozy as the evening approached. We had expected bad weather, 'but when was the weather good?' was my reasoning and I just lived with it, as most people did. Then, Cherry said she felt bad about not inviting Duncan Mohr.

"So, do I," I said. "What if we also invite Ruth Beaton, the Midwife and seat them both together? She's younger than him and comes from a long line of respectable medical people and she's attractive in an older woman kind of way," I asked her.

"We can seat Kenneth on her other side to keep conversation going, but I'll have to ask Hugh Og first." He agreed only if Ruth Beaton was coming too and he was happy to pick her up and take her home, if Duncan Mohr wasn't. I wrote out those two invitations and Hugh Og did pick up the Midwife, who was excited at getting an invitation.

Duncan Mohr wore his best kilt with his matching waist coat, like he was going to meet Bonny Prince Charlie himself and everyone else just dressed up warmly for the weather, bringing milk or fruit juice with them. We both met them at the door with the usual kiss on the cheek that Cherry hated. I can't say I liked it either but there you have it, as one by one they came with wee gifts for the twins and admiring them and our home, if they had not yet seen it.

Both Islay and wee Alex took care of all of the gifts. Dinner was ready and Meredith had the menu written out for each guest. Yes, it was posh and Alex was impressed, I could tell, as was Matilda. When Hugh Mohr arrived, he had taken off the usual filthy jacket he was seen with each day and his blonde hair was washed and combed. He had new clothes and new shoes, but the Midwife didn't go home with Duncan. After all, there were three single men there, my brother Kenneth, if she liked them young, Duncan Mohr if she liked them old and Hugh Mohr if you liked them sexy in a gross, old kind of way.

Ruth Beaton went home with Hugh Mohr.

Our evening went well and the multiple musical instruments made for a lovely musical night and even Cherry finally loosened up and sang one of her lilting Island songs in their Gaelic of a particular brand. It sounded more like Erse, I thought. Hugh Mohr brought his bodhran, Matilda brought her uilleann pipes, John Grant's old fiddle had been passed on to Morag-Freya, who had been taking lessons, but no one knew the MacGregor song Griogal Cridhe too well, until Gillcrest took over the fiddle with which he was very accomplished and Morag-Freya sang it as she had learned it from her Grandmother. It was the first time that I had heard it since Ma sang it in Loch Insh and she then stood and sang the second half, bringing tears to my eyes. I had often neglected our MacGregor past and ancestors, so it made me feel a sadness of memories long lost and my Father fishing on the ice on the Loch.

I decided then to look into the MacGregor connection and ask Grigor more about it, but Hugh Mohr told us what he knew that night.

"That song would always make your Granny cry and when she sang it, the whole room would weep too. It was the only song that her Mither taught her, while grieving for her husband and her son Grigor Mohr, Grigor's Father. A very good man. The best," he said.

"Raise a glass to Grigor Mohr MacGregor," he said and raised his glass of coo's milk. Hugh loved his Highland coo milk.

58. The Pict People Conversation

I had hoped that Fergus and Patrick Hamilton, whoever they were, would be respectfully quiet the whole night, but they were just waiting for the right time to bring up their favourite topic, the Pictish people.

"Malcolm, Kenneth," Fergus began, "Your Grandmother, Isobel, respectfully wouldn't share much with us about her ancestry, but she did share the story of King Nachtain defeating the Northumbrians and we looked into it and the location of a famous battle that was near Loch Insh. Can you tell us any details about that, you being from Loch Insh?" he asked. "He is generally considered the first King of the Pictish people, who until then had never joined up together to defeat an enemy. Can you help us?" he asked.

Hugh Mohr looked across at me with a warning glance.

"All of you were advised to do a wee paper together with Gillcrest, weren't you?" Hugh asked. "Aye we were and we did. That small paper wasn't received well, so we are looking for additional information. Aonghus here has a stronger interest in Kilmartin Glen, in Argyle, which upset the powerful people there and we have been shot down and treated like criminals," Gillcrest added.

"That's true, I have had trouble in Argyle ever since its publication," he said.

"Then why do you write such controversial things?" I asked.

"The search for truth isn't always popular Malcolm, but we do not wish to drag you into this unwillingly, especially given you have MacGregor ancestry as well, so Fergus I'd rather not involve this wee family with such new beautiful twins," he said.

"All I know is that the Pictish people haven't died out, they are like you or I and simply joined bigger clans, as the Irish who created Dal Riata became more powerful. They Christianised, learned Gaelic and were simply Scots, as we all are. The MacMartins joined with the Camerons and so on. I don't know why you want to divide us because that's not going to create a better Scotland going forward. I don't want to add to disunity," I said.

"I understand. Thank you, Malcolm, you are right. Unity is what we need to break away from Britain," he added.

"If you say, I'm too busy feeding my family bringing in crops and breeding up my herds to worry about the past, although Nachtain was our Father's name and that is his picture there on the wall," I said. Then Hugh Mohr stood saying that he had had an enjoyable night, thanked Meredith and excused himself with the lovely company of Miss Beaton.

They left much to the shock of Duncan Mohr, who had been hoping to score a lady that night, so he left soon after. Fergus, Patrick, Gillcrest and Morag-Freya left soon after that, apologising for any disruption. The small party remaining then was Matilda and Alex, James and Susan, Bruce and Ma. who complemented me on how I handled the whole Pictish thing, which was confusing to Alex.

"Ma didn't tell me that we had Pictish ancestry," he said.

"I knew," said Ma. "I think it was always there, but it was never questioned as an oddity," she said.

"We are not an oddity, Ma. They are students who want information and they keep coming back to our family. Hugh Mohr warned me about him, so if he approaches you in his slimy way, you know now to keep quiet," I said. "Bruce, you now know his face, so please take care of Ma in this thing. They can be crafty," I cautioned. "I wanted you both to know who they were. I have no wish to create division in Scotland. We are many peoples from many countries like France, Norway, Ireland and the original inhabitants, all mixed up," I added.

"I'm so glad you have that maturity Malcolm," Alex said.

"Don't be so condescending Alex. I am not a wee bairn anymore," I said.

"Matilda, can I please ask you for English lessons?" Cherry said to change the subject.

"We didn't learn English on the Island and I have been learning it bit by bit, but my spelling is really poor." Cherry said and Matilda agreed, but they left soon after thanking us for the lovely dinner and thanked Meredith. Alex was shocked at the rebuke, but he shouldn't have been. James and Susan filled us in with how their pregnancy was coming along and were so happy now together.

"Do you have the carriage tonight?" I asked.

"Nae not this time. Patrick was put out that he wasn't invited and told us to ride our horses," he said unsurprisingly.

"I have had a few complaints about people who were left off the list. Why is our place so important?" I asked James.

"The Frasers were all put out, as was Grigor," I added. "Grigor I can understand, but not the Frasers," he answered.

"Grigor knows that it's because of Helen that he is not invited anywhere, but until she makes some major changes, people won't invite her around and how can you, when you just employed her cook?" he asked. "There would be a bun fight, like at those 'gatherings of the bairns'. I'm not going to one of those again until Nachtain is under control. What a little shite he is," he said. "Just like his Father Ewen," he added.

"Did you hear about the fight over the finances?" James asked.

"Nae," I answered.

"Well as you know, Aonghus wrote to them requesting that they pay Helen and Grigor back the money they both owed and there was a big fight over it. Poor Grigor won't see that money for a long time," he said. "Helen had all that money from her art and invested it unwisely without protecting herself and people are saying that Kenneth is the better artist anyway now and doesn't over charge like she does," he said. As the party dispersed and James was leaving, he said, "Malcolm, we can go shopping together again soon, can't we?" James asked.

"Aye, that would be much more fun than stressful chatter," I said and I watched them as they walked out into the cold night as Duncan Og brought their horses to them. 'God bless you, Duncan,' I thought.

59. *The Gossip Vine*

The following day the gossip vine from Craskie was received by midday. Ruth Beaton stayed overnight at Chisholm House with Hugh Mohr and as she was departing early in the morning, they were both seen groping and smooching on his front porch by Grigor on his way to the fields. News reached Fraser's Trading Post by noon and Glengarry by afternoon.

"The dirty dog," I exclaimed.

"He could have at least hand fast before doing it and making it so public, Cherry don't you think?" I said. Smiling, she seemed amused by the adult fornication.

"How do we know they didn't hand fast? They could marry this Sunday for all we know. Anyway, he is sexy for an old bloke. I can see why Granny loved him," she said.

"Oh Cherry, that's gross," I said. "The silver fox was more dignified, I admit, but not sexy," she added. "Cherry, stop!" I said, being unable to bear the conversation about the dirty old men. She just laughed and I heard Meredith laugh from the kitchen.

'Time to go to work and escape women's business,' I thought. What nonsense, old Hugh Mohr sexy? Yuck! It's a scandal and I introduced them. After finishing all of my work, the two grooms, Duncan Og and Iain, were busy working with the horses chatting away and they seemed happy but laughed at something and of course I assumed it was the gossip.

"You two have heard about Hugh Mohr and Ruth Beaton last night, I suppose? I didn't encourage immorality, let it be known," I said to them both.

"What do you think they did Malcolm?" Duncan Og, the younger one said cheekily. "My Grandfather was all dressed up last night thinking he was taking a wee wife home, so I have to thank ye Malcolm, it's the first time he has looked defeated and by that disgusting old Hugh Mohr," he said

They kept on laughing, imagining the goings on and him a religious lad. I was disappointed.

60. More Than Clan Gregor

I decided to get on my horse and take a ride to see Grigor about those ancestral connections on the Clan Gregor side. Saying my farewells to the ladies, off I went thinking it would be more peaceful at Craskie, but I was very wrong. I tied up my horse and as I approached their lovely oak front door, the arguing from the inside between Helen and Grigor could be heard all over the farm. Hamish was strolling past and said,

"I wouldn't go in there if I was you, my friend. There's lots of china being thrown around, you might be hit by a flying teacup," laughing to himself, he came up to the veranda and thanked me for a wonderful evening the previous night. "Other than that pair from the University of the pesky nuisances, it was great," he said thinking his play on words was clever.

I was shocked by the screaming from the inside, but he was obviously accustomed to it and was going to get on with his day, until I said that I did need to see Grigor briefly.

"In that case my friend, you need me, so stand behind me, Helen can be dangerous," he said. I heard her yelling demeaning things at Grigor like he had never been a landowner and it was only because of her that he was and then Hamish opened the door and as predicted, a Turkish china bowl came flying out and he shut the door quickly. It smashed against the solid oak, naturally.

"Well Hamish, I might just leave it with you then when things are quieter. I was only going to ask Grigor about our Clan Gregor association, so my bairns can be fully informed. Can you please tell him I was here for that reason only and if he needed a quieter place to talk, my place is open to him when he is less occupied," I said.

"Malcolm," he said. "My wife, Cora might be losing her job this week. The Glenmoriston school is closing down now that the Islanders have all gone as well as the cleared ones. She thinks that the wool waulking should never have been shut down, leaving them all without jobs. Can you help us buy that table that's around the side here from Grigor to go to Hugh Og's back veranda, where we now live? Cora has heard of the suffering of the women who followed Isobel-Mairi to Inverness and wants to start up an exclusive hand sewn tartan business over there, if your Ma agrees. The empty house on New Farm could house those four or five women. Can you get the table and ask your Ma if she can allow those women to live in her house?" he asked seriously. "We are thinking of breaking them out of the Mill where they are being kept virtual prisoner. If you want to help, that would be appreciated too. Hugh Og and I thought it could be done when both Isobel-Mairi and Ewen are here at one of those gatherings, leaving only that ugly former head groom, also named Bruce, to shoot at, if necessary," he said in a secretive way.

"Count me in," I said.

"Ma will agree, don't worry. Isn't Bruce married to the head spinner Milread, Dougal's' sister, who owns the only spinning wheel?" I asked.

"Aye, that's how we know all of this and she wants to escape from him too," he answered.

"Right, let me mull it all over," I said.

"They may have to divide up the two farms between Grigor and Helen. Does Hugh Mohr still have the money to buy that half being Grant Farm including the big stables and the oat crops and the top half of Craskie, but keeping the old growth forest, the cemetery and the Chapel? This bottom half is only Craskie including the house, the goat shed, the small stable, a few crops and the garden and some old growth forest. Do you think the forest would be at risk if they divided and sold it?" I asked.

Hamish was too shocked to even think of it divided up and sold.

"What if you all put your pennies together and bought it from them or at least from Helen, then she can move in with Isobel-Mairi for the rest of her life with what she is owed," I said.

"I don't know Malcolm. I thought buying the table was a big deal, but now this is something that I had never dreamed of. I couldn't hurt Grigor with his crops quite frankly, but if there was a way for Helen to leave, it would be ideal," Hamish said.

"I'll leave the options with you, my friend and don't forget fishing this weekend," I said, as the argument raged inside.

"Does he ever hit her?" I asked out of curiosity.

"Nae, not like Padruig would have. She'd be dead by now, as would Isobel if she had shown any disrespect to him. Times have changed for the better, but Helen is out of control and I have felt like strapping her with a leather belt over my knee myself," the big man said, surprisingly.

I was close to Fraser's Trading Post, so I dropped in to buy some more wooden barrels for Ma's preserving, as well as salt because we had a few too many goats and I wanted goat's meat included in the mix. The Fraser's staff, who knew me well by now, said they had passed on the message to John and Anna and they were looking forward to meeting the twins.

"Thank you, John, you're so reliable for local message keeping," I said.

"Aye, it's the best part of the job. I heard your party went so well that you even got Hugh Mohr a girlfriend," he said, smirking as I departed. Then I decided to go back and ask 'Mr know it all' what the problem was with Helen and Grigor.

"Now, where to start?" he began.

"Helen's daughter, the flighty one who married that big bastard, ripped her off is the main problem, then they tore the guts out of Craskie staff and left them in a right mess. She's not paying it back and when Grigor tried to get the money back, he failed, so of course it's all his fault, not hers for not drawing up a proper contract in the first place, according to Helen. They've lost over ten thousand pounds, so far on the Mill, I have been told," he said. "Helen can't manage anything whether it's the school, the farm, the finances and now her marriage is on the rocks. Of course, none of it is her fault, she claims. She says it's all her sister's fault, the twin. That must be your Mither lad. Sorry, I shouldn't have said that," he said.

"That's alright. Better I know what's being said, but how is it my Mither's fault?" I asked.

"She inherited 'New Farm', leaving Helen having to pay for grazing, as well as losing the two houses that she built," he said.

"My Ma is a legitimate child of both Padruig Grant and Isobel Grant," I said defensively.

"We all know that lad," John said. "It's just Helen and her mad ideas," he added.

I left a little shocked, but I was glad that my wife was nothing like Helen. I was mulling over Hugh Mohr and his new love interest Ruth Beaton and couldn't help but feel the solution lay in Hugh buying the top half of that property. If it weren't for all of the years that Grigor had put into Craskie crops, I would have ridden up to his house and put it to him, but I decided to mind my own business, until I saw Grigor if he did come to my house and ask him. The idea of a farm overseer for both Alex and I came into mind and Alex had an empty staff house. So, I mounted up after having tied the barrels on rather awkwardly and rode home in a cautious canter.

61. Planning the Breakout

I dropped the barrels off to my pretty Ma, feeling bad about the gossip.

"What is it son?" she asked with Bruce listening in.

"It's not pleasant, can I tell your husband Ma?" I asked.

"Nae, son you can tell us both. Come in," she said getting bossier by the day. I told her first that Cora wanted the table from Craskie on her back veranda and intended to start up the wool waulking again with the initial women who had left. I didn't tell her that we would have to break them out of the Mill, but I think Bruce knew there was something serious afoot. Can the four or five ladies have temporary residence in your third home on new Farm Ma?" I asked.

"They can," she said. "When?" she asked.

"This Saturday, but best you don't mention it to anyone at all because of Isobel-Mairi," I said. "Okay, what else son?" I told them both what I had encountered at Craskie Farm and wanted to talk to Grigor about dividing up that property to sell. Unable to divorce, their options were to separate and divide the land before it was all worthless. I also thought it wasn't a silly idea to hire Grigor to oversee both Alex and my farms. I explained that Hugh could have enough money for his top half or the bottom half, especially now he has a new love interest. Bruce was curious.

"This is not all bad son, if you think of it as a good solution to a nasty situation that could get nastier. So far, he hasn't hit her, but what if he does and she drops dead and he's blamed," he said, standing up looking concerned.

"So which idea do you think is the best one Da?" I asked. "First, as you say, get that table and sort out those women and if you need me to help you break them out then I'm in," he said.

"Bruce, who said they were being kept prisoner?" Ma asked.

"Your son's eyes, my darling. Look at them," he said. I was embarrassed that I was so easy to read, but I was glad of his support against that nasty Bruce in Inverness, who was built like an Ox and had a potty mouth like no other.

"Are you going to break them out of the Mill alone then son?" asked Ma.

"Nae, Ma. Hamish and Hugh Og and Hugh Mohr are in on it with guns and now Bruce and me. Our own security, Duncan Mohr will have to stay here to protect you all in my house Ma on Saturday morning. Okay?" I said.

"What about Matilda?" she asked.

"I could ask her to go to my house for the English lessons but don't tell her anything," I answered.

"Why not?" she asked. "Well, P-P-P-P-Peter from the tartan shop is the leak here Ma," I answered.

"Oh, Alexander Og will be so upset," she said. "Aye, now I have to get back to Cherry, Ma," I said.

62. The Women Are Rescued

Saturday morning could have easily turned bad if anyone had leaked that we were all on our way with the Team to load up the women and their luggage. Ugly Bruce, as he was called, was tied up yelling Gaelic obscenities while we departed and I assumed someone would find him once we were gone. Those women were desperate and very grateful at being rescued. I had left them enough food for a week to cook for themselves and we all departed. I was pleased to be home with Hugh Og too, who was looking forward to eating dinner. I was surprised to find that Grigor was waiting for me and as we walked in, we must have looked as guilty as hell.

"I won't ask what you've been doing," he said. "But thank you and what did you need to know about Clan Gregor Malcolm?" he asked. Over a delicious dinner we all talked and asked relevant questions concerning the history of Clan Gregor and proscription.

"I wasn't allowed to be baptised. No Priest could baptise us as a MacGregor, nor could we own anything in our names. It was years before proscription ended and finally, I had my legal name on the Craskie Farmland deeds and when Ma built the Chapel a lot of us MacGregors, including me, were baptised," he said. He told us about the big hounds trained to hunt them down, so Ma got him a dog to kill any hound that came near him.

"I really miss her," Grigor said.

"Any questions family?" he asked. "Can you show me the MacGregor brooch Uncle Grigor?" asked Islay.

"It's so pretty," she said.

"What does it mean?" she asked.

"Royal is my race. We are from royalty. A long time ago," he said patiently and pinned it back on his plaid.

"When you are older, Islay and I pass into the other world, you can have it," Grigor said.

"I am your great Uncle, but you and your brothers can call me Uncle," he said.

63. Grigor's Dilemma

It was then that I asked him to join me by the fire to speak of other more current matters, which he took seriously.

"You have taken the women out of the Mill then?" Grigor asked.

"Aye, we have. They were being kept prisoner there," I said.

"I suppose you know my wife and I are no longer sharing the marriage bed, so to speak?" he asked.

"Aye, figuratively speaking. I have had a few ideas for you. Do you have a solution yet?" I asked.

"Nae, but I do have one offer. Hugh Mohr offered his house and land for me to buy, as he is moving in with Ruth Beaton. Their wedding is on Sunday and you and I are invited," he said.

"If I can find three thousand pounds and a good lawyer, then I can buy his house and land and not lose either of Grant nor Craskie Farms. In the meantime, I can just move in there to avoid a murder or accidental death. What are your ideas?" he said.

I talked with Grigor for nearly two hours and the family long moved off to do their chores.

"I suppose I always thought it would come good eventually, like it did when Ma was in charge, but it just gets worse by the day, then by the hour. My wife is not mentally well, in my opinion. Her mind is not what it was. She hasn't coped without her Mither and has lost most of her money, so I could never kick her out of the family home," he said

"Do you know from whom I could borrow that kind of money?" he asked.

"Aye, me, if we do it legally, like with an Edinburgh lawyer, not Aonghus. Then you will own Chisholm House or Charlotte House – I heard about your beloved Ox. Then Hugh signs it and hands it over and you move out. No land division needed, so you will be entitled to own the rest of the farm when your wife passes away or vice versa," I told him.

"Great idea," he said.

"Well, all the best Grigor, to you and Hugh Mohr," I said.

"Thanks for introducing the two of them," he said. "Who would have thought he'd keep on going like a randy old dog? He gets more than me for sure," he said. He took his leave after I wrote to the solicitor with his signature on it, with his repayments set at twenty pounds per month over ten years.

He may have to hire out his stables to other people for stabling to afford the repayments.

As he was about to leave, he left me a box.

"By the way, this box here is from me in gratitude for saving us more than once," he said. "It's a box of Turkish china that has never been opened. I'm not really sure what's in there, but it was a box of china stolen by those Irish years ago when it hadn't been unpacked by that home helper Agnes that we had, who slipped it to her boyfriend. I thought it would be safer with you, as Helen has taken to breaking all the china. I heard that you were there when that lovely bowl hit the door," he said.

I smiled as he left and I was glad we had returned to good family relations.

When I told Ma and Bruce that I was lending him all that money, Bruce was horrified at how much it was and worried Grigor wouldn't be able to pay it back. Ma, on the other hand, said she owed him and so she wanted to give it to him as a gift.

Questioned on that, she said "Grigor gave me a husband who I love and who loves me and it's the least I can do for such a gift of love. You don't have to tell him if you don't want to, but it's better you do, then there's only land title deeds required," Ma said.

"Hugh Mohr, Grigor and the lawyer can meet us here and I pay Hugh with signatures and no repayments." We all met, as Ma had suggested, with a lawyer from Invermoriston, not Edinburgh, who was competition to Aonghus.

The house was renamed Charlotte House, Craskie Farm, Glenmoriston and Grigor MacGregor was the new owner of house and land. Helen had parted with the table without it being known, as it wandered off during the night and she didn't notice it missing and when Grigor moved out, she didn't even ask him what he was doing. So, he just collected everything he owned, including the wedding gift of weapons from Padruig Dubh Grant and the painting of the Ox.

Hamish told us on one of our fishing trips that he was crying as he took his wedding gift of weapons from the old house that he had loved so much. He had thought he would always live out his life with Helen, his fae folk wife he used to say, but the disappointment at their inability to cope together anymore showed on his face. His deep sadness and his disbelief at how it was all still panning out with Isobel-Mairi, was hard for any husband or parent to take. I asked Hamish which weapons he had. There was a French pistol with ammunition, so secretly Hamish removed it from his house, along with the ammunition and hid it until his friend was in a better condition. We were all worried about them both and suggested that the gathering of the bairns be cancelled indefinitely while issues were unresolved. That way at least Isobel-Mairi no longer came onto the property.

Craskie Farm then became much quieter.

Grigor remained up the top of the farm most of the time nearer his precious crops and successfully started to rent the stables for income for himself. He grew his own fresh kitchen vegetables. He still had access to all of the Craskie animals for his meals that he now had to kill and cook himself, but it kept him busy. The wool waulking women took it in turns to clean his house and make his bed and sometimes cooked too. James often dropped in to visit him and their relationship improved. Helen found it harder to keep busy but started painting about six months into their separation.

The big house built by loving hands of friends, while Padruig was overseas, was loved for so many years by Isobel and so many people who had passed through there joyously, whether they were staff or family, and the occasions were spoken of in whispers around Glenmoriston until their deaths. Even though both parents had provided for their children and their grandchildren, it didn't prevent its inevitable failure and the house was now silent. Not the sound of children running upstairs, nor the fiddle being played or the uillean pipes or Ma's MacGregor song, or an argument or Ma's continuous grilling of the staff to do this or that or had they done this or that and had this animal been fed. Silence. Just the sound of Helen's own footsteps walking into her Mither's room, where she now slept. She was eating less, but still using the herbs and the potatoes. She was making some coin from selling a few coos or a few goats or the milk and cheese, but that was her life now.

She considered sewing again, but changed her mind and gathered it all up to give to someone one day.

"Ma, why did you die?" she wept to herself nightly. Sometimes she was seen walking to the Chapel to pray and talk to her Mither and that brought her some peace. One day finally, a letter came from Aonghus saying that Isobel-Mairi had sold the tartan shop to pay her back for as much as the shop sold for, which only amounted to half that she was owed, but it was better than nothing. In addition, it added that she would repay from the Mill ten pounds per month until the debt was fully paid off. There was no apology nor well wishes to her Mither and her Father, but it was a start. Immediately, she told Hamish who still worked there that she felt a lightening of her heart as all of that money was her life's work. She sold a few more paintings to John Fraser along the same old lines of Culloden, which would always hold a niche market and she was an expert on the topic, so if anyone could paint Culloden, it was still her.

Kenneth stayed away from painting Culloden and she stayed away from insects, birds and forests.

64. Some Marriages Do Fail

Grigor and Helen's marriage was not the only failing marriage, as Jean and her English husband fought it out. He decided to return to England, but before that as they were both Catholic and had failed in their attempt to divorce the first time, they both converted to the Episcopalian faith, if only temporarily, but to try to divorce again. Eventually, they succeeded and she kept the house and her son, Benedict Junior, and he kept the practice, which he sold to yet another Doctor. Benny Junior would visit his Father after he was no longer being breast fed, thereafter his Father wanted to see him every Christmas in London. Jean would have him on Hogmanay. The travel costs would be paid by the Father.

Ugly Bruce MacKay and his wife Milread were successful first time before the Courts, due to battery and Milread having been kept prisoner without pay for her work in the Mill. Bruce MacKay wasn't the only one on charges for the imprisonment of the workers. Milread and her child stayed in the house on New Farm awaiting the new business to start and when it did it was very popular locally, as no one liked Isobel-Mairi and hadn't wanted to buy from her. They had orders that would keep them busy for two years, so long as folk had their own sheep and this time Cora taught the songs to a younger lady too, so she could be replaced one day as her Mither was.

Ma liked the business operating there and the women living there, if it still suited them and after they started earning, she then started taking wee rent from them via her husband Bruce MacDonald. It was a long time before Helen even realised that they were even there and making tartan again with a lot of her Mither's dye recipes, but she said nothing.

If she went to Fraser's Trading Post, they didn't pass on any local gossip to her, unlike me, who they never stopped telling all the gossip to. Anna and the aging John Fraser with his son Simon and his wife and my cousin Beth did eventually come to dinner and it was the most boring night ever, but interesting on some levels where John told me facts like Padruig considered killing Isobel when he arrived home from Quebec for the 'shocking crime' committed against her by the militia and British dragoons. Her crime was not telling him about it and lying about the wounds she had [2]. I was glad not to have had the bad temper of that man and hoped no one in my family inherited his violent tendencies, despite being equally known for his popularity and heroism. I was confused why John wanted to be invited to my house, given our wide age difference and we had absolutely nothing in common. He was a decent enough old man, as was his son Simon, who achieved some projects asked of him by Granny, like having the narrow Drover's Road widened in Glenmoriston and the Glenmoriston Post Office built. So, I asked if he could do the same with our old narrow Drover's Road that ran alongside the Cherry Farms and build a Post Office nearby us and hopefully a Church too, as it was too far to Craskie if someone just wanted to pray. He had a negative response to the Church and cautioned we might end up with a fanatical group coming to Glengarry.

"If it was just for prayer, it was better to build your own Chapel, as Granny did," he said.

He did say, however, that there was more likelihood of getting a new school now that there were so many children in our area without a school. Families were having to send their children into the cities to board once they reached high school, he told me. It was surprising what statistics he knew about Glengarry. Most people home schooled their bairns, as did we, which we told them and Matilda helped us out by not only teaching English to my wife, but to Islay and Alex as well. Simon offered teaching materials from the government, which covered all subject areas including maths and even French and Latin, which he could post to me. I was very grateful for that. I wanted my bairns to be educated, as well as clever on the farm.

Simon did advise us how to obtain cheaper or free schooling through scholarships as well, so our children could even go on to university. There was a shortage of Doctors, so he recommended my young Alexander go into medicine and I said I'd already wanted to do that, but he had to show an interest first. It was a nice dream to think our Alex could one day be the Doctor for Glengarry. Islay was annoyed that women couldn't attend the university to study medicine as yet and asked if they could try to change that ruling. She was a bright wee thing and if she didn't study medicine, I suppose law was an option. She was certainly argumentative enough. The twins were too far off to think about. Anna brought over lovely expensive looking rattles for the twins and for Cherry and I, they brought carry backpacks for a bairn, so the bairn could be carried on your back while you milked the goats or were going for a walk. So, we had one each to walk around the farm with a twin each on our backs. It even had a nice wee hood to keep off the wind and the rain. I could even ride my horse with one of the twins on my back. They shared news about Fraser country that was also rewilding in small pockets like Matilda had done on Alex's farm and a lady author had moved into a house in their area and was a prolific writer on Scotland and its historic past. I put him onto those two nuisances, who kept annoying our family and maybe they could team up with that lady writer.

65. *The Praying Mantis and the Rabbit*

I asked my cousin Beth, who bred Highland Ponies, how much it would cost for two wee ponies for Islay and Alex and the cost was too high, so I let that topic alone. 'The Grants sure know how to overcharge,' I thought. They perused Kenneth's art-work and were delighted at the lightness of it.

"No gloom or doom," I heard Anna say and she purchased 'a praying mantis' painting and the famous 'rabbit' that I had dreamed of as a wee lad and took Kenneth to it to paint in Loch Insh. They were shocked that Hugh Mohr was married again and living in Glengarry with Ruth Beaton.

"Famous people, those Beatons," he said about them and was shocked that Grigor Og was no longer living with Helen.

"Padruig would turn in his grave," he said about that.

"The best place for gossip John, if ever you need to know any-thing is your own shop," I told him. "I rely on them for passing messages to and fro and furnishing me with the latest news," I hoped that telling the owner might not then stop the flow of information, but it didn't. He noticed the Turkish china we had, which was an incomplete set and said that he had bought it for Isobel when Padruig broke her antique china ware given to her by the late Uncle Allan MacDonald. Upon hearing that Helen was smashing the Turkish china and throwing it at Grigor, he felt it better that we had it and was flabbergasted.

"Maybe drop in to see Helen," I suggested, "She must be lonely I imagine and she doesn't like my family," He agreed that Helen alone now in that big house would be daunting after its lively past.

"What a shame," he said and they left fairly early as the weather was building up and they had a long way back home to Stratherick and the old man needed to keep warm as he walked slowly to his carriage leaning on his son. 'This winter could do him in,' I thought. And it did just that.

John Fraser died after a big storm two weeks later, but he had visited Helen before he passed accompanied by his wife Anna, also aging fast now. In his Will he had left Islay and Alex a highland pony each, which were delivered with their saddles, bridles, halters, brushes and lead ropes shortly after the Will reading. Duncan Og was put in charge of them and he asked to start teaching them how to ride, to which I agreed. My brother was happy to have sold a few paintings to the Frasers and was sad when the old man died.

"Kenneth," I said, "You need a lassie who likes what you like, like a lady scientist who needs the drawings of the insects she sees. So, a Zoologist is what they are called, I think. How about we ask Gillcrest in Invermoriston? James and I can take you shopping with us and we can all meet up with Gillcrest and ask him where to find a lady zoologist or entomologist, who does not drink. Are you in?" I said.

"They won't like me being a diagnosed alcoholic. What if they want to go to the pub every week? People do," Kenneth said. He wasn't confident anymore about getting a lassie, but he came with James and I who always enjoyed the day out shopping, finishing up with dinner at our favourite tea house. On this occasion we invited Gillcrest to meet us at the tea shop. He was so pleased to see us all and we all hugged and he sat down and ordered his dinner as well. It was such a lovely tea shop and the waitress was cute and Kenneth looked like he was enjoying himself. Boldly, he spoke up to Gillcrest saying,

"I am looking for a lassie who may be scientifically minded, as I love to draw insects and all kinds of animals. If there were wolves here, I'd paint them too, but it's so sad there aren't any around anymore," he said.

66. *Ivy Fraser*

"I thought you might know a lady scientist with a zoology or entomology interest, as well as a handsome young man interest, who doesn't drink or hang out in pubs. Do you?" Kenneth asked.

"I know lots of many scientists of course and we have meetings regularly in Inverness and sometimes Edinburgh and there are several lady scientists, many of whom are zoologists and entomologists. There is one lady who came to mind as you spoke because she's looking for an illustrator for her book on 'The Insects of the Highlands of Scotland'. She is unmarried, but a wee bit older than you Kenneth. Do you have an age preference?" he asked.

"Not really, so long as she is understanding about no alcohol. I don't mind if she's a bit older. How much older?" he replied.

"You are mid-twenties, now, aren't you?" he asked. "Aye," Kenneth answered.

"She's either twenty-nine or twenty-eight, it's hard to tell as she's young looking and tanned from the outdoors like Matilda was," he said.

"I am seeing her this afternoon about bugs in the hospital. You could meet her today if you wanted to meet her in her professional capacity. She can be abrupt around men to keep us all at bay you see," he answered. "Do you want to meet her and tell her you are an illustrator? You could invite her to your art studio to see the other insects you have drawn or painted and it may be that you become just good friends with a good job as an illustrator or you get yourself both a lassie and a job or just a lassie. Up to you both and your chemistry, isn't it?" Gillcrest said.

"The best part of it is Kenneth, she is tee total," he said.

"Really?" Kenneth said. "Aye never touches a drop. Hates all alcohol unless she is preserving insects, so that is where you may need to be careful and don't touch her wee bugs. She has trays and trays of them," he said.

"I had never thought of that," Kenneth said.

"Me too until I was a student with an older student doing his last year in entomology and I was his volunteer. I became as sick as a dog handling those bugs because as you

Ivy Fraser

know, I rarely drink alcohol," Gillcrest said, "but I suppose I could have used tweezers to pick up the wee beasties," he said smiling.

"What's her name, clan, birthplace etc Gillcrest?" I asked.

"She's Clan Fraser of Lovat. Most of her bugs are from her Father's own lands in the Aird. Her name is Ivy, she's kind of short like Ma was, with nice red hair, freckles on her face, but pretty and Catholic, born at home in the Aird," he said. After we finished up James was excited, but poor Kenneth was getting nervous the closer we got to the hospital, which he remembered only too well. I hadn't thought of that and he wanted to turn around and leave.

"No Malcolm, I can't go in there," he said and he was shaking all over.

"Gillcrest, we are going to have to cancel. James just realised that we have to get the carriage back to his Father. Can you please send her to Kenneth's Art Studio? This is his business card?" I said. I apologised and we could barely keep up with

Kenneth bolting for the carriage. "Never mind," I said. "If it's meant to be, she'll turn up in Glengarry one day," I said.

Poor Kenneth was pale and was still shaking as we left Invermoriston.

"I'm sorry brother, I didn't think of the hospital. Please forgive me for upsetting you," I said. I just wanted to squeeze my brother tightly so he would stop shaking, but slowly as he was further away from that hospital the more normalised, he became.

"It was hell in there wasn't it brother?" I asked.

"Aye," and looked away with tears rolling down his cheeks, so I could not bear it and I held him to my heart.

"You are my heart, my life, my brother. I love you. It'll be alright," I said.

"If bug lady turns up, well and good, if not forget her," I said. "'Bug lady' became her nickname and she did turn up on a pony and cart just when we had forgotten all about her, which was good because Kenneth had painted more bugs in that time. The cold weather didn't agree with him, so I'd light up his fire in the studio because he would get carried away with what he was doing and forget to light it. She strolled up to the door and knocked with us both inside just before I was due to leave.

"Hello, I'm looking for Kenneth MacNachten, is he here please?" she asked.

Her voice wasn't at all abrupt, in fact she was polite and kind of sweet. Maybe she just liked bossing Gillcrest around. I excused myself and decided to tell Ma and Bruce that Ivy was here and they wanted to see her. Ma had buns freshly cooked from her oven with jam and cream and a fresh big pot of coffee.

"Bruce, get the cups and plates and a tray quickly," and we all went together to the art studio to meet her. "Smoko time," yelled Ma and we all sat down to coffee and yummy buns with jam and cream. Bruce was a spoiled husband and was gaining weight. Ma introduced herself, "I am Marion MacDonald formerly MacNachten, Kenneth's Mither, as well as Malcolm's Mither and this is my husband Bruce MacDonald," she said proudly. Standing up to meet them Ivy said,

"I am Ivy Fraser, Mistress, pleased to meet you and thank you for this lovely morning tea. I was hungry. I'm here admiring your son's artwork. I hope that's alright? I need an illustrator for my book on Highland insects and Kenneth already has some of my rarest wee beasties that I can never find. Are you his manager Sir?" she asked.

I saw Ma kick him and he said, "Aye, I am and you may call me Bruce. What are you offering my son?" he asked. "For a book this encyclopaedic size, I can pay him two thousand pounds and he would receive royalties from every book that sells," she said. "I'll have that contract drawn up if you can give me all of the details once you and Kenneth know what those are. For instance, how many drawings or paintings and what quality paper and so on. When you two sort out everything, you will need to sign up the agreement or he would be wasting his precious time. He also needs a down payment for his needs, half up front and the other half at the completion," Bruce said.

"Well Kenneth, you do have an excellent manager, I will go to the bank and get that money for you now. I am happy you are the perfect illustrator for me," she said.

"I'll come with you dear. I know the bank manager and we can transfer it to Kenneth's account. Kenneth, do you need cash for purchases son?" Da asked.

"Aye. Da can I come as well, so I can pick up more paint and paper?" Kenneth asked.

"You need an easel too, don't you?" she asked. "I'll buy you one," she said.

"One more thing," Bruce added. "We are dry farms here, strictly no alcohol of any kind," he said.

"Good for you. Well done. I don't drink myself, but my wee beasties are preserved in pure alcohol, so better you don't touch them, unless you are wearing gloves or using tweezers. More than a few students have become ill from handling them, preserved in their deceased state," she added.

"If you have bairns, you best warn them too not to touch them for the same reasons. Some people don't have a reaction to them, but some do and I especially worry about the bairns. If I have the insects here with me, I'll store them high or locked up, if possible, in case you do have a wandering bairn," she added in a responsible tone.

"There are wandering bairns, as you put it. Malcolm has two who come in frequently, Islay and Alex and if Jean comes over, she has a son Benedict who must be over one year old by now and into everything. Matilda has two, Moses and Sarah," he said.

"Someone's religious then with those names?" she said. "Matilda converted to Catholicism to marry her husband Alex," Ma explained. It'll be a while before Malcolm's twins will be wandering around, so I will keep them out of your hair. How about we get Duncan to help keep the bairns out while they're working, Bruce darling," Ma asked.

"Grand idea Mither," he answered.

That evening after completing all my tasks with my coos including the birthing of a new calf, I went inside to wash and for the first time in months, my wife had my bath ready for me. The water was piping hot and she washed my long black hair and threatened to cut it jokingly. She scrubbed my long legs all the way up my thighs to my genitalia and that was nice. She was particularly gentle with my bollocks and I just let myself enjoy it, like Bruce was, being that spoiled husband. She washed up and down my general, so it stood erect of course, but instead of responding to its demands, I let my wife finish scrubbing my entire body including my back. It had been a long time and finally my wife was back to normal, thanks to Meredith. She spoke sweet things into my ears in Gaelic and washed up and down both of my arms and scrubbed my hands and each finger and even clipped my fingernails while still in the bath.

"Are we expecting guests?" I asked her.

"Nae, my darling, I am expecting you and the General to come and play after I have dried you off," she said. I picked her up in my arms as she giggled and while still naked, I walked off to our room carrying my wife to continue our love making. It was a shame that both Hugh Og and Meredith saw my nudity, but my mind was only on entering Cherry. They took care of our guest Duncan Mohr too, who thought it was hilarious watching my ass wander off down the hallway carrying my wife. My wee ones just told him Mummy and Daddy were playing, 'Mummy, Daddy Games.'

"Well, your parents are both handsome people, so I can understand why they would like to play those games," he said to Islay.

"My Daddy is handsome, isn't he?" she asked the silver fox, who had to agree.

"Aye, he is the most handsome man on these farms, then Uncle Kenneth. Then who do you think is next?" he asked the wee lass.

"I think Uncle Hugh Og is next," she said. "Am I handsome too?" he asked her, as she ran her fingers down the deep furrows in his brow and down his cheeks and said, "Nae Uncle, you look like old leather that someone forgot to put some oil onto."

Very honestly, she wasn't trying to hurt him, but there was the honesty of a bairn.

"You are the sweetest wee bairn that I have ever met," he said in response to her honesty then I came out pulling up my pants once I realised, we had guests.

Duncan Mohr MacDonnell

67. Duncan Mohr and Jean

"Malcolm, your wee daughter just told me that I was the most handsome man on these farms," and Islay laughed at him saying, "nae I didn't Uncle." Duncan Mohr was getting attached to my wee ones and then I saw Jean, my cousin, sitting in the corner looking a bit red faced. She must have seen more than I had planned on anyone seeing.

"Hello cousin Jean, I wasn't expecting you," I said.

"Sorry Malcolm, I saw more than I had expected to see, but it was only from behind," she said.

"I found this lass wandering around looking for your front door, so I brought her in to see you," said Duncan.

"Meredith, can we please all have coffees and buns or something yummy like that?" I asked. "Coming up Malcolm," she smilingly replied, then we all chatted and drank our coffee with cream buns when I realised that Duncan quite liked Jean.

"I just came around to see the twins Malcolm and to let you know that I am now divorced and if ever your bairns need any school lessons, I am now available. I am back home with Da. I have decided to sell that house in Glenmoriston," she said. Duncan butted in.

"Don't be too hasty lass. You might meet a silver fox like me and remarry sooner than you think," he said.

"Even if I do Uncle, I don't want to live there. The new Doctor might want to buy it and it could sell for enough for me to buy or build something here in Glengarry nearer Da and my wee Chestnut horse," she said.

"You could build a new house on my land if you wanted to, sweet lady," he said.

"Duncan, she's not interested," I said.

"Oh, yes, she is Malcolm. The silver fox is a sexy bloke, I hear. You could do worse Jean. At least he is Scottish," Hugh Og said hoping to off load the silver fox away from his wife.

"Well, I'd best be off with my bairn Malcolm, it's getting cold," she said.

"I'll take you down to Alex my dear Jeannie," he said, smiling with his missing teeth at her.

"Bye Cherry, Meredith and Hugh, Malcolm and Kenneth. You can take me home Duncan," she said and she linked her arm into his and off they walked, like an old married couple.

"You don't think he'll score do you?" I asked. Meredith laughed.

"I do. She likes him," Hugh Og had never been so relieved to see the back end of someone. Duncan was with Jean, who did need a Fatherly figure after all she had been through with that pig of a Doctor Browne. I must admit I didn't think that marriage, nor his practise would go so badly, but the sentiment towards the English was deep and not improving. With poor Jean having been raised in Nova Scotia, she hadn't known of the deep feelings on both sides. I was wondering about Helen's paintings of Granny's beasts on his wall in the waiting room and felt like snitching them somehow, but I would have to ask Grigor I suppose. He had the painting of Granny's first goats and I knew my wife would love that, but I couldn't start thinking like a thief.

Kenneth worked hard over the next six months with so many insect drawings. It made my skin crawl. Some of the bigger bugs were pretty and it was amazing that such pretty colours could be given to bugs. Kenneth and Ivy worked well together and they just chatted away about the subject matter correcting any small detail. One of her bugs was unable to be found and my brother slipped up and revealed that maybe I could find it in a dream. He knew immediately that he shouldn't have said it, so we covered it up with 'it was a coincidence', 'it was pure luck', 'I was making it up to entertain my wee brother' and so on.

"Don't worry Malcolm I'm a bit fae too, but this one has eluded me," she said. Once she described it and its favourite habitat, I knew that darn critter would come in a dream, so the next day I told him where to find it, but not to reveal it was from a dream of mine. Just pure luck.

That bug completed her collection and all of the illustrations. The book was published and my brother was paid handsomely. He didn't expect to see her again after she gave him a signed copy of the book because he asked her for another free one signed by us both to be given to our Ma and Bruce, who managed his affairs. She did that but went on her way, as people like that do and he was thankful to be drawing and painting portraits of people or lochs and forests again. He never imagined that he might miss her company but he did and she never imagined that she would miss his company, but she did. 'After all, she was a Fraser from the Aird whose family wouldn't think much of a family like us,' he thought until one day he was painting outside our house during a brief moment of sunshine, in order to capture the colours of the Ospreys' wings as two of them flew overhead.

68. The Proposal

Then some people, unknown to Kenneth approached him and Duncan Mohr came running.

"Sorry Sirs, Madam, identify yourselves," Duncan said as Kenneth quickly picked up his painting to go inside.

"Oh my, what marvellous security you have," they said.

"Aye, Sir. We are Frasers of the Aird, parents of Ivy Simone Fraser. We have come to speak with the young man named Kenneth MacNachten, who worked with our daughter on her book recently," the older man said.

Red faced and with our hearts racing, we entered the house with the Frasers introducing themselves seeking out Kenneth. I excused myself to find our parents.

"I have to get our parents, excuse me," I said. "Meredith, can you please give our guests coffee or tea?" I requested and ran as fast as I could to get Ma and Bruce, who were working with the goats. They didn't have time to wash at their place, so they washed their hands at my place, pretending to be calm and introduced themselves to these Frasers and asked what the problem was. They were not confident as one would expect from Frasers and started by saying that they liked Kenneth's work in the book.

"So, you are Kenneth?" the father said.

"Aye, what did you expect me to look like?" he asked them directly. "What's the problem? Is Ivy alright?" Kenneth asked.

"Oh aye, she is alright lad, she is well, but has asked us to visit you and your parents," the father said.

"Oh aye, why?" Kenneth asked. "Did she leave her bugs behind?" Kenneth added, not imagining that they could be there for a personal reason, but Meredith was listening in and came in and whispered in his ear and left again. Duncan didn't leave and neither did I. Islay came out and asked who they were. Cherry had been resting with the twins, but with all the noise they had both woken up and she came out and started breastfeeding them both.

"Don't mind us," Cherry said.

"Not at all, Mr and Mrs MacNachten, are you?" They asked Ma and Bruce.

"Nae, we are Mr and Mrs MacDonald, but we are his parents. I'm his Stepfather," said Bruce. "What can we do for you? We must get back to the goats," he said becoming impatient.

"Our daughter wants us to ask permission of you, Sir and Madam, if Kenneth would be interested in courtship with Ivy," Mr Fraser said.

"What is your name Sir? My name is Bruce," he said.

"Sorry, my name is Simon Fraser and this is my wife Patricia Fraser," he replied.

"They're already great friends, so I assume you are referring to marriage and if so when and how much dowry are we talking about?" Bruce said bluntly.

"Ivy is my only daughter, so we have amassed two thousand pounds for that purpose. We hoped to have more, but a lot has happened and my two sons needed their university fees paid. It would be given to you as his only living Father. Is that correct?" he asked.

"Aye, that is correct, this is Kenneth's deceased Father on the wall here, but Kenneth is loved by me as my son," Bruce said firmly.

"Da, can I have something to say here please, respectfully?" Kenneth asked.

"Aye son," Bruce answered.

"If Ivy wants a relationship with me, I would like to talk to her in private please and the business side of things I can leave to you all. You must know, Mr Fraser, that I am a diagnosed alcoholic, so there can be no alcohol, even at a wedding or a dinner party. Can your family cope with that, without judgement because I don't need people looking down their noses at me?" Kenneth said boldly.

"I have not drunk any alcohol in two years now. I will only marry a woman who will support me and prevent any individual from her family and friends introducing alcohol into our marriage and onto our farms. It's easy for my family because we are not drinkers anyway, but a lot of Scots can't get through their day without a dram of whisky or an ale. That having been said, any family that I involve myself with, has to abstain from any form of alcohol. Can you all do that?" Kenneth asked bravely.

"I am embarrassed to say lad that the delay in meeting you has been over this issue and that's why I was so surprised to see how healthy you looked, compared to the rest of my family," he said. "I cannot stop the Frasers from drinking their own whisky, so we have discussed how it could work and it's not ideal, but my daughter wants to break away from us all who drink alcohol and hand fast with you and eventually marry quietly where the bulk of the drinkers will never know, until it's in the paper. She is prepared to give us all up which makes me miserable as she is my only wee lass, but I know she can't bear to be without you," he said then wiping his eyes.

"Can you speak with her with these unhappy terms? I would follow all your rules as would my wife, but my sons won't, so my wife and I can be present at any important events like marriage, birth of a child and so on, but the rest of them wouldn't know where you all live, if you prefer," Mr Fraser said.

"Mr Fraser, these farms are dry farms for everyone. No-one here has a problem with that and I don't like how you are speaking to and of my son in such a divisive and condescending manner. He isn't the problem, you all are, so as Kenneth has asked, can he please talk with Ivy and we can take it from there. Now can you please leave before I lose my temper?" Bruce said.

"Aye we will leave. I am sorry and we will ask her to speak to Kenneth herself," he said.

"The dowry?" Bruce asked, "is not enough. I will consider it if it's double that," he said and the Frasers left.

Bruce was fuming and I haven't seen him like that. Ma took his hand and they held each other briefly then he apologised to Kenneth.

"Oh my God son, you poor lad, how dare those pompous bastards speak to you like that. Are you interested in Ivy son?" Bruce asked.

"It's okay Da. Thank you so much for your help. I did like her, but I knew there would be problems with her family of Frasers from the Aird. Like you said, 'pompous bastards' and if anyone was alcoholic in the room today it was him and his drunken wife. I could smell her from over here. Could you?" Kenneth asked.

"I could," Duncan Mohr agreed.

"I reckon just talk to the wee lassie. I mean she's not young. You'd only get a maximum of one or two bairns out of her, so where's the value?" he said bluntly.

"Oh, Duncan that's harsh if you like someone. Maybe Kenneth only wants one or two," Ma said.

"That is a good point Duncan, value and all that. What if she's sterile?" I said.

"I think that Kenneth should chat with the lass and point out all of the down sides, as well as the up sides. Matilda was old when she married Alex wasn't she?" Meredith pointed out.

"She was even older than Ivy," I said.

"If Ivy ever comes here Duncan, please just let her in but not her family. Frisk her as usual though. These people could be carrying those wee flasks in their topcoat pockets. The family can sit outside and I'll ask her why she didn't tell me herself and put my family and I through this embarrassment," said Kenneth.

"Why is it embarrassing son? You are the one who they have hurt. They're the alkies in my book and if they don't come up with a lot of money for you, they can't have my son anyway," he said with firmness.

"Oh Da, that's funny, paying money for me?" Kenneth said.

"Aye money for you to keep his expensive daughter. At least you have your own home already lad if you do like her. I suppose you could hand fast and just get on with it making a baby really quickly before she runs out of eggs, so long as she signs the 'dry farm agreement' that everyone here has to sign. Duncan has one on him all the time, don't you Duncan?" Da said. "Aye, I do," Duncan agreed.

"For what it's worth lad, I thought the two of you were an item working together. You have shared interests in bugs and insects and illustrations. She admired what you did and you admired what she did. You might do another book and become a famous couple who do stuff together even if there's only one bairn," Duncan said thoughtfully.

"I'll keep the Frasers off your back and if needs be, if they are a real problem, I'll bring in Hugh Mohr with his long rifle, so they know we are serious about protecting our own lad. I won't have them speaking to one of you like that and if Bruce hadn't spoken up for you, I would have. My blood was boiling," Duncan said.

Hugh Og put his hand on Kenneth's shoulder Zer and Meredith came around and hugged him but briefly.

"Uncle Kenneth, I'd marry you if I wasn't your niece and I'm sure I could have tons of babies one day because I'm half Islander. I'm sorry that I can't marry you Uncle Kenneth, I think you are lovely," Islay said.

Duncan whispered to Malcolm, "Keep an eye on your lass Malcolm, when she's a bit older, the lads are going to swarm around her. Now I'm off to speak to Hugh Mohr about this in case it escalates from here," he said and rushed off.

69. Let's Go Fishing

Hugh Og said, "Let's go fishing Kenneth, Malcolm. Cherry, you all good if you lose your hubby for a wee while?" he asked.

"Hugh, it's never a wee while, but of course go fishing. I'd love to eat some fish tonight. Kiss me my darling," she said to me with a passion that I wasn't expecting.

"Malcolm," she whispered, "I am so grateful that you are mine. I love you so much," she said. "I love you too my beautiful Islander lady," I said. Hamish and Bruce were surprised at the unplanned fishing trip, but thrilled and Cora was happy about it, but Ma wasn't happy to be alone and said she would spend the evening with Cherry. When we all galloped off, I felt free from worries and the weather was much better for fishing. No black clouds were rolling in, thank God and I was grateful for so many things in my life, my health, my wife, my bairns, my home and land and all my coos, good friends, our boat and good relatives, as well as good staff and a cock that stands up straight. Life for me was simple unless I had one of those weird dreams and with that simplicity there was happiness.

I caught so many fish that evening and so did Kenneth and we were all pleased with our catches. Hamish had set up a smoke house to smoke fish when we caught too many for those lean times. I can't say I was fond of smoked fish, but when salmon was smoked it was delicious, so I aimed for the salmon season. Of course, on board our boat, all the gossip from Glengarry to Glenmoriston was swapped with Grigor's condition discussed in detail, which was on the improve, despite his loneliness. Charlie, his apprentice, had moved in with him. Helen was still painting only Culloden paintings and passing them to the Frasers Trading Post now that John was dead to give them to Simon to sell to a group of collectors on the topic. Craskie farm was only just surviving, but at least it was on the upward now, but Helen no longer spoke to or of her husband Grigor. Jean, Alex's daughter was now dining out on occasion with Duncan Mohr and it looked like a relationship was growing. If anyone could be hurt, we all thought Duncan might be stung if she found a younger man. Kenneth told everyone about the Frasers of the Aird and Ivy Fraser.

Few of us wanted to give advice again except Hamish who hadn't been there during the day and he knew a bit about those particular Frasers because of his security work, but said he would make further enquiries, especially concerning her two brothers.

"What do you know Hamish?" Kenneth asked.

"I know those brothers are drunken brawlers in every drinking hole you care to name. Colin and George Fraser get frequently drunk from Inverness to the Isle of Skye. These are not the Stratherick Frasers, although they're tough like the Stratherick lot have always been in warfare but hide it well like sipping tea from bone china one minute then slashing someone's throat the next. Just like that old bloke that died recently, John Fraser, he was one of those tea sippers while probably planning your death at the same time. Deadly bloke he was in my opinion. He and Padruig knocked off a bunch of Militia on board that ship to Quebec, responsible for slashing Isobel with bayonets. So, don't underestimate them with knives. Get Duncan Mohr to frisk them for knives as well as grog if they turn up and you will need Hugh Mohr if they do, they're a nasty pair," Hamish said.

"Those are Ivy's brothers?" Kenneth remarked. "I can't believe it. So what University were they attending?" he asked.

"They have never seen the inside of a university, to my knowledge, not for the lack of finances, but too drunk and disorderly," he said. "They're just waiting for their Father to die to inherit that land in Beauly and take the easy road, to my knowledge, but I will ask around for you. It's a shame it's them that Ivy is related to. I hope you really like her, sometimes you have to escape fate like that fish whose line we cut, too risky to find out what could happen," Hamish said.

Hamish's word gave me the chills and I wanted to get home just in case they turned up unannounced to all of the women and the bairns in my house.

70. The Plan

Bruce had a bright idea before we turned the boat around to leave Loch Ness. He asked how far we were from the River Ness and the Beauly Firth.

"You can see The River Ness, Da with your own eyes there where the Loch appears to narrow then around the corner beyond there, so to speak, is the Beauly Firth," I said.

"Didn't those Frasers say they lived around here somewhere?" Bruce asked.

"I know they do," said Hamish.

"Their house faces onto the Beauly Firth but backs onto the River Ness on that peninsula near the mouth. If we stopped the boat up there thirty yards away, you could walk into the back of their house," said Hamish.

"What are you planning Bruce?" Hamish asked.

"Me? Nothing, but if Kenneth wanted the lass, he could walk into their place and after secretly locating her, accompanied by Malcolm of course, when he sees her, he could tell her to meet him at the Chapel at Craskie Farm in the morning when the Priest arrives and marry the lass. Then, without telling the parents, he would be married to her and they couldn't take her away like the Murray brothers[4] took Lord Lovat's wife that he raped that time," Da said. I had no idea who he was talking about being raped and why Lord Lovat's wife was taken by the Murray brothers and so on, but his message was clear that Kenneth could get a message to Ivy now and marry tomorrow morning. I thought it could work as I looked across at the wind-swept rear of the big house as we approached. I was nervous, I admit, but Kenneth was keen to get to Ivy without raising the attention of those brothers and he wanted to marry in the wee Catholic Chapel and we weren't even Catholic, but I married Cherry there too and they didn't even ask first if we were Catholic. I think that was because everyone else was Catholic there and so they just assumed that we were too.

The men moored the boat silently and we didn't speak again. Both Kenneth and I snuck up to the rear of the big house and tried to see where she was. It wasn't much different to sneaking up on rabbits. Then he saw her. He moved so fast and silently, it was amazing seeing my braw brother in action. I wasn't as braw, I am sure. He managed to gain her attention and I saw her eyes grow wide. Without disclosing our location, she came outside.

"Kenneth, what are you doing here?" she whispered.

"Ivy, marry me in the morning at Craskie Farm Chapel at nine o'clock and don't tell your folks. Just ride your horse and say you are going to Church, if you want to marry me. Do you?" he asked.

"Aye," she said smiling and we slinked off into the darkness and she went back inside to pack her things and find a good enough dress to get married in. They were married at nine o'clock the following morning. Her Mither may have been a bit suspicious because she gave her a lot of money for the Church collection.

The two of them galloped off home, as we all did in case, we attracted an attack from the Fraser brothers. Meredith had prepared a wonderful wedding feast consisting of a lot of fish and Ma provided goat's milk. That's a healthy wedding feast and no one turned up to steal away Kenneth's bride. They moved into Kenneth's lovely home now covered

in more paintings than his art gallery had. About one month later Bruce received the dowry he asked for Ivy and banked it in both their names but asked them not to waste it on anything frivolous. "It might be needed to replace an entire roof one year or one child's education, who knows?" he had said to them. Either way, it was clear that the parents knew she was with Kenneth and made no attempt to take her home, or criticise the way that she left and married him without including them. I think that in time Kenneth and Ivy may soften up, especially if they have bairns and include her parents, but not her brothers.

Hamish had said they were arrested again one weekend, so they were not changing.

71. My Culloden Dream

I dreamed again of a younger looking Padruig Dubh Grant, but this time he was with his friend Grigor MacGregor, Grigor Og's Father and another younger man with yellowish blonde hair whom I didn't recognise at first. Padruig had the same long legs like mine, lean like me too and he wasn't wearing a plaid. He was wearing long black tough looking pants and a black long-sleeved shirt, but he carried a plaid and a long rifle, as well as knives attached to various belts. Grigor was wearing a traditional plaid in dark camouflage colours of browns and black with a splash of mauve or teal with leather belts and knives. They were with a younger woman dressed oddly with the three of them. I suppose she was dressed a bit like Matilda, wearing long dark blue tough pants, not a skirt, with a blouse and an odd-looking waist coat. She looked at me and then they appeared annoyed, as I had entered into their dream space accidentally. She was younger than them and attractive with very long brown hair in ringlets and I wasn't sure what any of it meant other than that they were all on Culloden Field together and I did see that she held the MacGregor brooch in her hand, covered in mud. Padruig Dubh was standing protectively over them all and Grigor MacGregor told her to pin the brooch onto her clothes. I was sure that she wasn't Scottish or

English, although she would have Scottish ancestry. She had a foreign name that I do not recall and she was unsure of herself in their wet and muddy environment and she looked cold.

Then she vanished so quickly, it was as if she had never been there.

Grigor MacGregor looked happy that she had that brooch and he was of the firm opinion that she was Clan Gregor, but unable to prove it due to all of the broken ancestral lines caused by proscription. Maybe that's why he gave her the lost brooch from the field. It wasn't like any of my other dreams that were warnings or at least more specific like finding Kenneth's rabbit. I didn't think Cherry would understand this dream, so I sat up in bed and tried to identify who the third man was. Then I realised it was Hugh Mohr Chisholm as a younger man with two of the Seven Glenmoriston Men together on Culloden Field and that seemed significant, but I didn't know why, nor who she was. The twins had kept us up a lot last night, so maybe I was just overtired. New bairns are a lot of work when they are wee. At least Cherry was a natural Mither and had plenty of milk for them both. Maybe I could see Hugh Mohr about the dream after all my work today, I thought.

"Cherry, do you mind if I go and see Hugh Mohr after all my work is finished today?" I asked. "Nae darling. Please take Ruth some eggs from me. I have six in a wee box in the kitchen," she said.

Breakfast was always delicious and nutritious these days with our fresh eggs that Cherry was very proud of and breakfast was always complete when Kenneth and Ivy joined us as one big family with all of our bairns and Hugh Og and Meredith. A knock on the door revealed Duncan Mohr and Jean and her son Benny, who were all looking happy so early in the day. I thought that Hugh Og no longer had a thing to worry about with the silver fox whose hair was no longer silver. He had put some dark colouring in it to appear younger. I invited them both in for breakfast, so I could enjoy being with my family longer before my workday started or any Duncan drama.

"Eat first Duncan," I said. Islay was eating her eggs and giving us all an education at the same time on the old former Kings of Scotland because she had found her name Islay there. Between Jean and Matilda, my bairns were getting a great education with all of the books that were sent by Simon Fraser, my cousin Beth's husband, which just kept on arriving every week. I put aside a room upstairs near where Ma and Bruce slept if they were here. It was a big room in which I built a lot of shelves for all the present and incoming books, so it became the home-schooling room.

"Look Daddy, Uncle Kenneth's name is here as a King of Scotland and his brother or son was Uncle Grigor and his son was married to one of us, a lady who was a MacNachten" she said. "Really?" I made a mental note to read that book, but I assumed she was referring to King Coinneach MacAlpine. So, we are royalty on the MacGregor side and the MacNachten side. Pity about the Grants.

We also received notification that a Post Office was amongst the list of government buildings to be built in the upcoming year in Glengarry, as well as a school built up to grade seven with huge spare land allowing for a high school to be built later if the need arose and until then it was for a sporting field. I was thinking grazing land. Thanks to the efforts of Simon Fraser, who had spent government money on buying an entire farm for the school, the Post Office two blocks away, so walking distance for my wife but not too close for noise from a school. He was already widening Drover's Road and sealing it, but I wasn't sure what that entailed which upset my coos a bit with so many strangers coming up close to them. Duncan Og was earning his keep taking care of the coos not the horses, leaving Iain and Dougal, the junior grooms, to mind the Clydesdales. I apologised to Hugh and explained that it was only a few days more.

72. Love is All Around

Once I had eaten enough, having been ravenous, I asked Duncan Mohr if his news was good or bad. One never knew with him. He could calmly announce a disaster, so I always braced myself for his answers.

"Jean and I are hand fast," he answered, "so I just didn't want you all to think either of us were being immoral. I would never give Jean a bad reputation being from such a respectable family. We have both agreed that we will see if it still suits us in twelve months, so we will go the whole one year and one day without any Priests involved. After the trauma of Jean's divorce, she doesn't want a permanent marriage until we are both sure of each other. I don't mean that I am not sure of Jean, but this is a compromise as a temporary marriage. I would like your approval as my employer Malcolm. Jeanie, God bless her and her wee lad Benny and I, will live on Alex's farm. In my spare time, I will build a new home on my own land, so I don't disturb my son Duncan and his wife, Joanna," he explained.

"Duncan Og, your groom has been informed as have Alex and Matilda, because I had to ask Alex's permission to see Jeanie. I love her but she has suffered under that brute of an English Doctor, so it might take her a while to get over it and I want to protect them both. So, I'll probably be with Jeanie for about six months on Alex's land until the home is built to Jeanie's liking with everything for wee Benny there too," Duncan explained in detail "and it won't affect my work."

"Congratulation's cousin Jean," I said smiling.

"Congratulations Duncan, I hope you will both be happy together," Cherry said. "Love is all around Malcolm, isn't it?" said Cherry. "Look how many folks are falling in love, like Kenneth who even stole away his wife. It's so romantic to see Kenneth and Ivy every day and now new love with you and Jean. I wish we could find a lady love for Grigor Og, don't you?" she said. "If Hugh Mohr can get a new lady, then Grigor could. He is at least still handsome," she said.

"All the time I worked at Craskie, I never saw Grigor so much as look at another woman," Meredith said.

"I don't know," said Hugh Og. "Like you said, love is all around and maybe a lady just finds her way to him," Hugh Og said.

"Sweetheart you are such a romantic" she said and they kissed each other, "What about the Catholic part?" she asked. "Can you hand fast on top of a marriage if you can't get divorced?" she asked.

"Well, it's our Scottish tradition, so we can modify the rules, can't we?" I answered.

"I don't know," Duncan answered. "I doubt it. But I am sure I can find Grigor a woman. He looks in need if you know what I mean," he said. I gathered he was referring to sexual frustration.

"Has he ever had lady friends?" I asked.

"Nae," Hugh Og said.

"We could employ a cook for him who is in need too and let them get friendly," I suggested. "One of the wool waulkers probably fancies him," Meredith suggested.

"I'm seeing Hugh Mohr later on today, so I can ask him for a suggestion, but I'm no good at match making," I said.

Hugh Og had a lot of deliveries today and said he may be home late and was also meeting with a young man, whom he wanted to train as an offsider with him as a teamster. Cherry was seeing Matilda for English lessons in our house for her as well as Alex and Islay. I asked Cherry to ask Matilda about those blue pants from my dream and the origins of the fabric. Meredith asked if she could have a look at the herb garden to see if it needed more herbs, which it most likely did. Meredith loved to add more flavour to food as well as cater for everyone's health. She asked Hugh Og to get tomato plants from Craskie and gave him a wee list of other herbs. She had learned a lot from Granny, so I was very grateful we had Meredith.

Hugh asked me if I wanted any of the paintings from the Craskie house because Helen was selling things and might even sell the two portraits of Granny and Grandda and the Team before they vanish off the wall. Naturally I wanted them all.

It was a long hard day with the crops and all the animals and I even squeezed in riding lessons for Islay and Alex. They loved their new ponies and I was so glad I didn't have to pay for them. It was still confused why Old John Fraser left those pure-bred ponies, one male, one female, to my family. They could breed in competition with his daughter in law's business and I didn't want more ponies than we had bairns. Maximum six ponies. I thought Hugh Og's bairns and the twins could all have a pony and maybe wee Benny, if his Father doesn't fetch him back to England, which in my mind was what I had expected. I never believed that he only wanted the bairn just for Christmas with Jean having him for Hogmanay. If I was truthful with myself, I believed he would take his bairn to London for Christmas, but never return him to her. It would be better if Duncan Mohr was to get Jean with child as soon as possible, or she may suffer dreadfully.

I arrived at Hugh Mohr's house that he now shared with Ruth Beaton after work, allowing an hour to talk with him if he wasn't busy. He was pleased to see me, as was his new wife, Ruth and I found them gardening together. Love was definitely all around and it made me feel joyful. I told him the whole dream as it made no sense to me.

"Well lad you have described the field perfectly for someone who has never been there, even the smell and the dampness, so I don't doubt that you somehow went there and crossed a time barrier of some kind. The brooch is important to whomever the woman was, but I have no idea who she was and no lady would dress like that," he said.

"They might in the American colonies or New Holland?" suggested Ruth.

"That's possible," Hugh Mohr said, "but why did she just vanish like that?" Hugh asked.

"Fae folk is what my Mither would say," she said.

"They can do that," she said completely believing in it. "Were the men surprised that she went 'poof' like that?" she asked.

"I was one of those men, sexy lady," as he smacked her bottom and sat her on his knee.

"Nae, they were not surprised in the least. Like it was a regular occurrence. You looked a bit sad to see her vanish. Grigor Mohr was happy about the Clan Gregor connection, like he had found more than a clan buddy and maybe even deeper than that. He was expecting her back I think, as all three of you all were. She disappeared because of me. I think I wasn't supposed to see her," I said.

"Padruig looks like you. Do you believe me now?" he asked.

"Aye, but not his facial expression. He is so intense and as mean as hell," I said.

"Did he have the expression of a hunted man?" Hugh asked.

"Aye, I suppose he did," I said.

"You may also have looked like that if you had lived in those times Malcolm. Thank God you didn't," Hugh Mohr said with a sad reflectiveness that I had never seen on his face before and I decided to leave them both to a much happier night together. He didn't need to remember Culloden Field again.

"Thank you both for your insight," I said.

"Anytime Malcolm, you are always 'the welcome one' around here," Ruth said.

"Oh, and by the way, Duncan Mohr is hand fast with Jean. No church marriage because Jean is still recovering from the divorce and there may be troubles with the bairn ahead, but anyway they are happy presently, especially Duncan. I hope she doesn't break his heart. He wants to build her a house on his farm," I said. "She's the needy one at present and he wants to take care of her," I said.

"That's really nice. I hope it works out for them both, but I am unsure of the bairn's future," Hugh Mohr said.

"Duncan should get her with child as soon as possible," Ruth said.

"That's what I thought. Can you tell him Hugh to do the deed to make it work?" I asked.

"I can," he said smiling and was very amused about the idea of Duncan Mohr getting Jean with child at his age. "The other matter was finding a lassie for Grigor. Can you help there too?" I asked.

"Anything else?" he asked a bit sarcastically.

"Nae. Thanks Hugh," I said and almost forgot to give the eggs to Ruth as I was leaving. "Oh Ruth, these are from Cherry. They are her precious hens' eggs. Really nice for breakfast," I said. Then I rode off to get home for a bath. Cherry would complain if I stank, so I wanted a good soak in hot soapy water and to shampoo my greasy long hair. After seeing Padruig Dubh's dirty hair in that dream, I was determined to improve my appearance.

"Hello, my darling, it's your smelly husband off to the bath," I said. And before she could block her nose or some other complaint from being amongst farm animals, I headed to fill up the water to boil for my bath.

"Darling, it's already done. I am in here waiting for you and the bairns are all fed and sound asleep. I'll wash your hair my precious one, even those small curly ones," Cherry said and I was in the bath like a shot with my wife. She knew how to make me feel like a man desired by his sexy wife. Hugh Og and Meredith would often repeat the things we said to each other to tease us both the next day and it even seemed to get them worked up and the squeaking of their bed was heard more often. If Bruce and Ma slept over, I didn't like to hear those sounds, after all she was still my Mither, but on the rare occasion, it did happen and I had to close over my ears and even that didn't help. Ma was a wild cat in bed and I hadn't known it. She really loved sex. It was embarrassing for me and Kenneth when he heard it too, but our wives all thought it normal and laughed at us as being a bit childish.

A few days passed, I was pleasantly surprised when Duncan Mohr had delivered some items of value and had left them on the dining table with a note from Grigor.

"Dear Malcolm, please accept these gifts from our family to be kept in your safe keeping as they are no longer safe at Craskie Farm. Affectionately Yours, Grigor."

They were the two portraits of Granny and Grandda, as well as the team of eight Clydesdale horses driven by 'Isobel of Glenmoriston'. I asked if Duncan could hang them where Cherry thought best. Not to be rivalled by Glenmoriston history, my wife also took out a painting from her old port from under our bed painted by her Mither of their wee Island. It really was a beautiful place. So, it also took pride of place in our lounge room and would add to the chatter at our next dinner party. I asked Kenneth if I could buy more paintings from him to put in each of the bedrooms. He had one of the forests that Matilda planted, so I asked for that one in my bedroom. I really loved it and he gave it to me as a gift.

73. Helen Suicides

On our next fishing trip there was the usual gossip from Craskie, although Glengarry was rivalling Craskie with its dirty old men remarrying these days. Apparently, Helen had been all cheerful and some even said manic and waving to everyone, including Grigor. She had given all of the last of all of her paintings to Frasers Trading Post to pass on with no details as to who the money they attracted would go to. No one dared venture inside her home, these days and pay day was always on the veranda each Friday, as usual. It was only when Hamish went to collect his pay, along with the ever-increasing line of unhappy workers that it became evident that Helen was either late or missing. No one had seen her on that particular day and so poor Hamish opened the big oak door, that had seen so many family occasions in the past, to the most horrific and unexpected sight. He immediately ran to the garden and vomited, while the other workers, out of curiosity, poked their heads inside the beautiful door and regretted doing so.

Helen was hanging by her neck, from the stairs.

All of us from the family attended the funeral that wasn't well attended. Isobel-Mairi and Ewen were absent. Grigor was devastated, but had the big house thoroughly cleaned by the wool waulking ladies for a fee as it didn't smell too good. He burned all of Helen's linen and many things that were irretrievable in their poor condition, including all of her clothing. He brought in house painters and had it basically sterilised, so that every inch of it was covered with an odd pinkish colour that he liked. He even painted the exterior of the whole house, be it wood or stone, in white paint like mine. He rented out Charlotte House to the new staff he employed, who had never met Helen and moved back into his old home.

Hugh Mohr was busy finding a lady for him. Grigor had already been grieving for his wife for over a year and now that she had passed, it seemed like a respectable time to have waited. If Helen had been going to go back to him, she would have years ago.

All the land deeds were transferred into Grigor's name, including Helen's land where the school was located. A far cry from the days of proscription when a MacGregor could not inherit that land. With my daughter's books on the Kings of Scotland and having some understanding of why the brooch of the MacGregor's was 'Royal Is My Race', I understood more why they, like the Picts, had been so persecuted. It was legal at one time to hunt down and kill a MacGregor. What a threat to the monarch of that time, as well as to the Campbells, they must have presented. I had never been a fan of the Stuart dynasty and I liked them even less as time went on. I felt sorry for families who were taken in by the Bonny Prince. I know that I would never have fallen for his charm. What a shame the

Camerons got the ball rolling. If only the Gentle Lochiel hadn't agreed to follow the Prince, maybe no one else would have followed him either.

The waste of human life of that time is mind boggling, as was Padruig Dubh's loyalty to the Prince.

Cherry attended Helen's funeral with me too, although I was worried it might affect her milk flow, but nothing ever seemed to affect her lactation and for that I was grateful knowing the bairns were so well fed by their Mither. My Mither, Marion with her loyal husband and my Stepfather, Bruce also respectfully attended, for Grigor's sake. They had grown up together and they had both buried Bruce's Mither when she was killed by the dragoons on the day of the burnings in Glenmoriston. It was only fitting that Bruce would stand by Grigor. Hamish was there too, looking grey. He wasn't yet over finding Helen like that. Both Patrick and James attended, but only James appeared upset. Patrick shook his head at his sister's final day. At least Helen already had a place in the Church in which to be buried, but some opinionated people, including Henrietta, said her suicide didn't entitle her to be buried inside the Chapel. I wouldn't know anything about that, but Granny had it ready for her and so it was used. The Priests were not told at first that it was suicide just in case they wanted her moved out of the Chapel.

I engraved her name on one of the wall plaques of the many deceased folk who had lived and died on Craskie Farm. It was quite the list and it would run out of space soon. I wondered what her Father, Padruig Grant would think of her hanging herself, after all of his efforts to establish her with her own school and Art Gallery, houses and land. Very few women had that advantage in life in this time period, as men were considered only to control the purse strings. Maybe Grigor should have been handed it all after proscription had ended. Padruig had objected to Grigor marrying his favourite child, but when they were married, he still didn't respect Grigor as Isobel always had. She adored Grigor like he was her own son, which was partly why I had forgiven him. Granny saw in him something we didn't. So, what Hugh Mohr needed to find was that kind of lady for Grigor who could see whatever that was.

Reflecting so much on family, as you do after funerals, Cherry was worried about me. I had to reassure her that it wasn't serious. It was just me needing to grow up. When she first met me, I was quite immature, I think looking back on it, but with marriage and fatherhood and the hard work on the farm, some of which was new to me and fights over inheritance, I'd had to grow up fast and there had been many funerals since coming to Glenmoriston and Glengarry.

"Why don't we go on that picnic to Loch Insh with all the bairns, Alex and Matilda, Kenneth and Ivy, and Ma and Bruce, Hugh Og, Meredith, and Hamish and Cora soon?" I suggested.

"I'd really love that Malcolm if we are all up to it. It might be a nice break away and leave the two Duncans in charge with Jean," she said. We planned it for a few weeks ahead when the weather would be nice and maybe even sunny.

Grigor was selling all of Granny's sewing material, cotton reels of many colours, French buttons and silk and her myriad patterns made on paper with her pins and needles and all the things needed to sew or embroider or knit with. I bought it all for Cherry in case she wanted to sew the bairns' clothing and save money. There was even some linen for men's shirts with two different patterns. Granny had been busy at one time sewing and selling her items with which to buy the farm animals. It was an incredible achievement for it all to be lost so easily by her daughter and granddaughter. Even Charlotte the ox was the end result of Granny's sewing.

When I looked at how severe her facial features had become from earlier paintings, it was evident that life hadn't been kind to Isobel from all of that hard work. She was still beautiful and somehow quite unique. I can't say that I had ever seen another woman who looked like Granny. Her eyes were even more piercing than her husband's. I did wonder why she hooked up with Hugh Mohr, even with their lost bairn when

Padruig and her were so well matched, despite the violence in their marriage.

74. Carmel MacPherson

"What's up with you two?" asked Hugh Mohr, who had let himself in without knocking.

"How are you Hugh, losing Helen?" I asked.

"I am fine, thank you for asking. I think that Helen doing what she did was predictable. Her Mither was that way inclined too when life became too overwhelming. I can't imagine my current wife, Ruth ever entertaining the idea of suicide. In Isobel's case however, I was the handsome rescuer with the blonde hair, so she changed her mind about dying and decided life would be just fine if I was there to rub up against. We did it in every room of the house and every out house and the forest," he said bragging proudly of his sexual exploits with Granny, right up to her death. Cherry had had enough of that conversation and tended to the bairns but not before saying

"Maybe that was just another form of suicide in killing her soul, Granny's love and devotion to Padruig was obvious. She was a broken-hearted soul and you took advantage of it, that's what I think," she said and left the room.

"What can I help you with my friend?" I asked, trying to overlook her comment.

"Ruth has found Grigor a lady if he likes her. Are you interested?" Hugh Mohr asked.

"Aye, who is she?" I asked.

"Her name is Carmel Julianne MacPherson, fellow midwife to my wife Ruth. She's Grigor's age or a bit older, but not ugly and lives in Cameron lands somewhere. Widow for ten years. All her bairns were moved to the Americas years ago. She has her own home. Don't know all the details. Ruth has told her the whole story and she is moved by Grigor's life story. She wants to meet him, so what now?" Hugh asked.

"Can you introduce them? I don't think Grigor would take me seriously with women," I asked.

"Hmmm maybe Ruth and I could drop around with Carmel taking a cake or whatever the ladies suggest and then Carmel could see him up close and decide if she does like him. The women could go to the privy together where Carmel could pass on her thoughts and when they come back in, we could have a signal of some kind being for yes, she likes him, or no she doesn't," Hugh said. "If she does like him, I know he needs a cook because he doesn't have anyone permanent yet, even though Carmel is busy midwifing. Grigor has emptied out Isobel's and my old bedroom because Helen had moved in there and he's using that as an office for his book work on the farm. I heard James is helping him free of charge. It's quite a good office space. Old John Grant's bedroom is where he puts any guests. He has moved himself up to the top floor. All the old paintings have gone, but Kenneth might be able to sell him a few nice ones of nice things or portraits. Kenneth has one of Morag-Freya that Grigor might like," Hugh said.

I agreed to all of Hugh Mohr's plans because I wasn't up to it and needed to take care of my own family. Hugh left with all his plans formulated. I mentioned the painting of Morag-Freya to Kenneth later on.

I was concerned about Hamish too and was keen to see him again on our next fishing trip before we all went to Loch Insh and I wanted to invite him and Cora too. Hugh Og suggested we take the team to Loch Insh to fit everyone that was coming into the carriage. We thought we should take a four or six horse team with a spare horse running behind in case one throws a shoe. The number of people coming was growing, as excitement mounted and Ma, Cherry, Meredith and Ivy were planning the food as well as the bedding in the carriage, because it would be the following morning before we all arrived back home from a journey that distant. The bairns would need to sleep overnight in the carriage as would we in turns.

Our next fishing trip was quiet. The two brothers, especially Hamish were unusually quiet. Bruce decided to address the obvious topic that everyone was avoiding.

"I suppose her body was a mess Hamish lad? I've seen men hung in the colonies, six at a time and the smell made me throw up as they all lost control of their bowels. It's not a dignified thing to speak of when it's a lady, but lad you are too quiet and it's not healthy. I understand that she jumped from the balustrade with the noose around her neck, is that right? Was her neck snapped or did her head come clean off? Some people do make a mess of hanging," he asked.

I heard Kenneth vomit over the side at the visual image. "Bruce, do you have to be so explicit?" I asked.

Hamish was careful with his answer and responded honestly. "Her neck was just snapped, but there was a mess naturally and it stank to high heaven. I was glad I wasn't asked to help clean it up, but that'd be why Grigor has had the place sterilised and painted. He had the floor tiles lifted too because they wouldn't come clean and so they've been replaced. Gruesome task. The officers who attended all threw up too and didn't stay too long. The staff there that day all decided to leave their jobs. And aye, they said she had jumped from the balustrade with the noose around her neck. It was lucky that Grigor hadn't lived there with her for a long while, because the officers grilled him for over an hour, in case he had murdered her, I suppose," he said.

"The lead officer and the doctor ruled it as suicide by hanging by her own hand," Hamish said.

75. Loch Insh with Friends

"Are you and Cora and your three bairns coming to Loch Insh?" Bruce asked.

"Loch Insh?" Hamish asked. "Fishing there too?" he asked.

"Why not?" I said. "Whatever we all want to do," I said and I explained our plans and his face brightened up. Hamish was coming with his family to Loch Insh, unless something unexpected came up. He wanted to teach his lad, Donald how to fish, he said. It made me enthusiastic to teach my Alex how to fish too. If it was warm enough, we could swim in the Loch too. I had missed Loch Insh so much. Both Kenneth's wife, Ivy and my wife would see where we were born and raised and that meant a lot to me and my brother. Our bairns too needed to know that was where we were from, not Glenmoriston.

Loch Insh Bell

Cherry wanted to see the Chapel with all of its its mysteries, despite me telling her that it wasn't the original Chapel which was burned down. Even the old bell they claimed could fly through the air or some such, wasn't the original bell, I am sure of it. There was, however one part of the Chapel that was genuinely mysterious. The old Druid stone at the porch front where my Grandda stood after hearing the voice of my Grandma Isobel, needing help to get home to Craskie. That was real. It somehow transported him to where Granny was in the Great Glen, just as she was falling from her horse. That story did involve her brother too who was Grigor's Father, Grigor Mohr. The MacGregor's keep coming up, no doubt about it. I wanted to stand or sit on that old Druid stone and pray, wherever they have put it now and in its odd bowl shape.

On the day, there was a lot of excitement to be visiting our birthplace and Islay was especially interested that she was half 'Loch Inshian and half Islander'. We had to explain that she was a whole Scot, who lived in Glengarry, so then she said it made her a Glengarrian. Her world was too small to view herself as just a Scot. The ladies were all carrying a big basket of food each and I didn't ask what was in them other than checking for flasks of coffee and tea. There were a lot of blankets, pillows and warm clothing for the latter end of the day and night. They even packed milking stools, so we could sit by the loch on a seat. Some of us packed things to swim in and for me that was shorts and we fishermen all packed hand lines for the bairns, as well as for ourselves.

I offered to help Hugh Og drive the team as James had taught me a little how to drive the horses. Hugh Og said he would teach me as we went, if I sat up top with him and his new off sider, Angus MacKenzie. He was only seventeen years old and was also responsible for loading and unloading the carriage. He was a dark-haired young lad who was good looking and intelligent, but importantly he was a good horseman already and had previously worked elsewhere as a groom. He was learning Erse upon Hugh's request, but young Islay was a bit too interested in him for my liking.

"He's cute Ma," she said to Cherry.

It was a wonderful journey from Glengarry to Loch Insh and I felt quite the expert with the team by the time we arrived. All the ladies unpacked things where we had decided to stop, which was right in front of my Grandda's old croft. I went and said my hellos to my old friends who now occupied it and they had found a few of Grandda's things that they gave me, con-sisting mostly of books and a diary of his found in the ceiling. They loved our team in front of their croft eating up the long grass and brought buckets of water out for them to drink, then left us in peace.

Our activities went full range from swimming, to fish-ing, to visiting the Chapel up on the rise. I dived into the loch first wanting to feel its familiar-ity and its coolness after the journey, while Hamish got

Druid Stone, Loch Insh

out the fishing gear and my wife wandered up to the Chapel of the Swans. I hoped she wouldn't start getting the dreams that I was susceptible to. I remember sitting on that Druid stone for hours as a bairn, inside its bowl, especially after Da passed away. As I wiped myself dry, Cherry came up to me and asked where it was that Da and I had fished in the ice. I pointed to the exact spot in front of the croft, only now it wasn't frozen.

76. Da's Grave in Loch Insh

Then she asked where he was buried and I was surprised that I felt sad, but I took her to his grave beside the Chapel as she was entitled to know. His gravestone was covered in beautiful decorations that Grandda had engraved. The headstone said his name was Nachtain MacGregor MacNachten, husband to Marion MacGregor Grant MacNachten, father to Máel Coluim and Coinneach. It was odd to see my name written in its original form. The MacGregor name keeps on coming up too. I didn't remember that Da was also Clan Gregor on his Mither's side and it was surprising that my Mither was told back that far that she had the MacGregor connection too. I felt sorry for Isobel all over again. What a life she had led, it was mind boggling. Then wee Islay came to my Father's grave and asked if this was one of the Kings of Scotland.

"Why do you think that Islay?" I asked her.

"Because that name is one of the Kings," pointing at Gregor.

"Can you show me that book again at home love?" I asked. "Aye, he was King of the Picts and King Kenneth was half Pict," she said, then off she ran. Cherry and I both looked at one another.

"So, we are Pictish then?" I said. "My name in Gaelic means follower of Saint Columba, so an early convert name to Christianity, when now I'm not even Christian. I wonder if my Father is disappointed in me?" I said. "I do remember him calling me Mael Coluim and Kenneth was called Coinneach. I even called him that until we both started school and the English teachers changed our names and disallowed

Gaelic to be spoken. However, none of us knew Pictish language," I added.

"Maybe you are of Pictish ancestory but not completely. Look at these drawings, these are Pictish. Can we get Kenneth to draw this grave with all these Pictish symbols? Maybe one day, it will make sense?" she asked. Kenneth obliged with his lady love Ivy, who was fascinated.

"Granny said not to tell anyone Ivy, so don't tell your relatives please. One day I think it will be something to be proud of do you think but not yet?" I said

Ivy promised to never disclose family matters but didn't think it was a big deal at all but didn't have Pictish ancestory herself. She was mostly French, Irish and Norwegian she said. We Scots are a mixture of a bunch of people, so it shouldn't matter if we had Pictish also.

Hamish had fun teaching Donald how to fish and didn't catch much, only a few wee fish. The ducks were catching more than him on this occasion. Alex then wanted me to teach him too, so the next generation of fishermen were being born as Kenneth painted the scene. It was time for dinner and the ladies laid out a spread fit for a king for sure and we all ate until our hearts content. Even the Clydesdales wanted to see if we were eating something better than them and one of them nuzzled me wanting an apple or a carrot or both, so it was both. Hugh Og was surprised.

"He is never that friendly. He likes you Malcolm, or is it Mael Coluim?" he jested.

It was nice that a big horse liked me and kept nuzzling my neck for more apples, so I gave him more. Most of us had walked around the loch, except where it was steep. Some of us had swum to the wee islands and back and some had fished. Matilda fell asleep with Moses on the grass. Uncle Alex then had the chance to talk to me.

"I've missed you Malcolm," he said.

"Me too Uncle," I responded. "How are you since your sister passed?" I asked.

"I'm okay now. I was shocked, naturally, at the time, but things over there were getting worse. I was glad that Grigor had moved out, for his sake," he said. "I heard that you asked Hugh Mohr to introduce a nice lady named Carmel MacPherson to Grigor?" Alex asked.

"Aye, did he tell you what he thought of her?" I asked. Alex then appeared pleased.

"Carmel really liked him and wants to be hitched, was what I was told. Grigor was shocked at a lady being interested in him, so she had to be very bold to get his interest. She kissed him on the lips passionately, so I'm told," he said smiling.

Alex had to stop there as his smile may have appeared rude as he gained his composure.

"Grigor realised that he was as horny as a dog and forgot to hand fast and the two of them were at it like rabbits in his house, so Hugh Mohr and Ruth, both thought it was better to give them privacy and went home, leaving them to it," he said. "I presume by now that they have hand fast, but no one knows that for certain. Anyway, well done Malcolm, that was a bonny idea. Craskie might be on the up," he added. "Helen was ill and I suppose if I had realised just how ill she was, I could have had her hospitalised, but I am busy like you and she didn't ask for help. James might have known more than us just how poorly she was, but because she opposed your family, he lost respect for her too, as did I," he added.

On the way home, Hugh Og took the reins in the early morning darkness, but he lit two lanterns on each side of the carriage to light the way. It was very dark and I was bemused at how both Hugh and the horses seemed to know the way home.

"I'm glad you know the way Hugh, it's not like there are sign posts saying, 'Glengarry this way'," I commented.

"Wouldn't that be amazing to have signposts to know the way. I got lost several times when I first started doing this without Granny. It was a scary experience until I realised that the horses knew the way, so actually we don't need to worry if we ask them to take us home, they always will but most likely only to Craskie until they have been in Glengarry for a longer period of time," Hugh said.

"They're like homing pigeons in a way then?" I asked.

"Aye, they can bolt at the first sign of home, so you can feel the pull on the reins," he said.

"I have had such a wonderful time, my good friend. Thank you so much for allowing us all to use the carriage and your Team. I just love these horses. I hope my lads grow up to be like you handling these horses like you do," I said.

"Say, the word when they're older and I'll teach them. No problems. I'd love that," he said.

The family were mostly all asleep in the back after a long but enjoyable time in Loch Insh. My two bairns wouldn't stop running around as well as play with and on the horses, as did Matilda's, Hamish's and Hugh's daughter, if they weren't fishing. They had all enjoyed each other's company playing games.

"This sure beats that silly 'gathering of the bairns' with Nachtain trying to murder one of his cousins," I said.

"Nachtain is like his Father. A violent person by nature. He had us all fooled when he married Isobel-Mairi," Hugh Og said, as the freezing cold air was becoming even colder.

"It's not going to rain, is it?" I asked.

"It can always rain in Scotland Malcolm, you know that. There are raincoats under the seat for us three, or you can go in the back if you like," he said.

"Nae, I'll stay here with you and your raincoats. You and Angus might need my help," I answered.

"How is it Angus, do you like your new job?" I asked.

"Och aye, I do. Hugh's a good boss. I love the horses and the old farmhouse on Cherry Farm is right comfortable and friendly," he answered.

"How are you all complying with the dry farm ruling?" I asked.

"I have never drunk in my life and to be honest, I am relieved that I won't be pressured by mates into drinking," Angus answered.

Angus was a good lad, I thought and the journey was uneventful until the Great Glen, which was eerie and we saw a few foxes run across the narrow road.

"Ma said this place had some bad ghosts, so to never stop here in the dark," Hugh said.

"How does one become a bad ghost?" I asked.

"I think they are ghosts of the English that we Scots killed during and after Culloden. They're angry that they were killed, I guess. They didn't like Ma for sure. She was sick after going through here alone on horseback from Loch Insh," Hugh said.

"Is this where she nearly fell from her horse?" I asked.

"Aye it was. Legendary story that one," he said.

"Did you all know that lady?" asked Angus.

"See? Legendary, even the young folk like Angus here knows that story," Hugh said.

"She was my Grandma, lad," I replied to him. "She had just been to see our family at Loch Insh and was on her way home alone in this darkness," I said.

To Angus it was a fascinating story, but to me I was back in Loch Insh, waiting for Granny to come back and get us all, as she had promised so we could all live together on Craskie Farm. Life can certainly throw some unexpected events at you and that was one that I would never forget. I might have known Padruig Dubh better, if I had met him then.

As our strong friend Hugh pulled the Team into Glengarry, we were all pleased to see the Cherry Farms and Loch Garry

Ranch. The lights at both farms had been lit by the two Duncans, but we entered at our end and Matilda's family walked home from there. Hamish was staying over for the day as we had planned, with bedding arranged for his bairns. Jean had hot food waiting for us all then went home to her farm with Duncan Mohr on her arm. Duncan Og assisted unhitching the team and brushed all the horses down and fed the tired beasts. Cherry carried both of the twins and I carried Islay and Alex inside and put them to bed, taking off their boots first. Bathe tomorrow was my idea. Wee Islay pointed at the book for me with the Kings of Scotland in it, as I was leaving their bedroom. She even remembers things in her sleep. I was hungry again and keen to see what Jean had cooked. It was a meat stew of some kind and we all scrunched up our noses a bit.

"It needs salt, marjoram, potatoes, onion, tomato, garlic, pepper that's all," said Meredith, who was a bit amused but too tired to add those ingredients, so we ate the awful stew and felt sorry for Duncan Mohr if he had to eat Jean's food every night. Cherry had the big water boiling, so I guess that meant that no matter what, I was having a bath, even though I'd had a swim in the Loch.

"So long as you rub me with that soap Cherry," and off we went to enjoy ourselves and we left both Hugh and Meredith to enjoy themselves.

"Come on upstairs husband," I heard her say, "I like you dirty," Meredith said. So, smelling like horse sweat and horse shit, she had him in every condition and she adored her big smelly man. Cherry on the other hand would only have me if I smelled like a rose. Hamish, Cora and their bairns had the entire first floor and they were active for the rest of the night, on and off. Kenneth had the only quiet zone, his lovely wee stone house, but Duncan Mohr reported the next day that we were all very active, including Kenneth and Ivy. The dirty old bloke just stood outside in the dark and listened to all the love making sounds. Jean and Duncan weren't doing it as much as all of us obviously. Poor old Duncan.

"Do you need any tips Duncan, so you too can do what we all do?" I asked cheekily.

77. The Old Books

I was curious about the old books and the things found in Grandda's old croft, especially his diary. I had a lot to read with the book on Kings, as well as these as I worked the next day. I sat amongst the coos, who gathered and mooched around me while I read. The diary was my priority. I was shocked at some of it and touched by some, but interested when it came to plans surrounding us made with Granny. If I had ever doubted the story, it was there in black and white and it was intended that we live with her and Padruig in the main house. Helen had her way in stopping that from ever happening and then taking her own life makes it doubtful where she was headed in the Afterlife. After being a good daughter, how could she let herself down like that? I will never know. The only certainty was how much she hated my beautiful Mither after she was told about us all.

Grandda's diary included the beating that Granny received the night after seeing us, performed by Hugh Mohr, so she would live through the night and seeing Padruig's capacity for meanness in my dreams, I believed it. I read up then on the Scottish Kings and decided to talk to Grigor about the MacGregors related to King Kenneth McAlpin. My Grandda's other books were in another strange language. I assumed it was old Irish, but I wasn't sure. There were some drawings too, like his old Druid stuff. I thought I had better keep that and the diary well hidden in my safe. Too much Pict or Druid evidence might hurt my children one day. Let the historians guess who we all were and make fools of themselves.

I was still sitting and reading when a shadow cast over me and I quickly closed the book that I was reading.

"What might you be reading then lad? Dirty women or some such in the privacy of the coo paddock, eh?" Hugh Mohr questioned. It took quite a lot of convincing that I had never read a dirty book on women, so I gave up and carefully hid them in my satchel to later deposit in my safe.

"I just came to tell you about Grigor and his new woman, Carmel," he said. "But it looks like you're reading something more interesting than Grigor's sex life, eh? What language was that I saw," he asked.

"Don't know actually. I can't read it," I replied.

"You're an interesting fella, young Malcolm, I'll say that. All the coos are hanging around you like flies," he said. I hadn't noticed what they had done, but they had come closer and closer.

"They're just friendly coos," I said. "Hmmm" was the guttural noise he made frequently doubting what you were saying but leaving it at that and carrying his long rifle, he wandered off between the coos with some difficulty. It did appear that they didn't like him as much as me, but I hadn't noticed that before.

I decided to drop the books back and then see Jean and ask how she was going with dirty Duncan Mohr. When she answered her door, she looked a bit better than usual. 'It can't be her stew improving her health,' I thought. I suppose we are all going to worry more now that someone has succeeded in topping themselves in the family and I thought Jean had looked more miserable than Helen had ever looked during her divorce. She invited me in saying Duncan was due back soon. She had heard about our picnic and was a little envious, I detected. I had never been close to Jean because we were all newcomers. I always thought her accent was odd being born in Nova Scotia. I asked her about foreign languages because that was her specialty and she was considering returning to work but asked me what I wanted to know. I wrote down from memory the hierographics from the old books and asked her what language it was. She looked puzzled and replied that it looked like ancient Egyptian, but it wasn't, so she thought it could be another ancient middle eastern language, like Persian although old Irish was there too, so she didn't know without going to the library or speaking with a linguist from Edinburgh University.

"No worries, Jean, don't do that," I said, as I took it from her. "How's it going with Duncan Mohr?" I asked.

"He's very sweet and attentive. I can't complain, but I am not wanting to have sex," she said openly. "I don't know why. I just can't get into it. Not yet anyway. Duncan is disappointed, I know but I can't help it," she said.

"My wife cooks up a hot bath and soaps me up and washes my hair and that starts it for us," I said. "Everyone's different but you could boil up the water and get the tub ready in front of the fire," I said. "The other thing you could do is have a stew of beef not venison and add salt, pepper, marjoram, tomatoes, onion, potatoes, and carrots. Taste test it as you go. Duncan likes his food," I said trying to remember all the missing ingredients that Meredith named. "He also likes his deserts like those cream buns with jam," I said.

"Will that make a difference in my wanting sex?" she asked.

"Aye, of course. You will see the look in his eyes if he likes the food. You will feel happier, so then you give him a hug and let him move his hand around and it'll take off for sure," I said.

"Oh Malcolm," she said feeling embarrassed and shy.

"You have to make another bairn Jean, you're so young," I said.

"Thank you, Malcolm, I appreciate your visit. I'll start that stew now, then the buns," she said.

I whispered to her to not wear any underwear to make access easier. She was giggling as I left. I passed Duncan as I approached my front door and I had a vision of Jean taking off her underwear and smiled to myself.

"I've been to see Jean about a language question, but you weren't there. She was missing you, I think, you dirty dog," I said.

"Was she?" he asked and walked faster than usual back to his house. With my fingers crossed, I hoped she'd taken all of my advice. I watched the clock to see how long he was gone, and he was having an extended dinner break. Cherry asked me why I was watching the clock and I told her about the advice I had given to Jean.

"Oh Malcolm, that's so funny. You are now the sex adviser and my bath even got a mention. I wonder if it'll work," she said.

"They have to make a bairn, so it'll work," I said.

"So, you tell people about our sexy baths, eh?" she asked as she crept up on my chest, opening my shirt and holding my member in her hand. Kissing my wife was the most erotic thing I needed to do to get 'the general' unable to control himself, so our sex life was very healthy. It was a pity Alex and Islay walked in wanting lunch.

"Mummy, Daddy can't pish in here on the couch," he said. "Make his pee pee point into the chamber pot. I'll get it Ma," Alex said as he rushed off for a chamber pot to ensure that I wasn't going to pish on the couch. I love how bairns think. They are so innocent.

78. Is it a Fairy Dun?

In my dreams that night, I was in snow-covered high country, riding a big horse droving coos and herding the last of the calves across a burn that they were afraid of. Their Mithers had already crossed over the fast flowing, freezing cold burn. I managed to round them up as the farmer was yelling at me to hurry up as I herded them across gingerly. I then saw their Mithers who had been looking for their calves, come running up behind the farmer who couldn't hear them coming up from behind him. I was waving and calling to him that they were running to their calves in a panic and to step aside, but he didn't understand me. The other farmer saw them coming too and pushed him aside from one of the Mithers, but he was still trampled by the second coo, who was frantic to reach her calf.

The home was a small farmhouse made of stone underneath a few huge trees in a picturesque setting where he was taken, bleeding from his head.

He had a concussion. One of the farmers was a Fraser with bright ginger hair, whose young wife was wearing a pink, long old-fashioned dress from her neck to her ankles. But she wasn't shy, she was quite bossy and almost rude, but clearly loved her ginger haired husband. Her name was Isobel. There were other people there, one whom I recognised from that Culloden dream. 'The disappearing lady' on that day was there too, only she didn't disappear this time. This was where she lived, and her husband was injured. It was remote, but they liked it there, it seemed and her efforts to assist him were unappreciated as he had a brain injury, I thought. It looked like four or five of them lived there, as well as that lady's bairns, a set of twins a boy and a girl, the young married lass who had long straight fair hair, different hair to her siblings and her own bairn, and a naughty young lad. An adult friend arrived with the last of the calves and helped her with her husband, who was cursing at his wife in Gaelic, and I don't think she understood Gaelic.

That friend looked like a MacDonald. Then I awoke.

I got out the map to see where that home could be. I estimated that it was Fraser country in the Aird, somewhere before Inverness. The burn and its shape were followed by a waterfall further down and it could be located easily, so I had to go there for some reason. I knew that I would be able to recognise the small home and the outbuildings and obviously there were coos there, as well as horses. I told Cherry, who asked me why I needed to go there.

"Was I worried about the man's injuries?" she asked. I knew he was going to recover, so I couldn't answer it other than I just had to go, and would she allow me to go with a friend if I left her under Duncan's protection? She agreed but didn't understand, so she packed up plenty of food and coffee and water for me into saddle bags, as well as that map and apples for the horses. I asked Kenneth to come with me and he agreed, so long as he could bring his sketching book, so he could commit it all to memory.

Kenneth and I mounted up on our horses with Hugh Og looking worried and asking why and where with confusion on his face.

"Just the Aird," I said. "Cherry will explain it to you," I said as we rode off together. It was lovely weather in Glengarry, however we had allowed for snow as we went higher and higher. Kenneth said he had never been to this part of the Aird. It was very remote and I had never been there either. I was just following the map, when I spotted the burn eventually in amongst snowy surroundings.

"This is familiar," I said to Kenneth.

"What are we going to do when we get there?" Kenneth asked.

"I'm not sure. The injured farmer looked like an older version of Grigor, so it's not out of the question for him to be a MacGregor, despite this being Fraser lands. She was the same woman from Culloden who had the MacGregor brooch and then vanished. The young lass looks like a Chisholm with that blonde hair," I said.

"This might be a hangout for criminals Malcolm. What if we stumble across bad people, then what?" Kenneth asked sounding concerned.

We arrived at the burn directly opposite the house, exactly as it was in my dream. The trees too were the same, as was the snow and the outbuildings and cattle mooching about behind the outbuildings. I asked Kenneth to take the reins of my horse when he objected.

"Malcolm, there's something weird about this place, like it's not really there or not real at all and if we go across the burn, we may never be able to return," he said seriously. At that time their front door opened, but they didn't or couldn't see us despite our visibility. There was a young lady with straight blonde hair who looked like a Chisholm. She wore a weird old-fashioned pink floral dress from neck to ankles. Her husband followed her and he had bright ginger with greying hair, carrying what was their young child who looked nothing like the father. The important fact was they couldn't see us. Kenneth then said.

"This place is too weird Malcolm. It's as if it's like another time zone over there or a fairy dun," Kenneth said. "I'm not going there and I don't want you to, either. Can we go home now please? I value my normalcy too much to risk weirdness," he said. I agreed with Kenneth. The other side of the burn was like another world. I remembered what was said by Hugh Og about bad ghosts and we both decided to leave because we valued our wives too much.

"Let's go back aways and eat that food that our wives packed," he said.

"I'll sketch it for you and those strange looking people, especially the girl in that odd pink dress" Kenneth said. "Who wears dresses like that these days?" he commented. Then we left. I didn't catch a glimpse of the injured farmer or the vanishing lady but there wasn't any panic, so I deduced that it wasn't serious. I apologised to my brother for wasting his time and he said it was not a waste of time if it meant preventing me from disappearing into some fairy dun. He really believed in fairy duns.

"You know those folklore stories where people can disappear for hundreds of years and don't always arrive back alive?" Kenneth said.

"Aye, but you read those books more than me, what's with the dress then in fairy land?" I asked.

"Fairies wear stuff like that," he answered. "That fabric would not be in the shops," he answered.

Cherry and Ivy were so relieved to see us both return the next day, after resting overnight in a shieling. Hugh Og demanded an explanation because next time he was going after me if I did that again. I had no idea they were all so worried about us. When I explained that it was thanks to Kenneth that I didn't knock on that door, suddenly Kenneth was the hero of the day.

"Honey, I can't have you taking chances with all of us depending on you," Cherry said.

"I'm curious," said Meredith. "Old Isobel would see her brother Grigor Mohr as a ghost in the house, even at the dining table at Craskie Farm. You do understand that Grigor is dead?" she asked. "Is it possible that like Old Isobel, you too saw him as a farmer, but a ghost just the same?" she asked.

"I don't doubt it. Padruig is dead too and I've seen and communicated with him. They are quite capable of communicating as dead people," I said.

"I sure hope I don't see Helen," Ma said.

"I'm curious about that dress," Ma said. "If we go to a textile factory, we could take the drawing Kenneth did to identify it then that'll give us the time period we are dealing with and where the fabric is from, the designer and so on," she said.

"I am not going to dismiss Malcolm's dream. I too want to find the message within it," she said.

"Very well said Mither," said Bruce. "Just because you had to come back son, doesn't mean you'll lose the message. We can take out the wee cart tomorrow darling if you feel like doing some detective work for our lad," he said. Then they left planning their day after milking the goats. They took the drawing of the dress, worn by the lass with them.

"It is a terrible looking dress, but they are country folk," Ivy said.

"Both country folk and Highland folk, that remote would be wearing warm, woollen tartan, it was so cold there," I commented. "She wore small boots, but she would be freezing cold in that dress," I added.

"It's not a real mystery if her husband just told her that he wanted her to wear neck to ankles pretty frocks," Cherry said.

"If my husband told me this is what you have to wear, I would wear it just to please him," she said.

"Or if she's dead, maybe she won't feel the cold," Ivy added.

That gave me the creeps to think that they were all not of the living, as we understood the living.

"Time to chat to my coos," I said. It was all getting to me.

Kenneth yelled out that he would do all the paintings overnight up at his Art Gallery, so as not to attract ghosts into their house.

"Or fairies," I yelled back smiling. My coos had missed me, so I fussed over them a bit and even brushed the big bull down to look good for his ladies and as I was telling him he had to look good for his ladies, I saw Jean coming in my direction. I wondered if she was already with child as her facial expression was glowing.

"Malcolm," she called. "Aye cousin," I said, pleased to see her and talk again of normal things. Duncan Mohr who had worked hard in my absence, had done the deed she said, no longer shy to impart this kind of girly thing to me. I needed to confirm it and asked how often.

"So many times, I lost count," she said, almost giggling at the memory.

"Malcolm, I have never had sex like that before. He is a wonderful lover," she said quietly. I gave my wee cousin a big hug. I was so pleased for her. I could never imagine the old fella as a wonderful lover, but it worked for them.

"Did you do the bath thing?" I asked.

"I barely had time to put on the stew and the buns and the water for his bath when he came bursting through the door beaming at me. I was instantly excited and poured in the water for him and undressed him," Jean said.

"Jean, you had better not tell me anymore or he might get embarrassed," I said.

"Oh, okay," she said. "But I can tell Cherry, can't I?" she asked. And off she went to tell Cherry. She was obviously bursting to tell someone, and I had to work with Duncan Mohr and take him seriously and not see him naked in his bath or whatever exploits they got up to, but I was happy for him and her.

All that sex talk was actually giving me a message from the General and to make it worse a wee coo nudged me hard, right on my cock. "Wo, not there!" I said, when Hugh Mohr visited me again while I was rubbing my cock from the pain it had caused.

"Still hiding in the paddock playing with yourself Malcolm?" he asked.

"I am not, I was nudged in my groin by one of the coos and it hurt," I replied.

"Hmmmm," was his response, disbelieving my story. "Heard you took off to the Aird yesterday. What was that all about? Bruce said he was going to research a pink dress that some lass was wearing," Hugh said.

"Aye," I said.

"Can you describe it exactly?" Hugh asked.

"Aye, odd frock that one. It was ruffled at the neck and the cuffs. It was neck to ankles long, pink, lightweight floral fabric, long sleeves, belt about the waist, buttoned from neck to waist," I said.

"Hmmm. Was the lass fair haired and tall with a red headed husband?" Hugh asked.

"Do you know them then?" I asked.

"In a manner of speaking. It was a long time ago. When Isobel was still married to Padruig, I had a fling with a lass who came out of nowhere and I figured there'd be no repercussions, so I had my way with her. If Isobel had known, she would have flown right off the handle, so naturally no one ever knew, except Padruig and the men," he said.

"The woman was a writer but somehow, she gave birth to a blonde wee lassie and they both turned up on my doorstep where I was living with another lassie for a wee while. A neighbour had shown them the way. She looked younger, different you might say, and I had never had a biological child of my own, so naturally I thought they were having me on and I sent them on their way with that neighbour who lived alone. He couldn't believe his good luck, so he wanted to keep them both. When I told Padruig and Os'sian about them, they came with a spy glass to watch her from a hill, overlooking that house and she was wearing a brooch that I knew was given to her by Grigor Mohr from Culloden field. Padruig said I was an idiot as it was obviously her and she may be dead, but living here with the bairn who may be alive. Don't ask me to explain that," he said.

"Anyhow as she grew up, we went shopping to Inverness, the lady that I was having the fling with was always complaining about not having enough clothing, other than the blue pants she always wore. The bairn loved pink floral and wanted that pink floral dress in every size. She didn't wear anything else. Her name was Isobel too," Hugh said. "Don't ever have a fling Malcolm while you are already having a fling, it gets too complicated," he said.

"Hugh, are you saying that lass is your daughter who's living in the Aird?" I asked.

"Biologically, aye. I didn't raise her for long, Grigor Mohr did, but that's another story that's too complicated to explain. He delivered the wee bairn too. I'm not welcome up there in the Aird and Grigor Mohr is long dead," he said and went on his way leaving me in shock.

The farmer was Grigor Og's father, Grigor Mohr MacGregor who I saw in the dream, and was not of the living. Both his and Hugh's daughter, Isobel may be alive but of that, I was uncertain, as well as her red headed husband. Her Mither would also be long dead, but maybe they all lived there together in a spiritual sense? I asked Cherry that night if she had sat on the Druid stone up at Loch Insh and she had. I hoped I wasn't going to have more dreams like that one that are interconnected between the dead and the living. When I told Kenneth, he was shocked that the lassie was Hugh Mohr's biological daughter. He too had sat on the Druid stone as had I.

"So, she might be alive then?" Kenneth asked.

"Not sure, maybe?" I responded.

"Can't you look up the Title Deeds in Inverness on that land and see who owns it?" Ivy said. "Ask Aonghus for free maybe?" she said. "It's the most logical way to find out, isn't it?"

We hadn't thought of that and felt a bit silly, so that was next when in Inverness or Ma and Bruce could do it while they're doing their detective work. I still had a sore cock. According to cousin Aonghus, that remote land in Fraser country in the Aird was owned currently by two people – John Fraser and Ali Grigor MacGregor. The fabric was French silk and was unavailable here and had never been made here, to their knowledge, but had been sold in Inverness, a long time ago. This meant that no date was available, but possibly after the first Quebec campaign that Padruig Dubh was part of. Ma also researched the tough blue pants and they were also neither made here nor sold here but came from the colonies of the Americas at one time, possibly New York. Both fabrics could last this long they said, especially the blue pants that may have had hemp in the mix of fabric.

"Who owns these?" they asked. They were curious too, being so old.

When Ma and Bruce came home with their information, I told them what Hugh Mohr had said. Bruce was shocked.

"That man has no morals at all. Having a fling with a married woman was bad enough, but then a fling on top of the fling producing a bairn that he couldn't bother raising," Bruce ranted. "Disgusting individual!" he said.

"Aye, he is that, but he is also game enough to be honest, which I appreciate Bruce. Poor Granny was deceived by him.

She must have thought that he adored her, while he was also off with the other unknown lady, who also didn't know about Granny," I concluded. Both women were deceived.

Cherry had been listening to us all and hadn't wanted to interrupt, then finally spoke up.

"Malcolm, you know all that sewing stuff that you bought me from Grigor, just before Helen died?" she said.

"Aye?" I said.

"I don't know if it's of any help, but in amongst all of those things was pink, floral silk, as well as French buttons and silk thread in pink, as well as a paper pattern in the design that you have described. Is this the same pink silk that you saw on the lass in the Aird and your dream?" Cherry asked.

Cherry passed me the exact same pink floral silk that her dresses were made from.

"Do you know what that means?" I asked. "Granny was making her dresses or selling them in Inverness where Hugh Mohr bought them," I said.

I had to see Hugh again with the sample of silk, the buttons and the pattern.

79. Hugh Mohr and his Flings

I found Hugh Mohr once again with Ruth doing some worthwhile gardening in her front yard and I asked him if I could ask him about that pink silk.

"The pink silk, eh?" he asked. "I suppose you've found it amongst Isobel's stuff and I'm caught out?" Hugh Mohr asked.

"Looks like it. Is this it?" I asked.

"Aye it is," he answered.

"Look Malcolm, I was doing the dirty on Padruig with your Granny and I was doing the dirty on Isobel, who was a jealous woman too and I was doing the dirty on this 'out of towner', whose name I can't even remember and her bairn, so I bought the clothes, made by Isobel sold in the shop in Inverness out of pure guilt and it would help her buy the animals she was purchasing with her sewing. I felt better all round, the bairn had dresses she liked, Isobel had the money she needed and no one was the wiser, until now and Ruth probably thinks I'm a bastard now. Do you love?" he asked.

"Oh, my Hugh darling, you are not the young randy fella you once were. You are mine now and I love you," she said kissing him.

"And I love you too Ruthy," Hugh said, kissing her back.

"Are you satisfied now Malcolm and why is it so important and why did you dream of her, do you think?" he asked.

"Oh, I didn't specifically dream of her. The farmer there was injured with a concussion by being trampled by a Mither coo. That was the main part of the dream. But the farmer is, as you know, her Father, the dead one, Grigor Mohr MacGregor," I answered.

"Thanks Hugh, I won't trouble you over this again," I said.

"I feel so much better now," Hugh said sarcastically. Then the message of the dream came to me. Grigor Mohr was worried about his son. I planned to visit him this week, which I did, and he was glad of the visit.

80. Uncle Alex Passes Away

Our lives in Glengarry were extremely busy over the following years as our four bairns attended the new school that was built beautifully, courtesy of Simon Fraser's influence on the Scottish Government. We were also given that Post Office that Simon promised, which was much bigger than the wee one at Glenmoriston. The old Glenmoriston School and Art Gallery that had been briefly enlivened by Padruig and Isobel Grant, sat sadly silent as a reminder to its demise. We concluded that it should be demolished and sold to Simon, so they could expand their neighbouring business, given the industrial revolution and the need for bigger and better farm machinery.

I wondered about how the opening of Helen's Art Gallery was the catalyst to the death of my Granny, whereas Kenneth's art gallery had the opposite effect of awakening the creativity of the whole area of Glengarry. Kenneth didn't claim ownership to art, he encouraged all young artists to learn and he would give lessons once per week. The Lochs, rivers and burns continued to be fished by the five of us enthusiastic fishermen, all of whom taught their bairns to fish as well. The team of Clydesdales moved to my place permanently and we all lived in the one house, other than Kenneth and Ivy who had one bairn eventually. She was a real sweetie and because she was born in April, they named her April Marion MacNachten. The Frasers were friendlier by then and visited their Grandchild, which was nice.

The Cherry Farms were doing well as was Alex's, but Alexander Og was doing more and more of the physical work now that his Father was tiring quickly. Ma was worried about her twin because she was as energetic as ever, as was I. She took him and Matilda and Bruce to some Doctors in Edinburgh who said that Alex wasn't well, but by the grave looks on their faces, it was more than that. My Uncle Alex passed away at seventy years of age from an unknown illness. The funeral was enormous to farewell a beloved member of our family and our community in both Glengarry and Glenmoriston.

Fortunately, Matilda had already completed her Doctorate on the environment, which had people moving in high places to do something about that finally. Both of their two children, Moses and Sarah, were brilliant students and both were university educated. Moses became a critical care surgeon and Sarah became an hydrological engineer, many of whom were required on some big water work projects. They spent most of their time in either Edinburgh or Inverness and Alexander Og ran Loch Garry Ranch with his Step Mither, Matilda. He was the sole inheritor to protect his future, so long as he cared for Matilda.

Family Tree - Alexander Grant

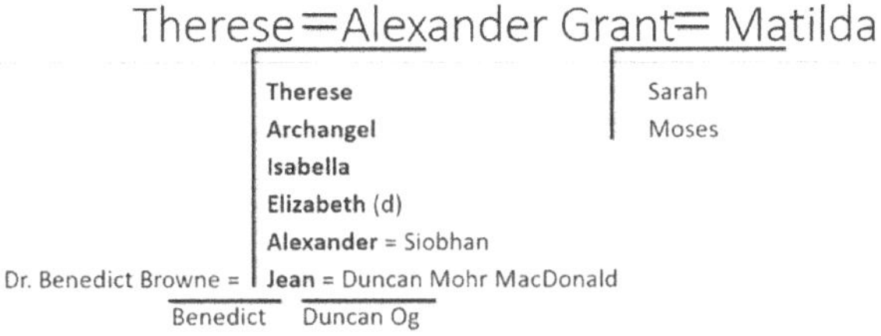

Peter had long lost his job when the tartan shop was sold and was never seen again. Alex Og then had lived a lonely life, so after poor old Duncan Mohr passed, Jean moved back into the main house with them both with her lad, also named Duncan, that she shared with Duncan Mohr. The wee lad was learning animal husbandry from Alexander. That had made life less lonely for both Alexander and Jean, as he had always adored his sister and they shared a common birthplace history in Nova Scotia. Duncan Og took on some of the responsibility for his Uncle, who was much younger than him, when his Grandfather passed away, leaving behind the grieving widow with the young bairn.

Benny had been removed from Jean by his English Father, years ago to live in London, as we had all predicted, but the lad was sent to visit occasionally at the expense of his Father. He had a very peculiar accent and wasn't accepted well on the farms, as well as being lazy, and despite it not being his fault to leave his Mither, I can't say that I had ever taken to him. Whenever he was there visiting, I generally avoided him. Loyalty to the Mither was my priority in life and I could not relate to their way of thinking.

As the coach left with him every couple of years, I breathed a sigh of relief.

My daughter Islay had always taken a fancy to young Angus MacKenzie, Hugh Og's offsider in teamstering and she was seen peering through his bedroom window as he was undressing by her Grandfather, Bruce. The lad was seventeen then, but well endowered and she was just six years old, but by the time she was thirteen years old they both asked us if they could marry and remain on the farm. It was a surprise, I admit and even a bit disappointing, as I wanted her to be better educated, but he was a good lad and would eventually inherit the eight-horse team from Hugh Og Chisholm, so we allowed it. Hugh Og only ever had the one wee lassie, Ferne, who didn't even like horses much at all and wouldn't inherit the team, while Angus was then a fluent Erse speaker to the Clydesdales. "The language of the horse," Granny had said.

Cherry and I both ended up having those disturbing dreams, as did Kenneth occasionally. We would all confer together as to any meanings needed attending to or just keep to ourselves. Some of those dreams helped people and some just revealed their deepest secrets. Some of those secrets were of the variety you would prefer to not know, like Hugh Mohr's daughter hidden up there in the remotest western part of the Fraser lands. Hugh Mohr finally passed away after an enjoyable older life without looking up his long-lost daughter, Isobel to our knowledge. He lived out his days with Ruth Beaton who adored her big man, no matter what his flaws or past sins were, and we can't ask for more than that from life. He was, after all, the Last of the Seven Glenmoriston Men and none of us could deny the impact that all seven of them had made during and after Culloden. His funeral was attended by so many, some of whom were dignitaries wanting to be acknowledged in the newspaper just to be seen at his funeral. Hugh Mohr had never met them, they were just wanting the publicity.

Culloden was no longer a shame factor for us Scots, but it was for the English.

81. Our Glenmoriston

There was reason to be proud that our Glenmoriston, small though it is, produced some of the most incredibly strong and powerful men of the Highlands, who were mostly killed off by their Laird and one of those who survived was one of my family, Padruig Dubh Grant. They did do their best with Glenmoriston, as did the MacGregors and the Chisholms and heroes they will always be and of that fact I am glad to pass to my children and my grandchildren. Helen Grant MacGregor let the team down, there's no denying that. I never quite understood how she chose to jump off her own balustrade with a rope around her neck, given all the privileges that she had been given in life. But she did and it overshadowed all the successes that both Grandda and Grandma had worked so hard for. The Catholic Priests were eventually told by someone about her death as a suicide and they then in turn asked Grigor for her to be removed from the inside of the Chapel or they wouldn't return to perform the weddings, funerals and baptisms that we all relied on.

Patrick Grant wanted Helen's grave that was inside the Chapel, put aside for himself, so it was most likely Henrietta who had told them. Rules are rules I suppose in a wee Chapel like that and so Grigor said that if Patrick and James dug Helen's grave in the graveyard, as well as one for him next to her, then they could move her body carefully as well as the tombstones for both Helen and himself. They would also then need to provide headstones as well, considering the graves would then be outside in the elements. They agreed also to pay for the engraving on the wall on the inside of the Chapel for both names to be done by me, as well as the engraving on both head stones that Kenneth and I both did together. James watched on questioning the merit of his parents' actions because they had always wanted those two graves inside the wee Chapel. The two graves inside the Chapel were then reserved for Patrick Grant and his wife Henrietta Grant.

Grigor Og MacGregor would still be buried beside his childhood sweetheart and wife at the time of his death in the graveyard, as well as Carmel beside him. Grigor was a healthy but aging man, still hand fast with Carmel, refusing to marry in the Catholic Faith again and living on Craskie farm, perfecting the soil as always, but maybe never forgiving Patrick and Henrietta. I continued to have an ongoing and good relationship with him, which I appreciated even more over time as I got to know the depths of the man few knew well.

82. Breaking with Tradition

Aonghus MacGregor

Before Uncle Alex passed away, he asked not to be buried on Craskie Farm, 'breaking with tradition' for the first time. He wanted to be buried near his wife, Matilda and family and so the first grave we all had in Glengarry was Alexander Grant. He loved the forest that his wife had created and asked to be buried under his favourite tree there, overlooking the burn. It was a peaceful location that wouldn't attract those bad ghosts, I thought, or arguing relatives. I had heard that Aonghus, my lawyer cousin, also was looking elsewhere to be buried at his time of death, as he was totally sick of the family arguments one after the other, some of which ended up in Court and he didn't want his peaceful time after death spent with the same arguing relatives, like his sister Isobel-Mairi and her husband Ewen, let alone his Mither Helen.

Aonghus had an awful job in my eyes, requiring a measure of toughness and patience that only the MacGregors could seem to summon for long enough to endure. Aonghus was listening to the continuous fighting over money owed, inheritance, disagreements over the names of businesses, treatment of staff, wages owed, or underpayment of wages and the list went on and on and on. Over too many ales one night, he disclosed all of the secrets of his law business dealings after drinking far too much because he, like all of Old Isobel's children, could not hold his liquor. His wife, Annabel had left him alone for just one night while she visited her Cameron family with their bairns and while he was left alone at the alehouse, his tongue wagged onward, without leaving out any details.

Unfortunately for him, a journalist from the Inverness Times was writing it all down in minute detail. Helen's suicide was not known publicly until then, but then it was known in every horrid and juicy detail, including the excrement on the floor that was unable to be removed thereby forcing the tiles to be replaced. Then there was the angle of her snapped neck with her tongue hanging out and her eyes bulging and rolled back and vomit coming from her mouth and not forgetting the smell of all smells that made grown men vomit.

Naturally, it found its way into the newspaper without naming Aonghus, luckily for him. It was in very poor taste, whichever way you looked at it.

Aonghus was a loyal family man who had been giving all of his family members free legal advice, especially his Mither while she lived, and Father who had been frequent callers on his legal opinions that took up a lot of his time but earned him no money. Only Isobel-Mairi gave him a few free items from the tartan shop when it was operational, but once it was no longer owned by them, he no longer received free items from them, just free legal advice from him was expected to continue. Before Helen's death, he had insisted that his Mither, Helen be repaid in part at least, on the debt owed to her. They then hated him as he began charging them if his services were required. The long list of relatives, some of whom he had never even met, continued to expect free advice from this well-educated, otherwise expensive lawyer and some of them were bringing charges against others in the same queue waiting to see him in his waiting room.

This resulted in an altercation on one occasion, requiring the Constable to come and break it up.

The last place he wanted to be buried upon his death, was Craskie Farm, I heard, especially now that there were legal issues with Patrick and Henrietta Grant insisting on the two graves inside the Chapel after Henrietta tipped off the Priests. He negotiated Grigor's deal in the cemetery with the two new graves which were to include head stones, as well as the tomb stones they already had from the Chapel, plus an allocated space for Grigor's new lady friend next to him, totalling three graves to be dug by Patrick and James. All the engraving was to be paid for by Patrick and performed by myself and Kenneth. What he didn't mention to them was that they would then need to replace the tomb stones in the Chapel with their own tomb stones once Helen's body was removed, along with her tomb stone as well as Grigor's. Helen's pre-prepared tombstone was paid for by Granny and decorated beautifully by her friend and second cousin, Gillcrest MacLachlan, who was now deceased.

Aonghus did not disclose to both Patrick and Henrietta Grant that the craft had been passed on to my Father, Nachtain MacNachten who passed it to my brother, Kenneth and I before his death and because our Father died young, we were both taught onwards by Grandda. May God rest his soul. As far as I knew, we were the only two people left in the region who could source and cut the stone, as well as engrave the stone with its many varieties of patterns and ensure that it was measured to the right size. It was a unique craft, I suppose.

That Sunday when the two Priests arrived, Helen's body had been removed, as they had requested and all of Grigor's requests were attended to thanks to Aonghus. The two Manor House business folk then thought that they were the new Lord and Lady of the whole district, without any official peerage of course, but attending Church that day was amusing like no other day. I hate Church personally, but to please my wife we attended on that day. What we saw was two big holes in the Chapel floor because they were no longer occupied or to be occupied by Grigor and the deceased Helen. They were then the graves of the living Patrick and Henrietta Grant, without tombstone lids to cover over the deep holes in the Chapel floor. The newspaper sent their writer once more to catch up on Craskie gossip and I saw him busily writing and sketching what he saw and heard. The Priest then asked to speak to Hugh Mohr, but he had passed away already, so he asked to speak to Grigor, but he said he had complied with their requests and removed his wife from her grave. Upon asking then whose graves they were, Patrick and Henrietta Grant were pointed out by several people. The Priest then spoke to both of them and said,

"You cannot leave the graves open during a Church service, especially one grave that has been previously occupied. Please cover it up like the others were. Someone might fall into one of the holes, not to mention the distress it might cause the family of the lady who was removed," he said.

The Priest's quote was in the newspaper too.

Patrick went out the back of the Chapel and angrily pulled off the two privy doors and brought them in to cover over the holes. Then the Priest expressed his distaste and decided to not stay overnight on the farm, as he always had done in the past and asked for the tops of the graves to be much better than privy doors, or the next time he would never return to be treated with such disrespect.

"Please install a proper tombstone lid on each one with the respective names of who will occupy them," the Priest said. He then gave a brief speech on respect for the Priests and the efforts they make to get to Glenmoriston like it used to be under the auspices of the Mistress, Isobel Grant Chisholm. He stated how disappointed he was with the disrespect exhibited for the dead, no matter how they died, as well as the Priests. Cherry and I were most amused at Patrick being told off and James looked pleased too. Susan looked too afraid to laugh or grin at their demise because she used to have a good relationship with Henrietta, but that had all changed after she was with child and was now happily married with her husband, James.

'Maybe it was time he and I went shopping again,' I thought.

Aonghus was contacted again by Patrick that week in Inverness complaining that Aonghus didn't tell him of needing the lids on the graves for the Church Service. Aonghus replied by saying,

"Just to let you know Uncle Patrick, I am charging by the half hour now for family as well as others and for every letter written, as well as any advice given. Do you want to continue this conversation as there will be a bill payable before you leave?" he asked.

Patrick paid the bill and stomped out enraged by the pup who dared to speak to him like that. He no longer sought out his advice on legal matters.

83. *Lord and Lady?*

When James and I we went shopping, he asked me how much the two grave lids would cost fully engraved in Caledonian Granite stone fully installed. "At the present time with the current cost of that stone, fully engraved would be at least two hundred and fifty pounds each, depending on how many letters you ask for and what design you ask for, if any," I answered.

He wrote down what would be written which included "Lady Henrietta Grant and Lord Patrick Grant."

"I can't do that," I said. "They are neither Lord nor Lady officially. Please James who asked you to have this written on their graves? That must be against the law?" I said. "Maybe get a legal opinion, I might be wrong, but it's a false claim unless they have been offered a peerage. Have they?" I asked.

"Nae. It was Ma's idea, she has this idea of being the Lady of the Manor," he said.

"Be careful my cousin, you have an honest soul, and she doesn't and you don't want her to drag you into hell," I said.

The rest of our day was enjoyable and I bought Cherry a new warm long skirt in tartan with a matching stole and a MacNachten Brooch. James was then inspired and bought Susan a long new tartan skirt and matching stole and Grant brooch. He dropped me off home with my shopping and I wondered how my news would be received by the horned Henrietta. 'The world would not miss her' I thought, we were all getting older after all.

I wondered if my wife and I, even in our spiritually dead condition, would continue to live here in Glengarry together. I decided to ask Cherry where she wanted to be buried. Most women had their shrouds already made with all kinds of decorations sewn onto them before their first bairn was born, but they generally left it up to their husbands where they would be buried. Cherry always carried a small bag of sand from her island, so that sand had to go into her grave too she had told me.

When I walked back into our peaceful farm, Cherry knew that I had something on my mind other than shopping, but I gave her the gift of clothing first, which she absolutely loved.

"Now my darling man, are you going to tell me what is on your mind?" she asked.

"Aye. You know how Uncle Alex is buried on his farm, breaking with tradition, which I agree with? Like Uncle Alex, I also don't want to listen to angry ghosts or relatives continuing their arguments into their Afterlives and there are so many now of our family in disagreement with one another. Alex wanted peace and so do I. Where do you wish to be buried my lovely wife?" I asked her plainly wanting a plain answer.

"You are a good man Malcolm MacNachten," she said caressing my face, "I cannot be buried on my island, as you know, but I have the soil I told you about to bury with me. So, I wish to be buried near you my love, wherever that is. I promised to follow you when I married you and I will. So, bury me wherever we are, be it here or Loch Insh or Loch Garry. I don't mind, so long as you are there with me. I have my shroud and I have my soil, so all I need is nearness to you my beloved," she answered. Cherry has a way with words that bring me to tears sometimes.

"Then, do you mind if we grow a few more trees near where the burn runs through our property then? Just the two of us can be buried there. I don't want to spoil the water if it ever widens or floods, so I suppose we can't be too close to the burn. Can we take a look tomorrow and chose a place for you and me? When we know for certain, we can ask young Angus and Islay to dig the graves when we die and I can make up the tomb lids in the next year," I said.

"Our Wills have never been rewritten either Malcolm since we married. Can we see Aonghus for that too? I hear he charges now, but it's worth it for peace of mind, don't you think?" she asked.

"Yes, we will do it all proper and legal like and let all our bairns know," I said. I went on to tell her about the gossip from James and Henrietta illegally wanting to call herself 'Lady Henrietta' and Patrick wanting to be called 'Lord Patrick' on his tombstone. Naturally I told her that I had refused.

"Those two are getting as nutty as Helen became. Be careful what he asks of you my darling and warn Kenneth too. He is so innocent he might believe that they are both Lord and Lady now. Poor Kenneth he is such a gullible sweetie," she said of her brother-in-law. "By the way, Bruce isn't well, it may be nothing your Ma said, but best drop in tomorrow with something healthy for him like a pot of my honey. I'll tend to the goats, so he doesn't have to do that," she said. "The nannies are so full of milk presently. It's quite the job separating it for cream then making the butter and now Ma wants to make yoghurt too," she said.

I was looking forward to our bath and I washed Cherry's long black hair and she washed mine. She had made some beautiful smelling soap and candles during the day with Meredith, so we both smelled like roses. Sex that night was more mellow than usual and we took it much slower and when Cherry reached her peak it was far more pleasurable than if I was too quick. I asked her if she'd prefer it slower all the time and she said she liked it however it came.

"I love you Malcolm," Cherry said.

"Do you think we will live on as spirits together here in this house like those people in the Aird?" I asked.

"Aye, if we want to. Do you want to, Mr Ghost?" she asked jokingly.

"Aye, it wouldn't be too bad waiting here with you for Judgement Day," I said.

84. Is Bruce Really Sick?

I visited Bruce and Ma the next morning while Cherry was busy milking the goats. He wasn't looking too unwell. He said he had just caught a cold and asked me not to fuss. There were too many people dying and I didn't want Bruce to die too.

"If you are too sick, I can't take you to see Grigor who wanted to see his old friend," I said. Of course, I made that up, but it cheered him up no end. "I'm seeing him today, but are you up to it Da?" I asked. Calling him Da also cheered him up no end.

"I'm up to it. I can go Marion. I'd like to see Grigor. I'm even dreaming now, like you Malcolm and there was something going on over at his house," he said.

"Okay, on horseback Da so we can get back early enough?" I asked. Bruce was out of bed so fast and his colour returned almost instantly, so much so, that even Ma was surprised.

"Ma, Cherry's milking the goats, can you help her with the yoghurt? She hasn't made yoghurt before," I asked.

"Oh, is she? Aye son, I can teach her how to make yoghurt," Ma dressed Bruce, which embarrassed him and we all went our chosen ways, waving to both Matilda and my cousin Alexander as we walked up to my stables.

It was pleasant saddling up our two horses with Bruce, as I had never been horse riding with him, so I ignored any slowness or tiredness, so he would feel the need to keep up, which he did and his 'illness' was vanishing by the second. Ma was spoiling him too much, but it made her feel good. 'Maybe she should babysit for us instead,' I thought. When we were arriving at Craskie Farm, we passed that dreaded old school still standing there in all its misery and that was one topic I hoped to address with Grigor. Both the school and its teacher house had seen better days and it was time to demolish them, if Simon Fraser buys what was Helen's land and was left to Grigor upon her death.

The Glenmoriston students could come to our school in Glengarry if there was a way to transport them all to Glengarry, I had thought. The gate was left open in expectation of my visit and I hadn't expected anything out of the ordinary. He had said that his friend Carmel was rarely there, as she was working hard delivering bairns, or caring for the Mithers. They had a sexual need for each other, but that was all because he refused to marry her in the Kirk. I tied up my horse when a young groomsman came and asked if he could stable them both and feed them as he took them. The farm was much tidier and quieter and it had a pleasant feeling as we went to knock on that big oak door.

85. Who is Bruised, Limping Zara?

Bruce knocked, then we waited a moment and a familiar face opened the door. Behind her were twins about four years old but lovely bairns, a boy and girl. They confidently said,

"I'm Ali" and the girl said, "I'm Fatma. Ma, say your name," Fatma said.

The pretty lady just stood there looking at me with the same feeling that I had.

"Have I met you before?" I asked.

"Nae, but you were in the Aird a while ago. Are you from the Aird?" she asked looking worried.

"Nae, I'm from Glengarry, but I think you might have a daughter named Isobel. The late Hugh Mohr's daughter? Is that right?" I asked.

"Who are you?" she demanded to know.

"I'm Malcolm MacNachten and this is my stepfather, Bruce MacDonald, originally from Glenmoriston, but now also from Cherry Farm in Glengarry. We are here to see Grigor MacGregor. Is he home?" I asked.

She looked surprised at Grigor's full name.

"What's your name?" I asked.

"Zara MacGregor," she said and let us in slowly and she walked with a limp and had visible injuries to her face and bruising around her right eye. She had obviously been beaten up and I didn't know what she was doing in Grigor's home. I could smell food cooking, so maybe she was home help with her own bairns living there with Grigor when I heard a wee bairn crying and the pretty lady hurried off to attend to the wee bairn.

"There's coffee over there," she said to Bruce and he started to pour out the cups when Grigor finally came up behind us.

"Sorry Malcolm, I was caught up in the oat fields. Hello, Bruce old friend. Let me wash my hands and I'll join you for smoko," Grigor Og said. He embraced Bruce, who was thrilled that the weirdness had diminished a little from the intense pretty lady, with the green eyes.

86. Grigor's Cook?

"Glad to see you finally have a cook, Grigor my friend. You've lost too much weight," Bruce observed. The lady was breast feeding her wee bairn in a couch chair, beside the fire.

"That's a wee bairn," Bruce commented. "Can't be more than one week old. He's not yours is he, you devil?" asked Bruce.

"Nae," the pretty lady said. "This is Causantin, my husband's son," she said firmly.

"He sure looks like Grigor," Bruce said.

"They'd be related," she said. "It's just the MacGregor family resemblance," Zara said.

"I've seen you in two of my dreams. One in Culloden Field with my Grandfather, Padruig Dubh Grant, Grigor MacGregor and Hugh Chisholm, where you were given a MacGregor brooch. Do you still have that brooch?" I asked.

She then looked at me like I was from another planet.

"Was that you who I saw?" she asked. She looked sad then and Grigor obviously knew her whole story and explained to her that I was one of those special people like the Sidhe, who could see things, but Bruce wasn't.

"You don't have to tell them anything Zara. Just feed your wee bairn lass and get back to the cooking or we will starve again," he said smiling. He compassionately put his hand on her shoulder and covered her modesty from us and ushered us over to the table to leave her in peace.

"Best leave her in peace my friends. She has recently suffered, so I have offered her my protection and shelter and a job cooking for us. She has two rooms with the bairns opposite my office and I've given her Old Isobel's things, like arisaids, plaids, skirts and boots and those warm slippers that Ma loved. I burned everything else of Helen's," Grigor Og said.

"Why was she beaten up?" I asked quietly.

"Her marriage is a good one, but that was until her husband's Father turned up and that is the result," he answered without giving details.

"What about her daughter, Isobel the lassie in the pink dress?" I asked.

Zara overheard me and said that Isobel was hit over the face also, but only once for trying to intervene, but she was alright and her husband, John Fraser was taking care of her.

"Do you all need our help. Can we go up to the Aird and get rid of that fella?" I asked.

"It's nice of you to offer, but you have seen our house. I saw you across the other side of the burn. We are all already dead Malcolm," she said.

"Sometimes we are visible and sometimes we are not," Zara said.

Bruce didn't know which way to look.

"When I first entered this world at Culloden Field, I was researching a book and I was alive then and I could return home to my life, but I was accidentally killed after being married here to Hugh Chisholm. When I was being prepared for burial by my clansman, Grigor MacGregor, he saw life inside my womb, that was moving. He then watched and waited, tending to my injuries until Isobel was born. He then delivered her and I became a younger version of myself. So, it was obvious that I was dead, but the bairn wasn't. The natural Father of Isobel, Hugh, rejected both of us, but that's a very long story and eventually I married Grigor Mohr MacGregor, with whom I have had four bairns, which I do not understand, because according to my religion, we stop reproducing once we die. Grigor has one of our bairns with him now because he adores our son, Hector. I escaped with just these three. Once Grigor's violent Father leaves, then hopefully Grigor will find me here, or I will go back when I am sure that his Father has gone. I love my husband with all my heart, but he was following some bizarre tradition of his clan, to which I refused to follow because we are also of two differing religions and cultures," she said.

"The midwife I had to see in Glenmoriston, gave me this address on Craskie Farm for a job, as I had no money and I didn't know that Grigor Og was a relative too, let alone the oldest son of my husband, Grigor," she said. "My bairns are half brothers and sisters to you Grigor and my husband is your Father. Does that upset you?" she asked.

"I am not totally surprised that my Father had another life after his life here, because he appeared to Isobel Grant, my Mither-in-law, as a spectre or spirit until her death, so how can I be upset?" Grigor Og answered.

"Please don't repeat all of this because I don't know what will happen. For now, can you all just pretend that we are all just of the living and normal folk?" Zara asked.

"Fae folk," he said, "And I am really happy to have siblings," said Grigor Og

"Fae folk it is then," she said. She could smile at Grigor Og, but the intense lady barely looked at Bruce and she was worried about how much detail that I knew, I thought.

Bruce then said, "When you arrived in Scotland, let's say, it's not too different to when I went to the American colonies as a youngster. I was a stranger, no money, no food and I didn't understand their various cultures or their languages. I settled with the Indians because they were more like us, I think. One feels like a stranger with no money or the wrong currency and no food, but your situation Zara, is even worse than mine was because you have dependents and injuries. You said you saw a midwife locally. Can you tell us why?" he asked.

Casting her eyes down, she pondered upon her reply.

"I have injuries to my private feminine area that has required some delicate stitching and that midwife said that Grigor Og had a lady friend who could check it each day until it was all healed. Is that alright Grigor? I am sorry that I didn't mention it, because it's embarrassing," Zara said.

"Of course, Carmel won't mind, especially now you have cooked the stew," Grigor said. Then when she finished feeding the wee one, I asked if I could change him, to which she agreed. She then tasted the stew to see if it was alright.

"Grigor can you please taste this and tell me if it needs more of something?" she asked as he tasted it obediently.

"Och, it's nice, really nice. What have you put in it to get that delicious taste?" Grigor asked.

"Just what's in your kitchen and your garden," Zara answered.

"It's like Isobel's stews. Those stews were intoxicatingly addictive. How much have you cooked?" Grigor asked. "In the future double the quantity of beef because I guarantee there will be men lining up for this," he said.

"Really? My husband never said my stews were any good?" Zara said.

"Well, he was ungrateful, wasn't he? That sounds like my Father," he said. "Can you cook cakes and deserts and bannocks and loaves of bread too?" Grigor Og asked.

"Aye, of course and do you have goats for the milk, cream, cheese, butter and yoghurt?" she asked.

"Aye can you milk them in the mornings? I'm too busy and can you collect the eggs too?" he asked.

"This is good isn't its fellas?" Grigor Og said, looking happy with his new arrangement.

87. To Demolish Old School

"I just had to put one thing to you before we are on our way Grigor. The old school looks dilapidated and I was wondering, given that you have inherited it from Helen, as well as the wee house, if it could all be demolished?" I suggested. "Some people need the bits and pieces like the windows and the doors, latches and knobs, as well as those oak floorboards. Hamish collects it now and sells it as a sideline business. I'll buy the oak boards and the windows in case we need another house on the farm because we've run out of the rock. If you do knock it all down, Simon Fraser could buy it all and Hamish and I could divvy up what we both want. The Frasers can add to their existing business with the industrial revolution as it is, with bigger machines needed for farming from America being made. It's just an idea," I said.

"We need to modernise farming and America is where they have all the new stuff," I added.

"What a great idea and you have earned the oak boards and the windows Malcolm. Come and get those anytime. I'll give you a set of keys and you can take what you like. Write it down and let me know when you return the keys. I'd love to see that place gone. It has caused nothing but misery for our family. It's like a curse. Simon might still want the fireplace to heat up his building, what do you think?" Grigor Og asked.

"Stuff Simon. I'll take the bricks and the stone from that fireplace too. Good Caledonia granite that and I need the hearth too," I added. Zara was busy making bread, bannocks and cakes and more stew, despite her limp and I was pleased for Grigor and I obtained her recipe too for Cherry. It was good timing for us to leave as Carmel arrived home.

Too many questions all over again. Poor Zara, if that was really her name. Bruce certainly did not look sick anymore, that's for sure. He had never heard tales of this kind in his life before.

Back in Glengarry, then Ma came running to our gate pampering Bruce as usual and he picked her up this time and swung her around to prove how strong he was. I hoped he hadn't put his back out doing that. Cherry watched on smiling as did Angus and Islay. We were happy and I told Cherry about the great stew at Grigor's house and gave her the recipe and asked if she could cook it.

'Hmmmm,' was the reaction. "Don't you like my stew, Malcolm?" she asked. I was then terrified that I had offended her and told her how wonderful her stews were and so on, when she finally told me that she was only joking and she would love to cook it if she knew what meat it was.

"It's just our highland beef, she soaks it first in something, I forgot to ask what, maybe vinegar?" I said.

"So, what was his cook's name then?" she asked suspiciously.

"Zara," I said.

"That's a nice name. Where's she from?" Cherry asked.

"Didn't ask love. None of my business," I replied.

Bruce was surprised that it was all going to be kept a secret but went along with it. Zara was just Grigor's new cook and Bruce saw a side to me that he hadn't yet seen. Just the same he was glad not to have to explain dead people to the living, who looked very much alive. Zara was a real curiousity and he wondered what her name really was.

88. Aonghus and the Wills

Cherry and I had planned to go to Inverness to update our Wills and we had an appointment to see Aonghus, my cousin, who was charging family now for his legal services. This was fair enough given how much time he had put into us all. He was more serious these days, if a lawyer could possibly become more serious, but the suicide of his Mither had obviously affected him adversely. He welcomed us both into his pleasant office and his secretary brought in milky tea to us all in nice china cups with saucers and silver teaspoons.

"Silver made in Tain" Aonghus said proudly of his teaspoons.

On his desk was one of those nice inkpots and feather things you see in that kind of office, which he saw me admiring too.

"It was from my Grandda," he said reflectively.

"What can I do for you both today? I hope it's nothing serious?" he asked.

"Just our Wills, cousin Aonghus. The last one we did was when I only had the one farm after we were first married, so I really should have been in before now. There's a share in a boat too that I have with some other men and I want my share in that boat to go to my son Alex," I replied.

"Yes," he said thoughtfully.

"There is a matter concerning you in our Uncle Alexander Grant's Will, regarding his farm called, Loch Garry Ranch. Just one moment before we continue," Aonghus said. "There's a Will reading for our Uncle Alex this Saturday at 2pm, at Loch Garry Ranch, but that part which pertains to you can be told to you now, especially given that it will affect the Wills that you are preparing today. Do you need glasses?" he asked.

"Nae, I don't wear glasses," I said.

"Malcolm, darling, I think you do need to see the eye doctor today, while we are here in Inverness," my wife said.

"Read it from here if you can read it and if not, I'll read it," Aonghus said.

The Will read: *"To my nephew, Mael Coluim (Malcolm) Nachtain MacNachten of Cherry Farms, Glengarry, whom I consider no less to me than as my son, I leave the land that was the half of the farm shared with Malcolm, left to me by Killian MacDonnell. Currently, the land I own is under oat crops and I believe he will better be able to cope with that work than my wife or my son Alexander Grant, who have both agreed to Malcolm inheriting that land. The land title deeds and division work has already been completed and is already in his name. There are two students attached to that work on the oat crops, whom I trust he will take on as they are free of charge from his cousin Gillcrest MacLachlan. Their names are available from my wife, Matilda Grant. There is also a knife that I wish to leave for Kenneth MacNachten, Malcolm's brother, that was from my Father Padruig Dubh Grant, made by the Algonquian people of Nova Scotia that none of my immediate family wish to keep in our family home. It is sharp and sheathed, but it is not a good knife for slaughtering or butchering animals of any great size. It might only be valuable as an artefact from the first Quebec campaign."* The Will read.

"So, Malcolm and Cherry, let's write up your Wills including this land that has been left to you Malcolm by Uncle Alex," he said.

We completed the work which took over an hour, including the share of the boat that I was leaving to my son, Alexander MacNachten. In my Will, I made it clear that the stables were able to continue to be used, beyond my death by Hugh Og Chisholm with his team of Clydesdales, so long as he continued to pay his rent on the use of the stables and pays the wages of one of the groomsmen, in accordance with my agreement with him and I provided a copy of that agreement. My own horses would go to my sons. The small stone cottage built for my brother is to belong to him for his whole life as well as his Art Gallery as well as the land upon which they both stand. Similarly, the stone cottage that my Mither, Marion MacDonald, lives in would belong to her upon my death with her choice of partner at the time. And it went on and on with so much intricate detail.

If I died first, the Cherry Farms would automatically go to my oldest son Alex, including the land left to me by Uncle Alex, which was mind boggling including all that extra land from Alex. I was born in a wee croft in Loch Insh into a family of little means and upon my Father's death, I never imagined that I could be sitting here listening to owning all of this land, when all around me, people were still being Cleared of tiny wee crofts.

The land Willed to me by my Uncle Alex, was not to go to Cherry, if I died first in accordance with his wishes, as he desired it had to go to my four bairns. I left the old farmhouse also to all four of my children to share, starting with Islay and her husband leaving a need for me to build another staff cottage for four men. It was then I noticed that Cherry's lips were pursed at the realisation that she wasn't going to inherit from me when I died. Cash on hand was also left to my bairns, but Cherry was only keeping her jewellery, clothing and to be accommodated unil her death if I predeceased her. I thought that maybe Cherry was disappointed in how much went to the bairns which was essential and I thought she had understood that in the way farms worked.

I thanked my cousin sincerely and passed on my condolences too.

I told him that his Da was looking a lot better now that he had a new cook, which Aonghus hadn't known about, so we exchanged some gossip and I paid a discounted bill. Aonghus was going to visit his Da then and see the new cook that he became curious about. A discount is better than full price.

Then Cherry took me to the eye doctor and I did need reading glasses after all, but so did she and we went home with reading glasses looking like old people. Cherry had an interest for reading books on the differing opinions of religions, especially in accordance with what happened after we died. We treated ourselves to cups of milky tea and cucumber sandwiches before leaving Inverness and discussed the massive land that Uncle Alex had Willed to me and what we would sensibly do with that but Cherry had no idea. It was four fields of oats and one fallow field. I decided that I could use that demolished old school's bits and pieces to build a storage shed for that many oats, as well as buy a few ratters, otherwise known as cats, while we were there in that town, which I was not too fond of, but some of the shops were nice. Cherry was far too happy about getting cats, so I stressed that they weren't for living in the house. I had an allergy to cat fur.

"They make me sneeze, we just need ratters and mousers," I said, so we asked a pet shop which ones to get for that purpose and went home with a whole litter of kittens, but I was dreading where they were sleeping that night. I also had plans to expand the goat house to increase the milk production, cheese and butter production from the goats. I asked Cherry if she was up to working on the goat's full time now with the bairns needing her less and one of the oat fields from that property was going to be given up for goats and whatever she thought the goats needed. She thought that Islay could assist her and Ma and build a real industry out of the goats alone, if I added to the existing building for extra goats and a specialised room for all of the milk separation and butter and cheese making.

My farm was a large industry now, so my staffing was important, as well as bigger signage over my gates for Cherry Farms. My mind was working overtime all the way home. I wrote to Simon Fraser who was up for a genuine Peerage, I had heard, so I wished him well in achieving that and asked him to achieve a few more things for us. The wee lane between my two farms now needed to be blocked off as a Public Road to become a Private Road, so I could move my coos in and out and not have any strangers coming onto either property. I asked him also if I could purchase the far end of it, thus extending my original Cherry farm where the goats were, expanding them across the existing road to where the oats storage shed would be built on the other side in the future, which I had just inherited from my Uncle Alex. I needed to maintain the first half of the narrow lane, as a lane for my coos when I had to take them to graze up the narrow Drover's Road. He reminded me that the laneway was a marker that locals had created for where the bedrock deepened so that oats could be grown on the land that had been left to me so long as I checked on the soil's ability to achieve that and whether the area flooded and became sodden. Just the same he agreed to my request but to put up a bedrock sign as a reminder.

I then asked him again to widen that narrow Drover's Road and thanked him for both the School and the Post Office and encouraged him to ponder over the idea of a sporting field in Glengarry for fusbal, with a covering overhead, allowing for the weather as well as dressing rooms and amenities. It could be for both the school and the community.

I also suggested that transport be arranged for any students from Glenmoriston, because the old school was officially being demolished and he may like to ask Grigor MacGregor of Craskie Farm about buying that land from him for the new farm machinery from America. Like in Glenmoriston, I asked him to have a low rock wall built on the opposite side of the road to keep out deer. I explained I was rewilding just one small corner of my old Cherry Farm with old growth trees, obtained from Craskie farm.

In case he didn't follow it all, I drew up a map indicating where everything was, with north indicated.

On my next fishing trip with Hamish, I told him what I needed from the old schoolhouse in order to build the storage shed for oats. I needed all the oak floorboards, the wooden exterior boards, the slate roof which had been newly built by Helen, the windows, the shutters, the new wide front door, with its nails, bolts, and locks and the chimney and hearth, but I didn't need anything from the teacher's house. That was all his.

He agreed, thinking I definitely had the better deal. He asked me if I needed help to build the storage shed for a wee pay and I asked how much. Suddenly, I had Bruce wanting to work on it too, then Hugh Og and even Kenneth for that wee pay. I was going to be broke this month. Jokingly, I told them I'd pay them in fish, but then I came to a figure that I could afford and they were all happy enough. The painters, however, were not as cheap as my friends and came in as soon as it was completed painting it white with two thick coats. I liked my storage shed design and the kittens, that were now cats, were catching the occasional mouse or rat and relegated to life outside in the storage shed. Occasionally I found the twins sneaking one in, but it went back out again.

I had sent my reluctant son Alex on to university when he successfully completed high school locally, after it had been built, thanks to Simon Fraser. Alex was studying medicine and wanted to specialise in both trauma care and Obstetrics. The really gross stuff. He was an intense lad with that surgeon look about him, I suppose. Life was not to be joked about and he rarely understood jokes, even if he was told something funny. I especially noticed that he didn't understand his Mither's, Island sense of humour that was hard to catch onto. She had given up trying to joke with him, because life was all too serious. He loved coming home from Edinburgh to be with us all and to meet his nephew, Nachtain Padruig, from his sister Islay and her husband Angus. He encouraged my twins to be educated too, so that Scotland wasn't left behind the rest of the world. My wee twinnies tried hard at school to please Alex, I think and learned every foreign language on offer, but as active as they were, their main interest would always be horses. I suspected teamstering and Hugh Og was still wanting to train them. They had learned Erse so they were ready and teamstering had my blessing. I could see my lads taking on the role of their Great Grandmither, Isobel of Glenmoriston and they would be the teamster lads from Glengarry, I hoped.

89. *Grigor Og Loses Zara and her Bairns*

I hadn't checked in on Grigor Og for ages as I was so busy, so I made the time and went there. Matilda dropped in a few buckets of beautiful red apples that had ripened, so I was pleased to know that Cherry would be busy cooking or preserving them while I was away. Grigor Og was without a cook again, but he had all of her recipes, so he was happy knowing he could cook it himself. He was still looking amazingly young for his age and healthy and strong. He had gained weight at least as a result of Zara's cooking.

"Are you going to tell me what happened?" I asked. He looked at me as if to assess whether he should and then he decided he would, if I didn't repeat it.

"I will not repeat your private business. I'm not like Fraser's Trading Post, who love to gossip," I said.

"One morning Zara had asked me about that Turkish China that was smashed and asked to see it. When I showed it to her in its millions of beautiful little pieces in a drum behind the house, to the left of the privies and she was so taken with it," Grigor Og said.

"It's so beautiful," she had said.

"She then asked me if I had an old bath or copper that I wasn't using anymore, as well as something like an adhesive glue or a cement substance. I got her what she needed as well as a small hammer that she also needed. I asked her what she was going to do with it all and she explained that she would cement the tiny little pieces onto the old ugly tub and make it beautiful again. So, the last time I saw her, she was gluing these tiny little pieces of Turkish china onto the tub, but when I came back from the fields for smoko, expecting to see her and see what she had accomplished with it all, she had disappeared. Their belongings were gone, but only half of the tub that she had started to 'make beautiful' as she said, was completed," he said.

"Come and look at it," Grigor said. Grigor took me out the back of his house where he saw her for the last time and the tub was still just sitting there as she had left it, unfinished but lovely. It was obviously an unplanned departure, but all her bairn's things were taken, as well as what he had given to her of old Isobel's. Their rooms had been left immaculate, as had the whole house apparently, but he knew it was unplanned as she was going to put a stew on after smoko.

"She had all the ingredients in the kitchen there ready, but nothing was cooking," he said sadly.

"And they were all just gone as well as her horse. I cried more for the loss of Zara than my own wife," he said so sadly.

"I hadn't even paid her the wages she was due. I don't know how to get it to her. Do you think she went back to the Aird of her own volition?" he asked.

"Her husband was your Father, so in my opinion, he came here after looking everywhere for them, then finally came here. He was clearly desperate to have his wife and bairns back, so that's a good thing. However, he knew that you had seen her in her poorly condition when she arrived, so he would have too much shame to present himself to you, in my opinion. He was most likely with Padruig and Alexander MacDonald," I answered.

"Why do you think that?" Grigor asked.

"They would have a method of disposing of people and indeed oneself, even if you are already dead, and my guess is the three of them or possibly two of them, with young Isobel out of sight, disposed of the huge monster of a man responsible for the crimes he committed against your Step Mither. She said her name was Zara, but I doubt that is her real name," I said. "How was her leg on the day she departed?" I asked.

"It wasn't fully healed but getting a little better. She was still limping. Carmel had dealt with the other matter and that was a lot better than her leg. Carmel told me that he must have had a cock the size of an elephant to do that kind of damage and I won't repeat what else she said. As for her leg, Carmel said that only a Doctor could deal with it, because it was beyond her range of knowledge. She was worried that there may have been a fracture and she had ridden her horse also with that injury, as well as working in the house walking up and down the stairs," Grigor Og said.

"Are you going to that part of the Aird anytime soon Grigor? If you do consider going, leave all your affairs in order before you go. By that, I mean your Will and so on. There's a vibe up there that if you go across that narrow burn near where the house is on the other side, then you may not return. It's like a 'fairy dun' according to my brother Kenneth," I said. "Can I ask you about her lovely artwork out the back?" I asked. "Can Kenneth put it up for display or sale in his Art Gallery? For a very high price of course, like two hundred pounds and call it 'Unfinished Work from a Fairy?'" I asked. "It'll do one of two things. It will either sell or it will attract one of her own who will tell her where it is and she or her friends may come to Glengarry. What do you say?" I asked.

"Oh Malcolm. God bless you. Firstly, I can't leave the farm to go to the Aird presently, but I will get my affairs in order with Aonghus. I am tempted to see that house in the Aird one day and if I do, will you come with me?" he asked. "And yes, you can display or sell that tub as artwork if you like. I can't imagine someone paying for it. I'll give commission to Kenneth then and the name is great. I hope to see Zara again, I really do. I miss the bairns too, especially wee Causantin. I felt happy with them here. But she must have missed her husband to have left so willingly. There was no sign of a struggle, just a hasty departure and I should be happy for Da, if that is his wife in his death. Those big green eyes. She really is a gorgeous looking woman," Grigor Og said.

90. *That Pict Stone*

'Maybe it was the right time for her husband to collect his wife before her Stepson fell in love with her,' I thought.

"Grigor, did Granny ever tell you about where she used to pray, other than the Chapel, to talk to those on the other side going back to the ancient ones? The ancestors, she called them," I asked.

"Nae, where would that be then?" he asked.

"Do you have an hour or so?" I said

"Aye, I do," he said. So, the two of us sauntered into the old forest and at the same time I talked about getting seeds from him for my rewilding. Lucky for me, he had already done that like old Isobel had and I could take them all today if I liked. As we entered further into the deep forest as usual, it became mistier and mistier, almost dark on this occasion. It was lucky that I knew the way and was familiar with all of its many shadows and sounds.

Finally, we arrived at the Pict stone and as I stopped Grigor looked at me questioningly. "Why have we stopped?" he asked quietly like as if he was disturbing something if he spoke louder.

"Do you see that stone there?" I asked.

"Oh aye, I can now, but I hadn't until you said it was there," he said surprised.

"Are you familiar with that type of stone?" I asked.

"Oh Malcolm, you are the stone expert not me," Grigor said.

"Look closer Grigor and rub off the moss," I suggested. As he looked at the foreign but beautiful looking markings, he realised that it wasn't just any old stone. It had writing on it from an ancient people.

"Oh my God Malcolm, it's Pictish! How did you know it was here?" he asked.

"Hugh Mohr was given the job at your farm as 'Keeper of the Forests'. Once he left Craskie farm he chose me who to disclose it to, under Isobel's strict instructions that no one was to know of its whereabouts or existence, especially the Museums and Churches. It has been protected since she was a wee bairn. I am telling you this because it might help you to speak with the ancestors. All you do is sit in front of the stone and wait or pray or talk to them," I said. "Kenneth and I both know of its existence," I added.

"So please promise to keep it protected and a secret, even from family members, until you can see a maturing of their understanding. For instance, Aonghus will one day be mature enough to know because the swans were a sign to Gillcrest MacNachten that he has Pictish in him like us and he will be ready one day, but not now yet though," I said

"What do I do?" he asked.

"We can both sit down and pray in your own way," I replied. As we both sat in front of the stone, the mist came closer and divided up into several mists that moved about like people do. I was praying for my family and thanking the ancestors for their assistance, but inside my head when I saw Grigor, he was weeping. I advised him to ask them for their assistance, so he did and he wiped away his tears, but it made me almost cry too as the feeling was way more powerful than the previous visit. He asked out loud,

"Was Zara really a dead person?" Much to my surprise one of the misty figures seemed to be reaching out to him. I heard his responses but didn't know what he was being told. Either way it exhausted him and he fell into a deep sleep and I did too. We awoke when nightfall was upon us then and all of those figures surrounding us seemed to vanish and then there was no mist at all. We realised then how late it was and strode back quickly to his home.

"Grigor my friend, we have much to speak of, but I must get home to Cherry and the twinnies. Do you want to come and eat with us?" I asked.

"Aye, that would be nice. Can I stay overnight then too?" he asked as he grabbed clean clothes, and we locked up his front door. He told the stable hand where we would be until the next day if he was needed and to let Hamish know and we took out our horses and galloped off home to Glengarry back to my anxious wife. I had strapped Zara's artwork to my horse securely and wondered what Kenneth would make of my taste in art.

Luckily having Grigor with me meant that I was not chastised for being so late and we all sat and enjoyed the stew that Cherry had tried to copy from Zara's recipe. There was lots of apple pie too with goat's cream. The stew was nice, I admit and better than on most nights, but it wasn't as good as Zara's. An improvement was better than nothing and Hugh Og and Meredith, both liked it, as well as Kenneth and Ivy. My wife had tried so hard to please me and so I showered her with praise and so did Meredith. Hugh Og said we were due to go fishing soon and invited Grigor, which I thought was a good idea to cheer him up now that he had lost Zara.

"What's this then?" asked Kenneth. Finally, he noticed the tub artwork just sitting in the lounge. "I really like this artwork. Who is the artist, Malcolm?" Kenneth asked. I looked across at Grigor and smiled. "Grigor had a friend named Zara who made it. It's called, "Unfinished Work of a Fairy," I replied.

"Really? This would sell for more than Helen's stuff. How much Grigor?" Kenneth asked. "It's a commission-based item obviously and I was hoping you could have it in your Art Gallery and if it sells, then I thought it could sell for two hundred pounds with your commission being twenty five percent maybe, if you agreed Kenneth?" Grigor answered.

Ivy was very impressed. "That's a good commission isn't it darling?" Ivy said.

"I don't know, but I accept that and it might not ever sell but it would be a marvellous talking piece and very inspirational for my students too. I love that name," Kenneth said.

"I'll make up the sign for it darling," Ivy said.

"I can make a nice wee box for it to be displayed on," Bruce suggested.

Kenneth's wee bairn April was looking at it and was in awe saying,

"Ma, a fairy made this?"

"Aye a fairy made it," Grigor Og said.

My wife was suspicious of the whole thing and in bed that night, she asked me who the 'fairy' was.

"Zara, the cook. Grigor said she was a fairy," I said.

"Wouldn't she be more like a house brownie if she was poor and cooking and cleaning, then leaves before he can pay her?" she asked.

"Now that sounds like you know more than me, about that kind of thing, so I'll go along with you. Whatever you say my lovely one," I said.

I just wanted sex, so it was no longer interesting to me.

"Now are we going to be serious or are we going to have some fun my sexy wife?" I asked. Tickling my wife in her sensitive spots always got her giggling and took her mind off things. My wife's breasts were always sure to get me going, lovely handfuls as they were with lovely brown nipples.

"These are all mine now," I said. "I no longer have to share them," I said with delight, as I penetrated her deeply and she squealed with delight. I was so horny that night I had to keep asking my wife for more and more. I wondered if it was the "fairy effect".

91. Zara's Story

Kenneth was unaware that Matilda and Ivy had sent out invitations to all sorts of people to come and see the latest in his Art Gallery, especially a piece by a new artist named Zara, who had made a piece called, "Unfinished Work of a Fairy". They sent an advertisement to the Inverness Newspaper hoping people in the Aird would read it, and they did. Grigor Mohr picked up his regular newspaper and saw the item advertised that his wife had been working on that day when he found her in the back yard of Craskie Farm. All of those living in the Aird in that house were made aware of the date that it was on display or sale for two hundred pounds.

"But I hadn't finished it and why would Grigor Og sell it?" Zara said.

"It was going to be a gift to him for helping us and they're calling me a fairy in the paper darling. That was just a joke, I thought. Are you angry with me Grigor? It's my fault" she said. The advertisements didn't have the desired effect, as Zara limped to her bedroom shaking and hoping her husband wasn't going to beat her. He followed her in with his belt, but his two friends, Alex and Padruig held him back and disapproved this time. They had missed her too in her absence with her beautiful cooking, as well as her many kindnesses to them. They reasoned with him.

"It's not her fault Grigor. However, if you like, we can steal that thing back from that Art Gallery in Glengarry, but she is not well enough yet for what you are planning. I want us to take her to Inverness to that doctor friend of Alex's to check that leg of hers. It's not right. It needs a doctor and then we can deal with this matter of the Art Gallery," Padruig said.

"Who is this Kenneth MacNachten anyhow?" asked Alex MacDonald.

"Zara, can you tell us who they are at least," he called out.

"Are you going to beat me Grigor?" she asked.

"Nae and come here, we all want coffee and some information," Grigor Mohr said.

All three of them watched her as she limped back into the kitchen to make the coffee with tears rolling down her face and trembling. It would be a while before she was fully recovered from the violent attack and any sign of violence made her afraid, causing her to shake all over. The last person she wanted to hate her was her beloved husband, Grigor. He went up to her while she was cooking the Turkish coffee over the fire and she was expecting the worse, but instead he held her in his arms as she trembled all over and she held onto him and cried apologising for upsetting him.

"Please forgive me Grigor?" she asked as his friends shook their heads in judgement of him.

"Of course. Forgiven. Like you say, it wasn't your fault," he said.

"Coffee please," the friends demanded. And Zara kissed her husband as he kissed her on the lips and she prepared a nice Turkish coffee for each of them. She took out the Turkish coffee from a tin and then put a big scoop of it into the long handled Turkish coffee pot with one teaspoon of cinnamon and three teaspoons of sugar with water almost to the top and put it over the fire. She brought it to the boil three times and then served it to the thirsty men.

Her husband rubbed her nice bottom with his hands and then squeezed it and kissed her neck, then felt her bosoms. Full as they were with milk, which he didn't mind. She asked, "Grigor, do you like my bosoms as much as you liked your previous wife's bosoms? Grigor Og said that you loved his Mither's bosoms and I wondered if you liked mine as much. Do you?" both Padruig and Alex looked away and left that to Grigor.

"Of course, I love them. That's why I'm holding them, isn't it?" he said smiling.

"Were Morag's nicer than mine?" Zara asked.

Grigor Mohr MacGregor

"Nae, yours are the nicest, especially when the bairns aren't sucking on them. I'll be glad when Causantin has stopped feeding, so I have them to myself again. Did Grigor Og tell you about his Mither's breasts, did he?" he asked.

"Aye he did. He said he loved his Mither's breasts too and would try to rub up against them or sleep in her bed when you weren't there, so he could feel them against his chest. So, I just wondered if mine could be that good," she said. Both Alex and Padruig by this time had nearly finished their coffee in wonderment of the conversation about women's breasts and Grigor Og's hidden obsession about women's breasts.

"Did he now?" he said sculling the hot coffee.

"Well, he should have married a woman with bigger breasts," he said.

"Aye, that's what I told him. He said his lady friend Carmel wasn't a buxom woman, unlike his Mither, so he was still looking for the perfect breasts on a woman for himself," Zara said.

"Now Zara, tell us please who the MacNachtens are," he asked impatiently.

"I had never met them, but I did see them opposite the burn here one day and in a dream, I saw Malcolm. He is a bit fae. They couldn't see me. I think it was both brothers, Malcolm and Kenneth, who were here before your Father arrived. Then at your son's house there was a knock on the door, to which I answered," Zara said

"Someone saw you there?" he asked in a terse tone.

"Aye," and she began to tremble again.

"How many people and who were they?" Grigor demanded to know.

"There were two men, one older and one younger. One was a friend of Grigor's named Bruce MacDonald. He was a bit dull, but nice enough. He said he was the Stepfather to Malcolm MacNachten and they were there to see Grigor about demolishing the school, I think. Malcolm, however recognised me from his own dream of Culloden when you gave me that MacGregor brooch. When I saw him briefly that day on Culloden Moor, I knew to leave and I did. He recognised me at Grigor's house as that same person. He asked Grigor questions, but Grigor wouldn't answer them and told me not to also and to just continue feeding Causantin," Zara said.

"It was decided that they would just call me a fairy," she continued, "So that's where that has come from on that old tub," she said.

"Do they know that you are actually dead?" Grigor Mohr asked.

"Aye, all three of them do and agreed to keep it a secret," she said. "Can I please sit down now darling? My leg's hurting," she asked.

"Can I see it?" Alex asked. With Grigor's nod of approval, he lifted Zara's long skirt to inspect her lower leg. Holding her leg in his hands, he moved it in various directions, which hurt with some movements and not others and the bruising had not gone away. The swelling had gone down a little.

"I think you may have a fracture in one of the two lower leg bones, but we do need to go to Inverness. Can I take her on my horse or you on yours, Grigor?" Alex asked.

"One of us will have to stay and watch over things here, even though John's watching over the coos and Isobel's feeding the chickens and the goats, we still need security here and two men with Zara. And don't open the door," Grigor said.

With that cleared up, Zara bathed with assistance from Isobel then dressed up warmly for the journey and was helped onto her husband's horse by Alex, who had strapped Causantin to his back, leaving Padruig behind.

The ride to Inverness required one stop for baby Causantin to be fed and changed and get some attention from his Ma, but he was asleep by the time the ride continued. They went straight to the Doctor's house, not knowing what reception awaited them, as he also had been a victim of Grigor's Father and was kicked out of the house after Zara had given birth to Causantin. They were surprised to see Sean, the Australian ghost who appeared to have moved in with the Doctor, whether he knew it or not.

"So, you are a Fairy now Zara," Sean said sarcastically, having read the newspaper too. She didn't have time for Sean, but no one could see him anyhow.

"Is Peter here?" Alex asked.

"He is for those he likes and he isn't for those he dislikes. Which category are you Mr Nudist man?" Sean added for effect.

"He's on my list," Alex mumbled to himself.

Then Peter the Doctor, who had been very fond of Alex previously, came out of his exam room.

"So, when you are in need you come to me and if not, you tell me to piss off? Is that it, Alex?" Peter asked.

"Let's go Alex, please," Zara pleaded.

Grigor then said to him, "If you don't fix my wife's leg, you'll have two broken ones," Peter knew that Grigor meant it, which made Sean laugh and we all went into the examination room together.

"All of you? Really? How many husbands do you have?" he asked.

"Aye, all of us, now fix it!" Grigor said pointing to Zara's right lower leg.

"How did you injure your leg Zara and don't say it was a farm accident?" Peter asked.

"The same asshole that kicked you out did her some damage too and I'm not in the mood to answer questions. Is it broken?" Grigor asked. Peter concluded that one of the lower bones of the right leg was fractured, called the fibula, but not severely.

"However, I do need to know how it happened in case there was crushing involved, meaning there would be a risk of blood clots if there was," Peter said. "Was it a crushing injury or not?" he asked.

"Aye it was," said Zara. Bringing the incident to mind, she then began to shake all over.

"And there's that too, she trembles sometimes since that day," Alex said.

"Alright, you will need blood thinning medications and eat lots of onions, which I have and you require splints and bandages to hold the bones in place for over two weeks," Peter said. They were due to go back to see him for it to be reviewed then. "I have the herbal tea here Alex or Grigor. You can give her this to calm her nerves, so whenever she starts to tremble, give her a cup of hot water with these herbs steeped in the water. If it gets worse than that, there is a medication that she could use to stop the trembles but, in her case, she shouldn't take that while breast feeding the young one, so it's herbs for now," he said. "As well as looking for what the trigger is that starts her trembling in the first place. For example, is it when you shout, Mr MacGregor, by any chance?" Peter asked. "And by the way the consultations here are no longer free of charge," he added just to get revenge.

"Nor is my Turkish coffee. That is if you ever visit again," Zara snipped.

"Will I be welcome if I visit?" he asked.

"Aye. Anyhow I'm an artist now. Haven't you seen an example of my work in the paper? It's in an Art Gallery in Glengarry," Zara said.

Grigor went to pay the bill and they both thought that Alex was following closely behind them with Peter, but they turned and he was still in the examination room with the Doctor. They had to wait for more than five minutes, then they both came out looking flushed in the face and adjusting their trousers. Peter then handed her the sticks that she would need to walk with too and he didn't charge them after all. Zara left feeling a little happier, leaving Peter gleaning over the advertisement saying, "'Unfinished Work of a Fairy' in Glengarry?" Alex left feeling much happier that his friendship was back on track with Peter. Grigor left feeling happier that it had cost them nothing, no matter what Alex had to do to achieve that.

The splints were uncomfortable, as well as the sticks he gave Zara to walk with. After feeding wee Causantin again, she suggested tea at the tea house before they left for home in the remote part of the Aird, but Grigor worried that there would be people who might recognise them all. So, Alex once again strapped Causantin onto his back and assisted her to sit comfortably in front of Grigor with the splints. It was going to be a slower journey back home to the Aird, but at least there was a diagnosis for that lower leg and treatment for it and those annoying trembles. Alex had to ride closer and occasionally adjust the position of her leg. Thanking both Grigor and Alex profusely, they all hoped that Isobel had cooked dinner for them all, as it would be slow going home with the splints on horseback.

On the way, they discussed that Isobel had hardly spoken to Zara since she had been home. Grigor said it was because she hadn't taken Isobel with her when she had had to leave and so he suggested that they buy her a big horse, now that she had outgrown her pony, which could be given to the twins. They needed to start horse riding lessons. He suggested that they allow Grigor Og to sell that tub artwork and to fetch the wages as well from Craskie farm, then they could buy Isobel a horse, a good saddle and bridle too, as well as long riding boots, pants and a split skirt, not in pink hopefully. Smiling at the 'not pink part', they agreed, so they would ride to Glenmoriston in a few days and hopefully get the money from Grigor Og without doing the long ride to Glengarry. That meant Zara would have to be the only one knocking on his door with the others not visible to him.

Thankfully dinner was cooked, because they were all famished and both John and Isobel had prepared a lovely dinner and cooked a loaf of bread too, while Padruig read his book as usual, justifying his position as security, so he just drank coffee and ate biscuits and sandwiches all the while in their abscence. He didn't even do any farm work.

"Uncle Padruig, can't you at least put the chickens away, as well as the goats while we cook, please?" Isobel had asked, but his answer was he had to follow instructions from the boss to make sure no-one opened the front door and to maintain security.

His hatred of farming was obvious. John put away the chickens and the goats as nightfall was falling and he spotted them coming across the burn and waved happily. He helped Zara dismount awkwardly with her sticks and then helped Alex with wee Causantin and carried the wee bairn inside. It was getting too cold outside for the wee bairn.

"The fires are all lit Ma and dinner is cooked," John said as he went inside. Grigor put both horses away and thanked Alex, as he rubbed his sore back and gladly went into the warm home. They all sat over the lovely dinner. The entire stew was devoured by them all, as well as the whole loaf of bread.

"Ma, I have some hot water cooking for your hot bath in your room. After cleaning up we'll go to ours for baths too. So glad your leg is going to get better," she said. It was the most she had said in weeks.

"Isobel darling, what colour horse would you like, if you had one, I mean?" Zara asked.

"My favourite is a palomino horse. My second favourite would be a chestnut mare around 15hh. Why do you ask?" she answered.

"Just wondering," Zara replied. The plans to go to Glenmoriston commenced in bed that night, until Grigor was unable to hold back his desire any longer, but as the Doctor had suggested, it had to be slow, gentle and careful. Peter had reassured them that reproduction was still a possibility because the midwives had done an exemplary job on Zara's private parts.

Zara and Grigor both enjoyed the ecstasy of love making, unable to be silent when the door opened to both Alex and Padruig just checking in to see if all was well as an excuse, staring straight at Grigor's naked buttocks.

"You lucky dog," Padruig said then closed the door. Bathing in the morning was awkward for her, with one leg held over the side of the bathtub, in order to stay dry. Padruig peeked in again using another excuse with her unable to move that leg.

"Do you need a hand to scrub any bits Zara?" said the cheeky man.

"No thank you," she said.

"You will need lifting out though, won't you?" Padruig didn't wait for the reply and lifted Zara naked from the bath and wrapped her in a towel.

As Grigor entered the room he said, "Just making sure she doesn't slip and fall over," he said, still smiling like only Padruig could when he felt like it.

Trying to get dressed with him in the room, standing on one leg was difficult. Grigor, thankfully put his arm around her waist, while they discussed when the three of them would leave for Craskie Farm.

"Grigor, there's just one thing you should know in making your decision as to who knocks on the door," Zara said.

"Aye, what's that?" he asked. "I might be wrong but are you unaware of how his wife, Helen died?" she asked.

"Will it make a difference?" he asked. "I don't know but if you have all the facts then you can make the right decision, is what I think," she said.

"Alright, you have my curiosity peaked now. How did Helen die?" Grigor asked. After explaining the gruesome details all over again, it was clear he had not known and was shocked that Helen would resort to that form of suicide.

"I'm sorry darling. I didn't want to tell you at all until it was clear that we were going back there and it might be of some importance to you. On top of that, Patrick and Henrietta had the Priests insist on the removal of Helen's body from the inside of the Chapel, so now her body is outside in the cemetery, as well as the empty grave for Grigor Og," Zara added. Grigor sat down then looking pale and sad for his son, as well as what had happened to Helen Grant, who had been so well cared for, at least in her older years.

"Grigor also told me that he had a complaint from Frasers Trading Post, to whom she had delivered what she considered master pieces of artwork on the Battle of Culloden. He explained that previously she had painted perfect pieces of the battle assisted by yourself and Padruig to get everything just right. However, on this occasion, she had delivered what he called were caricatures of Prince Charles and the groom whose head was blown off. She painted them like a child would paint with Prince Charles flying through the air as his bloodied injured horse reared, throwing him off. The people in it were all half the size of a normal person with an attempt to make a joke of Culloden, especially the Prince and that poor groom," Zara explained.

"So, John from Frasers marched up to where Grigor was living in Charlotte House at that time, with all six of the paintings. He said that in the wrong hands they would make all Highland Scots look like fools, so he gave them all back to Grigor and refused to sell them. That day was the day she was overly friendly to everyone, including Grigor and was looking a bit manic, some said. She killed herself that night," Zara explained.

"I'm sorry love. Would you like to see your son, or I can do it?" Zara said.

"How about we both see him, so the dirty little fella doesn't get ideas about you, my beautiful wife. I've already had to deal with that over breakfast," he said.

"What do you mean?" Zara asked.

"Padruig and Alex put it to me that they could be your husband number two and number three. I almost head butted the two of them. They tried to make me feel like an inadequate husband," he said.

"Oh, darling you know that you are all I ever want, but Padruig is getting too cheeky and Alex, lovable though he is, likes men. Can you stop that familiarity please or I can tell them that you are my one and only?" Zara said.

"I've dealt with it and Padruig won't be dragging you out of the bath naked again, unless you are drowning," he said. "He really needs a woman. We should ask around."

Time passed quickly and soon we were on our way to Craskie Farm in Glenmoriston to hopefully retrieve the lost wee wages as well as the money asked for on the artwork in Glengarry. Grigor Mohr dressed well for the occasion when he thought he would be seeing his son Grigor Og, as did Zara in a split skirt and a warm coat because the weather was coming over and it was expected to rain. Zara had her arisaid over her head in readiness, as well as to cover wee Causantin. Padruig was more subdued after being told he wasn't eligible to be Zara's husband number two or three. 'God only knows where they got that idea from when they knew Grigor was a Catholic and Zara was a Muslim,' she thought.

The front gates to Craskie Farm were open unusually, but convenient not to have to dismount for that purpose. Zara and Grigor scanned around to see if Grigor was outside or for any sounds that could lead them in his direction when they saw him sauntering, in his way down from the wee Chapel after locking its doors. He looked very lonely but not miserable and as handsome as ever as his dear Father. They were so much alike, more so than any of their other bairns and Zara lamented that Hector wasn't more like Grigor Og. Hector was such a naughty lad, who in his Father's eyes could do no wrong and he was going to be tall. Isobel wanted to accompany them this time to meet Grigor Og because she was related to him as her stepbrother through Grigor Mohr. She was in one of those pink favourite dresses of hers, covered with a warm arisaid for the weather. Grigor Og saw all three of them arriving and his face lit up no end and he began to jog towards them, as he summoned the groom to take care of the weary horses.

"Da, how can it be you?" he said, as he embraced his Father then was introduced to Isobel as their daughter, not mentioning Hugh Mohr yet anyway. "Zara, I've missed you so much and you left your wages behind. Please come inside and I'll get it for you," he said.

Her wages were in a wee paper bag and it may have been two pounds or less, but she did not count it. Zara had never earned a wage in Scotland before and to her it was precious, and she had no intention of spending it. Zara embraced Grigor Og warmly too. He was such a lovely warm person, she thought and an unappreciated soul.

"Son, obviously we can't stay, and it can't be known we were all here, do you understand that much?" Grigor Mohr stated up front.

"This is Isobel, Zara's daughter and my stepdaughter," he stated plainly as they went inside the spotlessly clean home. Grigor Og looked relieved to see her formerly badly bruised face was much improved, but sorry to see her leg wasn't yet.

"How long will it take to heal Zara?" he asked.

"Maybe a month or so with these splints. There's a fracture in one of the lower leg bones," she stated.

"I am so sorry about that," he said sincerely.

He went to prepare the coffee when Zara said that she would do it, so as she was making it, he was catching up with his Father. They were so glad to be able to see each other miraculously, even if it was just for a short time.

"You can come to the Aird," said Grigor Mohr "to visit." "It's not a fairy dun as some would have you believe. We saw the artwork in the newspaper. Can my wife have her share of that too, so we can buy Isobel a new horse?" he asked.

"Gladly," Grigor said and went to a draw and took out the one hundred and seventy-five pounds with Kenneth's commission taken out. He suggested that they take the drum of broken china today too, as well as the implements and glue, so she could make more out of any kind of thing lying around and call it something in relation to 'the fairy work'. He said he'd be glad to pick it up when he visited and leave it with either Malcolm or Kenneth MacNachten for the Art Gallery. Apparently, there was already a buyer for my tub. He said that it was a Doctor from Inverness. Peter someone, whose name he had forgotten. The Father and son enjoyed their coffees and each other's company, as well as passing on condolences for Helen and then we left with the drum tied securely to the back of Isobel's borrowed horse. Padruig had remained invisible, but was securely holding Zara's leg out straight, wishing that he could caress it. When she kissed her stepson farewell, it was the first time he had felt like her stepson.

"I'll miss you son and thank you for helping me," Zara said. They all departed before anyone started asking questions. On the snow on the ground, there were the hooves of his family departing, but there were hooves of four horses, not three.

92. *Alexander and Peter*

The "Unfinished Work of a Fairy" went on display in Kenneth's Art Gallery in Glengarry with so many people who attended to see it. A big SOLD sign was already attached to it when Dr Peter Heath walked into the unfamiliar surroundings. Alexander was assisting Kenneth on the afternoon and evening when Peter arrived and spent the entire time with him showing him all of Kenneth's work and packaged his purchase for him. They learned a lot about each other in that time and Peter invited him to his home anytime in Inverness. There were many disappointed customers at the Art Gallery who had all wanted the Fairy piece and looked sad as Alexander packaged it for Peter and carried it for him to his carriage. Alexander offered him coffee and cake before he left, inside his house, now that he and Matilda ran Loch Garry Ranch since his Father's death.

They were both lonely men, bachelors who needed a fulfilling friendship in their lives, but Inverness was a long way and he invited Peter also to spend time on the farm with him as he couldn't often leave the needs of the animals or the myriad things that came up on a farm. The two of them delighted so much in each other's company that Peter said that Glengarry would be a lovely distraction to his otherwise boring life and unpleasant clients. They planned for Peter to visit Alexander in two weeks' time. Matilda came in through the front door as he was leaving and was introduced and she wholeheartedly approved of him visiting the farm and staying overnight.

Both men had no idea how that one art piece connected so many people of the one family.

93. *Back in the Aird.*

"Ma can I please talk to you privately?" Isobel said after putting away the horses upon their return home from visiting Grigor Og MacGregor for the money needed to buy her a new horse.

"Aye, darling, so long as you have put away all of my fairy art stuff from Grigor Og," Zara said.

"Thank you Padruig, for helping me," she said. Padruig turned and hugged her warmly and helped her inside. Grigor Mohr was already checking the farm and asking John how things were during our absence. Grigor Mohr was such a good man and Zara adored him. All the goats were away already, as well as the calving coos as a storm was developing. She began to close the shutters on the windows, taking his lead when Padruig said he would do it and insisted that she went inside to sit by the fire. Followed by her daughter Isobel, who put the coffees on for everyone and stoked the fire, Isobel complained that John hadn't lit all of the fires and the house was cold, so she lit them and put bath water on before having that chat.

"What about dinner darling?" Zara asked. "Can we chat while you cut up that beef there and I can peel potatoes down here from my seat by the fire?" she asked.

"I'll chop up the onions and the rest of those vegetables then, or we will go hungry tonight," Padruig said.

"We'll need a loaf of bread too," Zara remarked.

"So, what did you want to tell me sweetie?" she asked. Padruig was listening so she told him not to repeat anything she said. He agreed but was confused at the change in her usual direct dialogue. "Ma, it's that nice man we met today. I like him and both he and I can have babies and he has a nice home and his wife is definitely dead," she said. "John is old and boring these days and I want children like you have," she added. "I want to move in with him, move out that other woman and have babies. Will it affect the ownership of this farm for you and Da? I'm not Catholic, am I?" she asked. Zara looked across at Padruig with squinted eyes like to say, 'definitely do not repeat this or all hell with be let loose'. "You can ask him to hand fast with me can't you and ask him if I can be his wife?" Isobel asked in her most direct way possible. Zara began hoping that Grigor would be outside for a bit longer, as she continued peeling potatoes and taking some of the vegetables from Padruig's hands that had stopped mid peel, like as if they were frozen.

Alex was yet to reveal himself, so it was just the three of them.

"My dearest Isobel, do you love the man that you met today, who is my husband's son, Grigor Og?" Zara asked.

"Aye, I do. He is so handsome, sexy and warm and cute and I think he would have a bigger penis than John's little weenie," she answered.

"Do you know how he feels about you?" Zara asked.

"Not yet. That's what you're for, isn't it?" Isobel said. Padruig then interjected,

"Let me help out. First of all, this land is not affected if you leave John Fraser and handfast Grigor Og, but your Ma has a bad leg, as you know lass, so would you agree to me going to ask him on your behalf?" Padruig asked. "John is Catholic though, even though you're not. Did you marry in a Kirk? Or did you handfast?" he asked.

"We all married the same day in a Catholic Kirk, but Ma said it meant nothing to her and demanded an Imam from her Faith, so that was done for Ma, but not me. John and I have only one marriage certificate and the bairn was baptised Catholic later also," she answered.

"Isobel, we really need to ask your Father. The Catholic factor is a problem because you can't divorce John, not that it stops people finding love, so if you both love each other, I support you. John might insist on keeping his son, however. Could you live without your son?" Zara asked.

"You know, Ma, that he is not John's son. He is Alex's biological son, isn't he?" she stated vehemently.

"Does John know that?" Zara asked.

"Nae, not really," she said

"Your Father is your legal Father, as he adopted you, if you remember and your biological Father attended to make sure that it was all above board. That being said, your Father needs to know all of these details and needs to be the one who asks his son, Grigor Og if that's how far it goes, not you Padruig. Thank you anyway, so please agree that after we cook the dinner and your Da has his bath, that you ask him nicely and I will help you. Padruig, can you find Alex and ask him about his biological son, Andrew MacDonald Fraser and fill him in?" Zara asked.

94. *Where Is Alex?*

Padruig searched high and low for Alex, who was always usually around. His horse was still in the stables and he was meant to stay on the farm while we were out. Eventually, he saw a shadow beside the burn with his flaming torch as the rain set in. It was hard to make out what it was at first. More like a blob that didn't move. He approached it warily, calling Alex's name and it did not respond. As he got closer, he saw when the lightning flashed that it was Alex slumped over beside the burn and as he got closer again, he heard him sobbing.

"What's wrong Alex?" he asked panicking.

"I woke up this morning feeling so lonely and when Grigor dismissed our idea to be husbands, I decided to go to Inverness to see Peter and he had left for Glengarry for that Art Gallery thing. That was when I saw them together," he sobbed.

"Who did you see together?" Padruig asked, bewildedly.

"Peter the Doctor and your grandson, young Alex Grant, your son Alexander's son, who lived in Nova Scotia all those years," he explained.

"Aye, he was the buyer for that fairy thing of Zara's. He was just probably picking it up is all," Padruig said logically.

"Nae Padruig, they are two bachelors looking for a friend and it looked to me like they really liked each other. I thought Peter liked me," he said, distraught at the realisation that he had been mistaken.

"Do you love your bairn more than that man?" Padruig asked.

"Aye, of course I do. What a question! I have to live with that heartache every day," he answered as thunder clapped overhead.

"You might lose him altogether if you don't pay attention Alex. Isobel wants to leave here and take Andrew with her. She fancies Grigor Og. Zara has her talking to Grigor Mohr now, which won't be easy, so you have to get it together and declare to John that he is yours biologically, so you can decide at least equally what happens to your bairn. Isobel wants more bairns and I don't blame her. Are you up to defending your rights as a Father?" Padruig asked firmly. Shaken into a new reality that he might lose wee Andrew too, he tried to recover from his misery.

"Aye, but can you help me? I'm a bit of a mess. I'll need to bathe and wash my hair," he asked.

"Do you like Isobel? I mean, none of us know if Grigor Og even likes Isobel. What if you two get together and forget the asshole's asshole as well as John Fraser?" he suggested. "I'll help you but do you like Isobel or not?" he asked again.

"Aye, but not as much as Zara. I suppose I do when she's not snippy," Alex replied.

"She wants a bigger cock than John's weenie, she told Zara, so all you need to do is walk in and flash your cock," Padruig advised. "John's weenie's no bigger than my thumb, so that wouldn't be hard for any man to do, but I'll have that bath and try and join the conversation. Can you at least get Zara to wash my hair?" Alex replied.

"Don't worry about all of the details, come on, get up Alex, you're covered in mud," Padruig said, as he helped his friend try to stand up and get into the house to bathe and deal with the emotional trauma.

In the bath, Alex was insisting on Zara's help, as she shampooed his hair, but she refused to scrub his feet. "Padruig, you scrub his feet then throw out all this filthy water please. Where on earth have you been my friend to get so dirty?" Zara asked.

"It's my soul that's dirty," he said miserably. The conversation at the table between Grigor Mohr and Isobel was getting louder and Zara was anxious to return to them both. She dried off Alex and dressed him in clean clothes, so he could put his part of the story forward with Padruig's assistance. Andrew, his wee bairn, was born to Isobel, but that fact was unknown to John. He was a surrogate Father, unofficially and that was why he had never left our home because he couldn't bear to be apart from Andrew. The problem was that John had never known and despite Andrew having dark brown hair, not the trademark ginger hair of that family of Frasers, he hadn't guessed, despite the lad even looking like Alex more and more as the years passed. The lad himself preferred the company of

Alex, who was very good with bairns. This was a real dilemma and none of the other bairns were happy seeing the adults carrying on like they were. Thank goodness the dinner was cooked to remove one stress and the bread would have been ready too.

Zara was as calm as she could be as she hugged her troubled and hungry husband from behind and served up dinner for everyone to calm the nerves of one and all. The bread was delicious and her eccentric family were slowly all calming down. All the bairns were fed and put to bed. They were all very tired, even Hector. It had been a long day. Zara started by saying that she now had the money for Isobel's horse, which Isobel could choose with Alex, as Zara didn't now have the time, if John agreed. She asked if Alex could take Isobel to Inverness with the money to buy the horse and the saddlery the following day, to which they all agreed taking her lead. It gave Grigor Mohr time to find out if it was even an option. Her husband needed a hot bath and she washed his hair and scrubbed him from head to toe, which relaxed him. When she was gently caressing and washing his genitalia, a smile crept across his face and she knew it would be alright. They would enjoy each other, then sleep.

An early morning start was required for the next day and so she woke everyone up for breakfast at five o'clock and sent Grigor Mohr to Craskie Farm and Isobel and Alex to Inverness. She also asked Alex to buy a few more milking goats, so she could start making cheese. The storm hadn't done any damage and all the shutters were opened once again. More vegetables were planted and some were brought in for meals that day. She knew to be better prepared next time.

Grigor Mohr had to make an invisible entrance into his son's home, where he was working in his office. When his Father spoke and then made himself visible, he was momentarily shocked but so pleased to see him again. Over coffee, Grigor Mohr explained that he had a question for him, which wouldn't take long and for which he was a bit embarrassed and apologised. "My stepdaughter liked you son and even though she is unhappily married to John Fraser with a son to Alex MacDonald, she wanted you son, being as handsome as you are, and the rest of her description included the required size of your penis. As a parent, I still have to ask you if you have an interest in Isobel?" he asked.

"I'm sorry Da, that would feel like incest because she is my sister, even though she is my stepsister," he replied.

"Can you please tell her that I am flattered at the attention, which I am, but Carmel will do for now and I don't want small children again, given she wants more children. I hope both you and Zara are not offended?" he said.

"Nae, it is just my job, as you remember talking to Padruig about Helen when you were a young lad. I appreciate you being candid and I hope it doesn't put you off coming to the Aird to see us?" Grigor Mohr said.

"Nae, I still want to visit you all. Da, can I ask you if you ever see Ma where you are in that world?" he asked.

"Nae lad. She kept a terribly sad secret from me before she passed and I only found out about it after her passing, which broke my heart and that was what killed me, so she avoids me, I think and I'm very happy with my loving wife," he answered.

Then he heard Hamish entering through the front door and had to disappear again.

"Have you taken to talking to yourself now Grigor?" said the big man, who had been loyal his whole working life to Craskie Farm.

"Coming fishing this afternoon then?" Hamish asked. Grigor Mohr then left with the knowledge that his beloved wife required before Isobel and Alex returned home from Inverness and he knew that Zara was up to something. Alex loved baby Andrew, who they had taken with them, leaving John alone with Zara on the farm, who was tinkering about with her fairy artwork as well as cooking and gardening. He thanked God for his wife.

Arriving home dressed in riding boots and a new split riding skirt on her new five-year-old big bay gelding with a white star on his face and four white socks, with fine saddlery, as well as the goats, both Isobel and Alex looked not only happy with the horse, but secretively happy about each other. The hope was that Alex had recovered from his perceived lost love and Isobel was going to be with child again, but this time, on her terms. Even if she ended up with both men, she wasn't about to lose Andrew and neither were Zara and Grigor. As days and weeks passed by, John stayed more and more outside with the coos and had accepted his lot, while Alex cared more for Isobel and her him. Zara no longer had to wash his hair, Isobel fussed over Alex as her belly revealed what they had also done that day in Inverness.

Padruig rolled his eyes each time Alex patted his new love's stomach, but there was peace, even though divorce wasn't possible. They had handfast, but whether that was legitimate if one was already married, they didn't care as they had found the love, they both desperately needed, as well as a bigger family. Grigor asked Alex to build on yet another room to our house that was no longer big enough for us all, so they drew up plans and decided on two more large rooms, both with fireplaces, so both men and Isobel and their bairns had enough growing room. There were enough rocks around the property to build on and on. Grigor had started praying more and thanked God that Isobel hadn't left with wee Andrew and for his wife.

After the Fairy Art event in Glengarry, it was noticed that there were a few rare onlookers to Grigor's house in the Aird, but who all stayed cautiously on the other side of the burn. We later heard it reported, that all some people had seen were the foundation stones of a house, like many of the clearances, but no home and certainly no people and thank goodness those folks stopped coming to look for the fairy. It didn't stop Zara from completing all kinds of fairy artwork that Grigor Og took with him after each time he visited to give to Kenneth to sell at his Art Gallery in Glengarry and along with the goat's cheese, Zara was earning more and more, which she gave to her husband Grigor Mohr to use for the farm. She only ever had a few requests of clothing for all of the family, including Grigor Mohr and the bairns and a larger cook pot for cooking or needs for the goats.

Grigor was so proud of his wife's unexpected income that he and John were able to replace the slate on the roof and more substantial shutters over all of the windows, as well as a few new beds and bedding. The next income from fairy art, as it gained popularity, were two more bedrooms and an upgraded laundry with a fire and a large copper in which to boil the linen, followed by a bigger fireplace in the kitchen to cook over.

The trips to Inverness, after the all-clear on Zara's leg, were more exciting being able to buy things needed by the household, including the barrels and salt for preserving meat, if there was a really bad winter. Alex took to farming now that he had decided to stay permanently and had planted a crop of potatoes with preserving them in a small structure, he built to keep them all in, once they had grown. He surrounded his crop, with the assistance of Hector, now a lanky teenager, with palisades in the event of deer coming in to eat it. Padruig was full of criticism, as usual and didn't assist and said they wouldn't grow in the Aird, but they did miraculously. They seemed to like the cold, not that any of the rest of the family knew anything about them.

Hector seemed interested in potatoes, which was even more miraculous to get him interested in anything. Once the first crop was ready to eat in all of their various sizes, we all helped Alex collect them. Taking care to leave as many to preserve as possible, we ate them for the first time with boiling them, just adding salt without removing the skin. Serving them up with goat butter alongside our stews on the first night was a worry to see if the bairns would eat them, so Isobel mashed up theirs. Grigor didn't love them but ate them very politely and congratulated Alex and Hector on their work. Zara did love them with butter, but asked Alex if they made a person fat, which of course he didn't know.

Either way, they were a huge success, and we were all proud of Alex and Hector.

95. *An Error of Judgement*

Hector was an odd child from early life and the strangest and obvious reality was that he looked every bit like a Grant, not much like a MacGregor at all and from Zara's side there was a lot missing on her family tree coming originally from a colony of England. Zara was unsure where all her ancestors were from, other than somewhere in both the United Kingdom, including Scotland, Ireland, and Wales and somewhere in Germany she thought. Grigor Mohr had revealed to her long ago in a dream, before they were married, that she was a descendent of Clan Gregor with some of those men under the ground in Culloden Moor, which gave her something to hold onto and the clan brooch meant the world to her.

Hector worried her, as he didn't respond to her as well as her other bairns did, if at all. He was adored by his Father, which was wonderful, but for a long time he was never punished at all and no one was allowed to punish him either. This meant that he did some awful things that eventually did lead to a spanking from his Da. In the early 1700's, where Zara's reading and knowledge base was, a young man who was difficult could be trained militarily by Lord Lovat, like Padruig Dubh was before the 1715 Rising, when he was all but fourteen years old. There was no such outlet for youngsters who were hard to motivate or difficult now. The most he had ever done was helping Alex with the potatoes, which was nothing less than a miracle.

Zara mistakenly asked Padruig over coffee one day if all of Clan Grant were in fact Grants, truthfully since their arrival in Scotland, or if they included other clans' people who had taken on the name of Grant. Not expecting to receive a bad reaction from him, Padruig asked, "What on earth are you driving at Zara?"

Glancing at the door, there was the hope that Grigor Mohr would not overhear this conversation because it was going to be about Hector, his favourite bairn. Grigor Mohr was over-sensitive regarding his imperfect son. Zara knew all about imperfect bairns because she had one of those in her previous life. Zara was hoping for some understanding about why the lad was the way he was and was already regretting having chosen Padruig to ask, but her reason was that Hector was more like a Grant than a MacGregor.

"Hector is more like you in appearance, height and mannerisms, as well as how you may have been as a young man when you were sent to Lord Lovat's to train and learn how to kill and so on," she said.

"How dare you talk to me about my childhood and how I trained, of which you know nothing Zara," Padruig answered.

"Didn't you train with Lord Lovat, for a time at least until it was removed from him and then weren't you with the Independent Companies? Is that true or are the facts misrepresented in all the books?" Zara asked.

"I avoided telling anyone anything over that period, so that all of that stuff would never appear in books of any description, so I don't know how you have this knowledge Zara and it really annoys me. You writers are always asking questions and writing it all down," he said angrily, showing his disdain for Zara herself. She decided to back off, realising her dreadful mistake.

"I am sorry Padruig. Please forgive me. I wasn't intending to hurt you, but I have and for that I don't have words to compensate. I just wanted to know if Clan Gregor may have taken your Clan name at one time, which might explain why Hector is the way he is. I am not a writer anymore and I am not writing anything down about any one of us, please know that. Do you forgive me?" Zara asked, but Padruig was looking over her head to her husband, who was listening to her. Afraid then of the consequences, Zara began to shake again for the first time in over a month.

"Get that tea Alex uses," Grigor ordered Padruig.

"Where does he keep the bloody stuff?" he asked. "I don't know. Get Alex!" he yelled. Zara was becoming worse and the tremble became a shake by the time Alex ran in and put on the water to steep the herbs that were in the upper cupboard away from the bairns.

"This helps also," as he kissed her neck. "Get away from my wife's neck," Grigor said. "Then there's this too. A gentle rub along her arm," teased Alex to illustrate the point. All of which made Zara chuckle at his antics and the tea worked wonders.

"Thank you, Alex," Zara said. "So, what brought it on Zara?" Alex asked.

"It was my foolish enquiry with Padruig, which upset him and rightfully so about our family, which doesn't concern him, so I must ask both my husband and Padruig for forgiveness please. I have made a terrible error of judgement today. I wanted to understand Hector is all," Zara said as her tears rolled freely.

"Don't you worry about young Hector, Zara, I know how to deal with him," Alex said.

"But he does look like you Padruig, not suggesting anything, but he could pass as a Grant, so it's not an unreasonable question. Now I've got work to do," said Alex as he left again.

"Zara, if you have something to say or ask about our son, you ask me. Is that understood?" Grigor Mohr stated firmly. He didn't reach for his belt.

"I understand," Zara said feeling deflated and humiliated and still no closer to understanding her own son, as Grigor also left to go back to work.

Then finally Padruig spoke to Zara.

"Some of Clan Gregor, during proscription took our name, as well as a few other names as well, but went back to Clan

Gregor at the end of proscription. There were some who had been Grants for so long that they stayed as Clan Grant and no one really knows the difference anymore," said Padruig.

"Your question wasn't wrong, but we all prefer the less they know policy," he said.

"Zara. Your books that you've written over there, are mine. I can read some English, as you know, but they're hard to read in parts as I am a native Erse speaker. Can you read them to us some nights if anyone else wants to listen? However, if the bairns are listening, you would have to leave out the raunchy bits," he asked.

"Aye, if Grigor agrees, Padruig. I'll ask him," she said and went to lay down for a rest.

Zara felt stupid for her mistake and just wanted to sleep. She awoke a little later to an amorous husband demanding sex as he lifted her skirt. He was a man who loved to enjoy her femininity with his face and tongue until it drove her mad with pleasure. It was this absolute power over the lowering and heightening of their love making that made him the most enjoyable lover. He almost always waited for Zara to orgasm first unless he was desperate and today, he waited and it was magnificent. Her enjoyment of his body was always on her mind, even when she was cooking or making her fairy art. It was all a sensual act of taking his penis in her hand and gently licking the tip which also drove him a little crazy, so that he entered her to try to slow down his ejaculation and then move in and out gently caressing her breasts and telling her things in Gaelic that she had never understood but it sounded so sensual, she didn't care. Holding her head, he asked her to look into his beautiful blue eyes and tell him that she loved him and she always did with a depth of emotion that brought tears to her eyes, knowing she had the best man in that world.

"Look at us my wife," he demanded. "That is who we are," indicating to his penis inside her vagina. Zara let out a cry of pleasure then came again as did he with his beautiful moan of a man in ecstasy. "I do love you, my Zara. You are all mine.

If I'm a little harsh at times, it's for our sakes as well as the bairns. You are all my responsibility and I will do for you all the best I can do until the Day of Judgment," he said with deep sincerity.

"I am so sorry for today. Have you forgiven me?" Zara asked. "Aye, but only if you'll let me spank you once on your beautiful bottom," which he did. Then Grigor was aroused again with the sight alone of her bottom and began love making again even though there were sounds of bairns in the kitchen and the smell of food cooking.

"Isobel is cooking tonight with Alex's help, so let's all pray it tastes alright. You and I can have a bath and then go out and see how much damage they have done to the kitchen," Grigor Mohr said. Zara was surprised to see that he had already cooked up the hot water for their bath, while she was sleeping and they both bathed together giggling like young lovers.

The kitchen was ready for them both with the table set and the food cooked and ready with even a loaf of bread that Padruig had cooked.

"Oh Padruig," Zara said, "was it really you who cooked the bread?" Zara asked as she embraced him from behind.

"How else were we going to have the book read?" Padruig asked. "Don't worry Zara, I've asked Grigor and he has approved except where it's too sexy for the bairns," he said all a matter of fact.

"Are you wanting me to read everything from the beginning, including the Prologue and the Forward?" Zara asked. "Aye, whatever that is," Padruig answered. "Are you interested in the books tonight? It will take a long while to read it all. Its over 460 pages long, including the Author's Notes and the characters both historical and fictional, that includes a piece on Padruig Dubh Grant of Glenmoriston," Zara said smiling.

"That's the bit I'd like you to read first Zara, so these gomerals will all know who I am at least," Padruig answered.

"There's a bit at the front about all Seven of you with my husband, why not that first, then you second Padruig?" Zara suggested.

All the bairns were fascinated that their elders were in books, most especially Hector, let alone that their Mither had written it. Grigor decided that Zara would read until the family all became too tired, then read again tomorrow and so on.

96. *Isobel of Glenmoriston*

We began to read "Isobel of Glenmoriston, Isobel's Story," on a stormy Friday night and the bairns were all tired into the second letter. The adults lasted longer into the fifth letter to be continued each day until they were bored with it, she thought. No one became bored with it and looked forward to the book reading every night, by the fire after the men washed the dishes and put them all away. Hector learned a lot about Uncle Padruig and Uncle Alex and had never imagined that they'd had infamy beyond his understanding of Scottish history, which was sadly limited.

Zara had been unable to keep him interested in home schooling on any topic, but the book reading was entirely different with the whole family involved, chipping in occasionally. Padruig was quick to correct Zara wherever she had the tiniest detail just slightly incorrect, which eventually drew a few "shut ups" from the rest of the family wanting to hear what came next in the story. Grigor Mohr gained admiration from the mention of his great horsemanship. The twinnies said, "Da, I didn't know you were a great horseman and now you are going to teach us, aren't you?".

They too were told to be quiet, so the story could flow on. Isobel glowed at the realisation that she was named after

"Isobel of Glenmoriston", the famous lady teamster of her time which drew some grunts from her former husband, Padruig Dubh.

"Was she your famous wife Uncle Padruig?" was a question asked by wee Ali which was received with a hmmmm from Padruig.

"Uncle Alex, what did you do?" asked Hector but answered by Padruig who stood and unashamedly gave an independent and glowing report of the skills of his friend.

"The magnificent fighter who was by his side and then was murdered by the bloody English," A few of the bairns then started to cry at that and cuddled Uncle Alex and we all thought it was bedtime for the bairns on the first night.

"Maybe we can skip over some parts?" Zara suggested. All in all, the reading was exciting for everyone.

In bed, Grigor said to his beloved wife, "I am so proud of your work Zara, sad though it is. Thankyou from the bottom of my heart. I expected to be forgotten, as all of us did when our society fell, but you have renewed it and given us back our lives and our purpose as well as our culture," he said with deep emotion. Zara slept beside a different type of man that night. A man who was proud of himself and his colleagues with all their various achievements, known only by themselves.

97. All About Hector

The following morning when Hector walked into the outbuilding where Zara did her 'fairy artwork', he had planned to empty out her large drum of Turkish china into the dirt and throw all of her collected rusty pieces, intended for fairy art restoration, into the burn but he didn't. He had wanted to destroy something of his Mither's, just because he wanted to see her cry, but after the previous night's book reading, he had begun to see his Mither differently. After all, the money she earned might buy him a horse too one day, like it had bought Isobel a horse. The twins, Fatma and Ali were before him in birth order, so he estimated one year for a horse and in the meantime, he decided to content himself with working with Uncle Alex on the potato fields, which he loved to eat.

He couldn't really understand why he wanted to see his Mither cry, but it had given him pleasure to see her upset and he enjoyed it when his Father had strapped her but now his Father no longer did that. Maybe she wasn't so bad after all, but even as a wee bairn he wanted to bite her breasts when being breast fed and had enjoyed seeing her cry in pain when her nipple was bleeding, once he had grown teeth. She stopped breast feeding him then.

Zara, in the meantime had to content herself with a folk lore story she had learned in the Highlands called 'MacFie and the Black Dog: A legend from the Isles'[7]. It was a very long story, but the gist of it was that the life from puppyhood into adult dog of a particular black hound dog, was that he was a useless dog. His former owner had said "the black dog's day will come" and so his loyal owner loved his useless black dog, rejecting his friend's advice to kill him, until the day when it paid off when the animal saved his life from a monster while on a fishing trip with friends. The black hound destroyed the monster, ripping off his hand and in the process, died himself. Zara then hoped that this old folklore tale from the Isles could apply to her much loved, but mostly useless son, Hector and his day would come, as it had with the black dog. Maybe she could ask Grigor Og to bring out some of his wonderful folklore books the next time he came and hopefully he even had that particular tale.

Each night and each reading brought its own challenges with the book's content, sometimes bringing tears, anxiety, anger, lust or joy, and revealing tragedies of the past. It had a powerful effect on all of its listeners, whether they were learning elements of Scottish history for the first time with its horrors, or if it clarified a mystery or if indeed it created one. Isobel from the book, once overcoming her despair was an inspiration to all of the family all over again to build up their own farm and work as hard as she had done. How she managed to endure life's myriad miseries of that period of time of Scotland's history, is in itself one of those small miracles never recognised in re-building Glenmoriston, joined later by her husband Padruig Dubh, who had been spirited away by the British to fight for them in Quebec. This was a sad and hard read for Zara, observing the realities of how life was for Padruig who was a dear and loyal friend as well as Alex and Zara's dearest husband, Grigor Mohr macGregor.

Both Padruig and his wife, Isobel had a complicated relationship but they produced three children, who in turn had their own children when life was easier. But despite all of their work and efforts, their daughter Helen still committed suicide a few years after her Mither's death.

That was the cloud that hung over Padruig's head of the daughter that he had adored so much, that neither parent could have stopped her from killing herself, neither did they blame Grigor Og. If anything, Padruig wanted to help Grigor Og if he was ever needed at Craskie Farm or seeing his other daughter, Marion who lived in Glengarry with the MacNachtens. Zara was glad of the readings in so many ways, for it brought their eccentric family all closer together and closer in understanding each other's hearts. Losing a life with Marion was a sadness Padruig kept to himself because of shame on so many levels, not to mention missing out on his Grandson, Malcolm growing up, who he really admired and loved.

The second book was a long way off with so many secrets revealed. The family were not ready for that yet.

Book 3 – The Greener Grass

Kenneth and Ivy MacNachten

Cherry Farms, Glengarry, Scotland 1800

1. *Getting it all on Track*

I inherited the land originally owned by Killian MacDonald, then inherited by my Uncle Alex Grant and myself.

Upon Uncle Alex's sad passing, the entirety of the lands, formerly owned by Killian MacDonnell, then all belonged to me, along with my original half of Killian's land and my small farm called "Cherry Farm". I continued to call both farms Cherry

Farms named after my wife Cherry. The land that Uncle Alex left me was all for oat crops, as well as one field that was fallow with no outbuildings at all, but it was all securely fenced with the longest wall being completely made of stone that was about five feet high.

The top end with a different neighbour was bordered only with palisades.

I had sent a letter to our friendly politician, now with a Peerage, Lord Simon Fraser, to own one end of the small lane that divided my two properties and make the entrance of that small lane into my own as 'private property,' which was achieved and it became approved and accompanied with its own sign saying:

PRIVATE PROPERTY. DO NOT ENTER.

I was then able to move my coos in and out of my properties and on occasion, when the need arose, would take the coos to graze further up the mountain, unencumbered.

Kenneth's Art Gallery visitors were all having difficulty parking their carriages on the very narrow Drover's Road that was still waiting to be widened, despite asking Simon twice to widen it, but 'patience was a virtue' my Mither always said.

That didn't stop me from writing to Lord Simon Fraser again, first thanking him for the private road accomplishment with a gift from the farm from my wife. Then I explained to him that the Art Gallery, to which he had already attended for the first item of 'fairy art', was needing the Drover's Road to be widened desperately, especially for the larger carriages. I explained to Simon that the 'fairy art' was an ongoing art phenomenon of both smaller and larger pieces, usually fortnightly, of many different sizes and prices and still commission based, because the artist was wanting to remain unknown, due to her shyness, but it was popular.

I was aware that now our Cherry Farms were going to be a larger industry, requiring more staff and more cooperation from within our families in order to save money. Therefore,

I organised a meeting for us all to be held at my house, so we could all discuss what was needed to be built, such as a storage shed for oats and larger facilities for the goats. The extension to all thing's goats included the addition of a sterile room, designed with one large window for the separation of the milk for cream, then making butter and the suggestion was to create cheese and yoghurt, if we had enough milking goats. For the goats we already had workers assigned being Cherry, Ma, Islay and Bruce. Cherry made aprons out of the linen from Grigor's farm, so the ladies working with the cheese especially remained clean. Each day, the aprons were washed and another provided to replace it while the first one was drying. Bruce also had a bigger apron, but not linen as it was of a greyish colour in a hemp material as he was also the slaughterer.

He gave his list of required knives or carvers to adequately perform his task.

Some friends had already offered to assist with the building, but not for free, as one would expect. There was a lot to build and the materials from the old School in Glenmoriston had provided nearly all of the materials required.

Then there was the need to examine just how healthy the soil was that Uncle Alex had been farming by bringing in my scientist cousin, Gillcrest Lachlan MacLachlan, who could in turn provide students, free of charge, to improve the soil for better output. We did have two of his students already, who were due to leave. We did need to examine each field, without completely stopping some existing oat crops from producing as they were, but reduce them in order to improve the soil in each field, one by one. It was an enormous task at hand and one that I had not been expecting to ever be faced with, not having been born a farmer.

I had to be careful not to completely crash the farm's economy. I also invited Grigor MacGregor to the meeting, who was well known for his soil improvement programmes and had also worked well with his son in law, Gillcrest. I needed raw experience to draw on and to advise me and those two people were the best people to advise on soil. My future plan was retiring the use of one of my oat crops from the old Cherry Farm where the goats would then be housed and cheese made with a substantial weatherproof building to deal with our storms, as well as the unexpected snowstorm that can, on occasion, bury you in.

There was no guarantee that Gillcrest would always be with us in our region of Glengarry as he was the Laird of the Lachlan Lands in Argyle and had been managing those affairs from a distance, while his Mither was still alive, but as his Mither had aged, it was a possibility that he might have to move there with Morag-Freya, who was against moving there at all. She had always loved her precious Craskie Farm and looked forward to seeing her Father there whenever she could, now that she was no longer a Nursing Sister, as her new wee lass grew.

Then there were the goats, which was my wife's favourite topic, along with my Ma and Ma's husband, Bruce MacDonald. Bruce was my stepfather, as well as Kenneth's and we had all grown to be very attached. Bruce called us 'his lads', so I am fairly sure Bruce loved us both, despite a rough start when he had first wanted to marry my Ma. 'Now he is a very spoiled husband who really needed more work or responsibility or he would lose his masculinity', I thought.

Managing the goat shed could be the answer to that.

2. Our New Security for Both Farms

Sadly, we had lost our security, Duncan Mohr who had married my cousin, Jean. She was now living with Matilda on Loch Garry Ranch with her wee son, also named Duncan with her effeminate, but capable brother, Alexander. I had noticed that cousin Alexander was spending more time with a tall Doctor from Inverness lately, who stayed overnight when he visited. I was going to ask Cherry what was going on with that man, apart from buying that fairy artwork the first time he was seen here. He looked English and was about thirty years old or older and a bit too friendly with Alexander for my liking, but it was none of my business, so long as he stayed inside the law.

With Hugh Mohr also passing away, our district lost our only two sharp shooters and experienced security. Hamish was security for Grigor at Craskie Farm and he was also coming to our meeting because he was one of the builders as was Hugh Chisholm, his brother and our Teamster, who still lived in our house with his wife Meredith and their bairn wee Ferne. They had talked of moving to a small stone home down by Loch Garry but didn't have the money yet. Those poor folks down there by the loch had been cleared and their homes were lovely but now empty, even though they required some modernisation and new roofs which had all been set alight to move them out.

'Maybe my Mither should buy all of those homes before some questionable organisation moves into Glengarry?' I thought. I did put it to Ma and Bruce to think about or at least buy a few of them and maybe we could even buy one, maybe Matilda could buy one too and then Hugh and Meredith could live there, and he would fish all day long on his days off.

I asked Duncan Mohr's grandson, Duncan Og, who was our junior groom, if he had security as a possibility in his future if I sent him to a course in Inverness, which linked all the security men up with each other to pass on information and keep each other informed, as well as upskilling with the use of weaponry and physical fighting, like boxing. He wasn't interested, but he did know of a friend who had already been a deer hunter for years and was a good shot with his long rifle as well as a very good fighter but hadn't done the course to connect up with the others and he wasn't sure if he also had the patience when nothing much was happening. To give me variety in choice he also said that he knew an older man, David MacLean, but not as old as his late Grandda, who had retired from the constabulary, so he already had the skills as well as another man also named Duncan MacDonald, his older cousin, who had all the skills and knowledge and was discreet.

After all, security men sometimes saw things that they wish they had never seen of their employer's family's antics.

Of his list, it was his cousin who he clearly wanted to work on our farms, so I asked him to bring him in the next day. My rulings for all staff still remained as strictly, no alcohol with the usual weekly search on the properties for any concealed alcohol and strictly, no intimacy or perving with any of the females living on the property of any age, or he might find that I was quite capable of rendering him incapable of ever working again. Duncan Og knew that I was serious about protecting all of the women and girls, even from themselves and still wanted his cousin to have the job, who was married with bairns of his own. I let him know that there was a certain odd-looking Doctor who was visiting Alexander on Loch Garry Ranch and he was 'a person of interest' if he misbehaved in any way.

I would also talk to Matilda about the shared cost of the security, so that both Loch Garry Ranch as well as both Cherry Farms would be covered by the one man. He could live on the property in the old Cherry farmhouse if he wanted to with his family. That was up to him and his wife if I approved of him first. It was sounding good, so I wandered down to speak to Matilda, who was thrilled at that news and both she and Alexander were also invited to our meeting as it might affect her.

Matilda asked me for my advice while I was there. It was concerning her Step son, Alexander, who coincidentally was rather 'taken' by a tall Doctor from Inverness who was English and with her knowledge of the English coming in handy, she didn't trust him with some false things that he had said and she asked me if she thought it was unreasonable of her to ask the Medical Board in London, who register all of the Doctors, if he was actually a registered Doctor, or if there were complaints against him in London or anywhere else in Great Britain. She was suspicious of him anyway and was worried about her sensitive Stepson. I agreed with her as I felt the same way and it was decided that she write that letter immediately, in order for its answer to be known before the meeting at my farm.

The agenda for our farm's meeting was becoming rather long, so I asked Ivy to write the full list of items to be discussed, as well as the full list of people who were expected to come, which would include the new security man, if I approved of him. I also asked Meredith if she could babysit all of the bairns for a wee pay, onto her floor of the house and read books or go to bed, but not to interrupt the meeting, as I was quite stressed organising the new industrial mood of our farm as it kicked off.

I had been so absorbed in farm work that I had been neglecting Cherry, but she had understood the need to focus on the farm and get it all working well, I thought.

That hadn't stopped Cherry from making a special dinner for us three men and the bairns together with Meredith and Ivy, so I wouldn't get worn out. The ladies had even made bannocks as well as loaves of bread, butter and cheese and a chocolate dessert that we had never had before. It was a steamed chocolate pudding that was a mixture of chocolate and flour and fine sugar with a chocolate sauce. I had never had a more beautiful dessert before, which they had kept a secret. I was so appreciative of the meal in its entirety followed by a hot bath that Cherry had pre-prepared.

Cherry wanted to check that that her 'general' was still working, so it wasn't long before my lover wife drove me into completely forgetting my worries and the stress just vanished. Her sensual touch and her demands on my body were answered with her usual expectation of my vibrant need for sexual activity. I loved my wife completely and as my penis entered her this time, I couldn't wait and it was like an explosion of my manhood into her without the usual consideration for her to orgasm, but I couldn't stop it as then, in that over sexualised state, I kept on going wanting access to every part of her, sucking on her neck and face then kissing her too roughly, which she didn't seem to mind and she even giggled at one time enjoying me, which kept me loving her more and more. The noises from our room must have made Hugh and Meredith smile, but later on we heard them really active too.

Maybe it was a full moon or something as I excused my animalistic needs. When we slept, I wrapped myself around her completely and I slept well.

3. The Meeting

Finally, the afternoon arrived for Kenneth and I to formally engage the meeting with everyone invited, who had been given the list of topics on the agenda to discuss. It was highly successful along with the newly appointed security guard for both farms, whose name was Duncan, as everyone in that family seemed to have that name. Being older than our stable hand, he was to be known as Duncan Mohr. He stood as erect as a statue and wore his Clan kilt, with shirt and waist coat.

Duncan Mohr never once smiled, especially when he was introduced to Cherry, Ivy and Matilda, but he had to know that Matilda was one of his bosses. He had taken it very seriously about the 'no intimacy ruling', which my wife Cherry was very pleased about and given that he was also handsome, the younger lassies needed to be put off him by his unsmiling demeanour. There was no doubting his skills in handling the latest in weaponry from France and he could kick box as well as regular boxing. He kept himself very fit by swimming in the loch and he went on regular long runs. I was hoping that we would never come to blows, because he would definitely win.

The letter that Matilda had received from London, concerning her enquiry about Dr Peter Heath, was also read out loud, even though Alexander was present. The answer from the Medical Board in London read as follows:

"Dr Peter Heath had been found guilty of 'assault with sodomitical intent', which was a lesser charge than sodomy itself, despite there being three complainants, one of whom escaped to tell the story. The laws for proving sodomy were extremely hard to prove, as it is punishable by death. That

particular individual, being Dr Heath, had an influential family, who enabled him to escape the loss of his licence to practice medicine in other parts of Great Britain, so long as he never returned to England. It was suggested to the Tribunal that he be sent to Scotland and remain there. If by some chance that he was found guilty once again in Scotland or any other part of the Realm, then his license to practice medicine would then be revoked permanently due to his predatory nature on young males and most especially injured males, who were unable to escape when approached." END

Poor Alexander's face went grey and unable to alert anyone to his own feelings, he chose to remain silent, although it was obvious to both his step Mither and I that he wanted to cry.

"Don't you worry about him, Malcolm. I'll kill the sodomite bastard," said our new security guard. I just thanked him for his enthusiasm, but we hoped that killing wasn't necessary. Advice overall was given to Alexander, who was known to be the Doctor's friend and to avoid him and to no longer invite him to any of our farms. I didn't envy both Matilda and Jean going home that night, explaining why there was a letter written to London enquiring about his new friend because his face wasn't saying that he wanted to avoid Dr Peter Heath, unfortunately, but we hoped that the law alone was enough to scare him from any further involvement. Just the same, it was a shock to all of us listening to that letter. Even I hadn't thought it was that bad and England just dealing with it by sending him to Scotland was what irked me. I wondered how many others here in Scotland had already been harmed by that man.

That was when Grigor Og spoke up and said that Dr Peter Heath was the Doctor in Inverness who had treated his former cook, Zara and had found that she had a broken bone in her lower leg, so it was a shame because his medical knowledge was sound.

"The Fairy lady?" asked Bruce. "Aye," responded Grigor Og. Then Kenneth had to interrupt them and ask to deal with the next topic on the list or it would take all night.

The goathouse was agreed on with its extension, including the new venture into making cheese, thereby needing at least twelve more nannies, which I would purchase. Islay was appointed as one of the milkers and she felt proud to be finally included into the working part of the farm. The cheese production was to be under the control of my wife Cherry, unless she became with child again, in which case Ma would take that over. Bruce was their overall manager with the birthing and breeding of the herd and when the need arose, the slaughtering of an animal. Ma felt proud of her husband having an important role that he liked, which also included collecting the goat hair for pillows and mattresses and maintaining the cleanliness of the facility and as a manager, his job also attracted a wee wage. None of us attracted a wage. Ma made the butter and Ivy made the yoghurt which she had previously done in the Aird, so all the farm was provided with enough yoghurt with every meal.

Ivy, who was taking notes like a secretary, also suggested that every time that Kenneth had the Art Gallery open to the public, that we erect a stall and sell any of the farms' surplus produce, such as the honey from Jean's hives, Ivy's yoghurt, cheese one day, oat cakes from the oat fields and any vegetables that may be in excess to us. The cash would then be managed by Ivy and given to that part of the farm from which they came, such as Jean's bees, who would get her cash, then she could buy more hives or simply pay for the needs of her bairn.

Everyone, including Kenneth, agreed to the stall idea and setting it up as a covered stall in case of bad weather.

Kenneth's only stipulation was that the farm goods absolutely did not creep into his Art Gallery. His customers could buy things as they were departing his Gallery and not when entering. The Art Gallery would then need a sign stating whatever all his rulings for entry were, to which the farm agreed to pay for.

The oat fields were next and so it was decided that coffee was in order before we started on that topic, which was an extensive one requiring time and concentration. During this time, however, Alexander quietly left and went back home to Loch Garry Ranch. I couldn't help but feel sorry for him and suggested that because Jean was no longer needed, that she followed him home too and comfort him and make him coffee there. He would need a shouder to cry on as that man had been grooming him, so while we could be pleased that it was stopped, it didn't take away Alexander's need for a close and loving friend.

Finally, we dealt with the large storage shed to be built for the storage of the oats, which my friends and Kenneth were going to assist in building and Ivy had written down their names. Hamish and Hugh being the main ones. God bless them. Then both Gillcrest MacLachlan and Grigor MacGregor addressed the group together, explaining first the need for the soil to be radically improved after having already tested it. They reiterated how much a greater yield there would be, as had been proven on Craskie Farm with good soil. They offered their assistance throughout that whole period, as well as the students from Gillcrest's science department at the Invermoriston Hospital. The lowest field, currently in fallow, was the one given up to the building for the storage shed and as such, that shed could be built as soon as possible before the weather changed. Then out of the remaining four fields, he suggested halving the current number and getting the Clydesdales to plough it all into the ground followed by a lot of manure as well as planting a nitrogen rich clover crop unintended for eating and also ploughed back in. Gillcrest said a lot of work was needed because the fields were all but deserts, according to his tests. I must admit those crops hadn't looked great, but it really required a professional and someone experienced to advise us before we turned it into the Sahara Desert. I then remembered what Simon Fraser had told me about the bedrock also and that then formed part of the conversation.

The amount of kelp from the coast would need to be three times the normal amount, as was usually needed due to the depletion of the normal nutrients found in our soils. Hugh in his paid capacity, was then asked if he could go to the coast with his second in charge, Angus for the kelp, so long as Hamish could start the building without him and it was decided that Kenneth and I assist Hamish for as long as was needed if Grigor allowed him leave for that purpose. The remaining two fields would then, although inadequate, be the only oats available from there, except my own two fields on the old farm, which already had good soil. Once the two crops were ready to harvest, one field would then remain fallow while it was worked on for as long as it took for that soil also to recover from years of neglect. If one of the first two were ready for either a summer or winter plant, then that could occur.

Grigor said that was when he could assist. Finally, when the last of Alex's old oat crops were finished, then it too would be ploughed into the ground and the cycle would start all over again. The aim being for there to be half winter plantings and half summer plantings all stored in the new storage shed. This also provided dry feed for both the goats and the coos, excluding the heads. The oat cakes could only be made at this early stage from my two crops on the old Cherry Farm, which was mostly needed for our bread, none of which was for sale as it would only just feed those living on the farms.

I decided against Ivy's oat cakes until we had all of the oat crops producing, which didn't please her, but bread for all the families came first, including staff who lived on the properties.

Our new Security man, Duncan Mohr, said also that he would remain on his own Father's property and bring his horse daily and wanted to know if there were questions, as he had to leave soon to do his rounds of the property before going home, then returning with his Hound that was needed at nighttime. He was talking to Grigor about the Irish incident at Craskie Farm and asked if I could ensure that in building all of the new buildings, that secure doors and locks and latches be included and suggested more outdoor lighting, obtainable from Frasers Trading Store.

He suggested new pole lights at the lane entrance between my farms where the new 'no entry sign' was to make that clearer that no entry was a serious matter which he could enforce. He also asked for more pole lights near the goats as well as lights that attached to the outside of the building to be used in times of birthing kids in the middle of the night, to which Bruce was thrilled, but Ma didn't want the lights too close to her windows or she wouldn't be able to sleep. The far end of the newly inherited land was all unlit as well and he suggested two things. He wanted the pallisades replaced with stone, if there was stone available and lighting between the two halves of my new Cherry Farms, being mindful of care for fire at the current time with the crops as dry as they were. He also said that all the new buildings would probably need windows that could be opened and closed in the roof exactly like Craskies stables had for lighting inside, as well as available torches attached to the outside of that building. I agreed to the 'roof windows' in the building for the goats if Bruce was very diligent to close them at night or during poor weather and the snows. I did not agree at first to those ceiling windows in the storage shed, but Kenneth thought it would be awfully dark without it and so did Hamish, so I eventually agreed and was given the name of that same clever builder who could achieve that.

Flooring in the storage room also needed to be completely dry and that same builder was the expert on that topic, but not cheap and Ma offered to pay for the flooring and the overhead windows as she knew I did not have the money left for all of that, considering that income from Cherry Farm would be reduced for a few years and we would all have to tighten our belts, make our own clothes, as well as no more shopping trips unless it was for essentials for the new buildings. Hamish started to feel sorry for me at the obvious cost as well as their wages and offered all the nuts and bolts from the teacher house that he had already taken. I was so grateful for that. I agreed to the eventual replacement of the pallisades on the top field, but money was short, so once the fields were earning, which was years off, we could build that stone wall.

Ivy was taking notes so that I would keep to my word I think, or maybe she thought we would all forget the many details. Either way, she elected herself a kind of secretary for Cherry Farms, so long as my Mither always signed off in agreement to it being accurate. She then suggested that we meet again every year to go over what was and wasn't achieved, as well as going over the finances and any other issues that came up in that time. I responded by saying that I would inform everyone when a meeting was to occur and no one else while in essence it was still a sound idea. That did put her nose out of joint, but she had gone too far. We were running out of time to even discuss the Team, so all I could say was that Hugh Chisholm's agreement had been signed off again for another year for the Team at the same rent and the same staff of one groom that he paid for as well. Angus, his offsider, did receive a wage and was married to my daughter Islay and they both lived in our big house rent free.

4. Loch Garry Homes

Ma quietly asked if she could raise one more topic before we all departed, which concerned the small homes beside Loch Garry that had been cleared recently and were up for sale.

Both Bruce and my Mither had gone down to see them all and assessed how much the renovations would cost and decided to buy them all with Ma's money, offering one to Hugh and Meredith once it was renovated at a wee rent if they both agreed. Her builder needed to replace all of the rooves on the houses and build on a laundry to each one of them, as well as new privies for all of them and new windows added with secure shutters. The inside walls, as well as the outside walls, all needed treatment with a type of mould and moisture free whitewash of some kind, perhaps lime, they would all then be rendered. They would all have separate titles now, instead of the crofts that they had once been, which included the small land on which they each stood. Front rock walls would be built, but not too high and the rear walls would be stone, as well but at least four feet high. She said that her plan with Hugh Og Chisholm and his rent paid over a period of time would pay off his house, resulting in his complete ownership of it.

One of the homes at the furtherest end of the row of homes was converted into having a commercial title, to enable a wee shop to open and to sell local goods and a baker had already

A Loch Garry Home

shown an interest in opening up a local bakery. One other of the homes was strictly put aside for staff for Malcolm's farm, paying a wee rent instead of living on the farm itself, if we had too many staff or female staff needed privacy. One other home was a gift to myself, and one other home was to Kenneth and Ivy, as well as one to themselves. That left two others that were unaccounted for as yet, but strictly not for tourists. Ma did not want our area to go the same way that Craskie Farm went with giving up the MacDonald Farm and converting it into a Manor house for tourism and all of the immorality that came with it, so she did want to know if Hamish wanted one. Either way he had first choice if he did, despite living on New Farm in Hugh's house currently.

She reassured Kenneth and I that it was of no cost to either one of us in the renovation process, as it was part of our early inheritance, to be held in our names and not our wives, hoping that, that would not offend either Cherry or Ivy. I knew my wife would not have expected that arrangement as everything else was in my name, but Ivy, being a Fraser, may not have felt the same way.

Loch Garry

On each small property there would also be a small stable at the very rear, only big enough for two horses and a tackle and feed room next to a chicken run, which would run alongside and in between each property with a small enclosure for hens at night. The homes would all have new rooves and new furniture and bedding, flooring and drapes as well as water plumbed to the kitchen and laundry. I looked across first at my brother Kenneth, whose mouth hadn't yet closed, then across to my dear friend Hugh Og Chisholm and then to Meredith, who both looked emotional and for the only time since I had known the big man, he could have wept at my Ma's generosity. He had to ask again for her to repeat what she had said and wanted her to clarify it three times, that it could be his very own. How much rent was the next question, as well as where exactly on Loch Garry which she explained and Bruce produced a map for clarity.

"Only wee rent," was Ma's shy answer.

"Can you please give me a clearer answer Mistress?" he asked politely.

"Is one shilling per month too much?" she asked shyly, hoping it wasn't too much.

"Nae Mistress, it is not too much, but then how long will that take to pay it off?" he asked.

"One-year lad," Bruce answered for his wife.

"My wife doesn't want to cause you any hardship nor Hamish either, if he is interested also," he added. "If you have no objection, I will pick up the rent on a monthly basis from you at your new home once the work has all been completed and you have moved in. But you haven't yet said if you will move in," Bruce said.

Both Hugh and Hamish decided to accept Ma's offer and asked Bruce if they could hug his wife, out of gratitude because not only was it their favourite part of Loch Garry, they would benefit and their wives would be pleased. She was so happy to be hugged by the two big men and to see them both so happy. The Chisholm brothers were both well known as lovely men.

"I hope you don't mind Hugh if we move out of your house on New Farm?" Hamish asked. "Nae, we can fish on our days off from the shore of the loch, as well as all of us going out in the boat," he responded happily planning their next fishing trip.

Grigor Og then asked Ma, "Excuse me, Marion, could I please rent Hugh's home on New Farm for Craskie Farm? I need it for female staff," he asked.

"That house doesn't belong to me brother, it belongs to Hugh, so you would have to ask him, but our rules are always the same, no drinking or other misbehaviour and they would need to tolerate the sounds of the wool waulking ladies singing," she answered. Hugh Og said Grigor could rent it for staff. Grigor Og then asked another question, if Marion could consider him as a renter or owner of one of the homes on the Loch too. She agreed to Grigor Og renting the last home on the loch and Bruce would deal with his contract and his rent. So, it was decided who all of the owners would be and the three rented homes would have a contract delivered by Bruce acting on Ma's behalf as her factor. Her lawyer would contact both Kenneth and I with the individual title deeds. No homes were then left unaccounted for, to which Bruce and Ma were pleased and decided the baker could rent the commercial property for a much-needed bakery. They needed a lot of time to do all of the work needed there on Loch Garry, as well as the new work decided upon for the Cherry Farms, including the goats, but they were both still energetic people, who felt excited about both of their futures with their new venture on Loch Garry.

Ivy said that we would all also receive a copy of the meeting's notes that she had taken on that afternoon and night. We were all hungry and just wanted to eat. Thank God we had Meredith, who had already cooked the stew and the bread. The bairns had been fed earlier. She hadn't yet finished the scones that she was making with the cherry jam she had been making for half of the day, after collecting all of the ripened cherries. Meredith was always thinking of what was next to be cooked and where she would obtain the ingredients. Her mind simply never stopped, so if we were out of sugar or something like that, it was a serious matter to be dealt with immediately.

I thanked everyone for coming. Meredith remembered all of the jars of the cherry jam and as everyone was leaving, they were each given a jar of home-made cherry jam. She asked for the jar back when they had finished. She wouldn't be Meredith if she hadn't asked for the jars back. Meredith was surprised that Grigor hugged her and thanked her. He had missed her, that was obvious, but there was no way he would get her back, I thought and she didn't leave our employ. If ever she had an issue, she would raise it with confidence and what made the difference was that we were all friends.

I really appreciated Grigor and Gillcrest's assistance and he was sending two students over for me to chose from to help me, then after all of the building was completed, he was sending the second student to assist Hugh in ploughing in the useless crops. It was a shock to Matilda, who hadn't taken an interest in the soil's condition and hadn't known that the fields were in such a poor state but I told her what Lord Simon had said about the bedrock so it was always going to be something we would need to keep an eye on, despite our border being where it was supposed to be deeper. She offered her assistance, if we needed her after she sorted out her family issues and I wished her well with Alexander. I asked her if it was an option for Alexander to be a mature age student and return to university and study whatever interested him if her Father could pay for it, but she didn't think she could manage her farm without Alexander, so that was ruled out. I wished her well and she said she was glad of the information from London, terrible though it was. She left me a copy of that dreadful letter from London about Dr Peter Heath.

Even I hadn't thought of all of the others that he had already harmed. I hoped one of them wasn't my cousin.

After dinner, I was too exhausted to take a bath, so I apologised to my wife and with all of the day's news and workload ahead, I prayed for help, which I rarely do. It wasn't going to be easy, but I had the best wife and friends and so maybe we just needed to go fishing and think of something else for a while. I thanked my wife, but I kissed her goodnight and wrapped myself around her again. She told me she was proud of me, as I drifted into a deep sleep. That night I dreamed of Padruig Dubh Grant, my Grandda again and he was aware that I was stressed and I called on him, but I don't remember anything else other than he had a sense of concern for me and my Mither, who was after all his only living daughter now. I hoped it was a sign that he could send me a boost of confidence and energy. That would be a miracle indeed.

5. *Locating Grandda*

The months passed into years when eventually we could all sit down at another meeting having achieved all of what we had set out to do. Even the Drovers Road was eventually widened thanks to Lord Simon Fraser, as those items from the artist in the Aird mysteriously kept coming through Grigor, although not quite as many as there once was. All of the oat fields were finally productive except one, which would always remain fallow and oats began to make Cherry Farms a profitable and going concern. I remembered praying about it all in the beginning and calling on my Grandda, so I thought I had better at least say thankyou somehow but wanted to visit that Pict stone to do that. I wasn't sure if he could be contacted there. It always felt like he was in that house in the Aird, where my brother, Kenneth had disallowed me to enter, out of fear that I could never return. He believed it was a fairy dun. One day,

I would go alone to search for a sense of my Grandda. I needed to locate him.

Our fishing trips were a sanity saver as well as a wonderful source of fish of many kinds, as I learned more about each loch from the brothers Chisholm, who were well settled in Loch Garry in Ma's newly renovated homes. The only complaint they had was the occasional midgie. Our big house was much quieter without Hugh and his family living there and I missed them I confess, but I still saw him every day with his Team or if we were working together and Meredith was still our wonderful cook. Bruce had taken his job as Manager of the goat farm very seriously and he looked younger and healthier for it, as he slaughtered beasts too for variety in our diets and would deliver cuts to us, ready to cook. Bruce was such an asset now to us all and I recalled the days when I even doubted allowing him to even meet my Mither to marry.

The emptiness of the house with only family living there had another effect.

Padruig Dubh materialised and on the first occasion I was too shocked to speak as I saw Grandda's spectre right before me. The next few times it was easier and I clarified that he did live in that house in the Aird and it was safe to go there because it was not a fairy dun. His wife from his life, Old Isobel, did not live with him, but rather a group of eccentric types like Zara the cook and her husband Grigor Mohr MacGregor and their children. He invited or challenged me, I wasn't sure, to visit him there, but he congratulated me on my excellent farming achievements but to be mindful of our next winter especially in Glengarry.

Finally, Ivy was able to erect that stall outside of the Art Gallery to sell Jean's honey and the first of our goat's cheese to promote it. The oat cakes were sold by the dozen too and as the sign read,

"Goods only to be purchased when leaving. No food or drink to be taken into the Art Gallery." By order of the Management.

Kenneth was doing very well with all of his art sales and 'the fairy art' always sold and so there were no complaints but because Zara was running out of the Turkish china, she had sent a message along that the artist might be 'retiring' as an excuse for running out of materials. Nearly all of Kenneth's customers also purchased goods from the stall, even surplus eggs if we had any, or vegetables, especially corn and each time the stall went up, everything was sold. With the new oat crops, we would be also able to sell bread in competition with the wee shop soon.

6. Alex and Siobhan

The biggest miracle on our farms was that Alexander met a sweet young lady who was the shyest creature on God's green earth, and she was as sensitive as he was. She was Clan Cameron and traditional, quiet, polite and so dignified that I could not understand how or where he had met her, let alone how he was attracted to her. She was pretty I admit, but I didn't dare to look too closely, else it arouse the wrong thoughts in people's minds. We did discuss her, naturally, hoping that it would last. Cherry commented that she was not the type to be seen with a male more than once, or her family would disapprove. I had to ask her then if they were betrothed because there was nothing official yet said to me anyway, even though she had visited their farm with her parents and escorted by her brother, at least five times. I was a bit offended that Matilda was keeping it all private. I thought the lassies' name sounded Irish, being Siobhan. She was not another red head and I liked her black hair, which was not unlike ours with blue eyes too. That was all that I knew and with my curiosity as it is, I paid them a visit, escorted by my wife, to ask them about the new lady in Alex's life.

Our security man, Duncan Mohr knew as much as I did, but was looking into her family for me. When Cherry and I knocked on their front door at a time when we knew she was there, Matilda opened the door and smiled knowingly as to why we were there. Cherry had a jar of cherry jam for them and we were invited in for coffee or tea. We were then introduced to Siobhan, who hardly spoke two words with her eyes cast down, but it was obvious that Alexander liked her as he fussed over her every need. It was the first time that I had ever seen him fuss over a female. Matilda let us know that her Cameron family had approved of the union, as they were both not that young anymore, being both as shy as they are and Alexander being a descendant of the famous Padruig Dubh Grant had impressed them.

The wedding was planned for one month's time and the service was at Craskie Farm's Chapel and the celebration was to be held at the Hart of the Highland Manor House, which Patrick and Henrietta were in charge of arranging. They were charging the Cameron family for the reception. Naturally we were both invited, as were both Kenneth and Ivy. It was the happiest that I had seen Matilda since before her husband had passed away and I felt her loneliness. He died way too young and unexpectedly. She blamed his early death on his many childhood traumas. He did describe the screams that he heard in his head saying that they were from the women who were being ravished, but it sounded to me more like the description of the banshee[1]. Either way, Alexander was without a Father and his oldest cousin wasn't me I thought, but just the same he asked if both Kenneth and I could be his wedding party. I think his oldest cousin might have been James. We were going to be wearing traditional kilts, so MacNachten kilts were accepted with the matching waistcoat. I owned a new shirt that I had never worn, so I was all set if they said we could wear boots, not hose. I hated hose, especially white hose when visible. Boots held all of my knives a lot better and they didn't clink when in my boots.

I was still having difficulty imagining Alex actually in the same bed with Siobhan and making bairns, but maybe I was being cruel to sensitive people, after all Simon Fraser was one of those effeminite types and he got married and had children and he's now a Lord Simon.

Then Matilda and Alexander looked long and hard at me to verbalise the unexpected.

Siobhan's Father was immobile with a war disability and had asked me to escort the bride down the aisle to be married to Alexander. I was so shocked when Alexander added, "Please Malcolm, it would mean so much to me." Naturally, I agreed so long as I could wear my boots with my family kilt and they agreed if they were clean boots. Matilda was arranging everything with Grigor and the Chapel with the Priest from Edinburgh, as well as Patrick and Henrietta and the reception. It wasn't going to be a huge wedding, but it also wasn't going to be too small either. Beth and James had a sister, Sarah too but for some unknown reason to me, she was never invited to anything. Maybe she was even more unpopular than we were when we first went to Glenmoriston. I thought to ask James one day on a shopping day.

The very aged Mr and Mrs Menzies were also invited and Matilda was hopeful that Alex and Siobhan would receive a nice wedding gift from them to help set them both up. They had already received her dowry of four thousand pounds Scots from the Camerons for their daughter. I asked if they were building them a new wee house on the property or renting Grigor's house by the loch but they hadn't yet decided. Matilda was working with the wealthy Cameron family to write out the wedding invitations. I asked if the dreaded Isobel-Mairi and Ewen were invited and they were, unfortunately but without their bairns. Morag-Freya and Gillcrest too, as well as Aonghus and Annabel were coming. It was going to be a family reunion too, of sorts. Maybe the ghosts would be there too?

That particular chapter of Dr Heath was closed, we thought, thank God.

7. Meanwhile in the Aird

Hector was strolling past Zara's bedroom window when he saw her climbing out of it ready to jump and before he could warn her about the five feet of snow outside of her window, she leapt and sank into the snow with it completely covering her. He ran over to where the snow ground was stable and seeing her hand waving out of the hole that she had created in the snow, he stretched his long arm to her hand and pulled her out with all of his strength. As she was coming out of the hole in the snow, she was gasping for air, appeared bluish and not really able to speak clearly. He dragged her to himself and then picked her up to where he thought they would return to the warmth inside the house, but upon hearing the two arguing voices inside, she struggled out of his arms and with what little strength she had left, she ran to the shed where she made her fairy art.

Hector then just thought he would tell his Father what had happened and where she was.

Inside the warm home, both Uncle Padruig and his father, Grigor Mohr were still yelling at each other with the twins Fatma and Ali both listening and Fatma was crying.

"It wasn't Ma's fault, I saw it all. Uncle Padruig grabbed Ma as she came out of her bedroom half asleep kissing her and grabbing her on the pussy. Ma was saying 'no Padruig, no don't,'" she said.

Ali confirmed that story to be true.

"Well, whatever happened in here with you lot," said Hector sarcastically, "Ma jumped out of her bedroom window and sunk into the deep soft snow but, but hey don't worry, I saved her while youz all kept arguing and she was too scared to re-enter here and she's in the shed now and bluish and shivering all over," he said as a matter of fact. "Don't feel you have to thank me or anything," he said as he warmed himself by the fire.

Isobel then walked in and caught the end of the story. "Is Ma alright?" she asked.

"Nae, of course not. She could have been stuck in that snow if it weren't for me," Hector answered. "What were they arguing about?" he asked.

"I told you Hector. Ma was smooched by Uncle Padruig and he grabbed her pussy, which she didn't want him to do, of course," Fatma said.

"Then when Da came in, he saw the smooching part and thought Ma was the guilty one wanting to smooch Padruig, but she was struggling and saying no the whole time. We both saw it, didn't we Fatma?" Ali stated.

"Then Da strapped Ma when he promised that he wouldn't do that anymore," Fatma said and started to cry. "I want my Mummy," she said. "Me too," cried Ali.

Their Father burst through the front door of their home carrying his wife, who was limp all over. Her face and hands were blue. He tried to warm her by the fire and rubbed her hands. Isobel assisted but said that they would need Padruig's help with his high body temperature. When Zara has had hypothermia before, it was only Padruig who could get her body temperature back to normal.

"Da, we have to get Padruig, despite the smooching thing. We can sort that out later," Isobel reasoned.

Padruig had walked back in, looking upon a situation that he had created and was in disbelief that she may not be able to return to normality and he was the hated one presently. He'd had a moment of being unable to control himself, as the lovely Zara was waking up, leaving her bedroom and he wanted to make love to her and now looking upon his crimes against the whole family, he sickened himself. He offered to assist as usual with her hypothermia from which she had suffered a few times before and it was only him that could fix that and everyone knew that, despite what had happened.

Grigor watched on desperately as his beloved wife was taking a long time to respond. She was breathing well enough, but he wondered if we needed to go to the dreaded Doctor Heath in Inverness when finally, she spoke.

"Grigor, I jumped into the snow and I kept falling down and Hector pulled me out just like 'MacFie and the black dog story.

The black dog's day did come'. Hector saved me," she said then fell back to sleep.

"What is Ma talking about Da?" Hector asked.

"Never mind son," he answered, "Ma's unwell".

But Hector's Day had come, whether his Father had realised it or not.

Grigor reluctantly agreed with Zara's body hard up against Padruig's for high temperature bare skin, as Isobel rubbed Zara's hands and fingers at the same time and wee Fatma and Ali rubbed her both her feet and toes. Padruig was wrapped around her as she lay unconscious, and her lips were beginning to show signs of being less blue. Zara was comfortable lying completely on Padruig's lap with his unusually high body heat gradually replacing her frozen limbs, especially her fingers, toes and nose. Padruig held his hand over her nose to prevent any frostbite and breathed warm air over her face.

"She could have been frozen to death in that hole Da, if I hadn't seen her jump. Those holes freeze over really fast," said Hector. "Da, why was Ma jumping out of the bedroom window? Fatma said you strapped her. Did you? And what did Padruig do to her to start it all off?" he asked. Hector was determined to have all of the answers from his Father, because he was the one who'd had to pull her out of what had nearly become his Mither's frozen grave. His Mither's grave may not have been located until the snow melted, unless he had seen her jump.

"I was angry and jealous son when I saw your Ma being kissed and touched by Uncle Padruig, for which she was punished and I see now that on the witness accounts, as well as Padruig's own admission, that your Mither was not in any way to blame for that incident. My reaction was sheer jealousy, out of my love for her and I could not bear it if she had feelings for another man and I know she doesn't. I wrongfully punished her and that is why she jumped from the window, but she can't have known that she would sink deep into the snow. She was probably only going to get her horse and go to Grigor's house. I am sorry son for that stress for you and we do owe you for saving her life," he explained.

"I kissed your wife just like Fatma and Ali said and touched her because I was so desperately lonely and suddenly in need of sex, as she just happened to walk in. May God forgive me. I am deeply embarrassed and remorseful to Zara especially, then you Grigor my friend and Hector and the wee twinnies. I am so sorry. I still love you all as my family and I hope you can all forgive me, please," Padruig said with difficulty.

"I forgive you Uncle Padruig, but don't do it again please or Da might hit Ma again," said Fatma.

"Da, you promised you wouldn't strap Ma again, so why did you break your promise?" asked Ali.

"It's not your Da's fault," spoke a weak Zara, "You have to respect your Da's decisions, whatever they are," she said. "Please don't blame your Father, he's a good man. I was silly for not knowing the snow was so deep and soft, so I sank," she said. "Hector saved me," she added then slept again.

"You are clever Hector," said both twins who agreed, as did Isobel. Both of Isobel's husbands, John and Alex were rounding up cattle to bring in under the shelter from the snow and had missed all of the action. Isobel had to cook again and this time asked if Hector could help her, which he did.

"Do you want me to leave your home Grigor, even if I promise that it will never happen again?" Padruig asked.

"We don't want you to leave, but finding a partner might be a good idea. My wife is particularly alluring and so any man would find her appealing and sexy. Even my son, Grigor Og thought she was sexy. So, I am not unreasonable in understanding how anyone would want to do what you did, but you are in a position of trust with our bairns too, so you can't let your manhood overtake your mind and you have an excellent mind that is unused, as is your body. We are all working, which helps work off that sexual frustration, so if you help around the farm more, it could be helpful all round, not that I am insisting because you need to feel what your niche is, if you want to. The stables and the horses need attention for example," Grigor said. "I am equally in the wrong by punishing my wife and not you. We were both caught up in an emotional whirlwind," Grogor Mohr added. "I pray my wife forgives me," Grigor said teary eyed. Zara was listening and reached out her hand to her husband.

"I love you always Grigor and you are forgiven. It is always your right to decide what you do," Zara said.

Zara was recovering slowly on Padruig's lap and the family worried that she may have gone into shock. After teatime the bairns went straight to bed leaving Grigor and Hector cleaning up.

"I have never done so much kitchen duty in my life before," Hector said. "I hope Ma gets better tomorrow morning." Then Hector too went to bed leaving only John, Alex, Padruig and Grigor.

"I'll not ask what happened, you can tell me when you are both ready," Alex said, then he joined Isobel in bed. John also said he was sorry for Zara's condition and he would make breakfast if that helped, then went to bed alone, while not complaining. Zara was clearly in pain and stiff as well as lethargic, but able to finally try to stand up and try to get to her bedroom, but her husband decided to carry his weakened wife. He wrapped himself around her to keep her warm covered in blankets with the fire going in their room and she was able to retain a core body temperature. 'She will need an egg for breakfast,' he thought 'with fruit juice and anything nutritional'. He hated himself for striking her until she reached for him in the night hugging him and touching him saying,

"I love you, Grigor," Then he slept peacefully. "I know you are a jealous man and I know you love me as much as I love you," she said.

Stiff and sore for a few days until it gradually wore off, she stretched her muscles each day with Hector, to hurry up the process and improve her muscular condition. He massaged her lower leg muscles too. Luckily her nose and toes were all saved. She had money put aside from the 'fairy art' for one pony for the twins and a horse for Hector and decided to ask Grigor if they could ride to Inverness and buy them to reward Hector for his good deed.

"So long as you ride with me. I am afraid you might fall off," Grigor said. And so, accompanied by Alex and Padruig, they went to Inverness and bought the pony and the horse, along with a few geese and this time Grigor agreed to having tea in a tea house, but he said it was this one time only, if she paid for it with the fairy money. She thanked Padruig for saving her nose and ordered sandwiches for all four of them, as well as tea or coffee and they left after having eaten a lovely lunch with their new purchases of two geese, two horses and an extra pair of gloves to keep Zara's hands much warmer.

"We'll also need barrels this year and lots of salt for preserving meat or we will all starve," said Padruig seriously. "Bad winter coming. Buy extra goats too, as well as geese and chickens," he said. So before leaving Inverness, the family bought all of what Padruig had advised, because he was always right about the weather. Nearly all the fairy money was spent, so Zara was hoping they had enough then to feed everyone. Sweet wee Causantin needed feeding on the way home and changing as well, because he suddenly had soft bowel motions, so the group had to stop.

"I had to feed him goats' milk yesterday when you were sleeping, so he's probably having a reaction to it," said Grigor.

"Causantin must also drink goat's milk as well now darling, so thankyou for doing that. He will need occasional pureed food as well. It is time that he was gradually weaned," Zara said.

"He is a ravenous bairn and one day he may be even taller than you or Hector," Zara responded.

"He sure stinks that's for sure," said Alex.

"You must have stunk like him when you were a bairn too, Alex," Zara smiled in response. The eccentric family all then went on their way home with Padruig assisting Zara up to her husband to hold tightly onto his wife who was still a bit stiff, most especially her fingers. Unfortunately, it began to rain but Causantin was well covered, as was Zara and the men all in their thick woollen plaids.

"Grigor," Zara asked in that coy and feminine way she had when he knew there was a particular request of him about to be made.

"I know that I said we shouldn't have more bairns, but I would like a wee lassie after all. Can we please try to have another wee bairn darling?" Zara asked.

The other men were listening with intense interest.

"Aye, we can but if it's another wee lad, will you mind?" Grigor replied. Zara was so thrilled at his response she tried to turn and hug him and nearly lost her balance in the process.

"Wait until we get home Zara before we hug, or you'll fall, and the horse will get spooked," Grigor said but he was smiling as were the other two men. He was pleased to have had such a request as that.

"I won't mind, I love all our bairns," Zara said.

"Then we should be growing more crops of food to feed us all, don't you think?" Grigor Mohr said.

"Do you mean like our own fields of oats for home made porridge and bread?" Zara asked.

"Aye, if it will grow in these parts, maybe only a winter planting and not the summer planting, but I'll ask my son Grigor Og. He's due to come around soon with your last 'fairy' money and that book on Folklore that you asked him for, isn't he?" Grigor Mohr replied. "Aye, on Saturday, unless that wedding, he mentioned was on that day. Do you know what date that wedding was?" Zara asked. Then Padruig butted in.

"Whose wedding is that and where?" he demanded. Barely able to hear above the rain and through their plaids, Grigor answered.

"A Cameron lass named Siobhan is marrying your Grandson, Alexander Grant from Loch Garry Ranch in Glengarry. The wedding reception is up at the place you built Padruig for your son Patrick. The service is in the wee Chapel that your wife built," he replied, enjoying adding the story that his wife had built the Chapel and Zara wanted all those details later at home. "I thought you must have already known about the wedding. You can go there and spook them all if you want to, but are there any of them that you communicate with these days?" Grigor Mohr asked.

"I've tried a lot of them, who do not respond, until I tried my Grandson, Malcolm MacNachten, from Glengarry, who did see me and he got the shock of his life on the first occasion. We have seen each other in dreams too. So, I've tried a few more times since then and it's a strict secret from his end and we can talk a wee bit now, unless his wife or bairns walk in and then I vanish and I'm back here," Padruig answered. "He's a bit fae is that Malcolm," he commented.

"Do you remember that old friend or second cousin from Loch Insh that Isobel had, named Gillcrest MacNachten?" Padruig asked Grigor.

"Nae, not really," Grigor answered.

"He reminds me of him, but not to look at, just his Druidish sort of nature. He looks like a younger handsome me," Patrick added.

"That's one of the lads who was by our burn that day looking at our house and who then decided to leave. It's his brother, Kenneth who is the artist that Grigor Og sells my artwork through," Zara added. "They look a bit alike, both tall and with nice long black hair, but Malcolm is the stronger in character of the two," she added. "And I agree that Malcolm does look a bit like Padruig as a young man but on the wall in his sitting room of his house in Glengarry, I have seen in a dream, a painting or drawing of another man, also similar in age to you Padruig, who is mounted on a beautiful horse intended for the Bonny Prince. That man was also the Grandda of both Malcolm and Kenneth. The name on it is 'MacNachten', possibly Nachtain, but of that I am unsure and the picture was a gift to Malcolm from the Menzies family, Matilda's adoptive parents, because that horse was a gift to the Bonny Prince in 1746. I think that poor horse died in the battle. Did it die Padruig? Because I actually don't know that as a fact, only that when the horse was shot in the shoulder, he reared up and the Prince fell off leaving his groom to give him his horse. In that process, that poor groom had his head blown right off," Zara commented.

"So, the two of you Grandfathers of Malcolm were on Culloden on that day, presumably and you both must have been like cousins, or at least closely related, because you are so alike. Same black hair with curls, the same straight back and really brilliant horsemen. He worked for the Menzies family at that time. The whole story is in a book at Malcolm's house and he hasn't had the time to read it. Perhaps you could ask to borrow that book and see how you are related to the MacNachtens or get Grigor Og to fetch it when no one's looking. It's in his office where he does his bookwork," Zara said.

"How do you know that Zara?" Padruig asked.

"I don't know," she said honestly. Even her husband was stunned at the detailed story and Zara seeing the painting on the wall in her dream. He knew his wife was special and had grown to accept the things she came out with, but it also annoyed him that with all those gifts, she still couldn't yet know the dangers of jumping into the snow. He accepted that was why they needed each other and they were so caught up in that story that they hadn't noticed how quiet Alex had become since learning of Alexander's wedding plans.

"When you go to that wedding of young Alex, I'll accompany you Padruig. I want to know what happened with that Dr Heath," Alex said.

"I know some of the story Alex, but you won't like to hear it," Grigor Mohr said. "When my son was here last, he showed me a letter to warn us off Doctor Heath, but I thought it might upset you and you seemed happy enough with Isobel. Was I wrong?" he asked.

"Nae, you're a good friend Grigor. Show me the letter when we get home, so we can enjoy the rest of our ride. I've bought my Isobel some pretty ribbons for her hair, so I am happy with her and my bairn coming soon," Alex replied.

The family was back to normal and it only took a day out and some chatting, a cup of tea and sandwiches and a new pony and a horse to restore balance. Hector and the twins were so elated. It was wonderful to see Hector throw himself atop his big new horse, even before he was saddled up. He galloped around the place and across the burn and back again, which was hilarious and Zara was giggling so much that she was forgetting how cold it was and needed her husband to pick her up and take her inside to sit by the fire, maybe feed the hungry wee bairn again, while he attended to the horses, the new goats and putting them all away as the night was going to be a cold one. The geese were housed inside Zara's fairy shed temporarily, but all were fed as John had already rounded up the coos and Isobel was cooking bread and stew and pudding for dessert for them all.

Grigor asked Isobel to have lots of hot water on cooking for those needing baths and to light all of the bedroom fires. Wee Causantin fell asleep on Zara's breast and she also fell asleep, so Grigor carefully and gently took him off his Mither's breast to put him to bed after his nappy change. At least their room was warm by then. He placed the bairn on his side, who frequently sucked his thumb and left a candle lit near the door where he couldn't reach it, if he woke up during the night.

Covering his wife's modesty, the whole family came into the dining room to eat and were ordered to wash their hands by the bossy Isobel.

8. The Wedding

I was dressed up for the wedding in my kilt, as was Kenneth and both our wives checked that our boots were clean. I was still taking a fly plaid too for outside, because the weather was much worse than we had anticipated. Cherry had made herself a lovely warm dress that had the MacNachten shawl and brooch. All the bairns were warmly dressed with wee boots as well and the Chapel was decorated with flowers that were provided by

Malcolm and Cherry MacNachten

the ladies from the Cameron Clan. I was getting nervous as the time approached but thank goodness Hugh had offered to drive us all in with a two-horse team, then the bairns and wives could stay warm in the back of his carriage. He offered to pick us all up at the end of the night. He wasn't offended that he hadn't been invited, but Hamish was there for security, so it would have been nice if Hugh was there too.

I should have become accustomed to the heartlessness of that family, but it still surprised me. I walked Siobhan down the aisle without any music playing, which was weird, so I walked slowly and then I left her with her husband to be, then sat down and that was it until we were the wedding party at the reception. 'This Chapel was a good idea of Granny's', I thought. 'How many people have been married in here now?' I wondered and 'how many Baptisms have there been?'

Matilda had organised a reporter from the Inverness newspaper to ensure that it was in the social pages of the paper. It looked like Matilda was trying to hide that her Stepson had ever been interested in men, so I approached the reporter and introduced myself.

"Good morning, Malcolm MacNachten is my name from, Glengarry," I said being the bold man, as I am known to be and then began my speech. "The woman who built this wee Chapel called, 'The Chapel of Saint Columba at Craskie' was my Grandmither, Isobel MacGregor Grant, also known as 'Isobel of Glenmoriston', the famous lady teamster. She is buried right there, inside the Chapel with a beautiful decorative tombstone cover and on the opposite side is her husband, Padruig Dubh Grant, one of the 'Seven Glenmoriston Men,' who also has a decorative tombstone cover made by my other Grandfather, the late Gillcrest MacNachten, who is buried in the Craskie Farm cemetary and his name is engraved on the wall plaque also," I said, hoping it would all appear in the papers.

I then purposefully pointed out all of the black marble plaques on the wall containing the names of everyone who was buried in our cemetary, be they family or those who had worked on the farm and been part of the Craskie Farm life.

"Just imagine what life would have been like if this Chapel hadn't been built with all of the weddings there have been, including this one today of my cousin, Alex Grant with Siobhan Cameron and all of the many Baptisms. The first bairn to be baptised here was Donald Chisholm, the oldest son of Hamish and Cora Chisholm," I said. "I am available at The Cherry Farms in Glengarry if you have any other questions. We have an Art Gallery there too, run by my brother, Kenneth MacNachten," I said. Then I thought it might be overdoing it as he was busily writing everything down that I had said and both Cherry and I left to go to the reception.

As we walked away, both Cherry and Kenneth were looking at me like I had to give them an explanation.

"It was spontaneous," I said. "That fella was just there and we could do with promoting our farms too, don't you think? On top of that, Matilda's motives are too obvious for people who know Alexander or that Doctor, so spreading other information about, I thought, might take away her obvious shame of her Stepson. He will know that she is ashamed of him and miss his Father more and we don't want another Helen on our hands, do we? Hopefully those two can stay married, even if he is hiding his true emotional identity," I said. "He doesn't love her, that's obvious in my opinion but it might work out," I added.

Both Alexander MacDonald and Padruig Dubh Grant were there at the wedding too, listening to every word Malcolm spoke to that reporter. Whether it appeared in the papers or not, didn't matter, it was his boldness and good intentions that they liked about him and decided that they had seen and heard enough and went on home to the Aird. Padruig wanted to do some work in the stables, now that there were more horses, provided that Hector cleaned up the manure for Zara's kitchen garden.

The reception for Alex's wedding was boring and Cherry and Ivy asked me if we could go home as soon as possible because they could see that Hugh Og was keen to leave with his team. Kenneth said his farewells, as did I and we left passing Grigor on our way out saying our thankyous to him as well. He asked me if he could borrow a book that I had on my grandfather MacNachten, who was the person that delivered the Bonny Prince his horse, which was gifted to him by the Menzies family. I had to stop and think what book that was for a while, then I remembered it and said of course he could borrow it, but as it wasn't mine, it could only be on loan for which I apologised. If it had been my own, he could have had it, but I had even forgotten that it was in my possession. The ladies and the bairns were all tired and climbed in the back of the carriage, as did Kenneth. I sat up top with Hugh, as Angus was at home with Islay, who had chosen not to attend the wedding. It was wonderful to be back home and despite living by the loch,

Meredith had cooked us more food, in case the food at the wedding was shite, as it often is at these functions, so I asked them to stay over and they did. We were all tired, but we told them all about the boring wedding party and Cherry told them what I had said to the newspaperman. It made Hugh laugh at the gall I had.

Cherry was quick to boil up hot water for my bath and so it was a relaxing time, while she washed me all over. I was beginning to be a spoiled husband, so I asked her if she was tired doing these things for me and her answer was to jump in with me with her hair clipped up to stay dry, so I could wash her too. That was driving me crazy, as I felt every inch of her lovely body. She was so beautiful to me that I was often still amazed at how we had met and handfasted on that same night. Going home married after just a few hours was still a family story told around the fireside and I pitied poor Alex who didn't have those same feelings for Siobhan and unknown to us, he could even feel sick at the thought of sexual penetration with a female. I had never wanted to ask him that.

"What do you think Cherry, if we ask Jean to keep a close watch every day on her brother and report back to me each day because all Matilda was trying to achieve was how society saw her family and not his very life?" I asked.

"Aye, it's a fine idea if Jean covers up her intentions from Matilda, so that it's not too obvious, then Jean should come to you. You are the boss around here now Malcolm, as young as you are, that is a responsibility that I do not envy. Your extended family may have a weakness where mental health is concerned, but additionally, there's too much focus on what people think. You, Kenneth and Ma are different to all of the family because you were all raised in Loch Insh," she said.

I dried down my long, hairy legs as well as my wife's shorter ones and tickled her delicate areas just to remind her what was next, but she knew and ran to the bedroom naked with me in pursuit to capture the love of my life. My Islander lady, Cherry. It was a nice slow motion as we eased ourselves then into the heights of ecstacy as she squealed her usual squeal indicating her orgasm. I allowed myself then to fully enjoy what the Creator gave us to enjoy with our wives. I loved holding her breasts in my hands and massaging them to suck on her nipples, which were a darker brown now after having bairns. When we were about to sleep, she asked me about that newspaper man.

"Malcolm darling, what if that reporter writes all of what you said in the paper? Will that be in tomorrow's paper do you think, and what effect will it have on our farms?" she asked.

I was too tired to think of all the consequences, I suppose, but I said that we should buy the paper the next day to see what was written there about the wedding.

"He might have left it all out or he might have included it all. So, I suppose, I'm not sure of the consequences, other than perhaps bringing Kenneth more business and I hope to have a lot of oats to sell this harvest, so it might help us sell the additional oats and potatoes we have and keep Hugh busy delivering it all. Ma said the shop by the loch is a bakery now, so they might buy our oats too, but my main concern was diverting attention away from Matilda's shame, so that poor Alex could try to be a normal married man and hopefully have a bairn one day. I think they should move out of the main house though. Don't you?" I answered feeling too tired to go on.

"Aye. I do. You are a good man Malcolm MacNachten," she said as she fell asleep in my arms.

The three barn cats were fully grown and catching mice and a few rats. Duncan Mohr suggested the best rat killers were actually owls, so he offered to build an owl nesting house that would be attached securely to the side of the oat storage shed. From their hiding place, the owl or owls spy on the unsuspecting rodent, then swoop down upon it in a deadly fashion and eat it. Duncan's owl house idea was so successful that we paid him to make three more and erect them around the property in differing locations. His big black hound dog that accompanied him at night knew where the rats were, so Duncan had the exact locations for the owl houses. His dog ate the rodents too which was gross but good to know. The storage shed had to be pre-prepared before harvest time and the last thing that I wanted was a mouse or rat plague, munching on our hard-earned oats.

"By the way," Duncan said on the day he offered to make those owl houses, "You are in the paper." I had forgotten after all to go and buy that darn paper. "I'll get mine from my saddle bag for you," he said.

Bruce had seen a few mice down by the goat shed too, so he also asked for both a cat and an owl house as well. Ma had alterior motives with the wee kitty and it spent more time in her house than the goat house. I actually witnessed an owl swooping down on his rodent prey one evening and I was impressed with Duncan's knowledge that wasn't connected to the swiftest way to kill a human being. I had long stopped listening to those conversations, but I imagined my Grandfather Padruig Dubh would have loved that kind of gruesome chatter. Even Hamish never talked about how to best kill a human being. I had employed one of a long line of killers, some who talked about it and some that never mentioned it, but all with the same name of Duncan from the same family.

The shed also had those prickly plants to lay the oats on when we harvested and it was coming up and I felt nervous, so I also asked Duncan to get Matilda to erect an owl house down in her forest that she had planted, maybe on the side of one of the bigger trees. Maybe the rats were also down there, was my guess and I was right and so she agreed to erect two, one in her forest and one beside her goats. Duncan Mohr handed me the newspaper he had promised and I was quoted word for word, so that the wedding itself even seemed less important than the historical context in which it had been held.

Of course, I liked that Cherry Farms and Kenneth's Art Gallery were promoted.

I was still meeting Jean every day, which just looked liked two friendly cousins catching up and no one, especially Alex, guessed that he was being observed and it was being reported back to me about his mental health. Then, happily one day she actually said that she had heard Alex and Siobhan making love with the bedhead hitting up against the wall each time he went for it. Her squeals were more like someone was being killed, she said as were his with the loudest of groans she had ever heard a man having and she had two husbands to compare that with, as well as her Father with two different wives, and so Alex's groan must have been a biggy. We both then concluded that Alex was safe enough to leave alone unless Jean had any concerns and she thanked me sincerely for assisting because her brother's sensitivity was only understood by his Da. I only hoped that the active night that the two of them had resulted in a bairn, but that would be wishful thinking I thought, but how amazing would it be to see Siobhan with child and all our anxieties of predatory males would be gone for good, one only hoped.

9. *Grigor Og and the Aird*

Grigor was bringing in his horse through my side gate and I wondered why he was visiting. I had forgotten all about that book he had asked about on the night of the wedding. I greeted him alongside my security guard and I introduced them both again to each other, so Duncan Mohr remembered him from that one night at the meeting and Duncan Mohr then went back to work with his unsmiling face that put most people off, but Grigor looked pleased that I had such a serious looking security guard. The junior groom came running and offered to take Grigor's horse and it was smoko time after all and I invited Grigor Og in for coffee or tea and cake.

"You're famous now Malcolm being in today's paper. People are talking more about our two farms than the wedding itself," Grigor commented almost laughing. "What were you up to?" he asked smilingly. I had to admit it brought on a bit of a wicked giggle. Over smoko my wife was most interested in it all.

"Oh Malcolm, will the Cameron family be annoyed?" she asked as she read it all in the paper.

"I wasn't thinking about the Cameron family, I was wanting my cousin to survive this arranged wedding by an overbearing Stepmother," I said, much to the surprise of Grigor Og, who wasn't expecting me to be that candid. "I have some good news today though Cherry. They have actually consummated the union, according to Jean," I said.

"You Glengarry folk are really different to the clicky Craskie Farm, as we have always been. You are more like a united nation of candid folk, who all work hard and I like the atmosphere around here," Grigor said. "I am here to pick up that book that I mentioned to borrow from you, if that's still alright. Is that the picture of your MacNachten Grandfather on the wall there and is that the actual horse given to the Prince?" Grigor asked, pointing to our painting on the wall.

"I'll get you the book and aye, that is my actual Grandfather MacNachten riding on the horse he was delivering to the Prince, gifted by a branch of the Menzies Clan. Although, it has to be said that they were known for playing both sides and covering up whose side they were actually on. But according to this story, my ancestor went through all kinds of dangers, and achieved getting the horse to him, as the story goes," I said, as I went to get the book from my office.

Handing the book to Grigor Og, I asked him who was interested in this odd story and incidentally, how had he known that I even had that book? Cherry looked upon our faces and decided to leave us men to whatever that was going to be about and went back to her sewing.

"I was hoping that you wouldn't ask those questions Malcolm but knowing you and your reputation it will do me no good to not disclose the truth, however odd the answer might be. So, can I ask you first that if the answer is or seems bizarre that we can still be friends?" he asked.

"Aye, of course. Fire away Grigor, it can't be that weird surely?" I responded.

"It's Padruig Dubh, your Grandfather, who wants to learn about your Grandfather MacNachten to see how you are all related. You have met Zara already, who was my cook and she explained some things to you. Do you recall her telling you that she was married to my Father, Grigor MacGregor?" he asked.

"Aye, but I confess to a lack of understanding about how she is married to your Father, who is long deceased," I said.

"They all live together, spiritually speaking, in a house in the Aird and Zara said she has seen you and Kenneth there looking at their house from the opposite side of their burn," Grigor said. "Do you want me to continue?" he asked. "Maybe it would be better if you came with me when I visit this weekend in the Aird, but its not for common knowledge. Anything you see or hear has to be between you and I, as a secret or they may vanish altogether and presently I enjoy being able to see my Father and you can meet your Grandfather. He told me he has been here in your house and met you in person, so it shouldn't be too much of a shock. It was for me at first, but not now. They have asked for a few books recently. One was a folklore book that I had and the other was in your possession," he said. "What do you want to do?" Grigor Og asked.

"I'll come with you to the Aird and meet my Grandfather, but I know nothing of my other Grandfather. That book belongs to the Menzies Clan, who will ask for it back one day, so anything of interest in the book could be written down by hand maybe?" I suggested. "What time are you going to the Aird on Saturday and what do I need to take with me and I do have one question. Is it definitely not a fairy dun?" I asked.

"I'm leaving very early in the morning, so we can get back to Craskie by late nightfall and it is definitely not a fairy dun, but they can choose to be visible to you or not. You won't make it back to Glengarry, so you can sleep in my house if you like, if Cherry understands that you have a night out with me," Grigor said. "Padruig heard you talking to that reporter at the wedding the other day, so he does want to meet you. He likes you and so did Alexander MacDonald, his friend and you only need warm clothing because its colder there, as well as water, a flask of coffee and an apple for your horse," he added. We arranged to meet at Craskie Farm before four in the morning on Saturday to give us plenty of time to get there.

"Please don't mention this to Cherry or anyone else," Grigor added.

Hector saw us coming first apparently, but I didn't see anyone. After both Grigor Og and I both confidently crossed the burn, that was quite fast flowing, we took both horses to a stable that I hadn't noticed before. Inside the stable were two small highland ponies and seven big horses. There was a tackle room for saddles and bridles and another big room for their feed. I was astounded that I hadn't noticed it from the burn. I took my things from the saddle bags, as well as that book Grandda wanted and followed Grigor Og, who seemed comfortable, then went into a house built of stone, some new, some old but solid. It had a small front veranda to keep the snow from the front door I assumed, as the snow was really deep and dangerous looking, if you weren't careful.

A couple of old horses wandered on past us, but just kept on walking. They looked as old as the hills.

Grigor Og tapped on the old door and Isobel, the girl who wore pink, came to the door looking pleased to see Grigor Og but then looking at me, she asked him who I was before she invited me in. Grigor Og was speaking in Gaelic the entire time, some of which I did not understand but it must have been their language of daily usage. She seemed to go back inside to consult first with whomever was in charge when I saw a red headed man walking across the grounds, herding highland coos and he waved in a friendly manner and I waved back.

"That's John, one of Isobel's husbands," Grigor Og said plainly. "He's a Fraser, but a nice man."

Finally, someone came to the door and it was Grigor Mohr. Both Grigor Og and Grigor Mohr greeted one another warmly and Grigor Og explained who I was and that I had the book that Padruig had wanted about the MacNachten gentleman who delivered the fine horse to the Bonny Prince in 1746.

"What's your name then lad?" he asked.

"Malcolm MacNachten, originally from Loch Insh, then had to move to Glenmoriston, but was moved on by my Aunty Helen, so I then moved with my Mither to my late Uncle Alexander's place in Glengarry. I live permanently now with my wife and bairns in Glengarry on my own farms, Cherry Farms," I answered. "Is there anything else you want to know?" I asked.

He called Padruig who said, "About time you made the effort to come here lad. Come in, don't just stand there looking awkward, do you have the book?" Grandda asked.

"I have the book belonging to the Menzies family that you may borrow but you have to give it back. Is that understood?" I asked.

"Understood lad. So, you are the mouthy one who was in the newspaper then?" he asked.

"If you mean, am I the one concerned about my cousin Alex's well being, married off to the Cameron lass, then aye that's me," I answered.

As I entered the house it seemed to become larger and there were more family members in there wanting to be introduced.

"We are the twinnies Fatma and Ali," said a boy and girl unidentical twins.

"Hello Malcolm, we have met before. I am Zara but I am busy preparing all of our lunches, so you'll have to excuse me," Zara said.

"I'm Hector and she's my Ma and that's my Da," pointing at Grigor Mohr said a tall handsome, teenage looking lad who was keen to be acknowledged.

"That's Isobel, my bossy older sister," Hector said. "That's one of her husbands Alexander, she's with child to him," he added. "She has another bairn who is asleep and so does Ma. My youngest brother's name is Causantin. Ma just bought me a horse because she jumped out of her window and sunk into the snow and I saved her, didn't I Ma?" Hector said boldly.

"You are my hero, Hector," replied Zara smiling at her son lovingly.

"Now all of you, can you please be quiet for a few minutes? Please, take a seat Malcolm," Grandda said.

Grigor Mohr had something he wished to discuss with Grigor Og about oat crops and whether they could do a winter plant there in the Aird. Grigor Og said he would bring his son in law to test the soil like he had done for me in Glengarry and they were then lost in soil and oats conversation, while Padruig attempted to ask me about the MacNachtens. I told him that my Da passed away when I was four years old, so when my Mither had to raise us, we had to move back to her foster Father, Gillcrest MacNachten. We had never known before that time, that we were Clan Grant on my Mither's side and we were expected to return to Craskie Farm, but Granny had a problem when she arrived back there after planning to organise our return, as well as building the wee Chapel.

"My Grandda MacNachten, who was our foster Grandda, put me on the Chapel building team and he was the one who let us all know that the return to Craskie Farm was temporarily postponed and that Granny was very sick. I knew there was a lot more to that whole story and my Ma was devastated all over again. Grandda told me his part where he heard her voice while he was sleeping, asking for help. So, standing on the Druid stone he was transported to her in the Great Glen where she was falling off her horse in her sleep and not only was he assisting her, but her deceased half brother Grigor Mohr MacGregor was also helping, so between the two of them, she didn't fall from her horse and awoke," I explained.

"We were not welcomed at Craskie Farm, Grandda, because Aunty Helen wasn't aware that she had another sister, the twin to Uncle Alex, and was very jealous of her, is what I was told. In trying to protect one of the twins from a perverted neighbour, it created another problem, but our family had a great life in Loch Insh. I can't complain about my life there and my foster Grandda was a spiritual man, who was so kind and gentle and who never spoke unkindly to my brother Kenneth, nor I. After the inheritance was finally sorted out from the thieving relatives in Glenmoriston, several times over, all was good in the world," I said in a matter-of-fact way. "You are also welcome to visit my wife Cherry and I in Glengarry. What else can I tell you?" I asked.

Grandda expressed curiousity about the man who had delivered the lovely horse to the Prince and so I wished him well in finding him in his world or it might be in the book, that belonged to the Menzies family.

"Perhaps give the book to Grigor Og when you have finished reading it," I suggested, "Or bring it to my place in Glengarry, if you like, but I'd like you to meet my wife. This is the first time that I have kept a secret from her and I don't want to do that again. You could also meet Kenneth, my brother and his wife Ivy, should you wish, not to mention your own daughter, my Ma, Marion MacDonald," I added.

Lunch was served and it was delicious, just as Grigor Og had described Zara's stews. Hector proudly showed me his new horse and we were on our way back to Craskie before the weather broke. It wasn't a scary fairy dun, it was just an ordinary family or eccentric family who lived in the past, but they were all likeable in their own different ways. 'We are not much different dead as we are when alive', I thought as we rode off.

I thanked Grigor Og for his trust in me, but I didn't think I'd be returning. I hoped to see Grandda again in Glengarry one day, but Cherry would have to be told about him somehow.

10. *Padruig Dubh Seeing Malcolm*

Padruig sat at the dining table virtually motionless but thoughtful after Malcolm's departure.

"Are you disappointed Padruig at meeting your Grandson here?" Zara asked. "Like you said, he is the mouthy one, so he says how it is. Did you find him too rude?" she asked.

"Nae, not rude at all, I liked the fellow. I was thinking how I could meet his wee wife without scaring her to death, so it might be a while before I see him again," he answered.

"You look sad, Grandda," said Fatma. "Why are you sad?" she asked.

"This book is all in English too lass and it might be hard to read, is all," he said, misleading poor Fatma and he went to lie down to avoid more questions of that day on Culloden Moor when he saw that horse given to the Prince by Malcolm's Grandfather, rear up with horrible injuries and the Prince was thrown off, as Zara had said. It just felt so odd to have been related in this way, to such a heroic man of that time who had been forgotten in history and even he had never known that his own family was directly connected, if only through a horse, partly due to never knowing he had another family member, who lived in Loch Insh. A beautiful daughter named Marion, one of twins, who had two sons, Malcolm and Kenneth, that had needed him. That's what made him sad.

Isobel and her Father John Grant had reason to protect the twins from that perverted farmer, his Uncle, but keeping it from him, Marion's own Father was another story altogether. Why had his wife, Isobel not told him that they were all living in Loch Insh? There had been so many times that she could have disclosed what her and her Father had decided to do after she had given birth to twins. His marriage was good at times with Isobel but terrible too, when these secrets came to light. It had been Isobel's intention to continue to care for the poor wee lass, Marion who was visited by both John and Isobel right up until the burnings of 1746, when the Clydesdale Team was lost from Craskie farm, along with everything else.

So, Marion had just been left there alone, without her real family and the MacNachtens took care of her throughout all of that difficult time and then they married her to one of their own, Nachtain MacNachten, realising that Isobel wasn't returning or maybe that she had died was a thought they may have had. Those two sons born to Marion, never knew that they were Grants and how it must have hurt them all, finding out after their father died, especially also then having to move to Glenmoriston upon the death of Gillcrest MacNachten, being removed from all they had been familiar with, as well as suffering a family then who rejected them and then having to chase down inheritance denied them or stolen by both Helen and Hugh Mohr.

It's quite an unbelievable story that the lad had endured and yet stayed decent, kind and honest with an intelligence and wit that Padruig admired. He was a young man with an old man's soul. Padruig wasn't sure how to make it all up to a lad who had obviously had to grow up fast with a toughness needed for all three members of his wee family, until they all married. Clearly, he had been protecting his Mither, until she too was remarried. He thanked God that Malcolm didn't hate him, but he also hadn't detected warmth from him, or a longing fulfilled. Malcolm had just wanted to know where his Grandda was to verify his feelings all along of where he thought his Grandda was.

Padruig was glad in a way that the MacNachten Grandparents hadn't taken over his role because they simply seemed to vanish from Loch Insh, perhaps dead or Cleared, so Marion's family all had to go back to Gillcrest, God bless his soul. He was pleased at least that his enquiries meant that he had no competition with other Grandparents. He was going to go to Glengarry, after all Alex was there at the other farm too, another Grandson who wasn't altogether manly, like Malcolm obviously was.

But Padruig had only one Grandson that looked just like him and that was Malcolm MacNachten. He was like looking into a mirror.

Padruig hadn't mastered Malcolm, Malcolm had mastered Padruig, without any fear of him. Malcolm had his number, he had figured Padruig Dubh out. For the first time in his existence, Padruig felt exposed. He wanted to sleep but his mind was racing as he went over that period when the twins were born and why it was that at least John would have told him where Marion was, after all Padruig was even in Badenoch, near Loch Insh when he handed the Prince over to Cluny MacPherson and his daughter must have been there, nearby with the MacNachten family.

Gillcrest MacNachten had even said to him later when they met that he had seen Padruig there in Badenoch taking money as they delivered the Prince over to Cluny. It made more sense now that he had mentioned the money when Gillcrest must have needed that money for his daughter, Marion. So, even Gillcrest must have known then that the Father of the child had never been told where she was. That might explain why the Camerons contacted Gillrest in the first place to open up that old wound. Marion could have been returned after that with her sons, but stupidly on the night Isobel went to Loch Insh to the family, alone on her horse, there was no understanding other than the building of the Chapel achieved, because Padruig ended up fighting with his wife, Isobel, as to why she had left to go alone to Loch Insh, without even taking Hugh Mohr.

Had his wife Isobel gone to Loch Insh to organise bringing the family back in the guise of the building of the Chapel, or inclusive of, in order to pay the MacNachtens back? She had given Gillcrest money on that day for the tombstone covers. Malcolm was one of the builders, he had been later told, who was just there to observe everyone, considering they hadn't been retrieved from Loch Insh to live on Craskie Farm. It was driving him mad going over and over it all and who was to blame for what. He wasn't blameless, as Isobel became ill after the beating that night and became too afraid to tell him then of their existence.

By then, it must have seemed hopeless to her.

Was it his fault that Helen had committed suicide believing in her exclusiveness as an only daughter? Had he spoiled Helen that much into believing in her own importance over everyone else, especially Alexander whom she was pleased had left for Nova Scotia, to her Mither's utter distress? He had never understood Isobel's grief for her son, until he realised that there were twins that she'd had to be parted from and under a heavy cloud of whether they had been the result of a rape or not in the minds of people, like her Father and even her brother. Isobel never believed that wee Alex was the result of that rape, so neither was the other twin, Marion. Maybe John thought that he, as Isobel's husband being violent as he was, would give up one of them to that pervert, after all being a wee pretty lass made it a realistic fear. John had lived through all of Allan's continuous perversion for years.

He hoped there was a special place in hell for the likes of perverted men like his Uncle.

Should he ask Grigor Mohr about that night when the information concerning that awful rape was extracted from his half sister and whether he thought that both children, Alexander and Marion were both products of that rape? Did he also have any other information concerning Marion and his grandsons? He decided to wait until the time was right and then ask his old friend for help. He heard Grigor come back inside from his work and chose to ask him then.

"Grigor my friend, can I please ask you for some information or advice? Since I saw Malcolm today, my mind won't stop grinding," he asked. "I'll even make the coffee," he said.

"Aye, I'll just let Zara know I'm back inside and hungry soon," Grigor Mohr said, as he went into Zara who was just writing out recipes.

"I'll start cooking if its okay to overhear your conversation," she said.

"Is it okay if Zara overhears? She's cooking tonight," he asked.

"Aye, of course," Padruig answered.

"I just have a delicate question concerning the night that Isobel admitted to the rape from my Uncle, placing Alexander's paternity then in question. You know now that there were twins born, Marion and Alexander, not just one child as we were told at the time. Is that what you have learned too?" Padruig asked.

"Aye, Marion is Malcolm's Mither, so that is old news," Grigor answered.

"Do you agree that it would be impossible for that perverted Uncle of mine to have a Grandson who is of the exact likeness to me, therefore debunking the possibility that the paternity of both my twins could have been the product of that rape?" Padruig asked.

"Aye, impossible for that lad to be anyone other than yours Padruig," he answered.

Listening on, Zara knew who Isobel had lain with on the day that he was asking him about on that night being discussed. Isobel had wanted to divert attention away from Hugh Mohr and her having an affair and while the rape story was true, it wasn't answering her brother's question as to who she had been with on that day.

"Grigor my love, Padruig my friend, I hope this is not too interfering, so I will ask you first. Do you want to know who Isobel Grant was having sex with at the time you were coming back from Quebec?" she asked. Both men looked aghast at what Zara had said.

Jumping up from his chair, standing between the two of them, Grigor responded.

"Only if my wife, Zara remains safe when you have this knowledge Padruig," Grigor answered as he stood up immediately to protect Zara.

"I understand," said Padruig. "Is this why you are avoiding reading more of your books Zara?" Padruig asked, lowering his head.

"Maybe it is, my friend. I don't want to hurt you. But on that occasion, it was Hugh Mohr Chisholm. They were having a love affair," Zara said. "She never stopped loving you either, which you must know as she stayed beside you until you passed away and drove the Team herself at her advanced age seated beside Hugh Og with your coffin on it. Even her horses were upset at the realisation that you were entering the earth. I am so sorry Padruig," said Zara and began to cry onto her husband's shoulder and he held her knowing how hard that was to say.

"I'll help you cook darling, what can I do?" Grigor asked.

"It's okay if Padruig needs you," Zara said.

"Come on, we can all do it," said Padruig. "I'm the best bread maker this side of Glengarry," he said looking relieved somehow and the three close friends put a beautiful meal together, while Isobel went around lighting the fires and telling John to bring in more wood or peat from outside. She was going to boil water in her Mither's room and change wee Causantin to bring to his Mither.

"Feed time Ma for Causantin. What can I do?" Isobel asked.

Zara kissed her wee one and sat by the fire when Padruig unexpectedly brought her a cup of hot coffee.

"Thank you Padruig, that's so nice of you," Zara said.

"It's me who should thank you for clearing that up and there's more I expect, so I want you to know it's okay to read it aloud. I want to know whatever there is to know," Padruig said.

"The bairns shouldn't hear it Padruig. It wasn't just a kiss," she said cautiously.

"So, we send them to bed when that stuff comes up," he said.

"I'm old enough Ma, aren't I?" Hector asked.

"I'll show your Father first son and ask his permission," Zara said, but spoken loudly from Grigor came,

"Bed for all the bairns, including Isobel!" during all of those parts.

"Okay with you John and Alex that Isobel goes to bed during those bits?" he asked.

Alex immediately understood that the other half of that love affair was Isobel's Father and was very quick to send Isobel to bed, but being opportunistic, John said that he would keep her company.

11. Malcolm's Craskie Nightmare

Cherry had been told not to expect Malcolm home and he was already missing her. Before they had even reached the farm, I started asking Grigor questions about the relationship between Padruig Dubh and Grigor's wife Helen. I asked him if they'd had an unnatural attraction to each other. He asked me what I meant by unnatural, but if I meant sexual, then definitely not.

"Helen did, however, worship the ground that her Father walked on. I was unable to tell her what I knew of her Mither's love affair with Hugh Mohr Chisholm because she would have shot her Mither herself with that knowledge," he said. "Her Father could do no wrong in her eyes and we were all well aware of his violent tendancies and no one is perfect and she felt that her precious Father, loving her as he did, put her above all women, except her Mither. She loved her Mither too and cared for her and never wanted to leave either of them," Grigor said.

"I knew well before anyone that Isobel and Hugh were in a sexual relationship, so I asked Ma and she admitted it to me.

I had seen them both making love in the lamb house, the forest, his house and all over the place on this property," he said, as we were riding in. The groom came out for both horses and we left him to care for them both. "Hugh even threatened to kill and eat my ox, Charlotte, once he knew I'd seen them, so I had to threaten his Collie dogs right back," Grigor said which sounded funny imagining two grown men threatening each other's favourite animals. "Hope you like beef stew, that is all my lady friend Carmel can cook I'm afraid. Just add salt or pepper if it's lacking. I like tomatoes in a stew," Grigor said.

"You have sheep here too, don't you?" I asked.

"Aye, we can slaughter you one tomorrow morning to take home to Cherry. Can she cook lamb then?" he asked as we walked into a nice smelling dinner. I was hungry.

"I don't know. We have never had lamb at our place, only goats," I answered. He called out to Carmel and asked if I wanted a bath first, which I did. I felt dirty going all the way to the Aird.

"Water's on, so I'll show you your room and we can pull your tub into your room then," Grigor said. It was odd being back on the farm that had rejected us and then had destroyed itself bit by bit.

After we had both bathed and put on clean clothes, Carmel said her goodnights and then went to bed upstairs and I was glad of that.

"How are things going with Carmel?" I asked.

"Ordinary, I guess, but she puts up with me and I put up with her, so it'll do I suppose," he said looking a bit lonely.

"About today's visit to the Aird, I am surprised that they all live so normally like we all do, but they're not alive. They still have relationship issues, emotions don't alter, the memories of the past don't alter and, in their case, they're still curious and learning some things. I don't know what I expected really, but not something that normal. Is that what you experienced when you first went there?" I asked. "What has been the most recent book you gave them other than the one I provided?" I asked.

"I loaned Zara and Da a book on Scottish folklore because after Zara fell into the snow, they all thought that she was babbling and not making sense, saying that the black dog's day will come. It refers to 'MacFie and the Black Dog.' It's a tale from the Isles, Cherry might know it. What Zara meant was that because Hector had saved her, in that case he was the black dog and 'his day had come,' meaning he had saved her instead of constantly being horrible to his Ma, so she bought him a horse with the last of the fairy money," Grigor explained.

"So, they even have normal issues with children too?" I asked.

"Well yes and no. It's important that you don't tell anyone that both Zara and Isobel can still have bairns because no one else in the Otherworld can. Will you promise me that?" he asked.

"Aye, but why can they and not others?" I asked.

"No one in that world is supposed to be able to reproduce, but because she died there accidentally whilst still alive, Zara was able to reproduce. She had only been researching for the books that she wrote and talking to the Glenmoriston Men for the book. It's too long a story but she married twice, first to Hugh Chisholm and had Isobel, so that's why Isobel is blonde, then Zara married Da after she had passed away, but was still able to reproduce and they are really devoted to each other. I am not sure what happened with the Chisholms, they won't say, but they are no longer with any of them," Grigor said.

"What books was she writing?" I asked.

"Isobel of Glenmoriston, Isobel's Story," he said. "The other book is short stories mostly but it introduces your story and herself with that false name she uses, but I don't have it. Padruig does," he answered.

"Do you have that first one?" I asked.

"Aye, you can borrow it. Excuse me now though, I have to sleep Malcolm, I am tired. Good night," Grigor said and took himself to bed.

I slept uneasily in that house, without my wife and awoke early and without waiting to eat or get the lamb that Grigor promised, I left for home leaving him a note and taking home that book that Zara wrote from another time.

12. The Wolf

I had dreamed of a really big dark grey wolf inside our house with the front door open. It was going to take me several hours before I reached Glengarry, but my horse was galloping most of the way and sweating from the exhaustion. When I finally arrived it was late afternoon, I opened the gate quickly to run to Cherry and the young groom, Duncan, came to get my poor horse and commented on the horse's condition.

"Have you seen Cherry yet Duncan?" I asked.

"Aye, she was with all the bairns and Ivy just a while ago visiting your Ma. She's back inside now," he answered.

"Duncan Og, have you seen a big wolf anywhere around here?" I asked.

"A wolf? Nae, there are nae wolves here, nae more, I hope Malcolm, but I will ask Duncan Mohr," he said urgently. So, I hoped the dream that I had had at Grigor's house was just a nightmare from being separated from my wife and my wee bairns. The twins were barely two years old. Cherry was overjoyed at the sight of me and emotional with it and I had to see if all the bairns were accounted for in my absence.

"Cherry, I can't spend another night away from you all, I had a nightmare that the front door was left open and a really big wolf was in here wanting to eat the twins," I blurted.

"Malcolm, it's now making more sense. Your Grandda Padruig, who I thought you said was dead, spoke to me in a kind of dream saying that the front door was open and to close it now because there was a wolf roaming around," she said.

"I jumped out of bed like never before to see if the front door was open and it was. I don't know how or who left it open, as we are still asking around. I rely on you each night to check all of the doors and windows Malcolm my darling. I am so sorry, it was my fault," she said with her voice quavering. I held her tightly.

"So long as you are all alright. I'll explain about Grandda over some breakfast. I haven't eaten yet," I said.

Explaining Grandda wasn't that easy, but I just asked her to accept that the Otherworld wasn't far away from us and maybe Grandda knew there was a problem at my house, somehow. Grandda knew that I was sleeping at Grigor's house. Then I had to explain where I had been for him to know that and that I had actually been in the Aird and one of those people there was Grandda, who I had been with. Dead people.

"You ask a lot of me Malcolm with your intuition at times and I have always accepted it because you have never been wrong, but you could have confided in me," she said looking a bit sad at the lack of trust.

"I am sorry, it was all Grigor's rules or nothing and then I was going to tell you everything. Please believe that. I have to ask you also not to repeat this to Ivy. Zara and her family of eccentric people, including my Grandda and Grigor's Da have found a way to live in that world, so who are we to judge them?" I asked. "Additionally, he helped you, so you too have a connection now with Padruig Dubh," I said.

"Now I have to track down that wolf and change the locks. Maybe there is a stray key that we are unaware of, such as the MacDonnell Family who used to own this property, or our old security man, Duncan Mohr, Jean's husband. It would be easier to change the locks and give keys only to select people who have to sign them in each day," I said.

"Meredith has a key darling, can she still have one?" Cherry asked.

"Aye but sign it in and out each day, so we know where all keys are at all times," I said.

"Malcolm, it might be symbolic rather than real, such as the wolf might represent hunger or oncoming famine due to a bad winter or some such," Cherry suggested and as it had already been suggested to me that we prepare for a bad winter that could be the only meaning hopefully, but it wouldn't hurt to track the wolf down if there was one and so in speaking to Duncan Mohr, I asked him to look for animal tracks near our house, like very big paw prints. He and his dog searched day and night and he wasn't sure of some of the prints that he found, but they weren't from his dog and he had never seen them before.

We concluded that there was at least one other large predatory canine of some kind and to be very careful to lock up everything all of the time. It was lucky that we already had bars on the windows, but human error was a factor that we could never be sure of. Going out at night was also a bad idea, as was slaughtering an animal leaving any blood behind for the wolf to smell. Harvest time was fast approaching, but this was an emergency and so I asked Bruce to arrange a meeting again at my house with the other farm present also to let them all know that we had a predatory canine, perhaps a wolf and all precautions were needed to be taken. The new part of the goathouse was spotlessly clean, but at the other end, where the slaughtering took place, would have to be cleaner I told Bruce, due to the smell of the blood. I loaned him one of the students to assist him in scrubbing down any surface where blood had been.

Everyone once again came to the meeting to learn of the canine or lupine predator, thought to be a wolf, but had already started preparing to kill it if they saw it, as well as their own house security, which applied also to the houses by the loch. Ma hadn't put bars on her windows there yet, so she was going to do that. Matilda thought I was overreacting and didn't take any more precautions other than locking her front door. I had my locks changed due to the unknown factor of how the door came to be unlocked and open in the first place. It was put to me by Islay that there was a mythical Scottish wolf which it could have been. She was going to read up on its appearance. I thought that if there were any confirmed sightings then I would write to Lord Simon Fraser to eradicate any wolves or stray dogs in Glengarry. In the meantime, I asked Ivy to take down any proofs that we had already, such as the paw print.

I was starting to sound a bit too panicky, so we left it at that so we could all get on with the harvest preparation. I did implore them all, however, to dispose thoroughly of any rubbish that might attract a hungry dog. I was glad of Duncan Mohr's attitude to it and his big hound. He asked me if he could bring another hound that he had at home, to ensure that the wolf could be killed by his dogs.

Duncan's Irish Wolf Hound

13. *Unhappy Wife*

There was my additional wee problem with my unhappy wife and so I asked Duncan Og to prepare the pony and cart the next day for me to take Cherry shopping with the twins to Invermoriston. Meredith cooked beautifully again, but now her husband rode his horse up to our house to pick her up in case she came across that canine. All the lights had been installed and lit for the first time that night across both farms and it was almost daylight in parts. The whale oil was going to cost me a lot, but we had to do it. Other farms were notified by notice through the post office to kill any predatory wolf seen in the area or big stray predatory dog. Before too long it was all over Glengarry that there was definitely a wolf, so the story grew in size and people were doing all sorts of things to protect their families.

Mostly arms and ammunition were being bought at Frasers because they asked me if we were preparing for another Rising in Glengarry and I had to tell them that it was just a big stray dog, maybe a wolf, that we were all after, because I also bought extra ammunition, as well as whale oil.

The next day I was dressed to take my wife shopping with the twins. The cart was ready with the horse and all it needed was my wife. She was dragging this out by slowly getting ready and not really smiling and just preparing to take whatever I had to offer her by way of an apology. It was annoying but funny too to see this side of Cherry, who was still unimpressed with me. I drove the wee cart and the twins both loved it, but she just sat there like a snob, without chatting the whole way in. When we arrived in Invermoriston, I took her to the loveliest lady's wear shop that I knew of there and she 'ummed and ahed' looking over nice dresses but not happy with any of them.

"Do you want to go to another shop?" I asked.

"Aye, another shop please Malcolm," she said. So, like a servant man, I took her ladyship to another, then another when finally, she wanted to go back to the first shop where she bought one of the first dresses that she had picked up. I happily paid for it because it meant the end of going from shop to shop, embarrassing myself. She knew how to punish me, for sure. Then we all went to lunch and the twins had icecreams for the first time and she ordered an enormous lunch for herself with fancy tea from India.

I was feeling the pinch by the time I was driving that cart home. I reckon that wolf had already come into my empty pocket. At least my bairns were happy but most importantly, they hadn't been eaten by a wolf and my wife did start to chat, if only a little, on the way home. When we arrived home Duncan Og was ready to take the horse and cart and, coincidentally Ivy was walking past and Cherry called out to her. "Oh Ivy. My husband bought me a lovely new dress today and we ate out in Invermoriston," she said. The twins called out too about their icecreams and ran inside. I think that meant she was over her huffiness. I was hoping for sex tonight as I had missed out last night with Cherry in that mood.

With the last of my daily chores completed being behind time, Duncan Mohr said he was bringing his additional hound over by nightfall, after his own teatime, for which I thanked him and wished him well with it all. I noticed he was also carrying additional weapons. 'No wonder folk thought we were starting another Rising in Glengarry', I thought. Kenneth and Ivy were locked up inside their own home, so I didn't disturb them and was pleased to enter my own home to find Cherry was back to her normal self, smiling and chatting like nothing had happened. It was her way then and better than throwing china plates at me, like poor Grigor Og had previously suffered.

Islay let me know over dinner that she had read up on that mythical spectral dog called the 'Cu Sith' [6] and had personally ruled it out because it was supposed to be green in colour, not dark grey, as I had described, even though the eyes sounded the same as well as its size, which was awfully similar. The locksmith had been, and the locks were changed and the new key system was in place and Meredith was cooperating just fine with it. Tonight, was going to be better, I hoped. Maybe after a hot bath? After Meredith's departure, I noticed water boiling and the twins had been put to bed. Islay and her husband, Angus were well and truly esconced upstairs.

Next thing, Cherry's hand came out of the room where we bathe, ushering me in, so I took the last of the water with me and entered a little cautiously. Cherry was already in the bathtub and in the water that she had already cooked up and asked for the last of the water without scalding her. She carefully lifted up her bare legs in an alluring manner to make way for that hot water and asked for the suds that were on the cupboard near me and to light more candles in that room, but to go back to the kitchen and put out all of those candles and smoor the lounge room fire.

There was possibly enough room in the tub for us both, despite my long legs. I thought I was getting all the right messages, but I was a bit scared to tell the truth. I wasn't sure if I should take off my clothes or leave them on, so I left them on and entered the bathing room.

"Malcolm darling, what are you doing in your clothes?" she asked. "Come on my sweetheart, where's my general then?" she asked and as I entered the bath water, up he went. Sex was definetly on tonight. After the soaping up of each other, ever so sensually as only my wee Island wife could do, we were already enjoying our love life in the bath, both of us making more noise than we should have been. Leaving the bath water behind, I was hoping it wasn't my job to clean the bath in the morning before Meredith arrived to both cook and clean the big house for us. Towelling down each other gently with the lovely soft towels that Meredith had left on the side cupboard, I carried Cherry to our room, interested in one thing, restoring the lovely sexual balance that we had always had. I was keen to please her and to make sure that her needs were met.

"I love you Cherry, my heart, my soul, my everything," I exclaimed with such deep and sincere emotion that I found it hard not to feel emotional. I knew that my happiness relied on my relationship with my lovely wife. We had the most exhilarating sexual expression of our love throughout the night and it was exhausting. I fell asleep first.

14. Harvest Time

Harvest time was in a few days, so I made all of the usual preparations. The wee cart was going to be needed constantly and I thought that one of the wheels needed attention when we went to Invermoriston, so with that in mind, I asked Duncan Og to organise the blacksmith or farrier to come around to repair it and to check all of my horses who may be needing shoes, so in passing I asked Hugh Og if his Clydesdales also needed a farrier to save money on the farrier coming to our farm twice. He was very happy to have all of them checked, as he no longer had a regular blacksmith. The farrier for Glengarry was an older and experienced horseman, as well as blacksmith and farrier who carried all of what he needed from farm to farm if he was told beforehand what was needing attention, which Duncan Og dealt with. It turned out that the squeaky wheel on my cart needed complete replacement, especially with the needs of Harvest time in a few days. My wife and Meredith had organised the geese for the after-harvest meal celebration tradition which some people still adhered to, but others had replaced geese with turkeys.

"Ye grow oats do ye?" the old farrier asked.

"Aye," I replied wondering why he asked.

"Ye got bedrock don't ye? Howd, you manage to get oats to grow ere then?" he asked.

"Apparently that wee road there is a marker where the bedrock is lower than in most areas of Glengarry, so we can grow crops as well as Old John MacDonnell, so long as we keep the soil in good condition," I replied.

Hmmm he responded and got on with his work.

My wee pony needed all four shoes replaced and he was feeling much happier afterwards. My own horse needed all four shoes also replaced. The farrier asked me what I had been doing with that poor horse.

"Nothing much, just a gallop here and there," I had replied.

It was that trip to the Aird that had finished off her shoes. My wife's mare's shoes were in fine condition and he praised whoever owned that horse. Angus and Islay both kept their horses there too, as well as my son, Alex who was attending university. He was coming home to help in the harvest, God bless him. He was still studying critical care medicine in Edinburgh and I thought we should have more bairns before Cherry was too old to manage a new wee one. I had already asked Lord Simon Fraser for a recommended local placement for my son, in about one year's time as he had all the contacts.

All of Hugh's beautiful Clydesdales were taken very good care of as the old farrier knew his business well and most of their shoes were replaced also, as well as the usual hoof trimming and the hair around their hooves, called feathers. Both grooms were invigorated into cleaning up each animal one by one by having a bath of sorts with soap. Both grooms then rode them around to dry them and they had their best day. I asked one of Gillcrest's students to come up and clean up all the mess made with the work being done and to muck out each stable. I thought that both Hugh and I could do with an additional groom and I put it to him so we were both going to look out for someone suitable as the new junior groom.

All of the nesting boxes for the owls were checked, as were the cats in the oats storage room and I checked every inch of the storage room, ensuring that the flooring was clean and dry, then asked Duncan Og to cut down the briars needed to lay the oats on, post harvest. I ticked each item off my list, including all of the scythes required and we had sufficient and while the farrier was there, he sharpened them all for me, but cautioned me too as to understanding that a sharp scythe can do some real damage to one of us if we were not careful in our handling of them. Alex from Loch Garry Farms was going to join in to assist us in the harvest, as was my own son Alex, Hugh Og, three students, my wife Cherry, Ma, her husband Bruce, Islay and her husband Angus, Jean, Kenneth and his wife Ivy, while leaving Meredith at my home full time to mind the twins, as well as prepare all the smokos and in between meals and the main feast along with Cherry, Ivy and Ma at the completion.

All the men were the cutters responsible for the scythes, followed behind by the women. There were nine cutters for all of those fields which was mind boggling that all of those fields would be cut down by hand by nine men with a mere sharp knife. I was hoping for advancements in farming by now. I promised myself to continue pressing Lord Simon to pursue any new farming methods and machinery from the Americas.

It was wonderful to see my son Alex again. I had missed him so much, but it was one of the things I felt we had to do

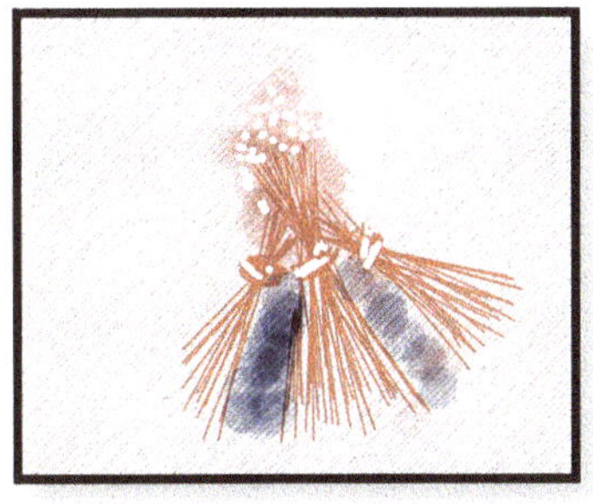

in educating at least one of my bairns, well. We all began the harvest after the lecture on how sharp the scythes were and the men started the cutting with myself going first. We were all followed by the ladies with their strings who bundled the oats into stand-up bundles into a stook. These were then collected quickly by Duncan Og onto the cart to be then taken into the storage shed before the weather changed. Each bundle was lain across the preprepared briars. We all cut and bundled field after field, only taking occasional smokos. With only one field to go, we had some lunch first, then quickly got back to work, worrying about the weather continuously.

When all the fields were finally harvested, the ladies were already cooking the geese that had been slaughtered that morning, but as they took a long time to cook, Meredith had not been able to leave that task along with my twins, who cooperated with her, thank goodness. The weather held out for us and we all thanked whatever God we all believed in and the area between Kenneth's house and mine was covered overhead with a sail to keep off the weather and tables were set up as a temporary feasting area. This was the first time that I had harvested this many fields of oats before, and it seemed like a first for Glengarry too but I already had orders coming in from the new bakery by the loch as well as a few military organisations, to name just a few. The oats later would then be threshed after which the oats would be delivered by Hugh Og's team of six horses. Naturally I had to pay him for that. Locals were impressed and even my neighbour, Old John MacDonnell was seen taking a look to see how it was going.

We all had our celebratory feast and I stood and gave a wee speech to thank everyone for their hard work. It had been a mammoth effort. They loved eating the geese and vegetable feast and the loaves of bread that Meredith had also cooked. My son Alex remarked that it had been the happiest he had been all year long, joining in with everyone to achieve a wonderful outcome of a beautiful crop of oats. The oats were well protected by the cats and the overhead window was closed tightly, with its doors closed and locked that night, I felt a huge achievement had been reached. It was gold to a farmer like me.

Both my son Alex and my cousin Alexander, renewed their acquaintance and my son was introduced to Siobhan. She had been too shy to join in, but she did offer to help clean up after the feasting. Matilda didn't come down to ask how it was going or to assist, but she had been odd since the night of the consumation of Alex's marriage. I concluded that she was just lonely and was missing her late husband. The following weekend, she travelled a long way back to Weem to visit her aging adoptive parents, who both died shortly afterwards, within a week of each other. She inherited their lovely home in the village of Weem and she decided to live there and hand over the farm entirely to my cousin Alex and his wife Siobhan. She had her lawyer draw up his total ownership of Loch Garry Farm. I congratulated him on being the owner and it felt better to be able to communicate with him, one on one about anything that would concern either of the farms.

15. *How to Reach my Grandda?*

Cherry went to the post office leaving the twins with me while she posted a letter to her Uncles in the colony of New South Wales, in New Holland and she looked a bit disturbed when she came home. I asked her what was wrong and she showed me a poster that was being handed out at the post office.

One of the local farmers claimed to have killed a dark grey coloured wolf that was a very large male, described as a lone wolf, most likely evicted from his pack. The description of the dead wolf was exactly the same as what I had seen in my nightmare. That was good news, but the existance of a pack wasn't. We were told the pack would not be in Glengarry, it could be miles away, possibly as far away as Glenmoriston. They could even be in the Aird and as I hadn't tried to communicate with my Grandda since he contacted Cherry to warn her about the front door, I asked Cherry if I should try to communicate with Padruig Dubh. I knew that he could somehow reach us whether through dream or in person appearing to us, which could be daunting.

I didn't know how it could work in reverse with me trying to reach him to update him on what occurred after he contacted Cherry, with the news of the dead Glengarry wolf and the possibility of a pack of wolves somewhere, possibly there in the Aird.

She suggested I sit alone in my office and relax and focus on his face or anything I remembered about him and simply ask to talk to him and see what happened. She didn't want to join me. It was too strange for her, especially if he replied. I locked my office door, so no one could disturb me while looking like an idiot talking to myself and tried what Cherry suggested.

I had to try several times when suddenly Grandda was just talking to me without my being able to see him.

"Malcolm, I hope you have disturbed me for a good reason," Grandda said. I first thanked him for helping Cherry and told him that there had possibly been a wolf around my house,  which had been shot now by one of the neighbours and my door had been open, as he had told my wife. However, it had been described locally as a lone wolf that had been part of a pack and had been evicted for some reason.

"That means that there's a pack somewhere, possibly Glenmoriston, or even as far away as the Aird. We couldn't be sure about that and I thought you should know, but if I was uneccesarily disturbing him, then naturally I apologise, as I had never tried this kind of communication before."

"You're welcome, Malcolm it was nae bother really. I was asleep and it was Zara and Grigor Mohr who came and woke me up to tell you about the wolf in your house with the door open. They asked me to tell you about that door, because I told them you were sleeping at Grigor Og's place that night, not Glengarry," Grandda said. "So, I tried to tell your wee wife who was hard to wake up, but she got a shock seeing me in her bedroom. Glad it all worked out. We'll keep an eye out for a pack round here, but we would have seen some evidence before now if they were here, so I'm thinking Glenmoriston is more likely. I'll tell Grigor Mohr to tell his son to look out for them. Now, I've gotta go," he said.

And he was gone.

There was something about having met those of the unseen world or whatever you want to call it. It left me each time with a sense of my own mortality, as well as what mark I wanted to leave on the world, as I knew it. When I went to sleep that night, I wondered about all of those things we hold dear and are important to us, like work and finances, as well as relationships. Did I have it right and in the right proportions? It would take your own death before you could see what you should or shouldn't have done, I suppose. It must be a particular kind of agony living and waiting for Judgement Day and not being able to undo things of the past. I did want to talk more with him about these things in the Aird again, but he didn't strike me as the best communicator or at least he was loathe to give too much away. I didn't know anyone like him, that was for sure, in life or death.

It made me disappointed all over again that we had all been banished to Loch Insh and I didn't understand the reason for a family separating twins at birth. Having twins of my own and seeing how close they were to each other made it all the more unimaginable. My Mither would have felt the loss of her twin, I was sure of it, even if she didn't know that was the reason for her sadness, growing up in Loch Insh, all alone without brothers or sisters. My poor Mither. I had always known to protect her and I did try and I loved her dearly and still do. I didn't want to share her at first with her new husband, but it eventually came together and she is happy now with him and he is a good man and he has turned out to be a good worker too on my farm.

Bruce had grown up with Grigor Og with another youngster at the time named Dougal, he said. They had met up when he first came back from the Americas but had rarely seen him since. He said the three of them had been together stealing tobacco from soldiers on the day of the burnings that they often refer to when this whole region was burned to the ground by British troops after the Battle of Culloden. The three of those lads were aimless too without their Fathers, so there were similarities between Bruce and I who had lost his Father to Barbados then to the Americas, which was when he decided to leave Scotland to look for him. He never found him because he had been hanged with other Scottish men, removed from their homeland.

Bruce and Grigor had watched his Mither pass away horribly in Glenmoriston on the day of the burnings, [2] so finding his Da was also dead, he had no choice but to stay on in the Colonies right through their war against Britain. His wife there was an Indian woman, as well as all of his many children and grandchildren. He left them well set up and independent of him once his wife had passed away, but I wondered why there were no letters to and fro with news from his children. Even Cherry wrote to her drunken Uncles in New Holland and received a reply once in a while. I would still be with my Father if he had lived and I always want to be with my Ma, married or not. Some people just think differently.

I wondered why Bruce didn't see Dougal anymore. Maybe it would do both Grigor and him some good to catch up. At least Grigor Og would be with the living. Tracking down Dougal wasn't going to be easy, so I asked Bruce up front where he was these days. He looked a bit disappointed momentarily, or just thoughtful of the dreadful past they had all shared. Then he reluctantly told me that Dougal wasn't far away, he just didn't talk much these days. I concluded that he meant that

Dougal MacDonnell was in Glengarry. I offered to have Ma over to my house to stay if both Grigor Og and he wanted to catch up with him perhaps in the wee house by the loch away from all of us. He looked momentarily interested or hopeful that the three teen friends would catch up but thanked me for my thoughtfulness and said he would ask Ma and think about it, as would Grigor Og.

"Did you have a falling out?" I asked.

"Nae, nothing like that. It's more like all of the things you want and need to forget, come flooding back when we see each other. All the horrors of that day become fresh again and I see my Mither passing away before my eyes with that gruesome facial injury that she died from. Grigor was there when she died, so somehow it isn't so bad if I see Grigor, but Dougal was at his house with his Mither, who then took me in. She was a widow too with very little money and many people at that time starved to death. Grigor's Da gave her money to pay for my upkeep and his family also assisted with clothes and food or else I too would not have survived that period of time with everything gone," he expressed with such clarity like it was just yesterday when it had all occurred.

"I am so sorry for your losses Bruce for both your Ma and your Da. If I have been interfering, I apologise but the offer stands if you all want to get together and I'll take care of Ma," I said. "Additionally, could I ask you and Ma to care for Cherry and the twins if I'm ever late or have to be away for the night?" I asked. "Cherry can't cope on her own, even if Islay and Angus are there, but if you and Ma were there, she would be alright. The mystery of the open front door has never been resolved," I said.

"Both Marion and I will always be available to move in if you were ever going to be late or away," Bruce said. I never needed to worry about Cherry again, he had said. I was thankful to Bruce even if I was held over at a meeting somewhere, I needed to know that she was going to be not only safe but emotionally cared for. As I was departing, I said that if Dougal needed a job, we did need more staff in the stables.

My three students had completed all of the threshing work, so the oats could then be transported to people and organisations who had ordered them, leaving enough for ourselves. I had bought some muslin bags, which were sewn up well, containing a weighed quantity of the oats and our first delivery was two muslin bags to the new bakery by the loch. When I was riding past later that day, there was a queue of customers as long as the entire length of the group of houses. It was a popular bakery whose baker ground up the oats himself and after installing big ovens of some kind, he baked bread for people who were coming from miles around. Our next two deliveries were to the military companies, who we had to please consistently as they were taking a risk with us in Glengarry.

The loose oats were taken in the carriage, as it had been in the 1740's driven by Hugh Chisholm with his assistant teamster, Angus, my son in law. These deliveries left us sufficient oats for all of our families on the farms if we had two plantings in the year, one summer and one winter. My son Alex was still with us on his leave from university, so he also accompanied Hugh and Angus to assist in the unloading. My wife made a dish from the oats by soaking the husks from the oats for a week, so the fine flowery part of the meal remained as sediment to be strained off, boiled and then eaten. The hay or dry feed that remained, helped with feeding the goats and the cattle, as well as keeping the stables and the goat house much cleaner.

Then the whole process started all over again to prepare the fields, which the students moved onto and when Hugh returned, he ploughed them all again with the continuous addition of the manure from around the farm. Matilda had complained about my piles of manure, but in one day, after delivering the oats was completed, all of those piles were gone, whether it was coo manure or horse manure or chicken manure. I needed a new apprentice for soil preparation like Grigor had with Charlie MacKichan and have that one person continuously working on the manure and collecting every valuable piece of manure from around the farms before the kelp deliveries arrived. Duncan Og was a valuable source of knowledge, because being young and growing up in Glengarry, he knew who was the right age and most of them were his cousins admittedly, but they were all good workers and knew to look out for rocks and stones. It was stressfull admittedly hoping our oat crops would be successful when so few of us were growing oats in Glengarry but we did it.

The money started coming in from the oats and my empty pocket was no more and I was able to buy new boots as mine were losing their soles. I suggested to my wife that we buy a carriage for our family with horse and harness too, if there was enough money after all of the buildings were painted. Not to mention taxes. I asked James if I could pay him to do my books for taxation this year, given the rapid jump in income. He agreed but asked me to hold off on the carriage until he had finished that work. He didn't want me to go into debt. It was nice to see him again and he worked in my office in the house. He had asked to stay overnight due to the distance back to Glenmoriston. We caught up over teatime and there were taxes to pay, but he sorted it all out and I paid it leaving me still in the clear for a wee carriage but nothing fancy. James even took me carriage shopping. James loved to go shopping.

Their business was quiet he said over lunch and told me that a reporter had been at their business looking for me from the Inverness Times, but he was at the wrong place. It was just about that dead wolf, so James thought he would be at Cherry Farms one of the days before the gossip column was due to be printed on the weekend. He was asking other questions which he hadn't answered.

"I don't know if I wholly trust that fella," he said. "He asked weird and inappropriate things about Aunty Helen killing herself. I told him to be on his way unless he was there to book a room or buy lunch. So, he left," James said.

"What weird things?" I asked.

"He asked if our ancestors could commune with the dead. Can you believe that?" James said.

"No. That's really out there and totally weird. Why did he ask you that?" I asked.

"No idea. We are too ordinary I had always thought," James said.

"Yes, we all are, especially now. The last hero in our family was our Grandfather and there's not going to be another Padruig Dubh for sure and not even he could do that," I replied, but I knew that he could of course. I was becoming uncomfortable about where that reporter was going with his questions and so I decided to tell Cherry not to let him in our house and to tell Duncan Mohr to disallow him entrance onto my properties unless I was there. I still went home happily with the new carriage and James was paid and he went back to Glenmoriston after I had mentioned that wolf pack to him.

During lunch he had mentioned that his Father was doing less and less as was his Mither and so he had to employ two other people to replace them, as well as their own security guard.

"Is Hamish not doing your security then?" I asked.

His Father, Patrick was always playing golf to get away from his Mither, so all was not rosey at the Hart of the Highlands Manor and Hamish was now only working Craskie Farm. Susan and James were getting along well and their bairn was healthy. He was proud of that, but worried where it was all going with his parents. 'Poor Hamish', I thought. He must have lost some income and we did need another security guard. The recent work had been overworking Duncan Mohr. Hamish was living by the loch in Glengarry now, so it would suit him to work for us, at least part time.

The family loved the carriage even though it was a bit small but big enough for us and it would only ever need the one horse. I just needed to build a small covering for it near the stable. I saw Duncan Mohr doing his rounds and showed him also and mentioned that Hamish wasn't working up at the

Manor anymore and would he be able to work with Hamish part time if I asked him? He was thrilled about having an extra hand.

"I like Hamish, he's one of the good guys. Poor fella going through all that shite at Craskie Farm. It'd be great to get him out of there altogether," Duncan said.

"I'll go see him then and by the way, there's a newspaper man asking odd questions. If I am not here, please do not let him in on any of the farms or answer any of his questions and make sure he stays away from Cherry," I said.

That night was a pleasant but disappointing visit to Hamish and Cora's place by the loch. It was lovely there. I didn't waste any time and asked him if he wanted to work at the Cherry Farms, given that James said he was no longer working with them. It was a surprise answer but Hamish turned down my offer.

"I have only ever worked at Craskie Farm. I would feel like I was letting Grigor down if I did that. But if Grigor sacked me, I would love to work here in Glengarry. Old Isobel gave me my first job ever on a half penny a day. I feel like she's still there every day. I know there are people who always go from job to job or place to place and when I lost the extra income from Patrick, even Cora suggested leaving Craskie, but I just can't be disloyal. It's not in my blood, I guess. But thank you, Malcolm just the same. You have a good system up there at your farm and Duncan Mohr gets paid better than me for sure," Hamish said. He apologised as I was leaving and offered himself if ever, he was let go or if Grigor sold the place, which he thought he should do.

I left feeling disappointed. Hamish was being underpaid for his many years of service and yet he couldn't leave them for better pay, even for three bairns and a wife who had also lost her job as a teacher in Glenmoriston. Grigor didn't appreciate what he had. Staff was a hard part of the job of running a farm, especially loyal staff like Hamish. Isobel must have had a special way with people to have made him feel that way and it took a long while for Hugh Og to leave Craskie. They had all shared a different kind of life together, especially when Padruig wasn't there and she needed those men, as she had needed all the others who had long gone since her death.

They were workers but friends and family too, who sat and ate together nearly every night and were never excluded from all family functions, right through to the grandchildren's lives. I talked myself into understanding it and also maybe changing how we managed my staff. Maybe we should have both Duncans in for meals. I wasn't sure how Cherry would feel about that. She wasn't one for trying to befriend staff and it was hard to get her to befriend Ivy and Matilda, who never liked her. There was Meredith who I could ask. She had no trouble leaving Grigor. I did ask Meredith, but she hadn't been at Craskie for as long as all of the others. Her first role was in the wool waulking group, before she moved into the house. But years and years of history had already occurred.

"It was that period in time Malcolm when people were desperate, losing everything and everyone, so even the smallest money was a God send or food from someone, let alone clothing, but everyone was desperate for shoes and boots, even Isobel. So, the people around you were more important then than now, maybe they were your very life source," she said.

"Or if you had lost a parent, maybe they replaced that parent and with Isobel, she was everyone's Mither. Those lads, Hugh and Hamish were the fisher lads, she called them, because they sold her fish first. They called her Ma. They lost their Father to drowning in Loch Craskie, so everyone had grief of some kind whether it was a parent, a son, a husband and some could not cope and took their own lives after the atrocities, which was sometimes a long while after the rapes and so on, that happened. They all did their best to survive, but they needed each other more is what I mean. Isobel wouldn't have had her house built at all if it hadn't been for the three friends who built it for her when her husband disappeared for nearly four years. Grigor Mohr, Hugh Mohr Chisholm and Donald Chisholm built it," Meredith said

"Do you need anyone Malcolm? You are so independant?" she asked.

"Aye, my wife. My very existance depends on her," I said.

"That is so romantic. I wonder if Hugh feels that way about me?" she said and went back to work.

I invited both Meredith and Hugh to stay and eat with us as my son Alex was due to leave in a few days. I talked about relations with staff and whether they thought I was doing a good enough job and they all seemed to think so.

"But what about Granny and how she ran Craskie, she was better at it wasn't she?" I asked.

"Isobel, or your Granny, was different. You can't compare a tiny wee woman who knew nothing about farming, except for the team and horsemanship with yourself. She was totally reliant on the men, whether it was their knowledge or their mere strength and so she had to keep in good with us all, when you think about how small she was, and without money, if Padruig hadn't sent them money and after Culloden, well you know that story and you know that he even left her in order to go and fight in Quebec, without building the house. He had thirteen years to build it and he still hadn't done it. All the men, no matter whether they were married or not, felt compassion for Isobel, especially when he beat her too after working so hard, as she did. I don't question a man's rights in his marriage, but he went too far which was why her indescretions were overlooked, in my opinion," Hugh Og said.

"She went too far with the indescretions I think. I was hearing all kinds of things people heard and saw, but we didn't dare repeat it or she would incur the wrath of her husband," Meredith said. "Then when your family, Malcolm, appeared out of the blue like you had never existed, it was too much, her husband should have known about you all, don't you think?" she said. "He was a brute, I know that, but he was still human, with a heart. It must have really hurt him to learn of an entire other family, who he had never known of. No, she went too far or whoever influenced her, like her Father, went too far," Meredith said.

"I must admit, it's interesting to learn about how it all came about, but I think Da actually wants to know how to better deal with staff like she did perhaps and it is a topic of conversation at university too at the moment, concerning staff relations, because the English have adversely affected the way in which Scottish families have always dealt with staff as family and not as serfs," said my son Alex. "The feeling there amongst scholars is that bosses should show more interest in each and every member on staff, know their names as well as their circumstances, pay them on time and adequately. It isn't necessary to have all of the staff seated at the dining table every night, as Granny obviously did for her reasons but occasionally, it would be advisable to keep good relations," he added. "In addition, allowing for staff to attend their family funerals or take off a day when sick or injured is reasonable. Injury at work is another topic of conversation that is quite heated there, as those types of injuries are said to be paid for by the employer. There will be a lot of workplace changes coming, you will see," Alex said.

"Maybe Granny was ahead of her time," Cherry said. "She ran Craskie Farm very well and she built a Chapel and that counts for something before God surely? Maybe she did feel guilty for those indiscretions, but it must have kept her sane too because she didn't end up like Helen," Cherry added. "I heard that she really loved Hugh Mohr Chisholm as well as her husband," she added.

"Cherry, I hope you will only love me and not some other loser," I said.

Having dinner with others was definitely way livelier and more informative than one on one. Islay and Angus were left a little dumbstruck that Granny had been indiscreet. They then helped clean up and went to bed early. I was hoping they would eventually have more family, but so far there had been no indication of it, unless the women were keeping secrets of course, as they often do.

I don't know if my own ideas on staffing altered a lot other than factoring in sick pay and injury pay, which so far had not occurred. I hadn't imagined that I wouldn't have paid for staff injured on the job on my farm. I asked Cherry in bed that night if we could have a weekly dinner with a few staff like the two Duncans or Dougal when Hugh was here next. She agreed, to my surprise that if it was something I was worried about then we should be better bosses and ask after their families and so on. It was a nice concept. So that's what we started to do.

My son Alex asked after Moses and Sarah, his second cousins, who had lived on Loch Garry Farm with Uncle Alex and Matilda, but they were still in Edinburgh to my knowledge, and they hadn't inherited any of Loch Garry. I explained to him that their Mither had passed it all on to the oldest son, being Alex, who was married and the two of them, Moses and Sarah would still inherit from their Mither, but it would be from the estate in Weem. It would still leave them both well off at their Mither's passing, but not to bring that on.

Matilda had been unhappy on the farm since Uncle Alex died and wasn't helpful or cooperative with us all, even over the wolf issue. She only ever complained about the smell of the manure or that I was overreacting to security needs. In the end she was very English and it was only her love for Alex that had kept her on the farm, as well as her one accomplishment of her wee forest, which was another complaint she had had when I asked her to put owls in her forest like I was accusing her of being a rat breeder in the forest by the burn. Sure enough, there were rats coming out of the burn that used to be pristine and so my owl nesting box was installed there, but she was really angry about how it spoiled the appearance of the forest. Now, thank goodness those rats are no more. Matilda was the biggest rat breeder and hard to communicate with or to take any accountabilty for and so with my cousin Alex now in charge, there was good communication between the farms, which is essential.

Moses and Sarah hadn't ever come back home for harvest time, like my son did and they stayed on in Edinburgh, even over holidays. They had no interest anymore in farmlife. He was sad that his half brother and sister turned out that way, but education can go either way, he said and that was the risk that farmers took in sending their bairns to higher education. Some of the students were embarrassed about their roots and lived in denial.

One thing I did know was that denial of one's roots is a long road back.

16. *The Morning Light in the Aird*

Zara was going about cleaning up the shed where she had been doing her fairy artwork, when her husband, Grigor Mohr spoke to her from a wee stool she had, near the entrance of the shed.

"Zara, I've hurt my ankle. Can you help me a bit?" he asked. Naturally she hastily took down her first aid kit that had some bandages and went to him immediately and sat on the ground in front of him, asking him which ankle. He indicated the right ankle, so in taking off his boot and hose, she thought it looked alright, as he lifted his plaid up higher. The sunlight was lovely that morning and captured the colours of his black leg hairs against his pale skin which looked beautiful as they glistened in the morning light. She wrapped up his ankle but was a little unsure of how serious it was, especially as he lifted his plaid further to reveal his thighs. Even though they were long married, she felt shy at how beautiful she found his long thin legs with the black hairs all the way up his legs, with not as many on his inner thighs.

"Is this how you look my wife in the sunlight, shy at the look of your husband who you sleep with every night?" Grigor asked.

"Grigor, do you really have a sore ankle?" she asked, as the smile crept right across his face.

"Your hands are on my thighs now my wife, it's not too much further is it and you can see what else there is in this light," he said so cheekily, as Zara ran her hands up his thighs, then knowing her husband had tricked her into this. Underneath his plaid was a wanting husband and Zara was a most desirous wife, who enjoyed his pleasure of her loving his manhood. With her head underneath his plaid, she heard him yell at someone who was coming into the shed and was told to "Feck off" in no uncertain terms, as he reached his peak of pleasure.

Taking off his wife's skirt, he lifted her to the work bench on which he placed his plaid for her comfort, so he was as naked as the day that he was born. Grigor entered his wife with vigour and love while first rubbing her clitoris. Despite their lack of privacy and having to yell at another to "feck off," the two lovers, enjoyed their love to the fullest with it all beginning with him tricking her into caring for his foot, so she was at the height that he wanted her to be looking up his plaid and at his manhood in that lovely morning light. Her shyness in that light was the invigorating factor in his enthusiasm for more and more sex, reassured him somehow that his wife really did adore him.

Inside the dining room in the farmhouse, seated in his usual place was Padruig at the head of the table reading a book with Alex to his left when Hector burst through the door saying he had been told to 'feck off' by his Father in the shed and they were doing 'it'. That did not impress Padruig, who loudly chastised the lad and told him never to disrespect his parents again in his presence or he would learn what for and it was none of his business what they were doing.

"Morning Padruig, morning Alex. I was going to do some work in the shed, but if you don't mind, I'll join you for morning tea," said John, looking pale and a bit rattled.

"What's happening in the shed then?" asked Alex.

"Better you don't ask," John answered.

"You see Hector? That's a respectful man," said Padruig.

In the shed, Grigor said, "You are so beautiful, my wife and I don't tell you that enough, but you are and I love you so much that it hurts sometimes," he said to Zara as they were amorously cuddling and then they began to dress again.

"Shall I take off the bandage then?" she asked.

"Nae, I want the memory of it, seeing your face looking at me like that when you were admiring me and then finally caught on," he said then laughed and laughed at his lovely wife.

"Are you hungry, we could eat if you like?" Zara said smiling at him.

"Good idea, fried eggs and those tomatoes you grow would be nice with toasted bread," he answered.

"Great idea, I'm starving hungry now too," Zara said.

They both walked into the house with all eyes on them, except for John, who hadn't dared to look them in the eye. He had never seen Grigor naked, let alone his wife as well. It was only Alex who had been previously known for walking around naked and not even Alex did that anymore since Isobel had put an end to it. Hector was bursting to say something but was terrified when he caught the look from Padruig.

"Don't mind us both. We are having a second breakfast," said Zara.

"You can make us one of those nice Turkish coffees, can't you Zara?" asked Padruig.

"Of course, Padruig when you ask so nicely, but we do need to buy some more the next time we are in Inverness," Zara replied.

"Then Alex and I can buy it next time, can't we Alex?" he said, as Zara busied herself with her husband's breakfast, who sat at the other head of the table looking very pleased with himself. A contented man, Padruig concluded, but much more than usual.

'Was doing 'it' in the shed somehow more exciting than the bedroom?' Padruig wondered.

"John, the shed is free now for you," said Alex and poor meek John left to go back to work.

Grigor and Zara's second breakfast was beautiful, as they both ate like horses as well as top ups on their coffees. Alex and Padruig just watched on at the new phenomenon of hungry outdoor love makers. Padruig wondered if this would give Zara her wee lassie that she had wanted. 'Grigor had to do something different to make a lassie and maybe that was all this was about?' Padruig wondered. Before too long Zara was feeling queasy in the mornings and vomiting up on occasion. She looked awful and felt awful. Her courses never came and she spoke quietly to Grigor one night in bed.

"Grigor, my darling. I think I might be with child. Do you mind?" she asked.

He smiled the happiest smile a man could have and held her face in his hands and kissed her wet eyes as she wept a little.

"I am so thrilled Zara and I hope it's a wee lassie, but I'll be happy with either one," he said. "We should find a new Doctor too, just in case I have issues don't you think?" she asked.

"Aye, we can all go to Inverness before you are too big and confirm it too, it might just be a stomach bug," he said jokingly. Zara held onto her husband tightly across his chest to reach his other arm and he rolled over and he wrapped himself all around her, as she needed to be held onto with the bairn she was carrying inside.

Padruig knew she was with child without being told, but others, even Isobel, were not noticing the changes in her and Grigor. This unborn child was obviously important to them both and that had to feel a bit scary in the first four or five months, when finally, Hector asked why she was so fat.

"Grigor, should we say something now?" Zara asked over dinner one night when everyone was present.

"Aye, we can if they are interested," he said cleverly.

"I'm interested why Ma is fat and was vomiting Da," Hector said.

"We are all interested Grigor and Zara," said Padruig.

"Zara and I hope to have a new bairn in three to four months time thereabouts, so please don't ask too much of my wife especially, carrying anything heavy or standing up for too long," Grigor said. "We are both happy about this new bairn, but at the same time we have to take all the care needed to bring the bairn into this world safely and I would like to ask all of you to help with that. Zara can't bring in the peat or chop the wood anymore, can you all manage with that?" he asked like a normal, but worried father to be.

"I'm sorry Ma for calling you fat," Hector said.

"That's okay son. I am fat and getting fatter by the day. You can help me with things, can't you Hector? You are my hero after all," she said and Hector hugged his Ma.

"Just ask me what you want Ma," he said. All in all, the family was very happy, while anxiety wasn't too far away. So many women had died in childbirth in their lifetimes.

"Do you have a new Doctor?" asked Alex.

"We have to go to Inverness to find a new Doctor," Grigor said.

"We'll go with you to help with Zara. Can she ride a horse now do you think, or should you hold her like you did before?" Alex asked.

"Can you ride now Zara?" Grigor asked.

"I'm not sure, how about I try it out and if it feels too uncomfortable, then I may have to go with you side saddle again, but that is hard on you darling," Zara said.

"If it's hard on Grigor, there's three of us, so don't be anxious about that," Padruig said.

"So long as you are warm and dry, we can't have you getting cold," Padruig added.

The farmwork came first, so it was two more days when all three men could leave the farm leaving it in John's hands, who didn't mind at all being left alone with Isobel and the twins. Hector had been given set tasks to keep them busy nearly all day, while Isobel was given two loaves of bread to cook, as well as an enormous stew and cake, as well as the following day's bannocks to keep her busy. The twins were given cleaning jobs of every room starting with their own, Hector's, Padruig's, Alex and Isobel's, John's and most importantly their Mither and Father's bedrooms, including changing the sheets. John had to do laundry on all the sheets, which meant boiling them in an enormous copper and pillowcases and clothes while his wife was able to hang them out in the brief sunshine, then bring them back into the drying room with the fire lit. He was also responsible for chopping enough wood to last a month, as well as collecting reliable peat.

They also had their dinners and smokos, so the day passed very quickly as the three men and Zara were in Inverness who did find a suitable lady recommended by a midwife, who also said she could come to the Aird if they couldn't get to Inverness. She was a lovely lady who was connected to the same midwives in Glenmoriston and Glengarry. Her name was Lillian Ross, whose husband had a horse and cart and took her to all of her ladies for miles around. Having previously had stitches in that delicate area, it did increase the risk for splitting, so the Midwife was warned to bring her stitching kit, however she advised it was preferable to cut before Zara split and so pain relief was needed, but Zara would only accept an herbal pain relief for the bairn's health. Reluctantly, she accepted that alcohol on any cut area was necessary. Grigor thought the Midwife was preferable to the Doctor, so Zara could still have the wee bairn at home.

The exact due date was helped by Padruig when the outdoor love making in the shed had occurred. It was arranged that Lillian would arrive in the Aird two days before that due date and stay overnight with her husband for as long as she was needed with the whole family, until the wee bairn was born.

Grigor insisted on assisting as he had before with the twins, as had Alex and Padruig, who said if the bairn looked like coming early, then he would ride up to Inverness to fetch the Midwife.

"You are so fortunate my dear, to have such a good husband as well as two wonderful friends," Lillian said. She touched Zara on her stomach ever so gently before we all left as if to talk to the wee bairn and spoke. "All the very best Zara, I know you are concerned, but please relax, love and enjoy your sweet bairn. I think it is a wee lassie," she said.

While in Inverness, both Padruig and Alex kept their word and bought a whole big bag of Turkish ground coffee, as well as ground cinnamon and sugar. Zara also asked those two men to buy another small coffee pot, so she could make more than one pot at a time.

"Just this once Zara," Padruig said, but they wanted to guarantee continued special coffees that they had never drunk until they had met Zara and now, they drank it every day. There was a Turkish shop in Invernesss that sold mostly china plates and lights but out of curiosity, Zara asked if she could see if they sold a particular sweet that went well with that coffee. Fortunately, they had lots of that particular sweet called Turkish Delight, so she asked her husband if he could please buy her just a few as a treat. He bought an entire box of them for everyone, which he thought was very expensive.

"Those people sure know how to charge. I'll nae buy that again at that price," Grigor said. "Thank you darling, its so sweet of you. Do you want to try one now?" she asked Grigor. He tried one warily looking at the foreign looking dessert. He licked it first then finally ate it. He liked Turkish Delight, but in seeing what he had, so did Padruig and Alex. Zara had to tell them to stop eating them, so they could be eaten with the coffee and even then, no more than two at one time due to the high sugar content and not just before bedtime, or it would be hard to fall asleep.

They made their way to their horses which had been stabelled, when the owner of the stables said that Zara's horse needed shoeing before trying to ride back to the Aird, but the farrier was just down the road behind the tartan mill, called MacKnights Mill, run by an ugly fella and his boss Ewen. Padruig went an awful colour and said he would remain outside while both Grigor and Zara went in to shoe the horse and he advised not to mention names such as Grant or MacGregor and it would be best to use a false name like MacKenzie from Kinlochewe. They were pleased to see that the farrier wasn't busy and could attend to the mare immediately and could check Grigor's horse too. Both horses needed shoeing, but their prices weren't too high because the MacKenzies were all good clients of theirs and were entitled to a discount. They paid up quickly and left as fast as they could, not knowing what the connection was with Padruig.

Padruig and Alex were in such a hurry to leave, the group were well out of town before anyone spoke of MacKnights Mill.

"That business is owned by my granddaughter Isobel-Mairi and her husband Ewen. They borrowed all the money from Helen and pulled out the staff from the farm and almost single handedly ruined Craskie Farm overnight. I set up that asshole of a farrier. I bought him a bloody forge and all. He is a Borderlander, whose last name is actually Armstrong, but due to the false information we had received from down there through Hugh and his contacts, we were not going to let the marriage go ahead, but Gillcrest MacNachten felt sorry for the man and took him home to Loch Insh, which was a mistake on more than one front.

He legally adopted the man and gave him his name of MacNachten, so in his documentation he can use that name.

Isobel-Mairi then had the bright idea of setting up the Tartan Mill and Tartan shop before the year of the sheep and convinced her Mither Helen to hand over all of that money she earned from the Art Gallery sales. Of course, I was dead by then, as well as my wife, Isobel. Marion's family from Loch Insh were the only legitimate folk with the name 'MacNachten', so young Malcolm as he was then, was as fiery as hell and disallowed them the use of it and fought Ewen and through lawyers and so on and my other grandson Aonghus was involved in the whole affair. He managed to mediate, and the name was changed to MacKnight, which was acceptable to both Malcolm and his brother, but they knew his brother Kenneth was the weaker of the two lads and plied him full of grog for free accounting, if they paid his rent and so to cut a long story short, they nearly killed Kenneth in the process. Call that revenge, I would say. He is definitely an Armstrong that piece of shite and I set him up on Craskie Farm. Kenneth was in hospital for over a month then joined his brother on the farm where Malcolm built him a home and that Art Gallery.That's not even with mentioning how Helen was supposed to get her money back, so that was another fight," Padruig continued.

"They did have a retail shop attached to the Mill, until it went through lawyers to retrieve her money. Family could go in for free kilts and so on, but not anymore. They had to sell the shop to pay back Helen about half of what they owed, then she killed herself. They still owe Grigor Og the money and Grigor owes Malcolm's Ma some money. Helen really made a mess of things once her Mither passed away and hated the only man who had ever really loved her, Grigor Og, poor lad. I am still sorry about that and ashamed, Grigor my friend. I am sorry," Padruig expressed emotively.

All of them who hadn't known the story were a little shocked to hear the details that Padruig would usually keep to himself.

"I am so sorry Padruig, that is a sad story. I do have faith in Grigor Og. He will do his best for those left with him, but I heard that after Helen died, the staff nearly all left except Hamish," said Zara. "He might have to consider selling the farm eventually, but hopefully not the old growth forest area where that Pict stone is located," she continued.

"How did you know about the Pict stone Zara?" asked Padruig.

"I wrote the book. It's in there Padruig, I'm sure we read that part already where Old Isobel used to sit in front of the stone when she was a lonely young bairn. Don't you remember that I read that part already?" she asked.

"Nae, but maybe you can read it again for me tonight. Will you do that if you are not too tired?" Padruig asked.

"I think my wife will be too tired tonight Padruig. It's been a long day. How about tomorrow night if it suits you both?" Grigor interjected, protecting his wife from any ill health or over excitement.

"My wife Isobel, is cooking for us all tonight, so hopefully we can all eat well when we get home after attending to the horses and have that nice coffee we bought and eat a few sweets with the bairns as well. Then off to bathe and bed for some of us," Alex said. "Tomorrow is another day," he added.

"Grigor, can I please ask for all of the family's opinions on both girls and boys baby names tomorrow night too?" Zara asked.

"Aye, nice idea darling," he said. "Are you still comfortable?" he asked.

"Nae, not really. It might be better if I pish first, then sit on your horse with you if you don't mind," Zara said. They all waited patiently while she pished behind a tree with Grigor holding up his plaid so no one could see his wife. He took her hand and gently led her to his horse while handing her horse's reins to Alex.

"Padruig, can you lift up my wife to me?" he asked.

He obliged, then they were all on their way to the Aird again.

Dinner was lovely and the twins had proudly cleaned up the house and John had worked hard all day. The coffee was beautiful, accompanied by the Turkish Delight sweets and the whole family was very tired and went to bed or bathed first. Zara had to bathe and Grigor helped her out of the tub and they were both ready to sleep.

Grigor was awoken by his wife screaming Padruig's name and Malcolm's name and some very scary incoherent fears, as she sat up in bed looking terrified. Padruig heard his name being called and came into their bedroom as Grigor was trying to calm his wife. It took some time to get clarity from her, but what she said made no sense to Grigor but did to Padruig. She said something like there were images of Padruig's face and then Malcolm's face then Padruig's then Malcolm's and so on without them being in the same room.

"Okay, Zara. You remember when you asked me to communicate with Malcolm about that lone wolf, so I did then he managed to communicate back with me after a few attempts to let us know that they had killed that wolf in Glengarry. That's all it's about. Malcolm and I can communicate now," Padruig said.

"They're not all dead. There are many more wolves here in the Aird. I saw a Mither wolf, a really big dark grey one, who was tired and had been running away from her husband wolf, I think. She had to rest and she had at least six wee puppies who wanted to suckle from her, so she lay down under a rock," which she drew for them as a landmark. "Then a huge wolf, maybe her husband came and stood up tall on that rock. He is really scary and mean. He was going to kill all of those baby wolves. Why would he kill those cute little puppies?" she cried and held onto her husband.

"He's here somewhere close by Grigor and we don't have bars for the windows. What about the horses? Do you think they're alright?" Zara asked.

"All the bairns Grigor, what if they go outside and find that big wolf and he kills them?" Zara was distressed.

Alex was woken up and thought the tea might be good to calm her down and made her some tea and came in.

"Come on Zara, have some tea so you'll feel better," he said.

"You have to stay calm to look after your own new bairn," he said.

"Thank you, Alex, you are right, but we need bars on the windows. There're at least six other wolves in the pack, maybe more," Zara said as she tried to calm down and the men took the conversation out of her room and sent Isobel in to relax her Mither. Padruig explained that Malcolm had told him all about Glengarry and the killing of that lone wolf and it was in the newspaper too. He told Padruig though that the wolf was a lone wolf, meaning he had been part of a pack, but had been kicked out. Malcolm wanted him to know that they could be here in the Aird but Padruig had dismissed the idea, for which he now apologised if they were actually here, according to Zara's bad dream.

"Are the folk in Glengarry already armed to track down a pack?" asked Alex.

"Aye, armed to the bloody teeth apparently. Gossip had started that because of their arms it was worried they were going to start another Rising," Padruig said.

"We need to do three things," stated Alex calmly. "Firstly, we tell the whole family here to take all precautions and close up every window and door and the bairns and women all stay inside. Secondly, you Padruig do what you do to contact Malcolm and ask him to arrange a wolf posse of armed farmers to track down all of these wolves. Thirdly, Grigor you get a tradesman from Inverness onto getting bars onto all of these windows and the verandas, as well as a locksmith to put bigger and better anti wolf apparatus for the house, the stables and the goat house. We four men can share in that cost if you all agree because it won't be cheap," he said. "What do you both say?" he asked.

"If the wolves are actually here, we could lose our whole herd of coos or goats, so I agree but in a different order," Grigor said. "Contact Malcolm first, I think to see if he can actually organise that group of farmers from Glengarry or if not, we are on our own," Grigor suggested.

"Do what you do Padruig, now!"

17. The Wolf Hunt

I said farewell to my son, Alex after we had all gone fishing the night before with Hugh Og, Hamish, Bruce and Kenneth, all having a night off to catch a few fish for all of the families after a busy season. Hamish was a bit awkward with me at first, so I just had to address it and tell him to come on over to us whenever he felt like it. There was no pressure to leave his job at Craskie and then he felt better. He mentioned that Grigor Og wasn't looking well these days as well. I was going to miss my big son, of whom I was so proud and that was more on my mind. He carried his culture with pride and was want-ing to work in our area near me. Invermoriston or Inverness hospitals were a possibility. I was waiting on a reply from Lord Simon Fraser to get him a good posting in our area, once his degree was completed in a short time.

Eating fish for dinner after catching them too, I stank like fish and needed a bath and then Cherry was happy to share the bed with me and she was my loving wife until Grandda appeared as a spectre in our bedroom.

"Malcolm and Cherry. Sorry to trouble you both, but it might be an emergency. You may have been right about there being a pack of wolves here in the Aird. We are not

equipped to deal with that many wolves. Zara thinks it might be the Alpha male, his female and maybe six others or more. She has drawn a landmark rock, so we could track the Alpha male who has killed the pups of his Alpha female, so that might explain why you had the lone wolf there. He might have been the father of those pups. We do not have enough men or weapons here to complete a task that big and dangerous. Is it a possibility that your Glengarry farmers, who are already armed, would be interested in coming here to the Aird to track them all down? We can vacate one bedroom or more for those men in this house, so long as they bring blankets of their own. Let me know tomorrow night," Grandda said.

"Okay Grandda, I'll ask the farmer who shot the lone wolf as well as my own security, who is very well armed. I'll let you know," I said.

And he was gone.

My wife had rolled over and sex was then off for the night. Cherry didn't like my dead Grandfather appearing in her bedroom at night.

"Cherry, they have an issue. The whole wolf pack is there," I said.

"They're already dead folk. Why does it matter to them?" she answered.

"You are not being very understanding. That's not like you. What's the matter?" I asked.

"You went out fishing with your friends and now you'll go out of your way for dead relatives in the Aird. How often do I go out? Just once," she replied.

"You know what Cherry, I never thought you to be a heartless person. You don't understand that there is life there. What about the horses? You don't care about them either? The goats and the coos that will be attacked by this pack of wolves. It's a serious matter Cherry for all of the farmers there, including Ivy's family in the Aird. If we choose to live on the land, we have to take all that goes with it," I said. I think we'd had our first disagreement and I rolled over too.

I looked up Old John MacDonnell, the wolf killer now as he was known in Glengarry, the next day.

After having already spoken to Kenneth over breakfast, I asked him to warn his wife's family and somehow get a message to

Ivy's brothers and let them know too, once we had it all sorted. Ivy's brothers had an awful reputation for drinking and brawling but they were also good hunters, as well as hating my brother for taking Ivy from them. Old John spoke with a slow gaelic drawl, typically a MacDonnell accent, apparently. He was keen to do the job and asked a lot of questions first about who lived in the house that I was referring to. I told him that women and their bairns, as well as old people and maybe only one man who could stay to defend the house.

"Who's that then?" Old John asked.

"That would be John Fraser, part owner of the property," I answered, hiding the identities of everyone else.

"Then lad, you need to get all the women, girls and bairns, as well as those old people out of there to a safe house in Glenmoriston," he said. "For many reasons. We will need more than one room and the men are not the types to be around the ladies. They can hunt and shoot and track, but no manners, if you know my meaning. If those folks are serious, then I can organise my MacDonnells, with their bad manners and no worries about the women folk. The only thing is, we will need is a male cook. Do you know one?" he asked.

"My cousin Alex can cook, but he would be leaving his new wife alone, but I can deal with that, I think," I said. "Those brothers of young Ivy, the mean beggars, we might need them too, being already in the Aird and armed as well as being good trackers, despite their foul manners. They sure can hunt. Leave Kenneth behind. They might accidentally kill him, if you get my meaning," I asked if he wanted a meeting and he said he would organise his MacDonnells, if I let Ivy's brothers know who can get other Frasers in on it too.

My responsibility was to get the whole family in the Aird to move that very day into Grigor Og's house in Glenmoriston hopefully, and give up the house in the Aird to a bunch of hunters whose language would make your ears burn, according to Mr MacDonnell. Hopefully by then, Ivy's brothers could be notified and motivate the other Frasers in the Aird with the map, drawn by Zara, which I had copied for Mr MacDonnell. Hamish was included, as was my own security, Duncan Mohr, with all of their weaponry and my farms were going to be managed by both Kenneth, Ivy, Bruce and Ma, who would move into my house with Cherry to keep her from fretting. Hugh Og was staying behind to care for all of the horses with the two stable hands and Meredith who was staying over in my house with Hugh too, to watch over the animals. Ma's main job was Cherry. I hadn't told Cherry yet that we were all leaving the following morning with the MacDonnells, to go to the Aird. Stopping only to occasionally drink or pish or eat what we had in our saddle bags.

The last person I approached was my cousin Alex.

"Cousin, how would you like to join in a hunt for a wolf pack up in the Aird? You'd be the cook for a lot of men. The family have had to move out of the house?" I said. "Siobhan can stay in my house with everyone else," I added. "Can your students run the place for a few nights in your absence?" I asked.

"Aye. Do I need to take the ingredients?" Alex asked.

"Aye, that would be bonny," I said. "Pack it all up then and meet us with the MacDonnells early tomorrow morning," I said. "Old John MacDonnell is in charge," I added.

Then I went home to quickly commune with Grandda with my office door locked. I filled him in and he said that Grigor was in Inverness organising locks and bars for the windows. As soon as he returned, they could all leave for Cannich, Glenmoriston, but most likely not until the next morning giving them time to pack. That way the tradesmen knew what they were doing too and could be paid, Grandda had said.

"Okay Grandda, well the man in charge is Old John MacDonnell, so it might be better not to have Alex there and I have quoted the only person present would be John Fraser, part owner of the property. I'll leave it to you to notify him not to mention all of you, even his wife Isobel," I added. "You are to stay in Grigor Og's house until the wolves are all dead, is that okay?" I said. "The other people that may arrive there too are Ivy's horrible brothers but good hunters, who can mobilise the Frasers too," I added.

Hugh Og had taken the boat the back way to the Aird and let the Fraser brothers know. They were not pleased to see someone from Glengarry, but keen to join in the hunt and were given the farm's location and where the Alpha wolf was last seen. Meredith was pleased to see her husband back home and uninvolved in the hunt, but he prowled my properties the whole night, she told me afterwards.

I had little time to pack my own saddle bags and to tell my wife that I was leaving the following morning, despite Bruce and Ma knowing already. I knew she would be unhappy, so I blurted it out with little delicacy. It wouldn't have made any difference anyhow, as she was firmly against the wolf hunt. I let her know that Bruce and Ma were moving in to look after her and Hugh and Meredith were staying too, but Duncan Mohr would be with me, as would Hamish.

"Why are you doing this Malcolm?" Cherry asked. "It's in the Aird, far from here. We can't just leave and go hunt wolves that you havn't even seen. What if they don't even exist and you all go there for nothing?" she asked.

"I know you are upset that I am leaving for a while, but it is a man's duty to do this to protect the whole community," I answered.

"Glengarry is our community, not the Aird. I disagree Malcolm," she said firmly, but I had to go, even though my wife was adamantly opposed to it. We left in the morning and it was an extremely large group of MacDonnells who were very serious, well armed and ready to go. Alex from Loch Garry was ready too and Siobhan had actually helped him put all of the food together. She was a bit proud of her husband I thought, unlike mine whom I couldn't quite understand on this matter.

The MacDonnells were hard to keep up with as they held a steady but fast pace and we didn't even stop for water, until we had passed Glenmoriston. My cousin Alex and I had been careful to maintain the Clan heirarchy with Old John MacDonnell as the leader of a serious looking group of tough men, some young, some older who glared at me on occasion. We stayed in the back of the pack of horses with Hamish and Duncan Mohr, riding fast onwards to the Aird. It wasn't until we had stopped to water the horses, as well as pish and have a drink ourselves, that Old John came to the rear of the men and said,

"Malcolm MacNachten, you are the only one here who actually knows this property, as well as the owner. I'll need you to ride up front with me now, until we get there. As I passed the MacDonnell men on their horses, they glared at me again, some just looked sideways at me while others looked positively hostile and when I reached the head of the group of the men, Old John MacDonnell said, "To my left lad," indicating I had to always ride on his left side and we rode off again at an incredible pace. I was learning a lot about the MacDonnells and it was an honor to be with these men. I was only nervous that Zara's dream may not have been exact and my mind was going over and over. 'What if we get there and there are no wolves?'

Then we arrived.

John Fraser was seen standing out the front of their house and we all burst across the wee burn and onto his property like a real force to be reckoned with. John in his polite way had been clearly told what to say and what not to say, more importantly and he shook Mr MacDonnell's hand introducing himself, as I introduced them. He indicated for their horses to be stabled in their stables and he invited Mr MacDonnell inside. Old John gave his horse to a young man who took mine as well and we entered. The house was empty of visible residents, at least that I could see. He told Old John that all the rooms were available to them except one, which was Zara's room, but he didn't say that he said,

"The lady of the house would prefer it if her room was not used." John had all the right polite language and there was coffee already brewing, as well as tea. When my cousin Alex came in, he got to work immediately and asked John Fraser where the fresh vegetables were after I had introduced him as my cousin Alex, who was the assigned cook. Alex also asked for a beast to be slaughtered immediately and butchered. John asked Old John if he could have assistance from one of his men and they got to work doing that, so that dinner would be cooked on time. All of the men drifted in, looking around curiously. They must have expected a bigger house or a somehow more expensively decorated one, I wasn't sure?

They chose where they were all going to sleep and they all checked out the entire immediate property, including the privies and what animals had been left behind. Zara's family had taken a milking nanny goat with them and the bairns must have each carried a chicken on their ponies and horses because there weren't many left of either the chickens or the goats. 'The geese seemed to be the same in number, but who could carry a goose on a horse to Glenmoriston?' I thought. The coos were mooching about watching on at all of the excitement. John Fraser told me that they had taken two coos with them as well, so they didn't eat all of Grigor Og's farm food.

Once Old John had sat down to drink his coffee, he asked where the rock in the picture was, drawn by myself. John explained exactly where that was, as he used to walk his coos through there, which he was no longer doing. He was trying to keep his coos closer to home now with the threat of the wolf pack. Old John seemed to like John well enough and asked about the other Frasers. John said that no-one except us had arrived yet, so he didn't know what was happening with those people. That was until we heard a ruckus from outside with many dogs barking and it may have been them, so Old John had his gun already out of it holster.

"MacDonnells!" he shouted. "Be prepared." All of them were armed and aiming their rifles and guns in the direction of the noise, so John Fraser went to the front door again.

"Gentlemen," he said. "I'm John Fraser, are you here to hunt the wolf pack?" he asked to around ten, very ugly, red headed and red bearded, mean looking men.

"Aye, we are, so long as Kenneth MacNachten isn't here. We are the Frasers, I'm George Fraser," their spokesman said. I presumed he was one of Ivy's brothers.

"Kenneth isn't here," said John. "Would you like to stable your horses with the MacDonnell's horses and come inside to meet the leader, Old John MacDonnell?" he asked.

The Fraser leader, George was accompanied by his bother, Colin inside and both Clan groups glared across at each other.

"I'm Alex," said my cousin, "I'm the cook, I need one of you to peel potatoes, so we can all eat tonight." One Fraser brother yelled to someone named Simon, "Come and peel potatoes!"

"You got coffee cook?" Fraser asked.

"Aye," said Alex and he gave him and his brother coffee and John told them which rooms were left available to sleep in, but once again Zara's room was unavailable. They were all satisfied enough that there was enough room for everyone and that food was cooking and obviously well organised by my cousin. They too were shown that same map, as well as the entire layout of the whole property and where there were caves, as well as other places that the wolves could hide.

It was too late in the day to start the hunt now, so it was decided how they would all hunt these animals and that the Frasers and the MacDonnells would separate coming in from different directions. Ivy's oldest brother George, was as Old John had said, "No place for a lady around them."

Thank goodness the guns were no longer pointed at each other and after food was being served up, starting with Old John MacDonnell, then George Fraser, then me. The focus shifted onto killing the wolves rather than each other and they had all found a place to bed for the night.

I was aware that this whole venture might be the end of my marriage and as I was looking thoughtful. Old John asked me "Trouble at home with the wife?"

I was surprised at the personal question and just how direct he was, but I did trust the old man and so I answered, "Aye, I do. Cherry didn't agree with my involvement at all in this and we had the first real disagreement in our marriage," I explained.

"Cherry is the Islander lass that came here with her two drunken Uncles, is that right?" he asked. "You should have married a MacDonnell woman, but its too late to say that now. I'll tell you what the gossip was when the three of them arrived. You would have been in Glenmoriston then. It was asked then, why would the loser Uncles send their familes to Edinburgh except the pretty lass, who could be an 'earner' for them? I know that sounds harsh, but those two men wanted to make money from her, was the general opinion, given that both of her parents were dead," Old John said.

"What do you mean an 'earner' for them?" I asked.

"We all thought that they were going to prostitute her, bit by bit, but along came Malcolm who married her. We all still thought they had something up their sleeves and you did help their fellow Islanders and we all benefited from that and all I can only say is that it was very charitable of you," Old John said.

"Mr MacDonnell, I think this has gone too far. It is true that her Uncles were drunkards and nearly killed me one night, so I will never defend them, but as for Cherry becoming a scarlet woman is unacceptable," I said, feeling terribly shocked at the mere suggestion.

"Only I would be brave enough to tell you lad, so you should thank me for what everyone thought," he said not feeling offended, but wanting me to know. "Does she still keep in touch with them while undermining you and ask yourself if what I am saying is true?" he said in the most disturbing way.

It was a horrible enough thought that she could have been a scarlet woman, but cooking up something else from the colonies was more terrifying than facing the Alpha wolf.

"If she wants to leave me, why not just leave, without undermining what I'm doing? That makes no sense," I said.

"She has to justify it to herself lad and I'm not saying she's leaving you, I hope not, you're a good lad, the best in fact, but if you ever need an introduction, I have a niece whose husband died recently and she would be a good wife to you. She can still have bairns, pretty in a MacDonnell way, dark hair, nice manners and a lovely and respectful girl. That's what I like. She's respectful," Mr MacDonnell said.

"Thankyou Mr MacDonnell, if Cherry leaves me, my heart would be too broken to please such a nice lass," I said with a sad heart and decided it was time to sleep.

If I had thought that the conversation with Mr MacDonnell over Cherry was more terrifying than facing the Alpha wolf, I was wrong when exactly that happened, as we all were all tracking the path of the wolves, finding plenty of tracks and evidence of their very real existance. We didn't expect them to be so close to the house and from that rock, but the

MacDonnells and I came face to face with the entire pack of wolves numbering seven, including the huge Alpha male. There was another injured female as well, so in total it was eight and we hunters numbered fifteen, some inexperienced who had never seen a wolf before, and others like Old John who was as calm as could be, shot the Alpha immediately sending the pack into a frenzy before the Beta could take charge. We had to take aim and fire as best we could, so I know I got one at least, I saw many others fall, but then the angry injured female came at us unexpectedly, nearly getting one of the young men who froze in fear and wet himself, poor lad. The MacDonnells were great shots and she went down.

That left a few wolves who ran off in the direction of the Frasers and we hoped that they would get them, while we made sure the ones we had, were actually dead.

"Does anyone draw?" I asked.

"I do," answered Donald.

"Draw the scene son getting the number of wolves correct as well as their location and write down who shot them," I said.

"You're quite the leader there Malcolm MacNachten and not a bad shot either," Old John said. "Well done lad," he said.

"Well done you too getting that huge bloody Alpha. I didn't know wolves grew that big," I said. "Is it too risky to follow them and risk being shot by the Frasers?" I asked.

"Aye, it is. Let's go back to the house and leave Donald to his drawing, so long as he has a rifle with him," he said.

"What have they been eating to get that big?" I asked.

"Our coos will make them big if they have no other competition and it looks like they've been here a while," Old John said.

"With only three wolves going their way, the Frasers should be able to deal with that, shouldn't they?" I asked.

"Hope so lad," he said calmly. I'm looking forward to my coffee and that cook you brought with you, young Alex. Well done, he's great. Loved that parritch we had this morning and the stew last night. He's something else," Old John said.

"His new wife, Siobhan was very supportive of him coming and helped him pack up enough ingredients, so he would love it if you told him that," I said. We didn't all hurry back to the house, as we all talked over what each other thought and what wolf each of them had shot, when the Frasers' dogs were seen whimpering back to the house, most of them injured and bloodied.

It didn't look good for their dogs at least, who then lay down licking their wounds.

"This doesn't look good, should we ride the horses down there?" I asked.

"Nae, coffee first," he answered casually. Alex was waiting for the first of the hunters to return, God bless him and he had cooked bread and cakes as well as another stew for lunch. I waived to my smiling cousin, who was very pleased to see me.

"How did it go Malcolm?" Alex asked.

"Better ask Mr MacDonnell, the famous wolf killer," I answered.

"You two are cousins, right?" Old John said. "Nice family, you are both lucky to have each other and I'm glad we have you in Glengarry, Mr Supercook," he answered.

"I killed the Alpha, Malcolm here killed two others, a few got away but we left them to the Frasers whose dogs don't look too well," he said too sarcastically.

"Coffee time Mr Supercook," he demanded.

"Mr MacDonnell, I have cooked you cake too," Alex said proudly and he served us all up coffee and cake. He was having his best time being included in the hunting party, however the cunning Old John went hunting often, so he had Alex on his mind for future trips, I thought. The last of the hunters came in, including Hamish and Duncan Mohr.

"You were lucky Malcolm," exclaimed Duncan Mohr.

"You got two. You've been hiding your skills. There was I thinking I had superior skills on the farm and I bow down to you as well as you sir, Mr MacDonnell, who shot the Alpha. Which one was the Beta do you think?" he asked.

"The Beta got away I think but he wasn't exactly the Beta, that's why I shot the Alpha quickly before he could be appointed," Old John explained.

The Frasers eventually came in two by two, reporting that they were attacked by three wolves and the two brothers, Colin and George Fraser had to be taken to the Beauly Firth to go by boat to Inverness, seeking medical treatment. They said they would take their belongings home with them now.

"Did you shoot the rest of them?" Old John asked.

"Oh, aye got all three, but ended up with injured dogs, horses and men, what about you lot then?" Fraser asked.

"Mr MacDonnell shot the Alpha male," said Alex proudly. "Coffee gentlemen?" Alex asked. "Nae lad, we'll be off to take the dogs home and our stuff. So, that's the whole pack then, is it?" he asked.

"Aye if you got three, then sounds like it. Was one male bigger than the others?" Old John asked.

"Aye, a lot bigger, the Beta you think?" he asked.

"Well thank you to all of you for coming up here from Glengarry. Mighty nice of you. Dangerous animals for sure," he said as he left looking tired.

We were all going to eat here again and sleep that night in Zara's house and then leave in the morning. I was going to go to Glengarry, via Craskie Farm, but we passed the family unexpectedly on their way back home, who carefully stood off to the side of the road hiding their faces, except for the bairns. Hamish was due to drop in to Craskie Farm any way, so I left him to it and kept following the fast-paced MacDonnells, who only stopped once to water the horses and the usual drink of water and pish, if needed which most of them did. No one made a remark about the people they had past and didn't guess it was the family from the Aird. I had surrupticiously held eight fingers to my Grandda, hoping that he would understand that we had killed eight wolves, as we cantered past them without any signs of recognition shown to them.

It was late at night when I finally arrived in Glengarry completely exhausted, as was my horse. Dougal, one of the grooms, was sleeping in the stable waiting for me, so he jumped up to take my poor tired horse.

"I'll take care of him, don't worry Malcolm. Did you get them?" he asked.

"Aye, our group got five and the Frasers got three, so we think that's the lot of them. How is everything here?" I asked.

"All good on the farm Malcolm. Not sure about the women folk. There may have been a wee arguement in your house between your Ma and your wife, so good luck," he warned.

Approaching my home, my legs felt so heavy and tired. I really couldn't face an angry wife, so I decided to enter quietly and sleep on the couch with a blanket to avoid the inevitable. Anyway, I had two days of hunting stink on me, so I had to bathe but it was going to be in the morning. I slept so well, calm even. Not like the usual stress I felt, so I only awoke when I heard Meredith preparing breakfast.

"Can you put on water to boil for me too Meredith? I must stink to high heaven," I asked.

"I am pleased to see you home safely Malcolm. You might want to know that Cherry and your Ma had words while you were away, but Ma won the argument. I'll get your bath ready before anything else. I'm proud of you, no matter what anyone says," she said.

I locked the door on the bathing room and soaked myself to relax more than anything, but I washed my filthy mop of hair that was getting long for those kinds of jobs and scrubbed my filthy feet. It felt great to smell nice again and to have a clean face felt like a luxury. I had omitted to take clean clothes into the bathing room, when I heard my daughter Islay calling to me, "Da, welcome home. I missed you so much. I've left clean clothes just outside the door for you," she said.

"Thank you, Islay. You are precious to me," I said, as I got out of the bath and was drying myself, there were increased sounds of the family all up and about. I opened the door quickly and grabbed my clean clothes and dressed before I would see Cherry. That MacDonnell lady did enter my mind and I wondered what it would be like with someone else, but quickly put it aside.

I wasn't expecting a barrage of hugs and kisses from the family, but it came from every direction. Even Hugh Og put his hand on my shoulder saying, "I am so pleased you are home safe. It's already in the papers about Ivy's brothers being in hospital in Inverness after the attack on them with their group only killing three of the pack. They gave all the credit of the organisation to Old John MacDonnell who tracked and killed the Alpha, but the paper was yet to speak to him," he said.

"The men's injuries were not life threatening but one of their dogs had to be put down. Two horses were also injured by the viciousness of the small group of disorganised wolves was thought to be because they had lost their leader. The horses were tended to by veterinarians in Inverness who offered their services for free, given the service that was provided to the community," Hugh added.

Poor Ivy was looking pale and came to me crying and thanked me. "You are so brave Malcolm," she said as she hugged me.

"You probably saved my brothers' lives," she went on.

"I doubt it Ivy, your brothers are very competent hunters and as tough as boots, but they got the Beta wolf on the run we think," I said.

The newspaper men were at Old John MacDonnell's place, according to Duncan Mohr who was in the house about to eat breakfast with us too. He said they were getting the details from him and the drawing by young Donald MacDonald which included me in the picture with Old John, so I left it all up to him and hoped they weren't coming here too. Ma and Bruce had taken on the new inclusive policy which I much preferred with Duncan there.

"Did Hamish get home last night?" I asked.

"I left him at Craskie Farm," I said.

"He stayed on at Craskie with Grigor Og and will be home earlier today instead, according to Cora," Hugh said

"I'm hungry Meredith, what's for brekky today?" I asked cheering up a bit but still not seeing my wife.

"Hello Malcolm," Cherry said as she came in with her head down.

"I'm pleased to see you in one piece compared to Ivy's brothers. I'm so sorry Ivy," she said. "Are you visiting your brothers in hospital?" she asked.

"Nae, not until they accept my husband," she answered. Kenneth was already on the verge of crying upon seeing me and when he heard his wife say that he couldn't hold back his tears and he first hugged her then he came and hugged me.

"Malcolm, I was so worried about you, I could hardly sleep. Were you attacked at all?" Kenneth asked.

"Just the once when the Alpha female decided to have a go at a few of us, especially the youngest of our group, Donald who wet himself, poor thing," I replied.

"One of the MacDonnells shot her and she dropped dead," I said ravenously eating. I was so hungry. Islay wasn't accustomed to hearing that kind of talk, so Ma asked me to tone it down a bit for her over breakfast until she had gone to do her work with the goats.

18. The Break-Up

"I heard there was a stramash here while I was away. What was that all about Cherry?" I asked, looking directly at her.

"It's all sorted out now Malcolm. Your Ma and I discussed an issue that we disagreed upon, that's all," she said.

"So, what was it that you ladies both disagreed upon, out of curiosity?" I asked.

Both Bruce and Ma had their mouths wide open at how casual Cherry had been to cover it up and Islay said she was ready for work, as did Angus and they both left. Hugh was very curious to hear what Cherry had to say and Meredith served him up a huge breakfast to keep him there longer and poured extra coffees into Bruce, Kenneth, Ivy and Ma's cups, as well as Duncan and even offered Duncan more breakfast and he agreed. So, they were all clearly going to stay a while to hear this out.

"All I said to Ma was that I disagreed with you leaving me and going to the Aird to hunt wolves that might not exist, but I see now in the newspaper that they did exist, so Ma was right all along and so were you Malcolm," she said. "Ma told me that I had to have more faith in you and what your choices were and to support you, even if I disagreed because that was my job as a wife, but I disagreed about that, so that's when we got argumentative," she said.

"Let me be clear here Malcolm," Ma said. "I told Cherry that as your wife, she had to be supportive as it was her role with such a hard job that you have, caring for so many people and not even expecting her to cook your breakfast. I cook my husband's breakfast and so does Ivy, so I asked her why she didn't now that she wasn't with child anymore," Ma said. "Additionally, I told her that her husband was special by going out of his way to save the lives of people and their livestock in the Highlands, wherever they lived, be it Glengarry or the Aird. I said that I was proud of you, so why wasn't she?" Ma added. "I am sorry son if I became emotional, but it made me angry that she wasn't supporting you when wee Siobhan was even supporting your cousin Alex as the cook, who was thrilled to go and help," Ma said. "Duncan's wife supported him as did Hamish's wife Cora, so Cherry was the only wife being unsupportive. I couldn't understand it and I worried that it might put your life in danger without her support," Ma added.

I put my arms around Ma and told her how many of us there were and perhaps meeting Old John would give her confidence. "The MacDonnells were a well-oiled machine and I was privileged to have been a part of the way that they conducted themselves and Old John MacDonnell was inclusive of me the whole time, even though I am not one of them, so with him I was safe," I said to make Ma feel better. "However, it was obvious even to them that I had a problem at home and that is embarrassing if the whole community here are talking about our marriage in a derogatory manner. And they have," I said. Then turning to Cherry, "Did you know what the gossip was here in Glengarry before we were married, about you and your Uncle's intentions?" I asked.

She looked at me blankly for a moment and then she said, "What are you talking about?"

"It was rumoured here in Glengarry that your Uncle's sent their families away to Edinburgh but not you, so that you could become an 'earner' for them and I am not saying that you were part of that plan, but it worries me that you still keep in touch with them, knowing that they were going to introduce you to prostititution, unless I had married you," I said. "Cherry be honest now. Did you know that they were going to introduce you into prostitution or were you completely innocent?" I asked.

"Are you serious about what you are asking me?" she asked. "You think now that because we have had a disagreement over wolves that suddenly I was training to be a prostitute?" she said. "Why did you marry me then if you thought so little of me and if that was what they were planning, I had no knowledge of it and wouldn't cooperate with them if it had been put to me," she retorted.

"I am a Mither of four children, I have my faults, I know and I disagreed with the wolf thing, but to suggest that, is extreme Malcolm and if that is what you men all talk about, then I am glad I disapproved. You like Mr MacDonnell, but I don't like him because he has called me a scarlet woman," she said.

"Then stop writing to your Uncles in the colonies Cherry. As your husband, I insist that you cease any further communication with them, because it is giving me a bad name," I demanded.

"They have invited me to the colonies. What will I say then to that Malcolm?" she asked.

"When was that and where is that letter? I wish to see it now, immediately!" I demanded.

"Ma, go with Cherry to collect that letter please," I asked. They both came back with the letter in hand and Kenneth, Hugh and I read it.

"This was one month ago Cherry and you just posted them a letter recently. What was your reply to your Uncles?" I asked, passing on the letter to Duncan to read too.

"I just chatted about the harvest and so on, but they had offered to pay my fare to go to New Holland. I thought it was generous of them," she said.

"You are married Cherry. You just said it yourself. You are a Mither. Why would you even consider leaving your husband? I have never mistreated you and I just bought you a new dress last week. Those places in the colonies are rough places where men do terrible things to women and there's venereal diseases there too, I have read that in the newspaper. I don't understand why you would disapprove of me going to track down wolves, when you were planning to leave me," I said.

"Not exactly leave you Malcolm, just visit my relatives in New Holland," Cherry said.

"Are your Uncles paying your return fare as well?" I asked, "And when is this supposed to happen?"

Both Ma and Bruce were finding it hard to control their anger and even Meredith was banging things in the kitchen a little louder than usual. Bruce stood up and said,

"Lassie, you will never find a better man than Malcolm MacNachten, for as long as you walk on this earth. If you leave him, there will never be an equivalent and maybe worse. You will find yourself in deep trouble over there, with no one to help you, with no money, no family, no friends. You are crazy to entertain the idea. You have been secretive all this time over this matter without asking your husband's permission or his opinion or that it had even been revealed. He only found out because of the MacDonnells and that's the reason you didn't want him getting too close to learning what was going on with joining them in the Aird. You are a little lying schemer," said Bruce. "Your Uncles are not paying your return fare, are they?" Bruce asked.

"Nae, they said I could earn money over there," Cherry answered.

"Doing what? Prostitution, Cherry, face it. Malcolm is right, they are grooming you to work for them as a scarlet woman, even though you are too fat in my opinion," Bruce said nastily. "Oh my God Malcolm, I am so sorry son, but I have to go before I say something that I will regret, to your wife," Bruce said and left and indicated for Ma to follow him too.

Ivy looked too shocked to speak, so she and Kenneth both left too giving their apologies to me.

Hugh Og then spoke up saying,

"I know what your Grandda would have done to Isobel and it sounds to me like your wife might need the strap, Malcolm. I am sorry my friend, but you deserve better than this. Cherry will not find anyone better than you on God's earth and this is a tragedy really. If there is anything me and Meredith can do, please just ask. If Cherry clears off, Meredith will still look after you, no worries there and I'll look after your son in law, there's bound to be fall out on this matter. All those Islanders might lose their jobs for a start," Hugh said.

"Did you never love me then Cherry?" I asked needing to know.

"Aye, I did Malcolm, but it is boring here and I don't have my own money. My Uncles said I would have my own money there," Cherry said.

"How long have you been planning to leave me then?" I asked.

"About a month," she answered.

"Have you thought how this will affect your son at Medical School or Islay in this community? I've been in conversation with Lord Simon Fraser to get Alex a good position and now if it known his Mither is off to the colonies by choice to be a scarlet woman, how will it effect his chances at a good job after all that I have spent on him to get a good job? Why would you do this to your own children? Poor Islay. What will Angus' parents say? Will they want him to leave her if you have that reputation? And what Mither can just leave her young twins? They are barely two years old without a Mither," I said.

I choked back tears of my twins growing up without a Mither and the reality of what Old John had said, finally sunk in. I was the only one who didn't know this about my wife in Glengarry.

"Were you already a prostitute when I met you Cherry?" I asked.

"My Uncles said if I was going to start costing them here, they would have to do something to earn money from me somehow and there was only one night when an old man, whose wife had died, wanted company and so he paid my Uncles to keep him company," Cherry said. "I'm sorry Malcolm, I should have told you, but then you wouldn't have married me. I thought marrying you was wonderful. I did love you but after so much farming and money going into the bairns or the farm, I was getting a bit unhappy is all, so I told my Uncles in a letter who suggested I go there," she said.

"Cherry, you are not as young as you once were and you have gained weight, as Bruce said, so even scarlet women are usually younger and slimmer, aren't they?" I asked.

"I admit I used to be prettier and slimmer, but they said it doesn't matter there and I'll get rich," she said.

"So, you do admit then that your plan was to go to New Holland to be a scarlet woman working for your Uncles?" I asked.

"Aye, but I want to divorce before I leave," she said. "Will you allow a divorce?" she asked calmy.

"Aye, you can divorce me and I will sign the papers before you leave, but you cannot have the twins or any money or property from me," I said, finally getting my brain to work. "Will you get a lawyer then or do you want me to organise the lawyer to end our marriage? You will get nothing from me Cherry, you know that. There is no sense in what you are doing," I added. "Was that old man who you kept company with, Old John MacDonnell, by any chance, hence your fanatic opposition to me going with him?" I asked.

"He was a MacDonnell and old, but I can't be sure, unless his wife also died around that time?" she answered.

"She did, so that answers that question. Was it sex you had with him or just company?" I asked. "He wanted sex," she said.

"So, all of the MacDonnells must have thought I was the biggest idiot that ever came to Glengarry," I said then realising my situation.

I was then unable to stop the tears and Duncan came over to me and ushered me outside for a while.

"Let's take a walk Malcolm," he said and we walked off some of the anger and disbelief and horror at my whole marriage being a sham.

"She was a scarlet woman before I married her Duncan," I said and leant against one of my fence posts crying. That was bad timing because reporters from the newspaper arrived. They wanted to know if I was one of the wolf killers but could also see that it was bad timing. I answered that I killed two with

Old John MacDonnell who was the leader. I then asked them to leave as I had work to do.

"Duncan, can you come with me to Old John's place and see if he's not too busy to talk to me?" I asked. Duncan told Ma and Hugh where we were going, then we left.

Old John's relatives recognised me from the hunt and I was allowed in to see Old John. He invited me to be seated in his comfortable office with Duncan.

"What can I do for you young Malcolm, the newspaper men have already been and gone," he said.

"I have a problem at home, of that you are aware that has grown somewhat in size and she now wants to go to the colonies to join her Uncles and also wants a divorce. My question to you is, were you the old man who she slept with after your wife's passing for money paid to the Uncles?" I asked.

"That was me, before she was your wife lad and I had no idea that you had any intention to marry the lass. If I had known, then I wouldn't have been there. I wanted you to know because the post office lady, my sister-in-law, told me there were letters going to New Holland and back again to Cherry from those same two men and so I had a responsibility to tell you that something was up," he answered.

"This is the name of the lass who wants to marry you and knows the whole story. A widow. This separate list are the women who have come in today wanting to marry the 'heroic Malcolm MacNachten', handsome property owner and the like. All MacDonnells. The sums of money beside each name are what each family has as a dowery for their lass. Some are widowed, some single, with a whole range of ages which my secretary has written down for you. So as soon as you have that divorce, the better, because you need a Mither for the twins, which they all know about and have agreed to raise," he said in a matter-of-fact way.

"You are not the first man to be stung Malcolm and you won't be the last. Here's the name of my lawyer to ensure your wife gets nothing, including the twins or the farm or any support money," he said in the most disturbingly matter of fact way. "I'm not a cryer, personally but I'd pick you for one, if you let it get to you, so my advice is keeping your friends like Duncan, Hamish and Hugh close, so you are never alone. Now deal with the business. See the lawyer and my sister-in-law is going to capture any other letters from those men and we'll follow the beggers' plans. If they ever step foot back in Glengarry, they're dead men. Don't you worry young fella, you'll have a good woman who can still have bairns. My recommendation is the one I mentioned who comes with the money. Now I have to do some farm work," Old John said.

We were ushered out then as I was riding my horse home, I suggested to Duncan we go to Invermoriston instead for a nice tea break, so we did and bought sandwiches and coffee. I learned more about the MacDonnells over tea and coffee, at least this branch. Duncan was hesitant at first, but finally he spoke up and advised me against using any lawyer representing Old John and I'd be wise to go to my own family's lawyer instead. When asked why he didn't want to get himself in a spot with them but only to say that Killian MacDonnell was hated for passing the land onto us in the first place and Old John would do anything to make my farm MacDonnell land again whether by marrying me to a MacDonnell or stitching me up somehow with his lawyer, so they could get my property ultimately.

"Those men are very loyal to him," he said. "Do you know why?" he asked.

"Nae," I answered. "Many of them are his bastard sons and I have a niggling feeling that we should be talking to that old midwife before she dies on us, to see if Cherry got pregnant to Old John too. Do you want to pay Ruth Beaton a visit?" he asked.

I was sure Ruth was dead, but she was still in her old cottage, only now she was nearly blind and very old.

"Malcolm MacNachten," she said without my announcing myself.

"Who is your friend?" Ruth asked.

"Hello Ruth, this is Duncan, my security guard," I answered. She invited us in shuffling past her magazines and books and her cat.

"Sit down, it's not everyday I get two handsome visitors," she said smiling with many missing teeth.

"I only have tea, will that do?" Ruth asked.

"Ruth we just had coffee, so I am fine. Duncan might want tea, do you?" I asked him.

"I'll have tea Ruth, no milk, one sugar," he ordered.

Once we were all comfortable at the table, I began to tell her the story and she admitted to knowing about Cherry before I married her but she thought I must have known, so didn't bring it up, naturally.

"What do you mean exactly Ruth?" I asked. "What did you know because she is leaving me," I added.

"I'm sorry to hear that son, really. I first met your wife when her Uncles called me in to terminate a pregnancy she had from a paid arrangement. You knew about the prostitution, I hope? It had been her first time in a paid arrangement organised by the Uncles and she was upset, as you can imagine, to then find herself with child. They asked me to terminate it which I did and she suffered a lot of pain and blood loss. She never wanted any more children she had said, but they all do," Ruth said.

"The father of the unborn, unfortunately was Old John MacDonnell, the one who killed that lone wolf recently. He keeps his bastards, all of them, like a private wee army," she added.

"He wasn't pleased when he found out, but there was nothing he could do about it," Ruth said. "Then you married her lad, so I didn't think I'd see her again but I did see her three more times. All terminations. Your bairns Malcolm. I asked her why when she was married and she said she had just had enough of raising children," she said.

"Then I was with my dear old Hugh Mohr, my darling man, for the last days of his life, and she came to me again for the same reason, to terminate your twins it was. It was Hugh, who upon hearing this, put his foot down and said, 'there was no way that she was killing Malcolm's bairns.' Those were his words," she said.

"So, I sent her home to have them and she did," Ruth said.

I was struggling to maintain a semblance of dignity.

"Ruth, I am going to divorce her. Can you please put it in writing to a Court of Law that Cherry MacNachten, a married woman of Cherry Farms, Glengarry, approached you to have the twins terminated and that you refused her this service?" I asked.

"Do you want me to add that she was also a lady of the night, lad?" she asked.

"Nae, just that, so she doesn't get the twins if she tries," I added. Awkwardly, she wrote down the details, with shaking hands-on paper and she even included the exact date when she was approached, where and who was present, even though he was now deceased. I left with my first piece of evidence against my wife of more than twenty years. I was stunned thinking that she had killed three of my bairns, who I had wanted so much and she was going to kill my precious twins. 'It couldn't get worse than this surely?' I hoped. I arranged to see Aonghus the next day saying it was an emergency.

I thanked Duncan profusely and gave him a pay rise. It was then that I remembered Zara and how I should contact them soon.

19. *Home and Wolf Free*

Zara walked into her home expecting a frightful mess, but surprisingly the kitchen at least was spotless. Isobel noticed the kitchen and all of the pots and pans being so clean.

"Ma, the kitchen is cleaner than we left it," Isobel said.

"Lucky, we took all of our Turkish coffee and sweets or there'd be none left, I warrant," said Padruig. One of the twins came running from their bedrooms saying, "Ma theres a dirty chamber pot in our room. Its full of pish," she said.

Fatma was told to get Ali to empty it for her and wash the chamber pot outside. Zara's room was still locked and undisturbed for which she was grateful. There was a note on the kitchen table that Grigor Mohr picked up.

"It's a note from a John MacDonnell who said that eight wolves were disposed of and inside the wee purse was a thanks to us for putting them all up," he said.

"How much darling?" Zara asked.

"It's lots of coins love. Fatma, you count it," Grigor said, which she did and it amounted to ten pounds and seven shillings.

"That's bonny," he exclaimed. "That will help towards those bars and locks that we had to outlay," Grigor said. It was divided up between the four men who had paid for the locks and bars. "That was nice of them darling," Zara said.

"Well, what is it, Malcolm? Or are you showing off now you that you can do this stuff?" Grandda asked when I contacted him that night. The office door was securely locked.

"Not funny Grandda. Nae, just checking in that you all arrived home and all is well. Then I do have other news," I said. "Well, there's no wolves here if that's what you mean. I saw you in the paper. You're famous now lad. Well, done could have done with you in The Rising," he answered.

"My wife Cherry is leaving me to become a prostitute in New Holland, I'm divorcing her, she had three of my unborn bairns terminated by Ruth Beaton, tried to get the twins terminated too but Hugh Mohr disallowed it, Old John MacDonnell has an army of his bastards and she was with child to him first, which explained her reason for not wanting me to go with him in case I found out she had been a prostitute before I married her. She's bored, hates farming, won't cook my breakfast, so she asked for a divorce and it just gets worse every minute of every day that I found out things that I never knew Grandda. I am upset, sorry. That Old John gave me a list of MacDonnell women to marry, recommending one who it turns out was his concubine for years with his bairns, not a widow at all and he is after my land, so I'm seeing Aonghus about the divorce tomorrow. What do you suggest I do?"

"Christ, Malcolm, I thought I had it bad with Isobel and Hugh, but sounds like you've even topped me. Go and see Grigor Og and take him with you as well as Kenneth, to see Aonghus in Inverness but keep him on track or he deviates a lot to his own woes. Get Grigor Og to divide up Craskie Farm into two, leaving only the old growth forest belonging to him but not to be farmed. The remainder of Craskie and Grant Farms have him draw up in your name only in his Will in case you lose the farm in Glengarry. He moves to that house by the loch if you do lose it. Fight for the divorce with Ruth's testimony, so you don't lose the twins and find a wife but not a MacDonnell wife for obvious reasons. Change the name of your farms to MacNachten Farms, immediately. Legalise the position of the Art Gallery on the property to be owned by your brother Kenneth and the land on which it sits, as well as his house in his name only and legalise your Ma and Bruce's house too on the same property in their names.

This division on the properties will deter Old John. Legalise the business name of your goats in your daughter's name, "Islay Goats" or something like that. If Hugh Og is keeping the team there permanently, legalise the name of your stables, not the team itself, in both of your names like MacNachten and

Chisholm Stables. Then marry but chose carefully. Zara and all of us will look out for you on that front. Let me know tomorrow how you go with that little shite Aonghus. Good Luck Malcolm."

And he was gone.

I had written it all down and I was ready to go to war it felt. I was going to leave Duncan at home to watch every move that Cherry made, while I was gone.

"Uncle Padruig, who are you talking to?" asked Ali.

"Does it matter son?" Padruig asked.

"Where's your Mither and Father?" he asked.

"Outside in the shed, but it's okay they're not doing it, Hector checked already," Ali answered. Padruig went outside to seek both Grigor Mohr as well as Zara for an opinion on Malcolm's issues. He asked both of them if his advice was correct as he was very worried about his Grandson.

"Malcolm is such a good man," Zara said. "I am shocked, why would she contemplate a terrible sea journey like that? It would take about eleven months with terrible food like hard tack biscuits and depending on the route they take, may not even make a stop for fresh food unless they go via South Africa. If they went to that country through the roaring forties, she might be shipwrecked on that western coast and never even make it to her Uncles in the colony of New South Wales," Zara said.

"A woman alone on one of those ships is unthinkable and ill advised by choice," she added. "She can't have any understanding of that long ship journey and what onboard shiplife is like, let alone what that colony was like in its early days there," she said.

"You are right Zara. Leith to Quebec was bad enough and from New York when I was finally able to get a ship back, I was as sick as a dog. Had the shits the whole way, as well as lice. Fun journey. I'm a Highlander and I barely made it on a shorter journey, so my guess is she doesn't make it there," Padruig said. "A lot of men died on my ship. Some just jumped off the side out of despair," he said. "But she still wants a divorce anyhow and he's going in to see Aonghus. My worry is if he loses the twins or if he loses the properties to the MacDonnells if he marries a MacDonnell," Padruig said.

"Grigor and I don't know any young available ladies, do we?" she asked.

"I might," Grigor said.

"Who do you know Grigor?" Zara asked looking worried about her husband.

"A MacGregor woman served me in Inverness the other day. She told me that she was looking for a good man for her daughter," Grigor Mohr said and Zara decided to walk back inside. She became upset that her husband was being approached by another MacGregor woman and being with child felt unattractive and wanted to cry. Grigor came in to reassure her that it was nothing to do with him and he had only been there for less than fifteen minutes.

"But do you still find me attractive Grigor?" she asked and cried on his shoulder.

"Zara, I am a one-woman man and you are it my darling forever and you are gorgeous," he said smiling at her.

"I just wanted to help Malcolm, is that okay?" he asked. Grigor Mohr gave the business address to Padruig with details spoken quietly for Malcolm, but not to give her their address in the Aird, only Malcolm's Farm.

Padruig apologised for not being sensitive to that issue, but it was understood that Zara was always like this when she was with child and was particularly touchy where her husband was concerned. Zara couldn't live without her husband, she felt. Being with child did make her possessive of him and she always wanted to know where he was. Padruig had to be careful talking about this topic. He hadn't experienced a woman who had really needed him and was seeing it first hand between Zara and Grigor Mohr for the first time in his life and it was nice that such love still existed.

For days after that, Zara repeatedly asked, "Where's Grigor?" and sometimes even Hector would take her to where he was tending the coos or birthing a calf or a goat, but on the day that he was cutting a goat's throat for dinner with blood spurting everwhere, she vomitted. She stopped pursuing him then around the farm but was constantly asking him how long he would be and where he would be. He patiently fell in line telling her all the details she needed. She was approaching eight months in her pregnancy and was carrying high and heavy and did as much around the house that she could manage. The new bairn was not going to be small and her midwife was due there soon. Everything was ready for their new bairn. Then Zara's waters broke.

"Grigor, my waters have broken," she said sounding a bit panicked.

The midwife's room was prepared for her and her husband but only just on time. Zara had asked Grigor and Isobel to stay inside with her sensing something. Alex decided to stay close also while Padruig watched on with concern. He knew she was going to have the bairn any minute. Hector was outside to watch out for the Midwife's wee cart as it arrived, which it did and he ushered them into the stables. He indicated to the Midwife that she was needed right away and her husband watched where the lad was stabling his pony and depositing his harness. The stables were locked up securely and he was satisfied that his pony was fed and securely in place and decided that the confident young lad named Hector, knew his horses and was obviously trusted around the property.

"I'm Hector," he had said to her husband.

"I'm Frederick Ross, the Midwife's husband," said Mr Ross. As Hector entered the house with Mr Ross, he was faced with Zara's door closed again and both Padruig and Alex looking questionally at him.

"This is Frederick Ross, the Midwife's husband," Hector said and he took him to the room that he would share with his wife for the night, which had been nicely prepared except for the chamber pot, which Ali remembered to rush in at that moment.

"Sorry, I forgot to bring back the chamber pot. It's been washed clean," Ali said.

At the dining table, Mr Ross was invited to drink tea because Zara wasn't there to make coffee, which he accepted. Padruig and Alex introduced themselves and reminded him that they hoped his wife understood that we did it the old way where the bairn was caught by the Midwife with them assisting, when Grigor Mohr got tired.

"I'll tell my wife if she doesn't know or she'll cut her," Mr Ross said.

"Lillian, they do it the old way love and the friends here assist. Alex and Padruig," he said.

"It's okay love, I've just been told," she answered as the obvious sounds of labour began.

The two men sat staring at her door anxiously with every agonising scream, not noticing the rest of the family and whether they were worried, but Hector was as he hadn't remembered Causantin's birth.

"Uncle Alex, is Ma going to die?" Hector asked.

Then Fatma began to cry. "Be quiet Fatma," barked her oldest sister Isobel.

"As for you Hector, if you upset her again, I'll box your ears," Isobel threatened.

"Watch out Hector, if Isobel is anything like your Mither, she can sure throw a right slap or punch," said Uncle Alex.

"Nae, she's not going to die lass. Who would we have to make the coffee if your Ma died?" he said, but it didn't help much as Fatma blubbed saying she would help to make the coffee.

"What lovely children you all have," said Mr Ross.

"Who belongs to who if I may ask?" he asked.

"Isobel, Ali, Fatma, me and Causantin and this new one coming are all Ma's," answered Hector. "Those two are Isobel's and John's and Uncle Alex. Andrew is the oldest and Donald is the youngest. Five lads in all and two lassies, so Ma wants a wee lassie this time."

"Alex!" screamed Zara.

"Good luck this time, I hope she doesn't hit you as much," said Padruig.

Zara was walked around the room with the two men either side in agony screaming with the Midwife on the floor. She called out to Isobel to come in to ready for the birth as the table for cleaning the bairn was all prepared for her to do her job.

"Isobel, help me with this too," she asked.

"She's coming," Isobel said and both women took the wee bairn carefully and it was passed to Isobel to clean.

"Padruig!" yelled Alex. "We need to get her to the bed now for Lillian to do the placenta, clots bit." Alex said.

All three men lifted her to the bed for the final stages, which had Zara still screaming and asking Lillian to stop and poor Grigor Mohr was an exhausted and distraught husband weeping on his wife's shoulder.

"It's nearly over darling," Grigor Mohr wept. His dear friends felt for the man who adored his beloved wife, whose welfare he had angst over. Finally, it was all over, the wee bairn was born.

"Grigor, Grigor, do we have a lassie?" Zara asked.

"Aye, my darling you have your wee lassie," Grigor answered choking on his every word as Isobel carefully handed the wee bairn to Zara when the Midwife was finished.

"Oh Grigor," she wept too, "look at our perfect wee lassie. Thank you, Grigor, thank you for our lives. I love you so much" she said. Lstening to the two of them was enough to make anyone cry. The wee bairn began to suckle right away.

"Both breasts," reminded the Midwife. "Isobel lass can you clean up? Gentlemen can we carry proud Ma to the kitchen onto a toul please Alex? Hector, make your Mither coffee now please," Lillian ordered.

Zara gave him all the instructions with Alex writing it down this time, so there was no more mystery over the coffee.

'Zara and Grigor were the happiest but most exhausted people on the planet,' Padruig thought but so in love while they both cooed over their new wee arrival. The family all wanted to take a look, but the midwife was in charge still and kept it from being too busy for Mither or bairn. 'It was the best coffee that she had ever drunk,' Zara thought as she gave her husband the last of her cup.

"Make some more lad," said Padruig, "Looks like you are second in charge of Zara's coffee," This time the exhausted Father got a whole cup to himself, while the two of them were in some kind of dream land of their own.

"What about the two of us too lad?" Padruig asked.

"Oh, Uncle Padruig, you didn't do much work like Uncle Alex did, but I will this time," he answered.

"Don't worry about me," said Isobel leaving out the back door with the dirty sheets.

"Fatma, Ali, make up Ma's bed clean, now please," Isobel ordered. It was lucky that dinner was already cooked as well as the bread, so that all the folk present could eat soon.

"Boil the bath water too lad," the Midwife ordered Hector, "For your Ma to bathe."

"Uncle Padruig can you drag the bath into Ma's room then please?" Hector asked, which he did with Alex's help.

"Now gentlemen, Zara's bath is ready, so Grigor can hold the wee bairn please and if you two men can help me take her inside, please?" she asked. Realising her clothes were going to be removed again, Grigor quickly stood up with the bairn and handed her to Alex and kicked him out as well as Padruig to undress his wife fully and gently assisted her into the bath. Instructed not to stay too long in case the heat brought on bleeding, she was assisted by her husband and scrubbed all over and assisted back out with minimal bleeding and dried.

"We'll still need a toul for inside the bedding Grigor, as well as inside her clothing," she said. The wee bairn was returned to the Midwife once Zara was in bed and she did all of her checks on the wee bairn ensuring there were no issues. "She might need to rest first Grigor, then eat," the Midwife advised.

He waited while the whole family as well as the Midwife and her husband ate their dinners, while Zara rested and there was peace in the house.

"Well done all of you," the Midwife said. Although hungry Grigor would not eat until he could eat with his wife and it was an hour before she awoke from her rest when she tried to get up. "Grigor," she called.

"I'm coming, you can eat dinner now love," he said.

"I'm bleeding a bit love can you ask her if that's alright?" Zara said. The Midwife reassured her it was normal and they both finally ate their dinner.

"I was so hungry," Zara finally said.

"Me too," said Grigor. "Having a bairn is hard work," he said as he smiled, thinking of his new wee lassie.

"Drink a lot of milk love," she was advised. "The best milk is from the Highland coos. I'll get her some in the morning John. You have a few ladies out there I can milk?" Padruig asked.

"Aye, I'll have them ready at the back door early in the morning for you Padruig," John answered.

"Will the bairn need any too?" asked Zara, "As a supplement until my milk comes in?" she asked.

"Ill advised. Goat's milk might be better. Do you have a Nanny?" Lillian said and Hector volunteered to milk the Nanny for the wee bairn.

"I'll do it now Ma," he said and went out the back door to milk the Nanny.

After dinner, the Midwife said that they would be leaving in the morning after checking on both Mither and the wee bairn and if she was taking to the goat's milk without too much trouble. If all was well, they would leave to go to their next customer expected any day soon. So, she was paid her wee money for her services and all was well the next day and Grigor said his prayers thanking God that his wife had safely delivered another bairn, but it would be their last. He couldn't bare to lose his wife and the anxiety of losing her was too much for him when he was confronted with her suffering face and wondered at the suffering of women bringing bairns into the world. He was Catholic, unlike his wife who was Muslim, but they made it work somehow but his prayers were not the same as hers or Isobel's and now he noticed that both Ali and Fatma were also following their Mither's prayers behind her. They prayed in Arabic often while his prayers were in Latin. Neither husband nor wife understood what each other's prayer meant, but they never made their differing religions an issue. He wondered which prayers if any that Hector would follow one day, but Zara wouldn't mind. That was their arrangement with each other.

Their wee house in the Aird had seen so many people come and go in the past few weeks with the wolf hunt then Zara's delivery, so the family were looking forward to some normality in their lives without anxiety or wolves. There was however the lingering concern about how Malcolm was handling everything and whether Aonghus had filed the divorce for him. It wasn't the first divorce in the family in his generation, so it was clearly part of Scotland's future. Malcolm needed a woman though, so as it was too touchy for Grigor to look up the MacGregor lass, Padruig asked if he would mind if he and Alex could approach her to tell her about Malcolm's availability, without involving Grigor, to which he gladly agreed and asked them to bring back a wee gift from Inverness for his wife from him. He described it so they could buy the ring from the jewellers. The two men succeeded on two fronts that day. They delighted a Mither searching for a decent husband for her daughter who was reaching twenty-two years of age and they achieved the ring in its correct size for Zara.

An inscription on the inside read, *"To my heart, my soul, my love, Zara. Yours always, Grigor."*

21. The New Arrivals

The MacGregor lassie was told of her fortune and where to go with her Mither and arrived at the gates of the MacNachten Farm, in Glengarry in their horse and cart. It all looked quiet until a stable hand met them. They explained that they were there to meet Mr Malcolm MacNachten, who was looking for a wife. The young lad's eyebrows lifted then he smiled, called for another man named Duncan and were allowed in.

I saw the cart with two women in it and wondered who they were, as Duncan Mohr came to me to explain why they were here. It had been a while now since Cherry had left and the divorce went through with alarming speed, thanks to the Midwife's testimony and Cherry would never see the twins again, nor receive maintenance or be entitled to any inheritance. All of the suggested land divisions on my property had gone through also, but I hadn't approached any women, to the dismay of the MacDonnells. My bairns had been informed at every stage and of all of the facts and it was going to take a very nice lady for them to accept another in their lives, but the twins needed mothering and Meredith had been doing most of it, as had I and Ma.

When they alighted from their cart, the older woman asked if they could please speak to me. They were well spoken and clean and appeared decent. So, I agreed. I asked Kenneth to be my witness and introduced him as my brother. The womens' names were of Clan Gregor, the Mither was Belle and her daughter, Ailsa. The Mither was widowed and her daughter was yet unmarried and around twenty-two, I thought.

"What can I do for you ladies?" I asked. The Mither got straight to the point with how much dowry her husband had left for his daughter, which was humble she knew, but was hoping to meet a good husband and my name was mentioned by two men in Inverness named Padruig and Alex. She wanted to know if I had yet found a new wife, which I hadn't but I introduced them to my twins to indicate that it wasn't an easy job raising these active wee bairns. Meredith took them back to play after that, but I asked if Ailsa could tell me about herself.

Ailsa began. "I was born in Inverness to both my MacGregor parents. I completed lower school and high school there, where I did well in all my grades. I am very good at English, as well as Gaelic and arithmetic. I haven't been to university because my father died. An apothecary gave me a good job where I have been working for five years and I have worked my way up to a senior role, but I would leave the job if I were to find a good husband. I don't have a problem with the man already having children, as you've already disclosed. Do you have any more children, other than the wee bairns?" she asked.

I wasn't expecting a question to come from her, but I said,

"Yes, I have one son at university and my daughter Islay lives here and runs the cheese making in the goat shed and it runs at a substantial profit," I said.

"Does the farm itself run at a profit?" Ailsa asked.

"Aye, it does since we've improved the soil and for the oat fields. So, come harvest time around here life is very busy. A wife would have to like being on the land and all that goes with being on the land. Have you been married before?" I asked.

"Nae, never," she answered.

"Betrothed?" I asked "Nae, my Mither has been trying to get me married before I got too old," she said, "But I've been too busy at the apothecary, which has late hours," she said

"So, have you had any bairns of your own?" I asked.

"How could I have had bairns of my own if I've never been married? Of course, not," Ailsa replied.

"What are you looking for in a husband then lass?" I asked

"I hadn't really started looking, so I don't know. But an honest man. Upright. Honourable. Polite. Hardworking. That kind of thing, I suppose. Handsome helps because if there are any bairns, then the bairns are handsome, but it is not essential," she said

"So, have you read about me in the newspaper then?" I asked

"Nae, were you in the newspaper?" Ailsa asked

"Oh, aye, that's okay. That's good. It was just the wolf hunt up in the Aird," I said

"Sorry, I don't know anything about that. I haven't really had time to read the newspaper," she said

Her Mither appeared disappointed in her daughter, like her daughter wasn't going to impress me at all with her lack of current affairs and started to drop her head, already expecting a rejection.

"My father died before he could put together a large dowry anyway, so I don't expect you'd be interested anyway. Someone like you. So that's okay. I don't mind if you ask us to leave. I'd rather leave than be embarrassed. Ma, can we go?" said Ailsa, expecting rejection.

"Nae, my cook is already making coffee. Did you not want to stay for coffee?" I asked

"Aye twould," said her Ma. So, we all went into the kitchen for coffee.

"Meredith, coffee please, for four," I said.

"Coffee is it, Malcolm?" she said cheekily

"Aye, t'is." Kenneth appeared to like the lass and started to smile at the situation and so did Meredith. I was feeling a little bit shy or something like that as well as under some kind of scrutiny.

"Well lass, after your coffee, I'll get Duncan here to walk you around the property and your Ma too, if she'd like to go. You can look around the property to see if it is a place where you can see yourself living. You can look at the house. Then what we'll do, in a week's time, is we'll meet back here again with a larger group of family who can talk to you, ask you questions, or you can ask them questions and see if they're still interested, or they think you're suitable or if I don't think you're suitable and so on," I said then turned to her Mither, "Are you related to Grigor MacGregor from Craskie in Glenmoriston?"

"Oh aye, distantly though. My late husband and I attended a funeral there for Grigor Mohr MacGregor, some years ago and another big funeral, at the same place for Padruig Dubh Grant," she answered.

"So, you're familiar with Glenmoriston then?" I asked.

The Mither answered that she was more familiar with Glenmoriston than Glengarry, as this was always a MacDonnell stronghold, she had thought.

"My Great Grandmother is Clan Gregor, so we have that in common and her name was Freya MacGregor, who went on to marry John Grant of Craskie Farm," I said.

"So, Mr MacNachten, were you associated in any way to Padruig Dubh then?" the Mither asked.

"Aye, he was my Grandfather and Isobel Grant was my Grandmither," I answered.

"Well, that changes things. It is very nice to have met you then, Mr MacNachten and I hope you take my daughter into consideration. You have a fine pedigree indeed," Belle MacGregor said admiringly then the ladies both looked around the house then were shown around the farms by Duncan Mohr. The following Friday afternoon and night was set aside for them to come back and meet the rest of the family and for each other to ask questions of one another and sleep in Ma and Bruce's house overnight, because of the long distance back to Inverness. The ladies then took their leave that day and there were no others who came knocking that week, thank goodness. Even Kenneth found it stressful, but I explained that I couldn't be left alone with any one of these women that may come knocking, or I may stand accused of something that I never did.

I had a disturbing dream one of those nights where I thought I saw Cherry on a ship bound for rocks and I put it down to that dance she did all those years ago. Either way, all the Cherry trees had to be chopped down and so I started to chop the first one and these were fully grown trees. It wasn't easy and the wood was hard. I thought I would just burn the lot of them. Then Duncan Og from the stables asked if he could help and he started chopping and then before I knew it, there were five of us chopping the trees down to their stumps which I began to dig up. I said to Duncan to just burn them and he said it would be a waste of wood for the winter so he could chop it into small pieces and stack them near the house to burn as firewood, once they were dryer and not green wood. Some of it also could be used for furniture making, he said. I told him to take it if he wanted to make anything from it, so long as it was all gone from my sight. I had planted them when I named the farms after the woman, I had thought I would spend my entire life with. Now they were a symbol of how naïve a man could be. So, the cherry trees all had to go. Eventually they were just big holes in the ground where the stumps once were and I was asked if I would plant more trees along that border.

"Aye, maybe apple trees like Alex has. I like apple pies. Never much liked cherries anyway," I said. Hugh offered to drive the cart to Invermoriston to pick up twelve small apple trees that grew the nice small red apples. Duncan Mohr said not to plant them in the same hole due to the loss of nutrition and to dig the holes in between the others, so I just kept on digging until all the holes were dug. Even Bruce helped. Then I thought to put manure in the deep holes and when Hugh arrived back with the wee trees that would take some time to grow an apple, that's where I planted them and filled in the other holes with the cherry tree stumps removed.

I was going to be rid of anything that reminded me of her.

Duncan Og said he had an idea for security for the gate if it was ever opened in the night while we slept. He had a lot of jam tins from his Mither that he connected up with a long line of thin rope. One end was attached to the gate opening and the rest ran all the way along the fence to opposite my bedroom window. I was confused until he put small stones into the tins and showed me how it would work. If someone opened the gate, it rattled every one of those tins all the way to my bedroom window and made enough noise to wake the dead. He said he would maintain it and always make sure the little rocks were still there. So, the youngest of the long line of security men was coming up with ingenious ways in security that didn't require killing anyone unless you woke up and came running with your rifle to shoot whoever was trespassing, I suppose. I was very grateful to him and we all ate together inside the house that day, after all it was lonely in there by myself. Meredith was the worrying kind and she was concerned about me. I had gone from a confident and happy person into a serious and lonely fellow. Thankfully my twins didn't miss her.

21. A Family Gathering

The Friday was arranged so that all my family could come to meet the two women, as well as inviting Grigor Og, given that they were all MacGregors. He in turn invited two of his MacGregor cousins, only ever seen at funerals, to vet these ladies. Ma wasn't confident about any of it, but Bruce was and I knew he wanted me to replace Cherry, sooner rather than later, or I could become too morose.

Thank goodness Kenneth and Ivy helped me out getting prepared for the big night of family stress time, which might result in my wanting her as a suitable wife, but so far, I hadn't felt anything, sexually speaking, towards the respectable lassie. Bruce sat down with a list of what I needed in a wife so that I could stay on track. He did that with my Ma. He wrote it all down first, so I added a few of my own as I did like my sex and I knew it was an integral part of my daily life if possible. I also wanted two more bairns and finish the family on that number or it could become unaffordable. Meredith and Hugh wanted to know where Meredith stood if I did marry, so I had decided it would stay the same except that hopefully the wife would do the mothering, the breakfast and hopefully most morning teas, but Meredith's wage would be the same because she would clean instead of cook or teach her how to if she couldn't cook. Either way, the two women would need to work together and Meredith was happy with that. I impressed on them that it wasn't a done deal at all, so there was no need to be overly concerned. I didn't think she liked me.

"That's just your hurt talking Malcolm. She likes you. I am sure," Hugh said.

We had a nice feast for everyone who was either a member of the family or connected in some way, including my cousin Alex and his wife Siobhan, Hamish and Cora, Hugh Og and Meredith, Ma and Bruce, Kenneth and Ivy, Duncan Mohr and his wife Mairi and the list went on and I left it to Ivy. Grigor and his MacGregors were staying the night because of how far they had come. There was cousin Aonghus and Annabel, Cousin James and Susan, Cousin Morag-Freya and Gillcrest MacLachlan, Uncle Patrick and Henrietta and all of the oldest of their children and mine. We didn't invite Isobel-Mairi for obvious reasons. My son Alex couldn't come but wanted me to inform him of all that occurred. Islay and Angus were going to be there too. Duncan's role was to ensure that a stramash did not occur and no alcohol made it onto the property or inside my house. The presence of his wife just made him look less intimidating to the two women.

Then the women arrived late afternoon when most people were arriving or had already arrived. Ma had dressed up, which was a surprise and so I actually changed my shirt when I saw how nicely she and Bruce were dressed. The ladies had a few other people with them, who they introduced as her sister and her brother in law, her brother and his wife and her Mither's brother and his wife. I was hoping there was enough room for everyone staying overnight, once the MacGregors arrived, which was soon after they arrived. Bruce introduced himself and my Mither and asked if everyone could introduce themselves. So that took a wee while. All groups chose to sit with their own and we all ate first and Meredith had cooked us a beautiful feast, which included chicken too. Bruce just started chatting casually at first, so that the groups would interact. He had a good way to break the ice with people who were unknown to each other. Surprisingly Ailsa's Uncle, Richard MacGregor stood to make a wee speech first thanking us for our kind hospitality and the cook for her food but got to the reason for them being there. He introduced Ailsa to everyone who looked shy and could barely look up, so her Mither had to tell her to. I saw Siobhan whispering to Cousin Alex asking to move places so she could sit near Ailsa. He agreed and some shuffling took place as Siobhan took her new seat near Ailsa.

Siobhan said something to Ailsa and was pointing to me. It was obvious that she was talking about me and she looked up and for the first time, I caught her eye. She liked me, I realised. But did I like her? She was pretty enough, but I wanted to hear her speak up. The MacGregor cousins then asked all of the clan questions to ascertain who was related to who and whether they approved of her with that knowledge. It seemed impressive, according to them, whoever her Father had been in life, who was a highly respected leader of some kind. He had been murdered, as it turned out, so he was too influential, according to someone they thought, so that family were approved of without doubt, according to them.

My cousins asked the usual questions about farm life and that proved to be an area in which she was severely lacking in skills.

"Skills can be learned," reminded Bruce. "I had never been a Goat Herd Manager in my life before, but Malcolm said, 'here it is, you're it', so I am the Manager and it has worked well," he said. "Malcolm has a way about him that says you can do anything and he tries his hand at anything and when he doesn't have the knowledge, he brings in the experts like Gillcrest here and we had the best crops of oats in the district this season," he said.

I heard Aonghus speak to his Father about whether his property, Craskie and Grant Farms would be willed to me or himself, Morag-Freya and Isobel-Mairi, which then drew attention away from the suitability of Ailsa, and I, as a married couple. He went on asking questions about the security of my farms with the efforts I had already taken to protect it from the MacDonnell interest. I answered my part which was that Old John had gone silent since the sign, MacNachten Farms went up, as well as the Kenneth MacNachten Art Gallery sign and Islay Goats Farm and it was well known that my divorce went through with lightning speed, without using his lawyer. I had obviously been given good advice. He had enough common sense to know by now that no MacDonnell ladies were going to be approached, no matter how lovely they were. The MacGregor ladies, however listening on to this question over the security of life on my farm, first asked to see a copy of my divorce from my ex-wife which was reasonable. The Uncle wanted to see my land deeds to prove my ownership and what the break-up on the land was and why it had been done. I was happy enough to reveal the land title deeds revealing all of the various divisions, but felt it was getting close to my emotions getting to me over what Cherry had done. Bruce asked me if he could answer for me what Cherry had done, thereby keeping my dignity intact. After his whole explanation with its gruesome details, including the termination of three of my wee bairns and attempted termination of the twins.

At that point, I had to stand up for a bit and pick them both up just to feel that they were still alive. And I thanked God for that.

After the horrible details were all exposed, the MacGregor cousins looked like they wanted to know where she was to kill her, as did a number of others like Duncan Mohr who had never overcome the shock of just how bad the reality for me was. I was going to have to live with it and keep my sanity with all my wonderful support around me, but I said to the lassie, "With this knowledge, I understand that I may not be your ideal man, so if you wish to leave, I understand."

"No Malcolm, you have my sincerest regret for your sorrow, but I have to ask if you would take her back if she returned to you?" Ailsa asked.

"Nae, never. It was hard for me to not harm her, as most men would have, but I do not hit women, no matter what. If she returned, she would be arrested for trespassing and there is no concern for you that I would take a monster like that back into my life," I replied. "My twins need a Mither. Can you see yourself mothering my wee bairns?" I asked. Ailsa surprised even her Mither then thinking of my wee bairns and she wept into her hands and nodded indicating yes.

Many others like Morag-Freya hadn't known of all of the messy details and were very empathetic and she came over to me and hugged me, as did many of the women, including Ivy.

"Where is she now?" asked Grigor's cousins.

"On a ship headed for the colonies, as far as I know which takes about eleven months to get there. It's quite possible not to survive these types of sea journeys, even if she disembarks in South Africa to return to Scotland, which we have catered for in our security. If she was to change her mind and turn around and come back, Duncan Og has put a security system on my gate in case she was to sneak in at night. This system which he can show you on the way out, alerts me if I am asleep. Additionally, I have full time security, Duncan

Mohr who is here tonight, while we are seeking another man to assist him." I introduced him then to everyone as my security. Up until then, they had thought that he was another family member.

"I heard you tried to get Hamish from me," said Grigor Og smiling. "I promise he is yours as soon as I decide on what I'm doing with Craskie," he added. "As for Craskie Farm, what will happen is that Isobel-Mairi will be excluded in the Will, due to what she owes the farm and you will be added with my two children, Aonghus and Morag-Freya unless they chose to forfeit to you," he added. "I would prefer it that you adults can work that out when I'm dead," he added. "If I become unable to work the farm, we would need to all meet again over that matter, but its not an emergency anymore with what you have achieved here already from what I can see," Grigor Og added.

We no longer discussed Craskie Farm and then the floor went over to the ladies' family to ask or me to ask. That was when Ailsa said, "What are you looking for in a wife? I want to know all the details," she asked. Bruce indicated to me to refer to my list.

"I have to be honest with you Ailsa, sex is important to me and I would expect sex nearly every day if not every day, honesty, love, trust, prepared to work hard in the seasons like harvest time, cooperation with me, consultation, no secrets. I would like two more bairns, no more, supportive of all I have to do here on this land but not only our property. If other farmers need assistance like the wolves in the Aird recently, I would expect support from my wife, because some things are dangerous like that was and I didn't have the support of my ex-wife. I also like my wife to cook me breakfast because it's a nice way to start the day. I also would like her to bring me smoko to wherever I am on the farms, as well as for whomever I am working with," I said. Bruce looked pleased with the list.

Ma asked, "Can you cook a good breakfast for a hard-working farmer?"

"Nae Mistress, I don't know what a man eats at all for breakfast, especially a hard-working farmer," she answered looking ashamed of herself. Bruce added, "All can be learned from Meredith or Ma. You are an intelligent lass, so it's only learning. I can even teach you if you like, but naturally if you have never been married, then you wouldn't know," he said. "Cooking bread is harder, so Ma can show you that, as well as separating the goat's milk that we bring up to the house each day," Bruce said.

There was a lot more dialogue that was quite exhausting when the MacGregors were first to ask to be excused to their rooms upstairs with Grigor, giving their blessings if Ailsa and I went ahead. Meredith showed them to their rooms. The Uncle was staying also in my house with her two brothers-in-law, who slowly went to their rooms and when Ma and Bruce were ready to leave, they took Ailsa, her Mither and Ailsa's two sisters with her. The Uncle had given his blessings also and thought it was going to be up to Ailsa and myself and advised that we get to know each other better. Hamish and Cora left to go down to their house on the loch with Hugh Og and Meredith to theirs, once the kitchen was all cleaned up. They also approved, but agreed we just needed to get to know each other better. Others like Morag-Freya and her husband Gillcrest were taking their coach back home to Invermoriston, but Aonghus and Annabel were sleeping in Kenneth's house and were leaving in the morning.

The overall opinion was they just wanted to see me happy and the twins cared for as the priority.

22. First Touch

We took it slowly over the months that followed and didn't rush into anything. Ailsa got to know my twins, Malcolm and Hamish well and loved them and they were taking to her quickly. I was liking her more each day, it just wasn't one of those magical moments when you are hit with lust as when you are nineteen or twenty years old. I talked to her about Loch Insh and we even took the horses down there for a lunch beside the loch with the twins. I showed her my Father's grave there and, on another occasion, she showed me her Father's grave in Inverness. I think there wasn't much more to learn other than whether we were physically compatible. I helped her up some stairs by taking her hand in Inverness one day and she seemed to like that and the feeling was pleasant and warm. I was losing that awful loneliness that I had felt after Cherry had left me and that was at least a start. We could converse easily now, without the earlier awkwardness. Then one day she asked me why I hadn't kissed her yet. I was a bit taken aback but I answered, "I thought you might be put off me if I was too forward."

"That's okay then," she said, so long as you don't find me ugly.

That's when it all began. I took her into my arms and kissed her softly on her soft lips but holding her so she couldn't escape my grasp and so I kissed her again and she seemed to like it. I liked it too. We walked to our horses, holding hands and she looked up to me and smiled, the loveliest smile that was captivating in itself. I wanted sex with her and I knew we couldn't blow it after all of the careful planning, but I hadn't had any sex for so long that I was bursting and I didn't want to embarrass myself by wetting my trousers.

I think I realised then that we were getting married and it gave me a jolt to the heart.

I turned her to me and asked her, "Ailsa, will you marry me?"

She answered, "Aye, I will. Do you think we need to handfast before we get to the Kirk part?" she asked.

"Aye, I do," I said.

"I am a virgin Malcolm, I am sorry if I am not experienced for you," she said. We handfast that same day in the privacy of a bedsit for hire in Inverness where fewer people would be interested in what we did. She was the sweetest, lovely young lady with all of her shyness intact and she gave it to me and I was honoured. She was enjoyable, but maybe I just had to let go of all of my pent-up emotions. I had hoped she wouldn't think,

I was a groaning animal, but groan I did as it was all let loose into my new woman. I had finally accepted that she was my new woman.

It had taken a while, but Ma took her time and both she and Bruce were happy in their second marriages. I searched around her sweet young body and it was delightful. There wasn't an inch of fat on her and her breasts were firm and perky, but not large. They would get larger with childbirth I thought. She had the slimmest waistline and she didn't mind me running my hands down both her sides to get her measured in my mind as my perfect woman, flawless almost. Her skin was the colour of coos milk before it was separated and she had little body hair except a few under her arms and her womanhood was as it should be, nice and bushy. I told her not to remove any of it because I liked it and she was very shy all over again. We kissed again, but until then, she hadn't dared to touch my manhood.

"Are you afraid to touch my manhood?" I asked her.

"Nae, can I do that?" she asked. My new wife was very new to sex and this was going to be wonderful as she gently held my manhood in her tiny hands.

"Firmly," I said. She brought on an ecstacy I cannot describe knowing that this wee woman had never had a man before and I had just taken her virginity from her and as she held my manhood in her hands, it released of its pleasure again. It was all new to her not knowing what was going to come out of my body and so there were frequent little gasps, but not of shock more of complete pleasure and interest. That was before I found her wee clitoris so she wasn't just sitting on the fence observing me. She was alarmed almost like, 'whats happening to my body?' and had an orgasm for the first time in her life. She became a fan of sex, so I needn't have announced it that night when I think back.

Ailsa loves me, my body, my manhood and what I do to her to enjoy sex.

The wedding was finally arranged at the Chapel on Craskie Farm, so long as the Priests weren't Catholic, I had stipulated. I liked the Catholics, but they put so many binds on a person that are too restrictive to human existance. I also told her that I wasn't sure that I was even a Christian. She was surprisingly pleased because she wasn't sure too, but we had to do the whole marriage thing in the Chapel, then everyone would know that Malcolm MacNachten had married Ailsa MacGregor. And so, an Episcopalian Reverand was called on and he was a pleasant but older man who was surprised to be called to Craskie, given that they were Catholics, he said. The turn out was huge. I left it all up to Ma and Bruce and they must have invited half of both Glenmoriston and Glengarry, even Old John MacDonnell, so he could see that I was married with his own eyes.

I could see Grandda and Grandma and all the eccentric family from the Aird, watching on too holding a new wee bairn. The reception was organised by my cousin James up at the Manor House and it was at full capacity. We both received lovely wedding gifts and of course I wore that tartan kilt that I had never worn from the day I went shopping with James and he was full of admiration at my appearance, as well as Ailsa who I had bought the MacNachten sash for her to wear over her French, silk wedding dress.

23. *A Shot to the Head*

I had left Duncan Mohr as security behind on the farm, despite wanting him there at the wedding. He was accompanied by his young cousin Duncan Og and our shared stable hand, Dougal. They weren't expecting any excitement like wolves, so as the evening wore on both Dougal and Duncan Og fell asleep in the stables. Duncan Mohr was doing his rounds, armed as usual. We'd had a rifle in the stables since the whole wolf problem had begun, but I hadn't expected it to come into use, now of all times when I thought a semblance of peace and order had fallen onto the farms. It was a bitterly cold night as Duncan Og slept, but he was awoken by the loud rattling of his tin can security alarm system. He leapt to his feet thinking I had arrived home, but realised quickly that the small round figure inside the gate, was none other than, Cherry. Both Duncan Mohr came running with his loaded rifle as did Dougal and Duncan Og, who took down the rifle in the stable.

All three rifles were pointed at the trespasser.

"Stop, or I will shoot!" yelled Duncan Mohr.

Cherry kept walking and said, "It's just me Duncan, I am back home now to Malcolm. I changed my mind about going to the colonies, so can you let me in please?" she asked, unbelievably.

"Madam you are a trespasser and you are no longer married to Mr Malcolm MacNachten who this night has remarried. Take your leave immediately or I will shoot," he said once again.

"Don't be silly Duncan, this is my home," Cherry said. Duncan then fired to the ground at her feet sending the dirt and dust flying into her face.

"If you do not leave Madam, I will arrest you for trespassing and will be forced to have you detained in Fort William, where you will spend the night in a jail at His Majesty's Pleasure," Duncan said authoritavely. Duncan ordered Dougal to light up the two pole lights, either side of the gate, which he did. Looking unwilling to depart, both other men prepared to shoot her as well when Duncan Mohr produced his rope, with which to tie her up. He ordered his cousin, Duncan Og, to get the horse and cart ready in case one of the rifles accidentally went off, and she was taken then as a prisoner, lying in the back of the cart, all the way to Fort William. She spent that night in prison and it was up to the authorities then what they would do with her. Both Duncans went with her there to Fort William, leaving Dougal alone to guard the property. He was nervous alone with the only rifle guarding the place, which was when I arrived home with my new wife, Ailsa in our carriage, followed by Bruce and Ma, Kenneth and Ivy.

I asked Ma to take Ailsa inside as I knew that if Dougal had been left alone with the rifle, that something serious had happened. I spoke quietly to him while he was shaking and he tried to empart what had happened that evening to myself, Kenneth and Bruce and I was grateful to all three of them. His appearance was unwell, to say the very least and he seemed very cold and the lad couldn't stop shaking. I decided with Bruce that he needed to come into the house, even if it alarmed Ailsa. The lad was poorly. I asked him to sit down on the couch near my new wife, but he was reluctant, because he wasn't clean. He had been sleeping a lot lately in the stables with the horses. One horse in particular lay down to sleep, unlike the others who all stood up sleeping. Dougal would sleep in between the horse's front and back legs with his own back against the horse's stomach to stay warm. I had only thought that one groom was sleeping there on the night of my wedding, but they both were there, fortunately.

He tried to tell his story of how the intruder entered and Duncan Mohr asked him to light up the tall pole lights, so he lit a torch from the building then took it to light them up. It was very bright then, he said but he felt odd and felt a stinging sensation on the right side of his head. He then started to see two or three of the intruder, and he moved in a wobbly fashion back to where he had been previously standing. He was trying hard, he said, to point the gun in the right direction, but his shaking was making it difficult. He was very pleased when we arrived home.

My new wife Ailsa sitting close to the lad was noticing a lot more of his physical symptons than us, who do not have a trained eye in the medical field.

"Malcolm, this lad is very cold and close to hypothermic. Can we first get him warm?" she said. We all did that in many ways. Meredith made him a hot tea, but Ailsa asked for a specific tea which would stop the shaking too, so she did that. Ailsa asked me to get him warm breeches, as his clothes were threadbare. I had to dress him up warmly but in so doing noticed how cold his feet were too. Ailsa asked Meredith to make up hot water to soak his feet, then put on hose once they were warm enough. Hugh Og looking on at his young groom put a lot of wood on the fire, so that the room was like a furnace for the rest of us. Angus was delegated to rubbing his feet until they were warm and my wife asked me for gloves for him.

I was starting to feel neglectful of my staff.

"Mistress," he said to Ailsa. "Why do I see three of everything?" he asked.

"Lad, were you kicked in the head by one of your horses?" she asked logically.

"Nae, but my head hurts," he answered.

"Do you mind if I search through your hair to look for an injury?" Ailsa asked.

"Malcolm, the lad's hair needs to be washed. Can you organize a basin of warm water for me?" she asked.

What she found was a graze that was bleeding on the right-hand side, but only a little.

"Did you know that you were bleeding?" she asked him.

"Nae Mistress," he answered. In her beautiful, expensive wedding dress, my wife lay him over her lap onto the lovely ivory coloured silk and asked if it was alright if she could cut his hair away from his injury. He agreed to that after we had washed it all.

Even his face was dirty, poor lad. Sleeping with horses wasn't a clean business.

Ailsa asked me for my shaving razor and some clippers. First, she cut a lot of his hair off, that fell onto her dress, then she shaved all around the full length of what she found to be the injury.

"It's a bullet wound Malcolm. He has been shot, but luckily, it's not too deep. Can you ascertain the angle that would have come from?" she asked taking charge.

"Do you have a stitching kit and some raw alcohol, not the drinking kind?" she asked which we did have for wounds.

"Lad, I am going to stitch it up and its going to hurt a bit. Are you a cry baby or brave like Master Malcolm?" she asked.

Ailsa hadn't seen me blubbing onto Bruce's shoulder a half hour earlier upon realising what had happened and the reality that Cherry did actually try to enter my house on my wedding night. While Ailsa was busy stitching up Dougal's head, I went outside with all of the described angles in mind and the appearance of his wound.

The shot had come from outside of my fenceline.

I searched carefully for evidence of spent ammunition, laying about in the approximate direction. If I had been a shooter, aiming at Cherry, I found the perfect spot. What my groom did was run into a fired gun aimed at her, which could have killed him. I knew then who it was. Old John's army of bastards who may have come down to investigate the sound of rifle fire at my place and saw her and then decided to shoot her, inside my property. With Dougal's bloodied hair in my sporran and the spent ammunition and carrying my long rifle, I wandered up the road to Old John's house. They recognised me and allowed me in, even though it was very late at night. I said I needed to see him immediately. He'd barely been home long enough from my wedding to be in bed, but he was and they got him up.

"Malcolm," he said, "I thought we'd seen enough of each other for one day," he said grouchily. "John, my stable hand, whom I share with Hugh Og was shot in the head tonight, this is his bloodied hair to prove it and these are the ammunition casings. They're from your blokes, aren't they?" I asked. "They might have been shooting at Cherry, who was an intruder while I was getting married. She's at Fort William under arrest. What do you have to say?" I asked. Calling in all of his out riders from that night, he asked all four of them who was responsible for the shooting of my groom.

Two of them looked guilty, one more than the other.

"Well, you idiots, which one was it? I'm tired," Old John demanded.

"It wa me, but he ran into my line of fire. I ad her in me sights boss," he said.

"What have I told you? Not on Malcolm's property, or his fenceline or anywhere near his gates, and you shot directly into his property, you fool? Go home to your Mither, hang up your rifle there. You don't have a job here, neither does your mate. You go home to your Mither too, both of you are half-wits," he said. They handed in both of their rifles.

"What are you going to compensate me with John? I have to buy my wife a new dress, pay the Doctor tomorrow when he comes and pay Dougal's wages while he sleeps it off, if he recovers," I asked.

Reluctantly, Old John went to his safe and took out a bunch of notes, "Will that do?" he asked. "Are you kidding me. French silk? That won't even cover the dress," I replied to the one hundred pounds offered.

He went back to his safe and angrily got out another bunch of money and gave it to me. It was around five hundred pounds.

"Will this do then?" he asked as he threw it down.

"If the lad recovers, it will, if he doesn't and he's still seeing double for the rest of his life and wobbling around like a duck, then it won't. You'll be paying his wages for the rest of his life," I said.

"Do you agree and it stays away from Fort William and put it in writing that you'll care for his medical and wages for his entire life, if there's no recovery?" I demanded.

"Aye and nice to see you too Malcolm, now good night. It'll be in the mail," he said.

Arriving back home, Duncan Mohr and Duncan Og were both at home and saw me coming from up the road.

"Am I glad to see you. What a night," Duncan Mohr said.

"It gets worse, young Dougal was shot in the head. Ailsa's dealing with it and I dealt with who shot him. Two of Old John's bastards," I said.

"Bloody hell Malcolm, I wondered why he was shaking, I thought he was just nervous," he said. "Come inside. You two must be exhausted. Your wife is asleep in Kenneth's old room. When you've eaten, you may as well join her," I said.

"What about your wee break by the loch with your wife?" he asked.

"Postponed is all," I answered.

"The kilt suits you Malcolm. I have to say it's a good look for you," he said and smiled.

By the time we had come inside, my wife had arranged for poor Dougal to have a complete hot bath, scrubbed from head to toe with his fingernails and toenails clipped and getting a lecture on hygiene from Ailsa, while poor Angus was doing the personal scrubbing part. When they dressed him again, he was almost bald, very clean, had stopped shaking or bleeding and asked to please go to bed in Kenneth's house, which was offered to him for the night. The Doctor was coming early to see him and he had to be clean, was Ailsa's plan. I checked the wound first and was impressed. Kenneth and Ivy took him home to bed and were going to see his wife in the morning to also talk to the Doctor before going on sick leave. I gave him his money for the sick leave and a bonus in both grooms' wages that week. Duncan Mohr also received a bonus for their work.

However, the hero was Duncan Og whose alarm system worked.

The Doctor said Dougal would need the week off work and Ailsa's skills on Dougal's head wound was praised. Cherry never returned to MacNachten Farms. An innocent farmer, unknown to her, had dropped her off, thinking he was helping out a helpless woman in the night and came forward to declare himself after he heard what had transpired.

My wife Ailsa and I did enjoy those days by the loch eventually and she learned to cook my breakfast and make the bread as well as the smokos and she loved farm life and being involved with all of its colourful characters. We had our first child one year after the wedding, a big strong lad who was going to be tall like me with a shock of black hair. Our lass also had the same hair but maybe not as tall. Alex my oldest son was given a position in Invermoriston Hospital and was a very popular Doctor. He moved into my house until he married Mairi, when Bruce, who was wanting to move to the loch, gave over his and Ma's house to both Alex and Mairi so they could still be close to us all. Mairi was a lovely bright lass who was working as a nurse at the same hospital until she was with child. After she left the hospital, she was working with the goats.

24. *Family Tree-Marion Grant*

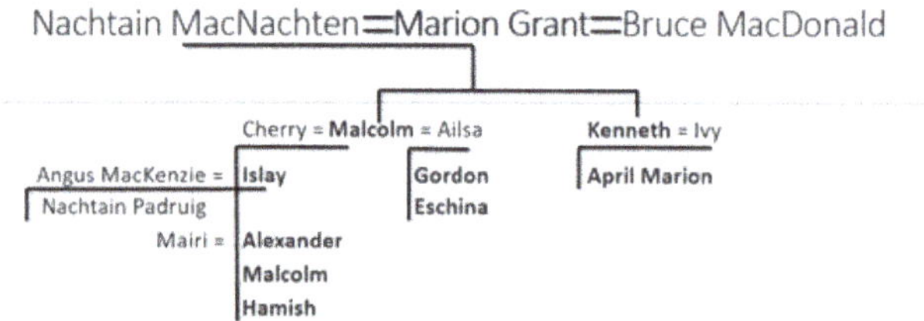

King George IV made a fuss over visiting Scotland and after already having allowed us Highlanders to wear our tartan again, the fool came dressed in tartan and there was an enormous rush on the Mills from the Clan Chiefs all to have their own tartans, leading to even more English control, but I wasn't surprised. Even Clans who had never worn tartan were wearing it. My unpopular cousin, Isobel-Mairi at MacKnight's Mill was making a fantastic income and she finally paid her Father back all that she borrowed from her deceased Mither. This enabled Grigor Og to leave Craskie Farm in the hands of his new Farm Manager Hamish, taking

King George IV

his money with him. I never achieved getting Hamish to work for me. Grigor's cousins all talked Grigor Og into moving to his house on the loch in Glengarry, to rest and go fishing with them occasionally.

He informed me that I was removed from his Will, considering my issues were sorted out in Glengarry. Considering his son, Aonghus was doing his legals for free, he rewrote his Will and with both Morag-Freya's and Aonghus' agreement, the farm was willed then to the deserving Hamish Chisholm, except the house that Grigor privately owned on its own title called 'Charlotte House'. This enabled him to come and go if he needed to or wanted to attend a wedding, a funeral or baptism, taking place in the wee Chapel, knowing that Hamish would take care of him, probably until death. Carmel was a presence in his life, but not one he could rely on. Cora was happy to move into the big house on Craskie Farm, as was Hamish and his family. He went on to do an amazing job of rebuilding Craskie Farm as Isobel would have done and its wealth grew astronomically.

Hugh Og felt happier to go between the two farms once again and he and my son-in-law, Angus were teaching my twins, Hamish Og and Malcolm Og, how to be teamsters at my request, while Ailsa taught them Erse and I saved up for the Clydesdales. One day, we would also have a Team with my twins running it. The twins are such bold and strong bairns with loud voices and completely fearless. They are very noticeable in Glengarry with their jet-black hair and handsome looks, as well as their boisterous over confidence. Duncan Mohr was teaching them to shoot as well, so my lads were going to be terrors one day to any young lassies. Ailsa and I hoped our new son, Gordon would become a lawyer one day, finances permitting. Lawyers were definitely an asset to our families. Our daughter Eschina loved cookery, but she was too smart and could study anything she liked at university. It wasn't unreasonable to have them both studying law and sharing the same law practice rooms. Islay took over the Goat Farm as the manageress, producing the best goat's cheese in the district. The new women on the farms all worked for Islay with the goats including Siobhan, Alex's wife, Mairi and my wife, Ailsa and Kenneth's wife, Ivy. They would all have their regular meetings and if more milkers were needed, they'd always find a lass. Angus took over slaughtering goats from Bruce after he retired to the loch. He always fitted it in with his teamstering and the twins spent a lot of time with him. I was so proud of my family now it was more the size that I had always wanted, starting with Alex my Doctor son, Islay, my goat manageress on the farm, the twins Hamish and Malcolm learning teamstering, then Gordon who I hoped to be a lawyer and Eschina who might study law too.

There was little doubt that my Grandma, Isobel Grant's presence could still be felt in Cannich and I imagine her wandering around at night still checking on everything, never leaving the land on which she was born. Hamish could feel her presence there and I wondered if he talked to her the way I talked to Grandda. It seemed now that Grandda was happy to wander around my farms in Glengarry at night when he's not in the Aird with his eccentric family. We often talked and he frequently gave his opinions about my bairns. He and Isobel had not chosen to be together in death and walked one another's chosen paths in the Braes and Glens of the Highlands, cherished by them both.

25. *Padruig Reflects*

Holding onto his precious books written by his best friend's wife, Zara, Padruig reflected upon the horrible secrets that had been revealed to him. It was upsetting even now, to accept that his wife Isobel had actually been in love with Hugh Mohr Chisholm and had carried his wee bairn until she miscarried the poor wee lass. God had not intended that wee bairn to enter the world with another man as her Father, inside his marriage. If she had lived, how could he have explained away a blonde-haired wee bairn when the whole family had black hair like him? The sorrow of his wife was evident now at the loss of the wee bairn to a man who was all but a child himself at the time of conception. What were they thinking to do that and risk their own lives, just before the march to Edinburgh in the Prince's army? His group of close friends were all supposed to be loyal to each other and he himself would never have performed an act like that on his friend's wife, no matter who they were. Wives were a taboo area for associated male friends, especially close friends and noteably when he was absent also in Quebec later on in life, when he had thought that his wife did love him. The wee bairn Fleur, had never been revealed to him in life, luckily for Isobel, he thought as he may have killed her as well as Hugh Chisholm.

Fleur herself was never to blame, as she lay inside the tiny coffin at her Mither's feet. Loss of her bairns was an issue for Isobel and one she could not bare in life and to carry that loss as well as her precious wee lass born to her as a twin to Alex must explain why she was heartless towards him as the bairns' Father. Meeting Marion before his passing was a shock, but being so close to death himself, there was no energy for rage, only deep sadness but happiness as well to meet the poor lass who had suffered John Grant's ingenious plan to protect her, to protect the twins. He knew only now just how much of a threat his Uncle had been and he wasn't there to help them, so it was hard to criticize John for making the decisions of a Father, instead of a Grandfather, while the actual Father was too busy to come home. Padruig had died in sorrow learning of Marion and her sons, Malcolm and Kenneth, his Grandsons. He knew he was carrying unfinished work from his life with him and it was only the communication now with Malcolm and being able to help him in his spectral form, that brought him some happiness, especially every time Malcolm had another bairn and now with a better wife. He was happy at least for Malcolm that he found out about his wife, so he too would not die in misery, like he had.

Contemplating his misery and getting unhappier in revelling in it, Padruig was interrupted by two of Zara's lads, Hector and Ali. Ali, despite his bigger size now as he grew sideways as well as up, sat on the floor like he often did, while Hector sat in the chair beside him.

"Uncle Padruig, can I ask you some questions please about our thing?" Hector asked.

"Now what would a 'thing' be lad?" Padruig asked knowing full well to what the lad referred.

"The man 'thing'," the lad repeated.

"Still got me. What's a 'thing'?" Padruig asked again.

"Me cock," Hector exclaimed with embarrassment.

"Oh, your cock. Now why didn't you say that up front lad? What do you want to learn from me that your Da hasn't already told you?" Padruig enquired, guessing that Grigor hadn't told him anything.

"Da gave me a clip over the ear when I tried asking him about me cock," Hector replied.

"Okay, what do you need to know lad?" Padruig asked.

"It's about how the farm animals doing 'it,' as well as Ma and Da and I want to know how my cock could do that," he explained.

"Doing what lad?" Padruig asked, drawing it out for as long as he could, to increase the poor lad's embarrassment.

"It," Hector replied once again.

"We have had this conversation before Hector, haven't we? There is no 'it' where relations are concerned. Are you talking about two horses mating or two lovers making love?" Padruig's command of English was improving and he enjoyed correcting someone else for incorrect usage.

"Making love then, Uncle Padruig," Hector answered with his head bowed down in shame, speaking much quieter than his usual loud and boisterous self.

"So, Hector lad, you want to know about making love with your cock? Is that right? Even though you havn't reached fourteen years of age yet, have you?" Padruig asked.

"Aye, I want to know how it works. How does it get in there?" Hector asked.

"Now lad, rules to this conversation are, I do not talk about the lassies, okay?" Padruig said. Hector agreed and Padruig was about to continue when Ali interrupted.

"I think I know," Ali said.

"Oh aye? Go on," Padruig said smugly.

"This thing happens to me in the nighttime where me cock goes hard and I wet the bed dreaming of lassies," he said very honestly. "So, when your cock goes hard, it can enter lassies," Ali said.

"Mine doesn't go hard. Its just limp. It couldn't do any of that. That's why I am asking. I have a limp cock," Hector bemoaned.

"You're not old enough yet lad, but you could encourage it along, isn't that right Ali?" Padruig replied.

"So, if I can get it hard then I can make love, Uncle Padruig?" he asked to clarify it as Ali was keen to show him how to encourage it.

"I suggest the two of you go to the privie to get that cock working and then go for it, lad," Padruig said encouragingly. From the kitchen, lots of sounds were coming from the privie they had entered when he heard that familiar sound heard all across the Jacobite camps he had lived in for years and in various military tents, even in Quebec when the men only had their hands to fulfil themselves.

Padruig patted himself on the back for solving yet another one of Grigor's problems, without him even knowing.

26. Grigor With Another Woman?

He wasn't quite anticipating the fallout of the big one that was just around the corner. Grigor had told him about the MacGregor woman in Inverness, Ailsa's Mither, who wanted to personally thank him for the introduction for her daughter to Malcolm MacNachten in Glengarry. He had all but forgotten about it and didn't know any details but as he saw Grigor come in hurriedly and wash himself as clean as a whistle and brush his mop of hair and tie it back, he grew suspicious.

"Where are you off too then?" he asked.

"That MacGregor woman in Inverness wants to have a morning tea with me," Grigor answered, as Zara entered with both wee bairns noticing her clean husband putting on a clean shirt.

"Did I just hear you say you were going somewhere? Where are you going?" Zara asked.

"I won't be long. It's just to Inverness," he replied avoiding her eyes.

"I can come too then to do some shopping, don't you think? I can strap wee Freya on my back and ride my horse now," she said very hopefully.

"Nae, I won't be there long," Grigor answered.

"Where are you going in Inverness then and what for?" Zara persisted. Realising now he had to reveal it, he told her that he was invited to the MacGregor woman's house for morning tea and he would come home afterwards.

"Then take us with you Grigor, so that MacGregor woman can see that you are a married man with wee bairns. One new one. That's what I think. Can I come please?" Zara asked. Grigor said nae again and was wanting to leave, so she asked for the address, which he gave her.

"Grigor just because she is a MacGregor, it doesn't make her better than me, you just think it does. She's a widow with needs and you are a handsome man. If you leave to see another woman, I will consider this unfaithful to me," Zara said harshly. Grigor left anyway, as he was expected to arrive at a particular time and his attitude toward Zara was the opposite to what it had been for their entire marriage, especially since the birth of wee Freya.

"You knew about this didn't you?" Zara said, as she shot an accusatatory glare across to Padruig and went into her room and Zara herself cleaned up, dressed and packed a bag for herself, Causantin and wee Freya. "You're feeding yourself tonight Padruig." Zara said. And she was gone. She got on her horse with Causantin strapped to her back and Freya to the front, with an additional belt around them so they wouldn't fall off. Before he was out of his chair, she was already crossing the burn on horseback, but not in the direction of Inverness.

Alex came in asking him where everbody was.

Padruig just said, "I'm staying out of it."

Arriving at Craskie Farm with the key she had been given on the sly, by Grigor Og, she rode up to the door of 'Charlotte House.' That was when the Team driven by Hugh Og drove in with eight horses, his offsider Angus and two young lads who looked like twins, arrived too. Zara had a better idea then.

Glengarry, where that woman's daughter now lives.

"If he wants to embarrass me, then I'll embarrass the MacGregor woman and her uppity daughter," she said to herself.

She walked over to Hugh smiling and asked if he was going back to Glengarry.

"Aye, I am as soon as I unload this. Why?" Hugh asked.

"I'm Zara, I need to see Malcolm. Can you take me to his house please?" Zara asked.

"Oh aye, are you Grigor's ex cook?" he asked.

"Aye," she said. "You'll have to ride up top with us and the twins," Hugh said. "I'm Hamish," said one bold twin. "I'm Malcolm," said the other. They were very agile, climbing all over the horses, the carriage and did what Hugh asked of them.

27. Zara Journeys to Glengarry

Glengarry was a long ride from Cannich as her horse trotted on behind, tied to the carriage. It was crowded up top with Angus and Hugh and her bairns, so the twins sat on top of the carriage part way and on Angus' lap part way. Ever energetic, the lads were both adorable in their own way and despite the strain on her back, Zara enjoyed seeing the world from that height, briefly allowing herself to forget, then it would burst back into her brain and she wanted to kill that MacGregor woman for honing in on her husband. Faced with losing Grigor, she was going to fight. What was left, if she lost her husband?

Wee Freya needed to be fed on the way and she instantly breast fed her, not thinking that she was in different company, until she noticed Angus looking at her breasts, so she covered her modesty. Freya was starving hungry and when new bairns want to be fed, there's no stopping that cry until they are fed, then fall asleep again. It was a much longer distance to Glengarry than she had realised.

"Do you want me to hold one of your bairns?" asked Angus.

"Aye, thank you, my back is aching," Zara answered. Angus was supposed to be assisting Hugh, but gooed over Causantin for the rest of the way and the twins held onto him too. He was clearly a favourite with the bairns.

"I'm Angus, Malcolm's son-in-law, Islay's husband," he explained. "I'm Hugh's apprentice and so are both Hamish and Malcolm," he added. Praising the lads was well received as they asked all the usual questions.

"Who are you, what's your name, where are you from, what are the bairns' names, who are you married to, where do you live?" they asked continuously. "Can we call this one Con and not Causantin," Hamish Og asked referring to the two-year-old lad.

"Aye you can, but only you two lads can call him Con, mind. His name is Causantin," Zara aquiesced.

"Why did you name the wee one Freya?" asked Malcolm Og.

"Her Father's Mither's name was Freya," she answered.

"You are pretty," said Hamish Og.

"You are much prettier than our Stepmither," Malcolm Og agreed.

"Lads don't be disrespectful of your Da's new wife," Hugh said and shut the lads down. 'I had to tread carefully then', I thought to myself. Respect to the person related to that woman in Inverness, trying to steal my husband, was going to be hard.

Hugh hadn't reacted to the twins' questions nor her responses, except on two occasions. When the answer to Zara's husband's name being Grigor MacGregor and not showing any disrespect to Ailsa were the only two perceived reactions, Zara decided that Grigor Og hadn't told him of their status, she hoped. Although his brother Hamish was the spiritual one, so he may have divulged some areas of question, but not that she was actually dead, let alone Grigor Mohr's wife, a lady they had both known as youngsters, when she was alive. Grigor Mohr's funeral was one that they had all attended and that day became memorable for eternity because Padruig became drunk after Grigor's body had entered the ground and he was overcome with grief at the reading of a poem written by Donald Chisholm.

He remembered bits of that poem to this day called, "Grigor of the Mist".

"It's true to say that Grigor, son of Grigor
Could recite the names of all the Scottish Sith.
His Grandmother taught him no English
Important only was the knowledge of the unseen.
Escaping as a deserter
Joining with the Seven Glenmoriston Men to live in a cave
Needed was he with that knowledge, through the mist
But of his sister, he knew naught."

That night Isobel had all of her china and glassware smashed up, as well as her dining table and chairs. Hugh and Padruig started the fight, but the whole family, excluding the women, joined in, except Simon Fraser, Beth's husband.

Poor Grigor Mohr, on the day of his funeral had absolute chaos reign in the Craskie house with Isobel bruised, but Hugh Mohr had a split lip and a black eye the next day, as did Padruig. Isobel was normally very forgiving, but Padruig breaking up her china and furniture was an unforgiveable act in her mind. 'It's funny what the brain retains and what it choses to release,' he thought, as he pondered the obvious death of Grigor MacGregor.

Hugh then asked Zara, "Are you familiar with the poem by Donald Chisholm called 'Grigor of the Mist'?" he asked. Zara said she was familiar with it and knew the last two paragraphs.

"Did you know that he was Isobel's half brother, being that Isobel was also a MacGregor on her Mither's side? Her Mither's name was Freya too. It's an uncommon name, don't you think?" Hugh was suspicious bond Zara only hoped that he wouldn't leave them by the side of the unfamiliar dark and winding narrow road.

"Grigor Og is my stepson, that is why I had the key to his house. It will be clearer to you in good time," Zara answered. The young woman sitting beside him didn't look old enough to have known Grigor Mohr MacGregor, Grigor Og's Father, but he decided against causing anxiety amongst all of his other passengers on board this night, to Glengarry that was becoming creepy. He was looking forward to seeing Malcolm himself, who would deal with it on every level.

The twins fell asleep spread across both Zara and Angus and Causantin was sitting on top of them, while Dorothia slept on. Then they arrived at MacNachten Farms, where the lights lit up the entry. The groom hurriedly opened the gate for them and the tin cans banged away, splitting the quiet of the night. Once the whole team was in, the twins seemed to know what to do and scrambled down. Angus aided Zara and wee Dorothia down, while he was still holding Causantin.

"Angus, take the team with Duncan Og. The twins and I will escort Zara and her bairns inside to see Malcolm," Hugh said decisively.

Hugh wasn't the only one pleased to arrive in Glengarry, while she rubbed her back and wanted to pish badly. Entering the lovely home was in itself an experience to remember, as Malcolm recognised Zara immediately.

"Zara, lovely to see you. What brings you to Glengarry?" Malcolm asked.

"Can I explain when I've used a privie or chamber pot please Malcolm?" she asked.

"Oh aye, I can take your bairn. This is Ailsa, my wife," Meredith was in the kitchen still waiting for her husband and Zara heard Malcolm ask Hugh for details and where his lads were, while she relieved herself finally and was then offered coffee or tea by a curious Meredith.

28. Zara Threatens

"Coffee please," Zara answered.

"Hugh said you needed to see me Zara. How can I help you?" Malcolm asked looking worried.

"My husband is Grigor Mohr MacGregor, as you know Malcolm and today, he was invited to Inverness to be with your wife's Mither, Belle MacGregor. I asked him many times to accompany him, but he refused and given she is a widow, I didn't wish him to be alone with her. He has never done anything like this before and our bairn is so new. I am here to ask if your wife can do something about this, if she wants her Mither's respectability preserved. That woman is poaching my husband. He's a married man with six bairns. Can you please send your wife to this address in Inverness to break up any liason going on there with my husband and to tell her to stay away from my husband, lest I lose self control?" Zara said, meaning it.

Zara was suddenly murderous with that woman in mind.

"I see. Hugh are you up to a ride to Inverness or should I ask Duncan Mohr?" Malcolm asked.

"You don't see anything odd in this story then, like Grigor Mohr is dead already?" Hugh asked. Stating the obvious.

"Aye, maybe I should explain," Malcolm said. "So is Zara," Malcolm said. "They are able to live in between worlds, but something has gone wrong here. He shouldn't have gone there on so many levels, it's serious," Malcolm said.

"But you have wee bairns?" Hugh asked.

"I died in this world during the 18th Century, but I was alive in the 21st Century. I was alive here initially and was researching a book and communing miraculously with the Seven Glenmoriston Men, but was accidentally killed, so now my life here is permanent. I can't go back home." Zara explained.

"Which of the men?" Hugh asked.

"Padruig Dubh Grant, Grigor MacGregor and Hugh Mohr Chisholm," Zara answered. "It's a long story, but Padruig has the books if you want to read them one day," she said.

Then Ailsa spoke, "Malcolm, I need to be taken to my Mither's house to protect her dignity. I will tell her that the man she entertained is married but will leave out the dead part, if you don't mind. No doubt you can explain it all to me later

Malcolm. Can Bruce take me in the carriage and stay the night that's left in Inverness? We won't be back before afternoon tomorrow. Can you give me some coin to pay stabling the horses?" she asked.

"Aye and I'll accomodate Zara in my house on the Loch. Meredith, please put a food parcel together for Zara and her bairns including paritch for the morning and goat's milk and cheese and bread and some of your stew?" Malcolm requested.

"Hugh please take Zara down to my house and ask Bruce to come up here to assist Ailsa into Inverness in the carriage. Can you also get Duncan Og to get the carriage out and tell him he is staying over there too?" Malcolm asked.

"Will your husband come to look for you Zara?" Malcolm asked.

"He has before but this time is unclear to me," she answered.

"He may have only been there to discuss an innocent clan matter Zara," Malcolm said hopefully.

With all the people aware of their roles in this exercise to save Zara's marriage, it only left contacting Grandda. Hugh left with Zara in tow. His day just became longer. Meredith went with him to go home. Life had become more interesting living and working with Malcolm.

The small house beside Loch Garry was delightful and Malcolm told Zara and her bairns that they could stay for as long as they liked, then when Bruce left with Ailsa, his home was quiet enough to contact Grandda.

"Grandda, it's me Malcolm. Zara is here if you are wondering where she is. What happened up there?" Malcolm asked. "Oh, I should have guessed you'd be involved in this.

Grigor came home late, I agree, but he still expected Zara to be here. He's beside himself with his bairns gone," he said. "So, is Zara okay?" Padruig asked. "Nae, she is upset and I've sent my wife to see Ailsa's Mither to keep her away from this lady's husband, which is fair enough. Why is he flirting with that old woman?" Malcolm asked. "Blowed if I know, but it's not my fault that he did it, however it is my fault that I didn't tell Zara about it I suppose," Padruig said. "You knew and did nothing to stop him wrecking his life? What's wrong with you Grandda?" Malcolm pushed and judged his grandfather's low moral compass. "You of all people Grandda. You know how painful this is. Zara is hurting and with a new bairn" Malcolm added. "So how late was he coming home from a morning tea?" he asked. "Around five o'clock. He had lunch there too. He said they caught up with things," Padruig said. "Is he leaving Zara then?" Malcolm asked. "Nae not leaving, but to be honest I'm not sure what's going on with him. He isn't himself. I thought he adored Zara, so it's strange and he won't say why he did it to her," Padruig said. "Is he coming to get her?" Malcolm asked. "Nae, but Isobel is frantic, so is Hector and Fatma and Ali who all want their Mither back. Can I bring her bairns to see her, even if he doesn't go to get her tomorrow?" Padruig asked with genuine concern. "We will all have to come on horseback. Where is she?" he asked. "On the loch, house three. Did he sleep with that woman?" Malcolm asked. "I don't know, but I will know. Alex and I will get it out of him," Padruig said with determination.

And he was gone.

29. The Standover

Alex and Padruig knew they had to do more than just chat to their old friend. He had loved his wife, was father of six bairns and yet he was throwing his happiness away. The two men prepared themselves and planned to approach him from different sides. They were then going to speak threatingly to him for his stupidity and for breaking up their home of happy people. Then Alex on the other side yelling threats at him for harming Zara, their friend. Then Padruig lunged and held him in a choke hold, with one arm twisted behind his back. Alex took to his neck threatening him with a dirk, demanding answers. "Did you sleep with the MacGregor woman?" Alex yelled. "Nae, I didna," Grigor yelled. "Did you grope her, smooch her, or speak any love talk to her, you dirty bastard?" Padruig yelled. "Nae, I did it to make Zara jealous, that's all. I didn't think she'd leave home with my bairns," he yelled.

The two men let go and Grigor wept. "I'm sorry, really. I'm so sorry. I was only there for morning tea then just wasted time in Inverness. I was hoping Zara would welcome me home, not go missing," he said.

"You should know her by now. How many times has she done a runner now or tried to?" Padruig said. "It's too scary without you for her, she wasn't born here, you nincompoop. She has to run out of pure fear without you, ever since what happened to her with Hugh and then your Father. I know that look of fear, and she had that. Why did you do that? What if this causes her long-term stress and she finds no one, with whom she can trust? She adores you and cannot be herself now, without you. You are everything to her, as well as her bairns. I can't understand anyone loving you, you asshole but she was too good for Hugh Mohr Chisholm and now she's too good for you too and I never thought that would be the case. I thought you were the best of us," Padruig said.

"I'm disappointed, but what can we do now? I'm taking your bairns to see her in Glengarry tomorrow morning, so don't panic if we are all gone, except John who is staying. It's up to you if you want to see your wife. This is the address by Loch Garry," Padruig said as he wandered off back to the house in disbelief that it was just a scam to make her jealous.

30. Inverness Night Visit

In Inverness, the carriage with both Bruce and Ailsa arrived with Duncan Og, in the middle of the night. There was a stable for the horse, so they first took him there to feed and drink before they knocked on Mrs MacGregor's door at three o'clock in the morning. Then Ailsa decided she would knock and call out for her Mither, so as to not alarm her with an unknown male voice. A male came to the door wearing only underclothes and said,

"Who are youz three and what do youz want at this hour?" he asked.

"I'm looking for my Mither please let me in," Ailsa said as she pushed past whoever that man was. Her Mither came tiredly from her bedroom half dressed.

"Ailsa, what are you doing here?" her Mither asked.

"Mither, please send your friend home," Ailsa demanded. Reluctantly, he dressed and went out into the freezing cold night air while Ailsa told her all of the trouble, she had caused by inviting a married man into her home, alone the previous morning.

Her Mither did not deny it and even said she fancied Grigor, but that he wasn't up for it at all, although it didn't sound convincing to Bruce. "A loyal one," she said.

"Mither you can't embarrass me or my new family like this, you must stay away from Mr MacGregor now. Can you please promise me that?" she pleaded.

"Yes, yes yes, now go to bed you three," she said adjusting her bussoms and showed them all where to sleep for the few hours left, they had before going back to Glengarry. Ailsa learned a lot about her Mither's secret life but wished she had stayed respectable for everyone's sakes.

"I'm sorry Da," she whispered as they fell asleep. Ailsa wanted to cry.

"It's okay lass, so long as its all sorted," he said. Bruce was one of the good ones, she thought and when they all awoke, they quickly washed, dressed, ate their breakfast without looking at her guilty Mither, then fetched the horse and carriage and headed on back home to Glengarry.

Marion and Malcolm escorted Zara with their belongings and food, to the wee house on the loch frontage, which was house number three in a row of six. It was on a small plot, as it had formerly been a croft. All of them were purchased by Marion MacDonald, Malcolm's Mither, renovated with laundries added and a small two horse stable at the rear, each also with a chicken run. Malcolm's was empty most of the time, so his chickens were at his Mither's chicken run. While Zara was to be living there, all of Malcolm's chickens were given back to her for fresh eggs in the morning. It was well furnished with a lovely big fireplace in the lounge room and a smaller one to cook on in the kitchen. In addition, there was a fireplace on the back verandah, which doubled as a drying room and there was a large copper to boil linen and clothing in. The wee house had been well reno-vated with thick white paint on all the inside walls and render on the outside.

There were two lovely couch chairs by the fireside and plenty of peat for the fires inside and a stores of peat outside as well. The dining table was at the rear of the house before opening the out-side door and it had a quaint, peaceful atmosphere. It had two bedrooms, one large one at the front and one smaller one at the rear, intended for bairns with three beds and a cot. In the larger room the bed was new with a beautiful goose down doona, as well as its own fireplace and tub for bathing. The water boiling bucket was strung across the fire in preparedness for someone to take a bath. The bairns' room did not have its own fire-place, maybe due to safety. It was plenty big enough for Zara, Causantin and the new bairn, whom she now called Dorothia. She didn't feel the same way about that MacGregor name any-more, despite Freya no doubt being a fine woman. It might upset her husband, but he didn't seem to care what upset her or the whole family anymore. She arranged the food that was given to her and was offered a milking goat too for her stay, which she accepted.

When they both departed, leaving her to arrange her new life, temporary as it might be, Zara was lonely. She had been accus-tomed to raucous laughter, loud boys running in and out, men making coffee demands and dinner talk, baking bread and making butter everyday routinely. 'What had happened to her life?' she asked herself. 'It was so sudden and unexpected that Grigor would seek the company of a woman and not just any woman, a fellow clanswoman.' She was angry with all of it, most especially the man whom she adored so much for going to that woman dressed up clean in a new shirt. Zara was all alone now just with her two young ones, so she got busy with the dinner, making bread, and putting some sheets in the wash. Mopping the floor and dusting down the shelves, she even missed her books belonging to Padruig. "We had such a nice life in the Aird and I think it's over," she said out loud to herself. Zara was beginning to see that her life as it was had ended and most likely her marriage too. She then sat in the couch chair and began to wail the loss of her spouse, as if she was attending his very funeral. She tried to pull herself together lighting all the fires and checking the copper to see if the sheet was boiling and it was. The bairns seemed happy enough as Causantin surveyed the backyard, then she heard him say,

"Da, Da." That was what he called Grigor Mohr.

Grigor was just standing there, observing her from the back-yard, dressed in another clean shirt and this time he was wearing a philibeg, the small kilt. He never wore one of those and what had he done with his old smelly plaid? She didn't speak first, after all he was at her new temporary residence. Finally, he spoke.

"Zara why are you here?" he asked. Of all things to say he chose that, so she turned her back to him and went inside with the bairns. He followed her in, looking silly in his new outfit.

"Did you buy another outfit to look good for Mrs MacGregor? Because if you think you look good, think again. You look ridiculous in it," Zara said.

"I know you are upset, but it's time you came home now to the Aird and cook dinner like you are supposed to," Grigor said.

"Would you like to tell me how it all went with the morning tea at Mrs MacGregor's house Grigor or does it embarrass you that at your age, you are still chasing women around when you already had a wife, you pig?" Zara exclaimed.

"I am not answerable to a wife who thinks she can dominate my every move of every day," he said angrily.

"No, you clearly think there wasn't supposed to be any consultation in our marriage of so many years, yet I remember us both happily consulting every day. I remember there being love, devotion, happiness, sharing our beautiful bairns, but you remember something different to me. Why is that do you think?" Zara said. "Oh, that's right, I'm not Scottish, worse still, I'm not a real MacGregor. I don't know who put these ideas into your head to break us up, but whoever they were, may God curse them to hell and back," Zara said, meaning every word.

"No one put ideas into my head, I just wanted you to feel jealous. I wanted to be admired again, that's true, but I have not been unfaithful to our marriage vows," Grigor said.

"Why did you want me to feel jealous? I am always worried for you, about you and where you are and I always wanted you back with me to love not hate, not like this," Zara said becoming emotional. "You have driven a wedge between us. That's not love. I have wanted you for longer than you will ever know because you are so unresponsive and I was never good enough for you. I see that now. That whole 'Royal is My Race' thing is too serious. We are just people, with feelings, worse still, we are dead people with feelings thanks to your friends," Zara expressed.

"Can I have a coffee at least?" he asked.

"I don't have Turkish Coffee, just ground coffee. Will that do?" she asked.

"Aye. This philibeg isn't mine, it's Grigor Og's. He told me to take off the smelly plaid and put on these clean clothes, but it would have been better to smell in my plaid," he said wishing he had never worn the thing.

"So, you stopped first at Grigor Og's house before coming here?" Zara asked. "That's low, even for you. Why did you even come here if your son was the priority?" Zara expressed with deep sadness. "You may as well leave, you are not here with the right motives or the right reasons, an explanation for your conduct or an apology for ruining all of our lives, as well as disrupting so many other peoples' lives too, like Ailsa, who I sent to see her Mither to stay away from my husband. Is that the jealousy you wanted with Ailsa and Bruce going to Inverness in the middle of the night?" she asked. "Jealousy is a dangerous emotion Grigor and it can get innocent people killed when others are just playing a game. Are you a child?" she expressed rudely.

Grigor grabbed her suddenly and Zara was shocked as he took her by both shoulders and shook her and yelled at her in Gaelic.

"You can't speak to me like that," Grigor yelled angrily. He then grabbed her by the throat. She was choking and unable to breathe when a quietness came over her as her legs could no longer hold her up. She slid down the wall he had her held up against, legs protruding forwards, when Causantin began to scream.

"Ma, Mamma, Ma," and he threw his wee body onto her as she fell limp onto the floor unconscious.

Grigor extracted his hands immediately, shocked at what he had just done. He went outside and it was unclear what he was doing, but Zara held her throat and woke up feeling dazed. In the backyard, he could hear some strange words from inside his head that were not of his own.

"May your cattle wander off at night,
May your chickens cease to lay
May the wolves eat your sheep
And your wife's face turn to mush...
by your violent hand....
Lost be your horses, your bairns and your life
Never again will love return to your marriage bed.
Only a wolf-like stranger can ....
Her face restore.

But love for you will be....
Never more."

It terrified him where it had come from and he feared a curse was already in motion.

In the far distance Zara could hear the sounds of many horses' hooves and thought they might be coming her way. It was hard to get up. 'Such an odd sensation when you're choking,' she thought. Grigor came back inside with a cool wet cloth and wiped her face.

"Forgive me please Zara, I am so sorry. I lost control of myself, are you alright?" he asked as he helped her stand up.

Zara limped over to a chair with Causantin following her. He turned to his Father and pushed at his legs. "Go way," Causantin said as a two-year-old trying to protect his Mither. Grigor heard the horses approaching as they stopped in front of the house. Zara peered out the window to see who was there. It was her family from the Aird. Padruig leading all of them. Isobel, Ali, Fatma and Hector followed by Alex. She smiled at them despite her discomfort and then went to greet them. Marion came over too and offered additional stables at Hamish's house that was empty now and he had offered it up to any additional guests she might have. Padruig, Alex and Grigor's horses could all go down to that stable, she instructed.

Isobel ran to her Mither and was relieved to see her, as were all four of her children. Zara ran her hands through Hector's mop of lovely black hair.

"I missed you so much son," she said emotionally kissing him too when Fatma began to cry. "Ma, Ma where did you go, I was scared without you?" she said. Zara hugged Fatma and Ali, both breaking down into pools of tears, then Padruig approached her.

"Zara, its wonderful to see you and it's nice enough here. The bairns all needed to see you, so it was my decision to bring them. I hope it suits you," Padruig stated, then in the afternoon light, he could see red marks on her neck.

"Are you alright? Are you fighting or have you made up yet?" Padruig asked.

"We haven't made up yet," Zara answered looking down.

"Your voice is a bit raspy. What's wrong with your throat?" he asked.

"Nothing. Just the damp air, I think. I miss my home. Malcolm said I could stay for as long as I liked but I miss home, I miss my bairns. It's just my husband who won't want me there," Zara stated.

"Has he said that?" Padruig asked.

"Nae, but I am not who he wants anymore, am I?" Zara cried and Padruig held her in his arms.

"I'll talk to him. He loves you Zara, but he's a bit confused right now," he said.

Alex came down from Hamish's house with Marion, who was explaining everything to him and giving him Hamish's keys.

"You've got Hamish's house tonight Padruig, but did you bring any Turkish coffee with you?" Zara asked.

"Are you serious? Would I forget the coffee when I am visiting you, the best coffee maker on the west coast?" he said smiling. Then they all went inside, except Ali who wanted to look at the loch.

Zara was preparing coffee for Alex and Padruig, when Grigor entered wearing his old plaid again with the shirt under it.

"Grigor Og gave me a philibeg to wear to please Zara, so I came here in it and she said I looked ridiculous." Grigor joked about himself trying to sound light and not the man who had just nearly choked her.

"What's with your neck Zara?" asked Alex. "New lover or someone tried to kill you, eh?" he added.

"Neither. I might be allergic to the loch or the midgies," Zara said concealing the truth.

"It was me," Grigor confessed. "I was overreacting and I hurt her, I think. I'm sorry Zara," he said.

"Coffee?" she asked. "Aye, bonny idea." Padruig was not happy. His facial expression was getting a little dark and angry, as was Alex's.

"Can we talk outside the back while the coffee's cooking Grigor?" he asked.

As they walked out the back all the bairns were exploring the wee house and deciding where they would all sleep. They liked it well enough. Ali came in saying he wanted to take a swim later. Zara heard a few thumping sounds from the backyard and a few groans, and the three men walked back in with Grigor a little worse off. They had beaten him for hurting Zara.

They began to relax with their coffees, including Grigor Mohr, when the sound of a carriage was heard.

"It's busy around here Zara," Padruig said. "I'm not used to all of this traffic," he added.

"Aye, the Aird's good for that peace and quiet until Grigor threw a man cannon into the family," Alex added. "I'd have the Aird any day. I'd get bored shitless living here," Alex said. It was funny to hear the usual banter and Zara was smiling again.

"I would too," she said. "It's very limited and there's lots of midgies," Zara added.

"Too cold for the blighters in the Aird, I reckon, almost too cold for you Zara. So, are you coming home?" Alex asked. Zara was suddenly sad again not knowing if her husband even liked her, let alone loved her. She felt like such an outsider.

"I've never felt like an unwelcome outsider before, even though I have always been an outsider with no Gaelic, but now I do. In my heart, the Aird is my home, but how can it be if my husband cares to look for feminine attention elsewhere? I don't know where to go. Maybe back to Craskie Farm where Charlotte House is big enough for all of my bairns and both Hector and Ali might even get a job there, now that they are old enough.

They could work for Hamish maybe? I don't know Alex," Zara said sorrowfuly, but not unreasonably.

"Zara, you do what you have to do for you and your bairns, but speaking for myself, I think we would all leave one by one without you there in the Aird, except for John of course, he'll always be there. You are what keeps us all together and happy and well fed. You are the best thing that could have happened to Alex and me. It's a sad thing to see you in yet another break-up. My grievances with Hugh Mohr Chisholm didn't help you with him in your first marriage, for which I apologise," Padruig said.

"But Grigor, once you two were married I had to see it with my own eyes, so I spied on you for a bit, then saw Zara with child and you were both so happy," he added. "I'd never seen Grigor happy like that," he addressed to Zara. "Not in life or death, so you had something that wasn't Scottish, Zara, it wasn't clan related, it was just your personality and the love within you. You care for everyone's feelings and have tried hard to please this man. I am witness to it. Alex is witness to it too, so unless it is a clan thing that has bugged you, Grigor, you had it made for eternity, I thought," Padruig said.

Grigor remained silent, listening to his friends' judgements of him. He was worried about that possible curse.

The knock on the door ended that reflective conversation and Zara asked Ali to open it. It was Ailsa and Bruce with his wife Marion. They were there to report on the night visit to Inverness. Ailsa was one for writing everything down in detail. She narrated the whole story from the near naked man at the door, to which Grigor reacted, right through to

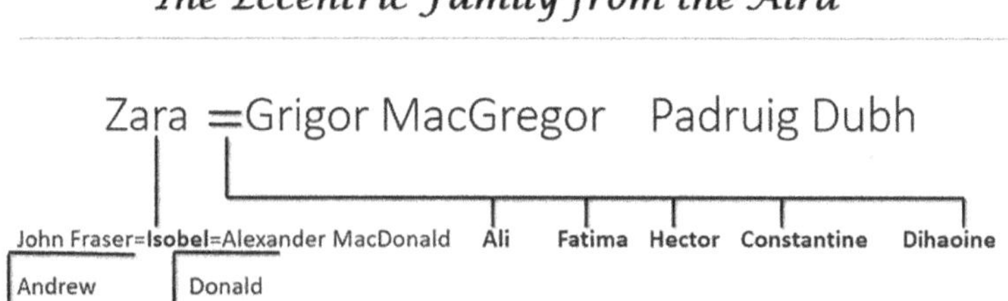

The Eccentric Family from the Aird

her Mither's admission to making a play for Grigor Mohr but that it remained unclear if he participated, despite her massive bosoms being frequently flashed at him. It was obvious that Ailsa was very embarrassed about revealing the secret life of her Mither's nighttime activities and she apologised to Ma, Bruce and Zara.

"Mr MacGregor," she added. "There are widows or just lonely people out there, who are jealous of what you have. If I was you, I would never be entertained by the like, despite our clan credentials, as it is never worth the agony and the trail of blood it leaves behind? Your wife has fought for you, by coming all the way from the Aird, then catching a ride on an uncomfortable team carriage with Hugh Og, Angus, the twins Hamish Og and Malcolm Og, as well as your own two wee bairns. I also have fought for you with my Da, Bruce here, by going to Inverness in the middle of the night. Malcolm has organised all of it and made this house available, as well as food. So, this is what I expect of you. I expect now that you will apologise to all those involved and the subsequent consequences, including these good friends of yours, your bairns, my husband Malcolm, and most especially your long-suffering wife, Zara, who must love you to do what she has done. I admire her for fighting for you, but now you have to prove that you are worth fighting for. Now if you'll excuse me, I have to go home to my husband and bairns. Have a nice day," she said confidently.

Ailsa was a force to be reckoned with, as were both Bruce and Marion. Malcolm had a good team on his side, that was obvious. As Grigor Mohr sat in his chair taking in the scene of that naked man in Inverness, he felt totally humiliated and fooled, not admired. He had to overcome his ego and admit that what he did was wrong.

"Zara will you please forgive me for upsetting you so much and forcing your hand, which finds us all here in Loch Garry? I apologise to all of my bairns too who have cried because of me. I apologise to both Padruig and Alex and I do love you Zara. I really love you so much it hurts. I know I have done the wrong thing by all of you now. I was such a fool when the woman was poaching me, like you said Zara and I should have either taken you there or never gone, then we wouldn't be here at Loch Garry. Would you please come home to the Aird as well as you too Alex and Padruig?" he pleaded.

"Is she safe with you now Grigor, since you choked her?" asked Padruig.

Looking totally ashamed of himself and unable to justify his actions, Grigor Mohr had to say that his wife was safe with him.

"Alright then, you won't mind signing this document here that I have written up in Gaelic, sorry Zara, whereby you promise that you will never harm your wife physically again in the future, but if you do, then you forego custody of your children, including the new wee bairn whose name now isn't Freya, it's Dorothia?" Padruig stated as he handed him the rough document in Gaelic.

"That also means that you pay for them if she has to leave you permanently next time," Alex added.

Both men were serious and had Grigor in a strangle hold that he could not escape from. He was being told to behave like a bairn in a classroom and it irked him and his MacGregor self, but he knew that they were right and wanted the best for himself, as well as Zara and the bairns with their own family situations, like Alex and Isobel who were keen to hug each other when the deal was done, so to speak. Isobel had been more upset this time than at any other time and could not bare another rough patch between the adults.

Alex was keen to sleep in Zara's house to keep an eye on things, as well as to sleep with his wife, who was feeling a bit fragile.

"Alex, do you want to sleep in here with Isobel and maybe Hector could go with Padruig to the other wee house tonight?" said Zara reading their minds.

"I'm staying in here," demanded Hector. "Ali can go," he added.

"Okay, that's fine with me. Would you all like to eat now before you go to your house?" Zara asked. They were all hungry, as were the bairns and luckily Marion had dropped in extra food when she saw the men arrive.

"I'll be glad to get back to normal food," said Padruig. There was a lot of agreement on that front.

The following day was the day of the departure for the whole family, but Zara asked first if she could visit Kenneth at the Art Gallery and thank him for selling the Fairy Art and ask if he had any other suggestions for artistic expression to sell in his gallery. No one else wanted to go to the Art Gallery, so Zara obtained directions from Marion and the next morning after breakfast, Zara started the walk, uphill through Loch Garry Ranch, which felt awkward being on another's farm. However, there were two women waving to her from their front verandah, so she walked across to them asking permission to walk through their farm to the Art Gallery. Their names were Siobhan Cameron Grant and Jean Grant MacDonnell, who were both lovely ladies and were lucky to have each other for company there. Zara didn't have that kind of feminine company in the Aird, except her two daughters, but on both Glengarry farms there were equal numbers of both genders, so it would be easier, she thought, to fit in bit by bit.

"I sell the honey here in big clay pots as well as small ones," Jean explained. "At first when my second husband Duncan died, I found it hard to make ends meet, so it was suggested that I grow bees for the honey. I was given one hive to start with, but I worried that the bees wouldn't like me, but they did and I liked them, so I got more boxes and placed them in different locations under different trees. The way it works around here on our farms is that we all have to produce something, then provide that free of charge to all of the residents. Then what is left over, we can sell when Kenneth has the Art Gallery open and now the people just come here to refill their clay pots, so I am making quite a pretty penny now," Jean said.

"Where do you get the clay pots?" Zara asked.

"That's from me," Siobhan added. "I had to find a way to provide too, so I took up pottery and made Jean's clay pots. I also sell all kinds of pottery at the stall on an Art Gallery open day," Siobhan explained.

Eventually finding the Art Gallery, Zara found both Kenneth and Ivy inside chatting and giggling about something. Their bairn was named April, but wasn't allowed inside there when he had fumey materials out used in artwork, in case it damaged her lungs. Zara introduced herself as well as excused herself, but was hugged by the amorous Kenneth who loved her Fairy Art.

"Welcome, welcome, please sit-down Zara," he said. "So, you have now overcome your shyness Zara?" Kenneth asked.

Slightly ashamed of her previous shyness, Zara asked him for advice. She wanted to know what he could suggest in the way of different art forms for her to complete, apart from the Fairy Art. Lots of ideas were thrown around as he demonstrated his artistic skills. He really was very talented.

"You could make pottery, like Siobhan does but in an artistic way, like sculpture," Kenneth suggested.

"May I also suggest that whatever money you make from it, is given to your husband because in your special case of your marriage, there was no dowry, like I received for my wife eventually, once April was born. We don't know what's inside people's heads, even though we may think we do, but you may find that at the bottom of your issues with your husband is money. He is a Scot after all. If you hand over your earnings, he may feel that it is justified and you will benefit from that, I hope. At the same time, protect the income of your bairns if they ever get work, because he might think he is entitled to that," Kenneth said.

It was a surprising angle that hadn't been explored and Zara was happy to take all the advice that she could get.

She then asked if Malcolm was busy. "He's over there with his precious coos. I think he's in love with them," Kenneth said jokingly and laughed. Zara said her farewells and let them know they were all leaving. Malcolm was amongst his coos sitting on a rock and reading a book out loud to them.

"Hello Malcolm," Zara called out.

"Oh, hello Zara," Malcolm answered. "I'm here reading to my ladies. I want more calves this year, I told them," he said. Zara hadn't known that he was quite the quaint character because he comes across so bold and strong. She thanked him for his assistance and hospitality and let him know that they were on their way back to the Aird soon.

"Not a problem, anytime. You are welcome here Zara," Malcolm said. "Have you sorted it out?" he asked.

"I don't think it will ever be quite the same as it was, but we have sorted it as far as we can for now, for which I sincerely thank you," Zara said. "Some things can't be understood I suppose, but not being Scottish there's a cultural divide perhaps where I don't understand a lot, especially when they are all speaking in Gaelic," she explained.

"Can you learn Gaelic?" Malcolm asked.

"I've tried. I'm no good at it and they laugh at me when I try," Zara said. "Not complaining, just how it is," she said a little embarrassed.

"I'll post you some books for learning Gaelic for bairns. It's easier to follow than the adult versions," Malcolm offered.

"Thank you, Malcolm. You are really a Saint," she said.

"Nae, just human family Zara. I know what it's like for you too. My first wife terminated three of my bairns and tried to have my twins terminated. If it hadn't been for Hugh Mohr Chisholm, they wouldn't be alive today," Malcolm stated.

"Hugh Chisholm was here?" Zara asked.

"Aye, he lived with Ruth Beaton, the Midwife. Did you know him?" he asked.

"Aye, he was my first husband, Isobel's Father," Zara answered, then she let Malcolm know she was on her way back home. Maybe via Craskie. Zara wondered if Hugh's ghost was hanging around Glengarry.

On the way back home, the group of horses and their riders made their way quietly in the direction of Glen Urquhart through Glenmoriston first. Zara wanted to speak with Hamish at Craskie Farm. The bairns were going to need a paying job and she could only think of Ali, as her oldest son who could work for Hamish now it was much busier and Grigor wasn't working the crops anymore. Kenneth had said to protect their wages, so she would tell Hamish that and if this whole scenario reoccurred, then she too would move there with all of the bairns, except Isobel, unless Alex followed them.

Zara was not confident that her troubles with Grigor were over. Grigor had not made love to her during the previous night. He turned his back to her and both of them found it hard to fall to sleep, but he did first eventually. It had felt so lonely to be in the same bed as the man who wasn't acknowledging her existance and she had felt rejected. He had not forgiven her for bringing his morning tea with that trollop to the whole family's attention. Then upon discovering that woman's night time infidelities, he had been shocked, but why? Why should it concern him now?

Zara was making a plan to first help her children from it happening again. They had suffered and they shouldn't have because of her and Grigor. It seemed to take longer than usual to get to Glenmoriston. They would not make it to the Aird until the small hours of the morning or stop by the side of the road after Craskie, she had thought. Craskie was coming up and she was nervous. She hadn't asked Grigor's permission for Ali to work away from home. She asked Ali to go in with her and no-one thought anything of it while they were waiting for her to see Hamish.

Hamish opened the big oak door and welcomed them both in. He was such a nice man. Zara asked if there was a job available for Ali at Craskie while living with him. Ali was surprised but not displeased. Hamish said immediately that he needed someone to work in the oat fields, if he could do that, which required him to do the soil course also in Invermoriston. He would earn a reasonable wage and Zara quietly asked him to put his wage directly into his hand each week or open a bank account in his name only. She whispered for him not to give Ali's money to Grigor.

"Can I leave my son with you now then?" Zara asked. It was heartbreaking to leave Ali behind, but as she approached the horses to get his, she had to answer the obvious questions.

"Where's Ali?" asked Grigor.

"He was offered a job here and I accepted, so I'm taking in his horse," she said.

Hector was furious. "What about me too? I can work too," Hector said. She had to take him in also then to talk to Hamish, leading both horses.

Grigor was dumbfounded. Padruig and Alex understood but were waiting for Grigor to explode. Hector was given a junior groom's job, but she had to make him promise to behave and to look after his wages. The first week she instructed them to buy work boots from Frasers Trading Post. The second wage to buy a warm coat and gloves. The third to save in a bank but not to give it to anyone.

Zara asked Grigor, as she approached him if he wouldn't mind if both lads stayed here with Hamish to work and mounted her horse to leave. Fatma and Isobel rode either side of their Mither, expecting trouble as they rode off in silence. They had to stop to rest and give water to the horses.

"Zara, this is not going to make him happy," Padruig said.

"I know, but the bairns will suffer again and I want and need them to be earning their own money," she replied. "They will be safe with Hamish," she added. It would remove a financial burden that was unspoken naturally, but a man obviously felt that responsibility and our farm wasn't like a big business, it only just fed us all. Zara expressed to Padruig that she too feared arriving home in the Aird when Grigor would make his feelings felt. Until then, they were dealing with a gloomy, unhappy looking husband.

31. Malcolm Explains

Meanwhile back in Loch Garry, before going up to Malcolm's house for an arranged dinner, Marion discussed her observations of Zara's whole family and friends with her husband, Bruce. "Bruce darling," she said. "You know when Zara's additional family members arrived, led by that man at the front, named Padruig, I felt a familiarity with him, but also the need to quickly arrange stabling for his horse and get the key for them to stay in Hamish's place. What I mean is I wanted to please him, not the husband. Which one was the husband?" she asked.

Bruce MacDonald

"He was already in her house remember? We heard them arguing a bit. He was the one with that dark beard and wearing that philibeg for a while," Bruce answered.

"There was something about him, I thought. He was so dignified. I really liked him, so caring for Zara's bairns," Marion added. "I'm going to ask Malcolm if I've met him before, maybe that's it," she concluded. The happy, older couple walked up through Loch Garry Ranch, as usual and into Malcolm's farms to get to his house. Kenneth would be there too, so she was looking forward to seeing both her beautiful lads as well as their bairns. Kenneth only had one wee lass, April, but Malcolm now had six bairns with the newest ones being Gordon and Eschina, with his new wife Ailsa, while Malcolm's oldest son Alex was now working as a Doctor in the Invermoriston Hospital.

Islay let them in when they arrived and the family was happy to see both Ma and Bruce. They were the most popular parents or in laws that anyone could have. Meredith helped Ailsa

Marion Nachten MacDonald

cook the feast to which she and Hugh were both invited, but he and Meredith were going home to the loch to spend time together. They had both been busy and a restful night was in order for them, so they left once Malcolm's family was all sorted. Over dinner was the usual time for all kinds of topics to come up and the obvious one tonight was Zara's family.

"Malcolm dear," Ma asked, "The man named Padruig who led Zara's bairns here, have I met him anywhere before?" she asked.

I was in a bind now with Ma asking that question because Padruig Dubh was her Father. Poor Ma, what could I say to divert attention away from him? I doubt Ma would understand that he was an other-wordly soul coming and going between worlds, as he has had to do in this emergency. He probably hadn't known his lovely daughter, Marion, was going to be there. Reluctantly, he honestly explained.

"Ma, that was Grandda. You met him on his death bed, but now he has resumed his peak physical condition in death and lives with Zara's family in the Aird. He is Grigor Mohr's best friend," Malcolm answered. Bruce knew about Zara and others but hadn't realised who Padruig was, or that he too was of the Otherworld.

"So how many of them are of this world Malcolm?" Bruce asked.

"I am not sure of the status of Isobel especially, who seems fully alive to me. As for the other bairns, I am not sure of them either and I think they too are unsure. As for Alex, Padruig, Grigor Mohr and Zara, they are all of the Otherworld," I answered. "I am now relying on you all as my close family, not to repeat this, as it might endanger their ability to function as they are now. Please do not endanger them in any way nor ourselves, if people think we are nuts seeing ghosts and the like," I added.

Kenneth and Ivy sat there in utter shock that they had been talking normally to a spectre who had problems just like the rest of us do.

"I feel like an idiot now," Kenneth said. "I told Zara that perhaps Grigor was unhappy about not having any dowry from her family upon marriage and to give any of her earnings to him to make up for it. I didn't know they were spectres. How could she have had a dowry if she was dead? I'm sorry Malcolm," Kenneth said.

"It's even more complicated than that," I explained. "Zara was first married to Hugh Mohr Chisholm and sometime after that was when she died but was with child to Hugh. That child is Isobel with that blonde hair that she has. Hugh had already left Zara, once he saw she was deceased, was the story and her only clan's person was Grigor, who remained behind to prepare her body for burial. The others all left also," I explained.

"What others?" Ivy asked.

"She had been researching for a book or two books and was in communication with them all, so at that time she was living with all of the Seven Glenmoriston Men. Upon her death, they all went their own ways. Except Grigor," I answered.

"Then what happened?" Ma asked. "Grigor saw movement in her womb and realised that there was life there that he had to preserve somehow, so he went about repairing all of her injuries and treating her as alive, so the bairn could be born, which she was and Grigor delivered her, even though her Mither was in a poorly, but conscious state by then with no memory of having died. It took a lot of explaining to her that she was no longer alive and unable to return to her other three daughters at her old home in her own time period. However, she grew fond of him and cared for the wee bairn," I said.

"Grigor was only thinking of Hugh then, who had to know that he had a wee bairn. The other changes that took place were her appearance, as she took on a younger form, the one you see today. I know this all sounds bizarre, but we will all go there once we die, and I hope I am still able to talk to you after I die. Finally, after she and the wee bairn were both ready, he sent them to where Hugh was then living high up in the mountains in Chisholm country, where unfortunately she met up with Hugh's wife, unknown to her, as well as a lot of his bairns. A local farmer had picked her up to take her there and when she told Hugh that Isobel was his, he rejected them both, not believing their story as her appearance was younger and he had thought she was dead. That farmer, who had his own agenda, offered her his home for a while," I said.

"Luckily, Zara always wore an identifying brooch, given to her by Grigor Mohr from Culloden Field. An old one. Hugh went to his other friends, Padruig and John MacDonald to tell them what had happened, who in turn spied on them at that house. It was definitely her, as she was still wearing that same brooch and there could be no doubt that the wee bairn was his, with all that blonde hair. They told him what an idiot he was and so on, to have rejected them both, but getting them off that farmer then wasn't going to be easy. So, they had to kidnap them both with John fetching her things from inside his house and that's when they all got back together again," Malcolm explained glossing over many details.

"What about the other wife?" asked Ma.

"Hugh always claimed that he had divorced her and remarried Zara in her religion too, but how true that is, I don't know because they were all Catholic," I said.

"So how did it end with Hugh?" asked Bruce.

"He was a playboy, was our Hugh, but he did love her and she loved him until she was with child again and his brothers were keen to break the law in so many ways, stealing here and there, including stealing a dowry, promising Hugh as the so-called 'single man'. Zara, who was six months with child, was ravished by one of the brothers, other than Hugh," I said cringing. "His Catholic older brother claimed that her being with child while unalive in her Otherworld meant that what she was carrying, was a demon to be rid of," I said.

"Oh," exclaimed Ma. "Did she lose the wee bairn then son?" she asked sympathetically.

"Aye she did and Grigor Mohr decided it was time then to leave them all, so he took Zara and wee Isobel up to the Aird and you know the rest," I said.

"No, we don't. If they left Padruig behind too, then how did Padruig and Alex end up with them now?" Ma asked.

"Alex followed them first, from memory and Padruig realising the whole group had split up and would follow Zara, so he eventually was accepted into their home in the Aird too, to become who you saw," Malcolm explained.

"Now how about coffee Ma?" I asked. Ailsa said she would get it and had been fascinated by the whole story, but it was a serious and sad one, that no-one was smiling over.

"When did she marry Grigor then?" Islay asked.

"When they reached the remotest part of the Aird, they met a farmer named John Fraser who invited them in. He lived alone and was glad of the company. They had already hand fasted at that time, but unmarried in a Kirk, until dialogue began between Hugh and Grigor to adopt Isobel and so the adoption and the marriage took place on the same day," I said then paused.

"I'll tell you more another day Ma. It's making me sad, I don't know why," I replied.

32. *Arriving Nearer the Aird*

Zara's group of horseriders had stopped again to rest in the darkest of nights. It was becoming much colder.

"It's going to snow," said Padruig.

"Oh no, it's so cold," Zara said. They rested under a tree where less snow was falling. Padruig began talking of the old stories of Scotland and their hardships and growing strengths and clan warfare and it lulled all three ladies into sleep with Alex beside Isobel to keep her warm. Fatma was cold.

"Grigor, can you keep Fatma warm?" Zara asked. Both parents were either side of her listening to Padruig rattling off the names of ancient kings and kingdoms, land gained and lost and gained again. Then surprisingly told the story of the MacGregors during Proscription and how many were beheaded by the Campbells. Stirring to his stories Zara asked,

"What about the Pictish people, they had kings too?" she said.

"Oh, Zara is getting back to normal. Can't forget the Pictish people, the first people of Scotland," and he spoke of their kings, their battles with the Northumbrians and the arrival of Christianity by way of Celtic Catholicism.

"Their argument was over the date of Easter," Zara said. "So, King Nachtain, who was the grandson of the one who fought that battle of Dun Nechtain I think, changed their date of Easter. He was a religious scholar also who should have been a Priest and he wrote to the leader of the Catholics in Northumbria to form a Peace Treaty by way of conforming with their type of Catholicism. Nachtain then wrote many letters to his Bishops who were displeased and even their hair cut was altered," Zara added. "But he created peace, that was what he was known for," she said.

"So, if I write you a letter then, will you eventually forgive me Zara and stop giving away my bairns?" Grigor asked.

"Oh Grigor," Zara cried into his arms.

"I do forgive you. My heart was broken into pieces. I am sorry now about Hector and Ali, but do you think they could work a while or come back home?" she asked.

"I want them home with us and the next time you give one of our bairns away, I'll be ripping up that agreement," Grigor said firmly.

"Alright," Zara agreed.

They mounted up again before the horses became too stiff and finally made it to their home in the Aird with smoke still coming from one of the chimneys. John was keeping one fire going. They all crossed their burn in single file almost in disbelief that they had finally made it back home. It really was home and alternatives could never replace one's real home. Stabling the horses without Hector was harder than usual with the work he did in there. Zara felt a pang to her heart at her hero's absence. She hadn't wanted Hector to leave just yet, but wondered now how they would receive the news of coming home and the disappointment Hamish also may feel.

Unsaddling her horse, Zara was deep in thought at what it would look like with Grigor going to Craskie and fetching his sons back. More unsettling for the lads, she thought and disappointing, unless they regretted taking the jobs. She saw how excited they were at the prospect of getting new boots and a new coat and gloves. Grigor didn't have the money for new boots or coats for them.

"You had something in mind for taking Ali there then?" Grigor came to her and asked.

"Aye, they need new work boots and new coats and gloves from Fraser's which is right near there. It would be easier than us going to Fraser's later, as it is next door to Hamish. I wanted them to have more warm clothing and footwear," Zara replied with a degree of disappointment.

Zara went on and told Grigor that she had talked to a few folks up in Glengarry about how to earn money in the Aird and Kenneth said to give anything artistic that Zara earned to Grigor, so it paid him back for not receiving a dowry for marrying her.

"I am in debt to you Grigor. I am sorry I didn't come with that money, only troubles for you," Zara said, still feeling inferior to other women since Grigor had that morning tea with another woman. Grigor was surprisingly unsure how to take in that new piece of information.

"Zara, have you lost your belief in our love?" Grigor asked.

"No, I would never stop loving you, but what I have lost is hard to put my finger on. It's more like I've lost you, your love, respect, concern, basically all that I had taken for granted that was part of our forever love. I couldn't survive this place, this world both physically and emotionally without you, so I knew that this time I had to fight for you, which is what I did," Zara said. "It hasn't made us happy and I don't know who I am to you now, I suppose. I have no confidence with what I can say or do with you. Maybe you might be happier with someone better than me. I can't speak Gaelic, I am just lacking in everything you respect and value," Zara explained.

Grigor was a bit awkward with what to say. Had he really done this much damage to Zara? Padruig was afraid of some permanent damage and maybe he was now looking at it.

"Zara, I didn't want to love you less by doing what I did, I wanted to love you more and you to love me more. I thought you'd still be at home waiting for me and you could have screamed any obscenity at me. Then I would be sure of us. But you were gone and this time you were really gone a long way, with two of our bairns. I was frantic, so you can understand my anger, can't you?" he asked.

"I don't understand you needing me to show that jealousy when you know I adore you, don't you?" she asked. "After the new bairn was born, I had to pay her attention, was that why?

Did you feel the new bairn had taken some of the love away from you?" Zara sked.

"Aye, maybe I was a bit jealous of the attention she got," he admitted.

"I am sorry Grigor that you felt that way. I was overjoyed at our wee lassie. It helped me overcome losing Sakina. It was like it had allowed her to be born in a way. It was a shocking loss of Sakina, you know that of all people. Only you knew what to do that terrible day to bring us here and marry and start over again and slowly recover," she said. "What will you have me do then now, I'm not sure?" Zara asked.

"Come inside by the fire with me before you get too cold out here, is the first thing we'll do," he answered. Zara and Grigor carefully walked over the snow-covered ground and when they both entered their warm home, despite the late hour, John was up preparing them all some hot food and hot soup and hot coffee.

Zara had been given honey from Jean in one of Siobhan's clay pots, so she put it on the table for them all to share too.

John was so pleased to see them all and welcomed them home too.

"Zara, I'm so glad you're back," John said.

"Where are Hector and Ali?" he asked.

"One of my ideas was to get Ali a job at Craskie for work boots and warm clothes and so on, but Hector wanted to stay there too. Grigor disagreed and is fetching them back tomorrow. I wish they could at least stay to get new boots and warm coats for this weather," she said.

"Aye, but they might disclose who we all are and suddenly we might get the newspapers here and that will be the end of our lifestyle here in this remote area," John said.

"Ali wouldn't do anything like that, but I suppose Hector could accidentally put his foot in it," she agreed.

"So, I am fetching my lad's mid morning after you tell me what has gone on with the farm John," he said. After a pleasant dinner with John, Zara slept without bathing before her husband joined her. He made love to her in a way that was just relieving himself of the built-up tension, but not to please his wife and being so tired, Zara decided not to bother asking for her own gratification.

33. *Arisaids and Plaids*

The early morning on a farm was always busy, but more so that day when a rider from Glenmoriston came galloping in across the burn with a large package addressed to Zara MacGregor from Grigor Og in Loch Garry, then he swung his horse around and left again.

"What is it Ma?" asked both Fatma and Isobel looking very curious.

"I don't know but it feels like clothing," she said.

"Clothing. Maybe something for us?" Fatma asked hopefully. Zara asked all of the men, including Grigor if they wouldn't mind if the lassies could open up the package and sort it out, to which they nodded in agreement seeing the looks on Isobel and Fatma's faces. With the bedroom door closed, both younger lassies were ripping at the package.

"Ma. Arisaids. There are arisaids in here, as well as men's plaids of differing clans like all those new designs they have made now. There's a letter too Ma from Grigor Og. Feels like coin inside too," Fatma said excitedly handing it to her Mither.

Opening the letter from Grigor Og, he had apologised for missing their departure because he had gone into his daughter's Mill to get these items for them all. The coin was from a 'pass around' amongst the family to help them pay their way back home. Zara went immediately out to the kitchen before Grigor Mohr left to give it to him.

"Grigor, this came from your oldest son, Grigor Og and others in Glengarry. When you get to Craskie Farm, can you please buy the lads working boots or they will be so disappointed?" she asked.

"Anything else?" he asked. "Coats and gloves for the upcoming winter, if there's enough in there." Grigor Mohr accepted the charity from his son gladly and went to see John about the farm before he was to leave.

When Zara walked back into her room, the lassies had put the goods into piles. Three arisaids for the three women. One was obviously MacGregor, one was one of the new MacGregor designs and the last one was uncertain but pretty, so Isobel wanted that one, so Zara gave it to her and took the new one for Fatma and gave it to her and Zara kept the older design.

"You can show your husbands if you like Isobel," Zara said.

"Nae, not yet. There's a MacDonald of Aonach here for my husband. Can I give it to him too?" she asked.

"Hold onto it for a moment and wait," Zara implored.

"This plaid is Grant Glenmoriston, so Padruig is the only Grant. That's for him. This plaid is MacGregor hunting, so that's for my husband. I'll hold onto that," Zara said.

"Which ones are these then?" they asked of two others that they were unfamiliar with and there was even a Fraser hunting tartan. Zara knew the Fraser hunting tartan must be for John, but the last two were for her sons, so she had to ask Grigor before he left.

"Now Isobel, give your husband his," she said as she strode out to the kitchen again.

"Padruig there's one plaid here for you from Grigor Og. It's nice, I hope you like it," Padruig was thrilled as was his good friend Alex when Grigor was walking in.

"My darling, this plaid is for you from your son. It's a MacGregor plaid. Do you like it?" Zara asked hopefully.

"Aye, its nice. Do you like it then?" he asked nervously. "Aye, I really do, it's lovely. Can I ask you please about the the two we are unsure of and John's?" Zara asked as she showed the two tartan plaids of a new design but MacGregor just the same.

"These are for Ali and Hector being MacGregor, that one is Fraser for John," he answered.

John was so happy Zara thought he could cry. His face went all red.

"Here my friend, from my son Grigor Og. It's for you, the only Fraser. I'll take these with me to give to my lads, then they won't mind leaving, will they?" he asked, looking doubtful.

"They love their Mither and their Father. Of course, they'll come home," Padruig said boldly.

"I need Hector for the potato crops. Tell him I can't manage it without him and the horses are all upset without him too," said Alex, exaggerating the truth like he always did.

"And Ali? What will you say to him if he has already enrolled in that soil course in Invermoriston?" Zara asked.

"You failed to mention a soil course in Invermoriston Zara," he said, looking towards Padruig for guidance.

"If he has already been enrolled, then leave him with Hamish as he is the oldest and arrange for weekends at home with us, that way all those boots will be paid for by him. If not, bring the lad home where he should be," Padruig said.

"I need someone to help me build a kiln so I can make pottery plates, bowls and art to sell, so he could be my offsider in finding clay of differing colours as well as build the kiln and help me sell what is art or surplus. Like a wee business enterprise," Zara said trying to convince everyone of its usefulness.

"A kiln. What a bonny idea. I wished I had one of those when all my china was stolen. I'll help you Zara if no-one else is up for it," John added.

"Good, we also need hives for bees to live in, to have our own honey. We need lots of those boxes which Isobel and Fatma can manage together to become productive," Zara said remembering that word productive after talking to Siobhan and Jean.

As Grigor was about to leave already mounted on his horse, Zara waved goodbye to him when he said, "So, are you coming then?" he asked. Feeling flustered Zara said she would and went about preparing Dorothia and strapping her to her back while John fetched her horse for her already saddled.

"Oh John, you didn't have to do that, you are not a groom, but God bless you," Zara said.

"Hurry up Zara," Grigor said impatiently. Then the husband and wife and wee bairn were on their way back to Craskie Farm at the northern most part of Glenmoriston.

Hamish was busy working as was the entire property, unlike when Grigor Og was in charge. When Grigor stated his intentions, Hamish just politely said, "Let's discuss this inside the house. Firstly, I have given both lads an advance on their wages for new boots to protect their feet. I didn't want any farm accident to harm their feet, so I got good ones from Fraser's, so that money would be owed to Craskie Farm if they both leave today," he said calmly and pleasant like he was talking about the weather on a sunny day.

Hamish had learned a lot from old Isobel, it was really remarkable.

"No problem," said Grigor who hated debt.

"I can pay you now," he said with confidence as he opened up his sporran to count out the money owed. He was surprised at how much the boots were, which didn't leave much in his wee purse.

"Both lads are really good workers and they have fitted in really well. Ali just knuckles down and quietly works while Hector jokes with his colleagues who have tried to belittle the newcomer with little success with all of his Gaelic obscenities, unknown by most of the youth these days," Hamish said. "It reminded me of the days when Padruig was alive with all of his creative Gaelic obscenities as I passed by the stables and listened to young Hector. Where did he learn those from?" Hamish asked.

"His Father," Zara was quick to answer.

"Okay then there's the soil course that Ali is enrolled in. Can we come to an arrangement Grigor?" Hamish asked. "How about Ali completes the course while still working for me and living under my roof, then asks the Professor at that course about what can grow in the Aird specifically and what to do in those snowy conditions?" he said. "At the same time, he would be working my soil and understanding the science of it all and once he is ready to go to plant crops in the Aird on your property, then he can be released from his contract?" asked Hamish. "What do you say?" he asked.

"What about Hector?" Grigor asked. "I need him at home," he added.

"Alright, he is released, but I want him, you and Zara to know, that there is always a job here for him with the horses. He will make a great horseman one day, like Grigor Mohr was," Hamish added.

"It's smoko soon. Stay for smoko and they will all come in here and you can talk to your sons or go first to where they are working to see them in their new roles," Hamish added.

Grigor decided that he and Zara would go and see both lads in their roles as they worked and Grigor was impressed at his sons' competence. He was even a proud Father. From the oat fields to the stables, he observed and spoke to them both. It was obvious that Ali did not want to leave but pleased to see his parents just the same. Hector, on the other hand, was persuaded with the promise of assisting more around the farm. He was asked to assist Zara with helping his sisters set up the beehives as well as figuring out how to build the kiln. The clay was easy he had said because he used to play with it and knew where various types and colours of clay were. Zara was pleased her lad was going to come home with them, but thought he might go back to Craskie sooner rather than later. We said our farewells to Ali once again and wished him all the best in his course. Zara asked him to bring back the knowledge to grow either oats or wheat and he would be in charge of it.

Before departing the area, Grigor wanted to take a look at what Fraser's had these days as they had expanded substantially into selling ploughs.

"We will have to buy an ox Grigor and borrow Charlotte's harnessing gear when we start ploughing," Zara said.

"Aye, we will," Grigor said looking at the new ploughs. The hand ploughs were a lot better than they used to be, but who could afford one?

"Farmers wait until they have harvested and sold most of their crop before they can buy an expensive item like this, but it helps to avoid taxes if they do," Zara said.

"How do you know that?" he asked.

"I grew up in a small farming community where my Father sold these things to the farmers," Zara said. Grigor looked then at the coats she had wanted for the lads that were waterproof.

"No way I'm paying that price. How expensive are these coats?" he exclaimed. Zara was feeling eyes all around them burning into them because of his criticism and she said, "Darling, I want to save some money." "Well, that's good!" Grigor said.

"Excuse me," she asked the man serving. "Where do I buy skeins of wool?" Zara asked.

"Up there in those houses. The wool waulking ladies. They have all that stuff," he replied gruffly pointing up the top of New Farm to the three houses that stood there at the top end of that grazing land.

"This must be the land that Malcolm's Mither now owns," she commented as they moved between the coos to get to the ladies' houses. Not knowing which door to knock on, Zara chose the centre house and a friendly lady answered the door.

"What can I do for you?" she asked.

"Oh hello, I was looking to buy skeins of wool suitable for knitting socks. Do you have those here?" Zara asked. Opening the door widely she confirmed they sold wool as well as woollen jumpers.

"Come on in," she said. "My name's Mairi."

Mairi had a delightful range of wool from which Zara selected and asked her husband if they could afford that for socks for the lads as well as all four of the men. He said he wasn't paying for the men, just himself and the bairns and his daughters if they wanted socks. Then Zara spotted the most delightful jumper she had ever seen. The wool was soft, not itchy and it was a pretty apricot colour with the head of a highland coo on the front.

"This is so clever. Did you knit this Mairi?" Zara asked.

"Aye, we can be creative now that we are out of that wretched Mill," she answered.

"Are you the ladies who were all rescued from imprisonment in that Mill in Inverness?" Zara asked.

"Aye, that's us," she answered.

"They withheld our wages too, so we were stuck until the men came and broke us out," she answered. "God bless them. We had to fight for our wages though from that Isobel-Mairi," she said.

"Malcolm MacNachten's Mither, Marion owns all of this and she got us all settled in free at first until we were earning. She still doesn't charge us much," she added.

"Hurry up Zara," Grigor said impatiently.

"You could all write a wee book on your experiences. A short story really," advised Zara.

"If you get it printed on cheap paper with a drawing of the wool waulking on the front cover, you could all earn an income from the book sales," Zara said. Grigor picked up the jumper with the highland coo on it and asked Hector if it would fit him and if he liked it as it was much cheaper than those coats at Frasers.

"Aye Da, it fits and there's two the same. I got one day's pay, so I can buy Ma one too, then we'll be matching," he said smiling and avoiding looking upon any unhappiness on his Father's face. Hector held the jumper up against his Mither.

"What do you think Ma, matching?" he asked.

"Oh, aye son," she said and held him tightly. "Thank you," Zara expressed.

Grigor grunted and counting out his money, there was enough to purchase two more jumpers with different designs. One for for Isobel and one for Fatma. One had a stag on the front and one had a baby lamb or goat. Their prices were awfully good and the family walked away carrying four jumpers and forty skeins of wool. They were given a discount on the skeins and she threw in a few for free because of how much the family had bought as well as extra knitting needles and tips on knitting socks.

"Thank you so much Grigor. That was a wonderful and worthwhile time buying what we needed," Zara said.

Grigor did look pleased to be thanked. They had left their horses on the farm while they shopped and went to collect them, finding that they had all been fed, brushed down, hooves checked, one shoe replaced then saddled up for them as they waited. Hector threw some dirty Gaelic words to his show off friend while he showed off his new jumper. He was going to be just fine in either world. The proud Father rode off with us carrying a different outlook on life. Thank goodness. Maybe his wee tantrum was nearly over, Zara had hoped sincerely. She hadn't had any decent sex in ages, it seemed and with only breast feeding on the hop as she had been for days, it seemed she would never get back to those enjoyable sexy moments the two of them had so enjoyed and were known for.

The wee bairn wanted to be fed, the moment the horses started to pick up pace and Zara had to ask for a slow pace while she fed her. Grigor and Hector talked a lot as Zara tended to the bairns' needs and also prayed silently for her marriage to be whole again, for her husband to find her attractive again and that Hector would be happy with leaving his brother behind. Before they started a quick pace again Zara said to her beloved son Hector, "You will be running stables one day. Malcolm's twins are going to be teamsters and are in training now as their parents save up for the Clydesdales," Zara said.

They will be the next team in the area who Hector would be dealing with and he would like them and would possibly be the only lad capable of dealing with those lively and Gaelic versed lads. When they arrived home, there was another parcel addressed to Zara, which Grigor insisted on opening this time. Zara showed no objection. It was the book Malcolm had promised on Gaelic for beginners for bairns, not adult as he had explained.

"You are going to learn Gaelic then?" Grigor asked.

"I'll try Grigor, but so far, I'm no good at it. Malcolm thought this book would be easier to learn from, so I could understand more of our conversations," she explained.

"You have involved a lot of people in our lives Zara. No more now. We need our privacy," he ordered.

"Aye husband," she complied and she felt that raunchy sex with her husband fly away on the wind.

34. *I Love You Sweet Grigor*

Zara decided to do something different for dinner that night and asked John for his old meat mincer to mince up the lovely freshly slaughtered coo meat. Hoping to do a version of spaghetti bolognese, without the spaghetti, she cooked up the mince with the many newly ripened tomatoes that loved life in the Aird. They had all ripened while they were away. Zara had carrots, onions and a garlic mixture she had made up when she had been to Inverness and actually found garlic in a shop. It was like finding gold, but now was the time to test it on these Highlanders. Without spaghetti, she decided she would bake Turkish pide with goat's cheese and her home-grown English spinach on the top, which would be ripped up by the diners then soak up the minced meat on top of it. That was the idea anyway.

Grigor Mohr MacGregor

Served up with Turkish coffee and a chocolate sauce pudding was her menu for the evening. She was busy for the rest of the day wearing her new jumper until she was too hot over the stove top. Zara asked Isobel to light up all the fires and bathe before the men came in. John was busy building the beehives with Hector assisting him and they knew where there was a wild hive up a tree, so before they knocked off, they were both getting that hive and setting up one of the boxes near the house, where it was warm. Zara gave both Hector and John midge nets for their faces in case the bees were unhappy. Fatma followed them to see how the bees behaved all the way back to the house. She was thoroughly excited about her new friends, the bees and John gave them some kind of blessing and instructed her to talk to them every day.

Zara taste tested her mince meat dinner, never yet eaten by her family. To her, the flavour was perfect in its proportions, with the addition of her herbs from the herb garden, thanks to Craskie Farm who had given her all of the initial plants to start her garden with. There was marjoram and oregano and others whose name she couldn't remember, as well as salt and pepper to taste. The family were all due back in at any moment, so she put the coffee on to be ready and set the table without anyone assisting. Zara had made six pides to go with it, unsure of how many were needed in this experiment. One by one they all drifted in at the smell of the coffee and she placed a big pot of the mince in the centre of the table with a ladel to serve it up with.

"Dinner," she called as she poured the coffees and took the breads from the oven as they all sat down. Padruig was first, Alex second, Hector and John third and fourth looking starving, then Grigor and the lassies.

"Whats this then Zara?" Padruig asked.

She explained to them what it was and spooned out the mince onto their plates or bowls in the case of Isobel's bairns, Donald and Andrew and wee Causantin and told them to rip some of the Turkish bread called Pide to eat it with. Maybe scoop the meat onto the bread. They were all seated, including Zara when she scooped her own piping hot mince on top of bread as they watched her eat it first. It was delicious, she thought and easier to eat than some of the stews that were a bit too chewy. Causantin was able to feed himself now and he was really happy with the new minced meat especially, as were Isobel's bairns. Grigor tentatively took a mouth full of the odd-looking meal ripping up the bread as his wife had done and then the other men followed. Alex really liked it.

"This is nice Zara, I like it. It's really tasty," he said so Zara poured him another coffee.

"I think it's nice Ma," said Fatma. "I love the unusual bread." she added.

"I like it too Ma. Can you share the recipe with us?" Isobel asked.

"Aye, of course. Glad you like it, but if you think it needs something like more pepper, then just say so then I can alter it next time," Zara said.

"Nae, don't alter it," Grigor said. "This is even nicer than your stews, wife," he said laying claim to Zara's achievement. She was 'his wife' once more.

"I have to say Zara, I've never seen or tasted anything like this before, so I was a bit scared at first, but I like it. Can I have some more?" Padruig asked.

Zara scooped more out for Padruig as more plates were held up for more, including the bairns. The last of the pide was ripped up and shared between everyone.

"Cook more of these, next time," Alex said almost demandingly.

"I admit Zara, I have missed your food while you were away and now this. It's amazing. I love it. I reckon cook more minced meat next time. I'll help you mince up the meat too if you like" John said. Hector came around and kissed his Ma and thanked her, saying Cora's food was lousy, so he was glad to be home with his Ma and family, especially for the food. Zara wasn't quite expecting to be lavished with any praise and love from her son and started to weap. She managed to choke it back to serve up the dessert.

"I have dessert too. Chocolate pudding," she said smiling. Her husband was pleased even proud of his wife and she was hoping that sex was back on their agenda after her bath.

"We'll clean up Ma," said Isobel, Fatma and Hector.

The bath water was cooking up nicely in Zara's room as she undressed ready to soak herself to both wash and to relax. As she was about to step into the lovely hot water, her husband came inside their bedroom looking upon the vision of his naked wife.

"Sorry Grigor, do you want to bathe first," she asked but he had that look in his eyes.

"Nae you first, while I just watch you. Are you washing your hair?" he asked.

"Aye, it's a bit smelly, even though I'll have to dry it by the fire," she said.

"Let me wash your hair then," he said surprisingly and took the jug and poured the water over his wife's head and began to wash it with her home-made shampoo and massaging her scalp. He hadn't done this for a very long time. Then he reached across her face to kiss her on the lips sensually, like it always used to be. She caressed his head as he reached into the bath at her delicate feminine areas to massage her sexually and spoke in that sensual Gaelic that she had never understood, but it always made her want him. He rubbed his hands up and down her slinky body now admiringly, as she had lost the baby fat. He wanted to touch every part of her like it was their first time together, exploring each other then he brought her to new heights without any penetration just rubbing her in the right place and the right way, gazing into her eyes.

These times are not silent and Zara saw that he wanted her desperately and he lifted her from the bath, held her to himself and kissed her repeatedly and dried her down and lifted her onto their bed. It was the most wonderful sexual experience since before the new bairn was born and the two of them revelled in their sexual needs for each other. Zara became a little game in the sexual excitement and as Grigor lay on his back, she sat on top of his erect member but then with the sensation of it, Zara stopped moving, so he lifted her buttocks up and down and then Zara wanted to just caress him laying bodily on top of him. She could feel his heart beating heavily and the warmth of his skin, then he flipped her over gently and became very vigorous in his love making until he was groaning loudly then reaching his peak and so did, she once again.

Emotions were running very high between the two lovers having had a difficult time in recent days and tears flowed freely. Grigor kissed away her tears as Zara wept.

"Do you still love me?" Grigor asked.

"Aye. I never stopped loving you and I can't stop loving you," she answered.

"Do you still love me, Grigor?" Zara asked.

"Aye, I do love you. There can be no other. You drive me crazy at times, but I will never stop loving you," Grigor answered.

"Am I still too fat?" she asked. "Nae, you never were. You are always beautiful. You should know this Zara that men envy me because you are with me, my wife and the Mither of all my bairns, except Grigor Og," he added.

"Are you tired?" he asked.

"Nae," she answered.

"Then massage me, wife," Grigor demanded, but his entire body was open to be explored with her fingers as she massaged him from his feet up to his face when she kissed him again, then ran her fingers through his beautiful long black hair. Placing her face against his cheek and laying pressed up against his body, she whispered sweet words to him as he fell asleep.

"I love you my sweet Grigor."

35. Bees and the Kiln

The bees were happy in their new homes and producing honeycomb but Zara moved them to the herb garden to pollinate the plants there. After saying hello to them she left them to Fatma who was in charge of them, while Hector and John were on the look out for more wild bee hives, they found another over near that rock where the wolves had been. The two of them collected that hive with some difficulty after Hector had climbed up the tree to get it. It was fortunate that none of the family were allergic to bee stings, but just in case, Zara had kept an old asthma puffer from her old life for anaphylactic reactions. It was very old now, but she hoped it would still work, if it was ever needed. After telling Fatma where her bees were, she pondered over how to make a kiln and decided it was way out of her area of expertise. She was no engineer, nor manufacturer of all things modern, unfortunately. John and Hector came in with a few stings that they treated and told Zara that the newest Queen bee was in her home and will hopefully work for us after he blessed them again. 'It must be a Catholic thing,' she thought so she asked about the blessing.

"Nae, its not Catholic. Just bee tradition," he answered. "My Mither kept bees and talked to them all day long. At the time I thought my Mither was going batty, but in talking to other beekeepers, I found it to be what they all did," John answered.

"I have to say Zara, you have come home with some good ideas and it's a bit exciting. Hector and I are having a wonderful time. My coos are missing me though, so we reckon we will look for one more wild beehive then leave it with Fatma. You and I will need that kiln to keep the honey in pots, so I'll help you with that after we retrieve the next hive as well as seeing to my coos," John said.

Isobel had slept with her husband John, on the night of our return, instead of Alex. 'John was noticeably happier than usual and much more energetic since then,' Zara thought. He never talked this much either. He must miss her a lot sharing her with Alex, but she never interfered. Zara's life was difficult enough as it was.

Grigor was building onto the existing stables to enlarge them somewhat. He must have looked at Malcolm's stables in Glengarry, because his design was very similar.

"Grigor, we need to paint these buildings too, don't you think?" Zara said.

"Aye, we do. Did you see all of Malcolm's buildings were painted white to combat the weather?" Grigor said.

"Is that the reason they were all painted like that? It was thick paint. Looks expensive though. I wonder if John knows where to get it cheap or free," Zara added. She remembered John's story of his earlier raids before he knew how to live as a spirit. He even stole chickens from the neighbours because all of his chickens died while he lay dying in the woods. Then Zara suddenly remembered the eggs that were waiting to be hatched, that she had been given in Loch Garry by Marion.

"Oh God. They'll be dead," she exclaimed as she ran to the stables where Hector was chasing around a whole lot of tiny waddling Scots Dumpy chicks.

"Ma where did these come from?" Hector asked.

"Oh, thank goodness son. They were eggs from Loch Garry, waiting to be hatched and Marion said to bring them here because they are visible in the snow, unlike the white ones that blend with the snow," she said. But she had forgotten all about them and they had already hatched.

"Do you want to care for them Hector?" Zara asked.

"Oh aye, they're so cute. I'll make them a warm house to live in and one day make chicks of their own," Hector said.

"I wonder if there's a boy chick with them to breed. How can you tell?" Zara asked.

"Oh, Ma. You know more about that than me," he said, then giggled. "You and Da happy again Ma?" he smiled.

"Cheeky lad," Zara said and hugged her son.

Grigor then came in to enquire after the emergency that she had run to, only to find strange little chicks running around.

"Was this the emergency?" he asked sarcastically.

"Aye, I forgot that I had them in my saddle bag, but they have hatched anyway. Hector is going to care for them. Better for our snow don't you think? I can never see where the white ones are against the snow," Zara admitted.

"So, that's why we have lost so many chickens is it?" Grigor asked.

"Aye, I'm sorry but I couldn't see them," Zara said.

"You need glasses Zara, we can see them just fine," Grigor said.

"Aye. Next time we are in town maybe if we have the money for glasses," she added.

"Grigor, can I tell you something please?" she asked chasing after him as he was walking out of the shed. Zara expressed concern over the possibility of Isobel's biological Father, Hugh Mohr Chisholm coming to visit them in the Aird. She had not known that his death had occurred in Glengarry, not far from Malcolm's farm where he had lived with Ruth Beaton. However, she was aware that her presence in Loch Garry may have stirred him up, spiritually speaking, as it had done in the past.

"Oh, well done Zara. We really don't need that problem," Grigor stated. Zara went on to say that she just wanted him to know, because she could feel him getting closer.

"If it makes you feel any better, my daughter from my other life did communicate with me in a dream and said that blonde men made her vomit. Blonde girls like Isobel are pretty, but he is ugly she told me," Zara said.

"Did she? Well, that's true. He isn't as manly like the three of us men," Grigor stated referring to himself, Padruig and Alex. Zara heaved a sigh of relief, so if he does turn up, Grigor's manly and good-looking self will confidently take over and not the insecure one asking if she still loved Hugh.

"Zara, thank you for telling me. That can't have been easy and I do appreciate being forewarned and I will tell Alex and John too to watch over Isobel more than they usually do and I'll chat to Padruig for a plan of action. Just in case," Grigor said and he kissed her nicely on the lips.

"By the way my wife, tonight can we have beef stew with tomatoes, potatoes and carrots in it and make a bigger than usual pot? And you had better get inside now to make two loaves of bread," said the husband not wanting Zara to be seen outside. He was concerned already.

"I was going to make a start with the kiln after John came back. Should that wait then?" she asked.

"If necessary, I'll help him build the kiln. I made one a long time ago, so at least I have the know how and there's no hurry on the stables, but there is with the kiln, if the honey comes pouring in. You can start making the pots inside the house or on the back veranda. Does Hector have the clay yet?" Grigor asked.

"Oh, aye a huge pile of it out the back of the house," Zara answered.

"What's Hector doing now?" he asked.

"Making a home for the wee chicks, so they stay nice and warm tonight," Zara answered.

"I hope this snowy weather puts Hugh off coming here," Grigor added. "Now go inside Zara," he said. He went back to Hector to give him his instructions after he had finished with the wee chicks. Zara went inside to start the list of his instructions.

"Bread so soon Zara?" asked Padruig.

"Aye my husband sent me inside. He'll talk to you later Padruig. I can make you coffee," Zara added.

"Oh, aye Alex is coming back in soon too," he added. "Well, I'll get started for all of you then, as well as the bread. Do you like tomato sandwiches?" Zara asked.

"I've never had one Zara, but I'll give it a try," he said smiling. The first loaf was going to be lunch and lunch was going to be tomato sandwiches, with goat's cheese if they liked with pepper and salt, Zara planned but there were also pickles in the cupboard that she had made of many flavours, so they might be nice too. Both piping hot loaves were ready when the three men were in full discussion over the potential problem. John and Hector, as well as Fatma came inside attracted by the beautiful smell of freshly baked bread. On a large platter, Zara had prepared all of the additional ingredients for sandwiches and started cutting up the hot bread. Hector tried to take it immediately but had to be told to wait or to help by buttering all the bread for her which he enjoyed doing.

"Fatma, can you add the slices of tomato please?" Zara asked. "Who wants cheese in their tomato sandwich?" she asked.

"Me," answered Grigor. So, they all wanted the cheese added, even wee Causantin.

"Pickles?" Zara asked. No-one was sure, so she placed the pickles on the side of the platter in two flavours. Corn pickles and fig pickles. Then closing over the sandwich, she showed them how it was done and started to eat hers with corn pickles. They all loved their sandwiches, despite their doubts.

An entire loaf of bread was eaten within seconds, so in beginning the preparation for round two, Padruig also began his dialogue of "your ex-husband this and that" coming here to make trouble.

"I divorced that man, which is more than I can say for the remaining six of you Glenmoriston Men who never divorced him nor even made him unwelcome. In fact, I don't remember him being punished at all for what happened to my wee unborn bairn, Padruig Dubh," Zara said very accusingly.

His inference of blame on Zara stopped right there when he said, "I'll get my own coffee then," he said.

"Nae, I'll get it. You leave too much mess behind," Zara stated. After making his coffee, Grigor indicated for her to sit on his lap to calm down, as she was visibly angry with Padruig. That was when John spoke up.

"Padruig, both Alex and I have a family relationship with Zara, so we should be calling her Ma actually, as she is our Mother-in-law. On the other hand, you don't, so shouldn't you be calling her Mrs MacGregor?" he asked, smiling to himself.

Grigor loved the idea that Padruig would have to call Zara, Mrs MacGregor, but knew that it wouldn't happen and John was just playing some kind of game to put him in his place.

"Mrs MacGregor. Aye, that's right, she is my wife after all," Grigor said holding onto Zara and kissing her neck possessively.

"My wife is not to blame for the behaviour of that individual of whom we were discussing," he stated and that was the end of it as far as blame was concerned. However, poor Isobel had to catch on as to what was going on.

"Is my Father causing trouble again?" Isobel asked.

"I'm your Father," Grigor stated possessively. "If you mean Hugh Chisholm, possibly and if you need to speak with him, I'll not stop you," he said a little sadly having always felt Isobel to be his and raising her for all the years of her life until adulthood, through to two marriages and two bairns, Donald and Andrew. He also delivered her into this world, so to think of her as another man's bairn, even though she was, would break his heart.

"I know you are my Da, but he hasn't seen his grandchildren, has he?" she stated. That made both of the Fathers of her bairn's prickle.

"Do you want to speak to Hugh then Isobel?" asked Grigor feeling hurt.

"Not really speak for long, just to tell him that I have two bairns now with John and Alex and he has no need to be concerned," she stated.

"He will leave if you give him a big meal and if I show him his grandchildren, I think," Isobel said.

"And if he doesn't want to leave?" Zara asked.

"That's where you experienced men in the area of conflict, assist and ask him to move on, politely at first, then not so politely and so on," Isobel answered.

Fatma was listening on and then began looking miserable and started to cry.

"I miss Ali," she cried. "If Ali was here, he and I would know what to do. Without my twin I don't know what to do," she expressed. "Can I go to Ali? Where is he?" she asked.

"He's in Cannich like we told you sweetheart and attends a course in Invermoriston to learn about how we can grow crops here," Zara said.

"Can lassies do that course too?" she asked. "Shouldn't we do it together Ma?" she asked. It was inevitable that as soon as there was tension in the family that she would want her twin beside her. Then John saved the day.

"If you were to leave too, the bees would miss you darling and they would all fly away. You are the Aird bee lady now. Ali would be so proud of you. I hope you stay so when he comes home on weekends, you can show him your bee family," John said empathetically.

"Do they really like me Uncle John?" she asked.

"Aye, they do. You tell them your stories and they like that. If you are missing Ali, you can tell them that and where he is and that he is coming home soon. Your Da is going to bring him home tomorrow aren't you Da?" he asked Grigor, addressing him as Da for the first time ever.

"Aye. Tomorrow afternoon sweetie, then you'll see your handsome brother again," Grigor answered.

"What if the cane toad turns up?" she asked. Looking quizzically at her, Zara had to explain why she had referred to him as a cane toad, which was a tropical toad that could puff itself up to look bigger, then spit poison to blind dogs or cats. Even birds that pecked at them were poisoned, so Zara apologised for calling him that, but Hugh did puff up and look bigger than he was.

"If he comes, it's up to your Da what happens and if he is not here then he will elect someone who will deal with it. Either way your brother will come home for the weekend," she explained. It certainly felt like he was close by and Zara started to cook that larger stew that was requested by her husband and asked for someone to peel the potatoes. It was a whopper of a stew in her biggest pot, large enough to feed two Hugh Mohr Chisholms. Hector had been sent to be outrider and even look for tracks in the snow knowing where he had previously hidden on the opposite side of the burn behind the widest tree.

Zara wondered if he would still be wearing that awful yellow coat.

John began building Zara's kiln, with Grigor assisting as Alex dug up his ripened potatoes and placed them into storage, as well as some in the kitchen. The corn was picked also before they were damaged by the weather as Fatma talked to her bees telling them all kinds of things. John had done a wonderful job of turning that situation around. The men didn't reveal their tactics to any of the women folk, but they were all obviously awaiting a confrontation.

Then Hugh Mohr Chisholm arrived, as bold as ever, not even trying to hide as he rode past Hector, expecting him to take his horse, as if he was his groom.

Hector ignored the expectation and awaited his Father's next move. Zara heard his familiar warning cooee to her and called both girls inside the house and into her bedroom, leaving the stew to simmer slowly. Zara hadn't yet added her usual herbs and spices or the tomatoes, so she had to go out the back quickly unseen to get those, then re-enter. Hearing the sounds of crunching boots on snow, she waited to see if the door opened, or if she had time to add the tomatoes. She chopped them quickly and threw them in without her usual care, washed the herbs and chopped them too and threw them in too, but as the door was about to open, she ran back to the bedroom and closed the door. All three of the ladies, with all the smaller bairns were gathered in there, including Causantin. Freya wanted a feed right then at the most inconvenient time, but Zara hurriedly put the wee bairn to her breast and Freya fed ravenously. Her name was still a problem as the family went between calling her Freya or Dorothea.

"Isobel, can you please light my fire? I don't know how long we will be in here and I let it go out," Zara asked.

"Is it him?" asked Fatma looking suddenly afraid.

"Aye it is, my darling but you need not have any fear. Isobel, are you still wanting to introduce your bairns to him?" Zara asked.

Isobel wasn't looking as bold as she had been at the table and was guarding her bairns like never before. Zara felt the sound of one of the men against her door and hoped it was one of theirs and not Hugh. Zara strained to hear their voices through the thick oak door wanting to know when and if any trouble was starting. She missed her hero, Hector.

"Ma," Hector called out. "You best check on the stew. It might be overcooking," Hector said. Opening the door then rapidly, it had been Hector leaning up against her door and he momentarily lost his balance.

"Son are you alright?" she asked.

"Aye, it just smells cooked Ma," Hector said.

Zara ignored all of the faces looking in her direction, except her husband. Grigor had the look of a man who could become fierce at any second, but not aimed at her, but at the family threat, Hugh Mohr Chisholm.

"Hello Zara," Hugh dared to say. Zara did not respond to him and just looked to her husband and went to the stew.

It was a little overcooked as Hector had said, but at least he had taken the bread from the oven which she had forgotten all about. All she seemed to be doing lately was cook and make bread. Zara noticed there was one man missing, John. What was their plan of action she wondered? All the men seated at the table were Padruig, Alex, Grigor and the unwelcome guest, Hugh and Zara was asked by her husband to serve up to all of them, including Hector when he also sat down, after closing Zara's bedroom door again. The stew wasn't her best, she knew that, but the men all ate it in silence and didn't even ask for their coffees, so Zara prepared her husband his coffee then Padruig, Alex and Hector and asked if Hugh would prefer tea.

"Nae, coffee it is for me too," Hugh answered. Zara just obediently made his coffee.

"Zara sit beside me," said Grigor after she had completed the coffee tasks. Grigor began asking me for my approval for Hugh to meet with our daughter, Isobel. Zara responded by saying it was Grigor's decision as well as her two husbands, Alex and John.

It was then that John Fraser entered, carrying a long rifle. Zara had never seen him carry a weapon and he looked like he could use that rifle and he was displeased at the presence of Hugh Mohr.

"If you want to see my wife, you go through me," John said sternly as he put the weapon up on the mantle piece above the fire, so the bairns couldn't reach it.

"And me," said Alex.

"My wife's name is Isobel Fraser not Chisholm and you have no rights over her as she was a MacGregor before she married me. This man, 'indicating Grigor', is her Father. Why do you want to see my wife, Mr Chisholm?" John asked, still looking sternly upon the face of the youngest of the 'Seven Glenmoriston Men'.

Zara hoped that John Fraser wouldn't go too far with the macho act.

"John," said Zara. "Would you like your dinner now?" she asked.

John did look hungry having worked hard all day long.

"Aye, thank you Zara that would be nice," John responded and sat down.

"I am here to visit Isobel with your permission, is all, but I won't stay long," Hugh replied a little taken aback. "Do I have all of your collective permissions?" Hugh asked, sounding a touch sarcastic. Grigor stood up and opened Zara's door and asked Isobel if she wanted to see Hugh and if not, then to stay in there with her bairns. Isobel came out sheepishly with both her bairns, Andrew and Donald. Their Fathers both immediately stood up and scooped up the child of their respective marriages. Andrew would be tall when he grew and his younger brother was catching up and could be as tall as Andrew. Neither of them would be as tall as Hector would become, Zara thought.

"I just came to say hello to you Isobel and to ask after your well being and I see you have two bairns too, so it's nice to meet them too," Hugh said. Neither Father was about to release their bairn to the man who should have been their son's Grandfather.

Grigor had been their Grandfather for their whole young lives and the odd blonde haired man was not appealing to them.

"I see there's not much trust left here anymore and I suppose I deserve that. However, I do wish you well Isobel with your wee ones," Hugh said and passed some money to Grigor for his grandchildren, which surprisingly, Grigor would not accept. Hugh then stood to leave and thanked Zara for the meal, to which she found it hard to respond, with her eyes cast down. Despite being a serial womaniser Zara understood why they had all loved him once. God only knows how many women he had actually engaged in a sexual relationship with, believing in his manhood and his gorgeous looks.

He galloped off into the cold dark night that was threatening to snow again. Hopefully that was the last time that the family would ever hear from Hugh Mohr Chisholm. But Zara was wrong.

"I'm sorry about the stew," Zara said. "It could have been a lot better. Can I get anything else for you all as well as poor Isobel and Fatma?" she asked. "You must be starving hungry by now as well as your bairns and my sweet, sweet wee Causantin," Zara said, kissing him on the cheeks. Their new wee one, whose name they could not yet decide on, wanted her feed too, so Zara sat by the fire with her on the breast after serving up her daughters and the bairns.

"Grigor, we need to decide definitely on a name for our wee lass because we keep going between the two names. Maybe we could think of another name altogether?" Zara suggested.

"What about Dihaoine? Meaning Friday, the day on which she was born," Grigor asked.

"I love that name," Zara responded.

"Thank goodness for that," Padruig commented. "You could always have the other two names as second and third names. Dihaoine Freya Dorothia MacGregor," he suggested.

"Grigor, that's a really fancy name. Would you like that for her Baptism?" Zara asked, "Then we could all wear our new tartans," she said. Fatma was happier once the tension was over, looking at her wee sister in a new light.

"Dihaoine," Fatma repeated.

"Have you eaten enough everyone?" Zara asked. They all wanted to finish off the last of the stew with Zara still apologising, but at least the bread was lovely.

"You saved the dinner Hector," Zara said proudly of her son and as Hector turned to kiss his Mither. Grigor said sternly, "Not on your Mither's lips son,"

"Aye Da," Hector said with a cheeky glint in his eye.

Sleep that night was unsettled. Zara lay on her back watching over to the window where her husband had stood for the last half hour, looking for any movement outside. His gaze was not his usual brand of seriousness or anger, it had a gloomy feel to it. He then turned to her and said in conclusion.

"It's not over yet. He's coming back with his two brother's next time. His hatred and jealousy for me is intense, I can feel it strongly from wherever he is right now. I'm the Grandfather, the Father and the husband, which are all the roles in which he failed with this family, especially with you and Isobel," he stated.

Zara felt scared as to what that could mean.

"Do you mean they want to do you harm or myself, Isobel and Andrew and Donald?" she asked.

"I can't say for sure, but I need to talk to both Alex and John. I think their intention is to dispose of me completely, probably down the waterfall in pieces. That is the sort of hatred he has, as well as does the older brother, Alexander. Donald would just follow his brothers," Grigor said.

"You were going to Craskie today to collect Ali, right?" Zara enquired. "Would it assist you to know that I have the key to Grigor Og's house and permission to use it there on Craskie? One plan could be, instead of Ali coming home, Fatma, Hector, me, Isobel, Andrew, Donald and one of you could stay there, with Hamish's knowledge, until you think we are safe again?" Zara asked.

"Aye, it would be safer there, than here because he has mapped out how many we are by visiting and noting all of our vulnerabilities," he added.

"So, did he come on a reconaissance mission, not a visit at all?" she asked.

"Possibly, I hope I am wrong, but that's what I get from it. He wants me out of the way, to get to all of you," Grigor responded. "Hector will have to be your bodyguard from now on, until its over," he added. "I'll talk to Alex and John. John probably won't leave the coos, so most likely it'll be Alex who goes with you or just Hector?" Grigor added.

"What about you Grigor, can you come too? I can't lose you," Zara said as she began to fret. "Poor Hector is only fourteen, he can't hold off a full attack from those three," she said. "I'll talk to the men and Hector and we will have to prioritise the safety of both you and Isobel, the lassies and bairns, especially Isobel's bairns," Grigor stated.

"Go to sleep now my darling and I will sort something out," Grigor said.

"Grigor, please promise me I am not losing my husband," Zara said.

"That's the part that I am worried about," he said.

Eventually Zara slept uncomfortably. Grigor came to bed late at night and made love beautifully and she didn't ask what had been decided between them all, but Zara had always been able to rely on Grigor's insight and decision making, based on what he saw in his visions. Hector was serious in the morning and sat beside his Mither and shadowed her around the kitchen, so he was taking his role seriously. Alex had been cleaning his weapons, sharpening his knives, even his sword and ensuring that he had enough ammunition. Padruig was preparing for war, as they all put on their plaids and Zara packed enough food for several days, starting with cooking bread and stew again to provide for both those who were staying and those who were leaving.

The lassies were all asked to pack some warm clothes in their saddle bags and anything they would need for possibly a week. Zara was pleased she was still breast feeding at least to alleviate any problem feeding Dihaoine. The Turkish coffee was offered to Zara, but she declined it as she knew how much the men loved that and they were risking themselves to go up against all three of the Chisholm brothers. Their friendship had lasted for so many years in life, but in death, after Padruig knew of his wife's love affair with Hugh Mohr Chisholm, there was no love lost there anymore, nor loyalty.

Padruig hated Hugh now for breaking down his marriage but in reality, Isobel Grant was saved by Hugh Chisholm. Padruig could never satisfy a woman and Isobel Grant had learned that early in their marriage.

It was decided that John Fraser would lead the family group in single file, after all, as he knew a narrow drover's path beneath the mountain ranges. Taking that ancient path, they would not encounter others along the way, nor be seen and it went all the way to the back of the Craskie forest. It meant trespassing a wee bit onto Patrick's land before opening the gate into Craskie from the mountain end. Zara collected her son Ali from Hamish who looked surprised at the change of plan, but

Zara carefully explained it all to both Ali and Hamish as Cora listened in.

Hamish promised to keep an extra patrol on the farm keeping out any uninvited guests and Ali joined the family temporarily in Charlotte House. Hamish also lit all the pole lights around the property. Before she departed, Zara remembered Charlotte's old yoke and harnessing gear used for ploughing and asked to borrow it all once we bought an ox. Hamish said he'd get it all ready for them when they were departing. He said Zara could keep it most likely, but he would double check with Grigor Og next visit. Cora gave Zara fresh butter and cream and goat's milk as well as a nanny goat on loan for their stay. The family were told to help themselves to hen's eggs when needed, which they did the following morning.

36. *Brutal Battle in the Aird*

Padruig Dubh Grant was a fearsome fighter in his day as was his off-sider, Alexander MacDonald. Alex had died young, but Padruig had lived to a ripe old age. Grigor was a dependable guerrilla tactics-style fighter. Those who died at his hand knew nothing of his presence until he was right upon them. He moved swiftly and silently. Between Padruig, Alex and Grigor, this time around, the mood was even more vicious than in their younger years, as their family was being directly threatened and they had already seen what could happen to Zara from one of those brothers. The three of them donned their plaids and covered their faces in soot, so any moonlight wouldn't shine up their pale skin. Weapons well prepared, they had strung a rope made of a metal substance spread across between the largest tree on the house side of the burn all the way to the stables. This would, in theory, decapitate anyone who crossed the burn on horseback. They were hoping to get all three in one go, then dispose of them down the waterfall, once and for all. If that failed, Grigor was up that same tree with a rope, aimed to hang anyone that the wire missed. If the hanging or decapitating was incomplete, they were all carrying swords and dirks to complete the dismembering of the bodies.

A shovel was left behind the tree to shovel away blood-stained snow into the burn, so bairns and wives were none the wiser. All their guerrilla warfare was extremely successful. Bloody but successful and all the body parts entered the fast-flowing burn to be taken down to the waterfall in many parts. The affected snow was shovelled into the burn, as planned and the wire taken down, as well as any other evidence of a battle having ensued in the Aird. All without a shot being fired. They would never trouble Zara's family again. Grigor asked Alex to pass on the message to Isobel once he was washed up, but the following morning was decided upon. The mens' horses were also taken as booty and coin they had on their person. Padruig said his horse was getting on, so he claimed a four-year-old bay gelding that appeared well trained in avoiding trees in the forest. That horse came with a beautiful saddle and bridle set, as well as saddle bags. The booty in the saddle bags was interesting also, which they divided up. Zara needed a new horse too, so Grigor claimed the lovely white and yellow mare for his wife. John's old horse needed replacing too but Alex said he would take one of the new ones, a black stallion and John could have his old chestnut.

Those men had come with a vengeance and a plan to dispose of Grigor and their eccentric family of the Aird proved that they still had the fighting spririt in them. Alex fetched the family the next day, this time being able to use the normal route away from the base of the mountain. He'd had a fear since childhood of avalanches and had never trusted the movement of snow. Snow was building up on the mountains and he thought it wiser now to stay further back in case of an avalanche. The family had slept reasonably well in Charlotte House and Zara explained how she wanted the yoke and harness to go with them, intended for use for deep ploughing with an ox. The hand plough that Grigor Og had used was there too, but the team would have to deliver that later, she asked Hamish.

John managed to carry all the harnessing on his horse as they moved back home yet again and returned the goat to Cora.

"He's the pits and now he's in bits," chanted Causantin. "Who taught you that?" Zara asked her sweet innocent two-year-old son. "Hector did Ma," was his reply. "Stop saying it. It's not nice," I said to him.

"Grandda, it's me, Malcolm. Can you see me?" Malcolm asked. "I had an awful dream last night of blood and gore out there. Are you all okay?" he asked. "We are son, but the others who

attacked us aren't," he said with myrth. "But we scored a few horses out of it," he said, very pleased with himself. "Who attacked you then?" Malcolm asked. "The other half of my old gang looking for trouble. Disposed of now," he said as a matter of fact. "Well, that's good I suppose. I'm glad you're safe. There was something in one of the saddle bags of value," Malcolm said. "Might be gold not sure, but the saddle bag had a stag's head on the front. Glad you're all safe."

And he was gone.

"Grigor, which one of us scored the saddle bags with a stag's head on the front?" Padruig asked. "Zara did? Why?" Grigor asked.

"Best get it, she might have scored," Padruig answered.

Grigor knew not to question Padruig if he seemed to be talking to himself, as it was always Malcolm. He asked Zara for her new saddle bags for a moment. Zara gave them both to Grigor as she hadn't yet opened them up and there was something inside. Grigor could not believe his eyes when he saw three small gold bars at the bottom of one of them.

"You have done well out of the booty my love," he said sarcastically.

"What do you mean?" she asked.

"You have gold bars in here," he replied. Looking upon them. She was shocked. She didn't want to touch it in case they were stolen.

"Oh Grigor, can you take care of that please? I only wanted those pretty saddle bags and comfortable saddle and my beautiful new horse. Thank you darling. They're yours," she said in earnest.

"It's gold Zara," Grigor said.

"Please Grigor, you melt it down or something. It's yours. Although, I do have an idea," she said smiling a cheeky smile.

"Consider it payment to you for my dowry," she said and they both erupted in laughter. It was rare to hear both of them laughing, so it drew interest.

"My wife paid me her dowry," he jokingly bragged.

A builder could now finish the work on the stables instead of him.

37. The Old Crohn

One of her two daughters whom Zara was unable to see face to face anymore could vaguely communicate occasionally through dreams and the oldest of them had painted Grigor Mohr, Zara's husband. They too had visions of her life in her world with her eccentric family in the Aird.

"My oldest daughter painted a nice painting of you," Zara said.

"I know, I've seen it," Grigor responded. He was able to zero in on whatever they said when they thought about him, let alone paint a painting of him.

"Do you like it?" Zara asked. "Aye, I do," he answered smiling, knowing he was part of an even bigger family and world of which he had little knowledge or understanding.

Rubbing her back again, Zara had to lay down for a while lying flat, hoping the aching pain would eventually go away. It had been like this since the day Grigor went to Inverness without her to meet Mrs MacGregor. John was walking past Zara's bedroom noticing Grigor rubbing Zara's back and asked if she was alright.

"Aye John, it's nothing. Just my aching back," Zara answered.

"I came across an old woman who might be able to fix your back, aways from here. I took my coos too far one day and accidentally entered her property, so I knocked on her door to ask permission to graze my coos," John said fearing she would be angry with him. "Instead of being angry, she was pleased to have my company and invited me in to drink tea with her. I had a small injury from a coo horn on my arm and she fixed it," he said. "I think she could fix your back easily," he opined. "I'll show you how to get there, but leave you both in privacy, what do you think?" he asked. It was agreed that John would take both Zara and Grigor to the old woman's small home, deep in the forest, the next day.

"She's not a witch, is she?" asked Zara over dinner that night cooked by Isobel.

"Just an old Crohn maybe?" Padruig said. "A wise woman, eh John?" he asked.

"Healer of sorts, I thought" he answered.

"Ma, please don't go there," pleaded Isobel. "What if she puts a spell on you both?" she asked.

"I hope it's a back-healing spell then darling. John wouldn't tell us to see a harmful person would you John?" Zara asked.

"Nae," he said, "but I have only met her the once," he added.

"How much does she charge?" asked Grigor.

"Naught for my arm," John answered, but she might charge.

"Can I take some of your honey please Fatma as payment?" Zara asked.

The next day, the three of them left seeking out the old Crohn, leaving both of Zara's wee bairns at home with an unhappy Isobel.

"Do you want me to follow them love?" asked Alex to his beloved wife.

"Aye, I do. Thank you, sweetheart," Isobel said, as she kissed him passionately. John led the party of three for miles into unfamiliar territory and Zara asked him not to leave them there unescorted for the journey back, in case they got lost. When the house finally came into view, it was just an old stone cottage, with a thatched roof, with only one working fireplace, it seemed.

John approached the door and knocked, considering they were already acquainted.

"John, dear lad. It's so nice to see you again. Who are your friends? My, my, my. What a pretty lady," she said as she touched Zara on her face.

"Please come in my friends. You would be Zara's husband, Mr MacGregor?" she enquired without being told their names. She already knew them, but Zara assumed John must have told her about who he lived with.

"I'll wait outside Mistress, it's a private matter they wish to discuss with you if that's alright," John said.

"Nae John, it's cold outside," she responded.

Zara asked first if she could ask about her aching back.

"Aye," she answered. Answering to the description of the pain without touching Zara's back, the old Crohn said. "Your pain is referred pain from your heart through to your back. You have experienced a broken heart recently caused by yourself, Mr MacGregor. You thought Mrs MacGregor from Inverness was better than your wife, having been born Clan Gregor, but you do not know what I know about your wife. You should consider yourself a chosen one by God to take this incredibly miraculous woman. You were weak but it will never happen again, will it Mr MacGregor?" she asked in a stern way that insisted on Grigor's respect for Zara.

There was no indication that he wouldn't do it again, which was a worry.

"You were jealous enough to dispose of a man recently who wanted to take her back to himself, were you not? There is another man who lives with you who loves her too, but will not take her from you, he will care for her if you are disposed of and you can both trust him with this love. Now Zara, with the knowledge of why you had the pain, you need to forgive him. Can you do that?" she asked.

"Aye Mistress," Zara said. The old Crohn bent to kiss Zara on the hand and hoped they would meet again soon for herbal remedies and the like.

There was no charge, but Zara left the appreciated home-grown honey for the old Crohn. They were all pleased to leave and make their way home coming across Alex by surprise, who claimed he was hunting for a hart. Silently, their journey took over an hour without the usual banter. Alex was curious and wanted to report to his wife and so asked. "Zara, what happened?"

"My back is feeling much better now, thank you Alex. She seemed to know everything about us," she added.

Grigor said nothing and was still angry at himself for his Inverness antics being so well known. John also was too afraid to repeat any of what was said, especially the disposed of ones as well as the additional man in the house, who was alledged to be in love with her. Who was that he wondered? Had to be Padruig? Surely not but who else? He wished he had been left outside in the cold.

"Alex," John asked quietly. "Would you know of someone who is in love with Zara in our household, apart from her husband of course?" he asked.

"Are you serious?" Alex exclaimed.

"We just decapitated the last man who threatened just that, so please don't accuse anyone inside our home of the same thing else Grigor will have him disposed of before you know it," Alex replied with the sound of fear in his voice.

"I wasn't accusing anyone. The old Crohn said that, not me," John said defensively.

"Then she's a troublemaker," Alex responded.

"She said he would not act on it until Grigor was disposed of," John said.

"There's only you, me and Padruig that it could be. You can rule me out. I'm in love with our wife, Isobel. You wouldn't be in love with your Mither-in-law, would you?" Alex asked.

"Nae, that's disgusting," John answered. "So, what about Padruig then?" he asked. "You are closer to him than I. Can you warn him about what the old Crohn said so that he won't do anything that would suggest that he is in love with her?" asked John.

"Padruig would not admit to it if he was and I have to admit that the deeper side of Padruig is unknown to anyone. He plays his cards very close to his chest if you know what I mean?" Alex explained. "After Old Isobel broke his heart like that, multiple times, he wouldn't let himself fall in love again, in my opinion even if his admiration was obvious. I mean to say, we all love Zara, but you are talking about sexual love, I take it?" Alex asked.

"I suppose so. She didn't say the word sexual, but that's the implication if one is in love," John replied.

"Okay. I'll forewarn him, so there's peace on the home front. Padruig wouldn't mind a romp in the hay with Zara, if I'm honest," said Alex.

"What did the old Crohn mean when she said she knows who you are and I can't see your value?" Grigor asked.

"I truly do not know Grigor," Zara said.

"Well, watch out little lassie. You might get more than just enjoyable sex tonight," Grigor stated. Zara was happy with that.

"You are the sexiest man in the world my love," she said.

"So long as only you think so, my wife and no man will come near you, just so you are warned," he said with a threat to whomever did come near her.

"Can Hector still massage me occasionally darling?" she asked.

"If he starts getting an erection over his Mither, I'll strap the lad. So, for now it is, but he is developing his manhood rapidly," he said. Zara had noticed how fast Hector was developing and how he would sometimes show off his manhood to Fatma, so she could see how big it was and when it became hard.

She thought better of telling her husband that.

"Do you think we should marry Fatma to a lad soon Grigor? John has a sixteen-year-old relative who passed away in an accident and he is still living at home, but he is lonely, he told John," Zara asked.

"Does he have red hair?" Grigor asked.

"Really bright ginger apparently, so if they could have bairns and they may not, considering that he is not of the living, then their hair would most likely be red," Zara answered. "He is a good horseman, cattle and goat handler who was raised on a farm here in the Aird. His name is Simon, of the Lovat Frasers," Zara said. "Simon Robert."

"I'll agree to meeting him is all. No promises," he responded.

"This week-end Ali is coming home with a friend too. His name is Iain Ross, he is seventeen years old, employed at Craskie as a groom, he's an orphan with brown hair but he might find us a little too weird if Fatma liked him. Then there is Padruig to consider again, I suppose. He needs someone and they love each other in a family way?" Zara said.

"Padruig? He's too old surely and that would be weird if he was my son in law," Grigor responded.

"Well, either way do we have an agreement to look for a suitable match for both her and us?" Zara asked.

"Aye, we do. She is old enough and lonely now without her twin, thanks to you," Grigor said. He was still bitter that Zara took the initiative to send Ali into work.

"He's not costing you now though darling. His course is free, his food is provided, as well as his accomadation and one day he will come home to grow food here on our farm, I hope," Zara said.

That night, Zara decided that they needed a more scientific approach to having children and what was obvious about her family was the women, including herself and Isobel both could re-produce, unlike anyone else in that world, which made life both wonderful, yet terrifying too, should they be somehow discovered. She spoke with Fatma and Isobel about this matter which was rarely mentioned as no-one wanted to feel threatened or abnormal. They decided on drawing up three charts, one for the fathers and mothers of the children and their status at conception, one for Isobel's bairns and one for Zara's bairns. A free page was allocated for Fatma's bairns. The idea was to look for any variations at any stage of life in case they had a shorter life span or something they hadn't yet thought of.

38. The Vanishing Act

The older bairns would often play with their ability to vanish and see who could do it better or faster. Up until that time, the wee bairns only vanished too if they were in the arms of the adult 'vanisher' such as Zara, but not independently, until they were Causantin's age, when they tried hard to achieve it and most often failed. The young ones all tried to be as good as their older siblings, but no one thought to practise away from the wee bairns because up until now they were unable to vanish independently, so we all thought.

Zara was dressing Dihaoine after her bath and was sweetly talking to her as she made cute baby noises and kicked her feet unwilling to wear her nappy. As Zara was putting the last of her clothing on, she suddenly vanished. Zara screamed. "Padruig, Padruig"

"What in heaven's name?" he exclaimed as he came running to her bedroom. Grigor was outside painting the stables.

"Padruig, Dihaoine's vanished, she's gone," Zara said as she searched all around the room. "Help me, please find her. She has gone," Zara screamed as she panicked as to where her child had gone. One minute she was there and then she was gone.

The front door opened and Grigor came inside carrying Dihaoine on his hip looking unimpressed.

"Zara what is the wee bairn doing outside in the cold?" he asked sternly.

"Oh, my God. My darling little Dihaoine, what did you do?" Zara exclaimed. "Don't disappear from us. Who knows where you might go?" she said. Grigor was confused. Padruig explained that the bairn did it herself. Zara hadn't left her outside coming to Zara's defence. None of the other bairns had ever been able to do that. Zara was giving her a strong talk about not vanishing from us, it was only to be used to vanish from the living ones. The wee bairn was pleased with herself and didn't think that what she had done was wrong.

"Heta, Heta," Dihaoine spoke. "Wanish," she said smiling.

"Go and get Hector," said Padruig. "Hector, have you had a hand in this?" Padruig asked.

"I didn't think she'd be outside in the snow. I'm sorry. I just showed her how to disappear like the rest of us," Hector said.

Hector got that strap his Father had threatened for endangering the bairn's life.

As life normalised on the farm, the eccentric family couldn't know what was around every corner, but they had done their best and for Zara the love for her bairns was what kept her motivated. Zara wasn't to know that a simple visit to see the old Crohn would change her life forever. Either way she wasn't to have any more bairns, so a visit to the old wise woman was a necessity to prevent another pregnancy, through herbal remedies.

That night Zara had a nightmare of no consequence to them, Grigor thought, although he comforted his wife when she woke up screaming. No doubt Dihaoine vanishing had destabilised her, he thought.

"What was your bad dream about this time Zara?" he asked patiently.

Causantin's Cave, Fife Coast

"It was a handsome young King of old Scotland. His name was the same as our son, Causantin. He was a beautiful, tall man who was beheaded by dark haired Norseman on a beach, then they stuffed his body into a big cave. It was horrible. His men all abandoned him," Zara sobbed.

"You can visit King Causantin's grave on the Island of Iona, one day, then he'll leave you in peace," Grigor said.

"Really? Can you take us there one day or that cave?" she asked.

"It's hardly a priority Zara. Where do these nightmares come from? Have you been reading history books on early Scotland or something?" he asked.

"Nae, I don't know who the early…" Zara stopped speaking.

"Maybe there was another King too. Who was his Father then?" she asked.

"King Kenneth MacAlpine, first King of Alba but an unpopular decision from my line. Why?" he asked.

"I might have dreamed of him too, but I can't remember it now or why," she said.

"Good, then can we sleep?" Grigor asked. He wasn't to know that those spirits were active in his area now and it wasn't the young and handsome King Causantin, it was Causantin's Father. As he tried to drift into sleep again, those strange words, like in a poem, came back to him that were in his mind when he was in Loch Garry. The words were of a curse. The odd thing was that they had no sheep for wolves to eat. They also now had no wolves, that he knew of.

Why would his wife dream of that family in particular, if she had never read about them, or met any of their descendents, he wondered as he tried to sleep? He knew his wife was bound in mystery, but at times he could understand it, but not this. He hoped it had nothing to do with what he thought was that curse and he knew Padruig would not understand that and neither would Alex nor John.

He just hoped that his wife wouldn't visit that old Crohn again. People like that could put curses on someone who they didn't like or were being paid somehow for an outcome, for self serving reasons. The outcome of that curse he heard in his head, was the end of his marriage, which terrified him.

He wanted to sleep and forget all of it. They were happy now. Everything was back on track. 'She loved him. He loved her. It was ridiculous to worry over nothing', he told himself.

Grigor made love to her, to feel her love again and then fell back to sleep while lulled in an uneasiness, he couldn't quite put his finger on. Zara would always be his, wouldn't she?

Secrets of the Braes and Glens

Authors Notes

The Seven Glenmoriston Men

<table>
<tr>
<td>
Hugh Chisholm</td>
<td>
Alexander MacDonald of Aonach (d.1751)</td>
<td>
Padruig Dubh Grant of Craskie</td>
</tr>
<tr>
<td>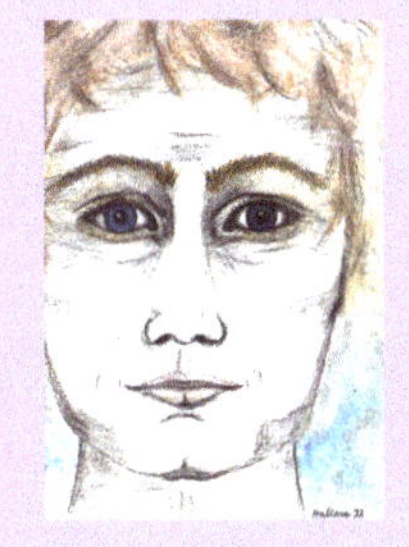
Donald Chisholm</td>
<td>Alexander Chisholm (d.1751)

(Chisholm sons of Paul Chisholm, tenant at Blairie)

John Campbell MacDonald of Craskie</td>
<td>
Grigor MacGregor</td>
</tr>
</table>

The Oath of Fidelity and Secrecy

(Translated from Erse)
"Their backs should be to God
And their faces to the devil:
That all the curses the Scriptures did pronounce
Might come upon them and their posterity
If they did not stand firm
To the Prince in his gravest dangers
And if they should discover
To any person, man, woman or child,
That the Prince was in their keeping,
Till once his Person should be out of danger, etc."

The Seven Glenmoriston Men

The Seven Glenmoriston men kept to their oath of Fidelity and Secrecy, and it was not known to anyone until about a year after the Prince's eventual escape to France, that those men had had any knowledge whatsoever about the Prince's whereabouts, with the exception of Cluny MacPherson of Glenalladale of Skye.

The Seven Glenmoriston men previously had been famous for refusing to give up their arms, which was required by a new law introduced by the Hanoverian rulers after the Battle of Culloden. The Seven Glenmoriston Men had taken an oath one to another and held to their Highland way of life. They were all very strong and courageous men, Hugh Chisholm only being seventeen at the time. A famous incident occurred where British troops were being guided through Glenmoriston by Donald Fraser stealing sixty Highland coos belonging to Padruig's Uncle, Allan MacDonald. Although they were only seven men and the British forces outnumbered them with sixty soldiers and thirteen Scottish militia, the British became so frightened of their fierceness, that they threw down their weapons and many ran away in fear. Padruig Dubh Grant communicated with the leader of the Militia and decided not to harm them. After the coos had run away, the British Major gave in to their demands and ordered the militia to round up the coos and hand them over to the Seven Glenmoriston Men.

The British Major was quoted as having said, *"they weren't men, they were devils"*. Padruig also demanded some of their food, which was given to them.[3]

Secrets of the Braes and Glens

Authors Notes

Acknowledgements

In researching this ongoing story, following 'Isobel of Glenmoriston', I designated the task to my assistant, T. Zayn Al-Abidin, to map the Scottish Clans of the 1700's who lived in the Highlands, including areas especially around Glenmoriston, Glengarry and Argyle. I would like to thank my assistant for her technical support.

I thank my assistant T. Zayn Al-Abidin also for driving in deadly road conditions at times in Scotland to search for the graves of the historical characters of my books and I found two, I believe. Padruig Dubh Grant in Drumnadrochit, Cnocan Burraidh and Hugh Chisholm in Clachan Comar Burial ground. Thanks also to historian, Hugh Allison for leading us to Hugh's grave. May their souls rest in peace. There have been storms that have closed access to roads, car accidents closing us off from Orkney for a time, storm Agnes that closed us from Dunnottar Castle for a short while but we made it each time. The rain storms towards the last days of this research trip to Scotland, were unexpected, but we limped finally back into Glasgow, albiet a bit bruised, but importantly with necessary corrections or additions in the upcoming novels. My journey throughout Scotland has been a book in itself.

I thank Mr David Chambers of Stravithie Castle in Fife, Scotland, for directing us to a genuine Druid site called 'Duninos Den'. I was not expecting to find something that unique and ancient with David's willingness to empart old knowledge with a genuine appreciation of King Causantin's Cave. King Causantin was one of the earliest Kings of Scotland once it united with Pictland and he was known for preventing a permanent base on the east coast of Scotland for the Vikings, which was his ultimate demise.

In Inverness, I need to thank Leakey's Bookshop for accepting "Isobel of Glenmoriston" into their vast collection of amazing books and I hope it can take off from there, as well as the following novels in the same series of books including "Secrets of the Braes and Glens".

Thank you also to the Curator of Clan Cameron Museum in Achnacarry, Catriona Fleming for adding my book to their library for visitors to peruse and order from that, if there is an interest, which is a wonderful show of support from Clan Cameron. It is an honour to be included.

To my artist daughter Halima Karger, I sincerely thank for her beautiful portraits throughout my books of my characters, both historical and fictional. Her work is truly beautiful and her support is greatly appreciated, as is caring for my cat when I am away. Halima is the eppitomy of patience when I request of her something she has never known of or seen herself before, so just from my descriptions she has been able to bring to life so much of the books that would otherwise be misunderstood or lifeless.

Other people who I wish to thank are Tracy and her husband, from the Carindale Copy and Print Store, for her expertise in colour prints. The Gaelic Society of Inverness, Scotland, have also been supportive and I thank Mr Iain MacIlleChiar for his knowledge and emails as well as his hospitality in Scotland. I still am of the opinion that Alexander MacDonald of Glenalladale from Skye was a Captain as well as a poet even if he is also known by another name, Alasdair and was well known by the Seven Glenmoriston Men who happened to love Erse poetry.

For constant editing and corrections that seem never ending, I thank Halima and Alice at Angel Key Publications.

Two medical practitioners have given me medical information relative to some delicate areas, so I am extremely grateful to them for sensitive topics, most especially Dr T. Copland in relation to miscarriages in my lead character's particular circumstances. I apologise if it has offended or distressed anyone who has lost a child in that way. Many thanks also to Dr J. Wright for giving me direction and suggested a course in Forensic Sciences for writers to ensure accuracy.

For agricultural advice on Glengarrry in the Highlands of Scotland, I would like to thank Mr Keven Gallagher from Ardgarry Farm in Glengarry and informal information on the bedrock in Glengarry and ongoing advice concerning Glengarry.

To Daniel Whyte of Strathmore Woolen Company, a big thank you for staying open for us to persuse the tartans of Scotland, as well as Allison his offsider in their assistance with the tartans we needed or were interested in. I have learned a lot from going directly to the woolen mills of Scotland, including Loch Carron Woolen Mill who hadn't heard of an arisaid until they met me. An arisaid is the equivalent of the great kilt, which was what my main character Isobel and her daughter wear in the books, being the heavy woolen hand spun garment worn by women in 18th Century. Daniel and Allison from Strathmore are the loveliest people and I hope they are more recognised for their efforts to keep up such an important part of Scottish cultural heritage.

I wish to also thank the owner of the Morangie Hotel, Mr John Shearer in Tain, where we stayed in Ross Shire who emparted his knowledge of the area and of the Clearances that took place there around Strathcarron.

To Bruce Fummey we give a big thank you for supporting my book 'Isobel of Glenmoriston' and to our historian Hugh Allison from Nairn for swapping my book for his book called 'Culloden Tales' and for his many curious stories of old

Scotland and of the Jacobites, in particular his weaponry of that era and his demonstration of their uses.

To the community of Pitlochry, we thank not only for their Highland Games but for their directions to the Pictish historical stones. The Sentinal stone and the Dunfalandy Stone. This small town also was one of the friendliest places that I visited in all of Scotland, although I missed the cabar toss that our Queenslanders are so good at.

I can't forget our local coffee shop in Brisbane, Australia, Zaraffas and thank them for allowing us to use their spaces and in particular Ashley Byers for his support as well as all of the other lovely ladies on both Instagram and Facebook and our cat Cosie who waited patiently for my return. Our Australian support base has been more important than you would ever know. May God bless you all for making my journey that little bit easier.

To everyone who has purchased a book or accepted a gift of one, thank you and I hope you like the direction the future books take into fantasy, with the introduction of new characters.

To Glasgow taxi services, thank you for returning my lost bag left in your taxi.

Secrets of the Braes and Glens

Authors Notes
Character Names, both Fictional and Historical

Beaton, Ruth- Midwife in Glengarry. Delivers Malcolm Og and Hamish-Hugh. Marries Hugh Mohr Chisholm in later life and he moves to Glengarry. She reveals to Malcolm Mohr MacNachten what Cherry had intended.

Browne, Doctor Benedict – son of Doctor Browne Senior. Buys a medical practice in Glenmoriston. Marries Jean Grant, daughter of Alexander Grant and Father to baby Benedict Alexander and builds a new two-story home with an emergency room. Divorces his wife Jean Grant and returns to England.

Browne, Benedict Alexander – known as Benny. Baby son of Dr Browne and Jean Browne nee Grant. The Father moves to London after parents' divorce and might want the child to live there.

Cameron, Annabel – wife to Aonghus MacGregor. Trained nurse. Daughter of Donald and Janet Cameron. Commences the 'Gathering of the Bairns', on Craskie Farm each week. Mother to Hugh Cameron MacGregor. Works in law office after marrying Aonghus.

Cameron, Donald – Father of Annabel Cameron. Husband to Janet Cameron.

Cameron, Janet – Mother of Annabel Cameron. Wife to Donald Cameron.

Cameron, John – Grandfather of Annabel MacGregor and treasure hunter.

Camerons, Lochiel of the – Charles 21st & Donald 22nd Lochiel, lived in Achnacarry, adjourning lands to MacDonald and Grant lands. Assisted Alexander Grant in purchasing a farm on MacDonald lands. Married.

Cameron, Siobhan – young lady who marries Alexander Og Grant of Loch Garry Ranch. Very shy lady. Becomes Siobhan Grant.

Chisholm, David – Father of Hamish and Hugh Og. Husband to Mary. Drowned in Loch Craskie.

Chisholm, David – son of Hamish and Cora Chisholm, brother of Donald and Mairi

Chisholm, Donald – one of the Seven Glenmoriston Men. Son of Paul Chisholm. Brother to Alexander and Hugh. Migrated to Canada with his family, where he died.

Chisholm, Donald Og – son of Hamish and Cora. First baby to be baptised at the new Chapel. Brother of David and Mairi, learns to fish at Loch Insh.

Chisholm, Eilidh – fictional wife of Donald Mohr Chisholm. Ravished during the burnings of 1746. Stays sickly and dies young.

Chisholm, Ferne – daughter of Meredith and Hugh Og Chisholm

Chisholm, Fleur – miscarried daughter of Hugh Mohr Chisholm and Isobel MacGregor Grant Chisholm.

Chisholm, Hamish - one of the fisher lads. Brother to Hugh Og. Son of the widow Chisholm, later the widow MacDonald. Husband to Cora MacKinnon. Father to Donald Og and David. Employed on Craskie and Grant Farms and the Glenmoriston School as security. One of the men who go out fishing together with Malcolm and Kenneth.

Chisholm, Hugh Mohr – one of the Seven Glenmoriston Men. Son of Paul Chisholm. Brother to Alexander and Donald. Fathered a miscarried child with Isobel Grant, named Fleur. Lived and worked on Craskie Farm. First husband to Zara

MacGregor and fathers Isobel. Married Isobel Grant after the death of Padruig Grant. Blamed for planning the theft of a portion of Marion Grant's inheritance.

Chisholm, Hugh Og – one of the fisher lads. Brother to Hamish. Son of the widow Chisholm, who was later the widow MacDonald. Husband to Meredith MacKenzie. Employed on Craskie Farm as head groom then later runs and manages the team as head teamster. Moves team to Glengarry. Good friend to Malcolm.

Chisholm, Mairi - son of Hamish and Cora Chisholm, sister of David and Donald

Chisholm, Mary – became Widow MacDonald. Mother to both Hamish and Hugh Chisholm.

Chisholm, Meredith – daughter of Alexander and Ferne MacKenzie, wife of Hugh Og Chisholm. Employed in the house at Craskie as well as wool waulking. Leaves Craskie job to work in Glengarry for Malcolm MacNachten.

Chisholm, Paul 🌿 – Father of Alexander, Donald and Hugh. Tenant at Blairie/Blame

David, Alexander Malcolm – Lawyer to Grant family. Sells his business to Aonghus MacGregor in his old age. Witnesses abuse to Isobel while at Craskie Farm.

Father Francis – Catholic Priest from Edinburgh who performed the funeral Mass for Padruig Grant

Father Michael – young Catholic Priest from Edinburgh, who preaches in the new Chapel St Columba at Craskie and brings coal to Isobel from Culross.

Forbes, Bishop Robert 🌿 – Bishop of Ross and Caithness, Episcopalian Church, Leith. Collector of witness statements of survivor's post Culloden battle through to 1775. Died before it was published.

Fraser, Andrew MacDonald – child born to Isobel Fraser

Fraser, Anna – wife of John Fraser of Stratherick. Mother of Simon Fraser. Lives in Stratherick.

Fraser, Colin – Drunken brother to Ivy Fraser. Lives in the Beauly Firth. Joins in wolf hunt and is injured.

Fraser, George – Drunken and dangerous brother of Ivy Fraser. Joins in wolf hunt and is injured.

Fraser, Isobel – daughter of Zara MacGregor and Hugh Chisholm, later adopted and raised by Grigor MacGregor. Referred to as the snippy one. Marries two men, John Fraser and Alex MacDonald.

Fraser, Ivy Simone – 28-year-old Entomologist, works in Invermoriston. Author of a book on insects, seeks out Kenneth MacNachten for illustrations for her book. She is hopeful for a romance and marries him secretly and becomes Ivy MacNachten. They have one child, April Marion MacNachten.

Fraser, John Og – Farmer in the Aird and husband to Isobel Fraser.

Fraser, John of Stratherick – Father of Simon Fraser. Husband of Anna Fraser. Militarily affiliated with Padruig Grant. Fought in the first Quebec battle. Owner of Fraser's Trading Post. Dies in Book two. His son Simon inherits his property upon his death.

Fraser, Robert – 78th Fraser Highlanders, Quebec. Friend and superior officer to Padruig Grant.

Fraser, Simon 🌣 – Husband of Elizabeth Grant. Fictionally, son of Anna and John Fraser of Stratherick. Became a politician.

Fraser, Simone-Anna – daughter of Beth and Simon Fraser

78th Fraser Highlanders 🌣 – formed by Simon Fraser, Master of Lovat. Fought and won in Quebec Campaigns against the French.

Grant, Alexander 🌣 – son of Padruig and Isobel Grant. First married to Therese. Six children including being Jean and Alexander. Loses two children in Nova Scotia. Fictionally, marries Matilda MacMartin upon his return to Scotland and fathers Moses and Sarah. Buys a new farm call Loch

Garry Ranch and accommodates his twin Marion and her son Malcolm.

Grant, Alexander Og – youngest son of Alex Grant. Fictionally moved to Scotland from Nova Scotia. A chef as well as competent farmer specialising in animal husbandry. Sensitive nature misunderstood by Malcolm.

Grant, Beth – daughter of Patrick and Henrietta Grant. Married to Simon Fraser. Fictionally begins her own business breeding Highland Ponies. Mother of Simone-Anna. Known as a snob.

Grant, Bruce – son of James Grant the elderly neighbour. Moves to South Carolina and purchases land with his brother Craig. He marries an Indian woman and has many children.

Grant, Craig – son of James Grant the elderly neighbour. Sells the farm to Padruig. Moves to South Carolina and purchases land with his brother Bruce. He marries an Indian woman and has many children.

Grant, Freya – mother of Isobel Grant originally from Loch Insh. Wife of John Grant. Mother to Grigor MacGregor from a previous marriage. Also, Clan Gregor. Murdered by British troops.

Grant, Helen – daughter of Padruig and Isobel Grant. Fictionally, wife of Grigor MacGregor and artist. Mother of Isobel-Mairi, Aonghus Grigor and Morag-Freya. Grandmother to Nachtain. Fails to succeed in running the farms after her Mither's death. Separates from Grigor. Commits suicide.

Grant, Henrietta – wife of Patrick Grant. Mother of Beth, James and Sarah.

Grant, Henrietta Og – baby daughter of James and Susan Grant

Grant, Isobel – b. 1702. Wife to Padruig Grant. Mother to Patrick, Helen, Marion and Alexander. Miscarries Fleur. Fictionally, Clan Gregor. Daughter of John and Freya Grant.

Grant, James 🌿 – son of Patrick and Henrietta Grant. Fictionally, married to Susan Chisholm. Assists Malcolm MacNachten in dressing correctly to propose to Cherry. Runs business with his father.

Grant, Jean 🌿 – youngest daughter of Alex Grant, who fictionally moved to Scotland from Nova Scotia, wife of Dr Benedict Browne, mother of Benedict Alexander Browne. Hand fasts with Duncan Mohr MacDonald after her divorce from the Doctor.

Grant, John 🌿 – father of Isobel Grant. Fictionally, husband of Freya Grant. Leaves an inheritance for Marion.

Grant, Moses - son and 8th child of Alexander Mohr Grant and son of Matilda MacMartin. Studies university then inherits Weem Menzies estate.

Grant, Padruig 🌿 – b. 1701 known as Padruig Dubh. Husband to Isobel Grant. Father to Patrick, Helen, Marion and Alexander. d. 1786. One of the seven Glenmoriston men and notorious.

Grant, Patrick 🌿 – son of Padruig and Isobel Grant. Husband to Henrietta. Father to Beth, James and Sarah. Fictionally, inherits the Hart of the Highlands Manor House and succeeds in business with his son James Grant.

Grant, Sarah – daughter of Patrick and Henrietta Grant. Married to Duncan Forsythe. Mother of Robin.

Grant, Sarah – daughter and 7th child of Alexander Mohr Grant and daughter of Matilda MacMartin

Grant, Susan - Clan Chisholm. Married James Grant, son of Patrick Grant. They divorce after birth of one child.

Grant, Therese 🌿 – wife of Alexander Grant. Six children. Fictionally, went to live in Nova Scotia permanently. Divorces Alex and remarries.

Hamilton, Patrick – friend of Aonghus from Edinburgh University, veterinarian. Journeyed to Loch Fyne with Morag-Freya and Gillcrest MacLachlan.

Heath, Dr Peter – Effeminate English doctor based in Inverness. Family Doctor. Befriends both Alex MacDonald and Alexander Og Grant. Matilda discovers he was charged with assault with sodomitical intent in London.

Johnson, Captain Stanley – Captain at Fort Augustus involved in collecting the stolen goods.

MacDonald, Allan 🌣 – Uncle to Padruig Dubh Grant. Fictionally, husband to Margaret. Later husband to Mairi Chisholm. Advisor to Isobel Grant.

MacDonald, Bruce – childhood friend of Grigor Og MacGregor, moves to South Carolina, marries an Indian woman then returns to Scotland in adulthood after her death. Marries Marion MacNachten. Becomes close to Marion's sons, Malcolm and Kenneth.

MacDonnell, Donald – young hunter who attends the wolf hunt in the Aird and draws the picture of five deceased wolves including the Alpha and the MacDonalds who killed them with Malcolm MacNachten

MacDonald, Donald Og – Isobel Fraser's youngest son, born to Alexander MacDonald. Brother to Andrew Fraser. Name officially was Donald Fraser as a child of the only official marriage of Isobel Fraser, later altered to its traditional format of Domnall.

MacDonald, Dougal – childhood friend of Grigor Og MacGregor, marries an heiress in Glengarry.

MacDonnell, Duncan – groomsman at Craskie Farm recommended by Killian MacDonnell.

MacDonnell, Duncan – new security man for Cherry Farms and Loch Garry, 30 years old, married with children, skilled with weaponry and fitness.

MacDonnell, Duncan Snr. – marksman, hired as security for Glengarry farms. Grandfather of Duncan of Craskie. Has a love interest in Jean Grant after her divorce whom he later married and has one child.

MacDonnell, Old John – elderly, cunning wolf killer from Glengarry. Led the group to kill the pack of wolves in the Aird. Powerful leader in Glengarry who eventually becomes close to Malcolm MacNachten through mutual respect and love.

MacDonnell, Killian – door neighbour of Matilda and Alex Grant in Loch Garry. Formerly taught the Gaelic language to Matilda whilst in London.

MacDonald, Lillian – washer lady for Cherry Farm three days a week.

MacDonnell, Margaret – wife to Allan MacDonald.

MacDonald, Mairi – wife to Duncan Mohr MacDonald, security guard to MacNachten Farms

MacDonald, Mary – wife of Joe MacDonald. Washer lady to Isobel. Helps deliver Nachtain.

MacDougal, Dougal – Senior groomsman for the Clydesdales after Bruce MacKay moves to Inverness, brother to Milread. Marries the widow MacKichan taking on her two sons, Charles and Henry. Lives temporarily at Chisholm House.

MacDougal, Fergus – Aonghus' friend from university, member of Pict club. Travels to Loch Fyne with Gillcrest and Patrick Hamilton. Contemplating writing a joint paper on the Picts.

MacFie, Amelia – Joseph MacFie's daughter from the Isles, fifteen-year-old home help. Interested in romance with Kenneth. Loses her job and moves to New Holland with her family.

MacFie, Joseph – mature aged student working for Alex Grant at Loch Garry Ranch. Formerly of the Isles. Befriends Malcolm MacNachten and successfully introduces his niece, Cherry to him for marriage.

MacGregor, Ailsa – second wife of Malcolm MacNachten. Devoted wife who has two more children with Malcolm but her mother creates an enormous problem with Grigor Mohr MacGregor

MacGregor, Ali – oldest twin son of Zara MacGregor. Begins work on Craskie farm to learn how to grow oats and perfect the soil. Later marries April, daughter of Kenneth and Ivy Fraser MacNachten

MacGregor, Belle– Mither of Ailsa MacGregor from Inverness. Widow. Known as a trollop who temporarily breaks up Zara's marriage owing to a curse

MacGregor, Aonghus – son of Grigor MacGregor Og and Helen Grant MacGregor. Husband to Annabel Cameron. Became a lawyer in Inverness. Highly intelligent and shares an interest with Fergus about the Picts. Manages all legal matters for the family farms and new business.

MacAlpin, Coinneach – mysterious old gentleman whom Zara meets at the house of the old Crohn. He identifies Zara and has regal Pictish ancestry.

MacGregor, Causantin – third son of Zara MacGregor and Grigor MacGregor

MacGregor, Dihaoine Freya Dorothea – youngest daughter of Zara and Grigor Mohr MacGregor in the Aird. Very expert at disappearing, even as a tiny baby.

MacGregor, Fatma – twin with Ali, daughter of Zara MacGregor and Grigor MacGregor who live in the Aird. Fatma has temporary marriage that doesn't last with an unalive Simon Fraser.

MacGregor, Grigor Mohr 🌼 – One of the seven Glenmoriston Men. Fictionally Father of Grigor MacGregor Og, husband of Morag, half-brother to Isobel Grant later to become Isobel Chisholm. In death becomes the husband of Zara MacGregor with whom he has many children.

MacGregor, Grigor Og – husband of Helen Grant, son of Grigor MacGregor, Father to Isobel-Mairi, Aonghus-Grigor and Morag-Freya. Hard worker and soil perfectionist on the farm. Influenced adversely after Isobel's death. His wife Helen commits suicide and he forms an attachment with Carmel.

MacGregor, Hugh-Cameron – baby son of Aonghus and Annabel MacGregor who attends the gatherings of the bairns each week.

MacGregor, Isobel-Mairi – daughter of Grigor MacGregor Og and Helen Grant MacGregor. Wife of Ewen MacNachten. Mother to Nachtain Grigor MacNachten. Leaves the farm to open a mill and tartan shop in Inverness during the year of the sheep. Causes trouble for her Mother Helen and Craskie Farm.

MacGregor, Richard – Uncle of Ailsa MacGregor

MacGregor, Zara – Grigor Og's temporary cook. Mother to Ali, Fatma, Hector, Causantin and Dihaoine who live on a farm in the Aird with husband Grigor Mohr MacGregor. Part of an eccentric family group who are no longer of the living. Mother to Isobel Chisholm, Grandmother to Andrra and Domnhall. In total Mother to six bairns from two Fathers.

MacKay, Bruce – the groomsman for the Clydesdales in Inverness, husband to Milread and Father to Robert. Starts work at Craskie but moves with the family to Inverness to work with the horses and the Mill.

MacKay, Milread – born MacDougal. Wool waulker and spinner, sister to Dougal MacDougal, wife of Bruce MacKay and Mother of Robert. Moves to Inverness to work in new milling business spinning tartan for Isobel-Mairi MacNachten.

MacKay, Robert –baby son of Bruce and Milread MacKay.

MacKenzie, Alexander – Father of Meredith from Kinlochewe. Husband of Ferne MacKenzie. Refused to attend the wedding of Hugh and Isobel.

MacKenzie, Angus- Offsider to Hugh Og, Teamster. Young and very handsome. Cousin to Meredith from Kinlochewe. Islay likes him then marries him and has a child living in Malcolm's house in Glengarry.

MacKenzie, Ferne – Mother of Meredith, wife of Alexander MacKenzie.

MacKenzie, Mairi – cook to Coinneach MacGregor, from the mountains.

MacKenzie, Padraig Nachtain – son of Islay and Angus MacKenzie, grandson of Malcolm MacNachtain

MacKichan, Alexandria – mother of Charles and Henry. Cleared from her croft to live on Craskie Farm. Marries Groom Dougal MacDougal.

MacKichan, Charles – 16-year-old student. Son of the widow MacKichan. Apprentice soil specialist to Grigor Og for soil movement. Older brother to Henry MacKichan.

MacKichan, Henry – 12-year-old son of the widow MacKichan. Younger brother to Charles MacKichan. Assistant to Hugh Mohr.

MacKinnon, Cora – daughter of Mairi and Donald MacKinnon (dcd), wife to Hamish Chisholm, mother to Donald Og, songstress, schoolteacher and wool waulking.

MacLachlan, Gillcrest Lachlan – Laird of Lachlan lands in Argyle. Husband of Morag-Freya Grant. Head scientist specialising in crop yields by perfecting soil. Father of Patricia Fleur. Lives in Invermoriston.

MacLachlan, Morag-Freya – daughter of Grigor MacGregor and Helen Grant MacGregor. Became a nurse at Invermoriston Hospital. Wife to Gillcrest Lachlan MacLachlan to be a Laird's wife. Mother to Patricia Fleur. Introduces Aonghus and Annabel Cameron who later marry.

MacLean, Murdoch – farmworker cleared from the Islands. Friend of Joseph MacFie from Loch Garry Ranch, Glengarry. Helps Craskie Farm get back on track. Uncle to Cherry who marries Malcolm. Moves to New Holland after hurting Malcolm in a fight.

MacLean, Joshua – Islander and farm hand on Cherry Farm in Glen Garry. Known as Joe. Uncle to Cherry, wife of Malcolm. He moves with his family to New Holland.

MacMartin Grant, Matilda – adopted daughter of Hector and Elizabeth Menzies. Born to a crofter family on Craskie Farm. Educated in London. Degree in biology and botany. Marries Alexander Grant of Loch Garry Ranch and has two children. Establishes old growth forest on the land.

MacNachten, April Marion- first and only child of Kenneth and Ivy MacNachten. Lived on Cherry Farms with her parents. Fraser Grandparents begin to visit her. Marries Ali MacGregor and moves to Glengarry to farm.

MacNachten, Bridei – baby son of Isobel-Mairi MacNachten and Ewen MacNachten, younger brother to Nachtain.

MacNachten, Cherry – formerly MacLean of the Isles. Marries Malcolm MacNachten. Mother to Islay, Alexander and the twins Hamish-Hugh and Malcolm Marion. Niece of Joseph MacFie and Murdoch MacLean. Worked as a chef and a prostitute before marrying Malcolm. Files for divorce to leave her husband for the colonies. Is shot through the head on her return.

MacNachten, Eschina Isobel – youngest daughter to Malcolm and Ailsa MacNachten.

MacNachten, Ewen – born MacThreynfhir or Armstrong – adopted son of Gillcrest MacNachten. Husband to Isobel-Mairi. Father to Nachtain Grigor MacNachten. Blacksmith and farrier at Craskie Farm. Ventures into business with his wife in Inverness. Has a fight with Malcolm. In debt with Helen MacGregor causing troube for Craskie Farm.

MacNachten, Gillcrest – adoptive Father to Ewen MacNachten, foster Father to Marion Grant, second cousin to Isobel Grant, Loch Insh, Foster Grandfather to both Malcolm and Kenneth MacNachten

MacNachten, Gordon Padruig– youngest son of Malcolm and Ailsa MacNachten. Hopes that he will attend university.

MacNachten, Hamish-Hugh – twin son of Malcolm MacNachten, Glengarry. Marries Fatima.

MacNachten, Islay – daughter of Malcolm and Cherry MacNachten. Wife of Angus.

MacNachten, Kenneth – Son of Marion and Nachtain MacNachten decd, younger brother of Malcolm, Grandson of Isobel, trained as a stonemason, becomes educated as an accountant paid for by John Fraser, takes up being an illustrator and an artist. Marries Ivy Fraser.

MacNachten, Malcolm Mohr – Son of Marion MacNachten and Nachtain MacNachten decd, older brother to Kenneth, Grandson of Isobel aand Padruig Grant, trained as a stonemason. Lived with Alex in Loch Garry Ranch. Marries lady from the Isles, Cherry MacLean. Had four children, Islay and Alexander, Hamish and Malcolm with first wife. Divorces Cherry and marries Ailsa MacGregor and had two more children, Gordon and Eschina.

MacNachten, Mairi- Nurse and wife to Malcolm's oldest son Alexander, a Doctor in Invermoriston.

MacNachten, Malcolm-Marion – twin son Malcolm MacNachten, Glengarry.

MacNachten, Marion – Twin sister of Alex Grant. Concealed twin daughter of Isobel Grant. Raised in secret by Gillcrest MacNachten in Loch Insh. Is returned with her two sons, Malcolm and Kenneth to Craskie Farm and re-unites with her twin brother, Alex. Meets Padruig Dubh before his death. Is moved to Loch Garry Ranch due to the clearances. Marries Dihaoine Bruce MacDonald. Later lives on Malcolm's farm and on retirement buys cleared crofts to renovate on Loch Garry.

MacNachten, Nachtain [senior]– deceased beloved husband of Marion Grant MacNachten, father of Malcolm and Kenneth. Died from pneumonia when Malcolm and Kenneth were both young, in Loch Insh.

MacNachten, Nachtain Grigor – born to Isobel-Mairi and Ewen MacNachten. Boss baby in the group

Iain MacNeil – Islander and groomsman on Cherry Farm, Glengarry.

MacPherson, **Carmel Juliann**- Midwife in Cameron lands. Interested in meeting Grigor after the death of Helen, then successfully get together.

MacPherson, Ewen of Cluny 🌷 – Laird of Clan Chattan and Clan MacPherson, contemporary of the gentle Donald Cameron of Lochiel

Menzies, Elizabeth – adoptive Mother to Matilda MacMartin later became Matilda Grant.

Menzies, Hector – adoptive Father to Matilda MacMartin later became Matilda Grant.

Menzies, Kenneth – The Editor, Inverness Times Newspaper, Scotland. Bought Clearance painting off Helen through John Fraser.

Ross, Frederick – husband to Lillian Ross

Ross, Lillian – midwife from Inverness, connected with the Glenmoriston and Glengarry midwives who attends the birth of Zara's daughter, Freya Dorothea

Shaw, Ann – housekeeper of Malcolm Law Rooms, Inverness

Shaw, Donald – the one-eyed veteran of Culloden battle, collects stolen bawbee from Isobel. Attends Padruig's funeral.

Stewart, Reverend John 🌷 – Episcopalian Reverend in Inverness. Sorts out many family issues,

Stewart, Mrs John – wife to Rev. John Stewart in Inverness.

Wool Waulking Women

Isobel (until retirement), Helen, Mairi MacKinnon (until dc'd), Cora, Meredith, Isobel-Mairi, Morag-Freya and Milread [until it moves into a mill in Inverness].

Secrets of the Braes and Glens

References

1. Britanica (2023) Banshee in Celtic Folklore, https://www.britannica.com/topic/banshee

2. El-Fatah, Zaynab (2023) Isobel of Glenmoriston – Isobel's Story, Brisbane, Australia

3. Forbes, Rev. Robert (collected 1746-1775) (published 1895) The Lyon in Mourning, Vol. III, Edited from 1746-1775 Manuscript by Henry Paton MA, Forgotten Books, University Press, Scottish History Society, Edinburgh, UK. Pages 101, 103, 106, 108, 109

4. Fraser, Sarah (2013) The Last Highlander, Harper Collins Publishers, London, UK.

5. Harper, J. R. R. (1966) The 78th Fighting Frasers: A Short History of the old 78th Regiment or Fraser Highlanders 1757-1763, DED-SCO Publications Lmt, Laval, Quebec, Canada.

6. Liath Wolf (2021) Cù-sìth: The Faerie Dog of Scotland (Scottish Folklore), Liath Wolf Channel, YouTube, https://www.youtube.com/watch?v=UyhFtHo9Xew

7. Liath Wolf (2023) MacFie and the Black Dog: A legend from the Isles (Scottish Folklore), Liath Wolf Channel, YouTube https://youtu.be/o38fO4FqTMU.

9 780645 868968